Edwin Ahearn

The Arbhal Sequence

THE WAR

THE WAR

i

At Kamsilat

Slowly he was invaded by consciousness of comfort, warmth and smooth linen, clean smell of a real bed. Stretching out bare legs the dim aftershadow of aches was pleasure in itself, soreness of a climb and long marches, of sleeping on bare ground had ebbed away, and his wounded knee gave only a very small throb.

He seemed surrounded by stillness, and drowsed mind slowly allowed that silence was what he was used to; here was a quiet tempered with faint noises of human activity; feet padding in the hallway outside his door, the very distant clash of plates and cutlery, a regular thumping from another quarter, which after a while he identified as the dull, steady sound of a carpet being beaten. Boisterous voices came trickling to him. This was the Great House at Kamsilat, and the sun was well up, brilliant at the window, white22r than it ever was on the other side of Arnan.

Not yet letting himself get up he worked his face down into the bolster and lay putting events in order, long sail towards sunset and so into darkness, Sarnak watchful at the helm, till they picked up the gleam of Kamsilat's light-tower, visible for miles out to sea. A lantern went up to masthead, and swift-oared boats came first to challenge, and then to guide them to the wide mouth of the Navu, Sarnak keeping up a constant patter of coaxing and occasional abuse for the ship. Amid flares and lanterns they docked smoothly; Dolvid went to fetch Aëlu, and could readily picture her waking smile, quick to fade. Then there was Rodlakh taking excessive pains with routine matters, seeing Galt's men would be accommodated at the barracks, wounded cared for, arranging for guard to be mounted over the boat's costly cargo. Tired exasperation gave way eventually to recognition Rodlakh was trying to put off a task he dreaded, going to the Great House with the news about Sebhal.

Horses appeared for them; as sky paled they rode behind lantern-bearers past big stone warehouses, across a broad cobbled court, up a way that wound to and fro, mounting from the harbor. A wide space where ways met, guarded gates, a climbing driveway among large trees. They came to the shallow steps and high carved wooden doors of the Great House. Saidhan had not been wakened, and Dolvid, by then almost asleep as he stood, could remember Doleni grave at the door, Aëlu embracing the mother with both dignity and warmth. The last picture, before a soft-footed steward led him away to where he could lie down, was Doleni's face going rigid, as Aëlu gave the news about her husband, the other's son. After looking for confirmation to Rodlakh, who was stiff and ill-at-ease, Doleni covered her face with both hands when Aëlu wrapped arms around her.

Meat was cooking somewhere, mutton or lamb. Sitting up, he found a robe placed on the oaken chair beside his bed, soft slippers under. Getting up, he went to the window.

He was above the courtyard behind the Great House, but first his eye leapt to the forest, now in the freshness of early leaf, ponderous Kamsilat oaks and soaring ashes straight as fretted pillars of cut stone. Along the ridge behind the nearest belt of woodland he could discern beeches by the silvered sheen of their trunks, and there was a knot of low-spreading *tovrelunal* with their bronze leaves. Nearer the walls containing the Great House were big elms, dense horse-chestnuts readying their candles of waxy pink or white. North and west the great oaks marched up the hills till they were met and checked by regiments of cone-bearers marching down.

Impossible the sentimental twinge of homecoming he felt could be real; there was nothing approaching these stands of trees to be seen east of Arnan. In the south, Ninkufu, his original home, there were no forests, but in that mild climate firewood was not much needed. and some large trees went unmolested. But he left there when he was six, so it might be that, as with mountains seen from a distance, forests fulfilled a necessary dream not anchored in any real memory. Stories, too, had forests, where men wandered, losing their way or their wits, meeting with lovely, perilous women, stumbling suddenly upon lost realms, encountering talking bears and cats that flew: in those dim and trackless lands anything was possible, and here in the Forest of Kamsilat imagination had its homecoming.

Down within the low walls of the earthen courtyard there was a flurry of unwarlike activity. Women of the household were combing out a shaggy mass of unbleached wool hung from a carding-frame. Not far away two or three boys were picking twigs from a great stack to tie into new birch-brooms, and with their teasing causing giggles and blushes among the younger carders of wool. Downwind, not only carpets but a large green-and-gold tapestry were hung for beating, and there were beaters of every sex and size down to tiny children. Extreme right in front of the stables bigger youths soaped saddles and harness, with a few horses being groomed; at a glance the picture of peace.

But fear of sudden attack was there. Even the broom-makers had small bows near to hand, stacked in tripod with a sheaf of arrows beneath. A gangly lad scrubbing out a vast beechwood barrel had his sword stuck into the hard ground in easy reach, while beyond the walls where the terrain rose, archers could be seen lurking in cloisters of the forest fringe; evidently all precautions had been redoubled since the abduction, and any new raiding-parties would not have an easy task.

"If you have slept enough, women can bring warm water." Rodlakh had come into the bedroom. "There is a meal being prepared."

Turning from the window Dolvid was unsure whether he should make deference now they were no longer in the field; he did not, and remained in doubt, partly due to Rodlakh's new appearance, dressed in a loose robe of plain linen over breeches and shirt of an officer here in the West, facings scarlet but with no sign of rank. He had shaved the light growth of beard and his hair was brushed out; posture was alert but not tense, shoulders held level and open. Here at Kamsilat it was absurd to recollect this prince had hoped to go undetected as a junior officer named Vol.

"I just spoke with Arvat. He is very eager to see you again." That was not unlikely, but it appeared he had introduced the subject so as to ask, low-voiced, leading Dolvid back to the window seat, "Do you think he could be the Patriarch's spy here?"

"Arvat?"

He was wound up for this. "Well, but we cannot relax our guard because of old friendships, or who anyone's father was. I know he was your apprentice, and what you taught has been valuable here — not just writing, but couching our official letters in appropriate language, interpreting laws and decrees. Still — "

"A son of Arvus serve the Patriarch? The father was a Deniant who used to chide me when I would not agree the *Atarlum* should be disbanded altogether — that was in the years when you could have such views and remain a true *rabhsayani*. Arvus certainly served your father faithfully." He had been murdered in the murky, new days of Ban-Sila's reign, when the realm was changing brutally from the gentle years of Lambarr.

"Arvat now holds his father's death was a conspiracy among other Deniants, who were angry Arvus went on serving *rabhsayum* when Ban-Sila came to power."

"That is preposterous. Arvat cannot have forgotten the *Kímukan* Zhinladh hunting him, too, that day — Zhinladh, son of Zhival, a faithful adherent of the *Atarlum*. They hate Deniants, and Arvus was one in charge at the Treasury, who wanted them to pay their fair share of taxes." Making Deniants the murderers was exactly the sort of farfetched, over-elaborate, mysterious and completely wrongheaded theory Arvat always seized on when he was a student of history.

"What is the evidence?"

"I cannot say," misunderstanding the question. "He has said some Deniants were overheard saying — "

"No, the evidence against Arvat."

"I am not saying he is under suspicion, only asking if he should be. He has been known to send letters secretly to the Mainland."

"To his sister. She is married to Rhunilat, you know." Arvat might be afraid his loyalty would be questioned if he were to write openly to the wife of a *bôdh'loiki* at Ban-Sila's Residence — and now was suspect because he wrote covertly. But Rhunilat was no policy-maker, as they had seen at Kadon Dinul, was not in the inmost counsels of the *rabhsayum* he served.

"Ban-Sila's realm," the brother, bitterly. "Where a man has to write secretly to his sister."

But when Arvat was questioned about the passageways he must have guessed what was intended with the information. If he was the Patriarch's spy why was the passage not blocked, or a trap set for the intruders? When they eavesdropped behind the Oak-Wall carving, the *Atarlum*, as represented by at-Zhâlai, already had news out of Kamsilat later than the departure of Sebhal and Rodlakh, Aëlu's abduction.

Rodlakh shook his head, apparently no more eager than Dolvid to hunt down the spy, a cold kind of warfare. Yet he or she could do a great deal more harm; Dolvid wished exposure was possible without the execution that would by tradition follow.

An answer to his question could, however, be found: if *g'Asalladh'* knew Sebhal meant to penetrate the Residence, He would assume the object was assassination, and might decide the *Atarlum* could hardly lose, succeed or fail; either the West would lose its leader, or if Ban-Sila was killed the Patriarch would bring forward young Orbanak, and hope to control him.

Rodlakh still wondered about Arvat: he had shown signs of discontent, and was known to have meetings in out-of-the-way places with officers in the Army of the West. "Edarron is one, senior half-squadron in Sebhal's hearth-company. His loyalty is beyond any question. He says Arvat had nothing of importance to say when they met — then why at dead of night in a drink-shop? They could meet openly here, or over at the barracks. Edarron is a bachelor," he quickly clarified, "but his taste is for women."

Thinking it through, the answer was evident. "Let me question Arvat about this, *Valrabh'*. If, afterwards, I am satisfied he is not the spy, will you accept that, no details?"

"I would trust your opinion." But Rodlakh was perplexed.

"So long as actions remain loyal, lords should not become too inquisitive about words spoken privately. Just as no one should want to know what his friends say about him behind his back."

As his way was Rodlakh paused on this with his head cocked. He nodded, and the subject tailed off. Dolvid was nagged at by the feeling larger questions were being put aside.

After a tentative knock two women brought in steaming water and rough towels, a third carrying underlinen and plain, well-made suitings. Rodlakh sat on the bed while Dolvid gave himself a thorough wash.

Messengers, Rodlakh said, had been here the day before yesterday, from *g'Asalladh'*, though they would not say so straight out. Imagining they still held Aëlu, they had terms for her release unharmed, but not before rebellion in the Northeast was put down, the Colony having given no assistance to Shumat. "These people knew Sebhal had spoken with Shumat's envoys."

"When? They knew more than I have — " on the brink of instant annoyance.

"At the beginning of winter. There was no secret about the meeting as such; it was after that the Colony joined with Shumat in a message to the *rabhsai*, telling him the Decree of Preference would be unacceptable to the Armies of the West and the Northeast; we believe that was why Ban-Sila put aside the Decree and took up the Loyal Oath."

"As often as we tried to read Shumat's intentions," in bewilderment, "you told me nothing about this meeting. If I am to be your *Bôdhrai* — "

"Be my friend, and take any title you like," plainly distressed. "I wanted to tell you, and was ashamed to."

Dolvid already regretted his rush of pomposity, and the unexpected word brought him up short. "You declined a realm."

"A pact made in my absence."

He and Sebhal had been together at the Frontier when messages came from Kamsilat that made Sebhal return eastward earlier than planned; he had stayed so as to go with a patrol to see Shâl Mines and its precarious road beyond the Frontier. Returning to Kamsilat some days later, he heard about the envoys from Shumat, one an army man, "an Owani, at least his name was, Onebhai, an officer called out of retirement."

"Onebhal, I know him well, or did." Well-respected, lean, laconic, survivor of a dreadful wound at the Pass of Perus.

From those meetings came a name, the Free State of Arbhal, uniting all those who stood against Preference, with the Colony and the Northeast as its twin pillars, and Rodlakh as ruler. But he, while he would stand out against the Decree, refused to be a part of mutiny or secession, and long harangues by Sebhal had not changed that, though eventually he agreed to lend his name as a supporter of the Free State, so as to present Ban-Sila with a united ultimatum. "I did not want armed uprising, only the threat of one — but Shumat has struck on his own. His envoys said they would begin an open struggle only if they could see no other way, but Shumat could have waited till we had confronted Ban-Sila, Sebhal and I."

"But you must have known declaring a Free State would lead to war. And that in two halves, divided by the whole width of Dramal and Ân, the Free State could not survive."

Rodlakh nodded glumly. He had known, but been so convinced his brother would see reason, the threat of war had seemed pure surmise to him, less than real.

In anyone else, this would have been naive beyond belief, but what Dolvid saw was Sebhal's duplicities. Beyond all doubt he had meant to murder Ban-Sila, and then present Rodlakh with decisions already made, armies in the field. And about the meeting with the men from the Northeast Rodlakh, plainly, had only what Sebhal had told him; knowing Shumat it could only have been Sebhal who invented the Free State and urged the uprising, perhaps he who had summoned the envoys to Kamsilat.

"I told Sebhal he would be a better leader for the Free State. But he maintained my mixture of bloods was needed — as if my blood is any different from Ban-Sila's! By that rule, a good Gabhani would rather have Bolan than Sebhal."

Dressing, Dolvid found someone had judged his size with a good eye. It had been years since he had wanted to face a looking-glass.

"Aëlu is sleeping. I hope she sleeps out the day, after all she has endured."

The meal was served in a small and comfortable room opening off the main hall. The Great House was built of stone, substantially rather than with any memorable distinction, but inside Dolvid continued to be impressed by the lavish use of woods for covering and ornament. Floors, big areas of wall, staircases were all a mellowed and pleasing contrast with the dressed stone of either Residence at Kadon Dinul, or with the Summer Palace of the Patriarch. Undoubtedly warmer in winter, too.

Saidhan, smaller than he once was, stood to greet Dolvid, and thank him for his part in the release of Aëlu. He called her `our daughter,' touching, when grief over Sebhal's death was so fresh. When they were seated the old man unexpectedly started to chuckle. "Drin b'Afon, hah? Well, a thousand years is long enough for any legend. It would have been good to stand beside you on the walls, there — these legs of mine, Dolvid. I have not become old, but they have shut me up in the body of a stranger, no strength, all aches and twinges."

"*Asai*, there would not have been any rescue at Drin b'Afon without men trained as Galt and his soldiers are. The Army of the West is Saidhan's right hand; you were with us on the walls."

A slow look. "A little of that with Ban-Sila could have saved you a lot of trouble, Master."

Dolvid was not sure whether he was offended, but Rodlakh said, "If you want flattery, Grandfather, you had better try somewhere else."

"Your pardon," he bowed. "Laluvoi, late in life, above everything, did not want to be made a fool of by her vanity, as she said the elderly can be. If I guard against flattery, I can tell myself I am not so old — a case of being made a fool of by vanity, hah?"

The first course, evidently meant only for the men, was a rich oatmeal porridge, laced with cream and sweetened with preserved blackberries. While they ate Saidhan wanted details of the Island, especially strength and quality of the troops they had faced. Since the Mainland was everyone's preoccupation, Shumat's uprising, and what the Colony's next move would be, there was an unreal quality about their talk of officers in the *Adanum Plakh'*, the Island climate, the excellence of the cream here in Kamsilat.

With that course cleared Doleni came in dressed in plain brown robe of mourning, steel-grey hair worn simply, her back straight as ash-trees. She had always resembled a younger Laluvoi, and while that likeness had not diminished, she was also becoming very like Saidhan, aging in his direction, so if both lived another dozen years the once-great difference in their ages would be near vanishing. There was no sign she had wept.

When they all were seated again Doleni broke off a piece of barley-bread. "Food for a war-camp," disgusted and apologetic. "We are under siege, you know. But for our grandson's tricks — the elder one, I mean — we could give you good wheat-bread."

"This seems good to me, *Asayu*." True, after days of arid kiln-bread, steadily staling.

"Yet you knew the tables of Kadon Dinul, in the gracious years. We shall not taste that graciousness again, not while Banak-loi holds Sword."

"Madam — " Rodlakh began a quiet protest.

"He was Banak-loi to my daughter. When the Patriarch gets tired of him, he can come here, and be Banak-loi again." Distaste sharpened Doleni's sharp nose. Most of the resemblance to Saidhan was in the tilt of her head, and how the patient corners of the mouth were always threatening a smile. A caution against trusting too much in what faces conveyed; Doleni had acquired her look of unembittered acceptance mainly by living across the table from Saidhan, and not necessarily by being resigned and unembittered.

The main meal arrived, a platter heaped with fragrant chunks of roast lamb, a large earthen pot of beans over which lamb-drippings had been spooned, also pickled cabbage and dark beetroot. Again as in the cellar at Burantal Dolvid was conscious of a shadowed *mai* surrounding the eating of meat, but it might be he had imagination to spare. Doleni did not believe bereavement called for fasting, and served herself with a large piece of lamb, though in the end she did not eat much.

"I was always opposed, you remember," she said when all plates were filled, "to this Mainland venture."

"We were all opposed to it," Rodlakh said.

"It took our son."

Saidhan cleared his throat. "He was a soldier for thirty years. Every day we have lived with the chance of his sudden death, you, and I, and Aëlu . I am not saying that makes it less grievous."

"And in the end, a thief's death, killed not by *jinzal* or in border-wars, but in a street-brawl with one of the creatures of the *rabhsai*'s new following."

"Sebhal died bravely, nonetheless," glancing to the two younger men for a confirmation. "Regardless of who had the weapon, we cannot ask more than that."

Doleni closed her face on him, as if she had long ago decided there could never be a bridge between her real world and his mannish fantasies.

"And we are still debating whether or not we're at war with *rabhsayum,*" turning to Rodlakh, or on him. "How many more good men are going to be killed for nothing? But for his loyalty to the House Arbhai-Navu, to you, *Valrabh'*, Sebhal might have been *rabhsai*, and all Banak-loi's nonsense about Old Owan dead. True? If the Army of the West had combined with Shumat's men — "

"In due course, madam," Saidhan said.

"Do we go on talking about *accommodation*?" with withering scorn.

"No, madam, we do not. We cannot make plans till we have up-to-date news from the Frontier."

So, it seemed, the decision to join Shumat's revolt had already been taken; Rodlakh's face was agonized but determined. As for the Frontier, there had been a renewal of disturbing rumors, but Nolimas, acting commander there, was on his way east, and should already be in Banakit; he would be expected in Kamsilat late tonight or tomorrow morning at the latest. Saidhan also noted that if the expedition had not gone to the Mainland, Aëlu could not have been rescued, since by the time they knew where she was the guard in Drin b'Afon would have been made far stronger.

After the main course had been cleared, some preserved fruits brought in, a squat, broad-shouldered man appeared in the doorway, asking to speak with Saidhan. Dolvid remembered him at quayside last night, Vinosai, under-warden of the port (as *Nim'*, Saidhan was also titular warden). His face was fleshy but flat, sharp Owani nose the pointer on a sundial.

"Your pardon, *Asai*," he said in a near-whisper when ushered in. "I must tell you there is a ship standing offshore with our patrol-vessels watching. A ship of Kargul."

Saidhan half-stood, hand going to where hilts would be if he was wearing a sword. "What is its business?"

"They do not desire to make port, *Asai*, only to land passengers."

"What passengers?"

"A lady of Kargul, and perhaps her servant, *Asai*."

"What lady?" Rodlakh's eyes met Dolvid's, and they were both thinking, however improbably, of Âna.

Vinosai could not answer, but knew only what he had been told. A couple of armed men had been seen aboard the Karguli ship, but only the two women asked leave to come ashore.

Saidhan, baffled, turned to Rodlakh. "Who can this Karguliyu be?"

"It occurs to me," with admirable calm, "she might not be of Kargul at all, but the girl Âna, who was at Kadon Dinul, and who rode with tokens of Kargul. She — " he struggled to characterize Âna without bringing in Sebhal. "She is with us in heart."

"This would be the one who came with news about where Aëlu had been taken? Well, bring her ashore, bring her ashore so we can see."

"Wait, Vinosai." On his feet, as Dolvid was, Rodlakh said he would ride with the under-warden. "How could Âna be here, and so soon?"

Dolvid could not work it out in a moment, but he too wanted to be waiting at quayside.

"Even if our visitor is Petakoi," Saidhan, with a sour twitch, "I would think the *Valrabh'* sufficient to welcome her. I want some words with you, Master."

"Of course, *Asai*." He sat. Rodlakh, in theory, could have overruled him, but there was no sign it occurred to him. If Âna was really here at Kamsilat (counting days, it did not seem possible, not in a Karguli ship) Dolvid supposed he would see her quite soon. Without another word Rodlakh went out; Vinosai barely reached his shoulder.

"A useful man, and lucky to be alive." Vinosai had been manning the light-tower in the illness of the regular keeper on the day of Aëlu's abduction, some of which he witnessed. He also saw the boy, his helper, shot down when sent to raise the alarm, and Vinosai had barred the door to the light-tower till friends came.

Dolvid was less than fully attentive. Two and a half days on Kamanta, not four since Tan Lughsai, just three from when Âna would have started back for Kadon Dinul. That left scarcely enough for the crossing, even if he could invent a reason for a vessel of Kargul to bring her here. Still his chest would be quieter and stomach calmer if he could be riding with Rodlakh for the port.

When hot *raminat* was brought in Doleni left to arrange for beds. As the last plates were cleared, Saidhan asked, "Do you remain a chronicler of our lives, Master?"

Seizing that opening Dolvid suggested if he was going to be a few days at Kamsilat he would need use of a small private room, and writing materials, so he could draft an account of the most recent happenings.

"Arvat can see to that." Saidhan, with a casual air failing to conceal deep interest, asked about his projected book concerning the rise to power of Banak and Laluvoi. "Laluvoi, I understand, intended you to have her private journals."

She had promised them, but Dolvid was already in exile when she died after a year of grievous illness, and he supposed the bequest was forgotten, or else cancelled by the *rabhsai*.

"Laluvoi never forgot a promise. One of the last letters she dictated asked me to take charge of the documents, hoping they could come to you in better times. They arrived here in a great wooden box which we left unopened."

Alarmingly Dolvid's eyes filled with tears. "I might have seen her one last time," Saidhan reflected, "if this reign had not been, or had been different. Our friendship, you know, went back a long lifetime." He opened a flask of the tawny southern wine often drunk with *raminat*, sweetish and smoky, and filled two small glasses. "Can an age be bitterer than letting Laluvoi die and not have her oldest friend there to touch her hand? Or putting such a burden of choice on youthful shoulders. That's a good boy, becoming a better young man, would you say?"

"I marvel to watch him grow."

Saidhan's satisfaction was rueful. "This girl, Âna, who may or may not be with us — she was my son's mistress?"

"Does Rodlakh say so, *Asai*?"

"No, he does not. You need not be discreet, Master; Aëlu is not going to hear any of this from me. Was she?"

"As I understand."

"You mean, yes. There was no child?"

A new idea. "I'm sure I would have heard. No."

"I hoped there might be a son. Fourteen years and no child — I do not blame Aëlu, but it is hard."

Carefully Dolvid reminded him Saëdhu, late wife to the late *rabhsai*, was equally Saidhan's offspring, and her surviving sons were as much his grandsons as a son of Sebhal's would have been, not only the disappointing Ban-Sila, but Rodlakh and Orbanak, too. But Saidhan had wanted succession in the Colony to be assured, and his family names to be remembered in a Selvan or a Saidhsila.

But this connected with a marriage, also long barren, far in the past, Laluvoi's, to the then-Heir Valplakh, son of Thral-Sivu. Though alert for any fresh details Saidhan, then a young Household officer, might give, the main outlines of the story were very familiar to Dolvid, the territory covered by his book *The End of the House Gabh'Owan*. Laluvoi was not eighteen

when married to Valplakh who was said by some to be half-
witted, certainly with some unappealing personal habits, so
that Laluvoi for so long did not conceive was less surprising,
perhaps, than that after twelve years she did.

Formerly, with most others, Dolvid had believed this
conception had ended in a stillbirth, after Thral-Sivu and the
Heir had been lost and Laluvoi fortunately saved in the
Disaster of the Ní-Tilagh. Then, from the actual report of
Captain Saidhan he had discovered a child, a boy, born weeks
early, had lived a few feeble days at Kir.

So as to go over this, it began to appear, was why Saidhan
had detained him, as if there would not be many more chances
to amend the record. Yet there were still truths he would not
say right out. He had loved Laluvoi, yes, but then everyone
who saw her fell in love. Something akin to Rodlakh's
adoration of Aëlu, then, and Saidhan likewise had enormously
admired the older warrior his Laluvoi ended by marrying,
Banak. He spoke now about the dazzling simplicity of Banak's
warmaking, his skill with weapons, his iron will. "He had no
need to be afraid of Laluvoi."

"Who had, then?"

A laugh. "Master, if you can tell me something more to be
feared than a beautiful woman who knows your mind better
than you do, don't ask me to face it — and I have fought *jinzal*
without flinching."

"Yet Banak might never have come to the Sword, if the
Gabh'Owan Heir had managed to live."

"If it was the Gabh'Owan Heir. What would you say,
Master? After twelve years with that worm-brain?"

He said nothing, waiting. Was Saidhan giving him the
news, tame by now though treason then, that Banak and
Laluvoi had bedded together while her first husband was alive?

On the contrary, he wanted to make the point that Banak,
though he loved Laluvoi, would never have begun the war for
her sake, nor for his own. He was a loyalist, who brought
armies speeding south because of the Heir he supposed Laluvoi
was still carrying. "He could not know the child had already
lived and died when he joined the battle, and then it was too

late; the war was between him and Tobhsila for Laluvoi, as she knew it would be."

A whiff here of conspiracy, ancestral forerunner to Sebhal's plan for outflanking Rodlakh's scruples.

But Banak, according to Saidhan, might have refused Laluvoi even after they had won, if he had known she had conceived outside marriage. After all these years what he called Banak's folly continued to gnaw at him, because he otherwise admired Banak so much. "Her husband, the Heir, dribbled down his shirt, and was known to nod off in the saddle. Washed only when flies gathered too thick." Yet Banak, Saidhan said despairingly, wanted to see Laluvoi as the spiritless sort of woman who could content herself with Valplakh.

"That was never Banak's right mind, that Gabhani streak, from his grandfather. He could be shocked by nature, a man of fifty. You have Gabhanil friends, Master? Do you understand this illness of theirs?"

This, from the man considered the best Owani friend the Other Races ever had, was a tempting bypath, but Dolvid was not to be put off the scent. "The baby, the one born at Kir, must have had an Owani father."

"So far as could be told, with anything so small and malformed."

"No, I mean Laluvoi must have been sure the father was Owani." Obviously she could not know the child was not going to survive, and the intent was to pass it off as Valplakh's son; if the father's blood were anything but unmixed Owani the risk would be too great.

Saidhan did not dispute this, but Dolvid was going to have to make do with hints. He admitted to plotting with Laluvoi to deceive his admired Banak, but brushed aside the thought another man might have conspired to seize power for himself. Laluvoi, he said, knew that to rule the realm, the days of Owani exclusion were finished. Her blood, her standing with the Great Families, the love she had earned, must be united with Banak's strength and skill, the trust he was given by the Others — a *rabhsayum* of all the people.

"But you, sir, were in love with Laluvoi."

"Oh, who was I?" sidestepping the plain question again.
"We were all in love with Laluvoi. However you write it,
Master, there will be too much sanity in what you say. Greed
for power and love for a woman, one loyalty at war with
another — we were all mad, you should try to keep that in
mind."

This, quite abruptly, became the end of their talk, with
Saidhan excusing Dolvid, if he still wanted to join Rodlakh at
quayside. Tantalized, despite eagerness to see Âna, he would
now have tried once more to get answers to his questions, but
the suggestion had the flavor of a command.

Belatedly, he did his best. At the main door a respectful but
assured file-leader made him turn back for the weapon
everyone who went unescorted was now required to carry.
With the sword he had won from the *Adanum* he was armed
better than going over the wall at Drin b'Afon, and surely
better-dressed, all but boots, the same well-oiled and battered
pair. Dolvid went with very slight limp, his wound well closed.

The grounds rightward of the main gates seemed to go
down all the way to the bank of the Navu, whose glint could be
seen through trees. He took that direction, passed over a
narrow bridge, one of several by which these paths were
carried across the main road east and west, here slotted in an
abrupt cutting between thickly-grown banks. On the far side
the path meandered in deep shade under great trees, and he
saw he had made a mistake coming this way; there was no way
downstream to the estuary, and the track he was on remained
thirty or forty feet above the river, bending to the right and
becoming a pleasant, well laid-out walk, with what would have
been, less his impatience, a fine view to the wooded far bank of
the Navu, its white and brown houses tucked in among trees.

About to return the way he had come he saw not far ahead
the riverbank swung right, and the path climbed to a new level;
by following it he might be able to circle back. On an upper
path a pair of archers were keeping close watch on him. He
waved, but did not get a reply.

At the head of steps where the two paths became one he
saw a woman's figure waiting, dressed like Doleni in mourning

brown, but slenderer and more youthful, Aëlu. Approaching, Dolvid gave half-deference, and she acknowledged with grave humor. The steady eyes, however friendly, brought back Saidhan's words about beautiful women who knew one's thoughts.

She asked if she could walk with him, and he was too flattered to hurry away. Nothing was said at first; he had no need to shorten his normal stride. They came to a high point, windswept and strangely wild for its place, with a view all the way to the circling cliffs that bounded the forest-vale. Southward the forest mounted in jumbled steps, forms of high mountains indistinct in the distance. Nearer, they could look over the roofs of the port to where Navu opened into Arnan. No ship was to be seen in the river's mouth.

They spoke about the *Mankh'*, and she enjoyed his imitations of at-Aval's high-pitched squeak, the prolonged vowels in at-Keliukh's emphatic speech. She had known at-Keliukh well, since he was the one who had taught the apprentice *nôd'yanul* their smatterings of history, poetry and lore supposed to equip them for talk with men of all callings from any corner of the realm: Dolvid remembered a girl named Embhu, exquisite among horrid little castings of classical learning, leading him to malehood. It could as easily have been Aëlu, whose term at the *Mankh'* certainly overlapped his.

She turned serious. "Are we going to war?"

"If not, war is coming to us. It depends on Rodlakh."

"Poor Rodlakh."

This contained a comment on his youth. "I am glad he cannot hear you."

"Yes," she admitted, after a parleying of eyes. "But it is not real; he is in love with his own dream, Sebhal's lady, the hero's helpmeet."

"He is seeing more that is real than he did a month ago."

"So am I." She went on to complain, not bitterly, of how women often had to know men's minds better than they did themselves, to refuse what was not asked without belittling. "I am flattered, too, and that makes it all the harder; he is handsome, accomplished, his rank could hardly be higher. And he comes to my rescue, fearless, sword in hand, just as in romances. As you did — " she gave his hand a quick squeeze.

"Listen to me, is he going to need my sympathy? He will know younger women by the dozen, and still be short of thirty-five when I reach the seventh seven. But I wish there was still a *margú* here in the Colony."

An oblique tribute to Rodlakh's attractiveness, presumably, that women were worried by his virginity. Aëlu, or Sebhal's carrying-off of Aëlu, was the reason the *margú* in the Colony had been closed.

Turning to the abduction, he questioned her about the number of men who had seized her that day. Four, she said, while a fifth stood close by. Others, unseen; her guard had been shot from ambush.

"Did you ever see more than five together?"

"Not before Drin b'Afon. I was blindfolded at the boat when others came; there were eight in all. Why?"

"Something about the tale I heard, at second or third hand, which seemed over-certain about the numbers involved. More than five, but you could not know there were not — a thousand."

"I was sure we had been invaded."

She did not ask for details about his suspicions, and they began exchanging tales of the *Mankh'*, till they came near the Great House, and Aëlu composed her face earnestly, saying there were some who might not understand laughter at such a time. Before going in she waved her thanks to their pair of shadows, the archers, who grinned shyly. Yet nagged at by anxiety to see Âna, this was all unreal.

The Great House was built to a pattern common for its period, with a many-windowed front hall running the entire breadth of the building. Several doors and corridors opened off this great gallery, and at the center, directly opposite the entrance, five steps mounted to the double doors of the main inner hall. Here, passing guards in the shallow vestibule, Aëlu and Dolvid discovered a tableau. On the middle step Saidhan and Doleni were side by side, looking down to where a woman in a long travelling cloak of hyacinth blue was kneeling on the polished oak of the floor, deep auburn hair flowing to her shoulders. Off to the side Rodlakh was standing, very princely, and a few paces to the rear of the kneeling figure, another woman also in travelling clothes, clutching a well-stuffed cloth bag and apparently terrified; she was in middle life and obviously a servant.

Saidhan was saying, "...you may if you wish remain as our guest. It is quite true Aëlu is safe — see." He gestured. The kneeling woman turned her head, and was not much beyond a girl. Perhaps drawn too firm for what some would call true female beauty, her features were those of baKargul in their handsomer version, but there was also some of Petakoi's purposefulness about mouth and chin. Her mother, Petakoi; Dolvid murmured, "Kamin-Tarú." He had never seen her before, but it could only be Tovakh's daughter, Kamin-Tolagh's younger sister.

"Was there a change of plans?" perplexed. The voice was pitched low, deep in the throat for so young a girl. She seemed to realize what should be said: "Oh, but this pleases me greatly." Her pique was less studied; "Why do the message-riders of Kargul bring nothing but news gone stale?"

In some ways the artificial, puppet-play nature of the scene put Rodlakh in his element; he stepped forward to raise Kamin-Tarú with a graceful hand. "Your messengers would have done well, cousin, to have this latest news so soon. The Lady Aëlu is here without leave of her captors."

"Oh." Hardly surprising Kamin-Tarú was bewildered. Dolvid, as something sure in this mysterious event, was working out more than one way the two were cousins. For a start, their grandmothers, Laluvoi and Faëlu, were first cousins, but there was a further line through Saidhan, who had a great-grandfather, Tebadh, in common with Kamin-Tarú's grandfather.

With the question of her arrival left hanging, introductions were ridiculously ordinary. She and Aëlu made half-deference to each other, Kamin-Tarú saying how glad she was to see Sebhal's lady safe, "though it makes me look foolish."

Saidhan, some note in his voice not altogether sincere, explained Kamin-Tarú had come to offer herself as a counter-hostage for the safety of Aëlu.

"I was at Peframi when word came of your capture — " opening her wide eyes to the full. "It made me wild. That is no weapon in a war, the taking of wives. I came so an exchange could be worked out, but now it seems this was not needed."

"No less generous for that." Aëlu also adopted the high-flown style, but with a glint in the corner of an eye. "This may be herald of better days between Kamsilat and Kargul." Saidhan's face was showing flat disbelief, and yet, the girl was here, that could not be argued with.

Introduced, Dolvid made deference, then met the large eyes with green in their depths. Their sensual appraisal was a hand tugging at him. At first he thought she colored her lips, then saw she did not; her skin was pale, generous mouth bright as berries on a rowan (*karganprova*, Kargul's own tree). "Dolvidh," she said, restoring the dropped aspirate. Surely he was too experienced, too soured to be muddled and assailed by the glance of a girl? He suspected Aëlu at his elbow was amused by his fluster.

Doleni took charge, inviting Kamin-Tarú to be a guest for a while.

Kamin-Tarú thanked her. "My ship has sailed — it seems I must stay," ending on a laugh not pitched as her speech was, but clear like a small bell. She was charming, Dolvid decided.

"Is this your baggage?" Doleni asked, a steward having taken the cloth bag. Rodlakh mentioned a larger bale, left at quayside, which a porter would bring. Though Kamin-Tarú did not give an immediate impression of height, next to Doleni it could be seen she was tall, and she went with a loose-limbed, looping walk that moved the long cloak in ripples.

"Strange embassy," Saidhan arched one white eyebrow. Rodlakh said he had known at once who it must be, when he saw the hair, but she had declined to explain her errand till she was brought to the Great House. "In the midst of her chatter, I could not frame proper questions." At that Aëlu made a faint, indescribable noise back in her throat, and Rodlakh gave her a sharp glance, probably fighting back one of his blushes. "She came here, fell to her knees, and said she was our prisoner. The rest you heard and saw."

Aëlu, though it irritated Saidhan, could see no harm in taking Kamin-Tarú at her word; ungracious, she offered, to do otherwise, so long as there was the least chance she had told the exact truth. But Saidhan insisted there was something she wanted, a job she had been sent to do; the baKargul had never before objected to any weapon they could use. His fatigue was evident.

"Have you heard? word has come from Nolimas, and he will be delayed at Banakit; he was overtaken by a fresh report from the Frontier, which he wants to unravel before coming farther east. He did not send on the report, though — perhaps it is too complicated for our declining powers." Now very old, he shuffled a few steps down the hall. "When Doleni returns — oh, never mind."

Aëlu went to him, all compassion. He tried to fend her off, then allowed her slender, insistent hand under his arm. Mouth close to his tufted ear she murmured, and Dolvid heard only the last word, " ...pain?"

"No, I am not unwell. Tired, only tired — this day... "

She gave the others a look to say she could cope with this. Gently she led Saidhan to one of the doors. "Sebhal's death," Rodlakh said when they were gone, as if apologizing for Saidhan, "affects him more than he can admit."

He tried to conjecture about the puzzling actions of Nolimas, whose loyalty and conscientiousness were beyond doubt, but Kamin-Tarú's intentions were filling his mind. She seemed an unlikely spy.

The girl, not yet nineteen, had surely been away from the narrow mountain-valleys of her province even less than her brother. She might actually believe this was how people behaved — that war was carried on as in the romances, chiefly by grandiose gesture.

"She has hardly lived in isolation. Not her. They say she has bedded a hundred men."

"They would not necessarily make her an expert on plain dealing. A hundred."

He was not going to give up that number. "More, I have heard." He gave a leering chuckle that did not suit him. "That is all to the good for the next one — practice makes for better sport. So I have been told."

"Perhaps you can find out — " marvelling at the self-assurance that let Rodlakh disown the knowing laugh: at the same age Dolvid would have fought all the *Adanum* sooner than admit any deficiency of experience. "Her eye is interested."

"In me? What makes you say that?"

"I saw it — curiosity, admiration." He might have said, measurement, and inherent in Kamin-Tarú's gaze.

"What do I do with the admiration of Kamin-Tarú baKargul? The last thing I want from that house is admiration." Nonetheless, his voice trembled a little, and he wanted to hear more. "What value can be put on the regard of a girl who has found so many to admire?"

Dolvid observed, without real conviction, that experience would give Kamin-Tarú more discrimination. "I myself would be proud — "

"Would be, or will be?"

"Her choice, as I see it, would be you." This, if taken in any exclusive sense, was a flat lie, but in a good cause, from the standpoint of policy as well as Rodlakh's education. Still, praising Kamin-Tarú was causing his own interest to warm, an animal urge that could exist independently from his disappointment over Âna.

Rodlakh, harried, exhaled heavily. "We have no attention to spare for these games."

To prove it, he went on a ride westward as far as First Bridge, hoping to meet up with Nolimas, or word of him. The Great House fell quiet, and Dolvid sought out Arvat.

A small, scrubby beard was new, otherwise he was not very different from the sixteen-year-old of seven years back, small and slight with quick changes of expression. He wore a coarse robe like a scribe's, and as in his apprentice days, carried a small leather satchel on his belt. His fingers were ink-stained, as always. "Seven years, and you have changed not a bit," he lied. "I told the lords, if anyone can lead you to the *rabhsai*, Master Dolvid can — or is it to be *Bôdhrai* now?"

"It makes no difference." They spoke briefly of the intervening years, and it was new that Arvat was an uncle, Tellis having borne a son about two years ago. Arvat had always known, so he said, that Dolvid would rise again. "As

Bôdhrai, perhaps you could put in a word for me in the right quarters."

"I do not think you need my word." Arvat had his place here, and apparently much of his time was his own. "You seem to be in favor."

"Ah. I may be. I lack the evidence, Master." He rubbed his thumb across two curled fingers. "I am not like you, Master — have you asked what you will be paid as Rodlakh's *Bôdhrai*? I knew it; nothing changes you. You could have been wealthy on little gifts from the grain-magnates, instead of which you bought parchment for the *rabhsai's* work out of your own salary, isn't that so?"

"I need some parchment now — " wondering whether he could ever attain age or rank to be given some respect. Lesser counsellor to two *rabhsais*, now chief counsellor to the Heir, past the middle of his thirties, still no one hesitated to mention what a fool he was.

Arvat was handing him a dozen or so sheets of paper. "Skins will do very well."

"Paper is cheaper than skins, Master, on this side of the Arnan — someday, everywhere."

He would have to get used to a land where wood and what was made from wood were commonplace. But this paper needed a massive crushing mill and several bleachings; he told Arvat about a man from the flat country down by the Kôbh who had perfected a way of making paper from, chiefly, linen scraps and raw flax, and the result, to judge by the sample shown, was smoother, whiter and more uniform, and probably cheaper made in sufficient quantities, because it took far less work. "If I had been at the Old Bronze Residence, I would have — " Dolvid began, and broke off; he did not permit regret for what was gone. Instead, he asked about Arvat's dissatisfaction.

The young man complained he was paid less than a half-squadron leader in the Army of the West, he who drafted messages for the eyes of the *rabhsai* himself. Just because he had been given refuge here at a time of need did not mean he had to be grateful all his life for any bone he was flung; what if he wanted to get married? He had nothing to offer a wife. "I don't mind the duties as such. But old Saidhan thinks anybody should be proud to serve the Great House at Kamsilat, day and night. The army ought to pay him for the privilege."

"Is this how you talk in your meetings with officers?"

"What meetings? I may have tilted a cup, now and again, with some of the officers. My evenings are my own, not so, if there isn't some work needed? Who has been complaining about this?"

Time for his guess. "I mean, the clandestine meetings you call, to discuss what the Army might do for its own welfare, if Kamsilat were to reach an accommodation with the *rabhsai*."

Very many years ago, accused of selling scraps of used parchment from the Bronze Residence, Arvat's face, as now, went through the whole range of available responses, from denial to offhand dismissal to defiance. "The big lords make fine speeches, but it would not be their lands lost if Preference came to the Colony, would it?" He sounded a great deal like his firebrand father, who never lost an opportunity to give warnings about the motives of those in authority. Arvus, however, had remained both loyal and likable. "No one," the son resumed, "has anything to say against Saidhan *Asai*, but he's near ninety now, isn't that so? After all, Master, soldiers are simple men and give their love to any lord who carries a good lance, sometimes forgetting their own best interests."

"And you have made it your job to remind them."

"They will not need it if Preference comes. They'll have to fight for their own, no matter what the lords agree to."

"Do you suppose Rodlakh does not know? He as much as said that to the *rabhsai*'s face."

"Ah, but if Saidhan were gone, and Ban-Sila offered Rodlakh peace with overlordship of the Colony — "

"He has refused all that and more — " angered by the sly, knowing look Arvat wore. "I was beside him when he did. He could easily have crouched behind his brother and done nothing, and he risked his life for your interests. Rodlakh has lost the most of anyone, not just standing and titles, but family. If your simple-minded soldiers trust him, he has earned it."

"You are really upset," astonished by this sudden eloquence.

"I wish I could make you see what a disservice you are doing — to yourself, to begin with. You know *g'Asalladh'* has a spy at Kamsilat?"

"Several, I don't doubt."

"One in particular that is aware of what goes on in the Great House." When Dolvid added the spy had probably made feasible the abduction of Aëlu, and Arvat now was a suspect, he was stricken, and protested that Saidhan, Sebhal and Rodlakh had all commended his work. He would never do anything to harm the Colony, his home now.

That was the desired opening, and he told Arvat that sowing the seeds of dissension, when everyone's fortunes were going to depend on mutual trust, could harm the Colony beyond what any spy could do. Natural enough for officers to come to Arvat to discover what they could about the mind of the Great House, and just as natural he would bask in the feeling of importance those meetings gave him, but there was no excuse for creating uncertainty about the good intentions of Saidhan and Rodlakh, their determination to stand firm against their people's dispossession.

"Some things," he appended lightly, "are true, and have to be said, even if they cannot be spoken without sounding pompous."

"I wish I could be with you again, Master," unexpectedly. "Could I not change from Saidhan's service to Rodlakh's? You have not told him your guesses about my meetings? You are not going to tell him, now that I have stopped."

"Not if I can assure him you are not *g'Asalladh's* spy. The best way to do that would be to uncover the real spy, who must have been part of the abduction. You remember the keeper of the light-tower was ill that day?"

Arvat thought. "Yes, a bellyache, I remember. Under-Warden Vinosai brought the news to the Great House. He was keeping the light."

Dolvid asked him to find out all he could about the illness of the normal keeper, to do so discreetly, and report only to him.

"Do you suspect — "

A warning palm held up. "If I suspect anyone, it might be dangerous once he guessed. This is between the two of us."

Arvat nodded calmly, all the excitement in his eyes. As a boy routine tasks had tended to make him bored and mutinous. Given a job he could see as important, and see the end of, his energy was inexhaustible, life serene. He was the same as everyone.

Pens sharpened, ink mixed, he sat near the window in his bedroom, forearms resting on a light desk, the kind taken by the wealthy or important on journeys or campaigns. He had headed a page with *The Island*, walked about the room, looked out in the corridor to see if anyone was passing, and come back to stare out of the window at a steadily clouding day. Long ago he had found events taken part in were hardest to record, and with his lonely exile so decisively broken, he was acutely conscious of a body wanting action — of being bored by his own brooding company.

His mind, moreover, was filled with the new information Saidhan had come near giving about the War of the Widowed and Banak's accession. His history would be changed, though there were some things he would never write down. An immutable element of the tale, part indeed of folklore, was that Banak and Laluvoi fell in love when she was seventeen and he captained the escort that brought her to be married to the unthinkable Valplakh. He, Banak, waited thirteen years for her; that part might be true, but after hearing Saidhan's account it was an open question whether Laluvoi *ever* loved Banak, or with the eye of statecraft chose him as her co-ruler of the realm. That sounded chilly, and it had to be kept in mind where the hint of this view came from, Saidhan, already befriended by Banak, a young officer with the Household when Laluvoi conceived. Named to command the escort when the royal party went south, suddenly given horrors to face and terrible choices to make, he came of age in a crucial week. What most haunted Dolvid was Saidhan, besieged at Kir, fighting to keep Laluvoi out of the hands of Kargul, scheming with her, as it now appeared, to catch Banak with a benign deception — and watching his own son barely live and soon die.

Forcing himself to consider nearer questions, Dolvid was soon unsure whether he was recording new history or pondering policy. *To delay,* he scribbled, *may cause Shumat's defeat, or driven east of Pass of Perus; Bolan and Tovakh believe Army of West hamstrung.*

A sound from the doorway turned him. Kamin-Tarú said, "Oh." She was dressed in a long, rippling robe the shade of midsummer cream, throat and bosom very white by contrast. Without at once knowing why he saw she had just bathed; only afterwards could he cite misted dampness of hair worn loose, faint pink of nostril-rims.

"Pardon, *Bôdhrai* — the door to my bedroom was left open a chink, just as yours was. I can get lost very easily." She laughed and her teeth were perfect.

"Not at all, *Asayu.*" Four or five paces inside, Dolvid held his place, neither barring the way nor inviting her in.

"Can you — " She was interrupted by a woman's voice calling from farther down the corridor. "No, no, Mansi. Everything is good. Yes, do." A distant door closed. Kamin-Tarú matched Dolvid, giving no sign of advance or retreat.

On the dressing-table there was an amber flask and a pair of small glazed earthen cups, and he offered wine.

"I do not want to disturb your work, *Bôdhrai.*" She was across the threshold. "Have you been here in the Colony, Dolvidh? No one mentioned anything about you."

"I have been here — " he totted it up. "Fifteen hours, not longer."

"Was Rodlakh away, too?"

"We came this morning." He made up his mind to impress her. "From Kamanta."

"Then you had something to do with the release of Aëlu?" He had kindled a slow green flame, and her hand was trembling as she took the cup of wine. "How does a boat sail against the wind?"

The wide-eyed abruptness delighted him. Taking a clean sheet of paper (it seemed a monstrous extravagance) gave him the chance to shuffle away conjecture on the mind of Kargul, of her father. He drew diagrams to explain close-hauled sailing and the principle of short tacks, and as she bent to watch moist hair spilled over the back of his left hand. Her scent was warm yet fresh.

"You're nice. People who know things usually can't be bothered explaining them to me. You have no wife?"

"Not now." He felt the approach of touchings, but was astonished when she leant forward to bite him lightly on the muscle under the ear. Then she pulled away, and moved swiftly to shut the door. Returning, keeping contact, eyes to eyes, she sat, or coiled, onto the bed. "You only have one chair."

"You swim?" steadying himself with words.

Uncoiling she nodded, eyes brilliant. "I love swimming."

As he watched her long motions his initial idea, *cat*, had been replaced by *otter*, skin gliding over loose-knit bones, an otter not with its landbound ungainliness, but looping and gliding free in its true element. Kamin-Tarú, altogether aquatic, let her head loll back till her feet circled up, floating onto the bed. Her hair spread in sundipped ripples either side of her. "Do your eyes tell the truth?"

"I can't help my eyes."

"Good. Well, then?"

There was some early clumsiness, unfamiliarity, together with the eternal awkwardness of translating instant, unimpeded attraction into the more reluctant language of space and motion. Once they had touched, however, there was no question there would be consummation. For which Dolvid must become part of her fluent world, in which he felt like an eager dog, threshing and splashing where she was effortlessly at home. Yet he was sure she enjoyed him, and she said so, teeth together. For once he was clear this began nothing except the sport of bodies matched; taking Kamin-Tarú with unencumbered joy he could release her with no regret.

"I liked that," with deep conviction. "I do like you, Dolvidh." He was sure that would remain the proper order of priority. Riding the storm a second time he almost drowned in grateful wonder at the newness. That might have been what she was trying to express, sentimental, but Kamin-Tarú was a marvel of absolute being, seeming to combine a man's restless, fickle wish to sample everything good to see with the practical sense of a woman who elects, clear-eyed, to follow her own nature. Ten years ago, and if this bedding had come after months or days of yearning, he would have managed to find some of either terror or gloom in the wholeness of it. As was and he had become, there was nothing but delight: he could almost declare his love in gratitude for her not needing declarations of love.

When they had reached the quiet shore she pretended for a short while to be asleep, while he was busy memorizing her. Opening eyes wide she sat up and began gathering clothes, not in sudden modesty or fear of interruption, but because there were too many joys she had not tasted for any lingering over sticky heeltaps.

Leaning across him so he could tie the drawstrings of her robe she asked, "Was Sebhal not there at the rescue of his lady?"

"No." She had seen Doleni and Aëlu, both in brown robes. Sebhal's death could not be kept concealed for long. Dolvid tightened the bow, and kissed her where neck curved into shoulder. "I am glad you did, but why did you come to Kamsilat?"

She craned at him, faces so near her eyes blurred into one. "You guessed."

He had not; the question had been only to hold off hers. He supposed there was more than one way to volunteer as surrogate for Aëlu.

She sat back on her haunches. "But I have a dozen reasons. The one I gave, and that is true, taking a wife hostage is an evil way to make war, and if it is Kargul's way I am not proud of being Karguliyu. But, Dolvidh, I am so tired of being left behind at Inilun or Peframi with my grandfather, while my brother rides off to Kadon, and sports with the pretties of Six Provinces. Have you ever been to Inilun Barabhi, our great seat? But Peframi is even duller, nothing to do there, and the only ones who ever come are a few old atarlal, and they always ride on after a few days. But a raf'yalu of Peframi burnt dooms for me, and said I would have some pleasant parleyings with the chief of our enemies. Besides, I was afraid Rheduban might come back with Kamin-Tolagh still away."

"You are afraid of Rheduban?" Mention of her brother had sent Dolvid's mind off to Kadon Dinul and the same futile fears for Âna.

"You must call me Tú now. I shall call you Dol."

"As you wish, Tú-*Asayu*." He made her giggle before repeating his question about Rheduban.

"I am never afraid while Tam is home. He is not fond of anyone I go to bed with, and if I told him the truth about Rheduban, blades would rattle, that I know. But as things are, Tam could stay at Kadon while Rheduban rides back — my father, you see, wants to bring — "

"Stop, Tú." He put a hand on her lips, and she did stop, astonished. "Do not tell me anything about Tovakh's plans. As it happens, what he intends is known here, but if you say nothing it can never be said you betrayed your own kin, or we unfairly interrogated you. You understand?"

She stopped gently gnawing at his fingers. "Who does not know there is no secret safe with me."

Rheduban, she at length resumed, could not be trusted. He had her do things she would never choose. His liking was all for pain, his own, though it could as easily be hers. "When he first came to me he put a little knife in my hand, and said, plunge it into his back as he loosed the dart — kill him at that moment. He knew I could not do that." But he had kept the same small blade at bedside.

"A hard slap, or a bite that draws blood," with a practical air. "I can understand that when the storm is on, but that is not the same as brooding on pain instead of the joy, or daydreaming tortures. When Rheduban smiles he is thinking about pain."

He asked whether she had ever seen him with a copy of the *Epranda*, but could not describe what sort of book it might be. Nothing, nothing whatever could be done for Âna, and Dolvid would not let anxiety gnaw its way out of the corner of his belly where it was unsleeping.

"In Kargul, we are taught Kamsilat is full of murderers and blasphemers and cowards, but as soon as I was old enough to know Laluvoi was Saidhan's friend, I stopped listening to all I heard at Inilun. Did you know Laluvoi? A lovely old lady. So I came to the *jinzai*'s lair to find out for myself." She arched her neck. "So far I am pleased. Saidhan has been hospitable — " darting a glance to be sure Dolvid knew he was being teased.

"Who would credit his age? Old as my grandfather, who is nearly blind, and does not have strength for courteous talk."

Dolvid at the dressing table retrieved her wine, scarcely sipped at, and handed it to her. "You had not met Rodlakh before?"

"In the South, I believe, when I was just a baby. I had not heard he had grown so tall. Or his neck so stiff."

"That is just his shyness. There is a task that surely would not be too irksome for you."

"What task?"

"Rodlakh. He has not bedded a woman." Now he was there, using Kamin-Tarú to remedy Rodlakh's disabling inexperience did not seem as inspired. Extraordinary how nonsensical curiosity was bringing back Dolvid's desire, now her long legs emerged from folds of the cream-colored robe.

She made a sour mouth. "You are asking me to break the colt? Men please me, not boys." Swinging forward she put her hand alongside his neck, and lowered her head to butt him tenderly, bronze crown to his chest. He threw a loose loop of his arms around her small waist.

She declared, "Of all foolish things there are, wanting to be the first is silliest. Any sport is better with someone who has played before. Am I a joke? You are so eager to make a gift of me." Flattered, on the perilous brink of being touched, Dolvid had let amusement show.

"No, Tú, no. I laughed having heard so many men say the same." He would not tell her the last was Rodlakh, just hours ago, in echo or speculation.

A shadow of pouting stayed with Kamin-Tarú, and the problem was plain: many men must have begged her not to go on to the next bed, and he had done the opposite; she might be half-inclined to cling to Dolvid to complete the reversal. "You have given me great pleasure, and will I hope again." That was chilly, and he tried to atone by stroking her forearm.

She pulled it away, bridling. "Then he will not bed with you?"

He looked (and felt) blank. Everything was different in Kargul. She swung away to sit on the edge of the bed and begin arranging folds of her skirts with earnest absorption. She had been thinking, she said, it must be the same as with

Pivrekhan, a young soldier of the Karguli cavalry. Rheduban wanted the boy, but then he was in Tovakh's personal squadron, and Rheduban, after determining he was not *anib'anuli*, did not dare compel him.

"My father would not tolerate tampering with his soldiers, especially by Rheduban, who would never be a captain of Kargul, except for marrying Radaghi, who is as mad as he is." Kamin-Tarú took a deep breath and finished the story; Rheduban had her invite Pivrekhan to her bed, and later demanded a full account of what happened; he was amused to have Kamin-Tarú play the part of Pivrekhan while he was Kamin-Tarú.

"The rumor must be true, about his mongrel birth. He sickens me."

She might on her own have taken Pivrekhan, who she said was fresh-faced with beautiful teeth, and had already shown signs of interest (*As who didn't*, Dolvid wondered). Something was left out, perhaps that Rheduban could tell Tovakh too much about his daughter, though Tovakh could hardly be unaware of her reputation. She was genuinely unhappy. "Rheduban loses the boundary between what he does and what is done, he forgets which is himself. The pain that pleases him could as well be mine."

Dolvid gave her what he hoped was a comforting hug, and she said Pivrekhan was hurt, because she would not agree to any more of Rheduban's games. "I see now why women put up with only one man. It is hard to keep so many things in mind. What are you thinking?" Her tone changed completely for the question.

Nothing, he told her. Âna would come through, she must, unharmed. His powerlessness was exasperating. "But I am not Rheduban. If you bed Rodlakh, I do not want a report."

"What is it you want?

"Just that you introduce him to this simple and agreeable sport."

"Why? Is this part of a *Bôdhrai*'s duty?"

"Of a friend's, I hope." But policy came into it, too, because Rodlakh's inexperience muddled his perceptions.

"What if he says no? He might not need a woman, living so
long without knowing one."

"He is shy. In the South he was mostly with the elderly, and
children. All that is needed is a woman with the beauty to
defeat his shyness, and art to make him believe it all his own
doing."

"How is that possible?"

"You ask me?"

Kamin-Tarú frowned it through, hair flooding over one
shoulder. Slowly, she smiled.

At Saidhan's behest, escorted by a file of cavalry with
fluttering pennons, Dolvid and Rodlakh rode down to quayside
where a boat was waiting to take them to South Shore, the far
side of Navu mouth, where the sawmills, wood-yards and
papermakers were. Obviously, Saidhan wanted a conference
where he was sure they would not be spied on.

It had nothing to do, seemingly, with other news. Dispatch-
riders had come in from the West, and Nolimas remained
elusive; in consequence of fresh messages received he had
decided not to come on to Kamsilat, and was returning
forthwith to the Frontier.

Saidhan snorted and Rodlakh cursed. The dispatch had
been penned by an acting-captain named Wanildhai, with an
opaque style that delayed full comprehension; it appeared that
at the Frontier wagons and their escort from Shâl Mines were
several days overdue, and a relief-patrol had not been heard
from. It was a week since the Frontier fortress of Drin Navuna
had received any word from the Mines.

They were two to three dayrides beyond the Frontier.
Dolvid did not have experience to judge how grave the matter
of the belated convoy might be, whether dust-storms or other
natural causes might have delayed it. The tone of the dispatch
gave little clue, and Wanildhai added a long hearsay account
about two men 'of my own country' who had staggered in off
Landegh past half dead from exhaustion, thirst and hunger, and
confirmed rumors of *jinzal* using weapons and marching in
regular companies trained for the making of war. This was
what brought Saidhan's snort.

'My own country,' judging by the quaint form of
Wanildhai's name, must mean the South, Dolvid's birthplace,
Ninkufu — the other possibility, the Island, was hardly likely.
Why two men from Ninkufu would be wandering on the
western plateau was beyond all conjecture; Rodlakh's comment
was that men from anywhere saw strange things after a few
waterless days in those harsh lands.

The small, swift boat had Sarnak at the helm, and he gave
the knowing look of a fellow-conspirator, though he was visibly
impressed by the pomp of the company, the two fluttering
banners, Red Blossom for the Colony, the other Rodlakh's
personal standard, with a border of royal bronze, and his
device, *tovrelunai*, a bronze-beech, low and spreading, on a
white field. Since returning to Kamsilat Rodlakh had worn an
enamel token with the same device on a chain around his neck.
    Hearing he was among the climbers who led at Drin b'Afon,
Saidhan went to thank and congratulate Sarnak, while Rodlakh
kept his eyes fixed on the approaching shore. Nearest the
quays were low sheds where long-timbers were seasoned, now
largely empty for want of customers. Slightly upstream where
the hillside began to steepen there was a broad slipway down
to a basin protected by a mole, and Rodlakh said in normal
times logs were jammed into irregular rafts to be towed behind
ships to the carpenters of the Heartland and the shipbuilders,
especially of Zelkova, Kargul's great port on the Kôbh Estuary.
    But he kept his answers brief, and was abstracted. Dolvid
had to ask twice how those who normally worked with wood
were staying alive. Then he said the Colony had greatly
increased the size of its standing garrisons; most of the men
from the two large sawmills were now with the port militia.
    As regulars, they would have to be paid, and Dolvid
wondered how long the Colony, in the absence of timber trade,
the *rabhsai*'s payments for rubies, could go on employing the
needy as troops. Nearer the Frontier, many would be soldier-
farmers with the yield of smallholdings to fall back on, but
townsfolk would have to be supported out of the Great House
treasury.

"Debased coinage," he said to himself, and only realized he
had spoken aloud when Saidhan, back at his elbow, said, "Not
yet. It may come to that." Well rested, his face had the softness
of a baby's.

Once ashore, mounting the slope to the largest of the
seasoning-sheds, accepting his grandson's offer of an arm to
lean on, Saidhan felt able to share his secret: very early a boat
had arrived with the same officer of Shumat's as had been at
Kamsilat before, now all alone. Saidhan, having had enough,
as he said, of all the world knowing what was discussed at the
Great House, had sent the vessel to this north side of Navu.

"What is his errand now?" Rodlakh, trying again to shake
off preoccupation.

"We have not yet spoken, but it does not take much
guessing, does it?" drily, but with a quick, puzzled glance.

The long sheds were open at the ends to weather, but could
be closed with tarred canvas hung in rolls. In the courtyard of
the largest there was a mean little outbuilding, shelter, perhaps,
for an overseer or night-watchman. In a low-ceilinged room
with a massive oak table too large for it, the officer stood to
greet the Colony. Tall though somewhat stooped he had
changed in fourteen years, though not in the direction of
slackness; his hair had thinned back, but his aging was that of
leather; he was leaner and tougher-looking than remembered.
He had been a valued officer in the '28 campaign, a fierce but
prudent fighter till he was wounded, a patient trainer of troops
after.

"Onebhal," Dolvid said when the man had made his
deferences to the other two. "I see you have yet to begin
farming in your Bathrâd country." Onebhal's extreme
attachment to and partiality for the region of his birth had been
a standing joke of the Narn expedition; he could see no merit to
any other lands, and his eventual decision to stay "a while" in
the Northeast was a tribute to the beauty and fecundity of
Narn's small hinterland. His mixed and dairy farm, he now
said, was by the south end of Odis Combe, which Dolvid would
remember. "The Narn country has a way of claiming you, as
Captain Shumat says. He was speaking about you, sir, wishing
he could find where you were — we would have had good use
for your pen. Your pardon, *asayal* — " Onebhal turned in

apology to Rodlakh and Saidhan. "But this man saved my life at the Pass of Perus."

Dolvid had denied that too often, and could not do so again, though he felt the old shame drown him. He had not saved Onebhal's life; nearer truth, he had left him for dead at roadside, and the man owed his life to simple oversight on the part of a ruthless enemy.

"Do you come from Shumat now?" feeling Saidhan's restlessness, hoping to bridge over to the business they were there for.

"No, sir, I do not." Onebhal looked from side to side in a puzzlement itself puzzling. The man had never expressed himself with any ease, and had no doubt been given this part as experienced and trustworthy — and also as an Owani: Shumat would see the emblematic value of such a demonstration not only Others stood against Preference.

Onebhal went on to say he had not spoken face-to-face with Shumat since the beginning of winter, and had been living secretly with friends in the Heartland, waiting. Dolvid identified the peculiar quality in his voice; the tone of a man ritually repeating what he is sure is already known. But both Saidhan and Rodlakh were obviously baffled.

"Waiting for word from Sebhal," Dolvid ventured. The only answer, Sebhal acting on his own. Rodlakh made a face of thunder, but Onebhal was relieved to hear the question. He had been waiting, but then nothing came but some rumors about the *Valrabh'* with another man gaining access to the *rabhsai*, but then leaving him unharmed.

Onebhal, still assuming his hearers were merely being discreet, tried to convey his present worries by means of hints, and as Saidhan remained mystified could be seen to move towards uncharacteristic anger. "Captain Shumat, not knowing anything has gone wrong, will carry out his part, and that's suicide if he is not going to have what he was guaranteed. *Asai,* is there an alliance between us or is there not? I must have this word before it is too late."

"You mean, an alliance of intent," Saidhan said.

"I mean, the alliance, the alliance," Onebhal shouted. "The alliance that was made, the promises we kept — or was this only a way to destroy Shumat and the Army of the Northeast? Whose was this Free State from the beginning? and now — " Trembling, wanting to say more, aware he had already said too much, Onebhal after a frozen moment strode from the room. The door, a rough plank one, banged shut.

Saidhan was angry. "Is this Shumat's discipline?" icily. Rodlakh's lip-biting unhappiness, however, had a different source; this was going to be his hardest test.

To Dolvid it was plain and he said so; either Onebhal was insane, or else Shumat had received some specific assurances and perhaps even instructions from Kamsilat. Possible to imagine Shumat lending enthusiastic support to the declaring of a new state independent of Ban-Sila's rule, giving his complete loyalty to one who convinced him of its rightness, but the Shumat Dolvid had known could never invent such a plan, just as the Sebhal he had spent some days with certainly could. That much was readily allowable, and Saidhan approved, implicitly rebuking Rodlakh's over-nicety, "Certainly my son would have taken leadership of this Free State, if no other could be found."

Yes, but the Free State was only a decoy, invented to mollify Rodlakh and enlist Shumat. Trying hard to maintain some obscurity he suggested Onebhal's story in itself was evidence the expedition Sebhal had led was intended to neutralize Ban-Sila. Shumat would have to have been assured of happenings at Kadon Dinul to give his uprising a good chance of success.

Rodlakh returned to the story about persuading Ban-Sila either to change course or to leave with them, but that would have been tantamount to abdication, and who could believe Sebhal would not at least attempt getting control of the Household and then the General Cavalry, Ban-Sila gone? — trying to make that *gone* sound indefinite, but this was reconfirmation; Sebhal had meant to assassinate Ban-Sila, then defy Rodlakh not to accept the rule. Killing of the *rabhsai*, though dishonorable, would have been scarcely worse than inducing Shumat to begin an uprising on the basis of Rodlakh's fable of Ban-Sila as an innocent captive.

Saidhan was not yet willing to see how far his son had been ready to go. "My son commanded the Army of the West, yes, but he could not make any commitment for invasions of the Mainland, not without our assent, the *Valrabh*'s and mine."

Dolvid remembered the stammer that came to Sebhal now and again, in some way part of this. "It would be very natural for Sebhal to promise commitments he wished he could make; he was a long time in a long shadow, *Asai*."

"Shadow? Mine? He had feats and fame of his own, and I always thrust him forward: my reputation never kept the sun off his face. He — oh, never mind, all fathers are fools."

It saved breath and soothed tempers to talk about what Sebhal might have wished for and what Shumat's camp apparently believed, rather than what was.   On this unrecriminating basis Dolvid was soon permitted to go and find Onebhal, who was just outside, leaning on a rail meant for tethering of draft-animals. His long face was very yellow, and he looked deathly ill. He raised one dull eye. "I'll be whipped, I suppose, for my boldness. Let them, so long as I'm not delayed here. So this is the last home of justice!"

Dolvid did not think Saidhan would order the whipping of a man of Onebhal's age and distinction, but said nothing; with lords you could never be sure. Instead, he tried to convince the man Rodlakh really had not known how far Sebhal had gone in his dealings with Shumat.

Onebhal, growling, revealed the two captains had kept up a confidential correspondence, initiated by Sebhal, for well over a year; Shumat had ridden out to see Onebhal, then living in retirement, when the first of Sebhal's messages came. Shumat, "being an honorable ninny," Onebhal said, had complied with Sebhal's demand all his letters be burnt, though Onebhal had advised him to say he had done so, but keep some proof of Sebhal's part in these doings, in case it was needed.

"They were in a code, after the first, but if I had one of them here, these lords wouldn't carry on as if I made it all up."

Sebhal had begun by talking about influencing the *rabhsai* they had by a show of force; later he began to hint the brother, Rodlakh, had received the true spirit of Great Banak.

"What is the matter with that youth?" Onebhal interrupted himself. "Pardon me, sir, but everyone is sure he's strong for justice, an enemy to Preference, outlawed for it — he has got more friends than he guesses, but he has to claim them, or else they must look somewhere else for leadership. You are his *bôdhrai*, sir, can't you tell him?"

He wished he could want to. "We'll fight, I am sure. But Rodlakh would not deserve so many friends if he was just an ambitious younger brother."

"Very fine, sir, but Shumat and his men are going to be sailing to their deaths, unless we can either help them or halt them. I only hope I am in time, as it is."

"Sailing?"

Onebhal explained the plan, Sebhal's, he said, first to last. The raiding there had already been, in western Ân, was intended to accomplish what now it had, drawing large forces north and east ready for an expected thrust across the Dakbân into Dramal. Relatively small numbers left there would go over to the defensive, while most of the cavalry, commanded by Shumat, would embark at Sebira and sail along the north coast to make landing somewhere in the great bay, Klam Dramal. They would thus be in the rear of major forces of the *rabhsai*, and even if Shumat could not achieve a march on Kadon Dinul, he could take the key city of Dônshei, and in Sebhal's words, "put a stopper in the bottle," preventing those armies of Bolan and Tovakh from returning to fight at the capital.

Because to coincide with Shumat's incursion, "whatever could be spared," Sebhal's phrase, from the Army of the West, was to cross Arnan, make a landing south of Kadon Dinul, perhaps at Tan Lughsai, and secure the capital. Sebhal predicted if he could hold Kadon Dinul a week a new *rabhsayum* would be acknowledged everywhere except perhaps Kargul, which might have to be fought, but would have few open allies. A bold scheme, but it might have worked, so long as the new *rabhsai* proclaimed by the conspiracy had wide support.

But now, as Onebhal anxiously said, if the Army of the West failed to make its landing, Shumat would march on Dônshei to be caught between enemy armies. The uprising could not count on enough defections from the *rabhsai*'s forces, Onebhal believed, to offset the squadrons from Kargul. He was regretting the gamble of having come here, fretting to be back on the other side of Arnan, where he could make the attempt to turn Shumat back.

Returning to the others, asked whether he believed Onebhal's claim of collusion with Sebhal, Dolvid gave an even briefer account of Shumat's proposed landing, saying it would be insane for him to assail the Heartland unless he confidently expected allies, and the Colony was the only place to seek them.

"If we could ever get a man to come back from the Frontier," Saidhan remarked sourly, remaining exasperated by the dispatch from Banakit.

Rodlakh, for some reason, had all at once lost his doubts, asking Saidhan whether, if the rumors from the Frontier had any truth in them, it would be possible to assemble a force strong enough for a serious attempt on Kadon Dinul. Not hurrying his answer, he brought in several new considerations, most importantly that western parts of the Colony had numbers of men like younger Onebhals (though not of his race), smallholders who had served out their terms, but would return to arms again to defend their own country. If they could take over a good part of the garrison duty, and patrols on Landegh were cut to the minimum needed for security, the Colony, doing without escorts here at Kamsilat, might swiftly assemble as many as sixteen to twenty squadrons of *péfrapravádal*.

"That is most of the lances we have here."

"Yes, and what are lances here, unless there is really a great army, *jinzai* or not, waiting to be fought?" It might be Saidhan was biased in favor of the Frontier cavalry he had invented, mounted on small horses and armed principally with bows and short-weapons, but regulars here were used for escorts and kept in readiness for any big fights, doing far less of the day-to-day patrolling.

When he recommended landing in the vicinity of the *Mankh'*, both to avoid the well-guarded Estuary and to be sure of putting the *Adanum Plakh'* out of the fight, Rodlakh's resolve began to waver a little, and he muttered about the Treaty of the Wind Caves. Saidhan was incensed.

"The Treaty? Where was the Treaty when men of the *Adanum* seized Aëlu? You come from assaulting Drin b'Afon, and speak as if there is a valid Treaty?"

Dolvid, understanding how Rodlakh's instincts recoiled from these acts, nevertheless agreed. He knew another reason; Orbanak, the younger brother, now in the care of the *Mankh'*; if he could be whisked away to the Island, when Rodlakh and Shumat took Kadon Dinul *g'Asalladh'* could declare Ban-Sila deposed and Orbanak the proper successor, legally dubious but a wrangling-point for long wars.

"That's it," Saidhan exhorted. "You will have to blockade the *Mankh'* by land and sea, capture the gates of Kadon and take both Residences — I wish these withered legs of mine would let me be with you."

Rodlakh's turn for annoyance; he only wished he could go off on business as glorious and simple as Saidhan made it sound. But they would have the *Adanum* to face, not in a fight they did not understand, but the task for which they swore their Death-Oath, defending the Person of the Patriarch. Then there was the Household, where some he was sure would stay loyal to Ban-Sila; Bolan and Tovakh each with large numbers of cavalry, neither of whom would necessarily lay down arms if Ban-Sila was captured.

"If you wait till they defeat Shumat," Saidhan said, "they will feel strong enough to attack the Colony. You can never have a better opening than this, with the main forces far away from Kadon Dinul."

"Yes, but how many men are going to die before this is over? And it is a terrible thing, to ride against the lawful *rabhsai*."

Dolvid was ready for that, telling Rodlakh this might be the last chance to save his brother's life. There was that phrase of Petakoi's that had struck Âna, spoken as a slogan or watchword, *never forget how the people loved Plakhval*. Plakhval was the fourth *rabhsai* in the House Gabh'Owan.

Rodlakh bowed ironic gratitude for the information. "Plakhval the Good. Except for Plakhsila, longest-reigned of all, and like Plakhsila he succeeded young. That was when his father was forced to abdicate, Kanavakh the Horrible."

"He reigned seventy-five years. Can you cite a single thing he did to earn his name, Good?"

"Well," flippantly, "He did not cut small pieces off people till they died, or hang them up in bunches by Market Gate." Both had been acts committed by Plakhval's father, whose usual nickname was *Vakh'biSegh*, Blood-Red.

"Exactly. He was loved because he was not his father." Petakoi's intended parallel was clear; Kargul's strategy was to have all the excesses committed in Ban-Sila's name, so his deposing could seem a deliverance, with the installing, perhaps, of Orbanak, but with Tovakh as Protector. If Tovakh had the wit to begin with some token moderation of Preference, he too could achieve popularity.

"He is such a fool, my brother. He is hanging himself — and it might come to that; Tovakh might add to his popularity by hanging a new Kanavakh."

"Then that is our plan?" Saidhan took Rodlakh off guard with his apparent deference.

"You ask me? You are *Nim'* of Telnavu and Captain of the West."

"Under Ban-Sila *Rabhsai*, whose orders are that before relinquishing my titles I arrest you, and ship you to Kadon Dinul, respectfully but under heavy guard." He rose slowly, gathering all his dignity, and swung a fist across his body in the royal salute. "He is Arbhai-Navu, no other shall we obey."

Dolvid was still; this was between the old man and the young. Rodlakh squared his chin and accepted the charge, but without expression. When Saidhan sat again he was something near smirking, whether because he had cornered Rodlakh into taking responsibility, or with the simple pride of a grandfather who lives to see his favorite grandson grow up.

When Onebhal was brought back in Saidhan rebuked his bad manners and disrespect, but allowed that the temper of the times and Onebhal's devotion to Shumat were a mitigation. "But, Captain, I would not choose you for an envoy, except to the thick-skinned."

Shumat's plan, or Sebhal's for Shumat, would have to be modified, Rodlakh told him. A good plan, but the Colony could not gather its forces in time to support it.

Onebhal, with the air of the once-bitten, wanted to hear whether there was a plan the West would be a part of. Having accepted, last year, that Sebhal spoke for Rodlakh, he failed to recognize the bridge that was crossed when Rodlakh pledged his support for Shumat's uprising, and promised also the West would not enter into any negotiations with *rabhsayum* except jointly, with Shumat. Who, Onebhal said, had already given that undertaking to Sebhal.

"However, Captain," Saidhan said. "It would be good if Shumat were to work out a truce, so long as he withdrew well to the north and east, and did not agree to any disbanding of armies. If he could manage a withdrawal, obliging the main opposing forces to follow... "

"Understood, *Asai*." Onebhal was anxious to sail, but Dolvid doubted any of them really understood what they had begun. No one had asked, what then? If Ban-Sila's armies and allies were defeated in the field, what would they do with him? Force him to abdicate in Rodlakh's favor, keep him as the very puppet-*rabhsai* Rodlakh once called him? Would he be permanently confined, and if not how could he be prevented from intrigue with Kargul, with the *Atarlum*, the Great Families? By what legal right could Rodlakh dictate policy to a *rabhsai* duly invested? How, then, could this revolt stop short of Ban-Sila's death?

At the Great House they discussed complete closing of Shâl Mines so as to release not less than four squadrons of cavalry used as escort on the road there. This would be included in new and more forceful orders for Nolimas, and while those went west there was plenty to be done at Kamsilat in preparation for embarkation. All at once they were making nonsense of their cautious crossing of the Navu, speaking so openly here.

They would need an inventory, he contributed, of ships available for use and the capacity of each for men, horses and supplies. Before anyone else could speak, Dolvid nominated

three men for the job; Arvat, Sarnak and the Under-Warden, Vinosai.
    "You trust Arvat for this?" Rodlakh asked.
    "Oh yes, I trust Arvat."

    Later, after Doleni had led Saidhan away for his rest, Aëlu
fetched Kamin-Tarú, and there was soft, sad music of the
olútaloi, which both women played. Not so surprising, after all,
they had become friends, although to be with both in one room
seemed a torment for Rodlakh, till he saw there was not going
to be any catastrophe. While on the South Shore he had bought
a wonderfully delicate and detailed carved wooden flower,
something a woman, though not a woman in mourning, might
wear in her hair.

ii

Âna

Roofs began to edge up over the rise, first the Old Bronze Residence, then, rightward, the New Residence, and after that the tops of many buildings poking above the city walls. Any homecoming feeling must be nonsense and she denied it; in no sense did she belong here.

She met no difficulty at the city gate, and it might be that her way-worn, maculate appearance gave increased credibility to the provincial courier's armlet. On the dark-pink stone of the Avenue latening sun sent Âna's shadow bouncing ahead, and the Great Window burned fiercely as she came up by the Disc. Reining, she twisted in the saddle to squint against the sun and wonder where westward it might find Dolvid and Rodlakh. Sunset and daybreak had most often been her times for seeing Sebhal: full day belonged to the Colony and the Army, and night was ceded to Aëlu. Night and the moon; again she had Sebhal's dying words in her ear, the same tears pressing at her eyes. Yet she had never wanted all of Sebhal. That might be self-accusation, but it was true. She'd had a dream-Sebhal, affectionate yet invulnerable, a hero of legend such as no wife could ever sustain.

Very well, there had been a sense she wanted to say *he is only mine*, a circle of sorts she had tried to draw around him. At this moment she might be risking her life still trying; if Âna could be a warrior the policy-talk shared with Sebhal must be something real, not just pretense of a shared hearth.

Yet it came to her that in those talks she lost the Sebhal of her dreaming; he had become different in the last days before the expedition, outside her imaginings, and that change, far beyond dying words, made it hard to mourn him. Her fervor for justice had been real, and took Sebhal for champion, and the hero gradually showed he was sincere only about winning; rage over Preference, desperation of the poor, cruelties of the oppressor only counters in the game, factors to be weighed to ensure triumph, not so much for justice as for Sebhal.

Then she had done what she had condemned in other women, pretending her chosen must be just and virtuous, as if she had no fire of her own, only what was reflected. She had always despised men who wanted to treat her as precious but incapable, claiming the right to convictions of her own, sincerely held and passionately proclaimed. Truth was she wanted it all; the respect (worship, even) Aëlu was given as woman absolute, and the worth she, Âna, earned in the world, venturing where not many women of her blood had ever gone. At any moment, having won either kind of regard, she coveted the other.

Glancing up, she was almost beneath the Great Window, and that reminded her of a woman, small and fragile-seeming, who had earned every kind of admiration. Putting herself alongside Laluvoi could have made Âna laugh, but here it broke the tear in her eye; she was exasperated to feel its tickle go crawling down her cheek.

Without question she was waved in through the small gate; Kargul was ascendant, and no one would risk a challenge to the token she was wearing. Once in the courtyards where she might be recognized it was time for the armlet unostentatiously to be unclasped and slipped into her wide pocket.

In the Court of the Ram a groom came to take her horse's head. As she dismounted the stablemaster appeared out of the dim inside. Seeing who it was he made his face as fierce as he could.

"Your pardon, madam, you never told me you had in mind to keep the beast overnight and past. Who's going to be blamed if there's questions, that is what I ask."

Âna asked forgiveness, and listened penitently to a lecture about his wide responsibilities, the important lords and officials he had to provide horses for at any hour of day or night.

"It won't happen again," in a low voice, playing her winning tile: "Dolvid sends you his regards, Master Norlum." Dolvid had recognized his own former stablemaster in her description of this man.

He looked all ways, as if expecting Dolvid to appear, and was sourly sad to hear he was not back in Kadon Dinul. "Hoped, I did, that exiling of him had been gone into again. We all knew, all his people, that was never what they said. Bolan!" Norlum too was keeping his voice down, but here he spat demonstratively. He must have served under Bolan in the successful Narn Campaign, and his contempt was strange to her; all men who had ever gone warring with Sebhal adored him.

"There's few enough to equal Master Dolvid, I remember, he — " and Norlum would have told a detailed episode from the expedition, if Âna had not put a hand on his sleeve. Saying she must be gone, she gave what news of his hero she could, and put into Norlum's care the documents entrusted to her. The man promised he would deliver them in person to Faëdhal and no one else: evidently friendship with Dolvid entitled her to Norlum's complete respect, and she felt a fresh twinge of shame over her early taunts.

She remembered to hitch up her breeches and fasten her robe before taking a deep breath and stepping out across the stable court. At the head of the narrow stair two pikemen were on door duty, neither her round-faced young admirer. The taller guard, a sour-faced man in middle life, lowered his pike across her path, and demanded to see a token.

"I am of the Karguli suite."

The man continued to eye her way-soiled clothes and spattered shoes. "Orders are, if it is the Captain of the Household, he cannot pass the door unless he shows the tokens." She took this to be an overstatement.

"Send to Kamin-Tolagh baKargul; he'll — "

"The Karguli captain is still away from the Residence, madam." Love for Kargul was not on the increase, but as he spoke the soldier was staring past Âna, and ignored her renewed arguments for admission. His pike and that of his companion were sharply grounded. Behind, feet were quiet on the steps. A nasal, droning voice said at her ear, "Âna. You have been missed, sadly missed."

As she turned her eyes were level with bared front teeth. Rheduban grasped her upper arm with just the tips of strong fingers. Past guards who now made no move to challenge he propelled her inside.

Keeping the firm grip he loped through hushed corridors, and frightened her to muteness with a look when she started to stammer a mild protest. They passed a final pair of pikes where white steps led up to the doors to the Karguli Suite. "Yes, you have been missed," and it had changed from a sarcasm to a menacing question.

Not easy choosing her best story while trying to creep back into the simple soul of Âna Arlemirrs-daughter. If true Kamin-Tolagh was absent the crucial question was whether he had come back last night; if not it should be safe to let it be thought she had spent the night with him, somewhere in the field. But returning, he would have complained about her absence (not for her sake, but in the same way as he would be annoyed by not finding some desired boots, or anything else to be thrown away when tired of), and Rheduban would know. Any rational assessment of Rheduban was clouded over by the terror he carried with him like a cloak: with nothing to conceal her dread would be no less.

He relaxed his grip when they were in the common-room, and she knew on that arm there were four marks under and one on top. No one here except the serving-girl, Marra, setting out some new dishes on the long sideboard; she had a listless look for Âna. But she too feared Rheduban, making a long sidling circle to avoid passing near him.

Rheduban seized a dish heaped with sweetmeats, figs, crystallized fruits, small balls of nuts and raisins congealed with honey, tiny puffs of pastry filled with jam. Even in her near-panic she noted the dark beauty of sweet-soaked cherries, brighter luminosity of strawberries embalmed in syrup. Munching, Rheduban said quite affably, "Let us visit Kamin-Tolagh's own lair." He gave her a small push, and followed her through that door.

Not much was changed, but she despaired to see the empty place on the wall where the sword-belt would be hung. "Cousin

Tam is not here." Before opening the inner door Rheduban licked long fingers. Âna (who was sure Rheduban could not be any degree of cousin to Kamin-Tolagh) had no choice except to go inside.

"Not here, either." With finger and thumb Rheduban placed the largest of the sweets deep into his mouth. He stayed by the door while Âna, trembling, walked past the end of the bed, trying not to show fear. Possibly she could succeed with a bold line (after all, Rheduban let himself be flogged by a woman of Burantal). Breathing deep, she opened the double-door where the great mirror was. Grimy, her robe buttoned wrong, she was less beggarly than imagination had made her, dwelling on black-rimmed fingernails, lank hair.

"We shall have to be patient and wait for our Tam." Rheduban's complacency was sickening.

"I've got to have a bath." Next to the glass the robe of yellow shuzi was in its niche; she took it over her arm, and made for the door with a determined tread. "*Asai*," perfunctorily, as if leave was already granted. Breath was heavy in his nostrils. She was past him, at the door, whether she had seized the initiative or taken him entirely by surprise. But if he came after her to the bath there was nothing she could do about it.

He did not follow, not at once. Though its door was outside Kamin-Tolagh's quarters the bathroom seemed to be entirely his. No one came to interrupt Âna, who soaked away stiffness and grime, postponed apprehension, and would have lingered longer if there had been more water heating; she was chilled as she dried herself, and hunger told her it must be time for the evening meal. Perhaps Kamin-Tolagh would come back to the Residence for that; she kept listening for a tread outside that might be his. She lightly oiled her body, glad to be clean after long rides and a makeshift bed, and touched a little spikenard to her hair. Only four days ago capture by Kamin-Tolagh had been catastrophe, and now she was hoping he would come and rescue her.

Barefoot, having forgotten yellow slippers, she padded back, feeling sure Rheduban by now must have gone on to other diversions. The outer chamber remained empty, the peg on the wall without buckler. In the bedroom, against dying light a shadow, a figure in the window-seat, just as she had waited for Kamin-Tolagh when he first bedded her. The head turned sideways, and she took half a step backwards; there was the thrust of upper lip under the hard hook of nose: Rheduban.

"Âna." He made it sound as if he might have expected someone else. The bowl that had held his sweets was empty beside him on the window-seat. Very hungry, she wished she had looked to see if there were odd scraps of food with her pack.

She wanted to retreat for the common-room, but Rheduban held her with his large, light eyes. She had been stupid to come back here.

"Âna," mildly, "Who said you could leave the Residence?"

"Leave the Residence, Lord? I've been for a bath is all, sir."

The eyes narrowed. "Are you stupid, are you really so stupid?" He was asking himself as much as her.

He stood. "Did we not meet outside, coming from the Court of the Ram? Before we came here?"

"If that's what that place is called, sir." He was nearer.

"Well? Did I not see you yesterday, and was your dress not the same as today, only less travel-stained?"

"Yes, Lord." She became cunning. "Yesterday, Lord, the Lord *Rabhsai* spoke to me, and he gave me his gracious leave."

"And after that, you went out from the Residence, and you have only just come back."

"After the Lord *Rabhsai* gave leave."

"You were gone overnight. Who told you you could do this?"

"The Lord *Rabhsai*, Ban-Sila *De'*. He gave me his gracious leave, Lord."

Rheduban came a step nearer. "Are you telling me Ban-Sila, *Ban-Sila* gave you leave to stay away nearly two whole days?"

"His gracious leave, Lord." Wasted ingenuity, if Rheduban did not care whether or not she believed this preposterous excuse.

"Where did you go, Âna?"

"Tam, I mean Lord Kamin-Tolagh, he went off with his soldiers. He said he would see me soon, Lord."

"I asked where you went. Do you mean, you went after him? And did you spend the night under the stars, under the Star of Kargul?"

Now she had to be careful. She did not dare say yes. "I looked for Tam."

"And spent the night, where?" On behalf of the simple Âna Arlemirrs-daughter she represented, she felt a curdling disgust for one of his standing who would enjoy bullying a girl of no importance; he could not possibly suppose her whereabouts affected Kargul in any larger sense. He was leaning forward, and it was plain the object of this detailed interrogation was that it excited him, as talk about mating might most men.

She said, "I rode too far, Lord, and was caught by the curfew and the night."

"Is that a tale to satisfy your Tam? You rode too far where? in what direction? What are you going to tell him when he asks how you passed the city gates, and avoided all the patrols?"

"Tam won't be upset. Tam likes me."

Rheduban laughed. "Âna, there is greater charm in your eye than your tongue, but you are not the only kitten in the litter. You rode southward, then?"

Startled, her knees weakened, but she remembered Rheduban who evidently enjoyed showing off his knowledge of the province, had asked what direction Arlemirrstead was. Now he tried to find exactly where in relation to Tâl Abfekh and Burantal, a road he often rode. She invented a trail leading off south and west some miles beyond Tâl Abfekh.

"Then you spent the night in the bosom of your family. What was it you took them? Food? Clothes?"

"Lord, I don't steal, not anything. I did not go to Arlemirrstead."

Relishing his game Rheduban agreed she could never pass the post at Tâl Abfekh without tokens to show. He brought up her supposed friend in the cavalry, and whether he could be here in Kadon Dinul, since she also lacked tokens for passing the city

gates. "Are you sure you rode southward?" but he had no real
curiosity, interested only in her discomfiture.

At last he studied the ceiling, and scratched his body where
the ribs would end. "Can you guess what your Tam told me? He
said you would surely need to be punished. Do you know what
he meant by that?" The voice had a new quality, soft and sly,
with a tone she knew from somewhere.

"Does your father beat you, Âna?"

"No, Lord."

"Did he, when you were smaller?"

"No, Lord." True, her mother had seen to that.

"Never? You mean you never disobeyed him, so that he
thrashed you?"

She said nothing, but took note of the odd phrasing, which let
the question be heard in two ways, one completely mad, but sane
enough in the twilit world of the *Epranda*, where pain was
sought for its pleasure.

"Your skin is smooth." He reached out and took one of her
wrists, not clamping down, though she already knew how strong
those long fingers were. "Can you guess what I am going to do?"

Silent, she had identified the new note in his voice. When
she was — oh, no older than twelve — there had been a man,
Udanak, on the farm, a distant semi-cousin, simple-minded,
trusted with only the most brainless jobs. Once Udanak had
stood in the doorway to the barn, preventing her leaving. He
never touched her, but asked her about all the things men and
women did together. Till now she had completely forgotten that
terror, and now could smell damp earth again, musty feed-sacks,
see the sunlight that meant safety on the far side of her
questioner, the single narrow ray coming through a chink to
strike near the man's gleaming eye, as the wet croon went on,
"Have they told you all about swallowing manhood, then?
Would you — " and in the end she dodged past him and fled, and
never told anyone about it, but made sure she was never alone
with Udanak again. She could see no sun and open air on the
other side of Rheduban.

In a blandishing way he told her there was no need for Tam
to question her about where or how she spent the night; he,
Rheduban, could say he had given her pass-guard tokens because
she was worried with her family not knowing where she was,
that she had been to Arlemirrstead and back —

"My mother, Lord, must be very fearful of what has become
of me. I hope I can go home soon."

The grip tightened on her wrist, and with as much thin calm
as he could command he tried to make her understand the favor
he was doing, forestalling Tam's anger. "Is that what I should
say?"

"Kamin-Tolagh *Asai* has been only kind to me." The answer
did not please Rheduban, but she was determined not to give him
his bargain, whatever her side was to be. Grotesque from the
start; she had never seen Kamin-Tolagh angry but could not be
more afraid of that than she was of soft-voiced Rheduban. She
was not sure acceptance or refusal made any difference, but as
Âna Arlemirrs-daughter she must continue to be obtuse about
what the real Âna had already rejected.

She was bad, he said, to repay kindness with deception, bad,
and should be punished. His eyes went to the bed where the
curtains were drawn back, and she realized he must have left and
come back while she was in the bath; the wide thong coiled on
the covers had not been there before. "A beating is what you
should have, my lovely."

She was being asked to concur. Not much acting was needed
to let her legs go boneless. She sagged to the floor, whimpering
a *No, Lord*.

"Oh, yes, pretty girl, you must be punished." He ceased
trying to haul her up, and instead pressed down iron-wristed,
bending over her to explain. He would tie her to the bed-pillar,
and she need not be afraid, he would not tie too tightly. Then she
would be beaten. He was tugging slightly again, as if expecting
meek compliance. "Come. You must take off your robe."

At a guess, the simple Âna would obey from habit, or
because she feared the consequences of refusal worse than the
beating. There were tales of Rheduban having women flogged

to death, and it could be that if she submitted to this ritual she might escape worse. No, and again, no, she would not collaborate in his game, and whether or not she was playing her part well no longer counted. Not if he had any imaginable right to punish her, surely not for his unhealthy pleasure was she going to be his partner; pain might be endured, but Rheduban wanted to use her, taste her — it was like his gorging of sweetmeats.

She was chilled to be asking if this was at an extreme what men in general called affection; Rheduban's voice had certainly become caressing, and it was his own lush appetites he was fondling.

He told her to be wise, and admit she deserved punishment; she became so much dead weight, and he was crazily averse to using violence, because she must acknowledge he was dispensing justice. Not letting go of her wrist he put the other hand at her armpit, and as if helping her rather than dragging her up, his strength raised her some way before he let her sink back.

Into her mind came a picture of her brother, years ago, tugging insistently at their mother's hand, trying to drag her off to see something she was too busy for, and here the same imploring turned into the same spasm of fury, sudden as a hiccup, twisting the face of Rheduban. Too enraged for phrases he muttered thickly of tearing and chopping, and the moisture of his vehemence dotted her face.

Once she had asked Sebhal about courage in battle, and he admitted that leading troops meant making use of shames men would die sooner than endure. Laughing, she said she would never be a soldier, and pitied men whose need for the esteem of comrades, commanders, tribes, families (it must often begin with fathers) lost them the power of choosing to live. And now she had small doubt Rheduban would kill her; one hand was pushing her chin up and back, while the other groped for the hilt of the little dagger he wore at his belt.

The finding and drawing of it calmed him somewhat, if calm was the word for his purring luxury. "The last throat I cut, the blood spurted in my mouth. Have you ever cut a throat, Âna?"

"No, Lord, no." The tip of the dagger pricked below her ear, as Rheduban shifted grips to hold her still. "Wait — "

Her mind found its way through this. Not numbed, it decided this could not be happening to her, or at least not now. It belonged far off, either long ago or yet to come, and in a very distant place. She could think with great speed and clarity, while watching herself. "Wait," she pleaded, distressed there was no interruption, Kamin-Tolagh did not come. But Rheduban must in some way know that, or surely he would not dare what he was doing.

For intolerable seconds the wide eyes glared into hers. He blinked slowly, releasing pressure on her, stepping back to contemplate her huddled body.

He inhaled deeply. "You say, *Lord Rheduban, I must be punished.*"

"Lord Rheduban, I must be punished."

"Good. Say, *My smooth body must be beaten well.*"

She repeated it in a toneless voice, words too dead for any meaning. Ignoring a proffered hand she used the edge of the bed to haul herself up, feeling how easily she could spit in the ugly face, and how certain that was to be fatal. He was trying to overmaster her with his eyes, and it took all her strength to look back without flinching. Sober, he would have known this was not possible in Âna Arlemirrs-daughter, but he was drunk on his own poison.

He told her to strip her robe, having taken the waist-tie from her. She loosened the robe and let it fall, level-eyed. He bound her wrists with the tie of yellow shuzi while she fought off faintness, insisting she would be victor whatever pain he inflicted; contempt could be used to drive away the terror of his personality, leaving only the practical fear of his bullying strength. After tying her to the bed-pillar, he reached for the wide leather thong, and she closed her eyes, clamping her teeth down on memory of his craven retreat from the Market Square at Burantal.

What followed the beating and his untying of her was the worst, and when he had discharged she was impatient with this vileness, seeing no reason why it should go on existing. He caught the hatred in her eye, and laughed. "She would kill me, Âna would kill me, given the chance. Is it that I teach you what you would much rather not know — a relish for pain?"

He rolled away to retrieve the little dagger, dropped next to the bed. A long thumb tested the blade, and he put the haft firmly in her right hand, wrapping the fingers with his left. Her wealed shoulders propped at bed-end, she gripped the knife, and Rheduban bent to nuzzle her body, deliberately exposing the wide, hard-muscled back, itself marked by old beatings. The knife sat lightly in her hand, and the keen steel would slide into even that sinewy flesh as into a ripe pear. She could come very near persuading herself it would be mercy, freeing this creature from the disease of its needs: he had dragged her into a gruesome world where there was no pity, and if she could could recall exactly the face of the dying Sebhal she might be able to stab. In her inaction were also practical considerations; if she failed to kill him the attempt would be her certain death, and if she succeeded she would have a dead Rheduban to explain, stretched across Kamin-Tolagh's bed.

Live, Rheduban raised his head slowly. "What should we do with you women, except flog you daily, night and morning? What good is it for a man to be stronger if he is made to fear using that strength? and when we say, *kill*, you will not — if you do not defeat us with your whimpering you will do it with refusing to weep. We shall have to kill you all, or keep you cowed with whips, or else end as your toys, when we have made the world safe for you." He took away the knife. "You understand none of this, do you."

He took up the leather thong again, but only to wind it. Reaching to grasp a shoulder, he turned her, and murmured a connoisseur's appreciation of his work; she feared sickly that his desire would rekindle, and could not see herself enduring another violation. But he stood again, telling her she would heal, he had drawn no blood, and it was only what her bright skin had earned, that it would have given his wife Radaghi great pleasure to witness, though she would not have wanted him to desist so soon.

Reclothed, sliding the knife back in its sheath he advised her, "You must not tell Kamin-Tolagh I beat you, otherwise I shall tell him where and how you spent the night. If he sees your welts, tell him your father whipped you when you came home; I shall say I gave tokens for that journey. Why will you not weep, Âna?" Before she could pull back he reached out to touch beneath an eye, confirming dryness.

He gave a little humming sound, and promised to have food sent for her, even if she was not hungry. "I am, now, I have a tremendous appetite. Another time, you can take the thong in those soft little hands, and see if you can make me cry for mercy."

When he had gone out she tried to wait to be sure he was not coming back, but could not hold back tears any longer, though the profound weeping would never reach the hurt in her chest or stomach. In a while Marra brought some food, and then Âna was bitterly sick.

When retching stopped she left the corner where the night-jar was, weeping again at what a sight she must make, firmly decreeing she had to stop this. She went for another bath, and needed long soaking, a lot of scrubbing to make some start on feeling clean. Her back was still throbbing when she came shivering back to the bed-room, but she had stopped smelling Rheduban on her body.

Someone had drawn the yellow bed-curtains and covered all but one of the *ôdul* lighting the room. On the near side of the bed she parted the curtains with care. The sleeper stirred but did not wake; Kamin-Tolagh, fully-clothed except for boots, his sleep that of utter exhaustion. She made her way round to the farther side.

She lay on her side next to the still form, cheek on the back of her hand. Coming back here had been senseless; not likely she would learn much more of any use, especially the things Dolvid had asked about: how was she going to uncover explanations for the Patriarch's great confidence? Unfair to give her such a task — she was washed over by a mixture of resentment and self-pity, as at Tan Lughsai, worse, and with good reason. As there, she had to remind herself sternly this was her task. That did not lessen pain or humiliation, nor improve her chances of surviving this second venture among enemies. The risks had been there when she elected to come back — was it that with Sebhal dead, the others gone to assail impregnable Drin b'Afon, it had seemed proper not to care about her own life? If so Rheduban had worked a harsh cure; he had shown her she wanted to go on living.

Rheduban had implied a lie; Kamin-Tolagh had not been back in her absence. Waking her with fondlings, asking how she had kept herself amused, he grasped her, heard her breath go jabbing in, saw and felt her wince.

He made her turn, and demanded, "Who has beaten you?" fingers lightly touching her back. She told him the story concocted by Rheduban; if she told the truth Kamin-Tolagh might fight him, and there was no certainty how that might turn out; she did not want Kamin-Tolagh killed or seriously injured, not yet, while he was her best protection against worse.

For an instant it seemed he was going to give sympathy, and then he summoned his swagger and gave a superior laugh. "Did I not warn you? I said you would be beaten unless you came home with gold. Though truth told, I think your father is glad of any excuse for baring your body, yes, Âna?"

"He was very angry with me, Tam."

"Oh, yes, I can see that." Tam was bright-eyed, hands unresting. Only to increase his own pleasure, true, but he was wonderfully adept at pleasing; there were ferocities and languors to make Dolvid's advice to her seem both cogent and very distant; here was sensation apart from past and future, consuming.

With a noise more groan than sigh Kamin-Tolagh rolled on his back and studied the shimmering yellow roof. "Rheduban," frowning, "why would he token your journey?"

"I said I wanted to see my mother." She saw no alternative to maintaining this story, which a chance word from one of the guard-posts she had passed could upset in a moment.

"He asked nothing in return?" Kamin-Tolagh shook his head. "One day I am going to have to kill Rheduban. My father should never have allowed it, his marriage. Filuvakh is a weakling — that is the lady's father, but it was my father's place to stop it. A man of Kargul — he is not even *Lekh'Owani* — it is said his mother had blood from the tribal west, where they eat meat raw, and make little cuts to prevent a woman's pleasure — you know about that?" Filled with words this morning Kamin-Tolagh went on about Rheduban, and she learned he had a younger brother, or half-brother, his own mother having died years ago, the great love of his father's youth. Propped on his side, stroking her dark hair, looking into her dark eyes, he said, "It is beyond me how any true man of Kargul and Son of Yoëlladhu could ally himself to a mongrel-woman."

Only in comparison with Rheduban had Kamin-Tolagh been a welcome sight; she was not going to muddle relief with liking again, or mistake less-despicable for good.

"A prophecy at Rheduban's birth," with a sneering face, "said he would come to the Chair of State in the end. My sister believes in these foretellings."

The distance she achieved took her through days and nights that followed. He was inattentive, not as that charge might conventionally be made by a woman — if she had wanted tribute in gifts and compliments, she would not have expected the blank dullness of Âna Arlemirrs-daughter to call it forth. Rather, this man was deprived of the faculty for experiencing a woman, any woman, she surmised. For a while they hung like trophies from his saddle-bow, and made no real difference to his life. For him they were not very distinct, one from another, except in superficial details he recalled; hair color, stature, whether thick or thin. A paradox his need for change came from an incapacity for perceiving it.

With his father gone he was sterner about duties, sharing captaincy of the Household with Kizhunai, still just a name; the only senior Household officer who visited the Karguli suite was a *kímukan* named Zhinladh, fat, with an overbearing manner and unending sympathy with Kargul's wrongs, as expressed by Petakoi, the necessary dominance of the Owanil and ordained servitude of Others.

She heard talk of reports from captains in the field; Tovakh wrote from Dônshei he and Bolan were moving north with the main cavalry, having already sent ahead reinforcements for the fortified places of Dramal. This might have been news worth carrying to Kamsilat if it could be done instantly, but was not worth her risking escape for, stale before it could be delivered. She remained docile and watchful, nursing fierce loathing for Rheduban, her teeth on edge when, in the common-room, he smirked as if he owned a part of her she could never retrieve.

Seemingly, then, her tenure would end tamely with Kamin-Tolagh sending her home. It was moving that way; he was nearly ready to be rid of her. The second day after her return he came back dishevelled from leading a patrol through the city , pleased with himself, humming his hunting-song, a scent clinging to him that was not what Âna had been using, nor any of the essences kept by the bath. Nothing in all this was as absurd as her faint feeling of a hurt she could not deny, or that Kamin-Tolagh later was more than normally solicitous of her pleasure. These were signs she should not want, especially that he was hesitating over moving on to newer delights. Next morning he was bad-tempered, making her bear the irritation he felt about staying at the Residence for an expected dispatch from his father. When it arrived in late afternoon it annoyed him more by containing almost no news; armies were camped on the heathlands that gave Dramal its name, and there was no fresh word of the rebels.

But she enjoyed the next news to arrive with at-Zhâlai, causing Petakoi's ripe voice to rise extraordinarily high as she demanded details and confirmations. "These blasphemers from the Colony!" she exclaimed, and then the discussion, in the Owanilú, became confidential. Âna, sitting at the firepit and playing with the kitten, heard enough to make her rejoice; Aëlu was safe and the *Atarlum* believed Rodlakh had been the rescuer, both had successfully escaped from the Island. No mention of Dolvid, but that should be all right; his death or capture would surely have been commented-on, and Âna was sure her straining ears could not have missed the name. Petakoi shook her head at impiety, while her son tried to be thunder-browed over a deed he plainly envied, with an outcome (she conjectured) he did not altogether deplore. At-Zhâlai was trying to explain *g'Asalladh*'s concern over the impossible promptness of the rescue.

Made obtuse by wonder, Kamin-Tolagh missed the point entirely, saying it would not be so hard to guess Drin b'Afon, knowing the *Atarlum* had Aëlu. "But to dare it," back over his shoulder, making for the table where he could write. "I want Rodlakh, sword to sword."

At-Zhâlai kept ineffectually trying; Rodlakh, they knew, was on this side of Arnan not three days before assaulting Drin b'Afon, which left no time for him to return to Kamsilat for the news about Aëlu, obviously his reason for going to the Island.

"As I always maintained, they did not drown, and there must have been a vessel from Kamsilat to meet them."

Smug At-Zhâlai vowed there would not be again; *g'Asalladh'* had ordered closing of the Strait, effectively cutting off Colony from Mainland. He had the means to accomplish it, a move long in contemplation.

Kamin-Tolagh, beginning a letter to his father in the field, wanted to know how soon this could be done, a crucial question, since release of Aëlu meant the Colony would no longer be powerless to act. If, before the Strait could be closed, the Army of the West managed to slip through, added troops would be needed for defense of Heartland and *rabhsai*. At-Zhâlai said not more than a week for the closing; in a large fleet some vessels might get past, but only a few. He would so advise the *rabhsai*.

"Does he know Aëlu has been released?"

At-Zhâlai turned up his palms. "I do not suppose, *Asai*, he ever knew of the abduction. Some things the *rabhsai* is spared." This brought a bark of a laugh from Rheduban, who had just come in.

"If he can be made to understand the situation has changed, he will let Kargul bring its squadrons from the south, to aid in defense of Kadon Dinul."

"The *rabhsayum*," Rheduban droned, "has not yet called on plenty of its own squadrons, the General Cavalry."

"Scattered among a dozen different garrisons. Not to be relied on in a fight with the Army of the West. Our squadrons are assembled, ready to ride, and loyal." Kamin-Tolagh thumped his writing-table with a fist. "If only Rodlakh would come, leading his farmer-army, I would show him lance-work. What was his chief weapon at Drin b'Afon?"

His mother, drily, "Whatever is the opposite of rashness, I suspect."

Yet in his father's absence Kamin-Tolagh commanded for Kargul, and Rheduban relished drawing attention to his inexperience. At last he asked Petakoi what would happen if, instead of Kadon Dinul, the Army of the West took this opportunity to assail Kargul? "Can the old man and the girl defend Inilun Barabhi?"

Kamin-Tolagh answered it would be nonsense for Sebhal to waste men in an attack in Kargul, but he would have Kamin-Tarú brought to Kadon Dinul when the Kargul' squadrons rode.

Petakoi said, straight-mouthed, "I do not want Kamin-Tarú here."

Kamin-Tolagh had started writing again. "You have made that more than plain. But if I am rash, what word do you have for Tú? I'll send for her."

"You need your father's approval."

"Oh, *Asayu*," Rheduban mocked. "Would you have them go sword to sword, the vanquisher of Drin b'Afon and the Star of Kargul without sight of a valued prize?"

Petakoi's face angered. Before she could answer, Kamin-Tolagh, staying remarkably self-possessed, said, "The prize, Captain, will be name. Rodlakh, you say, tamed Drin b'Afon — what about the conqueror's conqueror, then?" Unable to sit still, he went striding, hands feeling the grip of imagined weapons.

"If he comes," Rheduban said.

"How could he be left behind, if the West comes?"

"The West is not without its troubles at the Frontier." At-Zhâlai spoke so quietly he was paid no attention.

"The day we meet," through clenched teeth. "I hope Rodlakh has a good mount under him." Breath working in his nostrils he remembered Âna's existence, and came towards her, staring hard, with the look a cat sometimes has, as if instantly reverting to wildness.

"Go to my bedroom," with tremulous urgency. "Get yourself ready, I shall be there soon. Put on the rose-colored robe, and do not bind your hair." As she obediently stood up he brushed her arm with draped fingers. Rheduban was amused.

Perhaps the news about closing of the Strait was cue for an attempt at escape. Important, because as far as she knew there was no other safe sea-route from Kamsilat to the Mainland: the northern passage was narrow and easily defended, and southward from there to the tip of the Island was the Shoals, a terror to navigation.

With Sebhal gone and Rodlakh reluctant, she was not certain now that the Army of the West meant to come like a thunderbolt on Kadon Dinul; yet if the invasion was delayed much longer the chance might be lost.

She was comfortless between sleep and waking, irritated by bedclothes, the knees of Kamin-Tolagh, the noises his throat made when he dozed. She had hated the sour tone of the duelling with Rheduban, harsh and raw, not the ordinary buffeting byplay among men.

Nothing was in isolation, and she had been an inept dancer out of step with the music, so that Kamin-Tolagh asked what the matter was. She was preoccupied, escape filling her with despair over all the obstacles, and that was all one with the tenderness of her nipples, slight puffiness of her belly only she would notice, the sensation from toes to scalp to fingertips that she was holding down a scream. It would all be better tomorrow, and then Kamin-Tolagh would not want her in his bed: she was just as sure Rheduban would, and that was also part of the tense muddle, that she would be revolted by a man who, ignoring superstition, could, if she permitted him, give her exquisite pleasure. But he was most to be feared, and was it truly ignoring superstition? Rheduban went with deformed beliefs of his own, and the very fact that Gabhani and Owani were (for once) alike in banning coupling while moonsblood lasted would be Rheduban's chief reason for wanting it; there was no freedom in being bound to defy rules.

Soon she must ask Marra for wadding. Often that was just the sort of small, definite decision she could sleep on, but now she continued to stare at the yellow ceiling to the canopy. Perhaps Kamin-Tolagh would give her safe-conduct for her supposed home; with that she could reach Burantal, and Sett. Apparently by prearrangement Marra came servilely to rouse Kamin-Tolagh, and after he had gone, Âna slipped sideways into a churned sleep filled with monstrous dreaming.

Weather was no solace. As far as Âna could tell, shut up in the Residence, there had been some springlike days; she had seen quick, sparkling showers spinning in soft sunlight, and the breezes would be fresh and gentle. But now there came an unnatural warm, sleeper waking in disbelief amid the stickiness of high summer. Morning began with a hazed brightness that dimmed steadily to a sullen overcast; there could not be much wind, and the atmosphere was thick. By noon there were distant rumors of thunder, not from any direction that could be identified. Early, a wrangle had come between the two sisters, Finú and Radaghi, which Rheduban had tried to stop with some bad-tempered threats that soon had both women, wife and wife's elder sister, ranged against him. The comings and goings of Kamin-Tolagh were with the air of absorbed importance, and when in passing he tried to end the quarrel it flared up again; it had all begun with lost comb. Later, when Kamin-Tolagh came to bring Rheduban to a meeting of officers, Petakoi, also vile-tempered, recommended and all-but dictated an airing for the women, a spell in the Residence grounds.

Âna was not included, and so, other than the servant, Marra, was only one there when Kamin-Tolagh received a dispatch from his home province, just come by fast-messenger. Sounding a great deal like his father he let out a string of curses, while Âna, frightened, became inconspicuous. It did not matter; he had forgotten she existed, and after sitting to scribble a message decided to go out again with his own squadron. He took his cloak of shuzi oiled against rain, and left in a grim mood, with no word for Âna. Her sole clue to his anger was when Petakoi came back and read the same dispatch; her mouth set in a hard line and when Finú asked vaguely what the matter was, said only, "Kamin-Tarú, as always."

Like a toothache the day nagged on. Longing for Kamin-Tolagh's dismissal of her, Âna did not feel release of tight-strung nerves that usually came with moonsblood. For a while she was able to wander a little through the Residence, thinking about slipping out unnoticed, but while she could walk corridors unchallenged the outer doors were not to be passed without credentials. Back at the Suite she dozed a little, and after bathing her face in cold water went back to the common-room for some doggedly-swallowed food, while servants and the baKargul came, stayed and went as if in a dream, or as if deep under warm, brown water, mutters of thunder outside answered by discourtesies within. Kamin-Tolagh did not return, and late in the day with flutters of far lightning seen against a greenish sky, she slept again.

But for that same muffled drumming everything was silent when she woke. It seemed very late to her; the window was black. She was not sure whether the storm had passed while she was asleep, or was still gathering; outside the night could not be pierced. The wide bed was empty of Kamin-Tolagh, and she longed for sound of any human voice, feeling a thin, lost sadness. In the outer room, rummaging in the closet, she found a few pieces of kiln-bread and a couple of dried apricots which she pulled out of their embrace so they could be eaten separately. At the bottom of a pocket she scrabbled together a few of Dolvid's sunflower seeds, bringing a brief, wan smile while leaving her hungry. Straight from the flask on the desk-top she swigged some thin, sour wine, and could not stop thinking about the sideboard in the common-room, with its cold meats, fresh bread, compotes of steamed fruit.

That linked to another thought. It must be past midnight, and she wondered again whether she could slip out of the Residence by one of the doors that should be open. She still had the armlet of a Karguli messenger, and had done nothing to lessen its power, though she could not help thinking it would be straining her luck to use it again.

Sitting on the floor she stuffed her pack with all her campaign clothes and put the blue enamel clasp on top, then carried it to a spot just inside the door into the passageway. She opened the door and listened. All the baKargul ought to be sleeping, and the only one likely to come in would be Kamin-Tolagh. Slippered, she crept to the common-room door, which was open a crack. It creaked as she tried to open it noiselessly. The large room seemed deserted in soft *ôthu*-light, but over at the firepit, where there was no fire, a too-familiar, elongated face turned to see her.

"Well, now. Here is little Âna." Rheduban. Not able to retreat she held her ground just inside the door while Rheduban stood. He addressed someone else, farther down in the stepped pit. "You remember, the weekwife of Kamin-Tolagh."

Once again Rheduban's companion was the *rabhsai*, Ban-Sila, a perception which competed for her attention with Rheduban's word for her. That's what she was, a weekwife.

Rheduban was again in his toying mood. "Come, girl, show your respect. You yearn for company this hot night?" He stooped, spoke a few quiet words in the Owanilú about the absence of Kamin-Tolagh, and stepping up to floor level, strode to her. She refused to show how she shrank from his touch; he took her upper arm and ushered her to where she could make her deference to a scarcely interested Ban-Sila.

"Ah, now — Âna's hungry," (she must have let her eyes stray to the sideboard). In a caricature of courtesy he took up a platter and with deft movements filled it for her, including a lavish portion of Island smoked eel, about a month's rent, she calculated, for a poor tenant in the Nambalus country. Rheduban conducted her to the firepit, sat her down, handed her the heaped platter and went back for a fork. Board, standards and the tile-bag for a game of *zhabhu* were set out next to the dull-eyed *rabhsai*, and there were several open wine-flasks.

"This is a very hard game, Âna. Have you seen *zhabhu* played?" In the light of a single *ôdu* set on a lower step Rheduban's features were more grotesque than ever, his eyes full of danger. She was reminded of her first sight of him, racing for the *pefrai* to make his escape; he had on the same loose outshirt of purple shuzi.

"Lord, I have heard of *zhabhu*," and that was exquisitely funny to Rheduban. Having enjoyed it, he told her the tiles for this set, the *rabhsai*'s, were ivory, taken from teeth of an enormous animal found in far southern lands. In the Owanilú he confided to Ban-Sila, "A little farm-animal of nearer southern lands, but she gives some sport." Ban-Sila smiled mechanically.

They resumed play, and she followed better than they would have imagined; it also provided a chance to have some food. She would not have chosen the gathering, but it came to her that if her parents could know where and in whose company she was eating her costly meal, they would be most impressed. Next to the glittering notions of Residence and *rabhsayum* the reality was pathetically shabby. When there was talk about the northern revolt Ban-Sila's understanding of the reasons for it was vague as his knowledge of the lands, or dispositions of the contending armies. His only certain idea was the uprising must be crushed and its leaders punished, all of whom must die. He contemplated execution of all participants at or above the level of half-squadron leader. Rheduban hoped Shumat might be taken alive, and that Ban-Sila would consult him for ways the ringleader's death might be prolonged; mention of castration brought a small giggle from the *rabhsai*. That encouraged Rheduban to tell about a servant who stole some household articles and refused to say where he had hidden them; the story was so revolting it nearly made her give away understanding of the Owanilú, which, except when Rheduban had something he wanted her to hear, they continued to use, if not always correctly.

Ban-Sila wagged a forefinger to tell him even in Kargul such mutilations were unlawful, and Rheduban said, "The man was only some mongrel refuse." Ban-Sila gave an offhand nod, and that seemed strange when both of them (after Kamin-Tolagh's account of Rheduban's parentage) were, by their own standards, mongrel.

"How many troops will the *rabhsai* send to Kargul to keep this law?"

"Shumat first — one rebel at a time, Rheduban."

"Ha. Shumat would be strolling up the Avenue of Treaties if you had no *péfrapravádal* of Kargul to protect you. You to play."

Neither man was playing well, each intent on thwarting the other instead of enclosing territory that could quite easily be captured. While you could always use a turn for trying to dismantle an opponent's gains, this was seldom done until late in the game when a player faced imminent defeat. This game was coming down to where neither could win outright, although many tiles were left undrawn. When they counted *sibhul*, captured war-standards, the win went narrowly to Rheduban. Ban-Sila gulped down wine, and cleared the board to set a fresh game, with petulant movements of someone who did not enjoy losing. Outside from time to time pale lightning flickered; there was no rain and the night seemed swollen, a boil ripe for lancing.

"Unless we can bring up a thousand more Kargul' it is going to be Sebhal and Rodlakh strolling up the Avenue."

"Enough. This was raised earlier."

"Enough? Only if they are fighters bred in Kargul."

"I have told you, *we shall be advised*." This was the set phrase used by the *rabhsai* to put off decision; in a formal audience it would be a very rash suppliant who tried to continue debate after *ul an' yalil botadhayin* had been pronounced.

"With what advisors?" the suggestion of a sneer, and even in this place Rheduban's persistence affronted Ban-Sila, who glared. "In questions involving troops, with Bolan, with Kizhunai, my captains."

Rheduban grinned. He was playing *zhabhu* to win now, making his moves at once, waiting impatiently while Ban-Sila pondered a reply. Soon it could be seen he was trying to divide the center with a strategy known as Shaël's Scissor. "I can't see why you do not make me your Captain-General. Who plays *zhabhu* better?"

Though steadier and more solemn, Ban-Sila was not necessarily the less drunk. "Bolan is Captain-General designate."

"Ah, Bolan, Bo-lan-Ba-kir. Bo-lan-Ba-kir might get himself killed up north. But I meant to say, Captain of your Household."

"You go against Tovakh? He wants that for Kamin-Tolagh." Lower lip pinched between thumb and forefinger Ban-Sila looked for a weakness in Rheduban's line of standards.

"Petakoi, you mean, she wants it for her Tami — and who is he. You are forgetting who Rheduban is."

"Rheduban is beginning to forget who he is speaking to." Ban-Sila achieved some dignity here.

"We speak with Rheduban, us do," Rheduban mocked.

"Remember, your blood is not baKargul."

"Blood — ah, well, if we must speak about *blood!*" — he shouted the word, *seghu*, startling Âna and Ban-Sila, too.

"Enough, enough." He waved both hands in front of him. "Your liberties exceed... " The *rabhsai* used his turn to draw a tile. A blind one, and Rheduban exercised his right to remove one of Ban-Sila's key pieces.

"Kamin-Tolagh is — " Rheduban glanced sideways to see if she responded to the name. She looked up in alert vacuity, wanting above anything to be out of here, no less if it meant giving up any hope of escape tonight. This air was sweating and dangerous, threatened by worse than thunder.

Rheduban dropped into ordinary speech. "The joint-Captain of the Whores-hold. He has the *blood*, but I have put little sister through her paces — you should too, *Deghi*, you would not call her raw codfish. Tam! I would spin him out of the saddle while he was getting his lance up. I have flogged his woman, too — were you beaten, kitten?"

"Yes, Lord."

"Thrashed well?"

"Yes, Lord."

"Did you deserve it?"

"Yes, Lord."

"Will you have to be beaten again?"

"No, Lord, I thank you." Meeting his gaze head-on when he was in this mood might be risky, but she achieved it. With a barked laugh he turned away, back to the game, and made another daring move, threatening quick victory, yet vulnerable.

The exchanges with Ban-Sila went on, curiously like a quarrel with pauses; half a minute's silence might elapse but did nothing to take the tense, irritable edge off either voice, fingernails on slate. Ban-Sila's disdain of his attachment to the diversions of the *Epranda* outraged Rheduban, though he kept the tone ironic, asking whether the *rabhsai* found more he enjoyed in the antics of half-grown *atarlal* — this must be a reference to at-Zhâlai. "I have not forgotten what *diverts* the Royal Person."

Going back into ordinary speech, he turned to Âna, and asked what she would say if she heard the *rabhsai* had been known to kneel to Rheduban. This was dangerous, as the glitter of his eye told her: she did not want to learn anything about a *rabhsai*'s private pleasures.

"Oh, yes," Rheduban insisted. "And he can beg, too -- "

"Enough." Ban-Sila was stiff, but his tremor of rage could be seen. They glared, till Ban-Sila, with a quick flick of his wrist, splashed wine in Rheduban's face. Sweet wine, Âna supposed, recalling Tovakh's complaint. "Enough," the *rabhsai* ruled.

"Enough, enough?" Rheduban blinked wine from his eyes. "Before, you used to cry *more, more.*"

"We forbid you."

"*We?*" Rheduban shuddered to a precarious control, and found a cloth to wipe with. This madness was a badly-chained killer dog, and Âna wished for a way to stop it before catastrophe came.

"You change," Rheduban, sullenly.

"Play your turn."

"Let me study." He clawed out for wine. "Choices, hah?"

Having filled a glass he took a tiny sip, then with glowing eyes steady on Ban-Sila held the glass in front of him, delicately between thumb and knuckle. It stayed there while five could be counted slowly, threat clear. Plainly, too, Ban-Sila would not tolerate retaliation. Very deliberately Rheduban set down the glass, and with a hand like a whip moved one of his standards.

"Ha." Shaël's Scissors were almost closed, Ban-Sila at the edge of defeat. His hand went to the tile-bag, and he fumbled, sweating. A tile came out and was displayed; the Four Bees.

As the tile permitted, Ban-Sila began dismantling all the conquests of his opponent that were vulnerable. He had the quick, disdainful motions of a housewife removing bruised and overripe from strawberries spread on the kitchen table. This was the turn in *zhabhu* that could upset all skill and strategy, and as the *rabhsai* unmade all the best part of his game Rheduban closed his lips over front teeth, pressing so the red vanished altogether.

"You cheat — " a sudden roar, and he drenched Ban-Sila with thrown wine, batting the glass so it bounced, tumbling, across the *zhabhu* board. Both men came to their feet, and Âna swiftly sidled to the far corner of the firepit.

"You've got the Four Bees notched — I saw you feeling for that tile."

"Liar. Animal. I shall have you exiled for life."

"Cheat. I cannot bear a cheat." Rheduban's hand went to his small dagger. He sidestepped the *zhabhu* board, as Ban-Sila turned his head (after, she realized he had been about to call for his bodyguard, probably posted just outside the door). Rheduban's arm swept in a loose, almost casual curve, driving the knife into the *rabhsai*'s throat. "Liar," Rheduban snarled triumphantly, and clapped left hand on Ban-Sila's mouth to muffle the horrid noise which started deep. At the same time he let go the knife to crook his right arm behind a body abruptly limp. Âna had a full fist of knuckles in her mouth, stopping a scream.

She saw Rheduban's eyes, lit from below, become perfectly empty as he held the twitching body in his strange embrace. As the knees sagged he gradually knelt, lowering the body. Blood was spilling on Ban-Sila's face, stain spreading across his shirt. Rheduban loosed his left-hand hold, and the dead head rolled to one side, feet up on the lowest step of the pit. Pulling out his right arm Rheduban stood. The hands of the *rabhsai* were open and lifeless, and shining dark rivulets snailed across the tiles.

Far off, thunder growled again, and everything else came to a stop. Rheduban squatted to wipe his smeared right hand on the dead man's clothes. He threw back his head, mouth open: did she expect the baying of a killer wolf? There was only labored breathing, till he looked down and said, "Ban-Sila. Ban-Sila." He hid his face in his hands, and a sound began that could be either sob or hysterical laugh, and might be both at once, a hard, percussive sound he seemed unable to control.

Âna, forgotten and wanting to remain so, edged noiselessly away. After shock passed, Rheduban would inevitably decide to cancel her, only witness to an event not yet grasped, murder of the *rabhsai*.

After, it was easy to blame herself for the direction she took. The only safety she could imagine was represented by Kamin-Tolagh's quarters. She was in no state for calmly thinking her

options through; in this place she had been surrounded by
enemies, and it could never have occurred to her best chance of
safety would be to scream for help. But Petakoi, or worse,
Radaghi might have come before anyone from outside, and she
did not suppose either woman would have prevented Rheduban
from killing her. To make a dash for the steps up to the outer
door was not something she thought of, though Ban-Sila's
guards, if they were there, would surely want her alive for the
same reason Rheduban would prefer her dead.

Trembling, she stole back into the passageway, not daring to
shut that door behind her. Once in Kamin-Tolagh's outer room
she automatically picked up her stuffed pack and stowed it in the
wall-closet. Heart fluttering she passed the third door, and
perceived like any rabbit she had run to the end of the tunnel.

She leaned on the inside of the door, expecting to hear
Rheduban's approaching tread — though when he wanted he
could go like a cat. A soft chant began to sound in her head,
`Rodlakh is rabhsai, Rodlakh is rabhsai, Rodlakh — '

No question Ban-Sila was dead, no living head dangled so on
its stem. Rodlakh was *rabhsai*.

How long she stayed leaning against the door she did not
know. When at last she noticed there was something hard
digging into her back, it seemed it must have been doing so for
hours. Turning she discovered a heavy bronze bolt. With some
tugging it went home into a stout socket, part of a bronze plate
running the whole height of the door-frame. No one could come
in without breaking through the actual door, and that seemed to
be solid oak under bronze panels.

While she sat on the bed with a hand to her mouth someone
who had come on silent feet tried the door-handle. Kamin-
Tolagh, surely, would call out to her, and she supposed she
would open, although not convinced he would not find it easiest
to acquiesce in her death. The handle turned again, and no one
called out; she was able to imagine hearing soft footfalls moving
away. On the other hand she was quite certain of heavy
breathing just outside the door. Her heart, after one shocked

leap, had settled to a rapid drumming loud enough for anything, the rumble of thunder.

There was no food, and she was still hungry, not having been able to eat much under Rheduban's eye. Now she had breathing-space for self-blame; Rodlakh was *rabhsai*, and rather than prisoning herself she could have gone up those steps to where the guard should be standing. Those were heavy bronze doors, and anyone outside might not hear noises of Ban-Sila's murder, Rodlakh's accession. She could have been the one to bring the news to the Household. Rodlakh's Household.

The world had skewed; Bolan was Rodlakh's Captain and there was no reason for a war in the Northeast; Preference had died here tonight, or should have died. She wanted to giggle at the irony, the realm delivered from its plague by Rheduban.

Harsh, a brilliant flash came, and a huge rippling boom. She leapt, the windows rattled, and it came to her the storm had broken at last. Rain frothed at the glass; her heart tried to ease back into a less obtrusive gait, while lightning flashed without cease, battering of the thunder continuous. Something unmanageably heavy was being rolled overhead, and now and again came a curious whirring flutter, riffle of pages in a gigantic book.

She sat trying to make a calm in her mind, to ask why she did not and could not believe the realm precipitately delivered from evil. Rodlakh was *rabhsai*. Rodlakh was *rabhsai*, yes, if he knew he was, if Kadon Dinul could hear him proclaimed and see him invested. At Tan Lughsai Dolvid had endorsed the position that by himself Ban-Sila had no legal right to change the succession. The brother, Orbanak, was in the hands of the Patriarch, and the Household was half-held by Kamin-Tolagh. There was no knowing what the rest of the troops would do if g'Asalladh' proclaimed Orbanak; Kargul, the Families, the *Mankh'* had their friends among Household officers, and her uncertain impression of Kizhunai, the other joint-Captain, was of a follower, not one to stand firm for Rodlakh once Orbanak was installed.

That, if what she had overheard was more than a Karguli dream, meant Tovakh as Protector. Unless there was a strong popular movement in his favor Rodlakh was as far from *rabhsayum* as with Ban-Sila alive.

And even with support (perhaps from younger Household officers, joined by the rank and file) he would have to move rapidly to claim his capital. Soon the Strait would be closed, and the *Mankh'* would surely do everything it could to keep the news of Ban-Sila's death from the Colony, failing that, to prevent Rodlakh coming here.

She had been taught long ago the reign of a new *rabhsai* begins at death of the old; proclaiming and acclamation were only rituals to confirm what already was. For somewhat less than an hour she had been not a rebel but a loyalist, and so were Dolvid and Galt, Saidhan, Doleni, Shumat in the distant Northeast. She would try to speak with Kizhunai, but Âna's chief job was to carry the news swiftly to Kamsilat. Sett would help.

Like a huge ironshod wagon over cobbles the storm went lumbering away, brief compared to its daylong threat. She sat listening to nothing, wondering how far dawn was. When she at last went to the door it took whole minutes of savage self-goading to make her push back the bolt. That done she froze again, hand on door-handle defying her commands. Her mind conjured Rheduban crouched and waiting just outside, blood-thick knife ready, eyes lighted without a shard of human sympathy.

She opened the door. None of the deepest shadows could hold even a very small Rheduban, but she did not trust them. Going briskly to the closet she took out the pack, so she could dress in all her campaign clothes except heavy socks and stout boots. She resheathed her long knife at thigh-front, and less defenseless now, put the long rose-colored robe over it all. Under the light shuzi her body must appear oddly lumpy.

With the pack she left boots and socks inside the room while she went to use the earth-closet next to the bathroom. Emerging, she had made up her mind the pink robe was no effective disguise for her real clothes, so left it open up to the waist, making her knife accessible. Noises from the common-room sent her scuttling back inside Kamin-Tolagh's door. A voice, probably Rheduban's, then, as she shut the door, a high screaming and sounds that could not be guessed at, some thumps, and perhaps the slam of a door. The screaming could have been Marra, the serving-girl. She usually came early.

In the deep succeeding silence, Âna, overborne by weariness, went to the curved campaign-chair where Kamin-Tolagh had sat her down that first day. Pack to one side, boots to the other, she sat with knife held on her knees.

Not imaginable she could fall asleep, and she had no memory of allowing her eyes to close, yet she started awake to noise of many feet, the quarrelsome shouting of men. Among voices there might be Kamin-Tolagh's. She stood, and the forgotten knife went rattling to the floor. Retrieving and resheathing it, she returned for an instant to the bedroom, to see through that window the sky had turned pale: it was morning.

Telling herself everything would be all right if Kamin-Tolagh was there she went back out into the passageway, but before she could get to the common-room, its door swung violently open. The man there, booted, sword in hand, was not Rheduban. She recognized Freighanai, officer of Kamin-Tolagh's squadron. Behind her another door opened in the passageway, and she turned to confront the forbidding form of Radaghi, robed and blinking.

Freighanai said, back over his shoulder, "She's here, captain."

It would have meant nothing to do other than go forward, and Freighanai turned sideways to let her pass.

The scene for a half-minute was hard to comprehend. She had expected Kamin-Tolagh, but he was not there; other soldiers were, with drawn weapons, and seeing Rheduban in the middle gave the passing idea he had been arrested. Then she saw he was still armed, now with a long knife, and knew Freighanai had meant that 'captain' for him. The group blocked her view of the firepit, so she could not see whether Ban-Sila's body was there, but near the foot of the steps up to the outer doors a fresh corpse was huddled. By the plain smock and dark hair, it was Marra. Apparent how she had died; in the midst of blood-matted hair could be seen the silvered haft of the same small dagger that had killed the *rabhsai*. Âna could feel a sharp sorrow well beyond any liking she had managed to have for the sullen serving girl. She was young, and had died for nothing; did Rheduban really imagine he could keep Ban-Sila's death a secret?

He was haggard-faced in contrast to his manner, excited and even gay. "Have you slept well, dear Âna? Seize her."

She came deeper into the room, and as once before when pursued by this man's wife, put a chair between her and Rheduban; as she sidestepped a hand slipped from her arm, and she had just missed being taken from behind by Radaghi.

Some of the soldiers advanced. "Kill her," Rheduban said. Freighanai, approaching to take a captive, was halted by the brutal order, as was the nearest man to her front, the youthful Kambanal. He had no reason to love Âna, humiliated when Kamin-Tolagh lent her his *pefrai*, but protested, "Captain, this is the woman of Kamin-Tolagh *Asai*."

"Yes, kill her." Freighanai supported Kambanal, saying any killing could wait till Kamin-Tolagh came, but neither soldier dared interfere when Rheduban himself came forward with his knife ready.

Âna had already flourished hers to discourage the approach of Radaghi. As Rheduban sprang past the chair she used the blade to just turn a flat thrust like the one to kill Ban-Sila, and her point scratched the back of Rheduban's knife-hand; she saw the thin line of scarlet.

He gave a high-pitched cry. "It fights," tossing back his wild hair. "My kill."

Dirty patches on his face, dried blood, intensified the resemblance to a gleeful child. Far taller and with much the greater reach, he weighed the knife in his hand. Her back against the sideboard she wondered whether she could launch herself at him, and gave up any hope of living on. No help here, and no one would ever know what had become of her. It was sad, Marra too; a no one died and there were no questions. A fresh confusion of voices outside. While his wife watched eagerly Rheduban drew circles with his knife-point, enjoying this. He made a flicking feint at her face; their blades kissed lightly, just enough to spoil his intention of giving a defacing wound. Above, the outside door opened with a thud, as Rheduban drew back for a leisured backhand, laughing as his wrist pressed hers back, driving for her belly.

"What is this? Stop. I tell you, stop." Authority was there, and yet it was the voice of Kamin-Tolagh on the steps, sword in hand, red-brown hair dishevelled. "Stop him," he told his men, and as Freighanai on one side, Kambanal on the other advanced, Rheduban, with a fighter's caution, leapt back so she could not profit by the lowered blade. Sheathing, he turned to Kamin-Tolagh, who came down the rest of the steps followed by a handful of his squadron, all with weapons drawn.

"She must be killed," Rheduban said. Dizzy, she leant back against the sideboard.

Radaghi, near Freighanai, gave the officer's back a hard thump with the heel of her hand. "Why wait? Kill the slut." Freighanai blinked a little at the blow, but did not move, eyes on Kamin-Tolagh.

"She saw," Rheduban pressed his case. "She saw."

Though he had killed Marra, the steward who arrived with her had escaped; rumor of Ban-Sila's death was already loose in the Residence, and Kamin-Tolagh with his men had scuffled with some Household guards to reach here, hence the bare blades. But there was nothing to prepare Kamin-Tolagh for what he saw when he looked down in the firepit. His face whitened. "This you did?"

"We fought. The girl saw, she must be killed. Kill her yourself."

"What?" Petakoi, standing at the inner doorway, a commanding figure in her deep-green dressing-robe.

"This maniac," bitterly, "has killed the *rabhsai*."

"Rheduban is not a maniac," Radaghi, offended, taking these exchanges to a new level of unreality. Seeing she was not going to be killed just yet she sat down in the chair that had been her rampart, and tried not to think about the food just behind.

When Petakoi, stone-faced, had viewed the corpse in the firepit she demanded the details. Added to what she already knew Âna heard that some Household men had instantly made up their minds the *rabhsai* had died in a Karguli conspiracy; these Kamin-Tolagh's soldiers had clashed with, so far giving and receiving nothing worse than bruises. He had sent messages to summon the main Kargul' forces not now present, those quartered by Market Gate hostelry, but Kamin-Tolagh was also seeking a calm parley with the Household officers, and understood Kizhunai was at his Residence Quarter house. Just as he had told all this to his mother a junior officer came with fresh word Kargul had succeeded in seizing the Ram Court door and the stables, while Household regulars seemed to be gathering at the barracks, others having already secured the Personal Suite, where only some minor members of the Great Families were in residence. The desolate emptiness of Ban-Sila's *rabhsayum* came home; no trusted group of senior officials and ranking officers were there to take charge at Kadon Dinul.

"You have thrown away everything," Petakoi, icily to Rheduban.

"He was to die," Rheduban said, and Petakoi glared him to silence.

"Poor Ban-Sila." Plump, smooth-faced Finú had arrived to stand next to her younger sister. "Not thirty. That is a House, is it not, with misfortune for its chief heirloom."

She was knitting and unravelling her thick little fingers. Yet though Rheduban had sobbed for his own sorrows, and Petakoi was mourning the schemes of Kargul, this foolish woman was alone in speaking a word of grief for the fallen *rabhsai*. A link of sorts to at-Zhâlai, who had arrived and whose smallness now looked crumpled; his *Atarlum* training against display of strong emotions was laboring to keep him at the level of mere distress.

When Rheduban renewed his plea for the murder of Âna, Kamin-Tolagh asked him for what? when the whole city would know in an hour. But his mother saw farther. "Remove the only witness to the act of a drunken madman, and let a story about a Karguli conspiracy take root, is that it?"   Here they were speaking in the Owanilú, but Âna was newly struck by how peculiar their minds were, to continue talking about her so, not once having asked for her account of the murder. In Rheduban's sullen recounting the killing never came.

At-Zhâlai insisted the Patriarch must be informed, and asked for an escort so he could ride for the *Mankh'*. Kamin-Tolagh, with corrosive sarcasm, told him if the news was in the streets he would be far safer all alone than with soldiers of Kargul, the conspirators.

Rheduban said, "You seriously believe a rabble would challenge *péfrapravádal* of Kargul?"

"If you do not, test it; go and ride through the streets; you may save us a lot of trouble." Rheduban, seething, tried to stare down Kamin-Tolagh, but he was all cold steel this morning. He told the little *atarlai* there was no reason for him not to ride alone as any other day, but wondered what he could tell *g'Asalladh'*, when Kargul had no new plan.

On his dignity, at-Zhâlai observed it was not incumbent upon *g'Asalladh'* to wait for Kargul' deliberations; He would act according to His own enlightenment, His *aën'modha*.   At-Zhâlai's prediction was that a *Moradhilum* would be declared forthwith.

"Under my father."

"*Under* the new *rabhsai*, Orbanak."

"But with Tovakh as his *maëdhrai*," Petakoi, leaning forward.

"And, as you say, forthwith," her son contributed. "Some young fool officers of the Household were shouting for Rodlakh *Degh'asai* — at first I thought we had a simple rebellion." He nodded gravely in response to Petakoi's incredulity, while Âna's heart leapt.

"That succession was set aside by Ban-Sila himself," at-Zhâlai, petulantly.

"That — " Kamin-Tolagh again regarded the corpse — "may be one more thing even the *rabhsai* invested cannot achieve."

"*G'Asalladh'* can," at-Zhâlai said.

"With His allies." The news about Ban-Sila, Kamin-Tolagh observed, could be a long while reaching Kamsilat, and there should be ample opportunity to win over the Household. As a hope he spoke Âna's fear; if this younger brother was proclaimed and the elder failed to appear, Rodlakh's support would rapidly evaporate. At-Zhâlai, assuring them Orbanak was still at the *Mankh'* here on the Mainland, left, carrying for *g'Asalladh'* dutiful compliments of Petakoi and her hope His Enlightenment, on learning of events, would perceive the need of swift action.

Petakoi said she would write a message for Tovakh's eyes only; he must return at once to Kadon Dinul. Her son remarked he might be actively engaged with Shumat's forces and unable to break off; Kamin-Tolagh wanted the Kargul squadrons waiting in the south, in their own province. With Bolan in the north, he said, and the General Cavalry scattered among a dozen garrisons, Kadon Dinul could be taken by six squadrons and a mob, while a thousand Kargul lancers sat idle, ready to ride. Illegal for so much provincial cavalry to cross the Karguli border, but as with everything else since the death of Ban-Sila, impossible to say whether law would be enforced to the point of making war to stop them. Rheduban, saying the decision for those squadrons, whether and when to fight, could not be left to the under-captain now in charge, proposed to ride south and fetch the troops.

"You?" Kamin-Tolagh looked as if he would spit. "Show your face and we'll have the one thing we have to prevent, a general uprising." He was not making a joke.

"I had not realized what love there was for Ban-Sila," but today Rheduban's sarcasms were not going to be indulged, and Petakoi turned on him. "For love of Hrafi, go and wash. You stink blood." He was no pleasant sight, purple shuzi stiffened with black patches, both arms and his face smeared, fingernails of the right hand clogged.

"Yet it is true," Radaghi complained. "Ban-Sila was never loved." She held out hands to her husband, and he submitted to being be led out, one arm around her. With his going there seemed to be a general letting-out of breath. Yet, stupefyingly, the tenderness between the couple appeared genuine. Was it only that they knew and tolerated each other's monstrosities, and was that a definition of marriage?

"All the same, he is right about the need for someone to lead the southern squadrons. Who is there? Talfoyan? Yenughai? Only soldiers, no one to judge policy." Clearly Kamin-Tolagh wanted to be the one to ride south, but was not happy leaving the uncertain situation here. His mother, moreover, accused him of wanting to go, not just to bring back troops, but to search for Kamin-Tarú, who was missing. Petakoi showed no concern over her daughter, saying she was no doubt sporting somewhere with a new man, and must find her own way home, like a cat.

This must be the message that yesterday had put Kamin-Tolagh in his surly, distracted mood. "Why must it all come on us at once?" he demanded savagely. No one was paying Âna any attention, and she turned to begin systematically working her way through the remaining food on the sideboard, not replenished today. She rejected some tired fish.

Junior officers of Kargul arrived with mixed news. Servants and a few notables, including Rhunilat, had left the Residence with assistance from men of the Household. That same faction, among whom the noted Mixed swordsman Dorrmas was prominent, were calling for the *rabhsai's* known killer to be surrendered *to impartial justice* (the phrase made Petakoi smile bleakly). On the other side, the *Kímukan* Zhinladh had arrived, and was outside, waiting for talk with the baKargul.

He was admitted, the slow, fleshy man with short arms and a strut. Âna had distantly recognized his name on hearing it before, and now it came together; this was Zhinladh son of the big landowner and grain-magnate Zhival, and also the killer of Arvus. Âna had met the son, Arvat, in the Colony, and found him a negligible little man, not even able to make advances properly, but she knew the father, a Deniant, had been widely respected, Master of the Treasury in Lambarr's reign, and had offended the Families by trying to tax them equitably. So there was little question where Zhinladh's sympathies would be, even if she had not heard him before, fawning over the gloriousness of Kargul.

Numbers of Owanil among Household officers, he told Kamin-Tolagh in a voice too unctuous for a man who could hardly be forty, were set against the accession of Rodlakh, and ready to support Orbanak and a *Moradhilum*; they would not object to Tovakh at its head, since he was well-known to support traditional rights. Petakoi was eager to emphasize that side, parading her close friendship with *g'Asalladh'* and Kargul's long-standing commitment to the cause of Owan. But Kamin-Tolagh wanted only to hear how many lances Zhinladh could bring, and whether he could say where Kizhunai stood.

"He is wavering. He will be with us when he sees the best of his officers choosing right."

Presence of this senior Household officer persuaded Kamin-Tolagh he must fetch the southern squadrons. He did not alter when fresh word came from outside; many townspeople were in the streets, the Household faction with Dorrmas displaying (her heart gave a joyful leap) the Bronze-Beech banner, Rodlakh's personal standard. Those men had seized at least two city gates, Market and Harbor, and had turned back the last of the Kargul' troops from by the hostelry. "I was the one," Kamin-Tolagh, sardonically, "who gave gate-duty to regular Household, so as to keep Kargul together for patrols."

He was encouraged to hear there had been no actual fighting; the courier said Household men inside and Kargul outside the gate had mainly exchanged jokes and some familiar insults.

"They have ridden together, eaten together, gone whoring together, I don't doubt."

A terse discussion with his mother; they had no hope of holding the city, they did not have it, but Petakoi agreed the Residence could be defended, perhaps the barracks and Treasury, if enough of the Household were with them. She expected added forces from the *Adanum Plakh'*, once the Patriarch understood what was needed to bring about Orbanak's succession. The temper of the city would have to be considered, at all costs avoiding general uprising, while buying days for Tovakh to return from the north, Kamin-Tolagh to bring troops from the south. What Bolan might do was doubtful, but likely Rodlakh, if he came to power, would begin by deposing, possibly arresting, Ban-Sila's Captain-General. That, anyway, was what Petakoi would tell Tovakh to tell Bolan, and if he decided (as she forecast) to decide nothing, the General Cavalry would be as factional and incoherent as the Household, against the singlemindedness and rapid concentration of Kargul's forces.

Finú came to the sideboard and helped herself to honey-cake. "Who would be a *rabhsai*?" to Âna. "Or *rabhsayu*? Of the last six who ruled this realm, my dear, only Banak lived out his life and died in his bed. Be a farm-girl and breed strong children." This, though mad, was touching — and this woman was said to have best claim of any alive to be legitimist successor, setting aside Banak's irruption into power.

"Still, you will have lots to remember."

"Yes, Madam," triumphing over equal urges to laugh or weep.

Kamin-Tolagh was estimating he could be back with troops in nine days — eight, if fast-messengers went ahead of him and he found the squadrons ready to ride. He brushed aside his mother's question about whether he had slept, and then Petakoi said, "I see the girl is dressed for a journey. Take her with you. If she stays here Rheduban will find a way to kill her, and it may come about — " her voice dropped to where only Kamin-Tolagh could hear, but Âna could guess what was said; Rheduban would be more controllable as long as there was a live witness to the murder of Ban-Sila, as long as he feared Kargul might hand him over to justice to divert anger from themselves. While glad Petakoi had a reason to keep her alive, Âna was not sure she wanted to be shelved as a living threat to Rheduban, and it remained odd she was only the *idea* of a witness; still no one had asked her what she might say about the murder.

Kamin-Tolagh spoke through a crammed mouthful of barley-bread, telling her she must go away from Kadon Dinul, and not tell anyone what she had seen here. "It would be safer for you if you did not yet go back to Arlemirrstead. Is there somewhere else?"

"I have an uncle at Burantal, *Asai*," with a bold descent into truth.

"*Asai?*"

"Tam. I'd love to see my uncle."

"I do not blame you. If I were not in a hurry I would visit Arlemirrstead and make Arlemirr eat his own stirrup-leather. You will ride with us; we shall go by way of Burantal." After a moment he amended that; she would start off with Kargul, but their pace might be too much for her; she would be given a General Cavalry mount she must leave off at the post in Burantal. "I'll explain this as we ride," certain he had overtaxed her brain for the present.

Anxious to preserve this new-found belief in the chance of survival, she sprang up with every sign of readiness. He was going to his quarters first, and at the passageway door a newly-groomed Rheduban made a last quiet attempt to have Âna slain, telling Kamin-Tolagh it was not sane to let her live.

"The one, the one who saw," Radaghi chimed in, emerging. She and her husband must have planned together to keep their fangs sheathed.

Kamin-Tolagh gestured to where Marra had been stabbed. "We have had enough wanton slaughter. Rheduban will never face any charges, so long as Kargul holds together."

Inside he used earth-closet and a tooth twig, then decided on a wash. She used the time to discard slippers and put on socks and boots. She pulled the rose-colored robe over her head and left it draped across the chair, but when Kamin-Tolagh came back he bundled it up to stuff into her pack, then lifted her hair to kiss the back of her neck. "You will not be forgotten, little Âna."

Back in the common-room Petakoi came up, assuring her son she was competent to manage affairs here. "No delays, Tam," absently putting a hand on Âna's head.

With men of his personal squadron they moved at nearly a trot through the halls of the Residence, now silent. They came to the Ram Court door, guarded by men of Kargul. Out on the cobbles of the court most of the half-squadron that would go with Kamin-Tolagh was already in the saddle. Her mount was a chestnut *pefrai*, smaller than most, still a large horse. Placed between Kamin-Tolagh and Freighanai she clattered over cobbles under the blue banner of Kargul, through the south side courts to Pefrai Gate, held by Household men, either in Zhinladh's faction or else scrupulously neutral; Kamin-Tolagh was not delayed there.

The Avenue had been washed clean by last night's downpour; all the way to Harbor Gate no other horsemen could be seen moving, but there were little knots of citizenry at street-corners. As the Karguli troop came to the Disc some boys gathered on the north side of the Avenue set up a cry to be given Rheduban, the *rabhsai*-killer. Kamin-Tolagh tried them with his usual grinning wave, and some thrown stones fell short, skittering across the rose-colored Avenue. Those boys fled, jeering, but a smaller and braver group over on the left side kept chanting Rodlakh's name. Kamin-Tolagh shut his lips down tight.

Ahead and down the slope Market Place was deep in subdued menace, many people, no crowd but a loose skein of smaller gatherings, mainly watchful and serious. Most men and lads had staves if not knives or old swords, and Kamin-Tolagh muttered when he spotted some bows.

There was an effect of drawing back to permit passage of the tight group of two dozen riders, and a good number of mounted troops were assembling this side of Market Gate, breastplates bright. The formations were not symmetrical, and it looked as if parts of several squadrons had been hurriedly put together; apparently not only officers but ordinary soldiers were choosing sides.   Ignoring   the   mob,   Kamin-Tolagh   was   still   far outnumbered.

Level-voiced he gave the order for lances to be unslung, and at the walk they continued down the slope. Kamin-Tolagh told Freïghanai, "Half-files, right and left," and the formation changed to a compact four sixes. Some bystanders were drifting in behind, and Âna wondered about finding her moment to change sides; being killed in a street-fight by Rodlakh's supporters was not an irony she could enjoy.

Forty paces short of the gate Kamin-Tolagh called a halt. By the gate lively discussion was going on among Household officers, while their men sat unmoving in their saddles.

Shortly a senior officer moved out, flanked by lances and followed by a small knot of other riders, not all soldiers. Kamin-Tolagh turned with the order for lances to be slung, probably as token of peaceful intent, though it might also allow that quarters would be too tight for effective lance-work. Onlookers had mainly fallen quiet.

The officer was an Owani with a jowled face and ears that stuck straight out, and Âna, seeing insignia of a full captain, knew he must be Kizhunai; he halted, horse nose-to-nose with Kamin-Tolagh's. Among those behind him a tall but bowed man not a soldier was quieting his mount, and she was astonished to see Faëdhal, the Master of Tongues.

Just then he saw her, and frowned. She willed him not to give her away. If she wanted to be among friends it would be easy, giving a quick kick to her horse, to cross the space to the Household lines before anyone could stop her. But there was no assurance Kizhunai was going to be for Rodlakh: with Kamin-Tolagh, if they could negotiate this encounter, she would have safe-conduct to Burantal. Besides, her move would begin a quarrel, of no importance in itself, but quite foreseeably the spark to set off a fight no one wanted.

After an exchange of salutes Kizhunai, almost apologetically, began, "May we ask, *Asai*, where you are bound?"

"South, Captain. Why this stoppage?"

"The Household," Kizhunai maintained the formal, even ritual manner, "requires surrender by Kargul of the man accused in the death of Ban-Sila *Rabhsai*."

"As you can see, Captain, Rheduban is not with me. I give my sworn word he is not in my saddlebag." Amid chuckles Kamin-Tolagh became serious. "And the Household cannot require anything from me when my voice is half of the Household's."

Evading that, trying not to give offense, prompted quietly from behind by Faëdhal, Kizhunai said, "Who is your lord, *Asai*?"

"Mine? Tobhan baKargul, *Nim'asai*," he named his aged, almost inactive grandfather. "And over him, the *rabhsai*, duly invested and proclaimed."

"He is dead."

"Then his lawful heir."

Kizhunai again received some coaching from behind. "Do you then acknowledge Rodlakh Lambarrati *Degh'asai*?"

These two men had sat together to arrange the duties of the Household. Kamin-Tolagh was first to break the stiff mould. "We of Kargul," he began, then, "Come on, Kizhunai, you know there is going to be a quarrel over the succession. Rodlakh was outlawed. If I say what pleases you my father will disinherit me — the Council is going to have to argue out this case, not us soldiers."

From the group of officers behind Kizhunai a sour, sardonic voice called out, "Yet the Lord Kamin-Tola' won't stay for the debate?" The speaker, at once stared down by Kizhunai, was a tanned, effective-looking Mixed officer, short in the saddle but with good build and steely forearms; Dorrmas, she supposed, master of sword-fighting, enthusiast for Rodlakh.

Faëdhal now looked for Kizhunai's nod, and spoke. It was an extraordinary speech. "Lords, Captains, pardon me, I take no side in any dispute, only that the Captain Kizhunai has consulted me to be clear about what the law has to say on these matters. Not that I make any claim to be expert in law, but in language. However, to anyone who can understand plain language, the law here is quite clear. This so-called outlawry was never proclaimed in full Council, as law requires, and therefore if Ban-Sila *Rabhsai* is indeed no more, then Rodlakh *Asai* is our undoubted *rabhsai*. Your pardon, *Asai* — " Kamin-Tolagh had shifted irascibly in the saddle. "We have all heard Ban-Sila pronounced Orbanak his successor in Rodlakh's stead, but I fear that power is not among those the law places in the hands of the *rabhsai* acting alone — as is, I would offer, only good sense."

He appealed on all sides. "Lords, Captains, what confusion might there be, if a ruler with many children, as the late Lambarr *Deghi* was, could deprive one of the succession and confer it upon another, week by week, as one child vexed and another gratified him? Not to be thought of. Now, sirs, there has been no full meeting of the Council since well before — before, mark you — Rodlakh's departure for the Colony, hence well before his so-called outlawry, which equally, all due respect to our late Ban-Sila, possessed no legal force without due debate in Council. No, Captains, there can, in law, be no particle of doubt. Unless we have been misinformed and Ban-Sila *Rabhsai* is alive, our true *rabhsai* can be none other than Rodlakh *Deghi*." Breathless but complacent, Faëdhal settled back on his saddle.

"Tongue-master," Kamin-Tolagh was unmoved. "If *rabhsayum* were forged out of learned talk at the Bronze Residence, there would be no need for swords in this realm. Can you or anyone say what it would be if the Council met now and posthumously confirmed Ban-Sila's acts in outlawing one brother and making the other his heir? Dorrmas is right, I cannot stay for the debate, I am riding for home." Once again he asked Kizhunai by whose authority the way was being barred — a shrewd question, since obviously no orders could have come from Rodlakh, their asserted chief. Âna had been honestly impressed by the cut and thrust of this debate; Faëdhal, she supposed, could orate in that style while being tortured, but Kamin-Tolagh was a surprise. Where his personal vanity was not in the way, he could be keen enough.

Kizhunai tried once again. "Will Kargul surrender Rheduban for trial?"

"I have told you, I do not have Rheduban. Go ask at the Residence."

"Will you give hostages for him?"

This spilled out in a rush, and at the word *hostages* Freighanai, not waiting for an order, drew his sword. In a rush and ring of steel the half-squadron did the same, and seeing this the nearest ordered formation of the Household pressed forward, also drawing. Dorrmas sidled his mount to position at the front of this company, while townspeople all about gave voice.

Not noticed in the general stir, Faëdhal looked past Kizhunai and Kamin-Tolagh to meet Âna's eyes, his brows peaked high. She grimaced quickly, and ever so slightly shook her head, peculiarly grateful he did not think she was Kamin-Tolagh's woman by choice. He answered with a nod, just as faint.

"No. We shall not give hostages. Are we going to have to cut our way out of the city, through yesterday's comrades?"

That put it squarely back on Kizhunai. Behind him, Dorrmas, sword held negligently, crossed forearms resting on his saddlebow, appeared ready to give all Kargul a lesson with blades. Kizhunai was rueful.

"No, I cannot begin a civil war." He turned, waving for the way to the gate to be opened.

Dorrmas called, "But we will ride to the Residence, Kamin-Tola', and we'll have Rheduban, or there will be war."

"Silence," Kizhunai rapped.

Among townsmen pressing in on both flanks Dorrmas clearly had more admirers than Kizhunai. Disappointed growlings were nearby, some defiant shouting farther off, Rheduban's name was heard on all sides, and if the people, as many did in Âna's country, confused him with Kamin-Tolagh, civil war might have begun with an ugly mob-killing, one Kizhunai's men probably could not have done much to stop.

As was they made a narrowing funnel down to the gateway, and a grim Kizhunai rode side by side with Kamin-Tolagh as far as the gate. They did not speak; when Kizhunai drew aside and the two captains exchanged salutes it seemed both foresaw they would be enemies if they met again.

Angry jeers, big threats came from the crowd as Household men closed in at the rear of the Karguli half-squadron, good-humoredly keeping ill-wishers back. Âna, as she rode in under the archway, had a last glimpse of Faëdhal stretching his neck to peer at her, trying to read her looks. Out in sunlight again beyond the walls Kamin-Tolagh shook off ten years of anxiety. "Sheathe swords. Form files."

After a short pause by the hostelry they rode on, strength increased by the dozen men left outside when the gates were closed, but not a furlong down the paved road, Kamin-Tolagh, perplexed, called a new halt.

As if to himself, he muttered, "Is this right? If Dorrmas has his way, and Kizhunai rides on the Residence, would we not do better to aid in its defence?"

Beside, Freighanai. with his habitual gloom, twisted in the saddle for a look back at Market Gate. "Would they let us back in the city, *Asai*, without a fight?"

Kamin-Tolagh gnawed a lower lip. "If I knew where my father was — "

"*Asai* — " the boyish file-leader, Kambanal, spoke. He was, she now perceived, of better birth than most soldiers. "There are a hundred men left to defend the Residence, and we still have allies in the Household. Your lady mother, *Asai*, is captain enough, pardon me."

To Âna (she supposed precisely because she was not supposed to understand) Kamin-Tolagh said, "You see what it is. If I stay to help in this small fight, we may lose the larger one, for want of our idle cavalry." Setting out the dilemma appeared to help him; he gave a last half-glance back over his shoulder, and waved his riding on.

It was the last hour of morning, the day silver and gold, cool sun in a fleecy sky. She was amazed by her own resiliency; she was actually happy, with expansive joy of an animal uncaged. She filled her lungs with air untainted by conspiracy or madness.

Not long, and Kamin-Tolagh was asking her how much she had followed of the debate, and having Freighanai flatter him about his side of it. At Tâl Abfekh, a pleasant hilltop village, they rested and had some food and drink. The cavalry post was just past the houses, its nominal strength two squadrons, a *kímukan* in command, leathery with a skewed nose: she did not discover his name, but recognized the arid and weary voice; he would never know he had given her fictitious father a name. He was inquisitive as he dared be about the reason for this riding, and Kamin-Tolagh began vague and ended lordly in declining a direct answer, but was pleased they were running ahead of the news about Ban-Sila.

Rattling down the steep curve of hill they came to the rich bowl of farming country between these Arbhu Hills and the Burantali. "Where then is Arlemirrstead?" Kamin-Tolagh abruptly asked, and she waved an indefinite hand south and west. "Away from the road."

"Do not be afraid. What is it he grows, your father?"

"We have cattle mostly, Tam." True, but of Konatstead, not here.

He remarked he had been told what seemed to be true, that this was apple and wheat country.

"Yes, but our land is not as good, better left in grass, my father says. We have some grain, root-crops, too; after three years in pasture with cattle manuring the land — " she broke off, knowing that covering one mistake she had hurried to a worse one; she sounded far too intelligent, and was making Arlemirrstead too prosperous.

"And the calves have soft noses," she said, then made a rasping noise in her throat, pointing to the water-bottle at his saddle-bow. He unhooked it and passed it over, returning to brooding preoccupation, perhaps with events at Kadon Dinul, or perhaps with his missing sister.

In the crawling wagon of Arlimas this road had taken fourteen or fifteen hours to cover, but now just over half that, and she had no trouble keeping pace, though chafe of the saddle caused her to wonder how much she was bleeding, a question that had to be deferred. In late afternoon they were winding down between low, grassed downs, seeing up ahead the wide

eastward sweep of the road this side of the brown line of hills,
then Burantal climbing in its saddle, up to the right. Her heart
rose, and Kamin-Tolagh approved: "A handsome spot." This
was the approach that had given Burantal's situation its fame; in
tawny sunlight buildings sat the slopes with confident assurance,
as if there had been a treaty between makers of hills and houses.
She was reminded of a town she had known in the West,
Kreshavu, another place, though smaller, that could look down
on its valley with pride but not arrogance. But Burantal was also
much the older city, worn walls and weathered roofs soft as
velvet in the late glow.

Two gates gave Burantal an incorporated elbow of highway,
and at the bend, where the street that mounted for the heart of the
city emerged, there was the General Cavalry barracks with a
curve of crenellated wall; at its base long stone troughs were fed
by ducts from the hillside behind. As many as sixty horses could
be watered here at once, and it was a leisured evening scene with
Kargul' soldiers stretching their legs and swapping tales with the
garrison, who had become more amiable on learning these were
not Rheduban's troops, and were going to ride on after brief rest.
The men of Kargul, forbidden to mention Ban-Sila's death or any
of today's events at Kadon Dinul, must be hard put to invent
inconsequential news or recall it from duller days.

She dismounted and unslung her pack. Kamin-Tolagh was
already out of the saddle, talking with Freighanai, gazing up at
the hills. She could not simply slip away.

"Âna — " he stooped over her. "You know these parts?"

"A little, Tam."

"Shemugrân, that would lie over here?"

"More there," she said, turning his finger farther eastward.

To Freighanai he confided, "I wish I knew the way Rodlakh
came. We could miss Kanzan Tâl altogether."

Understood. News sent by fast-messenger from Kadon Dinul
would take the Great Stone Road, the Royal Way southward;
having avoided trouble so far by coming this way, Kamin-Tolagh
expected to find the news about Ban-Sila had beaten him to
Kanzan Tâl. He might well be thinking, too, about bringing his

troops back north, by which time Kanzan Tâl, a fortress city, could be in arms against him. But Dolvid said mounted men could not pass through Shemugrân, and after doing it on foot Âna believed him. She hoped Kamin-Tolagh would not try.

"Is your uncle far from here?"

"No, Tam. Utalai Course." That raised Kamin-Tolagh's eyebrows a little; in her desire to use as much truth as could be she had made her uncle too important: Kamin-Tolagh must know the gentry of Burantal, Mixed as most might be, lived on Utalai Course.

"What is your uncle?"

"I think a trader, when he may be. These are hard times."

"Can you stay with him?"

"For a while." It could not be that Kamin-Tolagh was deliberately prolonging this farewell.

From his belt he unhooked a small purse. "As I promised you."

She had been feeling shabby over her use of Kamin-Tolagh; without him she could not be here, plotting to defeat the ambitions of his clan. Her gesture of refusal was instinctive, but by far the worst mistake she had made. Utter bewilderment came into his face. "Your father, Âna. This is gold. With this you can escape another of his whippings."

"Then I thank you Tam." She gathered in his purse before he could revolt against his improbable role as suppliant. He seized her to give a fierce kiss. A few of his men raised a soft cheer, and whether begun with passion, embrace ended as display. "You will not forget me, hah, Ân'loi?" He struck a conqueror's pose and she loathed him, poor Kamin-Tolagh.

"I'll remember you. I thank you, Tam."

"Farewell. Good fortune." Tugged between bravado and sentiment he looked in her eyes, but then mirrored Freighanai's broad grin. When she reached where the road would mount out of his view, she turned; his final wave was for his men, not her, jaunty and self-contained.

Making her way up the broad slope of street she hoped there was no dark stain between her legs. If there was, let there be;

what was this fuss of secrecy and shame over what happened perhaps four hundred times to every one of half the human race? In some odd way it joined up with Kamin-Tolagh and his poses.

Burantal. It brought back the sweetness of lying with Dolvid, though she should not love this place where Sebhal died. Pausing for breath she was caught in an unexpected storm of sadness, not knowing what was self-pity, how much sorrow for — Tam, then; for the world. Perhaps none of that; she was terribly weary. She played a part with Tam only from outer necessity, never forgetting who she was. Somewhere must be a man brave enough to be himself.

She came to the intricate carved archway, the house with the sunburst on its door, remembering how she sprinted towards the sound of battle in the dawn of Sebhal's dying. The door was opened today by an astonishingly pretty girl, perhaps twelve, eyes black enough for a Froghu, dusky grape-bloom to the skin. "Yes?" A grown woman lurked in the dim behind.

Made welcome she stumbled in making a Gabhani guest-bow: she was dizzy, and the ache low down at the back of her head was one with sourness welling in her stomach. She could taste pain.

Morú, far away, told the girl, Morulis, to take Âna's burden. The phrasing made her smile, but the pack was meant; it was lifted out of her hand and Âna, seated in a wide chair, heard Sett was here and mending well. She could see resemblance between mother and daughter, though the mother was paler, showing a touch of Owani, as with her own mother, Âna's.

"Are you hurt? Ill?" A face that met life level-eyed. She had been a midwife, Âna recalled, achieving a tremulous *No* in answer to one of the questions, then weeping as she told about the strange parting, long ride, unrest at Kadon Dinul and her endless teeter on the cliff-edge of being killed by Rheduban, after he had murdered the *rabhsai*. About moonsblood, and wishing for friends.

Morú's interjections were few and mild; she said wise women had predicted Ban-Sila's end would be a violent one, but was more concerned about all Âna had witnessed and endured. She sent Morulis to tell Sett his niece was here, but forbade her to meet with him till she was rested and restored. "Come, we must stretch out in a nice hot bath — " this bright, chiding tone had often been used to coerce new mothers. "Plenty of lovely warm water."

The soap was yellow and suety, like the soap they made at Konatstead, homecoming indeed, after the oils and scented unguents at the Residence. The bathhouse of Untimarr was even grander than the one Falis, Nentirr's wife, was so proud of; here the peat fire was divided off by a stout brick wall so bathroom proper was neither smoky nor overhot, while above the fire the giant copper kettle seemed to be fed direct from springs on the hillside. Out of the kettle came a long pipe that ran through the brick wall and ended with a turn-spigot so the bath could be filled without using buckets.   Morú had sprinkled herbs, refreshing, though Âna in the hot water felt passingly like a piece of soup-meat.

She became drowsy, letting weary legs float, sore shoulders slipping on the end of the big bronze bath. Soon a girl arrived, not Morulis but the older daughter, Ondis, who was seventeen, less bashful and also plainer than her ravishing sister. She said her mother thought Âna might drink this now, and *this*, blessedly, was warm *raminat* with honey.

Ondis had also brought two or three robes and other garments, her own, since they were much of a size. She sat on a low stool next to the bath while Âna began drying.   "Your pardon, but coming from Kadon Dinul you perhaps have heard of a man Rheduban, a soldier of Kargul."

"I have heard of him," disgusted to feel the start of violent trembling, which savage plying of her towel brought under control.

Well, this Rheduban, the girl said, came to Burantal quite often, and once he had stayed here, in this very house, though she was not here for that. He was very ugly, and he came to do wicked things with a woman of Burantal, a woman everyone despised.

Having provisionally put herself in the same general range of years as Ondis she began to feel several centuries older. The *raminat*, however, was dissolving last jagged crystals of her headache.

"I'll show you her house, if you have the time. He gives her money." This was the final horror for Ondis — or rather, she expected it to be so for Âna, who had a small purse of gold resting on top of the clothes she had taken off.

Ondis was not clear about what the woman did for Rheduban, but understood men at their best would ask ugly things of a good woman.

"Monstrous. I wonder we honor them with so much of our attention."

"I have a friend, son to one of the Elders. Don't you think light-brown eyes are the best color for a man? If he is tall?"

"Light brown," gravely, "is a very good color, yes — " letting herself feel carefree.

"My father is also an Elder of Burantal. That's only a title, you see — my father is far less old than, well, many who are not even Elders. Burantal is an important city, but I wish I could have lived in other years — those of Banak-rai, who our Falcon-Netter saved, that is why we have the fountain. Nowadays there's so much hiding and whispering. Besides, men get killed for nothing."

As expected Ondis's clothes were a reasonable fit, a little loose at the hip, a little wide at the shoulder, a little tight at the breast. She finished tying a drawstring and faced the likable girl. "Take heart. You will be living in the years of Rodlakh."

"Who is Rodlakh?"

"Another in Banak's line — " adopting the proper lofty tone — "who found hospitality and safety at Burantal. Our new *rabhsai*."

A long and narrow back room was reached through a sliding door made invisible by the craft of a master-carpenter. Sett folded her in his arms, then proudly walked away and back to her by way of demonstration. There was only a faint limp. "Good to see you safe," then, putting her at arm's length, "but too thin, too thin."

The same could not be said of him, as he ruefully admitted; lack of real activity combined with the excellence of the food here was rapidly giving him a belly. "Two weeks today since the injury. Not bad, is it?"

She was stunned; two *weeks*! Just two weeks, and she was a different person.

Morú, Sett said, was a wonder with her herbs and healings. "I call her Lady *Ramidu*, and she scolds me for it — the *Atarlum* does not have many defenders here. Whenever she's tired of Untimarr, she can come to me — I say this when he's there, no harm in that."

None, she agreed; Sett's determination to stay unmarried was a recognized family joke. According to Âna's mother Sett in his early years had been 'disappointed' by a woman he had hoped to marry; since achieving prosperity he had become increasingly convinced any woman who showed signs of attraction had only his money in view; his urgent business journeys to escape entanglement were part of Konatstead legend.

To Sett, Untimarr was splendid, too, a joy to watch at work or talk with about woods, able to tell Nîv oak from Colony with the tips of his fingers. Already, Sett was looking forward to when he would be able to do some business in Kamsilat woods with the master-carpenter.

Where they were was an instance of Untimarr's skill, built as a whim, three rooms fitted in so cunningly you could circle the house repeatedly and be sure they could not exist.

"Some Household officers were in the house last week. We have not seen any more of Master Rheduban. Could it be he has lost his taste for whipping?"

She felt her back throb, and swallowed. "And gone to knives."

"You let me chatter on, and you've got all the news — I have been fretting for some word. Morú says it vexes my injury, but there's no poultice for that."

She began her tale, and her uncle's embarrassment soon gave way to wonder. Untimarr arrived, summoned from work on the other side of town, large, broad-handed, with a deep, confident voice and an easy courtesy that did not depend on forms. His pleasure at seeing Âna here was genuine as oak, and she was flattered by the gleam of warm bawdy in his eye, amused by the slight, intimate squeeze he gave her hand, as he innocently endorsed what his wife had told him about Âna's prettiness.

For both men (though Sett was used to it) she had gone contrary to all notions of what was proper for a woman. They must very well understand, though she did not belabor it, for what Kamin-Tolagh had plucked her from the fields, and how she had become so well-informed on Kargul and its plans, but neither made any comment, or seemed about to begin despising her. In her release from the oppression of lying and playing a part, away at last from the nastiness of the baKarguli circle, it all at once seemed to her the realm must be filled with good and kindly and generous people.

At the end Untimarr said bluntly, "They will never take Orbanak, ordinary folk. Nothing against the boy, but what would he be but the Patriarch's tame falcon? No, no — it's Rodlakh or war, you can see that."

Âna told him about divisions in the Household, perhaps General Cavalry as well, Kamin-Tolagh hurrying home to bring up a thousand fresh lances. "Let him. They say we can't stand against *pefral*, and that might be true if we're fools enough to wait in the open. Give them the crossroads and market-square — and let them try to grow their crops there, too. They cannot go everywhere on a front of sixteen lances; let's see them govern with a bowman waiting in every hedge."

As for General Cavalry he promised one garrison that would declare for Rodlakh; Untimarr would speak with officers of the Burantal squadrons first thing, and was sure which way they would go; they were men who had refused to take hostages when Rheduban was searching for his curfew-breakers. But the warning he gave confirmed her anxieties; Rodlakh, he said, would have to claim his own.

"News may already be on its way to him, out of Owan Sai. But I am going to Kamsilat to make sure."

"Alone? You can't do that, mistress." Sett, with long experience of telling Âna what she could not do, gave him a painful look.

"You must excuse me. I'm old-fashioned, yes, but Kadon Dinul ways do not suit all the realm, and Mistress Âna there are safer things these days for a strong man, as you know, than travel. Don't mind me, mistress."

He would go and speak to his friend at the Marionette Guild, Ondir, about banners. "What is it Rodlakh's colors display? A tree?"

"Bronze-beech," she said.

"Ondir will know. They have made many a banner for a puppet *rabhsai*; they'll welcome the change."

When he had gone Âna questioned Sett, who had once told her about a man with a boat in a village called Voruni, not far from Burantal. His name was Alkmas, Sett said, a strange man, but a fine navigator, who would help if he recalled past favors.

Near dawn, reassuring Sett there would yet be work for him to do, she slipped out of Burantal to the southward. Morulis, younger and prettier of the two daughters, led her by a backpath as far as a winding stair up the hillside, a way once used by those who garrisoned the watchtower now broken and decayed. Halfway up a path went branching off, leading through young woods and a tiny foaming watercourse, looping down to the road south of the hills. As Untimarr had predicted, she saw no one. Swiftly crossing the road she picked up a meandering and little-used track, which soon fell in beside the well-defined bank of a stream that could only be Shuburu, hurrying to Arnan. In about an hour she left mudflats by the stream and climbed a low eminence to look out on Arnan.

An age ago, before the Night of Owan, when Burantal was a camp guarding the Gap, Kadon just a gathering of hamlets and Dônshei the royal seat, when the Empire of Owan stretched from the Great Gulf, Flamûrai, in the West all the way to the Eastern

Ocean, there had been a busy port here, the outlet of Shuburu. She could not remember the name of that port, had never known why it had risen, nor the reason for its decline and death. Now it was only stumps of once-great buildings among weeds and bushes, the blackened remains of teeth in the very old. Where did hopes go? On a ridge the far side of where the port had been there was whitethorn growing, as very likely when the city was founded and in the years of its flourishing. Not those same bushes, but mayblossom came back, spring after spring, and in the end outlasted wrought stone.

Was it enough? Trying to imagine a world without her, she was not much consoled that she might hand down some of herself to children (though she could not see whose). She would want to be remembered by a few, with fondness, she hoped. All that was brave but futile, like building in stone. What else was there? Absurd to war against decay and oblivion, but what else was there?

This side of the mouth of Shuburu was the mean fishing-village, Voruni, but the house of Alkmas was said to be beyond the main huddle of houses, a short way west along the flat coastline of the bay. She skirted dwellings, where early starters stretched their nets or carried tackle down to beached boats. Soon she reached a stony stretch of shore where Arnan breathed and rasped in a slow rhythm, and mist hung on the far horizon. The one or two men she passed gave her glances of little curiosity; work-tough people on a bleak shore where there was small leisure for wondering about strangers. In a short while, tucked in a small hollow amid wiry grasses, she saw the turf roof of what must be the house she wanted.

Following a worn path on its circuit to miss a rocky patch, she was met by an odd-shaped man, stout at the top and spindle-legged below. With his straight-up hair and big, wattled nose he was like some ungainly wading-bird, his head keeping the rhythm of his looping pace. It was easy to see where his nickname came from, 'Heron.'

"Master Alkmas," addressing him as he came up. Reluctantly, when he had almost passed her by, he admitted that was his name. "If you're wanting fish, pay their price at market; I have none to sell." Sett had told her that Alkmas, who often had good catches when everyone else's nets were empty, suffered from perpetual suspicion an undefined *they* were trying to cheat him out of a fair price, and had been known to hold most of a big catch till good for nothing but to spread on fields as fertilizer.

"Master, I do not want fish."

"In the wrong town then, aren't you?" He laughed at his own joke; with his mouth, round, with thick projecting lips, his nickname could just as easily be *Tunnyfish*.

"I want you to take me to the Colony."

"Ah? Will midday suit you? You would not rather try the moon? Fine day for a sail, I grant you, but I am not running the Kamsilat Ferry." Hard to say the voice was high-pitched or low; it had odd twists and minglings. She did not find it unpleasant.

"My uncle, Sett, told me to come to you." She had one of his trading-tokens which she now displayed in her open hand.

"Kind of him." Now Alkmas really looked at her.

"He told me to enquire whether you were as crabbed as ever. He is at Burantal, injured."

"Ah? Broke his hand, did he, driving a bargain. Yes, all right, I see it, that's his token, good as a turd in any port on Arnan. What is it you want from me?"

"I have told you," she was patient. "To go to Kamsilat, speedily. They say you have the best boat. I have gold." She produced some, Kamin-Tolagh's.

Told what to expect, she was not discouraged by the objections Alkmas made. If he had the best boat he would hate to see second-best, let alone worst. He was just a fisherman, and had no supplies for such a journey. He wished people would leave him alone.

She shrugged up her heavy pack. "I have plenty of supplies, except water." The robe of rose-colored shuzi she had left behind; she wanted to have it burnt, but the idea of such waste had shocked Morú.

Alkmas grunted. "Oh, water. Whole riverfull of that, all it takes is somebody to fill up some barrels." He shook his head to complain about loss of a week's good fishing, with the brownfish about to run.

"Name your price," not willing to put coin after coin in the man's hand; she had already offered more than he could possibly make in a month's good fishing.

Nothing wrong with her price, it was the fishing; he hated to see good fish left in Arnan for want of somebody to take them. "This Voruni is full of fools who couldn't take brownfish out of their rain-butts. No, I do not want to go to Kamsilat. Outside law, that is, to take a man there, or a woman."

It had never occurred that Alkmas might refuse; she had not made any real second plan. Acidly she asked him for names of any braver boat-owners hereabouts.

"What do they call you?"

"Âna Konats-daughter."

"Konat." He showed recognition. "Nambalus way. Are you the one set straight two scribes about their spelling?"

"That was many years ago."

"Oh, aye, it was. Six you were then, and you're past seven now. What's your business with the Colony?"

"My business is my own, and urgent. Give me back my gold and I shall find someone else to take me. I have no time for chatter." After Rheduban she was not going to let mere rudeness intimidate her.

He was derisive, inviting her to show him anyone on this bit of coast who was certain he could navigate as far as, for example, Tan Lughsai. "If so, you'll be luckier than your uncle ever was. But if we're stopped by a patrol-boat, your tongue had better have a smoother side than that, Mistress Âna."

He was perfectly bland, as if all his refusals made up the natural way of saying yes. In good faith she could not conceal the added difficulties. "But there has been talk the Patriarch is going to close the Strait. How could that be done?"

"Been done before — closed, you should say, to rabbits who shit and run soon as they see a rammer. That's nothing; open or closed if I can't get through the Strait I'll join the *Mankh'* as mumbler-in-chief." H45e had turned back, and she was skipping to keep up with his stride.

"Lend a hand with some tackle, and we'll sail by noon, if that suits you." He halted to give a sly look. "I suppose you do not object to a slight smell of fish?"

iii

The Frontier

After an exchange of courtesies Dolvid told Aëlu, "I have discovered who is the Patriarch's spy here at Kamsilat."

She made an enigmatic face. "What are you going to do about that?"

"That is why I wanted to speak with you. I do not know." He had originally invited her to another stroll in the grounds, and when a shower spoiled that she came instead to the light and airy room put at his disposal ever since the warriors, old and young, had learned what he had done, beside write dispatches, in the Narn Campaign long ago. He was a quartermaster again, and had filled sheet after sheet with details of where troops were and their supplies would come from, inventories of weapons and munitions, of shipping. His chief window looked out on gardens, trees, and a gleaming slice of the Navu where it bent northward, but today clouds had come down to close off westward sight of distant, sharp-backed heights.

"Should I be told?" more inscrutable than ever. He had not known just what she would say, but had made a private wager she would not begin by asking the spy's name.

"*Asayu*." The title made her frown, but he was making a speech. "In history I have always deplored counsellors who knew better than their masters what those masters should know. It is an ancient plague. Hardly a minor advisor to a provincial magistrate who has not been sure his employer might do the wrong thing if he had all the facts. Often, they had the best of intentions, but those with responsibility for making decisions must be given — "

"*Bôdhrai*, we are not back with at-Keliukh; I follow you. If you are afraid Rodlakh might do something rash, given the spy's name, you could speak to Saidhan instead."

"And the other way about," he concurred. "Here is a man who is surely to blame for the deaths of the two archers, your bodyguards — well, you could say he shares responsibility for all deaths at Drin b'Afon and after. Worst of all, to my mind, he sent the apprentice lad at the light-tower straight to his death. That is hard to overlook."

"Who is he?" at last, and he told her, Vinosai, under-warden of the port. When she observed rather than objected that Vinosai had been many years at Kamsilat, Dolvid answered that would be true of a spy; Vinosai was trusted, worked at different tasks, was known for quiet ways and freedom from any scandal or controversy.

"But not with everyone. The trader, Sett, has never trusted the man. It was a joke he always told Vinosai he was going to Nambalus when he sailed for Klam Lughsai, or Kôbh-mouth when he was making for Irbat. One of his quirks — well, you have met him."

"Yes, and noticed one quirk in particular."

"His readiness — desire, could it be? — to seem less astute than he actually is."

"Exactly."

"The little niece, as I understand it — your pardon, never mind." Aëlu was not content with what she had learned about Âna, but put it aside. A grave charge, she said, against Vinosai.

One proved to Dolvid's satisfaction. He explained how Arvat had discovered that two days before the illness that put Vinosai in charge of the light-tower the usual keeper received a gift of wine for his birthday. He had not known who to thank, but recalled a visit from Vinosai who had a cup or two with him, just before he was taken ill. That was the tale used by the light-keeper to exculpate the wine, but it was easy to imagine ways Vinosai could have avoided drinking while making sure the other had some. No one had asked what had become of the undrunk remnant.

Far from the first occasion Vinosai had relieved at the light-tower, and quite possibly had used nights there to signal to vessels standing off-shore.

There was more to the case. Vinosai had not sounded the warning-gong when the abductors appeared — that was when he sent the apprentice to his death. His excuse was fear there would be an attack on the light-tower, and he made a strong point the gong was supposed to be sounded only in the event of an invasion. The question was, seeing some of the hostile force, how could he tell it was not part of a full-scale assault?

To clinch it, he had now done something which exasperated Dolvid with its stupidity, even though he had set the trap. Vinosai, asked to help with the inventory of shipping, had tried to leave off the list vessels in for caulking and scraping at Porrhaven, a small, rockbound harbor a short way down the coast. Arvat had described the place, where freakish tides made it convenient to maintain dry-docks, with gates like the locks on Dromladh's Canal. "When I asked, Vinosai said he had forgotten — effective Warden of the Port, and he forgets where ships go for repairs?"

"Why do you tell this to me?" It had seemed plain, though now he came to it the reasons were hard to express. He had no sentiment about Vinosai, who should die fighting alongside the *Adanum Plakh'*, his proper station. But trial and execution were unpleasant to contemplate, and there was a chance they could use Vinosai to convey to their enemies misleading reports of their intentions.

Aëlu, justly enough, supposed he had already made up his mind by himself, and repeated her question, what did he want from her?

"It is too large a burden. Someone had to be told I had uncovered the spy and done nothing about it."

"Someone who could not overrule you."

"Well, you could tell Rodlakh or Saidhan."

"Do you want to hear what I think?" She was amused. "If I went to Saidhan and told him all this, endorsing your decision not to move against Vinosai, I who am supposed to have suffered most in the abduction, it would surprise me if he did not also approve — he is a strategist. Then, well, whether or not to inform Rodlakh, how he might take the news, that would all be up to Saidhan *Asai*, not so?"

"Agreed."

"To think I could make such a plan all by myself." Her luminous eyes probed at his. "Dolvid, great house intrigue is not your best craft."

She had gone when Rodlakh arrived, sitting at once to begin unlacing his boots. Earlier Kamin-Tarú had been dressed for riding, but Rodlakh could not be accused of neglecting duties; he had just come from First Bridge, anxious again over lack of word from Nolimas. Ships were ready, many arrows and spare lances in hand. Supplies were no particular concern, since it was no wilderness they meant to overrun, but following the example of the Summer Palace they had saddle-rations packed ready in many small bags quickly sewn by a draft of wives and daughters; as Saidhan said, an invading army, all except the troops.

He came in a little later. Rodlakh had talked about the need for a proclamation, not as an advance warning of coming invasion, but to go ahead as a banner, announcing the Army of the West —

"Acts for the wellbeing of the realm," Dolvid supplied, "and the safety of Ban-Sila *Deghi*, and will count as allies all those who do not actively impede us."

From the doorway Saidhan's short laugh was sardonic. "Has anybody ever started a war except for the sake of peace? In '76 Tobhsila sent word to Nivu Din he came as a protector. Luckily it is a town that stands on a river." Retreating, the Kargul' troops had tried to burn the city, where of old much wood had been used in building. Buckets passed hand-to-hand from the riverbank had saved most of the town.

Rodlakh, flushing, said, "Murderers have said *welcome to this house*, but we do not stop saying it, or decide it is never sincere. Besides, I want more in the message than that." He did; phrases about taxes fairly apportioned and a law equitably administered, the desirability of settling differences through negotiation — much more than could be put in any effective proclamation. Saidhan, besides, kept counselling caution about what promises were put in writing before they knew what could be accomplished, and Rodlakh wanted to preserve legality, with no suggestion any measure would ever be imposed on an unwilling Ban-Sila. It was starting to become a wrangle when Dolvid ostentatiously put down his pen, and Rodlakh, taking the hint, asked him how long it had been since he had a bout at swords.

The sun was out again, damp patches in the yard drying, as they worked up a sweat with vigorous swordplay, watched by a few junior officers and some stablemen. Dolvid in his exile had taught the rudiments to a couple of boys, but his main fighting at Drin b'Afon had been with a knife, and he could not remember when he had last crossed blades with a skilled adversary. Rodlakh had quick hands, but at the start was lacking in concentration, and was surprised by how much Dolvid retained from the great teacher of his boyhood. As shadows began to stretch Rodlakh was pressing harder, frowning, and when they circled Dolvid saw there were two slender forms in the shadow of the door-arch, Aëlu and Kamin-Tarú. Rodlakh's conditioning was the better, and his sword-arm in practice; exchanges grew longer, and Dolvid was not unhappy when an interruption came. A dull bell gave a double clang as a hard-ridden *pefrai* came panting into the courtyard, flanks white-scrubbed, rider dusty and winded.

Before the messenger was out of the saddle Rodlakh had given his bated sword to one of the watching file-leaders, and was loosening straw-padded jacket and collar. The man, an ordinary soldier, made deference and handed over dispatches, scarlet-sealed.

"Nolimas." Rodlakh indicated to the man who had stood by with cold drink to give some to the messenger: *raminat*, now in abundant supply at Kamsilat.

Breaking seal and unwrapping, he quickly scanned. "*What?*" A second sheet, and Rodlakh read, muttering, then thrust the bundle at Dolvid. "Let us find Saidhan."

A sketchy idea of Nolimas as big and unsubtle was not much filled in by the dispatch, made of phrases cast in bronze that had served the military with hardly a change for centuries, robbing any event of reality. He expressed formal regrets over the death of Sebhal, news that had gone westward with Rodlakh's new instructions, since it had somehow become common knowledge at Kamsilat. After that, Nolimas flatly rejected the orders he had been given: it would be, he said, ill-advised and precipitate to consider transferring troops to other parts at such a time. Instead, the garrisons at Kreshavu and even Banakit should be made available to reinforce the Frontier. If feasible, he would proceed with the evacuation of the Mines, but to augment rather than reduce strength at the Frontier fortress, Drin Navuna.

Writing this, he was at Kreshavu, less than a dayride from the Frontier, where his new orders from Kamsilat had reached him simultaneously with fresh news from the Drin. There he had also met with and questioned a `duster' from off Landegh, who swore he had seen (but Nolimas wrote *observed*) a marching company of thirty to forty well-armed *jinzal*. So far Nolimas had not spoken with the other men, the traders, with their tales from the Farther West, but in view of what he understood of their account, and this new report, together with the fact that neither the original convoy overdue with its escort, nor the squadron sent out to look for it, had been heard from, he was on his own authority suspending all leaves, curtailing non-military duties, and preparing to begin a general westward movement of troops. Former soldiers farming in the Kreshavu country had been alerted for a possible return to the colors, and Nolimas urged the same be done with the more numerous pensioners in the Vale of Banakit.

`*Men with many years of service here,*' Nolimas wrote. He had started to cross that out, then let it stand, with re-emphasis: `*who have spent long lifetimes here in the West recall no such reports as these. The security of the Frontier remains the primary duty for the Army of the West.*'

"He is rebuking my inexperience — " the smile was very grim. "Forty *jinzal* marching in rows! Men who go wandering on Landegh catch the infection of impossible sights, as children do measles."

"What is a `duster'?" They had come back to Dolvid's work-room, and Aëlu had offered to wake Saidhan from his nap.

"A man of the tribes — they can smell water, it is said. They go out on Landegh for small amounts of gold — not veins or nuggets, particles mixed with the dust; they carry two small bowls and pour dust from one bowl to the other, taking out stones. The wind blows, and at last there is nothing left but a few grains of gold — a pinch of gold, with luck, for days of labor and weeks of journeying."

"And a lot of danger."

He nodded. "The wandering tribes let them be, help them, if they are lucky, when they run out of food or water. But the duster I met went white with terror, just at the word, *jinzai*. They are men unlike others, solitary, and in the end when they go out and do not come back, no one mourns for them."

"Perhaps we should envy them."

Rodlakh half-agreed, and his perplexity had nothing to do with war or *jinzal*. Dolvid waited to hear him assert the sport he was enjoying (as he surely was) with Kamin-Tarú was another expression of his love for Aëlu, or some such nonsense — nonsense Dolvid could easily have achieved at the same age. Everything was only itself, and if Dolvid lay with Tú while Âna was with Tú's brother, what? Symmetries too meant nothing else.

Returning, Rodlakh began to rail at the madness of basing vital military decisions on reports from a duster. "Why? Why does Nolimas have his attack of nerves just when everything is in the balance?"

"Insubordination," Saidhan, for the tenth time. He had listened to a reading of passages from the dispatch with growing irascibility. "Sebhal is gone, and you are being challenged to take charge."

While his waxed, Rodlakh's anger had waned, perhaps because he had come to a decision. "Nolimas is not going to have any troops moved up from Banakit; that could waste five days, going and coming back, not to say supplies — and their confidence in a command that marches them to and fro." He wanted new and countermanding orders to the military commander there, and a stern dispatch for Nolimas telling him to assemble all the strength he had at the Frontier, and to evacuate Shâl Mines if it took twelve squadrons.

"This would not have happened if we dared put in writing the purpose behind ordering squadrons east."

"Nolimas can give further reasons for doing other things," Saidhan said. "Weeks could be lost arguing this out, back and forth, and any chance for the Mainland will slip away."

"The only remedy is for me to be face-to-face with Nolimas. I shall ride for the Frontier at dawn. It can be done in sixty hours, killing no horses, and any fresh messages from Nolimas will reach me so much sooner. Dolvid, you will ride with me?"

"Of course." He had been going to claim the job.

After the evening meal they worked on together. The earlier dispatches had already begun the westward journey; fast-messengers would ride through night with lanterns hung at saddle bow, a change of horses waiting at every stage. Dolvid remarked how long ago he had first dreamed of seeing the Frontier, never seeming to outgrow his relish for remote and fabled places.

"Tú said the same, Kamin-Tarú baKargul. She is a splendid rider, but that is a hard road. Besides... "

"Besides." Last night, in his wide, unrumpled bed, he had begun to think he might have been too eager to usher delicious Tú into curing Rodlakh's deficiencies.

"Rumor," earnestly, "or gossip, has been very unjust to Kamin-Tarú." Dolvid braced for praise of her nature, paradoxically faithful, but instead Rodlakh was being converted to an Owani outlook. "Why should a woman, the same as a man, if it pleases her, not take pleasure where she finds it? Her brother is not condemned, or if he is it's with a laugh or with envy, and plenty of men, women too, admire his rutting. If a woman is made to enjoy more than one man, why should she go against her nature?"

"*Valrabh'*, what you say could easily come from your grandmother's mouth — Laluvoi's, I mean." Or Âna's, Dolvid silently added. It could not be long before Rodlakh brought him the news a woman's pleasure, he truly believed, was no less than a man's. Perhaps greater.

Suddenly in dark thought, Rodlakh said, "A hundred times a day I wish we had forced her to come with us."

Plainly, not Kamin-Tarú. Dolvid, astonished, said, "The cliffs at Drin b'Afon were easier." He was not joking.

"I cannot foresee where we shall meet her again." Rodlakh shook himself, a dog coming out of water. "Well, once again, we've got our job to do."

It was very early. A clammy sea-mist was making all the world a dull grey, in which people, horses, buildings, trees loomed as improbable clottings. Before going to mount, Dolvid encountered Galt on his way to the barracks, wearing the newly-conferred insignia of a full squadron-leader.

"*Bôdhrai*, where are we going to fight?"

"You are longing for the Frontier."

"Dry, there." He shuddered.

"We have to be prepared against the chance of an invasion."

"Ah, yes, *Bôdhrai* — " with the grin of a man who knows ships are not made ready to prepare a port's defenses. "We'll fight where we're sent, but if you teach a jackal to swim he's still no fish."

"You may well go west." There had been general agreement the best use of mounted bows was there. "How is Haun, have you heard?" The man had looked near death when they made port after the Island.

"He'll mend, he wants to be up and at the Frontier, his home. You are going there now?"

He nodded, not asking how he knew.

"Good road, *Bôdhrai*."

Hard to say who had risen to say farewell to whom. Rodlakh exchanged quiet words with Saidhan, while Kamin-Tarú, lithe under her cloak, hair soft in the mist, gazed up at Dolvid and hoped they would meet again. After mounting, Rodlakh took the girl's fine white hand in his. Wrapped as ever in her mysterious self-sufficiency Aëlu emerged from the doorway. "May I recommend, *Bôdhrai*, you shorten your stirrup?"

"I prefer them long for a full day's riding."

"You will find this is not the Great Stone Road to Kred Bakali. Three fingers shorter, I implore."

He checked resentment; she had seen Sebhal off on this journey a thousand times. Dismounting he shortened the stirrup, while she took in the leather on the right-hand side. As he was getting back up she put her hand over his on the saddle-bow. "Saidhan knows about Vinosai, and approves your plan. Now ride safe, *Bôdhrai* — and see he does the same." Rodlakh was bent down in the saddle murmuring to Kamin-Tarú. In the doorway was a tight-lipped Doleni, though what she disapproved of was debatable — it could as well be that Saidhan had interrupted sleep to be here. Rodlakh's acknowledgement of and farewell to Aëlu were correct, while Dolvid marvelled two women as different as Âna and Aëlu had both imagined he could do something to take care of Rodlakh. Among lesser watchers away to the left, shapes dim, Arvat gave a solemn nod, and tilted his head very subtly to one side, to indicate a squatter shape that must be Vinosai; Arvat had the job of watching him.

Unescorted, they went down the sharp slope to take the road where it ran in its deep cutting through the Great House grounds, this morning a dank tunnel roofed in grey. Soon they had been passed with salutes through the city gate, and with the day beginning to lighten were on a good road, following the curve of the river till that bent back southward, the road going on due west. They came close to the river again near what Rodlakh said was the two-mile stone, then left it to begin climbing, soon amid large trees; their next glimpse of the Navu would be where they crossed it for the first of many times, First Bridge.

Rodlakh remarked it was good to have a strong beast in this stage, where some pace could be maintained, as it could not in many rougher places to the west. But the stretch between here and Banakit also had the steepest sustained climb, a real test of a horse's heart and temper.

Dolvid's *pefrai* was the best he remembered riding, tall, black and deep in the chest, more clean-limbed than many, very sure of foot. He was called Enikai, suggesting the Owani *daënighai*, eagle.

They passed small farms cut out of the forest, the occasional house standing at roadside, many trails winding away into the trees. Now, beyond a band of dark cone-bearers they reached First Bridge, a massy structure of wood and stone across a deep, steep-sided gulch where the Navu rushed and thundered, though southward in less tumbled country they could see the river's shining and placid bends.

After pausing for a few words with soldiers of the guard-post here they entered a long, straight, testing climb, beginning of a series that took them up to where all sign of human habitation faded, trees fell away to bare rock or earth fissured and strewn with boulders. The sun was up, but colors here were austere shades of brown; they reached a dour, almost circular plain among circling brown hills, where there were dozens, hundreds of small hillocks, bare and sudden with rounded tops. The Froghul, Rodlakh said, held they were the work of sand-gods, but one small tribe living near Vonn claimed these were their lands, before the Owanil ever came west of Arnan — not before they returned, but before the First Empire, centuries earlier. In turn their legend said a people had this land before them, and lived in the forests, bringing their dead up here to be at the heart of these little hills. "But that would be before the world began."

Dolvid wanted to hear detail. This was, he said, a dismal enough spot for burial grounds. "If this is the country at their backs I do not wonder Frontier men fight so well for their farms."

Rodlakh assured him he would see better land at Banakit, and though there were barren lands beyond, Kreshavu was a pleasant place. "You will enjoy Kreshavu," kicking up his horse. "And we must be there by tomorrow night."

West of that town the road would pass very near eventual headwaters of the Navu, so for all the miles from Kamsilat road and river were lovers who could neither live together nor stay apart, long out of each other's sight but then intertwined again, or for a space content to be quietly side by side. In rocky country with uphill and downhill not gaining them any elevation the riders crossed the river twice more by stone-built bridges called New and Old. In part Old Bridge dated from the Age of the Shâls, and which was the ancient work was easily seen, lichened pillars rising indestructible and with a plain grace from the granite of the chasm, stone fitted together by masons with no living parallel. A wild, broken ravine where pale, contorted pines clung and rocks above suggested vigilant faces; what was said about the bridge was exchanged in hushed tones, and notwithstanding his deep interest in the stonework Dolvid was not sorry to put that place behind, with its brooding *mai*.

Beyond, going was more arduous still, road mounting in great irregular steps over ridge after keen-edged ridge, maintaining its westerly course, letting the Navu go off on a far northern meander while battling its own way across the rocky barrier. They would next see the river near Banakit.

They reached Vonn, an iron-hard hamlet fitted in among crags it seemed chopped from. A few patches of lean growing had been scratched out, and there were disdainful goats tethered by most of the houses. They stopped here to talk with quiet-faced, watchful but courteous men who brought them beer cool from storage deep in the shadowed stone; the day had never turned hot, but dust from the road had settled deep in throats. Rodlakh had to answer questions about Sebhal's death, while from the dusky insides of squat dwellings Dolvid was conscious of dark, gleaming eyes set in softer features, filled with curiosity about these important travellers. The clean air here caused him to tremble with anticipation which had no particular object. It came to him he was happy.

In the brief climb from Vonn dim memory stirred. "Are we somewhere near Vonni's Jaws?"

"We are there," with a gesture. "Look."

It was a cleft between dizzying cliffs where the road had been formed by filling with rubble. At the end of a steep descent the road bent back sharply to the right, cliffs against the sky like a block cloven by the stroke of a huge axe. They could be scaled, Rodlakh said, though not easily, from the village side, but from westward were unclimbable ("even for you spiders of Drin b'Afon, I think."). An age ago, Vonni, whose jaws these were, was a legendary local chieftain who rebelled in the reign of Shâl IV. Having allowed large armies of Owan to pass westward he "closed his Jaws" and with a few dozen men held this position against whole legions, till Larghai, coming up from the coast, forced his way from eastward into the hamlet, then a mere war-camp, named for Vonni, who even then held out on the clifftops till food was gone.

Dolvid bent his head back as they rode between sheer walls, and was glad this part of the Colony was at peace. If there was anything loose up there for the rolling, defenders would hardly need bows, and there was no nearby way of circling around. Coming to Fourth Bridge eastward from Banakit, it was said, if instead of crossing you turned north along the riverbank, you could thread a way past the mountains in the easier country where the Navu went, through water-meadows and marshlands, and come down into the wooded valley of Kamsilat from northward, after a week's journey. So the tale went; he was not sure anyone still knew that way, and there was no shorter one, or none had ever been found in the two separate sets of centuries when men had tried, First Empire and the present Colony.

Out of the Jaws the way was only by comparison more open, and they began a tedious series of twists and turns in a bewilderingly rough country. There were ridges yet to climb, but now the overall tendency was noticeably downward. On a steep upslope they overtook a loaded wagon, four horses straining to achieve the slowest of plods, driver cursing them on. At the top Rodlakh shaded his eyes, first sight of the Vale of Banakit, its

kindly green a glad shock to the eye after so much naked rock —
like crossing the wilderness of Naëni in the far Northeast and
coming at last to the fertile hinterland of Narn, though this was
not so lushly green as that bowl. By a long, straight slope, a
ramp, they came down for reunion with the Navu, which here
became broad and quiet-flowing. Southward, masses of brown
hills edged up as the riders jogged down. Here was Fourth
Bridge, a plain and useful span, and at its far end a miniature
fortress, the strong guardhouse with walled compound enclosing
both bridgehead and stables for mounts of the fast-messengers.
Once again guards were flustered when they saw who was riding
without escort, but calmed by Rodlakh's friendly wave; passing
through the arched gate Dolvid and he came to a nearly level
stretch of good road, bending hard left, then curving right to
follow the course of the Navu. Willows bent over the near bank
of the river, but the margins of the road had been planted with
grey-skinned beeches and airy poplars to form an avenue.
Ahead, past where the town must lie, the ground began rising
steadily once again, skirts thick with fir and pine mounting to the
hard outer bastions of true mountains, the direction of the
Frontier, of Landegh.

At a gap in the line of trees where a lane came in Rodlakh
grasped Dolvid's arm, and pointed southward, where domes of
arid highland loomed against latening sky. "Up there is Lunu
Tezh' Gate — you can see the broken watchtowers where the
saddles are. Since we claimed the Protectorate, only main passes
have been guarded, and then only with a handful. Men up from
the lakeside make their way through the Gate, for trade, or to
enlist in the Army of the West."
     "As Truni did." He was carrying the painted leather armband
taken from the young slinger's wrist at Drin b'Afon, hoping to
find a family to give it to.
     "The Lunu Tezh' men all know each other; some marry and
settle here, but they all have dreams of going back. They get
together and sing songs about that."
     "Do they dance?"

A keen look. "Sebhal said you had fallen in love with the Froghul — you wrote a book about them, too?"

"I should have the job over again; I was too young." Rodlakh was still curious, and Dolvid said a little about those few days when he was fifteen, still vivid, when he had stayed with the Froghul of Dramaru, at the Great Pledging of '21. After the long rough road he was wearily comfortable at day's end on this smooth and pleasant stretch, great horse moving under him, the feeling of something accomplished. For once he let sentiment claim him, and Rodlakh perhaps was puzzled by the note of elegy, sense of a vastly valuable treasure held for an instant, then lost forever; the companionship, those dances, the joy and pride in being accepted by a dignified people, even his own idiocy in misunderstanding what Tini-ra meant with her sad, earnest eyes, her nearness and touchings, her gentle courage in trying to break down his naive pomposity.

Rodlakh was wry. "You said your only pleasures were facts, ideas, words."

"These are words. I know better now."

"Know what better?"

"Self-preservation."

He indicated: "Here is the two-mile stone for Banakit. How is your mount? Has he got a run left in him?"

"If I let him he would gallop to the Western Ocean. I have been holding him in all day."

"Come on, then." On his chestnut Rodlakh spurted away. Crouched in the saddle they rounded a long curve, and there was the town, low walls, whitish buildings, stained now by the falling sun. Between well-worked farms and sparsish pasture the road ran straight for the gate set in its rounded archway, banner with the Red Blossom of the West coiling lazily in the southern breeze. A slow-trundling wagon, and by seeded growing-land Dolvid was obliged to rein in while Rodlakh swung past. Then Enikai bunched his muscles and sprang out as if fresh from the stable. At the mile-pillar Dolvid was wrist to wrist, and then past; on the brief paved stretch up to the city he slowed to let the *Valrabh'* catch up.

"A good beast," Rodlakh panted. "It is surely not the rider." The horse had been one of his personal string brought here when he came from the Mainland, and he asked Dolvid to take Enikai to keep. "Sebhal told me a man should never ride to war without a blade of his own, a horse of his own, and a woman of his own to wait for his safe return."

Dolvid thanked him, touched by the gift; he understood Enikai would have be stabled in Banakit for a while, since they would take fresh mounts in the morning.

As they went in at the gate an alert trumpeter sounded such a flourish the guards grabbed weapons and sprang to attention before finding out who had arrived. An unseen dog, small by its voice, began frantic chiding.

While most towns had their main buildings fronting or flanking an open square, often both marketplace and site of public meetings, the heart of Banakit was a low hill with a stand of fir on its sandy soil. Happ, commander of the garrison, was also town-magistrate, a large man, moon-faced and thick at the middle, several years past retirement age. He gave them a fine dinner with good wine at his official residence crowning the hill, where they would spend the night. He was affably skeptical about the rumors from the Frontier, recalling many past occasions when the excitable had been ready to predict doom.

Happ was proud that by cancelling leaves, paring escorts and garrisons providing them, levying added men to take over some of the routine, he had assembled nearly three whole squadrons of fighting troops, who would have gone eastward but for the countermanding order from Nolimas. Now, they were ready to ride east or west, as the captains decided.

That must be true, and all the senior officers watching the struggle between Rodlakh and Nolimas; with Saidhan aged and Sebhal gone the leadership of the West was a big prize. Yet in the manner of its phrasing Happ's comment was that of a junior squadron-leader resigned to the vagaries of those on high, rather than an experienced captain with wide authority of his own.

"He is sound," was the dry comment, as they set out again, sun yet unrisen, valley quiet in warmless colors under thin slices of hanging mist. Sebhal, Rodlakh went on, maintained men of Happ's kind were necessary at that level: for patrols, skirmishes, hunts he wanted young officers with imagination — Galt, for an example. But for a major war Sebhal always said he would want to know there were *kímukan* and under-captains who would be where they were told at the hour prescribed, no questions.

Dolvid, having taken a dislike to Happ, said, "Not presuming to differ with a war-leader of Sebhal's renown — " a curious way to say he was going to differ. He recalled instances in history when under-captains appearing where they should not be had won key battles, back as far as the fabled Larghai, who might have lost at Kaëfan Tufani, but for a departure from plan by his subordinate, Gaëladhai.

"That was a long age ago," thoughtfully. "Then, too, Sebhal never came to his big war. In a campaign, I might waste my temper and my spirit on men like Happ. If a thousand of these *jinzal* who march in formation came through Lunu Tezh' Gate tomorrow, he would ask for instructions. Well — " shrugging off the question, urging his new horse, saying this was a stretch where they had to make good speed against much rougher going later. With the river the road swung south in the narrow band of flatter land, and ahead the hills were great impossible thunderclouds piled against a morning sky pale and with sooty streaks of cloud.

Here in the Vale of Banakit they were hailed by other travellers and early-rising householders; a wagonload of farm boys on their way to plantings recognized Rodlakh and raised a cheer as the *pefrai*-riders swept by in gentle sunlight.

Soon the river was abandoned once again, and they were climbing lightly-wooded slopes fragrant with spring. Now their course was westward, and they came down to Fifth Bridge, a wide one, strong-built of stone, at its near end an extensive compound with ranks of empty wagons and long rows of stabling for *pefral* as well as draft and pack-animals. The reason for all this could be seen across the bridge, where the road, narrowing, clambered rapidly up into a land of pillars and spires, no more than a mountain pack-route from here to the valley of Drin

Navuna.   At this point all westward-bound goods were transferred from wagons to the backs of hill-ponies or tough little donkeys, while the fewer things going east, notably diggings of Shâl Mines and other rock crops from Landegh (some substances used by Heartland dyers, for example), often went from pony-back to a wagon.

Well back from the road over to the left, with a breathtaking situation at head of a deep ravine shadowed in blue, there was a handsome, lowbuilt structure, plainly a *margú*, even without the semi-circle of slender *ramminal* on its eastward side.   The *ramminai* was the tree whose leaves became *raminat*, but not these, which were dead, or nearly so.   The disused doorway was blocked by heavy timbers nailed in place.   More than a decade had passed since the *Atarlum* quit the Colony.

"This, then — ?" Dolvid began, and did not need to go on. It was the hostelry where Aëlu had been a *nôd'yanu*, till Sebhal met her, and shocked the Families, scandalized the *Mankh'*, and delighted many ordinary people by carrying her off to be his bride, she being just nineteen, with much of her indenture to run. It had really happened. Here was the site.

At the cavalry post attached to the compound Rodlakh listened to grievances of a squadron-leader who had been required to give up a file — his best, he said — from a squadron already under strength, to the assembling of forces back at Banakit. Now, he grumbled, he was responsible for day and night guarding of bridge and compound, the security of a long stretch of road, all with thirty-three men. "All respect, *Asai*, those men were needed here."

Dolvid did not know what could be Rodlakh's model for the patience with which he questioned, gently reprimanded, commended and satisfied the man, whose name was Idmas, asking him his opinion of Preference and whether he would give up his best men more gladly if they helped keep the promise Sebhal made, that Preference would never be imposed on the Colony. Idmas said it was not his place to question orders, but here Rodlakh demurred, saying it was indeed; if he saw the order as mistaken it was not only his right but his duty to question it, after first complying, as Idmas had.

"While I," he concluded, "have the duty to explain. If we continue to differ, you will have to swallow your grievances, or invent better arguments." Something here of his amiable father without Lambarr's frequent inconsequentiality, some of Sebhal's veiled steel, but none of the arbitrary expectations always lurking with him; not inexplicably the performance converted Idmas into an enthusiast, eager to be part of any expedition. "No one says," he burst out, "how our Sebhal died. We say there was treachery in it, and somebody's going to pay for it."

"We may live to see many debts settled," Rodlakh said.

The first day's journey had ended at evening; this day they did not come in sight of their goal till darkness was gathering. Tireder, they saw Kreshavu, perched on its low cliff down which a slender double ribbon of white water fell. In actual miles their distance was shorter, but the narrow, rough way slower going, a toiling plod up rocky hills and with care down slopes till backs and shoulders ached with the strain of holding their mounts. After Sixth Bridge the land softened a little, and Dolvid began to lose his feeling of confinement, of being condemned like a rope-walker halfway across to hold to one narrow way.   Then the lower point in a red-brown ridge dotted with low bushes, and they were looking across at Kreshavu.

Not a large city, facing south from its shelf, while down below the slender waterfalls merged into a single stream racing for oblivion in the Navu. Sable mountains hemmed every horizon, indigo cloud was layered above, and in the pale sky a single star, Aëlovoi's Handmaid, was icily brilliant.

Immediately surrounding Kreshavu the lands were barren, though Rodlakh said faint trails visible in good daylight led to green valleys, small and large, hidden among the dry hills, and terraced farms on wide, watered steps.

The westward road ran near the base of the cliff, and there was a small cavalry-post where a paved way led above to the

town. Here fast-messengers coming down from the Frontier
made their first change of mounts; it was now deeply-shadowed.
Rodlakh ignored a guard's challenge and pressed forward to
where in shafts of lantern-light a *pefrai* was being given a saddle
equipped with the gallows device where a lamp was hung for
night-riding. In a confusion of shouts and rattling weapons
Dolvid called out, "It is the *Valrabh'*," and then a young guard
was asking pardon, Rodlakh assuring him there was no harm,
cutting off discussion with a demand to know where the fast-
messenger was, the one intending a night ride. Just then, wine-
cup in hand, satchel over his shoulder, a broad, cheerful-faced
man came sauntering down from the little drink-shop where
ways met. When hailed, he was abruptly embarrassed and
unintentionally comical as he sought a place to put his cup, or
someone to take it.

Rodlakh did, sipped, and handed it back to him with the
comment he did well to keep refreshed.

Knowing the *Valrabh'* had started west Nolimas had told the
messenger to look for him, but forecast the meeting would be at
Banakit, or east of there. He handed over his dispatches, and
Rodlakh fumbled at a seal the color of dried blood in the dim,
then changed his mind, saying he might have something to add
for Saidhan. "Come with us to the hostelry," he told the
messenger, "and you can drink another cup while I read." With
enormous control he stuffed the documents inside his shirt.

Rodlakh's arrival at the hostelry, an older building that had
watched a town grow around it, was greeted effusively after
initial surprise. As he asked, one of the public rooms was
cleared, a scribe fetched and some cold meats set out with bread
and warmed drinks.

There seemed to be two separate messages. Rodlakh read the
longer, frown deepening, and handed it over without a word.

The superscription, *to the* Valrabh, *at Banakit or where he
may be found,* showed it had been written after Nolimas had the

news Rodlakh was coming west. Written in haste, to judge by
the scrawl, and breathless phrasing.

The end, too, of any notion Nolimas might be wrestling
Rodlakh for the Army of the West. He expressed joy and relief
that he was coming in person to the Frontier, urging him to have
a strong escort; nowhere was safe. `Our patrols,' he wrote, `have
met and engaged an ordered enemy. Those proceeding to relief
of the overdue convoy have found only a single broken wagon
and scattered belongings. Hope has not been abandoned that
the escorting troops may be pursuing a retreating enemy, and
may soon be accounted for.

No certain news from Shâl Mines, but rumor had them
besieged by a strong and well-armed force,`some have said, of
jinzal, or jinzai-like creatures.' Clearly Nolimas did not know
how to regard this, and complained all the Frontier was alive
with extravagant rumors. He enthusiastically endorsed Rodlakh's
orders to evacuate the Mines using what forces were needed, `if
indeed this may be accomplished without unacceptable
loss...range of the enemy bows is as great as or greater than
ours, though no match for our accuracy.' He ended by observing
the needed additional troops could come only from Banakit,
citing once again the madness of moving soldiery eastward at
this critical juncture.

Rodlakh was finishing the second and shorter message as
Dolvid set the other aside. "What does Nolimas mean, `an
ordered enemy? If his patrols have fought them, they can
describe them better than that."

"I only have the same words to read as you," lips stretched in
exasperation.

"You have met their writer, I have not."

"He has always written sense before." Rodlakh remembered
waiting scribe and messenger, and saw he was not behaving
wisely. "Read this," passing over the other sheet.

It was about the two travellers twice mentioned before, now
with names, Thuladh and Dhunival, brothers or cousins out of
Thenimala in Ninkufu, the ones who had spent weeks crossing
Landegh, and witnessed jinzal armies drilling and on the march.

Saying their story was important for Rodlakh to hear, Nolimas was sending them eastward so they could meet with him sooner; they would proceed here to Kreshavu and `await' the *Valrabh'* there ("Why," Rodlakh demanded, "does he talk as if I am riding at the pace of a fat *ramidu*?"); he was certain an hour's talk with the men would convince Rodlakh of the need to bring every man west to defend against `*such a threat as has not been since the Night.*'

"Sebhal used almost the same words. But why is Nolimas still dealing in hints?"

Knowledge someone else was baffled restored Rodlakh's temper. "He is afraid — you remember, Saidhan suggested it. Not afraid of fighting, not Nolimas. He has started believing what seemed impossible, and is afraid of ridicule. That is why he is sending on these men, Thuladh and Dhunival, instead of just their story."

Both fell silent, watched by scribe and messenger. Taken together the dispatches of Nolimas and earlier rumors seemed to leave no imaginable conclusion but that after fifteen centuries the fierce, brainless *jinzal* had taught themselves to band together, to use swords and bows — a creature already so fearsome that to deal with the teeth and claws of one *jinzai*, six fully-armed cavalrymen were not considered excessive odds. All very well to talk about hurrying every available soldier to the Frontier; what troops could ever withstand *jinzal* charging in massed formations? Or would find the courage to try?

Rodlakh sent the scribe away, and himself wrote a short note for Saidhan, saying only he had read all the messages, and would wait here at Kreshavu till the two travellers arrived tomorrow. If they started at sunrise, as Nolimas said, they should be here by midday or soon after, and remaining here would save time if Rodlakh had to write fresh orders for Banakit. He added a few words, to have Galt start westward with his men.

"The squadrons Happ has at Banakit?"

"Yes, write an order." Rodlakh called to the messenger to wait a minute. "They must be at the Frontier in two days to assist with the Shâl Mines evacuation, and Happ must find us two additional squadrons, I don't care where. Do not write that."

"— *begin assembling at least two additional squadrons,*" Dolvid wrote and read together, "— *ready for immediate service where we may stipulate.*"

Rodlakh took pen and signed his monogram. "And a man to take this to Nolimas tonight," he told the messenger, having written bare acknowledgment of the dispatches.

When they were alone Rodlakh began talking about a general levy, bringing back to the colors every man who had ever held a weapon. Hardly needed, he said, at Drin Navuna, where, because the fortress could not keep out every robber or raider, swords and bows were always kept close to hand.

"How many *jinzal*?" and Dolvid told Rodlakh what he knew; enough, it seemed, to lay siege to the Mines, enough to ambush an armed convoy, both of which actions indicated, as well as banding together, some cunning, an ability to think and plan.

Since Saidhan first formed his special cavalry, Rodlakh revealed, fewer than two hundred *jinzal* had been killed — and that was virtually all ever sighted, over thirty years.

Could *jinzal* somehow have bred with some other race, making these half-*jinzal* with human brains.

"*Jinzal* do not mate,"

"They have never been seen to."

"There are no females."

"None have been found." Dolvid was dogged; all breathing things were male and female, and if descriptions were true the fighting *jinzal* were certainly male. Why would they be either sex if they did not have both?

"On Landegh nothing is ever the same; who knows what might be true? Well — " On his feet Rodlakh did his wet-dog shudder. "If there is a *jinzai* army with *jinzal* bowmen we have enough that is real to scare us; we do not need stories children tell to frighten themselves. Would they attack defended walls? This siege — does that just mean the enemy is sitting on the road? If only we had moved sooner to empty Shâl Mines, a hundred, two hundred *jinzal* could be stopped at Drin Navuna, and if strays crossed the Frontier they could be hunted down."

He had made up his mind; they would use all their strength to open the road, and hold the gates at Drin Navuna to let in fugitives. After that, defend the Frontier with bows and lances, wearing the enemy down till they could be destroyed.

"What about the Mainland? about Shumat?" Nolimas talked about the coming of a new Night; if that began while Rodlakh was off challenging his brother's authority, what could anyone win?

"It may be we can destroy this band of *jinzal* in one battle, and there will yet be a chance at Kadon Dinul. But Sebhal should never have made such a guarantee to Shumat — he knew better than anyone there is always the Frontier, with its uncertainties. We'll know more after we talk to these traders."

Gnawing at his lip he continued to draft orders; watching his face, yellow in the lamplight, Dolvid wondered where the youth had gone, the one at Tan Lughsai, again before Drin b'Afon, who had not been sure the Army of the West would follow him — or, tormentedly, whether he should want them to. Rodlakh could not possibly be as confident in the exercise of power as he was now forced to appear, but over years the pretense would become habitual, become Rodlakh. That would not be all gain.

When Dolvid talked about getting word to the Mainland about war at the Frontier, he meant principally Shumat, to let him know the Army of the West would be delayed in coming. But Rodlakh seized the idea with return of some of his former optimism; if the danger was as grave as Nolimas maintained, Ban-Sila should be told. Bolan and Shumat, both made aware the realm might founder, would surely reach a truce so help could be sent. With two dozen squadrons of General Cavalry for reinforcements, he would not fear any imaginable numbers of *jinzal*.

Would you not? silently, but what if, let in to defeat *jinzal*, they stayed on to dispossess an Army of the West depleted in the fighting? Maybe Rodlakh could not imagine men who would think of turning threatened ruin to their advantage — but tomorrow, after talk with these men, what was it, Thuladh and Dhunival, would be soon enough to quarrel on this point.

Most important (and self-important) man in Kreshavu was the magistrate, Sovrai, a lifelong friend of Saidhan's, some said his natural son. He was in his sixties, not unduly deferential — or courteous — when wakened in early morning.

Dolvid had been up two hours after fitful dozing on his fears, the sensation all the world was changing, all policies and strategies, the disputes between Preference and justice, debates of *rabhsai* and Colony, *rabhsayum* and Kargul, coming to the squabbling of rooks for nesting-room in trees threatened by the axe. If rumors were true, then no one could tell what powers if any there were to stop the *jinzal* at the Frontier, at Arnan, anywhere.

Yet it was hard to believe the worst. He was afraid of *jinzal*, aware of the danger in riding on westward to meet *jinzal*, and yet without seeing them his fear was not increased by a tale of *jinzal* in armies, no more than it would be by *a squadron of panthers* or *a regiment of sharks*. The celebrated terror, *jinza'dazhai*, was of a creature that tore and slashed with teeth and nails and fought in a frenzy oblivious to wounds. That fear could not be increased by the discipline that made men march in ordered ranks.

"This Nolimas," Sovrai grumbled, pulling the collar out at the back of his robe where hasty dressing had trapped it. "Well, Sebhal, may he rest, thought the world of him as leader in the field, but who has ever known him get his facts straight in a dispatch? Would you not wager the Mines are besieged by ordinary raiders off Landegh, and these armies are just a large hunting-pack of *jinzal*?"

"Nevertheless, we must begin a general levy. I would not wager the life of the Colony." Sovrai was told he would have to use levies to take over garrison duties of the squadron to be taken away from Kreshavu.

"*Valrabh'*, you take a squadron from here, that means the road — "

"You will see a written order," coolly. "How is the stock of arrows?"

"Have you ever heard we failed to provide all that have been asked?" Sovrai was on his stilts, unnerved, as many would be, by what had come back in the body of Sebhal's soft-spoken, deferential apprentice.

"How many bundles are on hand?" — having found out in the past few days that arrows were bound in sheaves of two dozen.

"How many, *Bôdhrai*? It is not part of my duties to count them; there are always piles ready for shipping. As is, getting them moved up to Drin Navuna is more trouble than the making, so we have often said."

Rodlakh suggested, "Let us go to the workshops and make a count."

"So early? I scarcely think there will be anyone there yet."

"Then we must recruit and train extra workers at once, so as not to waste any daylight. If materials are needed they must be brought up from Banakit." He moved for the door. "No, no, have your breakfast, we can find our way."

"I was hoping you would have warm *raminat* with me."

"Later, perhaps."

"Nolimas, I wager, has been listening to sea-stories." The magistrate rose to bow out his visitors. "But Kreshavu will take all necessary steps, *Asai*."

Outside, Rodlakh began pacing deliberately. "It must be less than three hundred steps from here to the fletchers'."

The morning was bright and cool. Spreading very slowly from the heights westward, silver-edged clouds were no immediate threat of rain. As before, Dolvid noted the whiteness of light here in the West.

Kreshavu was no fortified town, and had no wall. Houses, except the oldest, clustered near the rim of the low cliff, were spaced out, most with small gardens or vegetable patches. Many small rills went in shallow troughs, often next to the flagged or cobbled streets. Trees were numberless, almost all planted by the dwellers, slender rowans and locusts, field-maples with their deep gnarlings, great age in miniature. Near the hostelry and partly overhanging it was a stouter tree, a good omen, Rodlakh's emblem, *tovrelunai*, with its smooth skin and coppery leaves.

At the workshops was a man-high heap of rough billets and some forty dozen finished arrows. The foreman, almost blind though only in middle life, able to shave and true a shaft by touch, complained his supply of feathers, which came from Banakit, was good for only a few days' work. Metal points, forged in Kamsilat, would also run low quite soon. If they had the supplies, the foreman said, there would be no trouble bringing in workers; half Kreshavu not with the army had done some arrowmaking.

The discouraging round continued with a visit to the stables, where Dolvid had a brief altercation with an officious horsemaster before getting an undertaking for an accurate count of all pack and saddle animals available in the vicinity, agreeing in return to look into the man's heated charge the stablings at Fifth Bridge overworked some animals so as to keep back the best, for what purpose he could not suggest. Rodlakh, meanwhile, had visited the armorer, and promised him more hands. All this was vivid reminder of the Narn Campaign; after fourteen years Dolvid was discovering the civil officials and suppliers of the Northeast were not uniquely obstructive.

Back at the hostelry he wrote and Rodlakh signed orders confirming the various instructions given; every clatter of hoofs sent Rodlakh to the window, but not till the second hour past noon did a half-file of cavalry came rattling into Kreshavu, with the lean, worn travellers in their midst. The soldiers' shirts and breeches they had been dressed in hung like slack sails on their fleshless bodies.

Thuladh and Dhunival were half-brothers. The elder, Thuladh, had an infection that drew his eyelid over the right eye, red and puckered like a cock's wattles; loose skin at neck and chin suggested he had been much larger on his frame than now. Dhunival, who needed help dismounting, limped painfully, and had his left hand and wrist bandaged. When they spoke, both had lost most of their teeth. Of the two Dhunival was the more obviously terrified, but both had with them the smell and feeling of fear, and jumped, wheeling, at the smallest unexpected sound.

After they had been given food and drink the storytelling was left mainly to Dhunival, while the elder brother looked on, grim-faced and despondent, making occasional additions or corrections in an ill-tempered voice.

The tale was fit for legendary rather than real histories. The half-brothers had been traders, working out of the southern port of Thenimala with their own ship, dealing mainly in wares bartered by the coastal settlements of Lower Vrobhan to the south and east — small quantities of spicewoods, precious stones, a few pinches of gold-dust. This was profitable trading, but erratic, and the brothers would have rather taken their ship to the southwest, where there were sweet fruits and popular spices, as well as larger amounts of precious metals. But except for the nearer islands that trade was carried on mainly by strange, low-built but seaworthy two-hulled craft of the Hrin, a people about which not much was known. They were master-mariners and in their distant homeland superb craftsmen in gold or silver; examples of Hrin work were occasionally offered at Kadon Dinul, always at beggaring prices.

Last year tribal wars had broken out along the coasts where the brothers usually traded, making it harder than ever to get anything of value in exchange for the glassware and dyed cloth they carried. After long debate they had decided to attempt a journey often discussed, not merely to, but beyond the Hrin lands. Hrin goldsmiths were said to import the metal they used, from exactly where was a well-kept secret — but even the actual Hrin lands, though they had traded with the realm for centuries, were not shown on any extant map.

Thuladh reasoned a stout seagoing ship could easily achieve any journey undertaken by the quaint Hrin craft, like a couple of longboats linked by a sort of bridge, where the living-space was, and room for the small cargoes they could carry. Shadowing Hrin routes, the brothers knew they must eventually come to places they had heard of, far to the south and west, beyond the dry and barren lands even the broadest days of the First Empire had not considered worth conquering. Some of the Hrin traders who came often mastered one or both of the realm's languages, and from a less-reticent ship's master the brothers learned they would have to sail well to the south in warming waters till they could round a far cape, then continue westward some days before bending north to make landfall on the farther side of a water that sounded as if it might be Flamûrai, the Great Gulf, at the head of which Shâl IX, twelve centuries ago, had fixed the western boundary of empire.

With a shipload of trade goods the brothers set sail, and made landfall sooner they had expected, on an arid east-facing shore. Then they continued south, reaching greener and less forbidding islands with men who, though they went naked and painted themselves, knew about Arbhal, and were eager to trade fruits and other foods. Asked about gold, they pointed south.

Rodlakh, keeping exquisite check on impatience, said courteously that in less hazardous circumstances he would enjoy hearing every part of their tale. For now, he would like to learn how they came to be wandering on Landegh.

They had in fact come, not knowing it, to what the First Empire called the Farthest West, beyond Landegh, beyond the utmost ancient frontiers. The brothers were at the end of their resources, after storms and sickness, a running-aground, after difficult repairs, an attack by fierce naked men who shot tiny arrows from tubes held to their mouths. Without rudder or mainmast, most of the crew gone, they broke up in hammering surf on a far shore, losing all but one of their men as well as a cargo Thuladh said included lumps of gold big as the top of his thumb.

All three survivors were weak and ill, with a disease of long-distance sailors, making their joints painful, gums sore and bloody. All lost teeth, and were unsteady on their feet, with painful boils and inflamed eyes. Too feeble for hunting or even fishing they kept to the shore, gnawing seaweed and wild celery, swallowing mussels raw. They became always thinner, but the

illness abated. Losing sight of the sea, which had been kept at
the right hand as they headed north, they wandered into a maze
of country where water was hard to find.

Dhunival paused here, breath rasping. His brother mumbled,
"We have seen the Valley of *Jinzal*."

Lunu Jinzalladhiyu, Valley of the *Jinzai*-Fathering, a legend
disproved over and over again, always coming back. In a year
where Drin b'Afon had been successfully assaulted, why not?
All that was needed was for the True *Rabhsai* to return out of
long exile — whatever that meant.

After a gulp of wine Dhunival could resume. In the dry lands
they had found themselves in a narrow and narrowing cleft. At
last, down to a slit, it ended in an abrupt drop, and there was a
sharpedged depression, level-floored, more hole than valley, but
a mile across.

"More," Thuladh said. "You know the hole left in thick
quagmire when a bubble bursts? That, only more than a mile
across."

Their first glimpse was almost enough to send them
scrambling down the scree where the cleft ended: they thought
they had run across a settlement of men. On the valley floor
were long stone buildings, certainly not a tribal village, regular
rows with made paths running between. But the ferocious arrow-
blowers of the south had left the travellers wary, and they
delayed, keeping a watch, trying to discover what men these
were. Soon, they saw *jinzal*.

"Many?" Rodlakh leant forward, but here Dhunival was
attentive only to recollection. They had seen *jinzal*; one, then a
few, then hundreds. Four hundred at least were living in that
hollow, and filled only a part of the long barracks buildings.

"*Jinzal* living in barracks?" Dolvid interrupted without
meaning to.

"Sleeping," Dhunival said. "Most waking hours they were
being trained."

The valley seemed not so much their home as a big war-
camp. The *jinzal* marched in formation, made ordered charges,
practised archery and pike-work, and fought mock battles.

"Mock," Thuladh interrupted, "only to say they weren't fought to the finish, and the sides marched back to quarters together when they were done. But there was plenty of real killing — real tearing, too. Those brutes would have eaten their own comrades where they fell, but for the whips."

Wielded, not by other *jinzal*, but men on horses who with those whips and trumpet calls controlled the creatures and were in charge of all training. They also wore cloaks of a shiny blue-green the *jinzal* might have been trained to recognize.

They lived at the far end of the valley, slightly higher ground with one large stone building and perhaps a dozen smaller houses with proper windows and trees around, well-made dwellings, Dhunival said, though he admitted they could not take in much detail for that, the far end of the valley.

"And the *jinzal* never attacked the men?" Dolvid realized how sound Nolimas's instincts were; none of this would have been credible written down in a report; told by these sick and harrowed yet matter-of-fact men, Thuladh with one hand cupped over his bad eye, it could not be disbelieved, not a word.

"Never that we saw," Dhunival said. Though controlled by men the *jinzal* were not in any other sense tamed, or anything but ferocious.

They had weapons, mostly cudgels and staves, some pikes and swords, those not archers. All the *jinzal* wore plain round helmets, and some had breastplates. They also worked siege-engines; a *zhin'pefrai* that could throw a heavy stone half the width of the valley (this was surely an exaggeration) and a machine without established name, a gigantic bow mounted on a wagon-frame, which shot an iron bolt with a force to knock down walls.

"What walls?" looking across at Dolvid.

Dhunival resumed, now with an air of apology, having left till last what was hardest to accept; the banner flying over the compound where the men were. The concealed watchers tried to believe distance, heat shimmer, their fatigue, even shared hallucination, must be responsible for what they saw, but in the end none had any doubt; it was the white banner, edged with bronze, the Sword depicted, royal standard of Arbhal, as it had been of Owan.

"*Rekh'rabhsai*," Dolvid interjected; he had just been thinking of it, the True *Rabhsai* coming back out of the far West when the need of the realm was greatest, a legend much older than the name usually joined to it, Lost Plakhan of the famous Bride-Quest, older, indeed, than the title, *rabhsai*.

"With a *jinzai* army?"

Dolvid hastily explained he meant that these men, whoever they might be, having learned they could train *jinzal*, having heard about the legend of the True *Rabhsai*, must mean to become its fulfillment. This created more new questions than it explained, but left very little doubt about what walls the siege-weapons were meant for.

That was further confirmed by the roads Thuladh and Dhunival had seen. The brothers and their remaining companion, bitterly debating and finally rejecting the wisdom of trusting themselves to men, even their own kind, who had *jinzal* for slaves, had cowered in the cleft, not daring to move, for thirty hours, till fear was overbid by thirst, and they crept away by darkness. Hoping they could resume their northerly journey, living off what they could find, they worked their way around the eastern side of the Lunu, and luckily fell in with a clan of tribal wanderers, who fed and adopted them. After a few days together there was a dawn encounter with three fierce *jinzal*, helmed, but with no weapons other than the old ones, hands, teeth and *tra'munu*, the so-called 'stoning-glance.' Not much was said about the horrors of this fight, except that several tribesmen died, together with the last man from the brothers' crew; there too Dhunival's hand was wounded, and at least one *jinzai* was disabled and left to die, as the nomad clan fled or scattered. Dhunival guessed the three *jinzal* must have been deserters or runaways from the Lunu.

Now the brothers labored in mounting uplands, and afterwards were able to guess they had wandered into the westernmost outliers of Kargan baDulfu, the immense unpeopled mountain country south of Arnan that closed the province of Kargul in on its southern and western sides. They quickly saw it was useless to challenge these ranks upon ranks of ramparts, and turned north again, skirting the stiffer climbs.

In a day or so they came unexpectedly on a road in excellent repair, which they might have followed but for their terror of fresh encounters with *jinzal*. Their caution was proper; hidden among rocks and brush they watched a company of about twenty *jinzal* go tramping west, flanked and led by mounted men with the same bright blue-green cloaks as at the Lunu, and the same banner overhead.

"What were they, what race?" Rodlakh asked. "Could you tell?"

"Ordinary men they seemed, *Valrabh'*." Thuladh's answer came out of Ninkufu, where almost everyone was Owani. Yet it was notable the brothers, no matter how desperate their case, never reconsidered their decision not to seek help from these men who trained and led *jinzal*.

The rest of their tale was confused; they seemed to have lost track of time, distance and direction, eventually wandering on only because they could not remember ever doing anything else. Their luck held; in their dazed state they twice almost walked into the midst of *jinzal* laboring at completion of roads like the first, these running northeast instead of due east. They recalled horsemen, the whips, and lying still under relentless sun for most of a day to escape being seen.

They were, they could not say how long, with another band of wandering Froghul, who neither helped them nor drove them off, simply tolerating their company, though shouldering them away if either brother came too near women of the band. This was normal; if one of the brothers had dropped from illness or exhaustion, the Froghul would have ignored it and gone on, not counting them as a real part of the band.

After nights of bitter cold the weather turned warm again one day, and the brothers were alone again in empty country. They stumbled on a road, better made than the others. Following its bends, dreamily discussing the prudence of doing so, they were surrounded and challenged by riders with levelled lances, a half-squadron patrol from the Army of the West. Too numb for joy or real relief they were brought to Drin Navuna, and when they could talk had told their tale to Captain Nolimas.

Rodlakh congratulated them on their safety, and asked for an estimate of the numbers of *jinzal* moving on Landegh. This was a hard question for Dhunival, who explained that wandering as they were they could not tell whether *jinzal* they sighted were the same ones as seen before. In the end his estimate was several hundred, maybe a thousand, and the elder brother chimed in with his habitual *More*.

With regrets for the need the brothers, already fatigued, were taken through the main elements of their story once again. When they had gone for a rest Rodlakh said, "How much do you believe?"

"All of it."

A nod of agreement. "A fight for survival, nothing else." Most of all, the siege-engines troubled him; they could knock down any walls, given enough time, and even Drin Navuna was not the certainty he had trusted in. "What is our plan now?"

It was very clear to Dolvid. "Kill *jinzal*."

Rodlakh began to become, if no happier, more animated. "We can do a lot of killing from behind strong walls, while they are knocking them down, and there is more than one set of walls. This is going to be a grim business, without much glory to it."

No question now about the general levy; it would be proclaimed at once. Messages for Happ in Banakit and a full report for Saidhan would be needed.

"And the *rabhsai*; Ban-Sila must be told. This threat is to all the realm; no room for squabbles among ourselves." Last night Dolvid was prepared to argue against this, but hearing the story told by Dhunival left him less certain. Ban-Sila and his circle must be made to see it would be catastrophe if they treated this as a chance to bring the Colony to heel. Perhaps Saidhan would go to Kadon Dinul, Dolvid suggested, once he heard what the danger was. Rodlakh was sure he would go, but when it came to drafting a summary of Dhunival's story they both came up against the feeling Nolimas had already known, and reached the same solution; the two brothers must be sent to Kamsilat to recount their adventures to Saidhan. He would probably want them with him when he crossed Arnan to get himself arrested as an outlaw — if troops could be found to lay hands on the revered Saidhan. Even Ban-Sila's habitual shutting-out of what was unwelcome could not work against the tale Dhunival told.

Those instructions given, Rodlakh began talking about mustering every arm that could bend a bow, which brought him back to arrows, and the need to bring in every scrap of stored food and feed so it could be kept safe and fairly distributed. The evacuation of Shâl Mines, if that could be brought off, would be followed by that from Drin Navuna of all those not a real part of the fighting force. Rodlakh doubted room could be found for them all in Banakit, but perhaps the great warehouses and seasoning sheds standing empty on South Shore at Kamsilat could be prepared to accommodate refugees.

Recalling again what Dolvid had done with the Narn Campaign of '28, Rodlakh, almost shyly, spoke of the need for someone moving freely between Kreshavu here and Banakit, Banakit and Kamsilat, making sure the fighters were getting all support they needed. There would be wagons and pack-animals to collect, supplies to be kept moving — someone would have to push and pull, bully and cajole, someone who had in his head a picture of the whole.

"That one is going to need an open commission, so he can decide matters on the spot, in your name and Saidhan's as *Nim'*, but without leisure to consult with you. Private property might have to be seized, captains and magistrates overruled — "

"Someone, then, who will not abuse his powers." Rodlakh lifted the chain with the bronze-beech medallion over his head, and looped it over his. "I know you want to see the Frontier, but that will not be at its best this spring. You will take the job?"

Dolvid felt honored, and said so, adding he would surely have to come up to the Frontier on one errand or another. Speaking, he saw why it had been mentioned at all. "But if they want to say I took the job because I was afraid of *jinzal*, I can't stop them. I am afraid of *jinzal*."

"Everyone is, or else too stupid. But they had better not talk about fear in front of Galt, or any of the Drin b'Afon men."

A pair of scribes standing by as copyists so orders could be sent to all officers at under-captain or above, all magistrates, Dolvid helped draft his commission, which would give him the right to commandeer soldiers as needed. "It takes a weight off me that you will be here," Rodlakh said. "I shall ride forward after we have finished all the dispatches and orders. I want those squadrons from Banakit rested here and on the road for the Drin before sunup. I hope Galt's squadron will be here soon. In hill-country those little horses do better than *pefral*." He grinned abruptly. "Yes. I am babbling. Better when I am back in the saddle."

Towards evening Rodlakh sat eating bread and cheese before taking to the road at the head of troops wrung painfully from the local garrison.

"What kind of men could ever break *jinzal* to their will? How could it begin?"

"What kind of men would want it?" — a mere token of contempt. Almost anyone whose desire was power would rejoice in a weapon like *jinzal*, if they could learn to control it.

"The Banner," shaking his head. "The Sword — who are their masters? A tide-pool of Owanil left behind as the Empire ebbed?"

It was hard to see how they could have maintained their colony through all the centuries since then. Besides, there was no legend of the True *Rabhsai* till long after, when Night was almost over. These men, ordinary men as Dhunival said, must be later renegades.

Rodlakh wondered if, after all, there was someone who could claim direct descent from Lost Plakhan. Dolvid, about to deny the possibility, changed tactics, telling him, as once he had told Âna, that it did not matter: Plakhan abdicated for himself and his line in perpetuity, leaving the unspeakable Kanavakh as Heir, and if that were not so it would not make any difference; the House Gabh'Owan was done with, Arbhai-Navu ruled; `True' had no meaning.

"True or not, a *rabhsai* with *jinzal* for Household would be hard to depose."

"Slavery, for those left alive to be enslaved."

"It has to be stopped here, in the West," starting to button his outshirt. "I wish I could see clearly how."

They went out where Rodlakh's mount was saddled and waiting, and he promised to send word from the Frontier when he knew more. They clasped hands, and Dolvid wished him good hunting.

"It looks as if there will be enough hunting to go around." He swung up into the saddle, and in a moment his little troop of soldiery was moving out. Notwithstanding all that was said Dolvid felt a stab of shame about being spared the fighting. Loneliness was in it, too, and sheer conceit, the feeling that if he was not there it would all go wrong. Âna would have urged him to insist on staying beside Rodlakh — here the established nag of guilt about Âna overlapped; now both his friends had gone into danger, while he would be the grocer. Not consoling to admit battle was a poor use of his proper talents: he would carry a lance more ineptly than the worst lancer, and his bowmanship would have given the Frontier archers rich amusement. No, this was not a war for personal glory, and for the realm's sake he was better used here. He went back into the hostelry despising himself.

Meetings

It might just be possible, Âna supposed, however unlikely, that the scruffy boy named Torr was in no way related to Alkmas; a couple of years helping run the boat might have turned him surly as his master without common blood as an excuse. Torr was about sixteen, and the corded muscling of his arms when they cast off was of a farm-laborer twice his age. As they made to come about he told her to move in a voice that informed her she was not only a nuisance but a contemptible one. Except for that sole curt order he said not a word to her till he came and asked for food. Alkmas was no more loquacious; grunts were an adequate form of communication between him and his apprentice.

Good manners must have nothing to do with seamanship. Though here and there in need of paint the craft, contrary to its owner's description, was scrubbed very clean. Its design was new to Âna; amidships instead of a long horizontal boom or square cross-tree of larger vessels the mainmast had a successful compromise, a long, oblique yard-arm that made the mainsail into a graceful curved triangle. Forward there were a smaller square sail and a jib, and the boat seemed uniquely capable of catching wind from any quarter. The two sailors knew their craft and each other, and they went skimming across the tranquil bay, dancing past fishing-boats becalmed or beating laboriously upwind.

Deep water reached, the breeze was firmly from the southeast. That seemed to satisfy Alkmas, who spoke: "Two days, not less, she'll be there. This time of year, she'll come more southerly, but we'll be in Kamsilat before she blows from the west." Without asking how he could know, she gathered he was forecasting a rapid passage. While Torr munched at cold meat and fresh bread from Morú's larder, Âna settled on deck, not letting anxiety about the Strait begin.

A buffeting blow roused her from dozing. Alkmas had thrown a folded blanket reeking of fish. Nobody, he said from the helm, could sleep like that, night breeze give you a stiff neck. Darkness had brought a chill, but the night was lovely, sea luminous under a half-moon drifting steady through clouds of indigo edged in piercing silver. Nibbled at from the right, a waning moon.

"What time would it be?" she called to Alkmas, who leaned against the tiller, gaze ahead unblinking. She wrapped the foul blanket around her shoulders, though there was a cleaner one in the pack next to her.

"Not midnight."

"Where would we be?"

"On Arnan, with no sight of land." For a minute he pretended not to know she was staring at him. "With this wind," he conceded, "we'll make the Southward Isles by morning. I can find my way among rocks."

If her face had showed worry he was wrong supposing it was for her own safety. Morning would be the second since the event from which everything now dated, discovery of Ban-Sila's death. Burantal may have declared for Rodlakh, but if Kamin-Tolagh had maintained his pace he must be close to Kôbh Crossings by now, if not already over and into the Paowanu Loi. When she came to the Strait he would be within the borders of his own province, messages having gone ahead to alert the cavalry he would lead back to Kadon. How many days it might take him to assemble those troops she had no guess, just as she did not know how far his father was from a return to the capital — nor how long it might take the Army of the West to be ready for a crossing of Arnan in force. What one policy, if any, might have emerged from factions in the Household was also unknowable, and the Household might hold the keys to both Kadon Dinul and

Residence. The only certainty was that Rodlakh would have to be prompt asserting his claim.

With a wag of his head Alkmas indicated the afterwell. "Sleep warmer down there, so long as we're not shipping water." That was a joke of sorts; the boat was heeled over to starboard but on the long, lazy swell only a rare curl of white was to be seen.

She went willingly, scrambling down to where in shadow she could discard the evil-scented blanket. Up against what she called to herself the downhill side the lumped form of Torr was snorting.

Bundling up the fishy blanket she threw it forward into deeper obscurity. She unpacked her own and the sleeping-bag, and not fancying being log-helpless if they started to roll decided to sleep on the bag rather than in it. Lying down, she was trying to get the edge of the blanket trapped under her feet when a hand shot out from the huddle next to her, catching her near the hip. Torr, one moonstruck eye glittering, walked on an elbow towards her. His blunt nose fit very well between middle and index fingers as she shoved him away, flathanded. The boy evidently enjoyed a show of token resistance; he gurgled a low laugh and resumed the advance, breath toiling.

She hissed, "Minnow, have you heard of Lord Rodlakh?"

"'Course." His face was near, and the tooth-twig was no part of Torr's daily duties.

"I am a close friend to the Lord Rodlakh," her tongue almost confusing it beyond redemption by saying *Kamin-Tolagh*.

After long, slow, complete digestion Torr said, "That's a fine, high lord." He may have thought she was presenting credentials, like a servant with a new employer.

"He is a great lord, and if you do not take away your hand, minnow, and go to sleep, I shall tell Lord Rodlakh, and he will have soldiers tie you up, so I can use a blunt and rusted knife to take away — " She bared her front teeth in the style Radaghi had acquired from Rheduban, then concluded with relatively leniency — "your ears."

Without a sound the boy sank back into his stinking bedclothes. Âna turned her face uphill and giggled, hoping he would take the shudder of her shoulders for stronger emotions. She chuckled herself to sleep.

It could not be much later when she was awakened. Torr must have begun his watch at the helm; a big-middled shape she recognized as Alkmas was squatting in the afterwell, looking down at her. After a while he shook his head. "No," he conceded.

"No," she agreed. The resigned downcurl of his mouth could be seen in the moonlight. He nodded slowly before stretching out beside her to sleep.

Dawn came with spray flying, a sharper breeze making the sea choppy. Âna fastened her outshirt, wished for a hot drink, made do with a mouthful of water, and found Alkmas back at the helm. As predicted there were the shapes of islands on either side, land indistinct, but each with a clear line of white where surf and cliff met. Alkmas allowed sailing was always rougher here. Farther north among the inner islands the going would have been smoother, but the prison isle where the eels were salted was in that group, and the *Atarlum* claimed the right to sink any craft that tried to sail too near.

"A ship made for war came chasing us while you were asleep. Showed no colors."

"We were too fast to catch?"

"Too crafty. You mark out a straight stretch of water with a following wind, that warship would catch us."

"You outsailed her on short tacks." She was amazed she had slept through it all.

Alkmas stared. "Aye, but he picked it all up from talk, your uncle. I remember when Sett didn't know a keel from a bowsprit. What could be your business in the Colony, then?"

Better to keep him cordial. "I am carrying news. Good news."

"Best news in the world, for the lords there's a way to make it mean more taxes for us. Last week I netted three one-eyed fish, three separate casts. That's not good."

"No indeed."

"Something gives meaning to things, think what you will. Not to say that lets us stop trying. Have to do all you can, omens or not."

As the scattering of islands dropped astern the sea calmed, and the wind, fulfilling Alkmas's prescription, steadied out of due south, their course continuing westerly, though she expected Alkmas to swing north at any moment. When the craft rode up on a swell she could see a line of distant land, blue on the northward horizon. It could only be the Island, Kamanta.

Midway between dawn and noon, day steadily warming, another mass of land reared on the port bow. "No island at all," Alkmas answered her question. "Tanu Moranti," the high headland projecting from the western shore of Arnan, nominally part of the Lunu Tezh' Protectorate, though uninhabited and tucked away behind great mountains, accessible, practically, only from the sea. Easing off a little into the wind Alkmas poked a foot at the dozing Torr, telling him to keep lookout forward.

The slap of waves became a regular stem-to-stern motion. On its new course the boat still seemed to be sailing at a great pace straight for the rocky coast. On the starboard side, too, land crept nearer, and soon the flat line of open water that was Filso Kamantani, the Strait. Alkmas seemed determined to sail past the opening, but probably was avoiding only deep water at midchannel. The Island's southwestern corner here was heavily defended, and when she made this journey with her uncle he had pointed out to her the bristling line of throwing arms, a dozen big *zhin'pefral* up on the cliffs, commanding, probably, almost to mid-Strait. The mainland side of the strait would be beyond the range of any, and that western side Alkmas evidently meant to sail, though the shallower water there was treacherous, with swirling currents and whole ranges of sharp rocks at or near the surface. That, she saw, was why Torr had been sent forward, and was now crouched, leaning out over the bow.

Cliffs had neared to huge, rough pillars with waves at their base shattering into mist. The gap had narrowed to a quarter-mile before Alkmas threw the tiller to run due north. Canvas was tautly trimmed, and Alkmas, one eye on the masthead pennon, did not appear troubled by the sucking back-eddies.

Rounding the bulge of the leftward cliffs they had been half an hour on this course, the way narrowing as Kamanta edged closer, when in open water at the approaches to the Strait were two black shapes low to the sea, fighting-ships, rammers, driven entirely by oars. When she told Alkmas his nod made plain he had been watching them.

They were near enough that she saw the oars of the nearest stir into action, as the sailless craft slid to intercept the course set by Alkmas. A trumpet call rang across the water, and the second rammer was moving more directly for the small boat. These fighting-ships were like insects skating on the polish of a summer pond; the sets of oars lifted and dipped in perfect unison. Taking in some sail Alkmas crept nearer the cliffs, the youth in the bow calling and signalling warnings as they passed close to or between hidden rocks. As the nearer rammer closed and the trumpet sounded again, Alkmas eased a little away from the cliffs, calling Torr to come and work the sail.

"What can I do?"

"Stay out of our way."

The long, dark ship was no more than a strong bowshot away. Figures of men could be seen on the central platform. A voice boomed out, "The Strait is closed to all ships. You must turn back."

"Island scum," contemptuous of the clotted accent. Alkmas called a sharp order to Torr, and the boat came about to starboard, settling on a new course, closer to the wind, making for center-channel and away from the narrows. The rammer circled to follow, staying outside their line, not attempting to close the gap, content to be obeyed and see them off. A mile northward the other was headed to guard the western side, and a third vessel emerged from the narrowest part of the Strait.

"I didn't reckon on three," Alkmas, when Âna told him. So far he seemed to be most entertained.

The nearest war-craft did not want to stray too far from its westernmost station; it veered a little southward, and the slender, beaked prow began slapping in the head-sea. By easing off gradually eastward Alkmas made the pursuer gain faster relative to their position south of the Strait.

"Where are you bound?" came bellowing. Alkmas, telling Âna to get down, came about very smartly to port and was running full before the wind, Torr encouraging the wings to spread, as the rammer, condemned to a wide circle, struggled to follow. More shouting came, and an arrow, nowhere close; the range would have been too long even if the rammer had not been making heavy weather of its turn.

Alkmas grunted satisfaction, but the gain was very temporary, with two rammers and the *zhin'pefral* ahead, and the one behind soon able to overhaul them once back on course.

For a while it seemed Alkmas saw otherwise, and would try to outrun the pursuer. Obviously either of the other two rammers could easily intercept, but Âna did not have the temerity to say so, and Alkmas quite suddenly changed course again, once more heading for the western cliffs. The following craft had settled to the chase, though gaining only gradually on the fishing-boat with a full spread of canvas and a fine following breeze. Soon the fighting-boat hovering up ahead went out of view behind the outthrust of cliffs.

Alkmas bawled for Torr to go back to his bow watch, and it began to seem they were going to sail on full-tilt into the rock face. Fascinated she watched how water slithered from stone, fantastic whorls of foam giving notice of wildly variable currents that could smash them beam-on into the cliffs. Fighting his tiller Alkmas relented, and now she saw what he was doing. Just ahead a line of rocks standing out from and running near-parallel with the cliffs left a narrow spumed channel. The fishing-boat could, if it did not go on the rocks, pass inside the reef, while the rammer, two oarspans added to its beam, could not. How that would help them escape altogether was a question Âna did not dwell on. The rammer behind was no longer gaining as the chop and swirl of the waters here interfered with rowing. Green-slimed rock was close on both sides; there was a slight rasping bump, and Alkmas's boat was inside the line of rocks.

After that narrow entrance the rocks diverged gradually from the line of cliffs, widening sea-room, though Alkmas stayed close in, watching every ripple of the sails. "Will they try it?" with a fearsome ghost of a smile, and as she watched she saw the fighting craft seem to hesitate, then swerve outside the line of the rocks, oarbeats picking up pace. Wind and sea were noisy here, but fragments of commands could be heard, and some erratic arrows came. Now the rammer would have been gaining fast, but the line of the reef was taking it well off to starboard. Yet Âna never forgot the other rammer somewhere ahead.

The rocky reef rose from the water, climbing into a kind of crazy stair that curved back to a rock-bastion about the size of the New Residence, divided from the opposing cliffs by only a few yards of water. On its outer side this stone islet sloped and tumbled gradually to the waves, but both sides of the narrow passage were knifed sheer to the water. Beyond, glimpses of the second rammer, headed downshore.

No decision to be made; to refuse the tight gap would be to let the first rammer cut them off back where the reef began. Torr came back to trim sail, and that allowed the pursuer to draw level. At a range of sixty to seventy yards the shooting was a little better, one arrow sticking in planking up by the prow, others splashing in the water nearby.

Amidships, Torr took up a pole, and she did not wait for any instructions, finding another and taking her station on the starboard side. A cry of trumpets came from the nearest rammer, as the fishing-boat, lurching and skewing, almost attempted the narrow gap broadside on. Alkmas cursed, fighting the tiller, somehow persuading the craft to resume forward way. Like a dream, Âna saw the beak of the second rammer just the other side of the narrow, coming on, and then she was stabbing out with her heavy pole as the fishing boat swooped between high walls. The mainsail flapped and spilled its wind, but current carried them between rock and rock. Breathless, she saw the fighting-ship up ahead was at the last declining the passage, turning aside. Waters slid down, and there was a loud rattling, splintering noise. The thunderclap of shouting that followed made her realize the noise had nothing to do with the fishing-boat. With a last attempt to spin thwarted by hasty pole-work, they emerged where cliffs fell back to make a shallow bay.

Alkmas crowed, "Broke some oars." Yes. Busy now trying not to go aground on the rock-bastion, the rammer's starboard oars were all in disarray, some with shattered blades; the helmsman, deciding at the last against the narrow passage, had left his swerve too late for the near-side oars to clear.

Âna expected their original pursuer would come swooping, now they were in open water again. Unbelieving, she saw the craft, ignoring its fellow's troubles, circle away, heading for mid-channel and a southerly course. On the far side, against the dark shore of the Island, the third craft was also moving southward. As her view cleared the jut of the near shore she could see why; sails of a ship much larger than theirs were visible, approaching the Strait from the south.

Though she agreed when Alkmas said their adversaries were after a bigger catch it seemed strange to her they would leave a boat that had openly defied them, unless there were other obstacles still to be met.

Alkmas had caught a breeze, and they were skimming across the inlet with the true narrows dead ahead. Here under the western shore they were far out of range of the *zhin'pefral* on the cliffs of Kamanta, which were no longer to be seen: the throwing-arms must be wound down ready for discharge.

Came a loud thud, but on the near side. Torr gave a yell; a large round boulder was climbing the air in their direction.

It plunged into the water not far off the starboard beam. Alkmas threw the tiller, not retreating but coming in closer under the cliffs. "Island shit-eaters. They've fortified the free side."

At its crabwise crawl the vessel had covered half the distance to the cape before another ugly blot of stone shot into the sky, the thump reaching them next. This was a nearer miss, rocking the boat, but of the *zhin'pefral* on this side of the Strait, perhaps only one could be brought to bear so close inshore. The fishing-boat was within fifty yards of the cliffs, here leaning back a little. Obviously, the rammers kept close under the cliffs so that any ships they could not halt were forced out into mid-channel; there probably was very little water that could not be reached by the big siege-engines from one side or the other. Desultory attack from a single *zhin'pefrai* was frightening enough, and Âna could imagine a dozen on each side darkening the sky with missiles; small chance any craft could pass unharmed through such a hail.

The course chosen had thwarted even the one; as Alkmas exulted, "Can't spit under your own chin."

In shifting winds they crept for the point. A rock went skimming along the cliffs above their heads, hit a bulge and sent a shower of fragments splashing into the water, missile itself falling harmlessly. Where the headland thrust out Alkmas had to wrestle with a wind that wanted him farther out in the channel than he was willing to go. In joy Âna saw the coastline of Kamanta bend back, the sudden expanse of open water without another sail. Gap between boat and cliff opened to perhaps forty yards, the western shore falling back even more rapidly. A scattering of bowshots came from above, wild in the whipping breezes, and as Alkmas regained control and tried to tuck back under the cliffs a number of boulders and lesser stones, pushed or hurled from the height above, came bounding and splashing down, though one fist-sized piece of granite made a loud rap and left a definite gouge on the foredeck, a pace or two behind where Torr was stationed. He yelped, Alkmas swore, and Âna was outraged. The stones shot by the *zhin'pefrai* had scared her, but even archery seemed less ugly than these rolled or tossed boulders and stones.

Which would not be renewed, as the point was left behind, and she saw her reaction was instinctive but wrong, exactly the process that gave sanction to killing with weapons: it seemed less horrid to stab a man than tear out his throat with the hands, and less terrible again to shoot him through with an arrow; elaborate weapons killed better, but kept hands away from the redness of guilt.

Alkmas spat and demanded what gave this *Atarlum* the right to kill him, or sink his boat. For the first time since the action heated up Âna really looked at Torr, and saw he was holding tight to prevent a whimper of fear. She tried to reach him with an understanding smile, but could not hold his eyes with hers, and knew he would resent any open comforting. She had only a slender margin of courage left for herself.

Behind, two thuds came in rapid succession. Wheeling she saw the boulders climbing on their course; Alkmas crowed to see how far to seaward they would pass. He was swinging back on the northward heading, and the strongest bowman could not reach them with a shot from the headland. Ahead the sea was wide and empty, and behind there was no sight of either rammers or the ship they had gone to challenge.

"Ten-thumbed idiots." Artillerymen, archers, the ones who navigated the rammers, impossible to tell which Alkmas meant. All of them, perhaps; he clearly saw most of the world, Alkmas apart, as inept. And they were through the Strait.

They made landfall in early morning, and the questions about what to do if she ever reached Kamsilat began to answer themselves, when she was recognized by the steersman of the patrol-boat that came to challenge. Loose-limbed, big-handed he climbed aboard to match Alkmas insult for insult; she had known him by sight when here before, had seen him again at Tan Lughsai; Sarnak. She got more answer than expected asking if he had not been with Rodlakh on the Island: engrossed in his lively and detailed account she had to settle for a quick summary of the rest when they reached shore.

From him she learned Rodlakh had left for the Frontier, and at her request he went off to the barracks to fetch Edarron, a half-squadron who had often brought Sebhal's messages when she was at her uncle's house, not far from the harbor, where she now went for a wash and to change clothes.

Edarron was in many ways typical of officers in the Army of the West, in which his father had served before him. A good soldier, Sebhal said, he was lightly contemptuous of the Kadon Dinul Families, flippant about the *Atarlum*, certain the West was invincible, an enthusiast for horses and weapons, willing to make tactical comparisons between Banak and Pir Kallikuk as cavalry-captains, though with what accuracy was unknowable.

Always puzzling; though he revered Sebhal, he had gone beyond hinting he, Edarron, was available to make up the difference there must be between her appetites and opportunities Sebhal had for satisfying them. He was good-looking in a way familiar to her, three parts Gabhani with Owani enough to tauten the features, and had the confidence of a young man who does not expect to be refused. Arrogant was a word that came to mind, though harsh for someone so well-mannered.

He came promptly, but she nevertheless suspected he had stopped to wash his face and groom his hair. There were commiserations to start with, and she thanked him, but did not give his warm-eyed sympathy much scope. Edarron was bound to perceive opportunity in her bereavement, and was obviously disappointed she needed him only to get admitted to the Great House, to a private meeting with Saidhan.

She had seen the old man riding, but Sebhal's sparse talk about his father had not left her expecting this restrained, grave courtesy and careful attention to her story. Nor would she have anticipated he would be so vulnerable to this new loss; he permitted himself to weep, and asked her pardon, reminding her he had now outlived his daughter, his son, and all but two of a dozen grandchildren. With a fingertip he lifted a tear from a fragile-looking cheekbone.

"One of those two, *Asai*," boldly, "is now our *rabhsai*. It must be the right one."

He reappraised her, and seemed pleased she was more than a messenger. "That one must have this news with no delay."

He was about to call for a scribe, but Âna said, "That is the reason I came to Kamsilat, to carry the news to Rodlakh *Deghi*."

That honorific, `High One,' usually reserved for the *rabhsai*, had probably never before been attached to Rodlakh's name.

Saidhan stared. "I would not deny the privilege to anyone who came here through such difficulty and danger, but Rodlakh is at the Frontier, or soon will be — he reached Banakit the day before yesterday, and was to go on in the morning with Dolvid *Bôdhrai* — I think you have met the man?"

"Yes — " she realized only afterwards she had been dismissive to the *Nim'* of Telnavu. Certain this was her task, only hers, she argued that besides the death of Ban-Sila there was a great deal, about the temper of the city, for example, and rifts within the Household, which she could spend half a day dictating to a scribe and still not be sure she had anticipated all the questions Rodlakh might have.

Saidhan smiled oddly, as if at something recalled. "Are you not tired from your journeying?"

"Except for the Strait, I did not do much else but sleep on the crossing, *Asai*." True, though the sleep had been mostly uneasy dozing that left her tireder.

"The Strait. And you heard about Aëlu, hah? Where is the Treaty of the Wind Caves, when the *Atarlum* is the home of bandits."

"A treaty can easily be stretched, if the Patriarch is allowed to make His own *rabhsai* and keep him close. That can save trouble over what is lawful."

"Aye, but it is not going to be Orbanak. Rodlakh is *rabhsai*, none other. If I send soldiers with you, you are willing to carry *rabhsayum* to him? It will be a hard ride."

"I have ridden the road to Drin Navuna before. I did not flag on the road to Tan Lughsai, nor delay Kamin-Tolagh, riding to Burantal. No, but it is true, *Asai*."

He spilled over into a chuckle. "I truly ask your pardon, my dear Âna. I was smiling for the sake of memory; twice you have put me in mind of another lady, who also liked to have her own way. I told her it would be a hard ride to the fortress at Kir, she being seven months with child, you see."

She did not know when she had last profoundly blushed. Saidhan pretended not to be watching her, bright, birdlike eye on the ceiling. "I am not changed. It is ridiculous to me I have to let others do the deeds. If I forbade your riding, it might be out of envy, hah?"

Now their arrangements could be swiftly made. She would have a half-file escort, and Saidhan, saying she could not hope to reach Banakit today, insisted she take some food here at the Great House before departure.

"The Lady Aëlu would want to meet you, and thank you for your part in her rescue, an important one.

"But only if you wish," he said, and Âna to herself, *He knows*.

"I have wished to meet the Lady Aëlu, *Asai*," blandly.

"No one told me, I guessed, knowing whose son he was." The eyes lost focus, and she would have wanted to comfort him, but before she could do anything he became brisker than before, saying nothing but Rodlakh's triumph could bring peace for proper grieving over losses.

"Rodlakh *Rabhsai*," savoring it.

It was meant as a thoughtful gesture, to have her escort commanded by an officer she knew, Edarron. With his self-regard, he would automatically assume she had particularly asked for him, and that made her apprehensive about the overnights of the journey. On the other hand Edarron was not offended to be commanding so few men, and that meant he had been told not its nature, but how important her errand was; she might use that to keep him at arm's length.

Yet in his eyes as she mounted she saw he would have to be refused all over again. It made her wonder about the whole idea of choosing. Men paused to look at her, but she did not include herself in the great beauties, as Aëlu certainly was. But also she was not among those, like the other one she met at the Great House, who proclaim their readiness for sport with every inch, every glance, every slight sway. So that men, like Edarron, like

Alkmas and his helper, Torr, like Kamin-Tolagh, she supposed, though he could enforce his whims, went through life presenting their case to every woman not actively repellent.

Yet when Âna's turn came, they behaved, for an instant even Alkmas, as if she should be flattered. Perhaps a hedge against refusal, which could be forgiven, if their fragile self-esteem demanded it must always be the woman who did not know what she was missing.

What puzzled her was how anything personal could be left. If Edarron said he wanted her, and she told him, not so, there was nothing in his wanting that was her and no one else, he would be offended, perhaps authentically so, speak flatteries, as if his having noticed her large eyes or slender waist gave him a personal claim on them and their possessor. Now, Dolvid — but Dolvid did not come into this: he had, she had found in their brief mingling at Burantal, an acute sense of persons, but did not bid with it, had somewhere agreed to accept without dispute what happened (or did not happen) into his bed.

She let her mind drift back to that other, standing in half-light, dressed in a robe a dusted shade of blue, cool-eyed gaze appraising her, as if to assess whether this newcomer, with her hair dressed, gowned instead of roughclad in shirt and breeches, might be a rival. A primal look, unmistakable as a man's lust, and that might be why Âna instantly knew who the girl was. Certainly not through logic; there was nothing reasonable about her being here. Nor was the resemblance to her brother immediately striking, though her lustrous hair was a golder version of his same alloy. Hovering at the threshold, Kamin-Tarú came in at Aëlu's invitation, and it could be seen she shared in the family grace; Âna felt a stab of envy for Kamin-Tarú's flowing walk, beyond any she had for Aëlu, whose calmly-worn beauty was outside imagination to possess. But what was Tú doing here? Where did she fit? Whether he knew, or was still wondering where she had gone, Tam must be frantic.

Edarron, agreeing they could not ride all the way to Banakit tonight, suggested they could make their halt at the cavalry-post between New and Old bridges.

They were past the two-mile post, climbing in pleasant open country. Âna considered. "If we press ahead, we could reach Vonn by darkness, or not much after."

He was skeptical. "Better wait, see how you feel when we get to New Bridge. You don't want to be all ridden out, do you." He underscored the words with a brief dip of his eyelashes. She made a patient face.

Dolvid's morning began with almost a battle. With Sovrai it would not have been unexpected, but the magistrate had caught the sense of urgency and had riders out at dawn spreading word of the general levy. Many returning to the Army would have weapons, those with bows bring arrows of their own, but not enough. This was becoming his waking nightmare: with a strategy of fighting *jinzal* from behind walls, bows would be principal weapon of the war, speed and accuracy of bowmanship chief hope of the West. But it wa childhood lore and sober truth that a *jinzai* was seldom killed by one arrow; ten hits, all agreed, might fail to stop one of the brutes; battles where five thousand arrows would not be an oversupply were easy to foresee.

He rode down the hill, where the Banakit squadrons were forming up after their night's rest. The tall young man who commanded the lead squadron was going to be paunchy in middle life, but at present his rounded face was far from soft. Dolvid asked him to take a half-squadron to the workshop of the fletchers, and have each man sling two bundles of arrows across his saddle.

"We are lancers, *Bôdhrai*, not bowmen."

"As I see. The arrows are needed at the Drin."

"We've got our own supplies to carry. Do you want to turn cavalry-mounts into packhorses, *Bôdhrai*?"

"Squadron, I would turn cavalrymen into packhorses if it would help kill *jinzal*. You are going to be facing more *jinzal* than your worst dreams, and the archers beside you had better not run short of arrows."

"I hope they will not."

"Do better than hope, help. The arrows are ready for you." He had been to the workshop early and found fletchers busy at daybreak. Four dozen arrows carried by each of a half-squadron would just about exhaust what had been made, and while workers continued to prepare shafts, they would hope metal heads from Kamsilat and the feathers from Banakit would arrive before stocks were completely gone.

Sour-mouthed, the officer was wheeling off a half-squadron to comply with the order, and Dolvid tried to work out where if anywhere he had gone wrong in dealing with the man. Whether they called him mad or despised him for a supply-train warrior, he was going to get his way; he had no need to be loved. But it was easier, and more was done, if what he asked was seen as proper and well-considered; if he had allies, not grudging servants of an imperious master.

He became genuinely angry with the brothers Thuladh and Dhunival, and that was unfair; only days ago they had staggered off Landegh, out of months filled with hardships and horrors, they needed rest and feeding, kindness, assured safety, and instead had become a living dispatch, relayed from interrogation to interrogation, put on the road to Kamsilat, and quite likely beyond there to Kadon Dinul and Ban-Sila. Unreasonable to expect them ready in early morning for further hard riding, but Dolvid fumed when he found them dawdling over breakfast with the sun already high. Holding annoyance in control he explained the urgencies in a stretched voice, and also spoke to the soldiers of their escort, threatening vague terrors if they failed to make Banakit today. That done, and with a feeling of utter dissatisfaction with his day so far, he set out eastward alone, wishing Enikai was moving under him.

After the activity stirred up at Kreshavu the quiet of the road was odd. Troops must be riding for the Frontier, supplies coming up, dispatches and replies to dispatches on the move, yet to be so undisturbed was disturbing, to ride an hour and more with nothing moving except his own shadow, and high, where a broken crag looked out over a lost and stony valley, a pair of eagles grandly wheeling. At Banakit, where he would sleep a few hours, a fast-messenger from the Frontier should catch up with the latest from Rodlakh: the slowness of news was going to be the worst part, he saw, of this job so glibly accepted: battle (as he knew from experience) could not be worse than the torment of not knowing. Not true; its horrors were worse than anything, but the grim wait for news had no compensating glories.

Afternoon was passing away when his eventless ride brought him down to Fifth Bridge, glad to be where the road improved. His eye was held by the deep cleft overlooked by the *margú*, all golden light and shadows of dusked purple, and only when he was across the simple, wide bridge did he notice a small knot of wayworn troops. They were on and about the long bench outside the compound guardhouse, taking refreshment from metal mugs, and Dolvid, tongue testing grimed lips, decided he would do the same. Before he could join them, he caught sight of Idmas, the squadron-leader here who had complained over losing his best men, deep in talk with another officer, dusty from the road. Then Dolvid's name was called. He turned in the saddle, and Âna was there among soldiers, mug in hand. Horses were lapping at the trough nearby.

His mouth silently made her name, Âna. Dismounting untidily he caught a boot in the stirrup, a treat for the cavalry men. Smiles vanished as the officer broke off his chat with Idmas, and seeing the token Dolvid wore had his men on their feet. He was a half-squadron, his hand swinging in vigorous salute as she came from brown shade into orange light into his arms.

"How many years?"

"Ten days — " proud of knowing exactly.

"We should not have left you at Tan Lughsai. There has not been an hour since — " breaking off so as to tell the officer, let his half-dozen men have their rest: they had been frozen in a tableau.

"I was stupid," trying to take her in with his eyes, remembering how serious she was, and how ready to laugh. "What more could you expect to learn?"

Dismay came as she was different after all, an assembly of features with separate names, eyes, nose, chin, lips, ears — surely his Âna never had such arched eyebrows? and then came a new joining, and there was only one name. Âna.

Drawing back to forearm length she took her revenge. "What if I told you I have changed sides? I am a loyal follower of the *rabhsai*. So are the men with me." Dolvid was bewildered; this was not her style for nonsense.

"Oh, Dolvid — " To her alarm, much more to his, she started weeping. The officer nearby took one step nearer.

He was holding her again. "No — " she unfolded herself, tears flowing freely. "Let us walk a step or two."

"Down to the *margú*." He had an idea it might make an overnight resting place for refugees.

They started down the short slope. She took a drowning breath. "Ban-Sila is dead. Rheduban murdered him. I saw it, I was there. Now Rodlakh is *rabhsai*."

"Well, yes, he would be, with Ban-Sila dead. Rheduban?" He did not need the perplexed look to know he was being numb and fatuous. "I cannot speak. Rodlakh is, now, is our *rabhsai*."

"If he will act," and some of her remembered, chiding tone was there. Of course: she could know little of the new condition at the Frontier, and remained prepared to debate Rodlakh's old scruples.

First: "Tell me about the killing, if you can."

She could, grateful at last to be a witness. Recounting her tale to Sett and Untimarr, as later to Saidhan, it was something she had heard about; words she had used then were useful now, but it became real, and Dolvid caught a glimpse of the fitfully lit, wine-soaked scene, Âna's despairing impotence against the plodding approach of disaster, the nasty offhandedness of the murder. He held tight to her hand, as she to his. "And now I am the one to take Rodlakh the news."

"What a time for this. Have you heard any news from the West?"

She cocked her head. In Banakit, where there were unusual numbers of riders on all roads, Edarron had been given a tale about a *jinzai* army. They had crossed with fast-messengers on the road, but their dispatches were sealed, and they too had only rumors to pass on. She had guessed it was just the same wild story dismissed before as exaggeration and panic feeding on gullibility.

"You would not say so if you had heard Dhunival and Thuladh. They are traders, hardheaded men of no imagination." He told her what they reported, *jinzal* in training or on the march, siege-weapons, the roads across Landegh, their masters under the Royal Standard. "Besides, men are missing, the Mines cut off. No, no, it is real."

She shook her head violently, hair flying, unable to believe the Colony might be crushed. "Still, he must go to Kadon Dinul."

"You know him. Do you think he will?"

She began arguing as if with Rodlakh; he would need only a token army to accompany him, four squadrons, even less — his appearance would bring over the entire Household (except perhaps a few officers in Zhinladh's faction), and the General Cavalry would follow, once he kicked Kargul out of the Residence. Only failure to grasp Sword immediately could defeat him. Besides, he could bring aid back to the Colony as soon as he had control on the Mainland.

A new question occurred; without belittling the skill of this Alkmas, it was clear they had come through the Strait largely by luck, of which appearance of a bigger adversary for the rammers was a good part. If Rodlakh sailed for the Heartland and his ship were sunk or captured —

"The Patriarch cannot keep up His blockade, with this war in the West."

"Rodlakh would say the same." Dolvid bit his lip, trying to work out new alignments in a realm suddenly rid of Ban-Sila. True, no one not here to smell the air of danger, speak with the witnesses, could ever believe actual survival of the realm was being settled at the Frontier. Then if the Patriarch heard of the war, He and His friends of Kargul, they would see it as a great stroke of unexpected luck, something to preoccupy the Army of the West while Orbanak was installed, Shumat defeated, Preference triumphantly established, Tovakh made secure as *Maëdhrai* — as *rabhsai*, but for the title. "No use saying no one could be so stupid: if He heard a whisper of our danger *g'Asalladh'* would dance for joy. So would Petakoi, you know that's true. By the time they woke up to their own danger it would be too late."

"What then?" despondently, not willing to acknowledge out loud he was probably right.

"Well, if there could be a swift victory here in the West — that is a dream." They had reached the front of the derelict *margú*, and awe of the *Atarlum* had evidently done more to keep the structure intact than the barricading of its doors, which could easily be torn away.

As they recrossed Fifth Bridge and walked back up towards the compound they turned over a number of alternatives; a direct appeal to Orbanak, in some way getting past any Patriarchal or other interference — a journey by Rodlakh in secret and virtually alone to Kadon Dinul. But if he did win over the Household, it would not mean any help for the Colony, with Kargul in the field as an enemy.

Dolvid laughed. "Does this seem unreal to you? — for us to walk beside a dusty road, settling the future of the realm? The *rabhsai* might want to be part of the discussion."

"You're his *Bôdhrai*. You are *Bôdhrai*." The distinction struck them both at once; a courtesy-title worn by many who offered advice had become an ancient post of power, a seat at the Council of Thirteen.

"Unless he picks someone else."

"Who else?" she challenged, but he was thinking that for the sake of peace, and alliance against a common enemy, it might be necessary to give out appointments to appease Kargul and the *Mankh'*. Âna would be offended by any notion of compromise with advocates of Preference, enemies of justice, and he was not going to quarrel with her. Laluvoi once said *the realm is the vessel that holds justice. If the vessel breaks justice runs away.*

"Well, while I have the office, I'll use it. We shall ride to the Frontier together; when the *rabhsai* learns he is *rabhsai*, he will want to consult. Your half-squadron, what is his name?"

"Edarron."

"A good officer?"

"Sebhal said so." She was wondering about this newly authoritative Dolvid, and went on marvelling as he altered Edarron's orders, telling him he would go back to Banakit and there take charge of a company of levies, which Captain Happ would assign. His field rank was to be full squadron-leader.

"Field rank? Then it's a real war, *Bôdhrai*?"

"Would you call a couple of thousand *jinzal* real enough? The count may go higher." Dolvid had unstoppered his little travelling horn of ink so as to scribble a message for Happ, followed by Edarron's new orders and rank. There was going to be, as Rodlakh admitted, a shortage of good officers young enough for vigorous command, and in this fight a regular file-leader might find himself leading a levied squadron.

Idmas, a wry smile covering deep hurt, said he had watched his own men ride through, as stiffening for a scratch squadron out of Banakit. Dolvid told him he too would be riding for Kreshavu, taking an additional file of his own men.

"That will leave only sixteen fit men for all duties here."

"Sixteen is too many. No need for road-patrols with so many troops riding; leave just ten under your most reliable junior officer, and go forward with all the rest." He would have an acting rank of *kímukan*, and use his regulars to lead files and half-files in a company made up otherwise of levies.

This breaking up of established squadrons was something Dolvid, citing the great Larghai, had advised Bolan against years ago in the Narn Campaign, but levies here would not be those raw recruits, but mainly men who had served before.

"Ride first thing," he told Idmas, who was failing to conceal delight. "Take any spare animals you have, *pefral* or smaller horses."

Seeing Edarron and his little band were mounted Dolvid called out to him to make sure when he reached Banakit that arrow-feathers had been sent west. Edarron saluted, and made a farewell to Âna, hand on heart, before wheeling away.

"Feathers?"

"War is made of little things. There was a fight Shumat would have lost in '28, if the enemy had remembered spare bowstrings. That was damp country, east of Yuvakh Din."

Day was waning when they took to the road again, sun dipping to the heights ahead. Wishing it could be Enikai, Dolvid had changed horses and taken a saddle lantern; pressing hard it would be near dawn before they could be at Kreshavu. Âna was confident she could ride on through night; she had managed brief rest at Banakit, where Edarron had been delayed, by a lamed horse and then by a largely fruitless attempt to get definite word about news from the Frontier that had turned the town into an opened ants' nest.

Crossing the level bridge she looked curiously at, tried to look into him, searching for a visible mark of change. Between them, she remembered, these things could be said. "When we met I saw you as another Rodlakh, everything muddled by too much considering."

"You saw him at Tan Lughsai; he can find his way when it comes down to yes or no. Since the Island, he is a different man — " stopping short of an admission he had been tutored in decisiveness by a youth of twenty.

"He will be fine as *rabhsai*." Alarmingly, that brought her near tears.

"He could be among the great, if he can survive this, and grasp his power." But the question kept running in Dolvid's head: without help from the Mainland, could the *jinzal* be withstood here? and with civil war breaking out, how could that help be found?

"Needs do change men. What about your Faëdhal with a sword buckled on, giving as good as he got from Kamin-Tolagh?"

"Tell me."

Riding was slow over the tortuous mountain way, and Dolvid admired her quickhanded persuasion of the tall *pefrai*. Often they had to go single file, and when they were side by side again picked up talk as if there had been no interruption. She told him a great deal, and where there was an obvious lacuna he did not question her. When it came to the morning Ban-Sila's death was discovered, he asked for all she knew or could guess about feelings at Kadon Dinul. Besides Dorrmas most of the younger Household officers seemed to be for Rodlakh, with Kizhunai cautiously occupying the middle, and Zhinladh openly supporting Kargul.

Dolvid made a sour face. "Zhinladh means the Families, and Kizhunai would wish to be Captain of the Household no matter who is *rabhsai* — he would tell you, he is a soldier, and does not make policy. I wish more of the Owanil had declared for Rodlakh."

"Why should they? With Rodlakh as *rabhsai*, Preference is dead."

"It must not divide by race. Saidhan is for justice, whether or not he benefits by it."

"Others, too. Your friend Faëdhal. You. Some of the Other Races do what they do out of their greed."

"Careful. You almost had a good word to say for the Owanil."

"I never — " She caught his eye. "Yes I did, and it is stupid, no better than *Lekh'Owan*. You cannot condemn whole races — Finú was kind to me, and Kamin-Tolagh saved my life, though that might have been policy. Dolvid — "

"Yes?"

She was struggling. "When we first met — I was very cruel. Because I saw you as worse than an enemy, a man with no convictions."

He could not accept that, and said so, gently. "Even under Ban-Sila men were not sent into exile for not having any opinions. No, you had to make me into an enemy. Because Sebhal had given you the job of killing me." It was said.

"Who told you that?"

He had worked it out systematically: if he was to guide them to the *rabhsai*, and if the assassination was going to happen, there would have to be at least tentative plans for disposing of the only outside witness. Sebhal would be busy, and that left Sett or Âna, and Sebhal would never have entrusted the task to Sett.

She admitted it had been talked about, but only if there was no chance of persuading Dolvid to endorse the principal murder. "I saw I could never do it soon after I met you. Never."

"I know." This was one of the parts where they could be knee-to-knee, except when meeting others moving east, one clump of which was the detachment of soldiery with the survivors of Landegh, Thuladh and Dhunival, in their midst. Seeing there was no longer any point to hastening them in the eventual direction of Kadon Dinul, Dolvid told the half-file leader to let the two traders rest at Banakit, and attach his half-dozen troops to the squadron being put together by Edarron.

Dolvid and Âna resumed their journey, again side by side, but for a long space nothing was said.

"Tell me about Laluvoi," at last.

He saw she meant not history but the Laluvoi he had known. He reminisced and the evening deepened, her questions came, soft-voiced. He lighted the lantern hanging from its frame on his saddle-bow, and noticed that with dusk his voice settled in his throat as hers did, new milk thick with cream, as if they shared one voice with one two-backed horse. Or perhaps they were being carried inside a circle of soft light that took in horses and riders, questions and answers. The world contracted to that, with a fragment of rough road rolling through the glow, an elusive curve of hillside, a lank, tattered weed rising like a mad beggar, hair wild and arms spread. It shrank to clop and slither of hoofs, chink of harness, voice of the Âna he loved. Their mission was desperate and this ride was part of that, but they could not go any faster and it was all incongruously gentle. Danger was ahead, urgency with them. Weary, each knew the other was mysteriously happy, and happiness was bound between them.

"Can you guess," now playful, "when I knew I could never do what Sebhal wanted?"

He recalled her first unhostile asking of questions. "In the Burantal Hills, when you asked me about the succession?" Strange to remember there had been discussion about the True *Rabhsai*, inconsequential then.

"Long before that. By then Sebhal was changing his plan, and he did not want me at Kadon Dinul. The morning at your house, when you made porridge." Well, but hours before he had begun to feel something more complicated than either annoyance or desire. Their hands came together and held till the next difficult stretch of road.

Pale yellow ahead, pale rose behind, above a luminous pale green, the sky was any color except blue when they came to the last ridge, across from Kreshavu standing on its dark cliff fretted with falling water. A few windows showed tawny lights, and it was gratifying to see lanterns and torches moving, both in the town and lower down, where the road ran by the cavalry-post. There where the way climbed up, many horses were tethered. Dolvid wrote a quick note for Rodlakh, and handed it to a guard, to go with the earliest messenger. A hasty scrawl at roadside was not the means for hailing a new *rabhsai*, nor for mentioning his brother's death; the note said only Âna was here, and they would reach him with important news before nightfall, after brief rest in Kreshavu.

In return he was given a dispatch in Rodlakh's writing, addressed to him, which he read standing beside his horse, endorsed, and resealed for forwarding to Saidhan. It was from the Drin. Rodlakh had spoken with men from small patrols still venturing out on Landegh, and several had sighted very large ordered companies of *jinzal*, some camped within a day's march of the Frontier. But the relief force for the Mines was being assembled, and Rodlakh was glad to see the Banakit squadrons, arriving as his dispatch was being penned. He reemphasized the need for every man who could hold a weapon, and asked Dolvid to find Galt. At the end he had taken the pen, not only to sign and address the dispatch, but to write the single word, *arrows*, across the page.

So it was true; Dolvid's heart felt clutched by a dismay that was like guilt. The account of the two brothers had not left any doubt, but he now realized he had gone on hoping there must be some mistake, even while fully accepting the reality of a *jinzai* army. The flatness of these new confirmations was the worst part.

Up above, the hostelry was almost filled. Dolvid had authority to evict some farmer come back to soldiering, stealing a last night in a real bed before the rigors of war, but short of that the hostel-keeper could offer only a single bedroom. Âna, head down, very like a sleepy kitten, muttered words he did not follow, about her father and a sleeping-bag, and then with a momentary return to clarity entertained and informed a crowded common-room by announcing one bed would be very good. Before, she had been trying to say that weary as they both were, not just one room, not merely one bed, but one sleeping-bag could be shared chastely enough to satisfy even her father.

The bed was a firm one, and in the beginning they took off only boots and outshirts, lying with arms intertwined. Dozes overlapped. The morning having become warm and moist, Dolvid half-waked to see her sit up and drag off her shirt, and he remembered that same impatient discarding when she had sat up beside Pir who was Sebhal who was dead. Starting there he drifted into a slack-walled muddle; he was Sebhal or was discussing plans with Sebhal, the boat-owner. If he failed to use right words there was some precious radiance he could lose.

He was awake, mostly so, and Âna came in smiles out of her
sleep.   They kissed as those who crawl out of the wilderness
drink, greed without end. Exhaustion melted to a rich languor,
unabashed whispering of nonsense. Her skin tasted salt, and the
warm scents of their bodies were a homecoming.

Loud pounding brought them through depth beneath depth of
sleep, at last into light. Naked together under a soft blanket, their
clothing pushed in wads all about them, they did not speak. Four
hours had passed; Dolvid raised his head to call thanks to the
serving-man who had wakened them. After nuzzling at a smooth
shoulder, he extracted himself, shivering, and soon went in search
of warmed water, then food to bring back to the room. When he
came with bread and cooked eggs, butter and warm milk, Âna was
towelling dry. Going to her pack for fresh clothes she turned
away from him.
     "Your back — " horrified.
     She reached back to touch the marks. "It is healing."
     Holding her, he heard the story of Rheduban and the beating.
She did not talk about the bedding, the rape, which had followed,
and her tones were calm, historical. He had heard a woman speak
about her body as if it were other than her, made for pain which
could never reach a self kept in uttermost private, but his wonder
was overcome by hatred for Rheduban. At the end he said, "I
hope no one kills him before I can get to Kadon Dinul." He did
not admire the pleasure it gave him to imagine being the one to
extinguish Rheduban.
     "Don't think about it now. Come back, Dolvid." She meant,
the tender Dolvid of three hours ago, but he could not aspire to
detachment from what was past and to come, sense of the now
that kept her wholly here. He was accused by eyes that pleaded,
and excused himself to himself; it was Âna who had unleashed
this other Dolvid by presenting him with something that needed
avenging. Before, when Sebhal died, she had given him the job
of killing Rheduban: he was not going to ask her pardon for
wanting vengeance for her violation.

He began to stand on dignity, and got as far as, "Forgive me if I cannot — " then saw he was being more than ridiculous; she was the injured one. In time to avoid making things worse, not to recapture their ease, he suggested they eat their breakfast, because it was a long ride to the Drin. That, too, was absurdly pompous; she had made that ride, he never had. The chill of self-consciousness closed on its own tail to become consciousness of that, and then of that.

She smiled sadly, putting fingers softly to his lips. Granted, the luxuries of their drowsed mating could not persist, but she hoped some tint would be left to color what came after; a mournful puzzle that he must withdraw into stiffness, changing all the world back to separate things, solid to touch.

He saw compassion in her eyes, but singleness of act and feeling had years ago gone beyond reach and he would never dare to follow her there; poses had defended him too long from the vulnerability of what he truly felt, believed, was moved by. He should be glad at last to have someone to see through all the masks and not despise what she saw, so long as the one was Âna. He could not rejoice; habit was making a new shield. "We have our work to do. What a year to be chosen by."

She mumbled rote accord, eyes suppliant, and yet he knew she was right, though all tales said his part, the man's part, was the harder, not to let love deflect him from duty. That was nonsense, her instincts were truer. He wished he could say, if they could love and go on loving, the realm, Rodlakh's *rabhsayum*, dangers and enemies east and west would be in their dream, which they could dream out as they elected. True, in that a moment, if not denied or amended by afterthought, was all time. He struggled for a beginning word, and Âna sneezed. It was a fit of sneezing, one starting another, and she knew there had been something turned away. Between fighting sneezes and trying to say she was sorry, his blaming draughts and dust, wrapping a shirt over her shoulders, they both began to laugh, and were taken by spasms of laughter uncontrollable as sneezing all through their hurried breakfast, where the sneezing forth of a shower of crumbs brought fresh laughter. They were still shaken by afterlaughs as they completed dressing and readied for the road. Hand in hand, cheerful, they came down to where the horses were quietly waiting, any ache of loss scarcely to be perceived.

Seen for the first time Drin Navuna was a surprise, no town at all, or hardly any. In the arid plain, the massive fortress plugging up the gap that wound between tortured mountains, a scattering of dwellings began to clump closer as they approached the mound where the road vanished into an archway with ramparts growing, cliff to cliff.

The fierce-toothed ridges Dolvid knew to be the margin of Landegh were not as tall as some of the less abrupt peaks the road had threaded, though higher in absolute terms. Each of the three main stages west of Kamsilat had a greater elevation than the last, and final descent into the Drin Navuna plain still left travellers far above the level of the Arnan.

The way was by means of a long, narrow causeway, becoming a bridge as it leapt across the ravine, joining rock to rock, its supports stone, sometimes stoutly bundled wood pilings, parts of the roadway made of many slender logs. Once the ravine was crossed there was a long, lightless cleft leading to a brief tunnel cut through solid rock, with double iron gates where all riders were halted. Past that, they rode down a gentler ramp, and the plain began amid low brown ridges. The curve of road followed where all wrinklings of the country converged on the Drin, guarding the pass as it had in the days of the First Empire, grey and black, forbidding. Much of the lower stonework with its fanciful carving dated from before the Night, and what had been reconstructed or added after the Return was strong rather than beautiful; this above all other defended places was a fortress with a job to do. Roads crossed not far behind the sheltering bulk of the fortress, the way that linked the watchtowers along the ridge swooping down to intersect the main road, and here was a slight gathering of some larger buildings, none imposing. Off to the left was the military commander's residence, a two-story structure built over an entranceway designed for something grander. Between this and the great somber walls of Drin Navuna was a wide expanse of parade-ground, surrounded by hardy trees.

Dolvid had no idea how many men could be quartered here. In addition there were barracks near the crossroads, and rows of small tents pitched in open spaces, displaying pennons of the various squadrons: there were stacked water-barrels and tethered horses, but though the smoke and scent of cooking-fires meant the evening meal must be near, few troops were to be seen.

From the hump where the roads crossed he could look down past the commander's residence and saw the reason; the space between there and the walls of the Drin was crowded with men, mounted and on foot, drawn up in their companies. They were completely in shadow, although the Beech-Tree banner of Rodlakh flying over the house remained in late sunlight. A general assembly; Âna said Sebhal would occasionally review and talk with the army from the terrace behind the residence.

Seeing the token Dolvid wore the sentinels at the residence entrance quickly lifted their levelled pikes. She led the way, hard left in the high front gallery, through a door to a little winding stair. In the corridor above there were further guards to be passed, before they came to a sparsely furnished rear hall across most of the width of the building, with doors leading onto a stone terrace. Rodlakh was just emerging from a small side-room, ready to go out to the troops, face resolved though showing lack of sleep.

"Âna. And Dolvid." Three strides and he caught up her hands. She seemed hesitant, and Dolvid felt a new shyness, as the vestment of *rabhsayum* came unseen to drape Rodlakh's shoulders.

Oblivious, Rodlakh hugged her, saying how good to see her safe. "I could scarcely believe the message, I thought someone must be imitating Dolvid's writing. Your news will have to wait, the men expect me — "

"You must listen." Âna stopped short, mute. She twisted to beseech Dolvid with a look.

"No, the news is yours."

"You are our *rabhsai* now," just as Rodlakh, frowning, was about to tell them again it must wait. "Ban-Sila has been murdered. You are the *rabhsai*."

He opened his mouth, went from Âna to Dolvid, declined to laugh at a joke in bad taste, while the gravity of it whitened his face.

"It is true." Occasion came to Âna's rescue, and she sank to her knees. "That he will accept my allegiance and my service."

He raised and kissed her, reciting numbly, "We, Rodlakh, accept and prize the allegiance of our friend Âna."

The pikemen holding the door for him to go out on the terrace was nonplussed, as Dolvid became second to take allegiance to their new lord, ignoring the Old Tongue, though at such a time its sonorities were ringing in his head. Rodlakh, in agonies to hear more, raised him, then drew Âna closer. Dolvid said he would tell the officers on the terrace Rodlakh would be there in three minutes.

Outside, he went straight to a big-framed man with a chin of granite, Nolimas, whose fist swallowed Dolvid's hand whole. "*Bôdhrai.* You might find a healthier season for your visit, but I see you've brought us back the Lucky One." He nodded at the window, where Âna's dark head was visible, Rodlakh's tall figure bent earnestly over her. That, Nolimas said, was the name some of the Fro' archers had given her. "I hope it is so, but I don't have much use for omens myself. Under-Captain Wanildhai."

Even with his own people, whose pale eyes often seemed focused elsewhere, Dolvid had seldom seen a pair this vague. The man was middle-sized and lithe, in his sixties, probably, with some of the stretched look of vigor retained. "A man scorns omens," as if dreaming, "believing it unlucky to be superstitious."

Not adding much to Âna's terse words, he gave these senior officers the news, Wanildhai's eyes a little wider, Nolimas with lower lip pushed forward: "Any other time this would be the best news for the realm since Banak's day. Rodlakh *Rabhsai*! Sad our Sebhal could not live to see it."

Dolvid appraised the assembled soldiery. A thousand and a half, he would say, regular cavalry on restless *pefral*, squadrons of mounted archers of Galt's breed, short in the saddle on low, tough horses. There were also archers on foot, as well as slingers and some pikes. Well to the front, centered on the terrace, was part of what must have been Sebhal's personal squadron, brown flag of bereavement draped beside the scarlet flower of the West, and Dolvid had a moment's pang, having sent an officer and others from this same squadron to take charge of levies. After the death of a famous warrior such units often fiercely resisted being broken up; almost till the Night came there had been a celebrated company still calling itself Larghai's Own, though by then Larghai had been dead four centuries.

Through the window he saw Rodlakh straighten, brush back hair two-handed, tug down his tunic, and make for the doors.

He would seize this moment. Seven years ago by strange circumstance, with everything in confusion after the Tan Lughsai catastrophe, Dolvid had been the one to proclaim the *rabhsayum* of Ban-Sila. If he had done nothing Ban-Sila would surely have come to power, yet the past persisted; his voice had given substance to that lunatic reign. A writer of history rarely speaks at its making, and now, having seen his one opportunity turn to the bad, here, against any odds, was a chance for amends. How many men, historians or not, had been able to proclaim a friend as lawful *rabhsai*, in the midst of those who had come to love him best? Nolimas had bellowed the troops to order, and as Rodlakh stepped out into the last of the sunlight, Dolvid spoke.

"At Kadon Dinul, Ban-Sila *Deghi* is dead." He was pitching his voice to carry, and there was a tense, absolute silence while this news was apprehended. "Succession now lawfully falls upon this lord, Rodlakh *Deghi, Rabhsai*, Rodlakh Lambarrati *bi-*Arbhai-Navu. See him! Honor him! Obey him!"

Unimaginable such a thunderclap could come from only fifteen hundred throats, the boom of welcome and approval that bounded from the walls of the Drin, and seemed to mutter away as summer thunder into the distant hills. Dolvid's throat clenched, and off to the left he saw a radiant Âna shudder in a vast sob of emotion. The soldiers beat swords together, pikes and lances on the ground, while some of the archers caused a curious low thrumming, stopping their bowstrings to make musical instruments.

A hand on Dolvid's arm, Rodlakh spoke into his ear. "Well done. Was there ever a *rabhsai* proclaimed with so few words of the Owanilú?"

In fact, his brother had been, but Dolvid merely nodded in the din, and enjoyed imagining Faëdhal's disapproval of these vernacular proceedings. Yet what could have been more ridiculous than to use a language not one in a hundred here could speak or understand?

Rodlakh had stepped forward, and raised hands. For seconds, it seemed the acclamation would not die down. A junior officer with an angry voice bellowed out, "Hear the *rabhsai*!"

"I thank you," he said. "My friends — " and in the new thunders this provoked, only those near him on the terrace heard the rest: "May I live to deserve such affection."

"A repeater," Nolimas rumbled. "We need a repeater." The junior officer who had yelled out before, evidently famous for his cavalry-drills, came forward to repeat Rodlakh's words, phrase by phrase.

He told them general assembly had been called, not for this, but to inform the men of the danger they and the realm were facing; there had been too many rumors. This other news had caught him unprepared, but — here Rodlakh raised his voice so no repetition was needed — "In this first hour, let us declare, Preference has no place in this realm; we absolutely repudiate inequalities of race or belief, now, and for as long as we may hold Sword." Each phrase of this promise was cheered; attracted by the tumult ordinary people had attached themselves to the fringes of the gathering, and against the brightness of the western sky the fortress parapet was lined with heads.

Using the repeater again, Rodlakh sobered his listeners with talk of imminent war. He did not soften his report; Shâl Mines, he told them, was under siege, and Drin Navuna soon would be. The fortress must be defended, but the Army of the West did not cower behind walls when those it was sworn to protect were in danger.

"Tomorrow, with many of you here, I ride to the relief of Shâl Mines. From those remaining we shall need increased vigilance, an even greater resolve to stand firm, and hold the gate by which we must return. Your courage, my friends, is not in question; it has been proved in a thousand fights. Now we must take pride in our discipline, our trust in comrades. This is our best weapon — " and again he waved aside the drill-officer to let his own voice ring out — "We are brothers." They cheered. "This is to be our sternest fight, and with trust in each other can be our most glorious victory." Applause swelled, and died down very slowly. When there was still, Rodlakh, not loudly but with no need for a repeater, said, "My thanks, my friends. Till tomorrow, good night."

"Live long, *Rabhsai*," Nolimas roared, as the shouts renewed, and trumpeters of the watch, without any order, made a brave attempt at the royal flourish.

Flushed and serious Rodlakh turned to go in, and applause brought him back; twice more the ovations made him return, before Nolimas had the trumpets sound, and those who had shared the terrace followed their young *rabhsai* inside, where the senior officers soon took allegiance, offering up and then receiving again their swords. Then Rodlakh, sending a man to fetch food and drink, called Dolvid and Âna to the small side room.

There were differences. For one thing, no one sat on the long leather-cushioned bench while he was standing. He looked from one to the other. "Oh, come," with half-humorous exasperation, and forthwith decreed they would never need leave to be seated in his presence, so long as they were among themselves. "Âna tells me you met at Fifth Bridge; you have done some riding since yesterday morning. After we have supper you can sleep, as I must. We do not ride for the Mines till the hour before noon, but I must be up at dawn."

Âna said, "How can you ride for Shâl Mines?"

"How can I not?"

Asked if the road was open Rodlakh gave the latest; there were *jinzal* but not charging as *jinzal*, lurking, waiting for the main prize; they, or their masters, must expect an attempt to relieve the Mines.

When she objected that riding out, therefore, would invite ambush, Rodlakh said the Army of the West was not without tactics of its own, knew the country better, and was going out in greater total strength than could possibly be anticipated. "The enemy is as likely to assail the Drin, believing we must have emptied it for this sally." He was gladdened by Dolvid's report on the troops, regulars and levies, that could be expected at Drin Navuna over the next day-and-a-half, in numbers if not quality more than replacement for the forces he was leading out tomorrow.

"Have you seen anything of Galt?"

"No. But he should have reached Kreshavu today, and by now is certain I am mad. I left word for him to wait there for further orders. I was sure you would want him to go with you to Kadon Dinul."

The expression went rueful. "How can I go?"

Dolvid was going to be obtuse and pretend the question was about means, but Âna flashed to the heart, instructing Rodlakh he must go. He had told the men of the West that Preference was dead, and that could be true only with Rodlakh holding Sword; if delay cost him his capital and his realm, the men here might defeat the *jinzal* and still end as losers.

"If we lose here," Rodlakh said, "the realm is condemned to far worse than Preference."

"Will your one sword be the difference between victory and defeat?" she had the temerity to ask. "You have officers, commanders here, but only you can do what needs to be done at Kadon Dinul."

"Good commanders, good soldiers — you heard me tell them we had to be brothers, and now you want me to say, you be brothers, I'll see you when it is over? They cheered me, for what? Asking them to stand in ranks to be killed? They are tough men here," turning to Dolvid. "Half of them must think they would stand a better chance taking to the hills with a hundred arrows and a bag of bread. They might be right, but they will do their duty,

and I do mine — be seen to do mine," he amended, foreseeing
Âna's next.

"If you won the *jinzai* war, would you be content with the
Colony for your realm?"

"If ever these lands could be made to feed themselves, we
could do worse." He took her hands between his. "How can I
know? Winning, would we have strength left to fight off Kargul,
if Tovakh came?" He told her his former plan, of a last appeal to
Ban-Sila, on the basis of the new danger, and somewhat
alarmingly went on hoping there might be accommodation with
g'Asalladh' — a truce, at least, while all factions allied against the
common enemy.

"*G'Asalladh'* would have His asking-price," Dolvid said.
"Such as your support for Orbanak as *rabhsai*."

"I would accept that, if it meant bringing the troops we need
here." Rodlakh hurried to appease Âna, who so far had advocated
with none of her former waspishness: "Accept it, with certain
guarantees against restoration of Preference. Even for the sake of
the realm's survival, I cannot bargain away other people's rights."

Âna and Dolvid exchanged silences. "Assurances made by
the *Mankh'*," Dolvid said, "can be trusted only if you are
bargaining from strength. No harm in negotiating, once you had
control of the Household and the General Cavalry."

"But then except for opening the Strait, we would not really
need them, and if we could make an ally of Kargul we could
dictate to the *Mankh'*. And if I had no need to go to Kadon, I
could afford to. Would you?"

"Would I?" — not sure what was being asked, to say what he
would do in Rodlakh's shoes, or actually to go.

"Your pardon, it is not fair to suggest it."

"I'd go, of course I would go, if you wanted it, and if it had
any purpose. Kadon Dinul is looking for a *rabhsai*, not an
interesting official of obscure birth."

"You will be *Bôdhrai*, if you accept the post."

"*Bôdhrai*-designate. The title needs confirmation in
Council."

"You know the history: has any Council ever dared not give a *rabhsai* the man he wanted at his elbow? I thought not. Well, leaving aside any mission, the title is yours for life, your life or mine, if you will take it. You could have less leaky ships to sail in."

"*Rabhsai*, with great gladness." That was meant, yet odd, when either of them might fail to live the month out, that Dolvid felt a pang for freedoms he, perhaps, was vowing away, work of his own, ten years from now, that might not get done because he was busy as *Bôdhrai*.

With only Âna for onlooker Rodlakh began whimsically high-flown, but ended in earnest, "We, Rodlakh, in our first appointment, name and designate Dolvid Vidukhat, friend and trusted counsellor, to be our *Bôdhrai*."

Thanking him for all the titles Dolvid again asked what he would do if he went to the Mainland. He could tell Âna was set against it.

"Negotiate, better than I ever could. You know Bolan, you are Shumat's oldest friend, you know Him who is now *g'Asalladh'* — you are going to say, that is no advantage, but He respects you even if He dislikes you; me he despises unknown. You have friends such as Faëdhal, and you said you knew Kizhunai. Besides, you are familiar with the law and all our traditions. You can even pick your way through the labyrinth of the Families, which is another Shemugrân for me."

Aware of Âna's eyes, he frowned it through. There were indeed things he might accomplish at Kadon Dinul if he could keep alive long enough to get them launched. He said, "This would require very wide powers, beyond, even, what you have already given me — plenipotentiary powers, to pardon, to confirm posts, to conclude alliances, all in your name."

"You have them, as long as you need them."

Dolvid grimaced, and earned a *Bôdhrai*'s salary for that day, telling him that when conferring such extraordinary powers a term must always be specified — he suggested forty days, but Rodlakh, saying he might be missing and his fate unknown, made it one hundred.

Âna, seeing there was nothing she could do to prevent this altogether, asked whether Dolvid was to be sent alone. If Rodlakh was lost, or believed lost, the Household would be Orbanak's, Tovakh or *g'Asalladh'* in real control, and Dolvid as good as dead.

Rodlakh agreed; an army could not be sent, but a guard would give added choice. He asked if two squadrons, a hundred men, would do any good.

Well, but a couple of ships had a better chance of getting through than a flotilla. "I would go with less than half as many, if they were the right men."

Rodlakh knew at once what was meant. "He will be missed here at the Frontier, too, but you have his respect, which not everyone can boast."

"How will you get through the Strait? With Alkmas, as you say, I had some luck. He must have sailed for home by now." When she last saw him he had been going to find somewhere he could swallow, he said, a couple of dozen oysters. His boat, in any case, was too little to take troops across.

"I shall not use the Strait."

"North Passage?" — a despondent face. It would mean waiting for the right tides, and in that narrow water any ship would be easy to intercept.

History was coursing like wine in Dolvid's veins. "*Rabhsai,* when one of your grandfathers, Saidhan, was besieged at Kir in 2876, your other grandfather, Banak, was here in the Colony, and came to Saidhan's aid with what seems impossible speed. He did not land to the south; he passed through Kadon Dinul, because he had Household troops as well as his own when he arrived at Kir. Counting days, he must have risked the Shoals, by far the shortest passage, if it can be negotiated."

"They say the Shoals are impassable."

"So also Shemugrân," determined to try it. Sarnak would be his helmsman, and he decided also to take Vinosai, as a way of getting him out of Kamsilat, and perhaps of inventing a use for him.

"Sett never cared for the man," Âna said. "Never trusted him."

"He is Under-Warden of the Port," Rodlakh said, but Saidhan would support the choice, and smooth the man down with blandishments about the critical importance of this journey.

"He was a pilot for the port of Irbat, after my years there, a shallow-water sailor. The mudbanks there shift constantly, and they bring large ships in with a smaller one ahead to guide them." More details were in Dolvid's head, but he did not bring them out, not to be secretive; fatigue and anxiety gave a bickering note to all the comments, making him tireder and less patient.

"Then you will attempt this *quest*," using the bookish word with intent, aware how ramshackle all their plans were, how unlike the sure deeds of legend. There was not much romance about grime, leaden eyes, *jinzal* by the hundred, perhaps a mile or less from where they sat, splintered factions and muddled loyalties at Kadon Dinul, or convincing young girls that how quickly they could affix sections of feather to shafts of wood might determine the realm's survival. "You will be the Voice of the *Rabhsai*."

"As best I can."

With something settled the carping mood went away. At a frugal meal with some good wine they expanded on their adventures, comfortable together, all three. Rodlakh and Âna no longer bristled at each other, and watching them Dolvid inconsequentially recalled when they had gone flickering together in half-light across the broad square at Burantal, how the slender youth and grace of both had wrenched at him, contrast with the reasons they were there some ultimate condemnation of this shabby time. But he was conscious of being the older only in consciousness, aware of how rare a gathering like this would be; if we live, he thought, we shall remember this evening, three friends sitting down to share food and talk. He was not sure what Âna intended, but in grim truth it was unlikely they would all meet again, and if through chance and miracle they did it would not be this; *rabhsayum* and its trappings would seize Rodlakh, and they would never be as truly themselves as in these outlaw weeks.

Rodlakh did his best to embarrass Dolvid over his part at Drin b'Afon, and Âna caught the teasing mood, saying wide-eyed

Dolvid's account was fraudulent. "He recounted the cliffs were climbed, not who led the climbing. In the battle he seemed safe on a rock nearby, making notes." She had in fact heard more from Sarnak.

"That is his conceit. We have to trumpet our own deeds; he knows others will boast for him."

"By your leave, *Rabhsai*, I did not hear the *Rabhsai* say much about swordplay. Ask the *Rabhsai* who fought and killed the commander of the *Adanum Plakh'*."

"Feasts are going to be shorter," she observed, "if the new fashion is to say as little as possible about one's own battle-feats."

There was some unfinished business; Dolvid wanted to deliver both a share of the prize-money and a personal memento, the leather armband, to the family of Truni, the young slinger. Rodlakh had a meeting with senior officers to discuss defense of the Drin, and said Wanildhai would know where Truni's kin could be found.

Here was a faint flawing in the mood of comradeship, the whisper of wind on a summer's day, sending wrinkles across a polished pond to bring thoughts of rain. Not knowing the terrain nor strengths and weaknesses of the Drin, Dolvid had no role at the meeting, that he understood. There was also Âna. After he had been told by Wanildhai to try at the little Froghu' drink-shop just past the cross-ways, it was sensible for her to decline the short walk. Road-weary, she would find hot water for a long bath.

He was numb with fatigue, but this might be his only chance to go, everything made perfect sense, yet when he slipped out into cool night he felt solitude and sorrow clutch at his throat, so he could have given a long, childlike wail of despair for what would not stand still.

Watchfires on every hill, flares and lanterns on the walls of the fortress, fires scattered through the encampments, made night recede. Dolvid could not banish a rueful reflection on the acres of woodland the war was going to consume. At their very first meeting Rodlakh had made the usual Colony gibe about the lack of large trees east of Arnan. Yes, but Dolvid had never convinced anyone the answer was, *we have burnt them*. Forests must diminish if every year more wood was consumed as fuel than could be grown; they could not all be fable, the early chronicles that had the eastward shores of Arnan thickly wooded. In the *Atarlum*'s defense, for once, it must be admitted the Growers had always tried to foster the planting of trees. Here farmers hated them for the wrong reason, disenchanted with any crop so long to show a return.

He walked back from his errand with better mood restored; he seldom had dealings with the Froghul that did not leave him happy. The aunt and uncle of Truni were owners of the drink-shop; Dolvid had preferred the aunt, the uncle having shown just a feathersweight too much interest in the purse of money, while the woman wept over the painted armband — it was true, however, she had the blood-relationship, sister to Truni's father, demanding bleakly how the news could ever be sent to the Lunu Tezh'. Both made the grief-gesture he would always associate with Tini-ra, scoring left forearm with right thumbnail.

As ever his fumbling command of a few words in their language gave pleasure beyond its merit, and he pleased them further by refusing wine or ale, asking for the sour brew of fermented goat's milk which all Froghul made, no matter how far separated by history or distance. Happily he had remembered to wear Rodlakh's badge inside his shirt, and with no barrier of rank a band of archers from a mounted squadron so far adopted him they tried to teach him a gentle-sounding song which he gradually realized was grossly indecent and very funny. These were mostly very young men, still with the hospitality that contrasted with Froghuli fierceness; there was respectful recognition of Galt's name, and no one was surprised when Dolvid told them the man would have `big words on true father-tales,' as history was called in that additive language.

Back at the commander's residence it seemed a mild intended rebuke that the door-sentinel had been instructed to keep special watch for the *Bôdhrai*, who was shown to where the bedrooms were. A steward led him to his own, surrendered a fat lighted candle, and when Dolvid asked whether the *rabhsai* had gone to bed was momentarily at a loss, as if offended no one had told him about Ban-Sila's arrival. Recollecting who was now the *rabhsai*, the steward a little shamefacedly confirmed he had retired. There was a message for the *Bôdhrai*; the documents he needed were drawn up and signed, and he would see the *Bôdhrai* at earliest light.

The soured mood was seeping back. Âna must be in bed, and it was unsatisfactory her head was not, as at Burantal, in the crook of his arm. In a dressing-robe he discovered Dolvid went yawning out, and in brief exploration encountered no one except servants, and a pair of guards who were polite but unhappy about his wanderings.

He headed back with a wild hope she might be waiting in his small room, dozing, perhaps, on his bed, ready to be wakened, dark eyes raggedly veiled. All he found was his thick candle smoking greasily. Calves ached and his sore eyeballs throbbed, but he knew sleep would not be captured without a struggle. He was angry and ashamed it could matter so much, that he could be brought to this infantile petulance with a world running for ruin. Self-accusing, he mortgaged a lifetime's distaste for superstition, trying to find the incantation to bring her.

The night became both long and terrifyingly short; for his own sake, and for his enterprise, he must attain some sleep, so he kept telling himself. Somewhere not far from dawn he slid into part-sleep, where *jinzal* were coming to take away everything precious, *jinzal* with whips. As at Kreshavu he was roused by knocking.

He had not heard Âna's plans, and in a few hours it had become impossible to ask. Mounted on a skittish *pefrai* he was not catching her eye this morning. Clearly she was going to start eastward with him, and Rodlakh had spoken about her staying in the Great House at Kamsilat. Dolvid wished she could be with him, but if Kamin-Tolagh had won or was winning the race there, Kadon Dinul could be a dangerous place, and if Kargul held it in strength they might take to open country, as Galt would unquestionably prefer; those hardships should not be forced on Âna.

In helm and breastplate Rodlakh gesticulated earnestly speaking to Wanildhai, who would remain as garrison-commander. In the various camps the morning call had sounded and the blue plain was crackling with small noises, ring of weapons and flatter clash of eating-tools, snort and flutter of impatient horses, voices calling out orders or queries, a short burst of harsh laughter. The underlying solemnity of this parting might be affecting Âna: when he remarked how quiet and private she was she smiled wanly.

Undiminished in ease, the *rabhsai* cantered to his friends, taking off the helm to sling it at saddle-bow, shaking out matted brown hair. Behind, two pairs of lancers edged and sidled uncertainly. Rodlakh glanced at them and turned back to the others. "Nolimas will not let me go five paces without escort. Yesterday I could ride off a cliff; if I do it today it means fifty-one broken necks. Are you ready?"

He brought up something Dolvid had mentioned, that in ancient days fire-arrows, hard to extinguish, had been used against wooden siege-engines. "Alvir found an old man who said he knew all about it — as far as he recalls, it is something to do with either saltpeter or alum. He might as well say, something to do with bows. Someone at Kamsilat might remember. If we win through to Shâl Mines and get back, we may have a long siege to withstand here."

The stores were good, he said, and he was willing to let *jinzal* scale the ridges and come down to roam in the plain if he could hold the Drin and the gorge, once women, children and the aged had been sent east. "I say the aged — it is going to be the very old; we have grandfathers with legs shrunken to twigs riding in to say they have not forgotten how to pull a bow. But we have to consider rations, too. Shall I ride with you to the causeway, then?"

Shadowed by the four lancers the three went trotting past the few houses and shops. Before the curving rise to the edge of the gorge there was a flat, open mile; they were tempted to race, but remembered the strenuous day ahead for the horses, and maintained an easy gait. A woman coming out of doors to scatter crumbs and see the day called out, "*Rabhsai*," and Rodlakh waved. In the gap between heights ahead a dull, poppy-red, painted sun had come up.

They came to arch and gates, the sharp turn through the cool tunnel. Another heavy gate swung back, and they were in the cutting, looking up to start of the first long climb, the road on its causeway bending across the wild gorge.

Little more had to be said. They were in dank shadow; Dolvid clasped Rodlakh's hand, wishing him good fortune and a safe return. Rodlakh returned the wishes, no more troubled at his prospects than before the final assault at Drin b'Afon, this young man going out to a fight with more *jinzal* than had ever been known.

Âna was on his far side. She had that same tense smile, and edged nearer so they could kiss. A low-voiced exchange Dolvid could not follow and wished he did not want to, ending with Âna's "I shall, *Rabhsai*," while he held her right hand between both of his.

"Good road," Rodlakh said, and Dolvid's mind had played him a peculiar trick; not in words but primed feelings he was saying farewell to the two of them, not Rodlakh to him and Âna.

"Urge speed on the levies you meet — " now for the sake of saying something. "They will be needed."

"So will you, here and elsewhere — " varying Rodlakh's words to the gathered troops, "Your courage is not in question, now you must show prudence. Your life is needed by many others."

He nodded in a way neither dispute nor agreement. "What?" when Âna murmured something so quiet it was lost in a burst of starling-twitter from the gorge. She shook her head. Wheeling his horse left-handed, Rodlakh achieved a jaunty wave, but the parting had left a great deal unsaid.

On the climb of the causeway Dolvid and Âna maintained quiet. Near the top end she halted to look back at the plain where mist and dust together were beginning to glow. From there it was single-file up the steep of the road; not a word passed for half an hour, when they emerged onto the level, rock-faces all around. A few stunted and contorted trees, some sort of pine, clung by their fingernails to granite speckled with lichens. It was full sun now, and Âna rose in her stirrups to take a deep breath.

"I looked for you last night."

"I was exhausted. I intended — " She stopped herself. "Dolvid, with the baKargul I had to tell lies beyond counting. I think better of you. I was with Rodlakh last night."

"So I would have ventured." He sought another subject, the tenacity of trees, an etched cliff-face with the look of gnarled bark. He would have been irritated if she had persisted with evasion, so must not now be angry with truth. But there was nothing else to talk about.

"You don't mind?" and he wondered why he was always being asked that. Attuned to him, she said quickly, "A snivelling question, do not answer. Rodlakh asked if I would bed with him. I knew the danger he was going into — "

"He reminded you of that?"

"Do you believe he would?" offended for Rodlakh's sake. She had been the one who could not keep out the fear he might not live through the next few days, and it made a difference, too, her assumption he was still virgin (though she should have guessed Kamin-Tarú's part in giving Rodlakh his new, unflinching gaze).

"Is he wearing his own sword today? The horse is his."

She came near rage: Sebhal's wise saw had annoyed her when first she heard it, and had nothing to do with this; Dolvid would never know how natural it had been to go to Rodlakh's bed, and how completely apart from any other act — or so it had seemed. "If I had known about Kamin-Tarú, I do not say I would have refused him."

"He is, after all, *rabhsai*."

She looked at him, trying to tell which one of the possible meanings he meant. For him the words had come out not properly considered; he could not say whether he was suggesting Rodlakh could have commanded her, or re-accusing the ambition she had once confessed to.

"He is, after that, Rodlakh," evenly, and Dolvid nodded assent, nearly managing to emerge from gloom into light and open space where they were all three friends.

Here was a difficult set of turns to negotiate, time for long thoughts. Âna went ahead, and when Dolvid could again come level with her he saw her set face showed disappointment. Brutally he asked in his head whether she imagined she could go straight from what they had at Kreshavu to Rodlakh's bed, leaving the world unchanged. After a solemn while he was forced to ask, why not? fighting down the bitter taste that did not belong here, but in the past, with Khalú. Smiling he said, "And has he asked you to be his *rabhsayu*?"

"Yes."

To his suddenly deeper silence she said, "Anywhere, there is only one person whose opinion I would value, and I cannot talk to him."

Dolvid's horse came near shying, as a large whitish butterfly, finding who knew what flowers in these bony heights, went dodging up. When the animal was quieted he said, "I would always rather be flattered than loved." She turned quickly, but the light irony was aimed at himself. "What did you tell him?"

"Truth — everything is uncertain. He understands, he said, it is most likely that he will not survive these wars. But he said — " hesitating, and then repeating Rodlakh's words in a rapid mumble. "He would go into battle singing if he knew I would consider this."

That nearly brought a laugh. "You would have to be hard-hearted not to agree to consider it, wouldn't you. How do you feel?"

She would rather hear about what he felt, but said, "It makes me giddy. It is not sane — so I told him. Me as *rabhsayu*? That is not sane, Dolvid."

"What did he say to that?" starting to admire his own control: in all this there were naked bodies, touching.

"He said — you cannot give any weight to what a man says at such a time. I might prefer flattery to love, too."

Not uniquely, he was feeling the tug of what she did not say. They talked, their language was plain, and still there was some key missing. Was it that while her words tried to describe, his sought to define? No, that was bookishness, but he felt impotent to bridge the gulf there was. Also he could not explore whether their morning in Kreshavu, magical for him, had brought her anything not there last night with Rodlakh; how could such questions be asked?

They were coming to a tough steep. He reined in his horse, putting a hand across to halt her, too. "Is it insane to think of you as our *rabhsayu*? No it is not. If — well, it is all ifs, and Rodlakh and me riding west and east are the biggest. But if there is any realm left to be ruled, and a Rodlakh living to rule it, you — " He was fumbling inarticulately, trying to shake off all poses. "He could never hope to find a better partner; the realm could not do better. That is not flattery, it is what I truly believe."

"Dolvid — " and he was moving forward again, leaving her in confusion. Last night, after Dolvid had gone off to look for the Fro' family, Rodlakh had been the one to speak, but she was not good enough at self-deception to pretend all initiative was his. Earlier there had been light touches of hands, searching glances she had not turned aside. Exasperation with Dolvid had helped her remember Rodlakh was handsome, but in finding all those reasons to share his bed she had not been prepared to go as far into muddle as the *rabhsai*'s precipitate talk of marriage had taken her.

When next they could speak she said, "What has become of Rodlakh's feelings for Aëlu?"

"Nothing. He would never marry her, and whoever he does marry will have to be reconciled to his adoration of unreachable Aëlu."

"No one is beyond his reach now."

"Unless he wants her to be."

Âna turned reflective, dwelling, Dolvid guessed, on how her former love had died speaking endearments for that same woman.

"Saidhan," factual-voiced, "holds that our next *rabhsayu*, for the realm's sake, cannot be another pure Owaniyu — he says so, when the last one was his own daughter." But Saidhan was not wrong; Dolvid could remember when the man he knew as *Menadhi*, now the Patriarch, used to gloat over how wives from the Island and the South had influenced the *rabhsayum*, and how in a few generations it was possible with wives of pure Owani descent to all-but breed out the taint brought by Banak.

Sharply, "Has he told this to Rodlakh? Have you?"

"No, no," seeing she did not want to be chosen out of policy, for the admixture of her blood. "Though Saidhan was fairly sure Rodlakh was one day going to be *rabhsai*, afraid he might want to be Aëlu's second husband. Now I think of it, he must have supposed I had some influence with him."

"Do you imagine you have not?"

"For who he chooses? Not a shred." For wife, that was; if it had not been for Kamin-Tarú, nominated by Dolvid to tutor Rodlakh, there might not have been a bedding between Rodlakh and Âna. Yet Kamin-Tarú all by herself might very well have taken on that challenge without a word from Dolvid.

Âna was thinking this period was a chaos, Rodlakh further confused by being new to the pleasures of mating; he might change a dozen different times in a realm at peace. "If I were to become *rabhsayu*, would we be friends?"

"I would hope so." Then he cautioned: "Short of treason."

"Treason."

"Marrying the *rabhsai*, she takes sash, whether or not it is ever seen. We cannot have doubt over who fathered the Heir."

They had arrived at the most difficult and precarious stretch between Drin Navuna and Kreshavu, uneven rock-steps and overhanging cliffs, where constant vigilance was needed; there could not be any sustained talk for an hour. She said, "What should I do?"

"What you desire."

"What do you want?"

"Your happiness."

For a heartbeat that infuriated her, no answer at all, one of those parries with which Dolvid held off life. Out loud she spoke words that had been in her mind going up the hill at Burantal, just after parting with Kamin-Tolagh: "When am I going to meet a man with courage to be himself?"

"You have," Dolvid was quick. "His name is Rheduban."

"He is a monster."

"His own monster — " shocked to see her eyes were bright with unshed tears; could just the mention of Rheduban be so painful?

When she spoke it was not about that, but she shook him with her accuracy. "Will you never be cured of what Khalú did not do?" Tears came to his eyes in admiration, or perhaps only recalled misery. By the sun it was just the hour when Rodlakh was to lead his squadrons out beyond the Drin, the fringe of Landegh.

He intended to ride on after a short rest in Kreshavu. Âna said she would stay. He could hardly argue, knowing how little sleep she could have had (barbs of pain lurked in innocent thoughts). For a couple of hours they were sharing the same room as before, and slept side by side, untouching.

A tapping came at the window, and after a pause, again. He had heard the same sound before without noticing, a scraping rattle, quite faint but intolerably annoying so long as he did not know the source. He pulled aside rough drapery, and saw the swaying branchlet with its glossy young leaves — the *tovrelunai*, Rodlakh's tree.

Dolvid knew quite well he could let loose rancor to corrode them, all three, and not doing so did not save him from the same gnawing bitterness, or worse. But there was something he was not understanding. She had made a choice, and if an action of hers caused him distress, that did not mean he condemned it for itself — he felt like waking her to ascertain whether she saw the distinction. In any case she did not need praise or censure from him; only a few days ago she would have been the one to assert that. Why change, and ask his opinion now? just when his feelings disqualified him? Rodlakh —

If he let it, this set of interlocking puzzles could obsess him. From this point to the end, which would no doubt be apparent when it arrived, he would work for the realm's survival. He kissed Âna's forehead as he left, but she did not waken.

For Rodlakh

At Banakit Dolvid caught up with Galt's squadron and did not know it. Lightheaded from lack of sleep he jogged into the tree-ringed town in its fertile vale not long past noon, the day after leaving Âna, and kept awake for conference with Under-Captain Happ, terrifying him (as he meant to) with talk of the women, children and aged of the Mines and Frontier country about to descend upon him. Leaning against the oak table Dolvid waited for the officer to stop saying what could not be done, declining to leave till he had promises of tents, clean water, latrine pits and careful rations of flour: Happ was confident the householders of Banakit would be hospitable, but Dolvid wanted nothing left to mere optimism.

Leaving there he went down to the stables to see that Enikai would be fed, watered, saddled and brought to the house on its fir-clad hillock in late afternoon. He afterwards discovered it was just then Galt was leading his men on the shaded road that led to Fourth Bridge and the long climb for Vonn.

By darkness the difference in pace between the short-legged hill-horses and Dolvid's *pefrai* was lessened; coming into Vonn past sunset he heard Galt had left two hours before, and was to pursue him unseen all through the night, having borrowed a soldier of the Vonn detachment to ride beside him with a lantern. His tall, squeaky-voiced companion kept reciting various available dangers, perhaps feeling he might be blamed if this important and taciturn dignitary suffered a fall, was waylaid, or managed to induce one of the rare venomous snakes to bite him.

When a hint of dawn lightened the sky he at last caught the sounds of horsemen ahead. At Old Bridge he sent his escort back, and coming to the New Bridge approaches he recognized the brothers Noldar and Guthdar, bows slung at their backs.

They gave him grins as he overtook the column. Noldar called, "Will we fight, *Bôdhrai*, will we fight? Everyone says we're going the wrong way. Squadron Galt has used up all his swearwords."

"If we don't fight, as I hope, we shall have a great victory." With a wave he spurred past, leaving them baffled. He had meant to ask about Noldar's bruised thigh; the man was riding without noticeable handicap. Passing familiar faces and as many he did not know Dolvid came up to where Galt was showing his orders to the guard on the bridge. The little squadron-leader gave a sober nod. "We've got a new *rabhsai*."

Passage of the bridge speeded by arrival of the Beech-Tree token, Dolvid told about the proclaiming of Rodlakh at Drin Navuna.

"That would have been worth seeing, and shouting for." The wariness was new; the effort not to show displeasure with how he had been shuttled to and fro, kept from his beloved Frontier when he was near enough to breathe its dust, was turning him into a respectful stranger.

"A grief you could not be there, and a measure of your worth."

"*Bôdhrai*, I had your orders, and I've read them. Is this true, we'll capture Kadon Dinul for our *rabhsai*?"

"I hope it is." He had written that no other men could be trusted so well for this job.

Galt began to rally. "If I'd been at his naming, I could not be here now; you were there, as a friend should be. They say our Saidhan was that kind of friend to Great Banak. The West always gives the realm its best captains, not so?"

"And has to fight hardest to make them strong."

He nodded, but was thoughtful. "That fight in the West. Pardon me, *Bôdhrai*, I would be less afraid if you were beside him. And — " he bridled modestly. "If my lot were there, too."

Dolvid felt he had never been handed a greater compliment. "The *rabhsai* said the same. His sparing you for my business tells you how important it is."

"Well, but we're fighters of *jinzal*. I never fought among houses, unless you count the Patriarch's house on the Island, and that I did not enjoy. What will we do at Kadon Dinul?"

"The less we do the better I'll be pleased. We shall see. Ride through the streets, maybe, and raise some banners. We may have to pay a visit to the *Mankh'*, and the *Adanum* might disagree with that."

Galt was scornful. "We'll shout *Here come the men who gutted your brothers on the Island*, and they'll scatter like starlings."

This talk was doing Dolvid good, but he tried to counsel caution. "They could be different men, doing their real job, defending the Person. And if Tovakh comes from the north and his son from the south, we might have twenty-five squadrons to face."

Pride did not reach to those odds. "But we will have others to stand with us."

"If only they can be gathered. That is our main task. Most of the Household, I would hope, and some General Cavalry."

"Sebhal *Asai* often spoke in admiration about Shumat, of the North."

"Yes, Shumat too." His mind groped out trying to guess where he might be, and Bolan, with all the squadrons under his direct command. A triumph if Bolan could be made no worse than neutral.

Galt asked about Tovakh baKargul, whether he wanted to be *rabhsai* in Rodlakh's place. Dolvid tried to explain the complexities of an alliance between Tovakh and the *Mankh'* that would probably try to make Orbanak *rabhsai* in name.

"Then Tovakh doesn't know the law?"

"The Patriarch's position is that Ban-Sila *Deghi* named Orbanak as — "

"Please, *Bôdhrai*, no more policy. We are Rodlakh's Men, the men of the *rabhsai*. You say that is law, it's our law, and whoever is not with us is a traitor."

"Let us say whoever is not against us is loyal. We are not going to be short of enemies."

At midmorning with no pause for removing signs of the long ride there was the first of several tense meetings with Saidhan, anxious for reliable news. Doleni and Aëlu also gathered to hear, and Dolvid knew numbly he was talking too much, detailed eloquence and plentiful opinion surging up from the bottomless well his lack of sleep had opened. Nothing was altogether real, Aëlu serving as his scribe, writing in a clear, rapid *Atarlum* hand the orders he and Saidhan settled on, Saidhan assuring him he would have Vinosai for the crossing, promising personally to look into the making of fire-arrows, asking him, asking Dolvid what he, Saidhan, could do to help the Army of the West, his army. Titles shifted worlds, and the old soldier was *rabhsayani* to the end.

The wearying Voice of the *Rabhsai* next spoke to an eager Arvat about taking over part of the duties west of Banakit that were to have been Dolvid's, to keep supplies moving forward. Arvat was wistful about Kadon Dinul, bloodthirsty when he heard Zhinladh's name, readily forgetting his newer theory about Deniants killing his father.

In the lists he had had made last week, he pointed to exactly the larger vessel Dolvid wanted, a trim, narrow-beamed ship, best-handling of its size on Arnan, so he was told. In more prosperous days it had been built to the specifications of its owner, Sett. Sarnak said he could handle her, and obviously could not wait to have his hands on such a highborn craft. He noted they would need oarsmen. Dolvid told him to get some experienced ones; Galt's men had done well on the crossings to and from the Island, but this was a longer voyage and a bigger ship, and he did not want the soldiers overworked before landing. Sarnak said he knew some idle whoresons whose arms would be none the worse for a stretching. Eight oars, of course, could not keep a ship that size under way with the load they would be, forty-odd men and as many horses, but were an indispensable aid to the fine-honed steering required.

But Sarnak was not glad when told he would be following the guidance of Under-Warden Vinosai, and while he nodded diplomatically his mood did not change when he heard about the man's experience in shallow-water sailing. He was better-pleased when told Vinosai would be in another, smaller boat, again when Dolvid took Aëlu's advice and let Sarnak share in their suspicions about Vinosai — suspicions only, he emphasized, recalling Sarnak could be impulsive.

Aëlu's misgivings (or, as careful *Mankh'*-bred self-effacement made it, the misgivings she detected in Dolvid) about using a probable enemy spy as his chief pilot were not altogether absurd, but Vinosai was not the sort to make his own death probable by running them aground; he would anticipate better chances to betray them when they reached the Mainland. He would navigate only through the Shoals, so there was no chance of his laying a course for one of the Island ports. Besides, Dolvid had a better use for him, not yet adequately foreseen, a place where Vinosai would be fed false information to give their enemies.

The dislike the man created among sailors must be to do with his function as port-warden; Dolvid, meeting him again, found him polite, a little cold, but most of all, unmemorable, so that it was hard to have any particular feeling about him. He was forwarded from Saidhan, and did his best blandly to sidle out of the expedition, saying he had not navigated in ten years, though he was virtually obliged to add (as he had assured Saidhan *Asai*) that he was ready to go anywhere and do anything if it could aid their cause. Many shallow-water sailors had greater experience than he. The fisherman Alkmas, with that odd cornerwise rigging of his, was as good as any. Only then Dolvid learned that Alkmas had not left Kamsilat.

"Well, *Bôdhrai*," Sarnak confirmed. "He couldn't, could he? They've got him locked up, after he got ugly drunk and bust up the *Pearl of the West*."

That, it seemed, was an oyster-shop down in the harbor. Oddly, Saidhan had not mentioned the incident, though he knew about it, having given orders that Alkmas, because of his services, was not to be whipped. He was being held now because he considered the shop-owner's claim for damages to be outlandish, and refused to pay.

Dolvid, having sent Sarnak and the modest Vinosai to prepare the large vessel, had Alkmas brought to the Great House. Except for the look of dazed, newborn cleanliness common to all sobered drunks, his appearance was exactly as Âna had described, his manner somewhat subdued, not so much penitent as puzzled by his fit of destructive rage.

About that, he did not quarrel with what he had been told, but had no independent memory of throwing a table or trying to make the owner, who had refused him more drink, eat oyster-shells. The man's mouth was already healing.

With Dolvid paying (surely overpaying) the damages, and writing a pardon, he agreed to his boat leading the larger one through the Shoals, reluctantly to accepting Vinosai's pilotage, and, if they succeeded, to return here bringing news of safe arrival. Getting a good price for his services, Alkmas became more of what he must ordinarily be.

"I'll need to rig a second jib. I don't suppose you can spare me some for the oars? My boy can work sail." Torr, he supposed, had been sleeping aboard the boat.

"See Sarnak at quayside — you will have to get together on signals, too; he will be at the helm of the larger ship."

"Sarnak? Well, we can all talk slow and plain. Look, if you want to sail today we'll have to be at sea in three hours; fifteen to north cape of Kamanta, and that's where we need to be by sunup. Even your Vinosai can't sail the Shoals by ear."

"That is not possible — " Aëlu had been fascinated by this man's rudeness. "The *Bôdhrai* must rest."

Dolvid said, "Can you be ready?" If *raminat* and speech could keep him awake till they sailed he would sleep aboard ship.

"Jib and all, I'll be ready while your Sarnak is working out which end the rudder goes."

If that was so, Dolvid told him, he could give a hand with loading the main vessel. Galt was officer in charge. Properly rested, Dolvid might have lost his temper with Alkmas. His fatigue was keeping him precariously balanced on a dream of effortless efficiency; sooner or later he would have to pay for this borrowing.

At the next meeting they discussed the *Atarlum*, and the hope that once enough swords were on Rodlakh's side to cancel out Kargul, the Patriarch would try to save the Treaty by lifting the blockade of the Strait.

"The Treaty!" Saidhan was indignant. "Ask Aëlu about the Treaty!"

"Ask me nothing. If we are going to let rancor govern policy, we shall never have friends. I do not suppose Rodlakh would mind Bolan himself at Drin Navuna, so long as he brought lances for jabbing *jinzal*."

Having seen on the Island how she was obeyed, it was no whim when he asked Aëlu if she could do something to prepare Kamsilat for refugees. The first from the Frontier would be trickling in next week. As many as possible would be kept moving to the eastward so that if and when survivors came from the Mines there would be empty spaces ahead of them. After that it might be necessary to empty Kreshavu of all but those needed for the war. He explained his idea of using the disused storage buildings on South Shore, and she agreed to begin collecting essential supplies.

"Sebhal," she confessed, as Dolvid at last was going for a wash, before preparing to embark, "Sebhal believed it demeaning to his position if his wife was seen doing hard work. As a girl I used to enjoy the keeping of bees."

She laughed at his astonished face. "Yoëlladhu had a secret; I was never stung, either."

While he was putting on fresh clothing Kamin-Tarú found him. She was dazzling in a free-flowing apricot-colored robe that took all its shape from her.

"I have missed you, Dol." He tilted his head, but did not labor for a gracious lie; except for her effect on Rodlakh, hence Âna, he had hardly thought of her.

"And now all these meetings I may not come to, great coming and going, boats getting ready, messengers — " Lazily her eyes were taking in the campaign-clothes, the Beech-Tree medallion. "Is it true Rodlakh is *rabhsai* now?"

A tricky point for her. He told her yes, the law was plain, but it would be the public position of neither her father Tovakh, nor in particular her mother Petakoi; he did not want her to be at war with her own family, and told her she could say Rodlakh had been proclaimed.

"Will you make war on Kargul?"

"It might come to that."

"My mother said Sebhal was the tool of Others and Deniants, and Rodlakh was Sebhal's tool. You are an Owani."

He was lacing boots. "True, and I am Rodlakh's tool, his *Bôdhrai*."

"Is this not our land? Hundreds of years before the Others came."

Others, he reminded her, were there before the Owanil came; their own earliest history said so: the Owanil fresh from Kamanta fought to possess the lands between Arnan and the mountains — her province, Kargul. He asked her whether she would want to give back Kargul, if descendants of those original inhabitants could be traced.

"No such descent could ever be proved."

"Have you met any Owani who could prove his descent from, let us say, Yuvakh Martyr?"

"We are the Owanil, that is enough, and the land is Owan. Why are you so cold, Dolvid?"

"I am very weary, and in a hurry." He found a lightly-oiled cloth for wiping the blade of his long knife.

"Take me with you."

"Where?"

"Where you are going. Rodlakh does not come, and you are as bad as Kamin-Tolagh. Now you are leaving again. I have been so bored."

"Why did you come here, with war boiling up?"

She pouted. "I told you, Peframi is worse, it is the end of the world, where only *atarlal* ever come; I have not a soul to talk to."

The oddness of this had registered passingly when said before. "Tú, why do *atarlal* come to Peframi?"

"I cannot say. Something with the vineyards, I suppose. That is all anyone ever talks about, there." Western Kargul, not a large city, but the wines of its gorge were famous.

She again begged to be taken with him, saying Doleni did not want her here (probably true), and he was the one who had pleased her best of any. Her head was to the side, hair hanging free, and if the color had been, as was always said, red, it would have jarred sourly with the robe's color. As was, the harmony was exquisite, hair a source of light. "I pleased you, too, do not pretend otherwise."

He was grateful she had not thrown her arms around his neck or nibbled at his ear, and spared a half-moment for recollected sweetness that meant nothing but itself. He told her how impossible it was to include her in his sailing, and put aside the bitter question about how much better than Rodlakh he had pleased her. That was nothing; Âna was more complicated than this grown child, who would always tell a man he was the best she had ever known, and not exactly be lying.

Continuing to answer Saidhan's questions about preparedness in the westward garrisons, Dolvid looked around for his sword, sure he had brought it. Full of reproach, Kamin-Tarú carried it to him; he reached out his hand, but she, earnest as any six-year-old, sank to her knees to pass the belt around his waist. He was embarrassed, Doleni hard-mouthed and disapproving, Aëlu amused but also touched; she and Kamin-Tarú liked each other.

Doleni said, "The girl, Âna, who brought us the news. Will she stay at the Frontier?"

Speaking across the burnished head Dolvid said she might be in Kamsilat tomorrow, or very soon.

"A pleasant, modest girl," Doleni wickedly remarked.

"Of modesty — " Saidhan was oblivious, "I am no judge, but that girl has a head on her shoulders. And very nice shoulders, too," he teased, and Doleni turned away in mock-exasperation; this, too, was a ritual.

Taking both of Dolvid's hands Kamin-Tarú rose and kissed his cheek. "Return safe, Dolvidh *Bôdhrai*," she intoned. "I may not wish you victory." This came from the sort of books he had most despised, with flowers drawn at the margins, stilted travesties of any actual history. Now he was moved: he saw the girl and her brother playing at warrior and wishmaiden in the lonely great houses of Peframi and Inilun Barabhi, Kargul citadels sad and sour with their false view of the past. Neither Tam nor Tú, probably, would ever see the perfumed gallantries and rote-learned flourishes came down in real life to wringing extra tax out of a struggling farmer, denying advancement to a man who did not have the right curve to his nose. Nevertheless (or all the more) Dolvid took the smooth face between his hands, and, as her books would say, saluted Kargul's fair daughter with a kiss.

The muddle would end, and he could slip into unconsciousness. At quayside in a damp and gusty wind he went over instructions with the two helmsmen and their deputies, for Sarnak another of the Drin b'Afon men, Muranak, heavy-faced and solemn, and for Alkmas the grubby and unkempt apprentice, Torr, whose amorous aspirations Dolvid had heard about from Âna.

Vinosai was late to the muster. At the least it must have crossed his mind he was under suspicion, and there was nothing for him to relish about the whole venture, but if he tried to miss sailing his days here would obviously be over, and aside from spying he had a comfortable bachelor's life at Kamsilat. Besides, he had instructed Arvat to pursue the man with questions about the running of the port in his absence, thereby keeping track of where he was; an hour before sailing he sent the brothers Noldar and Guthdar to fetch him, and they came riding down to the quay with half an hour to spare, everyone amiable. Dolvid did not see how he could be in the small boat without making it obvious he was keeping watch on Vinosai (and besides, he had heard Âna's description of the sleeping-arrangements), and so was obliged to give Alkmas some hints, amounting to an instruction to make sure they turned eastward well north of the Island.

Saidhan, overtired, had been forbidden the harbor by Doleni, while Kamin-Tarú had gone off to her rooms sniffing back tears; only porters and pack-animals were there to watch as they cast off, poling, then allowing the ship to drift down-current. By the time the major craft had cleared the docks Alkmas was already standing out in the Estuary under full sail. Near Sarnak Dolvid stood on the afterdeck and wondered if he would come back to Kamsilat — whether any of them would.

Though the road ended at Kamsilat port, a rough track mounted to the few houses above the Estuary, becoming the way that served the light-tower. Up where it started that climb Dolvid's eye was caught by a pair of bowmen keeping watch among clumps of bramble and gorse. Then he saw Aëlu, grey cloak flapping back in the breeze to show the dull brown of mourning beneath. Notwithstanding her escort she was the picture of solitude, standing on the cliffside, as perhaps she had stood to watch Sebhal's last departure. Solitude need not be loneliness, it could as well be self-sufficiency: there was nothing pathetic in Aëlu's stance, her face not readable at that distance, but the head high, hair lifting. Dolvid raised a hand, but if seen it was not acknowledged.

Sarnak said, "There she is." His voice had a note of joyless satisfaction, and he was not talking about the sun, now stabbing through a chink between dark cloud and dark horizon. Over to the right, not in view, must be the northernmost heights of Kamanta, while straight ahead the sea was like nothing ever seen, and he peered hard, wondering how much of the strangeness would go away in better light.

He had wakened before dawn when the course changed, veering east. On deck, Muranak was at the helm, face brooding under a swinging lantern, while a watch forward kept them in sight of the bobbing stern light of Alkmas's boat. When hints of morning came into the sky Sarnak returned.

Now the eye rebelled; the sharp spikes were islands, and others like rounded backs of sea-monsters could be accepted; nothing helped maintain that what was in between was water, a flat plain, surely, of limestone and gravel, streaked with a bruise-colored stone. Perhaps passage might, after all, be impossible.

As the small boat worried at the fringe of the Shoals looking for a channel, Sarnak, not willing to rely completely on the signals of Alkmas, had men in the bow and at each beam to warn of rocks and reefs. Soon the ship was among patches of yellow-green weed, passing a long sandbank where sea-birds sat in line, watching. A sudden deep where foam-streaked water circled, then jagged rocks, a dense cluster of pebbled islets, Sarnak reviling the pilot-boat for its choices, probably due in part to Dolvid's insistence on the need for a quick crossing. In calm weather, which they had, it did not seem the Shoals would be desperately dangerous for anyone willing to take time over it, finding a safe overnight anchorage. That would, of course, take away the reason for attempting it, and there would always be risk of an unwarned squall.

Vinosai and Alkmas together, determined not to cede back any of the eastward gain, dared a narrow way, and the larger vessel made nudging contact with rocks, grazed a sandbar. It was to be supposed, however, the pilot-boat was keeping in mind the far greater draught of the following vessel, a notion which Sarnak found forceful ways of expressing.

The journey went on with oaths and vigilance, many near escapes. In the forward hold the horses seemed tranced or half-asleep, all except Enikai, tethered between Frontier hill-horses, black and glossy, a raven among thrushes, and as bright-eyed, taking a wisp of hay out of Dolvid's hand.

The ship hissed and jarred to a hesitation athwart a long sandbank; hearts paused too. Like a hunter taking a jump Sarnak crouched holding the tiller, and straightened as the following wave came. The ship shifted, trembled, and with the next wave shook free; they were in the strait between two of the larger islets of rock, deep, clear water with no obstructions. Sarnak was happy, but in a quarter-hour the seas closed in around them again. With sun almost straight overhead they sailed into a heavy sea running southward, and Sarnak barely had room for his obscenities before he issued a string of orders, adding sail and extra men with poles prepared for fending. Galt for a while helped lean on the tiller, but seas were becoming more open, and chief hazard was isolated rocks; the smaller craft ahead no longer making its swift darts and circles in search of a channel.

After half an hour, still leaning against the press of the seas, Sarnak's long-jawed face became serene. "Alkmas can call me auntie if this isn't the current that comes down north of Pavani."

That was to say, the eastern shore of Kamanta, and would mean they must be nearly through the Shoals. Almost at once Sarnak had to pull hard on the helm to avoid a new mass of rocks, but soon he was forgetting all his vicious envy of the pilot-boat's nimbleness; they emerged into broader and deeper blue waters under a blue sky dotted with cloud. Muranak was awake, and Sarnak was happy to surrender the tiller.

"What I need," he confided, "is a good shit." He disappeared below.

As reminder of what might have happened in the narrow and treacherous waters, afternoon brought a sharp rainstorm, with slapping seas in the gusty winds; among rocks it might have been disaster, but now the worst was seasickness of some Frontier men, and fear among the horses. In the big seas the main vessel lost sight of the fishing-boat, but Dolvid was not unduly anxious, sure Alkmas had managed worse conditions than these, and that the two ships could navigate independently to Owan Sai from here. In less than an hour the storm passed, and as visibility improved they sighted the other boat again, riding well when both vessels crested together. As the seas diminished the round, hairy head of the lad Torr could be seen in place of the beaked one with the protuberant lips; like Sarnak Alkmas was giving himself a rest. It came into Dolvid's mind that as things were the scruffy youth might someday be able to boast he had laid a questing hand on the *rabhsayu*.

"*Bôdhrai*? *Bôdhrai*, fighting-ships are barring the way to Owan Sai." Dolvid rolled out of the bunk, reaching for his sword-belt. The deep modelling of Galt's face was picked out by the light of a single *ôdu* hung in the low entrance. Otherwise, darkness was profound, and the silence of the ship.

"What is the time?"

"Near dawn. Sarnak says we're just off the Paowan Estuary. I have the men standing to. These fighting-ships told us to heave to, while they send small boats."

"In whose name did they stop us?"

"None that was spoken, *Bôdhrai*."

Above, there was a lantern by the taffrail, but the ship was mainly dark. In deep shadow by the starboard gunwales crouching archers had arrows to their strings. Up by the waist the small boat of Alkmas had come alongside and made fast.

On the high afterdeck where Dolvid mounted, Galt had a cluster of bowmen watching to starboard, and there the lights of at least two fighting-vessels were doubled in black, swelling water. Not the low-built rammers preferred by the Island, these were massively made as a sort of floating fortress, with a stepped terrace running much of their length. They carried both bows and pikes, and were meant to fight by attempting to grapple, while well-protected archery raked an enemy. Most also carried a smaller version of the *zhin'pefrai* either forward or aft, but they were safe only aimed within a narrow scope, recoil making for dangerous wallowing, especially when stones piled on deck made the vessel tend to topheaviness. Broad-beamed, under full sail these craft were at best slow-moving and clumsy, but were used defensively, cruising a limited territory.

Sarnak said, "We could sail rings around them, *Bôdhrai*, but it's too easy to foul those chains." Behind them the fighting-vessels trailed big logs, barely floating under the weight of heavy lengths of chain that strung them together.

"It is good, Sarnak," having detected a note of unneeded apology. He could make out on the water between ships dripping oars, faces of steersman, a man standing in the nearest boat, probably the officer. Before any challenge could come, Dolvid called out, "Who is your *rabhsai*?"

Mutterings, and at last, "We are the Warden's Force, out of Owan Sai. What ship are you?"

"The ship of the *rabhsai*, out of Kamsilat."

"The *rabhsai* is dead."

Dolvid knew the voice. The man had transferred from the Household to this force, responsible to the Warden of the Port, although technically under the Captain of the Household. "Perimas. You were less certain when you brought us word of Lambarr's death in '35. You should have learned the realm can never be without a *rabhsai*." Dolvid remembered this man distraught and sobbing with the news of the Tan Lughsai Disaster, and was fairly sure he could be managed.

"Who is that?" sharply.

"Dolvid, *Bôdhrai* and Minister Plenipotentiary of Rodlakh *bi*-Arbhai-Navu, *Rabhsai*."

"What is — " but Perimas was overwhelmed in a burst of cheering, not only from the Frontier men, but from his own boats, and the larger ship behind. To Muranak Dolvid said, "Can we run a light up at the cross-trees, and break out the Bronze Tree standard?"

Perimas, when near-quiet came, said, "The succession is in dispute. The Patriarch — " and again he was interrupted, now by groans, menacing shouts. "Silence," Perimas hissed.

"Let me aboard, so we can confer."

"Prepared to take allegiance to our lawful *rabhsai*. Or else come aboard under *madh'loi*."

Perimas's blink could practically be heard. Presumptuous, offering truce to a man whose job was defending the port, but the Six Provinces were not going to be conquered with one understrength squadron; the best weapon was highhandedness. Policy was coming clear, and the tone was being set for encounters to come, many of them, he judged: he was not an invader, but spoke for law itself, the source of law.

Renewed muttering in the boats, and then Perimas called, "It is as a private person I ask to board, to confer with a private person."

Oh, no, Dolvid said to himself, no confidential talks and hedged bets. "The other is not here as a private person. Look!" In the yellow light of a lantern, the bordered banner with the Beech-Tree broke, floating, from the mainmast. Sustained applause came from every quarter, with officers in the fighting-ships trying to quiet their men.

When it died down Perimas was defensive. "I am under orders of Fonul, Acting Warden of Owan Sai."

Appealing direct to the men Perimas commanded might force the officer to take new allegiance, but the future of the army had to be kept in mind; encouraging men to dictate to their commanders was unwise.

Instead he suggested Perimas and his ships *escort* his to Owan Sai. Perimas would still have liked his private chat, but haggled instead over the term; Dolvid, content if there was no hint of capture, settled on *accompany* as a word acceptable to all.

Day came as the four vessels entered the Estuary between the soft hills of Dramal and the slighter rise of the Paowan with the familiar profile of Kadon Dinul, Residence distant but plain against the pale sky. "We sleep there tonight," he told Galt.

Easily outsailing the cumbersome ships of war, Sarnak came about quickly one-and-a-half times to lead the way into the basin of Owan Sai, and was told to take the space with the ornate pillars, the royal berth not even the *nim'* of a province would dare use without special permission. Alkmas meanwhile gave a lively exhibition, striking mainsail with exact timing so he came to rest against the short jetty, never touching oar or fending-pole.

This always seemed a mean spot to be the royal port; Owan Sai had hardly a building worth naming, and the waterfront was nothing but warehouses and small drink-shops. Once, Kadon Dinul was its own port; all the land between here and where Harbor Way climbed past the city walls must have been laid down, grain upon grain, by the Paowan River. A flat, scrubby land of coarse grasses and few trees; the slope beneath the north walls of Kadon had once been riverbank. Yet the port was a well-run one with ample dockage, hoists and winches for handling cargoes of every kind, large stables with wagons and draft-animals for the moving of goods. Only Kargul's main harborage, Zelkova, could rival Owan Sai as an Arnan port.

With Galt and two of his men, Kuno and Dalirr, Dolvid leapt down to the quay, not waiting for the gangplank. Someone handed down the standard of the *rabhsai*, and Kuno held it over Dolvid's head, till told to move one pace left, making space for an unseen Rodlakh beneath the colors.

Perimas, also with flanking men, approached, tall, long-muscled, but less than commanding as a figure. Seven years, and advance from half-squadron to *kímukan* had not much changed a face already lined when he was young. After perplexity he recalled the royal salute need acknowledge no more than that Rodlakh belonged to the ruling family. That done, Perimas looked straight at Dolvid, in enquiry rather than confrontation. Nevertheless, a war could begin here. Behind Perimas more of the Warden's Force was falling in, and behind Dolvid Frontier bows were vigilant.

Extending his hand he told Perimas this was well met, but the man's grasp was tentative. When asked for news from Kadon Dinul he was uncertain, too uncertain for someone who could be at Harbor Gate in less than half an hour; he embraced vagueness to evade commitment to any point of view. There were, he understood, three main factions all with supporters within the Household. Kargul held Residence, Treasury and Barracks, but only a handful of Household troops were with them, under Zhinladh. Both those groups endorsed the Patriarch's assertion Orbanak was correct successor to Ban-Sila, and they had many adherents among the Families. The bulk of the Household, under Kizhunai, held the streets of the capital, while advocates of Rodlakh, taking their lead from Dorrmas, were in firm control of all city gates and the Bronze Residence. Perimas "had heard" Dorrmas advocated storming the Residence in Rodlakh's name to arrest the *rabhsaidakradhi*, Rheduban, and drive out Kargul, but had also battled briefly with the *Adanum Plakh'*, who had tried to force *g'Asalladh's* entry into the city — here, Perimas almost betrayed his own sympathies when he offered that while Kizhunai had not been able to persuade either side to any accommodation, he had prevented spats and skirmishes from becoming something far worse.

If `accommodation' meant Kargul surrendering Rheduban while the others renounced Rodlakh, it was not surprising none had occurred. Yet Rodlakh's popularity with the soldiery could not, of its nature, go deep; his brief years had given him small chance for winning renown; most, surely, would have come to accept the revised succession, if the younger brother had been formally proclaimed. That Dorrmas had evidently prevented, till now. Kizhunai's levelheadedness had always been admirable, but in these circumstances preventing fighting was not a good in itself, when all it did was give Kargul the chance to gather its squadrons.

Of larger Kargul' forces Perimas had no knowledge, and about Bolan only an impression the magnate Khelagh, the Captain's father-in-law, had declared Bolan would support the Patriarch's choice, Orbanak. Here at Owan Sai Under-Captain Fonul had forbidden any support for Rodlakh, saying there was no *rabhsai* without *g'Asalladh's* countenance.

Dolvid reminded Perimas of the day he had come to the Bronze Residence with the news about Lambarr. "We do not wait for death of a *rabhsai* before we debate the laws of succession; Rodlakh became *rabhsai* at the moment Ban-Sila died."

Perimas did not speak, his dilemma plain, and Dolvid was going to have to deal with many versions of this. Fonul, the man who commanded Perimas, was an Owani of Family, and if Rodlakh's cause failed, all those who declared for him might be condemned as traitors. Dolvid wished he did not understand so well; Rodlakh was in open country among a thousand *jinzal*; there was no room for hesitation.

He shook the man by saying, "I am going now to relieve Fonul of his post, and take charge of his troops in the *rabhsai's* name. Will you speak your allegiance, and retain your command? Or live to be one of those who *might have* helped?"

Perimas wrestled with his doubts, half-glancing back to the troops who had cheered the Beech-Tree banner, giving threat its force. His hand went to the sword at his side; a rumble came from his own men, and behind him Dolvid was the creak of a bow.

The face of Perimas cleared. Feeding sword from its scabbard and taking the blade, he offered it, and started to kneel.

"Not to me — " indicating the space beneath the colors. Perimas shifted over, knelt, and spoke the same short allegiance as the officers at Drin Navuna; in Rodlakh's name Dolvid accepted it, confirming Perimas's post and returning the sword. As it hissed back into the sheath a deep noise of approval came from the Warden's Men. Dolvid hoped his relief was less evident than that of Perimas, all at once pleased with himself.

Vinosai was standing at quayside, a little detached from the disembarking soldiers; Dolvid spared a moment to congratulate him on his navigation of the Shoals. No reason for this not to be genuine, nor Vinosai's flush of pride, his murmured admiration for Alkmas's handling of the boat. Soon a plausible excuse had to be invented not to offer him a post shortly to be vacant and obviously suitable, Acting Warden of this port.

The quarters now occupied by Fonul were close by the simple stone arch commemorating the homecoming of Plakhan in 2707, the beginning of Harbor Way. Dolvid remembered coming here by night to find Saidhan, seven years ago, when the old soldier Narudhai (still alive, but in complete retirement) was Warden, and Arvat was being smuggled to the Colony to keep him safe from his father's murderers. A square stone house, flat-roofed, with four white steps up to a doorway, now joined by pikemen, who dipped their weapons in salute when they saw the standard borne by Dolvid's small company of horsemen, everyone whose mount was so far ashore.

Never admitting a possibility of being stopped he went up the steps in two strides. The pikeman to the right reached across, but only to open the door.

In the long, dim hallway a retreating servant put up a hand to fend him off. Two more guards appeared, and, not going to a weapon, Dolvid planted his feet with authority. At the far end of the hall a man in the doorway was fastening his breeches, while his white shirt flapped loose, slack jaw dropping in a yawn. That arrested when Fonul saw Dolvid, now flanked by Galt and Noldar. He was a flabby man, near seventy, a widower, once commander of the Tâl Abfekh garrison, a post he gave up as Ban-Sila's choice for magistrate there. His eyes were crusty with sleep.

Appearing to expect deference, he complained at this unannounced intrusion. Dolvid told him the *rabhsai*'s business could not wait, and indicated the colors; Fonul sketched a royal salute.

"I delayed only to hear Perimas's allegiance, having come here to — "

"What allegiance?"

"The Acting Warden might prefer to speak privately." If Fonul insisted on humiliation, that, too, was available.

"There is nothing to discuss in private. What is your authority here?"

"*Bôdhrai* and Minister Plenipotentiary to Rodlakh *Rabhsai*."

"Just a moment — it is by no means established — "

"Fonul, I have no time. This is only a visit of courtesy, to say I have taken charge of the Warden's Force, in the name of the *rabhsai*."

"Oh, and how do we address you, Minister?" Fonul sneered. "Are you not the *kaël'rolai* who sneaked into the Residence and threatened Ban-Sila *Deghi*, the son-in-law Khelagh got tired of?"

Beside Dolvid Galt bristled, but there was no margin for anger, though it would have been easy and delicious to answer, *and are you not the magistrate who took bribes from both sides in a land-dispute?*

Instead, "*Bôdhrai* is quite adequate. The world turns, Fonul; many a loyalist is going to have to be light on his feet. The *rabhsai* does not intend to penalize those who remained servants of the late Ban-Sila, even if they supported policies he means to repudiate. If you will swear new allegiance you can keep your titles, and retain nominal command of the garrison."

"Nominal command!" incensed: Fonul may have taken Dolvid's reference to lightness of foot as a personal gibe.

"Your name will appear on all orders, but they will not be valid without my endorsement. I cannot make any commitment about what the *rabhsai* might want for the future." The last was not true; any appointment not needing ratification in Council Dolvid had powers to confirm or abolish. Fonul, set for a long fight, did not recognize forbearance.

Noises from outside interrupted, tramp of feet, cry of voices. At Fonul's command the doors were thrown open. Light streamed in, and with it the name of Rodlakh. With twenty of the Colony men the Warden's Force in its entirety had marched up from the harbor, in perfectly ordered ranks, though there was no senior officer in sight. From the stock of colors kept by the royal port they had taken a Beech-Tree banner to carry, and were keeping up a chant, *Rod-lakh! Rod-lakh!* A small throng of early citizens, mainly dockside porters, were adding their voices to the acclaim.

Fonul, stricken, said, "Mutiny."

"A time for choice," beginning to see he would say that very often before this was done with. "They have chosen right."

Fonul, protesting he was their commander, retreated back into the hallway. The soldiery outside was not far above one hundred, with perhaps fifty or sixty townspeople added; they sounded a multitude.

It remained unknown what commitments or what private assurances kept Fonul from taking allegiance to Rodlakh, as he puffed over legality and the voice of *g'Asalladh'*, threatening his guards with discipline when they came at Dolvid's call.

Not encouraged by this first encounter with the Families, he pronounced an end to Fonul's duties and powers as Acting Warden, and personally removed his insigne. Outside there was a burst of cheering, and Dolvid left Fonul baffled, going out to meet Perimas mounting the steps. Worried, he tried a joke: "A

man should be at the head of his troops, even when he has to run
to catch them."

Dolvid handed him the bronze double-circle just taken from
Fonul, and told him to wear it on the right side, making him
acting under-captain. He also invented a new title to confer on
Perimas, Acting Commandant of the Port, under the *rabhsai*'s
direct orders; for now there would be no new Warden.

"Is this correct, *Bôdhrai*?"

"You will have it in writing." Dolvid held up his hands and
briefly addressed the soldiery, expressing Rodlakh's thanks,
assuring them only heavy fighting at the Frontier had kept the new
rabhsai away. In their self-congratulatory mood they were ready
to cheer his call for unsleeping vigilance, with *rabhsayum*
threatened by many enemies.

When he stepped down to resounding applause he was
questioning his own mood; an arrogance adopted in need becomes
a powerful intoxicant, especially when it succeeds. The resistless
effect of gathering power was what he had to make use of, but he
did not want to become the strutting cock he was obliged to seem:
he wished Âna were here to sober him with glances of
conspiratorial amusement.

Feeling harried by everything he spared some minutes at
Perimas's quarters going over ships and men available, making
plain the *unsleeping vigilance* of his speech was not just words.
Though Kargul normally despised ships for moving cavalry, the
ease and swiftness of a sea-journey might occur to Kamin-Tolagh,
if he was checked at Kanzan Tâl, and he would be able to find
vessels at his own port of Zelkova. Every attempt should be made
to prevent his landing at Owan Sai. With double watches four
ships could be kept on guard day and night.

"But Kargul has been our ally in the uprising."

Questioning out loud whether there had ever truly been an
uprising, Dolvid agreed these were complex times. The real
shock for Perimas was being told to extend his watch to prevent
any sea-traffic between the Island and the Paowanu *Mankh'*,
especially ships leaving Mainland for Island, to prevent the flight
of any person.

"*Any* person, *Bôdhrai*?"

"Any," emphatically. "If a Person of great authority should attempt the voyage He must be treated with courtesy but firm courtesy. The same is true for anyone of the Family." His chief fear was the prolonged war there might be if *g'Asalladh'* spirited Orbanak off to the Island, and declared a *rabhsayum*-in-exile.

Written authority given for all this and the guarding of Fonul, spared further humiliation by being left in residence where he was, The main part of Galt's men were already in the saddle, together with the half-squadron commandeered from the port. The morning now cool and sunny, they rode under the arch and began the climb for Kadon Dinul.

"A good hour's work — " Galt handed him something wrapped in a white cloth, a large chop of cold mutton. Between the last outliers of Owan Sai and the outskirts of Kadon Dinul the Minister Plenipotentiary tore greedily at the meat, and where the ground rose to the walls of Old Town a lean black dog was lurking by the road, ready to leap for a tossed bone.

"Will there be a fight here, *Bôdhrai*?"

"If there is not, we may make one." The wondering face recalled this was Galt's first sight of Kadon, and it was borrowing his eyes to be astounded all over again by this mountain-range of stonework with the Residence for summit, as much a legend as Karg' Kamanta had been for Dolvid.

"A great city."

"If it had a heart to match its magnificence," he was surprised to hear himself say.

They rode along the west walls to where the wide square opened, the Spear of Yoëlladhu at its center. Household lancers were in front of Harbor Gate, and others, dismounted, up on the mound beyond the Bronze Residence, across the road that led to the *Mankh'*. Most eyes were now on Dolvid's contingent.

Right beside the Spear he called a halt. He, Galt, and Dalirr, who had the standard, moved out a little, and a group of riders came down from Harbor Gate, allowing their banner to unfurl. It, too, was the Beech-Tree, and among officers was Dorrmas.

He seemed a very youthful man to have been renowned for his swordsmanship so many years. His face, open and forthright, was full of competence; without real friendship he and Dolvid had known each other, Dolvid believed with mutual respect.

For him there was no hesitation about giving the royal salute. "You've been sent by Rodlakh *Deghi*?"

Dolvid said quietly they should have allegiance spoken before exchanging stories. More formally, for all the nearby Household men to hear, he announced his title and powers, derived from Rodlakh's *rabhsayum*.

"*Bô'rai*," Dorrmas responded in the same ceremonious manner, stubborn to mispronounce anything in the Old Tongue. "You are empowered, then, to hear and confirm our allegiance."

They dismounted. Even reversing his sword and handing it up had marks of the dexterity that made Dorrmas a master. As before, Dolvid sidestepped to create the space filled with unseen power, and when he gave back Dorrmas's sword cheers went up from all the various companies of troops. With an upward glance Dorrmas said, "Wouldn't this please *g'Azalla*?" They were in the shadow of Yoëlladhu's Spear.

Two officers whose rank, squadron-leader, was the same as Dorrmas, but who appeared to have accepted his primacy, dismounted and took allegiance, and Dolvid, not wanting to spend the rest of the day at this, signified he would not hear individual oaths from any rank lower.

The account Dorrmas gave was not very different from what he had heard at Owan Sai; Kargul held the Residence with the support of some of the Household, more officers than men, the numbers diminishing as men kept slipping away to join the Captain Kizhunai. There was, however, a new faction; the `private armies,' as Dorrmas called it.

All big landowners had larger or smaller bands of armed retainers, the actual numbers hard to ascertain, since many of them were also farm-workers, especially at planting season, and harvest. Largest force of all belonged to Khelagh, who had apparently been the one to collect an irregular army, to assist, he said, in defense of the Residence. So far they had not been permitted to enter Kadon Dinul, nor attempted to force their way in, but were camped in the disused barracks of the Special Forces outside East Gate, several hundred strong, under joint captaincy of Lavsila, son to Ladh-Sivai, an important figure in the grain trade, and Ghuradh, Khelagh's only son.

The names made Dolvid smile; several years ago he had defeated both in an inept attempt to kill him. Still, these armed men could give Kargul some useful auxiliaries if Tovakh's squadrons started to arrive from the North. Dorrmas said, "Aye, by themselves, two squadrons of regulars could puff them away, but they can be a nuisance, and I have to waste men keeping watch on their rookery."

On this point, at least, he seemed to have a tacit understanding with Kizhunai, and even Dorrmas allowed it was harder for the Captain to condemn the private armies outright, related as he was by blood or marriage to most of their employers.

About Kizhunai's overall position he said Dolvid had better ask him; it appeared there was a daily debate of the issues at Harbor Gate. "I'm Pir Kallikuk if I can see where he has a position, except not wanting to offend anybody, and asking politely every day for Rheduban to be surrendered. I've asked him, does he think Kami-Toly has gone south for his health? If we wait much longer — "

"We shall take back the Residence today," hoping it could be done. The armed camp lurking outside East Gate only increased the urgency.

"I would have given it a try before now, *Bô'rai*, but my advisor was against putting Kizhunai in a corner." Dorrmas gestured to the Bronze Residence, where a white-haired figure, tall but stooped, was descending the front steps. With a firm, grave tread, a too-short sword swinging at his side, Faëdhal came to make deference. Offering allegiance he understood without needing to be told the business of the empty space, and when he fell to his knees an oath was at last given and received in Owanilú of the purest, a demonstration. Before handing Faëdhal up, Dolvid reconfirmed him as Master of Tongues, adding,

"Hereafter, with the rank of *bôdh'loiki*." Faëdhal had always resented his post had not ranked with lesser counsellors.

"I guessed, if that is the word, surmised, perhaps, we would soon be seeing you."

Politely but unmistakably, Kizhunai must be summoned to the Bronze Residence, under safe-conduct. Giving this instruction to Dorrmas he observed a reluctance, and the reason was not hard to guess. A squadron leader in command of a makeshift army had been making his own policy, defying the *Adanum Plakh'*, ready to defy the might of Kargul. Defying his commander, and now Kizhunai might be about to make peace, and Dorrmas did not know where he would be.

This was delicate; the split in the Household had to be repaired, and to encourage and reward insubordination was never wise; Dorrmas had saved the day, but Kizhunai, if he could be persuaded, was more important in almost every way to Rodlakh's cause. That said, those who had championed Rodlakh without waiting to be coerced or persuaded should have their place.

As a beginning Dolvid advanced Dorrmas to the rank of *kímukan*, and told him he was seconded from the Household to the *rabhsai*'s personal staff, removing him from Kizhunai's direct command.

"I did not begin this, *Bô'rai*, in hopes of a reward. What's right's right. But I do have a wife and the boys to think of. A man needs protection from his friends."

"You will get word to Kizhunai."

With a short, decisive nod Dorrmas remounted and loped for Harbor Gate, where a throng was gathering, both inside and out.

Dolvid swung back to Faëdhal. "Why are there no colors over the Bronze Residence?"

Faëdhal, mildly shocked, protested neither the *rabhsai* nor any of the Family was installed there. Proper, he maintained, for the Beech-Tree to be displayed by troops of the Household, which was held to pass to the new *rabhsai* at the moment of accession, the ceremony of allegiance being merely ritual confirmation of what in law already was. The edifices and royal residences, on the other hand —

"I thank you, Faëdhal. We are within our rights now to raise the colors?"

"If I understand your powers aright, *Bôdhrai*, the very second you set foot in the Residence — the Old Bronze Residence, I intend to say. Although I gather the other is to be in our hands before the day is out."

"Correct." Gratifying if everyone, especially the men of Kargul, accepted its inevitability as calmly as Faëdhal. "I want to hear your story." Indicating to Galt to follow, as he and Faedhal, as so often in past years, went together through the gateway and up the broad steps to the great doors, their clouded soft blue-green.

At one juncture, according to Faëdhal, followers of Dorrmas, having been reinforced by some contingents of General Cavalry who had marched in without orders from Tâl Abfekh and even as far as Burantal, were besieged by the *Adanum Plakh'*, as Dorrmas was laying siege to the more conciliatory Household men, who would have allowed the Patriarch into the city, something Dorrmas boldly refused. Meanwhile Kizhunai's Household kept up their bloodless watch on the New Residence, so there was a siege inside a siege inside a siege. "But for Kizhunai, Dorrmas would have attempted to break into the Residence on that very same morning the murder was found out — after Kamin-Tolagh baKargul left southward in the company of — um, well."

"Âna," reassuring him she was loyal to Rodlakh, saying if she had not brought swift news of the murder to the Colony he, Dolvid, could not be here now.

"Then you had no ship out of Owan Sai?" The vessel with full accounts of the murder and the situation at Kadon had sailed, at latest, on the second day after Ban-Sila's death, after which Fonul had not allowed any further ships for the Colony. That one must have been the sail Âna saw when passing through the Strait, the larger vessel the rammers had gone to investigate. Whether that ship had been sunk, captured, or forced to make port somewhere, it certainly had neither reached its destination nor returned.

In the provinces, Faëdhal said, as far as he could tell there was much confusion, with the General Cavalry presumably commanded from the north, wherever Bolan was. He had not been heard to declare for Rodlakh, as some garrisons were certainly doing. No doubt, Faëdhal said, Kizhunai, having seen the dispatches, could say more.

It was not the idea of Kizhunai reading sealed dispatches that made Dolvid stare, but the obvious implication. "Do you mean messages have been passing freely in and out of Kadon Dinul, the Residence, even?"

Faëdhal protested they had no authority here to question a royal messenger, nor open what was under a provincial seal, though in the case of Kargul a violation had been seriously discussed.

Now he was dizzied. "Actual messengers of Kargul have been coming and going?"

"As I say, *Bôdhrai*, we had no authority — "

"Yet Dorrmas, at your instigation, forcibly prevented the Patriarch from entering the city."

"Different altogether, surely, my dear Dolvidh? Perhaps we have come to regard this as a mere formality, but the fact remains each separate entry of the Patriarch into Kadon Dinul, under the Treaty, requires the *rabhsai*'s permission. There, as I told Dorrmas, our legal position was unassailable. But to interfere with a provincial message-rider without obtaining a royal order — "

"From this minute," writing the order as he spoke, "we shall read every word that goes to and comes from Petakoi." Dalirr took the document when barely dry, and went to find Dorrmas with it.

Faëdhal resumed his account; the battle with the *Adanum* here outside Harbor Gate had cost, he had been told, seven or eight lives before Kizhunai obtained or imposed a truce. After that, *g'Asalladh'* tried to proclaim the boy, Orbanak, out by Treaty Stone. The townspeople who went out of curiosity shouted down the *atarlal* who were trying to revive an ancient battlefield ceremony, and there was further jostling between the crowd and riders of the *Adanum Plakh'*, but no serious renewal of either fighting or the attempt to make Orbanak their ruler.

That was four days ago. The Patriarch, Faëdhal said, had written a note to Kizhunai, bitterly protesting the defiance of His authority and denial of His prerogatives, but had not tried again to enter the city.

Dolvid wondered what was in His mind. He was holding back, and that was puzzling unless He believed time was running in His favor, as it should, if His blockade had succeeded in cutting off the Colony entirely. Perhaps the *Mankh'* was encouraged by word from either father or son, Tovakh or Kamin-Tolagh, though it was to be hoped that the General Cavalry commander at Kanzan Tâl, without special orders to the contrary, had refused to let Kamin-Tolagh's squadrons pass. He wrote an order to that effect, even if it meant war, and added that Bolan had for now 'relinquished' the Captaincy; orders would be issued from Kadon Dinul.

When Dorrmas arrived he was sure the southward garrisons would all be with the *rabhsai*, if the men could have their say. "They would march on Kadon to raise the Beech-Tree. If Bolan doesn't come out for Rodlakh he'll have an army of three *kímukan* and an under-captain."

"I have a message for him, too, if I could be sure other eyes would not see it. There is no rebellion in the Northeast; Shumat should know the *rabhsai*'s first words rejected Preference in any form."

"Courtesy and tact," Faëdhal, sentimentally, "are second nature with him."

Dorrmas laughed, but then was serious. "I've told Kizhunai, the people are sick of bullies and they want Rodlakh. If he could have come and said a dozen words outside Harbor Gate, the city would have gone up like tinder."

"He wanted to, but war at the Frontier detained him." That, for now, would satisfy Dorrmas and others; in that faraway place there was always war, more or less. There must be no guilt over where he was leading these young officers and men, enthusiasts for Rodlakh, if he was no longer alive. Four days since he had ridden out beyond the Drin, and Dolvid could well be policy without principal, *Bôdhrai* to nothing at all.

He told Dorrmas the beginning of all strategy was to avoid bloodshed where possible, but they must have Rheduban out of the Residence. The underground way, common knowledge now, had been thought of early, but it had been blocked with rubble, the outlets inside the New Residence sealed the day after Rodlakh paid the unannounced visit on his brother.

"I was among the hunters that morning. Most of us were hoping we would come home with our bags still empty." Till now it had not occurred to Dolvid there might have been factors other than cleverness and luck in that escape; Kamin-Tolagh had been quite right to complain about the efforts of the Household.

Galt cleared his throat. "*Bôdhrai*, the *rabhsai* is *rabhsai*. His Minister must come in by his front door." Dolvid nodded gratefully for understanding of what he had tried to convey with every action since landing. "What about Kizhunai?"

"He did not say he wouldn't come," Dorrmas said.

Assisted by Faëdhal he went on drafting orders, and acted as unconcerned as he could manage. In this great bluff the failure to keep moving forward was a bad setback, worse if he let it show. Discussing dispositions of their tiny army he found the sixty men who had come with him from Owan Sai brought active strength in regulars to almost four hundred, with volunteer bowmen helping with the watch on the *Mankh'* road where the *Adanum* would come, as well as the camp of the private armies. If Kizhunai merely stood aside, a large enough force, Dorrmas said, to retake the Residence, and there were many men of Kadon who would take part if they were allowed to. This, with an internal shudder, was deferred; teaching a mob they could break into the defended Residence was no good start to Rodlakh's *rabhsayum*.

At the door a saluting soldier announced, "The Captain Kizhunai!" Dorrmas sprang up, and so did Faëdhal, surprise in his face. Dolvid, not directly facing the door, not turning his head to do so, stayed seated.

After five long seconds Kizhunai walked in front of him to make the royal salute. "*Bôdhrai*," in a flat voice.

Now Dolvid got up. This was a man who had risen steadily in rank over the years, never greatly distinguishing himself, never committing a serious mistake, demonstrably honest in that he was not enormously wealthy, though his origins were by no means poor. Once he had been senior to Bolan, and in retrospect his failure to step forward when Lambarr was looking for an officer to command the Narn venture was the juncture in his career when renown passed him by; unkind history rubbed his nose in that failure by making him the officer to greet the returning victors of '28 at Dônshei Bridge. In Kizhunai's defense, he had been caring for his first wife, ill that year, who subsequently died. He remained an officer who had risen near the summit by knowing how to obey, and the somewhat disdainful expression of youth was hardening into the resignation of middle life. With his waist his face had thickened, but his ears still stuck straight out. The hands were always a faint surprise, blunt, hairy and capable, the left now resting on his hilts.

"Kizhunai," remorselessly abrupt. "Your rank and titles cannot be confirmed till you have sworn new allegiance to the lawful *rabhsai*. You have been associated with actions casting doubt on the succession — "

"Others beyond my learning, *Bôdhrai*, are debating that." Kizhunai had a glance for Faëdhal. "My business is preventing strife till we have a ruling."

No one, granted, stood to lose more by joining Rodlakh's cause, if it ended in failure. At this delicate point, Dorrmas was nudged into taking Galt on a tour of the positions where troops were, and was obviously not sorry to leave.

Able to speak freely, Dolvid told Kizhunai warfare could be only delayed, not prevented, unless the realm was to be handed to Kargul and the *Mankh'*, which was what Orbanak's accession would come to. Kizhunai did not seem to have considered why Kargul would support Orbanak over Rodlakh — and that was flatly unbelievable in an intelligent man; clearly Kizhunai made use of being a plain soldier who followed orders, carrying out policy not making it, so as not to think about unpalatable things such as mutiny and civil war. When Dolvid told him the ordinary soldiers of the Household and General Cavalry could never be trusted to bring terror and dispossession to their own, which was the true reason why troops of Kargul had ever come to the Heartland, Kizhunai tried to maintain they had come to free royal squadrons for the campaign in the Northeast.

"But before Shumat's uprising was ever heard of patrol duties were being transferred to Kamin-Tolagh and Rheduban with their Kargul', and when the Household captaincy came vacant you were given only half, harnessed with the Heir in Kargul. If his father is named Orbanak's Protector where is your future?" Suspecting a wound rubbed raw Dolvid meant to be relentless.

"Kamin-Tolagh is not twenty-five — "

"I know," succinctly.

The picture he wanted to put in Kizhunai's eye was not a realm where the *Mankh'* and Preference triumphed forever; on the contrary: that could never be accomplished, but the stronger its proponents were allowed to become, the more ruinous the wars that would get rid of them. Ban-Sila's unexpected death and Rodlakh's accession might be last chance of knitting together a realm.

Here Kizhunai conceded a little. "For three years, *Bôdhrai*, I have been telling anyone who will listen, there are measures no soldier could ever enforce. Loyalty is not the question. Some of us — your kin as well as mine — think the ordinary people are there to be squeezed, like wine-grapes, and we can go on and on, tighter and tighter. It is crack-brained, who will your soldiers be?"

On the far side of Landegh someone making use of the royal colors had an answer to that question: *jinzal*. But the new view of Kizhunai as quietly protesting in private while continuing to do his public duty was an attractive one, although in reality, `anyone who will listen' might translate into his wife or one or two close but powerless acquaintances, hardly Bolan, or the Families at large.

"I am aware you have your allies and advisors. You will probably want to consult with them. Like you, I am not willing to begin a war among friends, but those in possession of the Residence are not and never can be that, for anyone who admires justice. Nothing is going to prevent Rodlakh's reign, but if a dozen Kargul squadrons arrive before we secure Kadon Dinul, a lot of lives will be wasted bringing about the inevitable. You have till the second hour past noon to take your allegiance, then we move." With what objective was abundantly clear, and perhaps Kizhunai would tell his men just to stand aside. Dolvid knew he had not yet struck just the right mixture of threat and promise — or rather, finding it, he was ashamed to use it, the obvious forecast that trying to be fair to both sides Kizhunai would end up necessary to neither. "We are going to work together. I want to talk to you about other troubles in the realm. The second hour, then?"

Kizhunai nodded, giving nothing away.

When he had gone Faëdhal cleared his throat. "If you will allow, this could have been forced on him, here and now. Not, may I say, that I have anything but admiration for your skill with him — "

"We do not need victories as much as we do friends." The new, deferential note was not as displeasing as he would hope. Such an easy trick, power: having decided exactly what you wanted you choked off your own feelings so as to make cruel use of other people's. It was giddying as drink, and as dangerous (in both senses) as having a *jinzai* for a servant.

With only copy-work needed for the orders and dispatches Dolvid left Faëdhal in charge and went outside. Resurrected habit made him use the side-entrance, and coming out into sunlight he could see from the mound of the Bronze Residence how the

Mankh' road had been blocked with a couple of farm-wagons lashed together and reinforced with barrels and boxes. High on the grassy bank above the road bowmen kept watch while eating midday food.

Just inside the gateway some junior Household officers and one or two from the General Cavalry were matching blades, very near the spot where Dolvid had been obliged to do the same with the young, half-mad Bolan, the first time they met. At a short distance Dorrmas was watching critically, his right hand restless.

Dolvid went down the steps and to him. "Would you give me a lesson?"

"*Bô'rai*, I've heard it said you should be the one giving lessons. Are you in practice?"

"No. I crossed swords with Rodlakh, with the *rabhsai*, at Kamsilat, once or twice. I need some honing. I have to kill Rheduban."

Dorrmas made a face. "That's a slippery *jinzai* for anyone not in practice. His blade's a crime, he swashes it all anyhow, but I or anybody else would give a year's pay to have his feet. Not to say, he's strong enough for three madmen, and has the reach to match. You want to knock off some rust, then?"

The two who had been fencing were catching their breath, and Dorrmas called for the bated blades and padded jackets. Both drew their own swords and stuck them in the ground.

Dolvid could not tell how easily Dorrmas might beat him in a real match. As a teacher he was looking for bad habits disuse always brings, not pressing home his own sequences. He was certainly a fine, straightforward swordsman, and Dolvid started to think the elaborate style he had been taught belonged to a former fashion, a past age of the world.

The feel of a sword began to come back, and both of them let out the reins a little. Whenever a wrist drooped Dorrmas would call out, "Your point?" and "Heels," when his weight settled back. With a long rally full of fine things they began to have an audience. Suddenly Dorrmas went right up on his toes and twinkled sideways, darting in with thrusts at odd angles. Dolvid laughed as, as much like Rheduban as height and build permitted,

Dorrmas jumped in with a slash, sprang sideways and then back, front teeth jutting, uncannily reminiscent of the Market Square in Burantal. From a region other than thought a deceptive sequence came back to Dolvid's hands; he had Dorrmas off balance, made him hurry a guard, and actually hit him, mid-breast. Scattered applause was heard on all sides.

"Kheval lives on!" Dorrmas saluted breathlessly. "How does *Bô'rai* feel?"

"Freer." Right arm circling at the shoulder.

"That'll be all for now, or you won't lift your arm when it comes to a fight. There's a woman next to the pie-shop can give you an oil-rub. If I can advise, fighting Rheduban be candle, not moth. The man admires his own dancing so much, let him dance. But you're not so rusty as all that."

They took off the stuffed clothing and picked up their swords. "Better," earnestly, "if you let me do Rheduban. No need for you to, and it would properly make my name for me. No offense to old Faëdhal, but we've just started to get some things done here, and somebody has to take charge, till the *rabhsai* can come."

Alone, he went to speak with some of the townspeople gathered near Harbor Gate with their sense of important things about to happen. Two shopkeepers and then a third demanded protection against the rioting they were sure would soon begin. A woman, questioned, said food was now a little less scarce but prices even higher than when Ban-Sila was alive. Some boys of about fourteen boasted they had thrown stones at Kizhunai's portion of the Household, and were disgruntled when he did not praise them for it. A rather older group, all for a march on the Residence, went to the gate and stared through the bars at the Avenue, before returning to repeat their threats.

He was not sure when or how it started to be common knowledge he was Rodlakh's *Bôdhrai*. At one moment he could saunter a short distance down Harbor Way, choosing whom he listened to. The next he was being pressed from all sides by men and women with questions and complaints. An elderly, nearly

toothless man was peevish because Ban-Sila had died without
revealing where he had hidden the singing tree. Others wanted
just to look, or quite soon to touch. Maintaining a genial air, he
tried to be polite to everyone. A simple thing, to withdraw from
gathering confusion, gently brush past reaching hands, resume his
stroll. Shouting though only inches from his ear a woman said
she had heard nothing from her son, who was levied, while a
pretty girl talked right past Dolvid, telling her friend this was the
rabhsai's friend, Rodlakh's man. Threading through was all very
well except beyond each blockage a new knot at once formed.

" — come himself, not sit in his palace over the water," a
craftsman was carping, and Dolvid made the mistake of turning
to debate him. His opening remark, that the *rabhsai* would be
here but for troubles at the Frontier, started half a dozen
discussions at once. Hot-eyed, a weaselly little man reached for
his outshirt, to demand. "Then tell me, why is the Household
divided?" Another tried to pull that man away, causing an
indiscriminate jostling. Dolvid's smile was starting to ache.

Pressure eased, and a shoulder came working through to his
side. "Some room for the *Bôdhrai* — " a firm, good-humored
voice, Noldar's. An anxious-faced Galt was regarding Dolvid
reproachfully, and he had Guthdar and Dal with him.

"What is it?" thinking there must be news.

"Nothing, *Bôdhrai*." The mouth made a stubborn line, and
his soldiers formed a wedge around Dolvid. The case was made;
with power he could not have casual wanderings.

Judging by the shadow of Yoëlladhu's Spear only minutes
were left. Dolvid drew back from the window, and went down,
fastening on his sword-belt. Faëdhal followed, and Dorrmas was
already opposite the front entrance, mounted and holding Enikai.
About a squadron of Household men were flanked by Frontier
archers, hill-horses pathetically small next to the big *pefral*. Galt
was in charge, reinforced by some of the Owan Sai men.

Both outside and inside Harbor Gate the curious had swelled to a crowd, but Kizhunai's men on duty there had withdrawn; if the other part of the Household meant to fight it would not be here.

Dorrmas, as Dolvid came up into the saddle, said, "If only they'll let us pass, we're more than enough to take the Residence. You won't be needed, *Bô'rai.*" Behind the Household men a contingent of General Cavalry from various garrisons was assembling.

"Let us move inside the Gate."

Unfurling of Rodlakh's colors brought a somewhat hesitant cheer from the onlookers. The gates were flung open, and riding in Dolvid heard in his mind the bitter phrase, *this cursed Kadon Dinul.*

Past the gate the lancers came up into a line of eight abreast, while Galt had archers at either margin, riding between trees and the buildings, where walkers usually went.

Up where the Disc was other riders became visible, and Dorrmas clicked his tongue vexedly. Also on a front of eight lances something near four squadrons of Household were coming at the walk, under the plain white banner, bronze-edged.

After a dozen further paces Dorrmas said, "Pardon, *Bôdhrai.* You are in the line of charge."

"Stand." he said. Dorrmas with a blink gave the command, a double disadvantage; his men were facing upslope, and sitting still to face cavalry on the move. Dolvid fiercely hoped the fight would not come, but if it did the flanking bows ought to be decisive.

The citizenry, except for a handful of the boldest, had faded back outside the gate. All was quiet; in the front rank of lances a soldier rubbed nervously at his eye with a knuckle.

With the approaching squadrons about eighty paces away, still at the walk, a rider, quickly recognized as Kizhunai, came threading between files to move out ahead of his men, standard-bearer next to him. At fifty paces, to Dolvid's relief, he halted his men, but rode on alone. Dolvid kicked at Enikai's flanks and went out to greet him.

Kizhunai met his eyes in a long, hard stare. In a profound surrounding expectancy, the captain dismounted, drawing sword to offer up the hilt.

Dolvid gulped down both tears and a yell of joy, gravely swinging out of the saddle to receive the sword. Rodlakh's banner came forward, and Kizhunai knelt to speak his allegiance and hear his rank and title confirmed. Dorrmas began tapping the butt of his lance on the reddish stone of the Avenue, and soon all his followers were doing the same.

Those who had followed Kizhunai raised a cheer, and men who had been levelling lances at each other spurred forward to hug, clasp hands, swing friendly punches. In the midst of this swirling reconciliation Kizhunai was hard-mouthed. "News, *Bôdhrai*. Four squadrons of Kargul should reach Kadon Dinul after noon tomorrow, and expect to be supported by the private rabble by East Gate. Tovakh is back in Dônshei. Everything he writes confirms what you tell me: he intends to secure the city. *The chief rabbit of the Household —* " he was quoting corrosively — "*can be persuaded it is no business of his.* Tovakh expects to be here in person, as soon as he can get up-to-date news of Shumat."

Mention of Shumat was much the most alarming part, with Tovakh as far south as Dônshei. He wrote, Kizhunai said, of Shumat retreating from El'tuf, and also that *our fearless ally is drifting in the North, with enemy miles to his rear.* This was obviously a reference to Bolan.

After leaving Kamsilat Onebhal apparently had not been in time to prevent Shumat carrying out his part of the plan made with Sebhal; having lured defenders north and east he had landed behind them. But something had gone wrong if he was now in retreat.

Kizhunai, asked who this message was intended for, showed some embarrassment. As many others before it was addressed to Petakoi, and without new orders it would have been passed on, like those others, unopened. At a guess, Dorrmas or one of his followers must have told Kizhunai of Dolvid's readiness to intercept dispatches, but how it came about was less important than the effect on Kizhunai, who was bitter over his own blindness. "Let us be glad," cutting short the captain's self-castigation, "we talked as frankly as we did. With the Household made whole again what chance is there for four squadrons of cavalry, with three hundred auxiliaries or three thousand, to force their way into the city? Let's smoke the other hornets from their nest."

With Kizhunai's men relieved from guarding other ways into the city, joined by most of those they had been keeping out, nearly five hundred armed men assembled in the space between Disc and Residence, Household troopers with many grins and handshakes sorting into proper squadrons. About a hundred went to invest the Barracks, their own; Kargul, expecting a fight, had already been seen to bring its men back from the Treasury to the Residence, and their light forces guarding the Barracks would have to surrender if once the Residence fell.

A holiday spirit was spreading; Dolvid asked Kizhunai to cordon off the townspeople below the Disc, and he used three half-squadrons to do so. The forces could be spared; best estimate of enemy strength inside the Residence was barely greater than one hundred, including their allies, Zhinladh's small contingent from the Household. Kizhunai's written demand Zhinladh resubmit to proper authority had already been delivered, and rejected without comment, but as the various royal forces were deploying in front of the Residence a scuffle broke out over to the right, where Pefrai Gate led to the courtyards on the south side. Shouting, the chime of weapons, the gate burst open and about a dozen men sprinted for the lines of Household troops, calling they were friends. Most of the fugitives were Household men, but there were also some youths of about sixteen, probably from the Families. Pefrai Gate was hauled shut by the defenders within, and any more who wanted at this last minute to change sides would have to find another way.

Meanwhile, under the Great Window, the central doors to the Residence were opened, and a double line of Kargul arranged themselves across the top where the Steps narrowed a little, armed with heavy pikes.

Laconically Galt asked, "Shall we shoot them, *Bôdhrai*?"

"Bend your bows, but wait for word." He tried to read what might be behind the grim faces of the Kargul'. The horse-obsessed traditions of his province made any Karguli reluctant to fight on foot, and here, unsupported by bows, they must see how foolish their position was. Karguli indifference or outright aversion to bows could cripple them once away from the open ground they regarded as the only proper terrain for battle. Over to the right, a dozen good archers along the wall by Pefrai Gate could have made it very awkward for the attackers, but as was, the royal forces, drawn back a little, could guard against any sortie there.

With Dorrmas and some others Dolvid started up the central course of the Steps, doubting whether the pikemen above were aware their breastplates, which might turn even a close-range shot from a light Owani bow, were about as much protection as a linen shirt against Frontier bows.

The Steps were in two flights, and on the level between they paused. Closest of the pikemen was within four lengths of his weapon away. Galt's men were on one knee, bows bent.

Dolvid called to the defenders, telling them they would not be harmed if they threw down their weapons. Some of them glanced back longingly at the too-distant Residence doors.

"Throw down your weapons," again. The Karguli officer directly above him complied, in a way, by pitching his weapon point first at Dolvid, who sidestepped. The pike clattered down the Steps, the Karguli officer drew his sword, and his final command was nailed in his throat by an arrow. Two men, starting forward, were also felled by archery; a cheer went up from the attackers, and Household men, dismounted, their swords out, started up the Steps. Higher, there was a little catch in the breath, giving the chance to make a last call for surrender. Some pikes went to the ground, while about eight defenders made for the doors.

Galt, quick to assess, called for the doors to be seized, and his tough, short men went forward, shooting as they ran. Sword out, Dolvid also went leaping up between the double row of bronze and gilded statuary. Pikemen fell or surrendered as the closing doors were wrenched back, by Dorrmas among others. In a comical vision, four men were holding a giant bronze bar, suddenly with no slot to put it in. They dropped it, as the attack surged into the Residence. Dolvid was with those at the front who came to the foot of the wide main stair, where, halfway up, a pack of Kargul' soldiers had their swords out. Dorrmas started forward, but Dolvid held him back; with the entrance forced there was no hurry. The Kargul' above shouted taunts, while Rodlakh's supporters streamed in below.

A crash of cheering from outside, was, as seen through the open doors, to hail the *rabhsai*'s colors now displayed. The rearing bronze warhorse, emblem of the Paowan, had a strangely delicate upraised hoof, and the standard-bearer had made use of the deep notch under the fetlock to hold the banner upright on the topmost step.

Most Household men knew the ways of the Residence, and a squadron-leader, borrowing a few of Galt's archers, went doubling down the corridor to the right with sixty swords, to bar the way to the stables and courts on that side. Certain the Residence could not be held, Dolvid let Dorrmas assemble his close-packed troops.

Again, he called for capitulation. Defiance came back from above. The archers with Galt let go a volley, and the Household charged with a fearsome yell.

Using their skill and some good judgment Galt with his favorite bowmen went on shooting as long as they could, but as the attack pressed upwards the angle became too fine. Fresh swordsmen charged; there was a lurch and a plunge as the topmost stair was attained. No longer held between balustrades, the defenders gave way.

Dolvid saw nothing of the running battles through the courts and around the stables on the south side; this fight on the stairs was the last concentrated action he was to witness at the Residence. The struggle became headlong pursuits and forlorn stands by brave, doomed knots of the Kargul' and their few allies, surrenders and treacheries, calls to single-combat and cries for assistance. Booming voices, clash and clang of steel, scuffling feet and the thud of heavy bodies echoed through the elaborate caverns of glass and carved stone. After, everyone talked about the half-mad battle-glee of Dorrmas, who laughed as he looked for his next adversary, but when seen again he was sane enough, though eager to account for all the enemy.

Not with him but with Kizhunai (who never unsheathed his sword) Dolvid plotted to have the Residence systematically quartered by groups no less than file strength; stupid to squander their advantage in numbers, by now very great.

Faëdhal arrived. He had failed to secure the tip of his scabbard and the uncontrolled swing of the sword tended to spoil the dignity of his march up the Steps. He looked this way and that as he climbed, sharp-nosed and complacent.

"If I may say so — " his legs were strong as ever, and he was refusing to be breathless. "They put up less of a fight than I anticipated."

After an incredulous stare, Dolvid softly struck the old scholar's shoulder with a cupped hand, then knelt to attach the scabbard-ties.

"No, *Bôdhrai*, no. You really must not — consider your standing. Ah, that is how they go, is it — " offended propriety yielded to interest in something fresh. "I suppose if one had to run — or, indeed, if there were a need to draw a blade in some haste... Yes, practical, very practical."

All reports coming back were of the collapse of any systematic defense. Arranging they should all meet again at the General Audience Hall, Dolvid left the other senior officers, contravening his own instructions, going to look for Rheduban with only a small, unbidden following, Galt with Dal and Kuno, Noldar and his brother.

He did not think Rheduban would be found in the Karguli Suite, where Household men had already gone, as he must eventually for speech with Petakoi. He, the *rabhsaidakradhi*, might have been expected to attempt an escape on the south side, or through the Rose-Stone Wing and so to the Residence grounds, but men were in wait there, and no word of his death or capture came. Nor had he been seen.

Crossing the General Audience Hall with a half-smile for the memory of stunned recognition of Âna, when he peered into this place from behind the great carving, Dolvid tried the small bronze-sheathed door that led to the Private Audience Chamber. Not locked, and the little room with its panelling and highbacked chairs was empty of life. From here, through a rounded archway, a short stair went up to the Personal Suite. Not quite knowing why, Dolvid was sure Rheduban was in this part of the Residence. He sent Kuno with a message for Dorrmas, asking for a detachment to be sent up the main way to the Personal Suite, the broad stair on the axis of the building. A third way, little used, required crossing the vaulted vestibule where steps climbed to three of the suites used by the provinces, and there men must already be on watch.

In the short cross-passage after the climb there was a clash with three men of Kargul, trying to gain that third stair. One man, having reached it and started down, heard boots, bounded up again, clashed swords with Dolvid, and went back down three steps at a stride. When some weapons appeared below, the man was frozen with fright, till Dorrmas came up the stair, disarmed him deftly, and held him in a powerful left-hand grip.

"Where is Rheduban?" Dolvid demanded. Terrified, the young soldier stared up at him.

"Leave that one to us, *Bô'rai*," Dorrmas advised, meaning Rheduban. He went on to say the battle here was won; at last count there were fifty-eight prisoners, many not expected to live, including the *Kímukan* Zhinladh, who had wounds from both blade and arrow. He had done most in trying to make a cohesive defense of the Residence, not Rheduban, who had not been seen by anyone. "And the dead not yet counted. I would not want the cleaning of this place."

Yes, time to have someone sent into the city to find where the *Bôdh'loiki* Rhunilat might be, so a start could be made in reordering the Residence and getting the servants back at work.

Dorrmas, hand and wrist red, one sleeve sodden with blood not his, climbed up to Dolvid. "You've sworn his death, then?"

A nod.

"Is it true he killed Sebhal? That's the rumor I heard. Never sword to sword, surely?"

"Bow against a hunting-knife. Rheduban did not know who he was fighting, and may not know yet who he killed."

"I'd guess your oath must be held by Lady Alalu."

"Aëlu — " not correcting his assumption. They were moving for the innermost parts of the Personal Suite.

"My wife says, if my tongue had one-tenth the skill of my sword-arm, I could go farther in this realm. *Bô'rai*, all I meant was, it is an oath you're bound fast by."

"It is." They went through a sitting-room with bright cushions and a wide fireplace, not cleaned out, into another ante-room, with long couches where guards or servants could sleep. Next was the bedroom, used by every *rabhsai* since Plakhsila, a light, airy space, with a great curtained bed empty and stripped. Facing the end of the bed was a heavy carved cabinet stuffed with books and documents, which he longed to explore. The room had a disagreeable odor, which did not come from the mustiness of old parchment, nor from clothing and bedclothing stored in presses. "Night jars need emptying," Dorrmas, sniffing. Perhaps food left to spoil: most servants had fled when the murder was discovered and Marra killed; no one cleared away remains of partly-eaten meals.

In the wall next to the head of the bed there was the sort of plain, low door that usually led to closets. This one was locked, and Dolvid remembered Ban-Sila, a light sleeper, complained early in his reign he could not find anywhere in the Residence that was entirely dark, and soon converted unused space into a second and more private bedroom, windowless, where morning and evening light never came. Above were fretted iron grilles over vents high on the wall, assuring air for the obscure chamber. There was nowhere this side for a key to fit. The door might be held on the far side by a simple bar, a turnbuckle, a hook.

"Ban-Sila's bolt-hole." Saying it confirmed conviction the room had to be searched. This door could be broken in, but Dorrmas said there was another entrance in the corridor beyond, a former storeroom as vestibule to the hidden bedroom, one of the places he had always had to post guards when he was in charge of the pike detachments, a rotating duty in the Household.

They went swiftly through the row of other rooms, study, dressing room, the one for breakfast. Galt pointed out a wedge of bread, not staled, and picked up a lancer's heavy gauntlet, lined in pale blue shuzi, slipping it on to show how amazingly long the fingers were.

Back at the chamber with the cushions a handful of General Cavalry men were staring with interest at their surroundings; what was familiar as home to the Household men was a legend to these from Burantal. Recollecting himself, their officer reported the Karguli Suite was taken, and three ladies found there were being confined. A minimum of force was used, although the chief lady had to be prevented from burning some parchments, and was now very angry. Except for a servant belonging to the Residence no men were taken there.

The hunting-pack, as Dolvid thought of it, went back through the ante-chamber and turned into the corridor. Not far ahead steps led down to the night-pantry where Dolvid and Rodlakh had almost been caught raiding. Amid the clump of boots and clank of weapons there was the faint, sharp click of a door gently tugged shut.

Sword out, he was to the storeroom door in two strides. Galt called a warning as Dolvid thrust the door open, and plunged into the dim, relieved by a single *ôdu*-globe over the inner door, standing half-open. As he went through this second door, and was in absolute darkness, Galt's reproach came, "Curse it, *Bôdhrai* — " and was understood; he had done just what he had criticized Rodlakh for, at the guardhouse in Drin b'Afon; against the pale-lighted entrance he could easily have been killed by someone laying in wait.

Eyes strained at blackness, and nostrils were affronted; the stench noticed in the main bedroom was much stronger here. The whole space was heavy with it, the smell of rot and the revolting sweetness of feasting worms.

Eyes began to steady and collect impressions. Against the ceiling, a faint checkering of light coming through the air-vents noticed on the other side. Swimming shapes were becoming firm; this was no great space, and much of it was occupied by a large, plain bed with no curtains. Near where bed and wall came together a pale globular form was hanging or drifting, and Dolvid edged forward, eyes twitching. Dorrmas muttered they would have light brought, but the intense murk was gradually ebbing. He was gripping his sword ferociously. The pale shape was not floating above the bed, but resting on a dull pillow; a head, but below the chin the neck seemed to end in a dark, ragged line.

He was looking at wounds and patches of discoloration on skin; the body continued, and there were feet he could reach out and touch. The putrid smell came stronger than ever, and he knew whose body this must be. He felt the acid choke of nausea rise. Galt beside him made a dry mock-spit, while Dorrmas uttered a horrified *No*, which turned into a real retch.

Behind them, leftward, there was a sound, a choked sob that in other circumstances might have been a suppressed chuckle. Very rapidly but as if in slow deliberation, Dolvid resaw Galt posting men on each side of the doorway. Neither of them were as near as that sound, while Galt himself and Dorrmas were close by, but to the right.

He swung around, just in time to see a tall wedge of light narrowing to an adze shape and vanishing, as the connecting door closed.

Before he was there he knew the door had locked. Instead of trying to solve that lock in the dark, he leapt for the outer doors, jostling Dorrmas, telling him they might trap the fugitive in the Personal Suite. Him: he had no doubt it was Rheduban.

Rounding corners he came to the first room, and as he did the door that led to the stairway was just closing. He began to have a dream-feeling, endless pursuit of an invisible something that cannot be caught.

Out between sets of stairs he gave a shout, seeing his quarry, who part-sworded, part shoved aside a Household man so as to make for the little stair down to the Private Audience Chamber. A vision of Rheduban stock-still, hair wild, lips peeled back from his front teeth, before he plunged down the stair. There was someone to help the wounded man, bleeding high on his body, and Dolvid clattered down after the fugitive, Dorrmas and Galt staying with him.

Rheduban had wasted no time in the little panelled room. Passing through into the Oak-Wall Hall, Dolvid saw him racing for the main doors at the far end. Before he could get there, a number of men appeared, swords in hand. Blades clanged, and Rheduban veered off and galloped for the door on the other side of the stone canopy. Dolvid and Dorrmas moved across quickly to cut off that escape. Rheduban aimed a hacking cut on the run, and was surprised by the firmness of Dolvid's stop. Swivelling to dodge again in front of the canopy Rheduban tried for the door he had come in through, but Dalirr, Kuno and others were there, others coming behind them.

Breathing hard through his teeth, Rheduban backed warily to the front of the Chair of State, trying to watch all directions. He swept his sword-point back and forth in a long arc as the Household men, at least twenty, approached from the far end of the hall. *As petitioners would*, Dolvid incongruously said in his mind, and Rheduban was standing where Lambarr used to when hearing suits.

"My kill — " loud enough to startle himself. He was not alone; Dal had his bow ready, and looked stricken. Rheduban swung slowly in his direction, the grin coming, and Dolvid marvelled at how insane this was, and wasteful; the object was that this creature be kept from doing more harm, and if he killed Dolvid in single fight it was not likely the others would meekly let him go. Âna's violation was what chiefly moved Dolvid, but he was conscious of acting out a convention of revenge not in his real nature; nor did that mean he thought any less of Âna, or abhorred any the less what Rheduban was capable of.

The Household men, constantly being reinforced by fresh arrivals, respected his declaration and were perhaps relieved to do so, hanging back, but Dorrmas let loose a curse, and was right. In a surge of childish self-pity Dolvid wondered how she would feel, now she had gone to Rodlakh, if he was to die avenging her.

He dismissed that: this fight had to be; if he let Rheduban be shot or overwhelmed by numbers there would be a loss he could never regain. Conventions could be aspired to.

He felt a shiver as the mad-dog eyes came on him; the tall, wide-shouldered man let out a laugh of pure delight. Lowering sword-point he walked straight at Dolvid, who with an effort snapped the eyelock, and made an elementary mow. Rheduban with steel wrists flicked his sword up to stop, replying with a fast, whipping backhand, half downward, that would have been finish for the novice that opening implied. Parrying, Dolvid tried a quick wrist-stroke for the throat, and the taller man had to hurry his blade, shortening his stroke as he fell away. He saw this was to be in earnest, and tautened out of his casual slouch.

Dolvid, certain now he was not hopelessly overmatched, came in with a series of quick, high half-cuts, sending Rheduban back with no chance for a clean reply, till he used his agility to spring clear, at once rebounding to lunge in from the left. Dolvid had to be quick to turn that thrust, and they locked hilts. Rheduban, fully behind his blade, took the advantage, pressing hard, and it was all Dolvid could do to prevent him slipping the lock on the forehand side, which would have been the end; he could not have recovered to ward the thrust.

The strength of that arm was too much for him; Kheval would say, 'step around your hilt,' but here it could not be accomplished by backing off; the wide-striding Rheduban was in balance, quick enough to whip his sword back and jab again.

Both fighters were grunting, while spectators, constantly growing in number, were marvellously quiet. Dolvid got his right leg planted, thrusting up and away with all his force, struggling up almost straight, ignoring the white steel near his eye. Rheduban was the one to abruptly release pressure and jerk his sword free for an elbowy short-arm jab at the face. Hearing a noise from

Dorrmas, knowing it had been close, Dolvid went ducking away, trying to open up some space for swordwork.   Rheduban followed, sensing a win, harrying him with cuts and lunges, high and low.   An inconsistency in the flagging of the floor made Dolvid nearly stumble; he went to the side without meaning to, and missed being spitted by pure chance, as the sword snagged loose cloth under his arm.   Their bodies banged together, Dolvid's left closing down on Rheduban's sword-arm, while his dropped shoulder forced Dolvid's weapon up and away.   From a corner of his eye Dolvid saw long fingers go snaking down to close on the hilt of a knife, long, not the ornamented *rabhsaidakradhi* dagger. The snorting mouth was near his eyes, and the corpselike aroma that clung to Rheduban was not surprising considering his recent choice of company.   Feet strained at the floor, and Dolvid felt rather than saw the knife start out of its sheath.

He sprang almost off the ground, flinging up both arms to release the clamp; Rheduban's turn to be caught off-balance.   Not waiting to draw the better knife at his back, Dolvid drove his adversary the width of the hall with a fierce head attack Rheduban used both blades to hold off, crouching and weaving.   At last there was noise from the watchers; this looked like Dolvid taking command, but he could not make a hit, and felt a hint of despondency even at the height of his attack.   After all, he might be overmatched; his best chance had been a quick finish, and if this fight went on long Rheduban's strength would win it in the end.

Right in front of the great oak carving Rheduban sidled away from three backhands.   He cocked his sword, and with a whirl the other way came in low with his knife.   He was within a fingerspan of impaling himself on the sword held hard for that purpose. Dorrmas (almost surely) again let out a cry, as Rheduban, also giving tongue, threw his body into a contorted twist to avoid the sword, left hand banging hard against ribs as the dagger swung behind.   They were both laboring for breath, and Dolvid felt despair surge; he had used nearly everything he had ever learned.

Rheduban ducked away with nimble feet in the space between wall and the canopy over the Chair of State, turning to parry as Dolvid could only follow; a ringing sequence of quick wrist-strokes as if their style was dictated by this narrower arena. Suddenly Rheduban lunged in, brought his feet together and made a jump back, letting his arms drop as if tired. Dolvid could hear Dorrmas advising, *candle, not moth*. He eased back in turn, setting himself. With a howl, Rheduban charged wildly, long blade and short both flailing.

Bobbing away with no chance for anything of his own, Dolvid steadily gave ground. Over-eager, Rheduban made two consecutive long thrusts, and was off-balance; any other should have been beaten there, but once more he was agile enough to roll his body away from Dolvid's counter, and to recover with a rapid, complicated flicker of feet that backed him from the middle of the hall to the front of the canopy. He giggled, and shaped for a new attack on Dolvid, who was getting breath, trying not to show how nearly he was done. Sword-points slithered and chimed, and then came a long, wailing cry, "*Rabhsaidakradhayin!*" From Rheduban's left a small, robed figure came at full run to drive a short, slender sword in behind his shoulder.

Rheduban lurched sideways just a little, eyes flickering down to where the point stuck out from the hollow of his long throat. Horror keeping everything else still he gave a sound like a sigh, like contentment. His legs went boneless, sideways collapse of the turned body dragging the sword from the hand of his assailant, at-Zhâlai, who stood weeping as Rheduban crashed at the base of the Chair of State.

In a moment the small *atarlai* was engulfed by soldiers who seemed angry at being robbed of a proper finish to the main fight. Dolvid, trying to blink away daze, needed three tries to sheathe his sword, while Rheduban was dying in a great deal of blood.

Galt was first at his side, and there were Dorrmas, Noldar, Guthdar, Faëdhal, all gathered near him, while others looked on from a discreet distance. Dorrmas gave his back a great thump. "Bad ending to a good fight." His eyes showed no duplicity, but so expert a swordsman must be aware at-Zhâlai's treacherous intervention had probably saved Dolvid's life.

Faëdhal, who had been worried, was babbling a little. "Here this *atarlai*, of the *Atarlum*, of *g'Asalladhum-lakh'*, what reason — "

Dolvid's breathlessness had come, and the sweat was cold on his back. Inside the ring of soldiers at-Zhâlai went weeping on; one man had him gripped harshly by the forearm, till Dolvid gestured he should desist. No one had touched Rheduban's body. Dolvid was empty, Rheduban was dead, and the realm ought to be cleansed of all evil, and was not.

Was it only the finish that left Dolvid numb and cheated, the notion such a fight needed proper consummation, even if it had been his own death? Here, he had been the intruder; Ban-Sila, Rheduban and at-Zhâlai were a small, intense personal story, nothing to do with statecraft or the clash of armies, its effect on the realm only incidental to the participants. Dolvid thought of Âna, and nothing was proved, nothing altered.

He rejoined Dorrmas. "Another hour or so, and I would have had him." He meant that as bitter irony, but Dorrmas said earnestly, "That double feint, *Bô'rai*, where you force the reverse and bring him onto your blade, would you show me that again when there's a chance? Anything human would have been skewered there."

Kizhunai was here, and brought cold *raminat*. "It is good there are not two of that one," nodding towards the corpse of Rheduban.

Petakoi, at her grandest, said, "Squadron-leader, I want to go to the stables."

Dorrmas was uncomfortable. Dolvid, with a deference, "*Asayu*, I regret that cannot be allowed."

"*Shilai ti-ani y'ôl?*" Petakoi recognized him as Owani, but her use of indirect address was calculated insult.

"*Kímukan*," giving Dorrmas his proper rank, insignia notwithstanding, "tell the lady of Kargul who I am."

"*Asayu*, you are speaking with the *Bôdhrai* Dolvid."

"*Bôdhrai? Ba-shilat Bôdhrayit ô?*"

This was beyond Dorrmas, and Dolvid said, "Of Rodlakh *Rabhsai*, whose rule you may hear formally proclaimed less than an hour from now. Petakoi *Asayu*, representing Kargul, can have an honored place on the Steps." Faëdhal had made this bizarre suggestion, and it would certainly have been a stroke of policy, but if she would not willingly appear, he was not willing to compel her. The scorn in her face, so far, was faint. He apologized for inconveniencing her, and said it might be possible quite soon to allow her to return to Inilun Barabhi, or go to her husband, wherever he then might be. For the present, however, she would be kept at the Residence, but without any other restraint.

Petakoi gave up the ill-advised attempt to cow him with her Owanilú. "By what right do you hold us captive?"

"You are a prisoner of war."

"Of what war, whose war?"

"The war your own province began, *Asayu*, with illicit seizure of this Residence, and acts committed in defending its unlawful occupation."

"And what about your Household? Are you going to reward these men for theft?" She reached out her hand for the sheaf of documents he held, some charred at the edges. "Those are my personal property."

"That is to be determined, *Asayu* — " letting his eyes wander around this common-room. The firepit where Ban-Sila had died, familiar from Âna's account. There, by the sideboard, Âna had very nearly been killed.

At the far end two women came in, evidently from washing; the small, plump one wiping stubby hands on her front. The other was hardboned and tall, but he knew they were sisters. Dolvid took a step or two in the direction of the firepit, and with his eyes asked Petakoi to follow. She did, not very readily, and he murmured, "Lady Radaghi must be looked to. Rheduban is dead."

Petakoi came down slowly from heights beyond reach, and seemed to see Dolvid for the first time. "You have murdered him."

"He died, *Asayu*, with a weapon in either hand. That is more than we can say for Ban-Sila." He could not tell whether tiles of the firepit showed signs of blood.

She kept her voice low. "Other than the distress of our kinswoman, this death is no great sorrow to me personally, or to Kargul."

"That I can understand." He recognized an opening move when he saw it.

"Then you must also know, *Bôdhrai*, the killing of Ban-Sila was nothing to do with the will of Kargul. It was the act of one madman."

"But Kargul was not in any hurry to give Rheduban up to justice, and men have died because of that. Yes, *Asayu*, yes. I am aware Kargul did not want the sudden death of Ban-Sila. It came too soon for your plans."

Leaving the documents with Dorrmas he walked past the startled Petakoi, past Finú and Radaghi. He wanted a look at Kamin-Tolagh's rooms.

"But surely, *Bôdhrai* — " Faëdhal's faith in his powers far exceeded Dolvid's own — "you have ordered the southward garrisons to refuse Kamin-Tolagh passage? I copied the orders myself."

"The order may be too late." If they had been alone Dolvid would have confessed he was far from sure his authority would be acknowledged at Kanzan Tâl, but with Kizhunai and Dorrmas and Galt there he remained omnipotent. "With his father, I am at a loss why Kamin-Tolagh is not already back here." Tovakh, in his letters to Petakoi, had expressed the notion more forcefully, assuming his son was taking time for all the women of the Kovilanu. Dolvid was gratified by further confirmation of Vinosai's treachery; the improbable story fed the man, about the Army of the West gathering for an assault on Kargul, had been passed on; Tovakh was insistent his son must ride for Kadon Dinul 'even if Sebhal burns Inilun Barabhi to the ground.' So Tovakh believed Sebhal was alive: Dorrmas explained the circumstantial account of his death had not come to Kadon Dinul till men from the Burantal garrison marched in to join him.

"You came not one day too soon, *Bô'rai*. Now the city's safe, those four squadrons Tovakh's sending are a nothing. If we had gone on squabbling, they would have caught my lads out in the open, while the ones at the Residence came out to fight." He stared coolly at Kizhunai, who looked back levelly at him: as well these two had shared a victory today.

Kizhunai said, "They should have fought us in the streets. *Péfrapravádal* are wasted as defenders on foot."

"The *Bôdhrai* was too quick for them," Galt said. "We had Owan Sai and were at Kadon Dinul before they could think properly." Already lectured by a newly-created *kímukan*, Kizhunai was ready to draw the line at small squadron-leaders from the West, but forgot offense when Galt added that it was the same at Drin b'Λfon, complete surprise.

Mouths generally came open, and Dolvid said hastily that story could be told at leisure, and that it must be the same once again at Dônshei. He meant to go there, leaving at first light, taking one hundred of the Household, under Dorrmas. Additional bows could be levied to strengthen the defense of Kadon Dinul.

Not a choice; he had to go, and did not dare take any more men away from the capital, no less threatened by the *Adanum Plakh'*, plottings among the Families, than by the inexplicably delayed Kamin-Tolagh. At Dônshei, as he explained, Tovakh had the better part of his army, and somewhere north and west was Shumat, who had retired in good order from a fight near El'tuf.

The full story could not be extracted from what Tovakh had written to Petakoi, but apparently Shumat had landed about a week ago, which meant that when Onebhal was at Kamsilat, demanding what had become of Sebhal's promises, Shumat was already at sea, and no message could have been in time to turn him back.

Though it was plain from Tovakh's writings the forces with Shumat were far from negligible, something else must have gone wrong with his invasion, besides Sebhal's failure to create diversion at Kadon Dinul. Perhaps some of Shumat's army had been lost at sea. It was necessary to open the door for him at Dônshei, not only for his sake, but for the realm's. Beyond the visible end of all schemes here on the Mainland was the need for sending help to Rodlakh.

Kizhunai was unsmiling. "The Captain-General is in the field against Shumat."

"Not for long. Shumat is the loyalist now, Tovakh the rebel."

Dorrmas, elated at the prospect of some real campaigning, wanted to be gone, to prepare his forces. Dolvid went with him to the door. "By all means, bring your own squadron, but be sure the other half-hundred has men in it who supported Kizhunai."

Dorrmas nodded comprehension. "Tovakh at Dônshei in strength? And you'll take the city with our hundred and Galt's forty — not quarter what took the Residence back from a handful?"

"I expect to collect troops on the road. Besides, I think we can decoy Tovakh away from Dônshei." Tovakh, who listened to what Vinosai told the Patriarch: he was beginning to have a clearer idea of why he had brought the man with him. Vinosai was still at Owan Sai, helping run the port, watched closely by Sarnak.

When Dolvid came back to the middle of the room Kizhunai said, "No disrespect, *Bôdhrai*, but it seems to me you cannot know which way Bolan will jump. Could he not stay allied to Tovakh?"

"Nothing is impossible. His rank and file will be for Rodlakh. What would Kargul do with a Bolan and no army?"

"In my judgment the same goes for the southward garrisons. Whether they will fight to stop Kamin-Tolagh is anybody's guess."

He could repeat the nonsense about his orders coming too late, but this was an honest man as well as an astute one. "There is a lot of confusion. It may be hard to know which orders to obey."

"Then, again without disrespect, these doubts were all there before we stormed the Residence, before — " He tailed off, but clearly meant, before Dolvid brought him over to Rodlakh's side.

"I have often noted, as an historian, you understand, that all power is the appearance of power. Otherwise, just to prove it could be done, you would have to kill everyone. If you had not joined us, I would have found some other way." And if Kizhunai felt he had been bluffed now, what would he say when he heard about *jinzal* at the Frontier?

"Oh, I am content — " Kizhunai looked it. "Hanging in the air between this power and that is no good for a soldier. We have to have some ground under our feet."

"True." Faëdhal had not spoken for half an hour; all the talk of armies and strategies might have bored or baffled him. "But, *Bôdhrai*, if one might put it so, *rabhsayum* is far more than an appearance of power, as the vestments are, the beechwood tablet, as the Bronze Sword was and Bronze Beech is. These are powers in men's hearts, and therefore more, not less than they appear."

"Good — " wishing he had this simple trust. "Knowing, I hope, enough of your heart, I would want you to be the one proclaiming the *rabhsayum* of Rodlakh from the Residence Steps. Would you?"

Faëdhal, with no loss of dignity, wept his gratitude.

Other minor officials of Ban-Sila's *rabhsayum* were beginning to present themselves at the Residence; most were of Family and would probably have preferred Orbanak's accession, but Dolvid heard their allegiance and gave them stations on the Steps for the proclaiming.   There were accounts to oversee, decrees and orders for copying and distributing, the striking of an issue of coinage in Rodlakh's name and with his portrait. In the *Song of Tales*, after victory came feasts and boasting, maidens adoring. Some of the Household men might have found the equivalent, but if stories described anything real those must have been simpler ages, when winning meant you had won — or maybe their idling after battle made ancient heroes fight the same war, over and over again. Rodlakh's men worked, and the meal at the Residence after the ceremonies was plain, its table-talk filled with purpose.

The proclaiming had gone as well as it could in the absence of the principal, and the scarcity of dignitaries to stand on the Steps. No provincial overlord, no Captain-General, no Master of Revenues; conspicuously, the *Atarlum* went unrepresented.

All these deficiencies were partially atoned-for by the crowd, startling with its size and enthusiasm. Magically, they had gathered in the Avenue as the sun broke out before vanishing in westward banks of cloud. The Families and Craft Families were there as much out of curiosity as any love for Rodlakh, and ordinary townspeople no doubt wanted to seize the chance of expressing their loathing for Kargul, their pleasure at being rid of Rheduban, news of whose death, embellished to suit his monstrosity, had gone through the city like a spring wind. But whatever the reasons for coming, the Avenue from wall to wall and from the foot of the Steps to beyond the Disc, was packed tight.

Faëdhal, like Rodlakh at Drin Navuna, was assisted by a repeater, a cavalry officer who needed all his knowledge of the Owanilú. Dolvid firmly insisted on popular intelligibility, and Faëdhal achieved a fine balance between that requirement and his own desire to be archaic and arcane: the proclaiming rang with rich music of the Old Tongue, and raised unquellable ovations with its plainer phrases. Not many spectators could have doubted Rodlakh, with all his styles and titles, had come into a power beyond challenge, though Dolvid stayed achingly aware the most important of missing participants might be lying dead on Landegh.

As darkness fell a drizzling rain came, but that did not prevent visitors of all kinds to the Residence. Not all were admitted, but Dolvid as Minister Plenipotentiary did agree to hear some of the outstanding suits, and two magistrates came separately to bring him cases they could not make a ruling in; one he passed on to Faëdhal for an explanation of the Law of Legacies, and the other he solved out of hand, with a formula he shamelessly ascribed to Plakhsila *Kímukoi*, who might have said it but in fact had not, *Where laws appear to conflict, the magistrate is at liberty to use common sense.* In between there were men and women with complaints about damage caused by officers of Kargul billeted in their houses, one with a rambling tale about a tapestry Rheduban was said to have borrowed, or perhaps it had been bartered for some silver ornaments delivered to a third party, who had never given up a half-share in some raspberry canes. Unsure of whether the woman wanted her tapestry back, compensation, or all the raspberries, sure she did not know either, Dolvid told her to go to a scribe and have him write what she expected from her suit, "and then we may unravel this tapestry affair." Puzzled, the woman then laughed excessively, and he supposed it would be quoted all over Kadon Dinul by morning as a select example of the *Bôdhrai's* wit.

For all this he sat on a plain chair set next to the empty Chair of State in the Oak-Wall Hall, Rheduban's blood having been washed away. Galt and some of his men watched with unblinking attention, and it occurred to him he was being guarded from assassination.

There came a tiny girl, no older than three, who ran to give Dolvid a circlet of spring flowers. Behind her, accompanied by a woman servant, his wealth worn with a smug reticence more ostentatious than display, with a walk where stateliness was decaying in the direction of waddle, short-necked and big in the middle, Khelagh. Dolvid had considered summoning him, but this was better.

His breathlessness was becoming chronic. "*Bôdhrai,*" he panted, after a jocular deference. "Do you not recognize your niece?"

The question was both idiotic and monumentally tactless: Dolvid was not sure of the rules, but did not think he could be uncle to a child of his former wife's brother, born after the divorce from Khalú. "Hardly possible I could, when Ghuradh was not married at my exile."

After a startled blink (the reinstated were not supposed to recall former disgrace): "Is she not pretty, then, my grand-daughter?" She was, but the female side of the family was noted for its looks, and Ghuradh, heir to the enormous wealth of this man, had his pick of the Residence Quarter, and was said to have chosen with a good eye.

The girl was under the canopy, and about to climb up the arm of the Chair of State. Before Khelagh's servant could recapture her, Galt came and took the little girl's hand in his. He had said something about a daughter of his own; Dolvid was ashamed of vagueness on this question.

"These are my wife's kin," he told Galt, and, as expected, it was taken as a sign vigilance could be relaxed. Oblivious to the alarm of the servant-woman he tucked the child up on his forearm and took her to see the Oak Wall carvings, which she traced with a stiff forefinger while he explained them with stories much more interesting than the facts. The serenity with which Khelagh pacified the servant was a little forced, but he had evidently decided Galt's mere touch was not going to contaminate his grand-daughter. Even the purest of Owanil families frequently had Other Races — though seldom men — to minister to their children, sometimes even as wet-nurses.

"Will the *rabhsai* soon come to Kadon Dinul?"

A telling concession. Like the officials Khelagh was here in case he had miscalculated, and Rodlakh could consolidate his power, but it was unexpected the magnates would abandon so soon the pretense Orbanak was the proper successor.

"He must dearly love his adopted home in the West."

"He has good friends at Kamsilat."

"*Bôdhrai*, you could convey to him he has more friends than he might suppose here at Kadon Dinul."

"That has been my experience," concurring sweetly. "And I am nothing but the *rabhsai*'s banner. Of course, one has to learn to distinguish between true friendship and simple self-interest."

Khelagh looked up and down, and Dolvid waved him to a seat. "The two, at best, can go together, not so? And a man is a fool if he cannot tell when time has come to change some of his friends."

Out of pure curiosity though he would never trust this man, Dolvid probed at the faint hint of accommodation. "But no one can go to bed a Deniant and wake up an *atarlai*. Especially if he has followers, he has to consider how far they will follow him, and if he has friends who will never change their views, he has to put a value on friendship and balance it off against any new advantage. But loyalties are not an investment, that can be switched to another line where profits may be better."

"Hm," Khelagh grunted. "A hard view — then minds never change?"

"Those who rule cannot worry too much about minds. They have to measure change by the things people do."

He meant to go on, but Khelagh interrupted, implicitly dropping the subject. "Khalú is at Kadon Dinul."

"As is natural, with Bolan away. Does she hear from him?"

"You have a message for her?"

"She could send my hope we shall soon meet — " just managing to find words to cover the chance of what might be a useful overture, while not quite revealing his inability to communicate with Bolan. But Khelagh's mind was elsewhere.

"*Bôdhrai*, Dolvidhai, if I may continue to call you so — " he stood, with a fresh half-deference. "I am only one among the Families wishing to offer every assistance — our homes are at your disposal. Your personal expenses must be considerable." Hand going to purse was almost visible.

"Not so, since I possess no property at present. But the offer of your home is generous; I may someday need to quarter troops with you. My regards to the Lady Linaëyu," Khelagh's wife, Dolvid's former mistress.

"Of troops," as if recalling a question. "The fiscal basis of the new *rabhsayum* needs careful thought, since taxation may be difficult while conditions are what they are. You are blessed with many enthusiasts for Rodlakh *Rabhsai*, as one sees, but the loyalest *rabhsayani* must eat, support his family... "

He could have laughed out loud at this clumsy blend of seduction and veiled menace, as if to say, without the Families the *rabhsai* would have no money. He hinted instead at the opposite, privileged leaders with no one left to lead, the few Household officers who had stood out against Rodlakh's accession deserted by their own rank and file. "Other things have run their course. If there were no Rodlakh, the realm he stands for would yet be the only one that can endure. This is a moment for saving what you can, not forcing ruin."

"Is that meant as a threat?"

"No, no. A man who predicts the storm is hardly threatening you with weather. I feel the climate of time, and I can only warn."

Khelagh, at a loss, again called attention to his beautiful grandchild, now being returned by Galt, opportunity for the one real piece of business involving Khelagh.

"She should continue to have a father." Dolvid explained the difference between men taken in the fight today, soldiers under orders, who would be treated well, sent home when prudent to do so, and private individuals such as Ghuradh and his friend Lavsila who chose to take up arms, arm others, against the *rabhsai*, and after today's proclaiming, could be condemned as traitors.

"That is inconceivable. You, *Bôdhrai*, could never allow it to happen."

He meant, to a former brother-in-law, and he might be right, though none of this family he had married into had spoken up for Dolvid at pronouncement of his exile. But the leaders of the collected private armies might never survive to their trial.

"They are going to get themselves killed, Khelagh, and there is nothing I can do about that. After we took the Residence today, I had to stop some of the officers from attacking the camp by East Gate." That was true; Dorrmas with blood in his mouth was hot for it. "They cannot last ten minutes against a few squadrons of regulars. Ghuradh is no fighter."

That established, he told Khelagh the camp must be disbanded, the men marched back to their respective estates by middle morning, or else the Household would attack. Khelagh, convinced he meant it, was dubious about how quickly the dispersing could be accomplished, when some of the men came from lands two days to the south and east. Dolvid, the approaching Kargul' squadrons in mind, was inflexible, till he hit on a minor improvement, and offered to enlist the two hundred best bows as auxiliaries at Kadon Dinul for the next few weeks.

He was not worried about buying treachery; most men in the private armies were of Other Race, and their bowmen would probably rather shoot at the cavalry of Kargul than at the Household.

Khelagh was again gathering to leave. "As for disbanding, I'll do what I can."

"Middle morning. I am sure this is within your powers, Khelagh." The sarcasm was intended: the irregular army would not exist if Khelagh had not called it into being.

Faëdhal toiled up the long hall grumbling about the stupidity of magistrates. "Firstborn is first born. If a will wants male inheritance only, it must say so, in those very words. Was that not Khelagh I saw, with his grand-daughter? He appeared less than happy, if I may so phrase it."

Siege

Always in the past she had loved Kreshavu. For start had been three days, unflawed, with Sebhal, in early days when he was her god, and his wanting of her had an urgency on the edge of anger to fill her with happy dread. Only later was it even thinkable to question whether he had ever shared her passion for justice, or she ever comprehended his yearning for sheer power; in the beginning they were two parts of a happiness.

Not all bodies though bodies were in everything; Kreshavu was for walks, buying food from strange-spoken townspeople with their friendly faces, dabbling feet (the Captain of the West did not do that) in clear, icy rills, for admiring looks from Sebhal's officers, which then seemed freely given.

What is first can only happen once, and yet at least one other big happiness (and sadness) belonged to Kreshavu. Now Dolvid had signed his note with love and ridden away without her, as he said he would: they would meet again, he wrote. And the town was a war-camp; the dust of its streets and dust rising from the busy road below was veiling the trees with a ghostly dull, hanging yellow in yellow light of lamps. Âna soon tired of noise and confusion and the rudeness they bred, and went back to the hostelry. There she was hailed by drinking soldiers who mistook her calling (or mistook her for having one, she amended). The hostel-keeper was soon there, brandishing horrid threats about the *Bôdhrai* and Rodlakh *Deghi*, and having left the men chastened caught her on the stairs to offer abject apology. Taking advantage of his embarrassment she made him find enough hot water for her to have a deep, lukewarm bath. After light food she slept through unsoundly till dawn.

In dull morning her mind was made up, not easily but with no doubting afterthoughts. If she rode on to Kamsilat Saidhan would be affable, she and Aëlu circle each other with only what they could not speak about in common; there would be nothing for her to do. Banakit had its vale and some paved streets as well as a carved stone horse-trough she admired, but busy with the needs of war would only be a larger, louder Kreshavu, and Kreshavu was intolerable. Drin Navuna would also be comfortless, but that mattered less in a place built for war, and once she reached the Frontier she would have no need for anxiety over what was happening there, no two or three or four-day lag between event and news. Rodlakh, with practically his last word, had forbidden her to be there in this dangerous time. That could be fought about when he came back from the Mines, as by Hrafi's good grace he surely would. *Mankh'* talk.

Except for soldiers everyone was moving eastward, but no one questioned her right to ride west. She met farm women and their children trudging for Kreshavu, drawing aside in narrow sections to let the horses pass. Packs, and the occasional pack-animal, were loaded to capacity, and among food, clothing and other most necessary things they all seemed to make space for household articles of little use or none, not valuable, but treasured for beauty, familiarity, happy associations — woven picture-mats, brass incense-burners, small figures of carved wood or wrought metal, the little clustered shapes of tinted glass some of the Froghul hung in windows to catch morning or evening light. Yet these were a sign of hope, and a bony-faced wife who warned Âna against riding west talked about the *jinzal* as one with storms, floods, drought, a natural terror to be endured; the families would survive while their menfolk conquered. Âna knew better the realities of this particular fight against *jinzal*, but felt comforted by the simpler view, and all day she saw resignation but never dismay in the face of refugees; some were boisterously cheerful.
She ate food in the saddle. Very near the spot where she had asked, pretended to ask Dolvid for advice and been told to do what made her *happy*, she overhauled a long file of slow-moving soldiery, mainly new levies. Spurring past in this part where there

was room, when she had passed about twenty men she came to one she knew, a regular, one of Sebhal's squadron who had been in her escort under Edarron. He told her the new *kímukan* was up ahead, but as the way steepened and narrowed it took her a precarious hour to come up to Edarron at the head of his hundred. To her he looked tired.

"Hail, warrior," she called out. He laughed, but his chest swelled.

"It will be a good *kímuko*," earnestly. "Not the Household for looks, but every man here has fought before. They'll fight. I understood you were to stay with the *Bôdhrai*."

"He is here in my saddlebag — " Kamin-Tolagh's joke, but usable.

"Then that could not have been him we met on the Banakit road, hammering eastward? You won't have much company at the Drin, madam — the women are all leaving."

"I shall be with the *rabhsai*."

It took Edarron a moment to put *rabhsai* together with *Rodlakh* and then he said it was the best news for the realm since Banak came to power, meaning, no doubt, Rodlakh's accession, not her pairing with him; in the interim his face could express an opinion he would not dare to in words, and she saw his view of her and could not comfort him. Where was consolation for Edarron in saying she would not have agreed to bed with him, even if his rivals had not outranked him? But she would want him to know, wanted to be sure for her own sake, she had not taken the men she had because they were Captain of the West, *Bôdhrai*, *rabhsai*. No need to agonize; all Edarron wanted was diversion and a boastable conquest, and some of that, anyway, he could find elsewhere.

Coming down to the gorge and its long causeway she felt the tingle of excitement or fear. Both far off and nearer signal trumpets were sounding. Where the plain was visible detachments of cavalry were on the move. The Drin prevented any massed incursion, but in all its centuries had never been able to seal off the whole Frontier; watchtowers guarded some lesser ways over the rim of Landegh, but there had always been a need for hard-riding patrols to deal with enemy who, singly or in small groups, found feasible climbs past main lines of defense. Such sweeps were a principal use of *pefrai*-mounted cavalry at the Drin.

An officer by the gate at the far end of the tunnel advised Edarron to keep his men closed up; there were *jinzal* loose on the plain, deadly for stragglers. Edarron stood in his stirrups in the rough, flattened space, trying to scan what he could of the ground between here and the Drin, while his long column trickled through the tunnel, forming close-ordered fours as they emerged. He licked his lips. "It's not like the old squadron. We've never fought all together."

Among the men scant news was circulating: Captain Nolimas and the *rabhsai* had both ridden out to relieve the Mines, and the Drin was now under the command of Wanildhai — they repeated the name, as if it could be a talisman.

At last in fours the column started for the Drin, watching on all sides. Soon, away to the right, there was a curved bare rib of hills where a file of regular lancers was going at a walk, helms and breastplates dazzling in westering sun. Like Edarron, their leader rose often in the stirrups to look all around, and when he suddenly fell the first impulse was to laugh at his clumsiness. Realization there was another reason came swiftly; farther back in the file a *pefrai* went down on his front knees, and now Âna could see arrows flying.

For the first time she saw *jinzal*. They were partly concealed by a fold of the ground, yet their heads were so high it seemed they must be mounted, except for the bobbing, plunging movement she had so often heard described and seen imitated, a *jinzai* at the run, powerful and tireless. Hunched shoulders were iron-muscled; under plain round helms the muzzle-like thrust of lower face where the long, tearing teeth were. They were carrying pikes or heavy spears, and from somewhere near their archers kept up the shooting.

Fighting their horses, formation gone, the lancers had left the spine of the ridge, turning to meet the attack. Big legs pumping the *jinzal* came on the skyline, and she heard the gasp of Edarron, as he saw the whole bulk of them, the crushing power they conveyed. He had seen *jinzal* before, but the numbers and their cohesion had rattled him. There were a dozen or fifteen in sight, and as many must be down in the hollow, to judge by the arrows that kept coming. One stray hit a running *jinzai*; it staggered but never broke stride and ran on with the shaft stuck high in the slope of its back.

Edarron seemed tranced. Âna, circling, begged for the sword of a mounted archer over-armed with knives and a brass-ended club, and, mouth gaping, he passed it across. "Are we going to sit by and watch our friends slaughtered?" furiously, and Edarron leaned in the direction of the fight, an order clogged in his throat.

On her *pefrai*, the same lean and splendid beast she had ridden out of Kamsilat, Âna started down the road-embankment by herself. Over on the ridge battle was closing, and the diminished cavalry jinked frantically to stay at weapon's length, to prevent tearing teeth from reaching them. The nearest duel was not a quarter-mile away.

"Âna — " Edarron, uncertainly, starting after her, still not committing himself.

"*Rodlakh!*" she shouted, but in anger, a curse for Edarron's reluctance. Beyond understanding, the muddle of fear, rage, desperation and impotence she felt, as she kicked her horse into a trot. She had gone twenty paces, twenty-five, when Edarron gave a roar, and only the action that went with it made his order intelligible; he spurred after her, and behind, in no order, the *kímuko* fanned out, *pefral* with the lances going quickly to the fore, the archers unslinging their bows.

Light on a horse bred to carry a fully armed and armored nineteen-span man, Âna heard thunder behind, and cooling a little let Edarron come up to her. Ahead the battle had broken into little fights, what remained of the original dozen lancers now hopelessly overmatched. An unhorsed man went down under two charging monsters, a third, the essence of nightmare, still coming on after getting a sword under the breastplate.

Edarron asserted control over his disordered company in the only sensible way; "As you will," bawled over his shoulder, never contemplating a charge in formation.

She was now among *jinzal*; being sane she was terrified, and did not know what she had come for. A rounded back was near her, its owner trying to snatch the lance from a mounted man. She aimed an awkward cut at the bunched neck, feeling that impact jar her arm, as the head turned, snarling. It passed, and she emerged on the crest of the ridge, where arrows were in the air.

Thorny backslopes fell to a small pond, and on the near side of muddy water about a dozen *jinzal* archers were under command of two horsemen as in the tale Âna had heard repeated, men in gleaming blue-green cloaks, fat late-summer flies on carrion. Strange the archers had not been sent charging into the fight now there were no clear targets; they were quick to fit an arrow and had good range, but their aim was unsure. Ducking away she wheeled hard left and came down from the crest, skirting confused fighting.

To say the creatures had been surprised by the new arrival would overrate the *jinzai* mind; in a sense everything surprised them, and their reactions made up for the lack of foresight or memory, cumbersome bodies swivelling with amazing speed, teeth snapping. One already tangled with two of the original file received a lance in its side, and could yet reach to break off the weapon. As the *pefrai* came near riding him down the creature reached up a hand to tear at the horse's hindquarters, and it was the following rider that finally felled the brute, using a crude smash of his sword.

The mounted archers as they came into the fight had no need to be instructed, circling the fringes, picking their targets. Some went to the crest and duelled with the *jinzal* archers below, shooting faster and straighter, quickly felling the cloaked horsemen, who had imagined they were out of range. Lanceless, sword red, a rider emerged from the fighting and cantered straight at Âna, waving madly as if to drive her away. Edarron, and after a glare he yanked his reins and hastened back to join in hacking down a wounded *jinzai* wrestling with three other soldiers, two unhorsed.

The fight, at a cost, would be won. Âna decided she had never been made for cavalry-actions, and enjoyed *jinzal* even less. Distaste for the whole gory mess reached its climax when with all fights done the cavalry made groups of four, three to remain with lances poised, while the fourth dismounted to hack at fallen *jinzal*, blood and flesh flying, till death was certain. A cold and brutal business, but far from wantonly bloodthirsty, as she saw when a terribly wounded *jinzai* could still close a vast hand over the ankle of the man trying to finish him off, and, having toppled him, raise its bloody bulk enough to fall on the man. The three lancers drove their points again and again into the humped back, at last bringing the creature down.

As he reformed some of his *kímuko* on the road, Edarron remained annoyed with her, and in his complaint all women were condemned. Her job, his Gabhani side insisted, was to bind the wounds and weep for the dead, certainly not to commit his men to battle. Blood gone cold, she would not have disputed the question.

He kept left shoulder pointed at her as he rode to report in at the Drin with only a small escort, leaving the rest to finish here; besides the *jinzal* there were their own dead and wounded to be seen to. It was the straight stretch rising to the crossways before Edarron said anything. "I did not expect to have to fight so soon. What a way to blood a new company."

She almost called it a victory, but it did not feel like one. If there were many bands of *jinzal* this size, some larger, how often would it be possible to meet them with six-to-one odds?

They stayed wordless on the brown plain no longer kept safe by the strength of the Drin. At last, greeted by trumpets under the hard walls, Edarron said, "I should not have doubted my men. You set a sharp spur."

Her smile felt thin. She was toughening since south of Shemugrân, when the sight of blood spurting made her retch helplessly. "I was a fool. I do not have the shoulders for fighting on horseback. Or the stomach." She had almost said, thighs, but knew Edarron would turn that into provocation.

"So. Nothing wrong with your heart."

Wanildhai had held every rank in the Army of the West except its Captain, carrying a lance in the reign of Banak-rai, and becoming part of the very beginnings of the special cavalry mounted on hill-horses, when he had been praised for his skill in training tribal men. He was in his forty-fourth year of service. He and Âna knew each other by sight, and she believed he vaguely approved of her, hardly certain she was a woman.

He had singular personal habits for an Owani, or for anyone, blowing his nose one nostril after the other into his hand, which he would then wipe on a towel kept by him for the purpose, an unimaginable horror by the end of the day. He scratched his behind or his privates without detectable embarrassment. Besides his maddening and probably painful piles, years of camp-food and eating in the saddle had made a windy ruin of his digestion, and he would often belch or fart loudly (and occasionally both at once), muttering *Come, now*, or *Wake the stinking dead*, as if to rebuke his offending guts.

He was said to be a good soldier; Sebhal had respected him as one of the few Owanil cavalrymen who understood the value of archery. When Âna arrived he addressed the ceiling, "At Kadon Dinul, they say — or so they say they say, I have not been there since Lambarr's day — they claim your Frontier fighter's no good behind walls, and all because some Froghu' auxiliaries, two hundred years ago, rushed from behind earthworks to grapple the enemy. I am worn out telling lamp-oil Larghais this is an army can do anything, anything. Front of the gate we're building the best heap of dead since *Konúrai*, and hasn't cost a scratch. Curse'em, we'll show you fighting behind walls."

Âna ducked as the whole Drin shook to a booming crash. "They do have some machines," absently, "for knocking at the door." Another shuddering impact came; *zhin'pefral*, she learned, were hurling huge boulders at walls and gate. Though strong the outer gate was already weakened, and there was little doubt more artillery pieces would come into the siege as soon as they could be set up.

Warned to stay off the ramparts Âna made her way through dim corridors, tunnels cut in stone, seeking a way to the first gallery. Where there was a sudden lighter space, a crossing of passages, she saw Edarron again. "Where are you to be sleeping?" abruptly.

He of course knew Rodlakh was absent, and also that he would be going out on patrols behind the Drin, and if occasion came, sorties in front. Not casually, he remarked his chances of survival were slight, that he had wanted to share a bed with her ever since sight of her, when she came to the door of her uncle's house wearing only a loose dressing-robe over her shift — how she was clad more than a year ago seemed to give him an especially good claim.

If she had felt any attraction there might have been an innocent charm in his arguments, though not in the last, when he told her she would be sorry for what she had missed when he was killed. There were two senses for this, and unfortunately he intended both.

Hot-faced, disliking the harried feeling, she at last broke away, and if she had not given him a plain *no* it was his fault for making it matter so much.

In the gallery archers sat commanding the gate at slits cunningly made, so angled that two or three bows could use the embrasure, though it would take a master-bowman to put an arrow through the slit from outside.

The Drin here faced not west but south of that. All prospects on Landegh were bony desolation, bare hills and rocky plains, cruel ridges enclosing tortuous folds of ground, wind-weathered cliffs, steel-hard shoulders thrusting up through parched plains. Where the Drin was placed all the higher ground tended down towards the gorge, where the road made its brave beginning on the hard journey for Shâl Mines.

Here were the many *jinzal* dead Wanildhai had promised, most evidently killed by multiple arrows in headlong charge against the outer gate, entrance to the courtyard, where a high front wall ran from rock to rock, the natural foundations of the Drin. To attack the gate it was necessary to enter a shallow bay of the fortress, with archers above and on either flank, and if an entrance were to be forced — and the gate's battered condition suggested that — there was another and far stronger gate in the front of the main fortress. Into that courtyard arrows and missiles of every kind could be rained down from all sides.

The assaults had come just after dawn, and now the *jinzal* were being held back, shooting mainly harmless arrows and setting up their artillery. Only two *zhin'pefral* could be seen, but there were others, including one that could throw rocks very high a tremendous distance; it was this that was doggedly hammering away at the upper works, the reason the ramparts were unsafe. The machines must need *jinzai* strength to work; the large stones came arching over as if lazily, and seemed to take long coming down to crash against walls or gate.

"Flyspecks," a junior officer nearby said. "Don't they know these walls have stood a thousand years?"

An underestimate for the lower courses, joined to the living rock in exact setting of immense blocks with no mortar used. Rebuilt portions higher could be damaged by sustained battering, and the air on upper levels was already thick with dust, but the defenders were confident of no collapse, and apart from the outer gate a year of pounding could not make a breach. Some, eager to resume the killing, actually looked forward to when the gate went and *jinzal* crowded in through the narrow gap. Others, gloomier, predicted if *jinzal* continued to work their way past the Drin and into the plain the cavalry could not hunt them all down, and the Drin would be cut off from supply. Drin Navuna had been besieged in the distant past, never taken, but whether artillery could pound a way in would in the end make little difference to men without food, or drink, or arrows to shoot. Âna had a haunting fear she did not tell anyone, that this was the year when everything changed; on the Island that other impregnable fortress had fallen.

No attack came through long night. When morning arrived no *jinzal* were seen except the distant ones working the two catapults, but the heavy battering resumed and redoubled. Though *jinzal* notoriously were panicked by flame, at mid-morning outlying farm-buildings on the plain behind the Drin were burning unchecked, and Âna supposed the shiny-cloaked men, the *jinzai*-masters, had brought the fire. Edarron was on patrol-duty on the plain, and she saw him when he came in for a short respite and shoeing of his horse.

"We can't hold any territory — too many places to conceal enemy, and too many of them here. They are going to wear us down, man by man."

After this talk Âna went to see Wanildhai. Impossible to have a discussion with his absent air, so she threw out her idea, better to cede everything to the enemy between Drin and causeway, except the smaller circle of buildings around the crossroads, and the road itself when anything had to use it. Whether or not she had influence, the attempt to fight *jinzal* everywhere in the plain was abandoned, and there were fewer casualties to count, though there would be losses while the road had to be used, and the *jinzal* gathered and charged, fierce and always hard to kill. Wanildhai sent word reinforcements coming up from eastward — replacements, as they were becoming — should be held at the barracks and stables of the Gorge, where they were safe, secure in their supplies, and intact, ready to join a counter-attack when opportunity came.

"Give up the Drin?" Wanildhai challenged the table in front of him. "I would, and hold the Gorge, if we did not have a gate to keep open." He gave a loud belch. There was no word from down the Shâl Mines road, and looking out on the *jinzai*-infested country her eyes filled with despairing tears; how could the four hundred who had ridden out survive with no walls to guard them?

Later that day *jinzal* managed to drag to heights south and a little east of the Drin a pair of *zhin'pefral*. After allowing one attempt by volunteers to dislodge them, costly in lives, Wanildhai would not authorize further attacks, although the weapons could reach the road between the crossways and the Drin, and the open space where the cavalry normally mustered. Stones soon crashed through the roof of the commander's residence and into the terrace of Rodlakh's acclaiming; these were probably stray shots, and there was no systematic attempt to destroy that or other buildings within range. The men directing the *jinzal*, plainly to be seen up on the skyline, looked instead for gatherings of troops or convoys of wagons under escort, and some damage was done.

Meanwhile at the front of the Drin the stoning went on, and so many big rocks were littering the space before the walls a soldier joked the *jinzal* were going to build a hill so they could climb on the roof. The courtyard gate was hanging precariously, but no charge came, and only the strongest archers could hunt for targets where the artillery was. One more day was endured.

On her third morning she woke to a new sound, a booming with a clang and a clatter in it. She lay a while in her bunk, in the quarters normally set aside for married officers, and the noise that had wakened her came again, heavy and echoing. She had slept clothed, and pulling on her boots and an outshirt, taking a fistful of oats and raisins to chew, made her way to the second gallery, over the entrance. Wanildhai was there already with other officers, and as the sound came again, here clang rather than boom, he sucked at his bad teeth, and said the traders had spoken about this.

Inside the southward loop of the Mines road was a long, solid slope of bare, coarse-grained rock, a single huge slab, beetled over by a rock generations of troops had called Gazhil-Face, not knowing they were keeping an ancient impiety alive: long ago, because of the pouch-eyed look of some wrinklings high on the rock, someone had fancied a resemblance to the then-Patriarch; the name was a faulty memory of *g'Asalladh's-Face*.

Beneath this bulge of rock the *jinzal* in the night had set up new engines of war, three of them, mounted like *zhin'pefral* on heavy wooden frames, but with long beams set crosswise, so they somewhat resembled an enormous bow held horizontally.

That was their function. Between the pair of crossbeams there was a deep notch, aligned with a forked support like a cut-off prop for a clothesline, up near the front of the frame. As Âna watched *jinzal* labored at turning a ratcheted wheel at the side, taking up a twisted rope, in turn bending back the crossbeams, slices from a young tree bolted together six thick. When the wheel could not be turned any farther, beams straining, a wedge was knocked into the teeth of the wheel to hold it. Three *jinzal* were needed to lay a heavy bar across the notch, tucking it into a kind of cup, probably leather, at the center of the stretched rope. The bar was not the shape of an arrow, but thickened at the tip to a blunt nose, making it resemble a slender stalk of asparagus, though other, bawdier suggestions were heard. This thicker head was what rested on the forked support at the front.

The elaborate preparations did not go on unimpeded, but the distance was at least two hundred paces, and the *jinzal* were in part shielded by a short, slatted roof attached to upright braces of the frame. When one of the creatures was struck down by an arrow (or, more usually, by several), the others, oblivious, went on working, but most arrows went quivering into the overhead shield, or stuck in the frame proper. There had been talk of fire-arrows, Âna recalled.

A hammer was whirled around and down, the wedge went flying, crossbeams sprang straight, and the projectile went flat and true through the gap where the courtyard gate had now been flattened, to strike the inner entrance to the Drin proper. A second of the machines was ready, and another of the blunt missiles came flying. This had been set askew, or else the launching was wrong; the bar struck the ground well short, and went clanging end over end, bounding to hit the walls, its force still impressive. After a next shot had sailed true to hit the gate, word came up it would not withstand many such blows.

All the best archers looked for stations to give them shots against this new threat, and there were hits to *jinzal* working them, so many that their masters had the most advanced pulled back thirty paces or so. Loud jeering went up from the Drin, but the great stones shot by the *zhin'pefral* were coming thick, making the ramparts unsafe. *Jinzal* archers were also shooting, some driven into the open by their masters.

"To draw darts," Wanildhai concluded, and gave the order to ignore these easier targets so long as the great iron-arrowed bows were manned. These, obviously, were hard orders to obey, as a bowman of the Drin saw his tenth arrow thud ineffectually into the shielding roof, with open targets a hundred paces nearer.

In the gully down to the left of the long rock-slope helms could be seen massing, *jinzal* being readied for a charge against the inner gate, or so everyone assumed.

The sun was high when these began to move forward, emerging up onto the Mines road. Control over the beasts was far from perfect, and out of bowshot the bright-cloaked riders could be seen making extravagant use of whips and sharp prods to assemble the companies, while the hoarse hooting of their short trumpets was continuous. The leading *jinzal* leaned into their lumbering trot, and with them they had massive logs with metal caps for battering at the weakened gate.

Breath snagged in her throat; *jinza'dazhai*, the celebrated terror. But this was new; she was among the first to see *jinzal* moving in a mass nothing could halt or turn aside. Long teeth were flashing, bunched legs working, while in the Drin officers used soothing but tremulous voices to persuade their archers to wait.

The charge reached the flattened courtyard gate, and as they jammed in the bows of the Drin twanged in chorus, shooting intense and accurate. Some of the rams were dropped, some felled *jinzal* were at once trampled down by their brothers; wounded, dying and unscathed some came on, and in the gate-towers men could hurl down rocks and burning lumps of tallow. In learning war *jinzal* had not lost their loathing for fire, and a

strange high-pitched whimpering greeted the flames. Some
blazing fat stuck on the forearm of one, and his squealing, as he
whirled in absolute panic, was horrible to hear, though some
defenders were greatly entertained.

One party of *jinzal*, while suffering losses, was intent only on
dragging away some of the iron shafts that had been shot against
the gate. In the courtyard the attack was clearly ebbing, and it
appeared that rather than the grand assault this had been partly to
test the defenses, but mainly with the object of retrieving the
projectiles. The cost was thirty to forty *jinzal* killed or cripplingly
wounded, a reckless kind of captaincy but not cheering, since it
suggested forces large enough to survive such waste.

While the creatures who could made their retreat in
obedience to new trumpet calls, and an archer on an upper level
was boasting he had shot one of the cloaked horsemen, a small
postern by the main gate was quietly opened. Âna was filled with
agonized admiration for men who would go out on foot to finish
off wounded *jinzal*. After sitting cooped, they went about their
job with deadly enthusiasm, and the enemy was sluggish in
response. A warning yell rose from the Drin as some twenty
jinzal climbed to the road and came at the charge. Those in the
sortie made retreat, and their comrades at the archery-slits covered
them with accurate bows. Leading *jinzal* fell and stumbled, the
killing-party regained the Drin and the postern-gate clanged shut.
Enemy trumpets recalled some dozen *jinzal*. It began a breathing-
space.

Behind, also, a lull came, and a fresh supply of new-made
arrows was convoyed across from the Gorge. Soon, however,
iron shafts were coming again. Now, the defenders when they
could, made quick sorties to carry these inside after they had spent
their force against or near the gate. But the ordinary *zhin'pefral*
were in the middle of inexhaustible supplies of the stones they
needed, and their duller crashing was constant.

As Wanildhai had forecast, the main gate could not withstand
the next determined assault. Beyond it was the long near-tunnel
through the heart of the Drin, hung at each end with a heavy
forged portcullis, and he had the first raised. When the gate was

battered down the defenders waited till fifteen to twenty *jinzal* were inside before dropping the portcullis behind them. Ironbound oaken doors into the Drin held, while archers systematically shot down the creatures.

Between portcullis and wrecked gate was where fighting was most desperate of all. The door to the stables was broken in, and horses whinnied terror while men on foot with pikes and lances struggled to hold back the oncoming enemy. Sore-fingered bowmen kept shooting, and when all enemy between the two drop-gates were dead, both portcullises were raised long enough for the squadron of cavalry assembled behind the Drin to charge into the fight, driving through the main gate and all the way to the courtyard entrance. Holding back any reinforcements, the enemy brought artillery and their bows back into the fight; the cavalry of the West was obliged to retire after losses, but their object was accomplished. Even while men and *jinzal* struggled and died in the enclosure of the courtyard, some men from the Drin were propping the main gates in place, using blocks of stone and massive timbers to restore a barrier.

The sun went down and as darkness came, swiftly as it did here, the fighting stilled. To a wonder no one would admit, the defenses had held, but Edarron said they would come again by night, when they could get close without loss; the bows so far had blunted every attack before it reached the Drin.

In the courtyard two giant fires were piled, and by that light and lanterns the battered gate was strengthened. It would have to be broken down from the inside if the retreat from the Mines came and was hard-pressed. Wanildhai said he was reducing further the cavalry actions behind the Drin, hoarding the lances and mounted bows for a sortie in strength when Rodlakh came.

If he came. She lay sleepless through a night with no renewal of fighting and forced herself to admit the *if* could no longer be resisted. The *jinzal* were limitless, and even stone and steel were not strong enough to stop them. She began to weep, and if too soon for Rodlakh and his companions, there were plenty of dead and wounded to grieve over here at the Drin.

In the morning she began what Edarron would have called proper women's work, tending the hurt, bringing food to those unable to feed themselves. In the large airy room that gave on the central courtyard, she thus missed what there was to see of Wanildhai's most daring counter-move: lancers and bows quietly led their mounts by difficult paths well north of the Drin, and came down, Wanildhai personally at their head, to smash at the flank of *jinzal* companies being assembled for the next assault on the gate. Quickly retreating, the cavalry drew away large numbers of enemy in pursuit, and then from the Drin men on foot emerged, bowmen and pikes, many carrying blazing torches. They assailed the siege-weapons, fighting around them with the *jinzal* and setting fires, the nearer of which archers on the ramparts could feed with balls of tallow stuck on their arrows.

When Âna, hearing the din, came to her usual spot for watching, the foot had been recalled and bows of the Drin were turned on *jinzal* coming in pursuit of scurrying men.

On the rock-slope mounted men in their blue-green cloaks were using their whips savagely trying to make *jinzal* face and fight fire. A cheer rose from the Drin when one maddened brute caught at a whip and pulled the man from his saddle, going for his throat with teeth. The end of that was lost to view when many *jinzal* crowded in, though not, as was hoped, to join the lethal mutiny. A new group of *jinzal*, better-trained or more disciplined, began beating at the fires with uncured hides, but someone from the Drin must have doused the largest of the *zhin'pefral* with lamp-oil and the flames leapt up fiercer.

Close-pressed, the remnant of retreating men regained the Drin, and Âna turned away. The sortie must at least have delayed the next assault, but many good men had been lost; they could not afford these victories.

When Wanildhai rode back, unscathed from his part in the thick of the cavalry action, he was of the same mind; this would be the last gesture, and now they would sit still and kill *jinzal*. A motto, ready-made to become watchword for the siege.

When she went back to where the wounded were brought, business was brisk, and she was dismayed to see Edarron in fierce

pain from a gaping spear-wound in his side. He had lost a great
deal of blood, and was hovering in and out of coma, but when she
was wiping his face he gave a feeble sign he knew who she was.
When next his eyes came clear he nearly smiled, and sounded
between his teeth something about dying with no one but week-
wives to tend him.

With every consideration given to pain and his sinking state
that sourly annoyed Âna. True, most women now assisting with
the wounded had been caught in the siege after staying to ply their
trade, and some were managing both, which gave them little
sleep. That seemed if anything praiseworthy; surely the stiffest-
necked Gabhani who ever gave such a woman his week's wages
then called her vile names ought to be glad week-wives could turn
to nursing, not offended the hurt were tended by whores. They
were for the most part conscientious and careful, with none of her
squeamishness at touching or disturbing wounds, and they were
surely warmer than the few women no longer young who took
care of the sick in less bloody times, and did not see friendliness
as any part of their healing.

It seemed the lives spent in the sortie had purchased a long
respite. Back with the wounded she heard a file-leader telling his
neighbor, "We've hurt them, given them more fight than they were
looking for. Who would take on the Army of the West, for
choice?"

"But they're not human, these. And where's Captain
Nolimas, where's the *rabhsai*, then, with best part of our best
horse, tell me that."

Âna wished she could be convinced there was no difference
between the steady loathing she had for this work of cleaning and
binding and wiping up, and what a soldier felt before he faced the
enemy. The bodies were either young, and their spoiling filled her
with a sick fury, or else old, wounds adding to the misery she felt
for the ugliness of time's more gradual ruin. As she tried to say
comforting words to men in pain, frightened by pain and the
glimpse of their own fragility, her mind was mostly elsewhere
altogether, with Rodlakh, or with Dolvid on his equally hopeless

mission — and then she would think of Burantal, or the night-ride to Kreshavu.

When she was attentive she started to recognize her deep resentment at being the one to have to do these things, and she could quickly feel hatred for the wounded, not only for being disgusting, but for having found an unfair way to claim her sympathy or pity.

In charge here was Pirron, a lean-faced Mixed; he and an old Froghu' well-woman with some healing skill were the only ones Âna had any talk with. There were some lads who had stayed on to fetch and carry, merging into one pinch-faced, openmouthed boy whose answer to any request or order was "What?" The lesser healers who gathered by the door to gossip and had little to do with their week-wife auxiliaries were worse than anything; perhaps they dwelt in such detail on the most horrible wounds in hopes of hearing ideas for treatment, and perhaps their obsession with the young and the handsome whose looks or limbs or manhood would never be the same was their way of expressing horror (certainly what they believed), but it all sounded like only slightly masked relish, and she went by their conferences with her head down, vowing she would not come back.

Her returning was an act of defiance. She did not think it was her duty, nor that she owed the service; she was sure she had no aptitude. Hers was a cat's perverse determination, and she wondered whether, in their hearts, cats were more abjectly compliant than the most fawning of dogs, knew it, and despised it, arching their backs against their own obedience, just as she defied her revulsion.

There were no new attacks, only a desultory stoning of the Drin, as afternoon moved into evening. An idea going the rounds was that most of the *jinzal* trained to work the siege-engines had been put out of action; true the full force of the artillery did not resume, but from the upper galleries it could be seen two of the *zhin'pefral* were burnt beyond repair, as was one of the other machines. For those, too, there seemed to be a shortage of iron shafts, now the enemy were no longer being allowed to reclaim them.

Behind the Drin as the sun slanted down a supply-train on its way was attacked by a sudden band of charging *jinzal*. Its force overturned one of the low, small-wheeled wagons peculiar to this country, but the convoy was well-escorted, and Wanildhai sent out a squadron from the Drin. The cavalry was learning how to use speed and numbers against an enemy that neither fought nor retreated as men would.

The rest of the wagons and pack-animals came safely to the rear court, where one cart was struck but only a little damaged by a stone from a *zhin'pefrai* on the heights. The fortress had received food, dispatches, arrows, and some forty men to fill losses.

"Men ought to be going out," Wanildhai explained to an oil-lamp, while Âna stood near. "Not coming in to share our hunger, if that's the worst of it. Five days, and no word — tide turned, mouse had drowned, is that it?"

The proverb here was sinister. "Many leaving the Mines would be on foot."

"Oh, aye. We may be winning." He tilted in his seat to break wind on a skeptical note.

She suggested it would save rations if some of the wounded fit to be moved were sent back with the wagons. Wanildhai readily endorsed that, and going down to help choose, Âna discovered Edarron would not be one of them; he had lapsed into a far deeper unconsciousness, his breathing slight.

She sat beside his mattress, and heard herself silently promise she would spend a night with him if only he would get well; it was as if he had gone to the brink of death to make her feel guilty about refusing him. She thrust that away, and went to see about others who could safely be moved. When she came back with fresh water for Edarron, he was dead.

She stared into the courtyard where a long-stemmed tree reached for the light, having shaded to death generations of its own lower branches. Unfair to be accused by the dead, because no defense had any effect. But life could not be guided by guesses about how long anyone had to live: that might have been part of what took her to Rodlakh's bed, but Rodlakh was a friend. She had no more chances to make Edarron see that difference; wasteful to keep trying out in her head other ways of saying it.

A night-attack was launched, with harsh blasts of blunt trumpets, and pounding of rams. Behind the Drin, as not till now, *jinzal* were where the roads crossed, and their masters brought blazing brands. The commander's residence would not catch fire, but a number of houses and shops went up in spouts of fierce flame, while Wanildhai watched glumly and declined to release a sortie in the dark, even if to save their own homes. Instead, archers crouched waiting for flames to show them targets to shoot at.

They had that at the front gate, fitfully lighted by torches burning in brackets along the walls, enemy crammed into the space in front of the restored gates. These were breached again, and there was confused close-quarter fighting, undecided when the trumpets began sounding on one repeated note, signal for retreat. Fighting broke off, not to be renewed that night.

She was wakened before light. Wanildhai, acting as his own lantern-bearer, was in the low doorway. She sat up, confused about what day it might be.

"News. From the *rabhsai*."

It took hold slowly. "From Rodlakh, Rodlakh *Deghi*?"

"A man slipped in by darkness — nothing in writing. The *rabhsai*'s forces are holding together after battle and loss, bringing back folk from Shâl Mines. Here tomorrow, or they should be. The *rabhsai* is not unhurt."

Muttering he had many plans to make and orders to explain he started to shuffle away. Âna grabbed at him.

Once Wanildhai had told her Rodlakh's injuries, as far as he knew, were not grave, she was able to see how kind he had been to bring her the news. She had no clue whether he heard her thanks.

Light came and there was a change. The faces of the archers as they sat at their slits were lightened by anticipation, though no one knew quite what to look for, whether the *rabhsai*'s column, terribly mauled, was riding here to its destruction, or was strong enough to scatter the besiegers and re-enter the Drin in triumph. In any event there would be something other than shooting arrows till their fingertips bled, waiting for the enemy to batter down the walls. So far the artillery had not resumed.

One visible difference was that apparently under cover of the night attack the *jinzal* had carried or dragged away many dead, of which most were their own kind. The explanation passed from man to man in a revulsed murmur, "Short of food."

Near her the same archer who had claimed shooting one of the horsemen commented, "If they had their way, they'd rather be breakfasting on you and me."

"Me, maybe," his neighbor said. "Not you."

A spell-breaker, greeted with an excess of laughter and almost at once a new catch-phrase for the siege, adaptable to many circumstances, *Not you!* — raucous joking that helped them not to dwell on comrades who had been killed or disabled outside the walls.

After the respite tempers were strained when the mainly invisible *zhin'pefral* resumed, aimed higher. After an hour a heavy section of uppermost ramparts cracked loose to go crashing down; it had been cleared of men long before, but to see the solid Drin begin to break was dismaying. One of the giant bows was shooting again, and its second shot opened the gap in the gate, inadequately patched after the night-attack. Since the *jinzal* would not again be trapped between the two portcullises, Wanildhai kept a squadron mounted in the tunnel, facing Landegh.

The expected assault did not come. No comfort; the main strength of *jinzal* had most likely been drawn off to attack the more exposed men under Rodlakh; except for those working the engines and a handful of archers none could be seen from the

Drin. She remarked pointedly to Wanildhai these were small forces to keep him huddled within, and a strong sortie now might clear a path for Rodlakh. He told the cloudy sky, "Take apples green, you will be worse off than hungry."

Back with the wounded, used to only the thudding of the *zhin'pefral* punctuating tense quiet, she heard cheering break out. Dropping a hunk of stale bread she had been gnawing, she ran back to her usual vantage-point, amid excited babble from the defenders.

Coming through a deep defile leftward Frontier archers were in murderous duel with those *jinzal* on the rock-slope beneath Gazhil-Face. Quite unexpectedly, Rodlakh came into view, urging his mount at the head of a long double-file of lances picking their way down onto the road, but turning away from the Drin. He was helmless and obviously wearied.

Now Wanildhai, not troubling with messengers, went down at the run to see the portcullis raised and battered gate thrown aside; some hundred horse went trotting out, while others were drawn up inside. At the same time fresh horse, largely levies, were crossing from the Gorge behind the Drin, and Ãna, seeing the workings of an elaborate plan, was hot with shame at having tried to goad Wanildhai.

Unfamiliar with the shape of Landegh outside her view from the Drin she understood not much of what happened that day, only that Rodlakh had invited ambush by the main *jinzai* force so he could come down behind them by way of a little-known defile, allowing Wanildhai to assail the rear of those left guarding the road. While these various actions were being fought the slow-moving, battered remnant from the Mines kept doggedly on, and its escort was able to delay new enemy bands coming up from the south and west, till Rodlakh could come to assist.

All she knew then was that after long, inscrutable quiet the wagons appeared on the road in mid-afternoon, and with women, children and wounded scrambled into the Drin, followed by detachment after detachment of troops, shielded by numerous

short charges and disentangling retreats by small, file-strength
bands of the cavalry. Men died at each fresh engagement, and
Rodlakh was in the thick of it all, untouchable, watching admirers
said, by any weapon, although Âna could see he was taking up the
reins shorter than his habit, leaning a little, as if in pain. She
wanted to scream at him he had done enough and more, and
ceased to breathe when he went out of her sight, or was turning
for a new counter-attack. He was one of the last to ride for
shelter, and archers on the walls, doing what they could to slow
pursuing *jinzal*, still managed to sound his name as he reached the
gates. Empty wagons were overturned to block the gap, and the
harsh trumpets again recalled the *jinzal*, which crouched away
under the bows of the Drin. Soon the artillery took up its
pounding again.

In the entrance-gallery the familiar face was slack with
overstrain; the wound, evidently from an arrow, was in his left
shoulder. Red-rimmed eyes stared without belief, and his words
of greeting were, "In the name of Hranakh, who told you to come
back here?"

"No one — " reaching out to steady him as he stiffly
dismounted and started a sway. "I came."

"That I see. I see that." Between fatigue and the vexation of
anxiety his teeth were chattering. "Why? Do you think the
fighters have not enough to worry them? When will you learn to
obey?"

Nearly blinded by her own quick anger she held clenched
hands straight by her sides till the spasm passed, then made deep
deference. "Your pardon, *Deghi*, I was wrong to come back.
After you have saved the realm you can see to my punishment.
Will he not rest now, and see his wounds tended?" She was
starting to weep.

Heavily Rodlakh put his arm across her shoulders, and they
walked together to the captain's quarters; Wanildhai, with them,
might be very slightly smiling.

Pirron, the gaunt healer came to examine Rodlakh's wound. The arrow had glanced from another man's breastplate, and not gone deep into the shoulder. It was sore and angry, largely from chafe of the shirt, but when Âna washed away the blackened blood there was no sign of festering. Pirron dabbed on some unguent, and left the binding to her.

"You have seen to the Captain Nolimas?" Rodlakh was muscled in the lamplight at day's end, but what chiefly struck Âna was how boyish he looked.

Pirron said he had done what he could, and twisted his mouth up as he did when deeply concerned. "His great strength gives us some hope, *Deghi*." Nolimas's wound, from a spear, was in the hollow of his right thigh, and he had been carried to the Drin on a wagon.

Unopened dispatches were handed to Rodlakh. Following conventions of wartime he went to the most recent first, and frowned over it. He tried the earlier dispatch, looking for an explanation. Dolvid, then, had sailed from Kamsilat, and could not possibly have slept four hours between the Frontier and the embarkation.

That was the straightforward part. To Wanildhai he regretted that the wounded and other slow-moving survivors from the Mines, having been looking forward to the Drin as their refuge, would have to continue their eastward journey before night fell. In that way they would not slow down the most vulnerable part of the main retreat, across to the Gorge and causeway, when the Drin was left undefended.

He expected more debate from Wanildhai, allowing it would be hard after their skilled withstanding of the siege, but now the full force of the *jinzal* would come against the weakened Drin, which no longer defended anything but itself, and would cost lives to keep supplied. The Gorge, with no real crossing except the long, narrow causeway, was as strong a position, or stronger, and its supply-line was safe.

Wanildhai readily acceded to a disposition Âna knew he had already proposed. "There, we can sit still and kill *jinzal*." He went off to issue new orders, leaving behind a soft ripple of farts.

Rodlakh sighed again, returning to the dispatches. Saidhan was or soon would be at Banakit. Dolvid had appointed Arvat to help with supplies, and Saidhan said it needed greater authority. "Doleni will be frantic with worry. Arvat must be at Kreshavu, and Dolvid — " he counted, thumb on fingers. "At Kadon Dinul, if it is going right."

Without warning Rodlakh plunged his face into cupped hands and sobbed bitterly. "I cannot... I cannot... " were the only intelligible words that emerged.

She went and closed the door to the small private work-room where they were. Rodlakh looked up with the haggard face often seen in a weary infant. "If I had been killed I could not send any more men to die."

Reaching for his hand, she used both hers to pick it up and press the back to her lips. She pushed hair up away from his face, and got a watery smile. Then he shook his head bleakly. "Tomorrow, to make space for the retreat, I shall have to order a sortie — how else is there to do it? I am sick, with sending men to their deaths. Nolimas is dying, and we have not yet counted how many did not come back. What chance has Dolvid, a friend? I cannot ask any more to die."

"You flatter yourself — " managing to be both stern and affectionate. "These men are not dying for you and your rule, and if you were gone it would not save lives. Here, they are fighting for their homes and their honor, the life of the Colony. Even the ones who have gone to Kadon Dinul are not risking their lives for you, but the justice you stand for." Her voice broke, and her grasp of Rodlakh's hand was to comfort her as much as him. "That is why you have to go on living."

"What men there are — " raising his head, mood abruptly altering. "What men in the Army of the West."

They had food in what had been Sebhal's quarters, and a fire was lighted, not so much for warmth as the pleasure of watching it. From time to time great stones came crashing against the outer walls, but did not spoil the reasonless feeling of safety Âna hugged. After writing a number of short dispatches Rodlakh wanted to dictate detailed accounts, his of the relief of Shâl Mines, hers of the siege here, in the form of a long letter for Dolvid, whether or not he would ever read it. Worth doing, he said, for its own sake, their gesture to history. Besides, fighting *jinzal* in the open field costly mistakes were made at the onset, and he wanted the tactics they had invented written down, so other forces of the realm taking up the fight would not have to learn the same lessons at the same unacceptable price.

He was going to bring in a scribe, but Âna, not wanting any intrusion, said she could do it, and did.

Storytelling was not among Rodlakh's primary skills; he tended to give general conclusions before recalling specific events: *We now know* jinzal, *even fighting in companies can be killed; what one man can control cannot be altogether indestructible to others. Their archery is far inferior to ours for accuracy.* The inadequate account of how the siege of Shâl Mines was broken Âna began to improve by asking questions, but then there was an interruption, an apologetic messenger, but a brave one who had volunteered to make the dash from the causeway all alone. The dispatch he had was from Banakit, and superscribed *With All Urgency.*

"Saidhan's hand," and she watched his face change as he broke the seal and read. A thumb to his teeth, he cursed softly, but after finishing the dispatch reread it carefully before saying anything.

"A new army of *jinzal* is heading for the Lunu Tezh' Gate from the south and west. They came over the hills at the borders of the Protectorate; it is wild country and we never dreamed a serious invasion could come that way."

The news had been brought by men escaping from the path of this second army, well-armed, and a large mass, certainly in the hundreds, possibly as many as a thousand. Saidhan had emphasized, *these are sober men bringing us this word, and the story cannot be doubted.*

"What could be more logical, now we see it? Force us to send every man westward to defend the Frontier, then cut the Colony in half behind them. If Banakit falls, we will be cut off, and Kamsilat virtually undefended."

She asked about the narrow passes that made up the Gate. Rodlakh said there were no forces near Banakit to do any better than slow an enemy. The same was true of the river; once an enemy came down into the Vale of Banakit the placid Navu there, with its low and level banks, could not stop them, though breaking the two minor bridges might delay them half a day. Boats or rafts could cross, and so could swimmers, new bridges could be made; impossible to defend the whole length of the left bank where Banakit stood.

Wanildhai, who had been summoned, knew those parts well, and agreed. The Gate would be a last chance to stop the enemy, if only troops could be sent there in time. "If that could be held a few days," he confided to the fireplace, "we could send cavalry, which won't be much use to us after we pull back to the Gorge."

Rodlakh had already decided they must send troops. "Saidhan on his own authority diverted some reinforcements meant for here, *if the* rabhsai *will pardon my taking this on myself,* he says, as if the most experienced soldier in Arbhal needed instructing."

"He has always been a stickler for due procedure, *Rabhsai*," Wanildhai, for once directly addressing a listener.

Rodlakh dreaded the *jinzai* army making for the Lunu Tezh' Gate might well be more powerful than the one besieging them here. "That is what I would do if I captained our enemies — send only sufficient force against Drin Navuna to make us rush all our men here, then strike for Banakit with the bulk of my army, giving me enough troops both to drive against Kamsilat and bottle up the Army of the West, simply by blocking Fifth Bridge."

"Or breaking it," Wanildhai supplied.

Rodlakh wanted every available lance sent eastward as soon as they evacuated the Drin, not waiting for slower riders; he would ride with them himself, leaving Wanildhai to manage the main retreat at the rearguard.

"The defense, that is, of the Gorge."

A very long silence, Rodlakh's face showing every shade of his hurt. "No," at last. He began to explain how they could not be sure of holding the Lunu Tezh' Gate even if the reinforcements arrived; there were too many ways through those hills. With Banakit sure to be lost the cavalry could fall back to defend the road to Kamsilat, but they would then be fighting on two widely separated fronts, with no hope of relieving or supplying Wanildhai, caught between two *jinzal* armies.

This clear exposition was hinting at a course so drastic it was hard for Âna to grasp, and even more so for Wanildhai, whose life had been defense of the western lands. Rodlakh had leapt to the conviction this was no war for territory, but only a duel of armies, one of which must be destroyed. He was proposing giving up, evacuating all the country west of Fourth Bridge, or even farther east, surrendering the strong defenses of the Gorge, Kreshavu and all the long road to Banakit, the wide Vale with all its farms and scattered dwellings, the towns, bridges, crops in the ground, so much that could never be saved or replaced. "It is a question of staying alive. The enemy wants to trap us, divide us, grind us down. Our only strategy is to be where we can do the most killing with the fewest of us being killed."

Wanildhai seemed stricken, but for Âna, Rodlakh might well have risen in a moment to greatness with his enormous daring, his ability to put aside so many instincts and emotions, the feelings of his men for their own lands.

"Vonni's Jaws," Wanildhai, suddenly, "we can hold them there till the sun goes cold."

"A place — " Rodlakh had been told the watchword for the siege, "for sitting still and killing *jinzal*."

He hoped relief would come in the end from the Mainland, and with their backs to a seaport they could never be entirely surrounded or cut off from the chance of supplies, unless there was a *jinzai* navy, as well.

Once the decision was taken details of what must be attempted seemed to invent themselves. Rodlakh's task with the regular cavalry would be to delay the enemy at the Lunu Tezh' Gate, and in any case to hold open the road through Banakit and its valley while its people were sent eastward, and the slower-moving retreat from the Drin and Kreshavu made its way, mounted archers guarding women, children, the aged and infirm. Wanildhai was sure his rearguard could sting the oncoming *jinzal*, and block parts of the road, break one or several bridges behind the retreat.

"This will be a business. *Deghi*, if he could come to the squadron officers and explain as he has here — otherwise they will be miserable about retreating so far, and from places that could surely be held. We've got half the farmers of the Vale of Banakit with us, and they'll see their lands left for these brutes."

Rodlakh told him to call a meeting for an hour from now, and she could not help contrasting this wonderfully decisive man with the one who had sobbed his powerlessness before the worse news came. He was in a desperate mood, but not one of despair; war was changing him, but he was still at his best where there was only yes or no for answer.

When Wanildhai had gone he confessed, "I did not say, there is a good chance these westerly parts of the Colony will not be retaken in our lifetime; Vonni's Jaws could be the new Frontier."

She had no answer, seeing he had made a bold choice, unable to tell whether it was the right one. He spent only a moment silent, then coolly resumed his dictation on the Shâl Mines evacuation.

When he had left for the meeting of officers she followed his suggestion, appending to the letter for Dolvid an abbreviated account of the siege here, trying to use exact, unemotional terms an historian would approve, her mind constantly picturing the lumbering *jinzal* invading the Colony proper. Storming the fortress they were fearsome and hateful, but the full obscenity of creatures that knew nothing but death and destruction was to imagine them in the water-fretted ways of gentle Kreshavu, the well-ordered farms of Banakit's green bowl.

When Rodlakh came back, "No matter what price we foresee, duty always asks more," was all he said about the gathering. He took up and read through what she had written, shaking his head sadly, then picked up the pen and with his mouth gaping in exhaustion added the latest bad news. `The Short Retreat is accomplished,' he wrote. `The Long Retreat is beginning.'

Letter finished and sealed they sat in front of the dying fire. "A week," numbly. "If we can keep Banakit open a week, there is a chance. I have sent Saidhan — " He lost the thread, and began elsewhere. "Dolvid may get us some troops. It is the only plan, really, to hold Kamsilat, and use the Jaws to kill — " His head jerked back with a snap her own neck felt.

"You must sleep, *Rabhsai*, in a bed."

After squinting contemplation of the dull fire he asked, "Will you come to my bed?"

"Yes."

"I meant, so to sleep with me — that is — " he was muddled. "I am too weary for anything but sleep. If I were not so tired I would want more, if that was your — "

"*Rabhsai*." She put a hand over his lips, shiny and creviced from the parching winds of Landegh. "It is good to sleep side by side with a friend; no need for anything more."

Dônshei

The water-meadows on the Paowan's south side were at their lush best, vivid green sprinkled with buttercup, cowslip and celandine. Dolvid felt a twinge of guilt, but could not do more for Rodlakh's cause by failing to notice a lovely day. On the north side there were the high heathlands of Dramal with their austerer aspiration to rebuke him with the stern task he was facing.

A productive morning. Sarnak, warned, had readied river-barges for over two hundred, nearly half of them Household under Dorrmas, with a squadron of General Cavalry, and some seventy scraped together from the other forces. It was also Sarnak who breezily reported that Alkmas, saying he would have been fishing the waters of the Shoals long ago if he had known how easy they were to navigate, had sailed again for Kamsilat with the news for Rodlakh. While at Owan Sai Dolvid had released the deposed Fonul, who now could do no harm, and having heard about events at Kadon Dinul maintained he had never taken a stand against Rodlakh.

It was not surprising the other Under-Warden had made himself useful; Vinosai had unsuspected kept his post at Kamsilat for years, and would not change his ways now, less so if he guessed he was under suspicion. Dolvid, saying they might be navigating the shallow and treacherous waters up in the Angle of the Paowan, asked for more of his help, and he was now in the stern of the broad-beamed barge ahead, in talk with glum-faced Muranak. His real purpose, if he took the bait, would come much sooner.

Sarnak gestured at what looked like dandelions in seed, sheep grazing high on the slopes of the northern side. "These Dramal herders must be mountain goats themselves, you ask me."

Galt was intensely interested. "They're kin, on my father's side. Is it true, *Bôdhrai*, they speak a kind of Froghulú, after a thousand years?"

"Not here, but farther north, or they did twenty years ago when I knew them. No doubt they still do."

"Stubborn as stale cheese," Sarnak said.

Each barge had two shifts of strong rowers, but all were rested for a while, when they halted near where a small and vigorous stream spilled into the slow and stately Paowan from the north. Crossing over to the second barge where Dorrmas was, making sure Vinosai was also in earshot, Dolvid explained this was the outlet of the Lurr, which meandered past the walls of Dônshei. There was a landing, and a trail of sorts that traced the course of the stream. North of there, and west of the hills, Shumat with his army, when last reported (by Tovakh), was moving slowly south, and they had to get word to him. Tovakh in fact might well be at Dônshei, but if a messenger kept to the trail he could work his way past the west side of the city, and rejoin the road north of there; Shumat, who had wagons and wounded, would have to be keeping close to the road.

"That would be the Irbat road, *Bôdhrai*?" Vinosai said, and Dolvid pretended only now to remember the man knew this country. He remarked there would be a chance of danger for the messenger, who would have to speak with some authority, so as to authenticate a written message.

Galt, a party to the plot, said he could find a man. "I would go myself, *Bôdhrai* — "

"You are needed to lead your fighters."

"Your pardon, *Bôdhrai* — " Vinosai's eyes, greedy for the chance of treachery, ended any faint doubts. "If Captain Shumat has outriders looking for enemy scouts — "

"He would not permit wanton killing. No, Tovakh's patrols are the real danger."

"I'd as soon run into the *Adanum Plakh'*," Sarnak said, and should have been kicked for trying too hard. Vinosai knew who the allies were.

Though he gave Sarnak a curious stare, he was too eager for the job to spend much thought on oddities. Then too, he would be uneasy every moment in the company of enemies. "Might I be the messenger? I shall not get lost, and I can evade detection, knowing the lie of the land. There is not much I can do with your forces, *Bôdhrai*. I am no fighter."

"With luck, we should not see any fighting till after we join up with Shumat's army, and that should be some days yet."

"Some days?" Dorrmas was startled.

"Five or six."

"Will I stay with Captain Shumat, then, after the message is delivered?"

"Just a moment. It is not decided you will be the messenger,"

"Well, if the *Bôdhrai* does not think me capable — " The man's flat face puffed with what was quite genuine affront.

Not too readily Dolvid allowed himself to be persuaded. A few oar-sweeps ahead was the broad, pebbled shore by the mouth of the Lurr. Now tilted and decaying, mooring posts were set here; almost within living memory there had been a crossing of the Paowan here, and a proverbial phrase, *Leak like the Lurr Ferry*, probably explained its demise. Listening carefully to final instructions, accepting a sealed document, Vinosai, joined by one of the small hill-horses, was set ashore. With a tight little wave of the hand he turned and led his mount over gravel to where bushes climbed a steeper bank. At a second try he found a way up, and passing among small trees quickly vanished.

The barge put out, and staying close under the north bank slowly crossed the mouth of the Lurr where water ran shallow and silvery over bright pebbles. Past a slow bend they came up to the other barges, using their oars merely to maintain their position against the slow current.

Once he judged they were out of sight of any possible lookout Vinosai could have reached by now, Dolvid had them return to shore, and make fast to crablike exposed roots of trees. He wrote out a second, genuine and simpler message, scarcely more than greetings and encouragement. To Noldar, who was to be the true messenger, he said, "When you meet Captain Shumat, tell him Dolvid remembers the three pretty daughters of Sebira." He made Noldar repeat it; Shumat would know that particular reference to the days of the Narn Campaign could not come from anyone else.

Half an hour having passed, the barge was allowed to drift with the current back to the outlet of the Lurr, where Noldar would use a way that set out somewhat westward of the one Vinosai had taken. More agilely than the other he vaulted ashore, and his horse followed him willingly.

Dorrmas was frowning, as the barge steered by Sarnak came near. "What was that?"

"Later." He climbed to the gunwale and leaped, and a man kept him from staggering as he landed.

They spent the night moored beneath the banks on the Heartland side, a couple of miles and a long curve downstream from Dônshei Bridge. Again to Galt and Sarnak, as to all muddled travellers, it had to be explained that while there was a small town there now, the name once had meant only the Paowan bridge to cross *for* Dônshei, half a dayride north. Better to tackle the garrison there in the morning. Dorrmas was hot to throw down challenges to all who had not yet declared for Rodlakh, but the policy would remain to avoid fighting, and keep the undecided neutral at worst: one reason for this river-journey was so as not to encounter the four oncoming squadrons of Kargul, which, with their potential allies defeated or dispersed, could safely be left for the defended walls of Kadon to deal with.

Not a cold night, and the barges carried braziers for small fires where the soldiers could heat drinks and warm their feet before turning in. Wrapped in cloaks Dolvid leaned on the rail with Dorrmas and watched black water, as he explained the two messages.

Vinosai he expected to go straight to Tovakh, who might already know about the man as a spy of the Patriarch.

Authentically, Tovakh would learn the Residence had been taken, and that there was a force in the field against him.

"As also the puny size of that force," Dorrmas observed.

That part might in the end be to the good. Dolvid had been very tempted to drop hints he was in negotiation with Bolan, to make Tovakh look nervously over his shoulder, but had pulled back from that, realizing Bolan might already be in Dônshei, and the rest of a good plan would be ruined by attempting too much.

The meat of the scheme was to allow Shumat to make junction with Dolvid at Dônshei, by making Tovakh quit the city, heading north and east. The spurious message Vinosai was carrying told Shumat to turn directly eastward, and use a herdsman's pass, one that actually existed, to cross the hills, and so stay well north of Dônshei, and come down to the Paowan River a long way upstream from here, where a sharp elbow of the river gave the country its name, the Angle. There he could meet Dolvid waiting with the barges, and together they would journey downstream and seize Dônshei Bridge, trapping both Tovakh and Bolan in the north, while Shumat with Dorrmas marched south on the Royal Way to deal with Kamin-Tolagh.

Not as confused as he sounded, Dorrmas asked how Shumat could know he was supposed to do all this, if Vinosai took these instructions to Tovakh instead. He agreed, of course it was all nonsense, but why would Tovakh move to intercept, if Shumat did not have the instructions?

Two answers: first, and the reason Dolvid had taken pains to give the message carried by Noldar its unimpeachable authenticity, he expected Tovakh to send Vinosai on to Shumat, so as not to miss the chance of waylaying that army when it descended, virtually single-file, at the eastern end of the herding trail. Also, Vinosai must be in doubt whether he was trusted, had seen the message written in duplicate, Noldar packing up supplies for a journey alone; there was even a chance he had watched the second landing from concealment. In short, he would assume a second dispatch, identical to the one he had, was going by another route.

"And you believe Tovakh will act on this?"

"At the least, he will have to divide his forces. Tovakh has been seeking a war to fight for half his lifetime; he is hungry for victories. What he ought to do is come down to Dônshei Bridge and hold it in force, but I would expect him to send most of his squadrons in hope of taking the celebrated Shumat in flank. If he missed that march he could still reach Dônshei Bridge before us — if we truly meant to join up with Shumat at the Angle, I mean. Let him just take eight squadrons north, and we can have Dônshei."

"With our three squadrons and the odds-and-ends, *Bô'rai*? That's a fortified city with strong walls."

"Just why we have to have it. We should add to our strength in the morning." He meant, from the Dônshei Bridge contingent.

"Doesn't Tovakh have allies — levies?"

"And we have Rodlakh's colors. Would you want to be a man of Kargul, shut up in Dônshei with levies from Kadon Dinul and Dramal, when the Beech-Tree comes in sight?"

Dorrmas enjoyed this, so that Dolvid could have envied the faith he instilled without sharing; it was all tenuous hopes. Then Dorrmas sounded a new objection. "Vinosai will surely tell Tovakh his lady is a prisoner at the Residence. Why wouldn't he ride for Kadon with all the forces he can gather?"

"How can he? According to the message Vinosai is carrying, that would put Shumat and us at his rear, with the chance to win over Bolan; he could be trapped between the walls of Kadon Dinul and all the armies of the realm." Tovakh's deep mistrust of what Bolan might do was in all the plans.

"What if the garrison at the Bridge resists us in the morning?"

"Dorrmas," adopting a weary tolerance not natural to him. "A moment comes when all ifs have to be bundled up and stuffed in your pocket, or you will not have a hand free to hold a sword. That is what you did when you came out for Rodlakh."

"I did not think at all, I didn't see a question. Rodlakh was *rabhsai* and Rheduban a murderer. If there was any debate Master Faëdhal was there, using a lot of words to say the same thing."

Dolvid nodded, and found a junior officer of the General Cavalry to question about the command at Dônshei Bridge, a rotating duty taken by senior squadron-leaders and *kímukan*, being part of the Kred Bakali command, which was Under-Captain Hinn's.

Seeing him smile the man did too. "You know him, *Bôdhrai*?"

"Doesn't everyone?" Hinn, a Mixed with no awe of the Owanil, had done well to prosper during Ban-Sila's years. In the years of dearth near the end of Lambarr's reign, when Dolvid, in his post as a kind of quartermaster for the province, had earned the lasting hatred of the big landowners, Hinn had been an officer of troops seconded to the effort to control the supply and price of food. Staggeringly vain, he had turned into a curious species of local lordling at Kanzan Tâl, becoming not rich in money, but a miser over hoarded power, bribed by flattery, riding on a saddlecloth of white shuzi.

He probably never knew it was Dolvid who ended his reign, quietly having him returned to normal cavalry duties. Blaming himself for not having asked about the Kred Bakali command, Dolvid sent one of the Household men riding by bad paths through darkness with a message for Hinn, who, properly approached, would surely be for Rodlakh.

With a soft double thud Galt vaulted from the next barge, having been making a round of the men and inspecting equipment. Remarkably, he had already won the respect of the Household men, who normally felt an ordinary trooper attached to the Residence was equal to anyone else's squadron-leader. "*Bôdhrai*, will there be a fight?"

Dorrmas shared the doubt. "Aye, what if Dônshei tries to keep us out? Will we fight?"

"We shall do what I have been doing. Everyone is given a fair chance to acknowledge the *rabhsai*. At the Bridge, no worse than too much talk. Later, we shall have to be ready for fighting."

Galt looked around him, though night was impenetrable. "This is a large realm our Rodlakh has come into. I did not expect to see so much of it in my life."

Not waiting for an answer from Hinn, in early morning the little army landed and made for Dônshei over grassed ways. It took a skirmish to get there, and it could have been a battle; two squadrons of Kargul cavalry tried to bar the way, with a large company of levied men, bows and pikes. After letting loose a few arrows and discovering Galt's mounted bows could outshoot them by a hundred paces, the levies, already exhorted to lay down their arms, declined any further fight. The Kargul' regulars, now greatly outnumbered, having lost some men to the bows, fled for Dônshei, and the royal forces, bypassing the crowd of sullen levies, followed at their steady march, leaving one dead and with three wounded.

In the hollow of soft green hills Dônshei first seen was a ripe and sculptured city. Dorrmas, never having been here, said it could not be a town of Arbhal, and that was nearly true. The outwalls, daunting as any erected when the First Empire flourished, with their deep, narrow slots, outthrust bastions smoothed into flowing curves, were unfailingly foreign. Here, architects of conquered Vrobhan had come as captives and settled as teachers; while it was acknowledged they had influenced all later building of the Empire, elsewhere what they taught was absorbed into the more austere tradition of Owan. At Dônshei the native manner remained as a memorial to the great land Shaël and his successors had plundered and razed.

For a further century this transplanted Vrobani city was, ironically, the capital of Old Owan, seat of the *Nímurai*, as the ruler's title then was, and center of all learning outside the *Mankh'*. Sixteen centuries later it retained a part of its splendid reputation, its distinct architecture, its remembered pride, and its own law.

Though he had lived here in his teens, Dolvid's chief memory was the later one of how the city took to its streets to cheer the returning victors of the Narn Campaign; speeches, flowers underfoot, the lovely women, and Bolan complaining as they set out again in the morning his brave warriors stank like weekwives, a bunch of frowzy violets.

Past scattered outlying houses the road swung left about a knoll, so the south gate of the outwall actually faced due east. Here, Rodlakh's men were awaited by the Dônshei Guard, with *Foi'kani* in their midst.

His title and position were unique; nominally sovereign he did not make deference to the *rabhsai*'s own person. He was the same man who had greeted Bolan fourteen years ago, but could not be expected to remember Dolvid. Then but not now he had put on his archaic ceremonial kirtle, but without it he remained the same small, rotund official with the incongruous, sharp face of a fox, lofty with self-importance.

The curled and curious Dônshei horns, rich-voiced, sounded flourishes to salute the Beech-Tree banner, and before Dolvid could say a word he was being proclaimed-to in the Owanilú:

"*Dônsheyit Dinun, bina koëlu, bina ga-foi dankegu, am-yalol rabhsayum ni-orabhai —* "

"This City of Dônshei, by law and by ancient and honored custom," Dolvid translated for Dorrmas and Galt, and continued to do so as the phrases rolled, "Makes alliance with *rabhsayum* not as subject, but an independent sovereign state, but those who ride under your colors are herewith extended our hospitality."

These words, while spoken by a herald, presumably represented the views of the official he sat beside. "*Foi'kani,*" Dolvid answered. "As Minister Plenipotentiary of the *rabhsai*, Rodlakh *bi*-Arbhai-Navu *Deghi*, I recognize and honor your city's ancient and singular standing." All this would be more sonorous in the Owanilú, but he was not going to parley in front of his troops in a language not one in ten could follow.

"*Bôdhrai —* " the *Foi'kani*, sitting straighter on a sleepy horse used his own arid voice to answer, following him into ordinary speech. "The City of Dônshei does not challenge your authority."

"As it may not." Behind, the army seemed small and tattered.

A slow blink of the deep, foxy eyes. "But even you must allow, these are uncertain times with your Council of Thirteen not having met, and *g'Asalladh'* Himself casting doubts on Rodlakh's proper accession."

It occurred to Dolvid that Faëdhal, given his powers, would have crushed this man, not knowing he was doing it. "Does *g'Asalladh'* sit in the Ivory Chair of Shaël? What is the power of one voice in Council to set aside rightful succession?"

A child's anxiety came into *Foi'kani*'s face. The chief families of Dônshei all had that same sloping forehead; these were the only ancient bloodlines that actually took pride in admixture, claiming a strain descending from princes of Old Vrobhan. Why princes and not stonemasons was mysterious. "The City of Dônshei desires friendship with all powers of your realm."

Sick of himself, Dolvid bared some steel. "Did the men who marched from here intend a hospitable welcome with their bows and pikes?"

"*Bôdhrai*, men from Dônshei are not always Dônsheyil. Bolan of Narn enjoyed our hospitality for a while, and those men were levies he had brought together and marched here."

"Are there others here in Dônshei?" Impossible the *Foi'kani* would be sitting here if Tovakh was at Dônshei, and equally unlikely Kargul had abandoned the city altogether.

"Under arms? No, none."

The tone was unmistakable, someone telling an exact truth he is aware will mislead. "Under arms. Then the levy is a farmer or a smith again, as soon as he unbuckles his belt or puts down his bow?"

"That is what the law of the realm says, your realm, *Bôdhrai*."

A point to him. "Under its *rabhsai*, sir. You have your orders, of course, from Tovakh baKargul, who left here at daybreak — " That was a well-founded guess.

"The City of Dônshei cannot be ordered."

"Threats, then — " trying to let sympathy for the man's awkward position moderate his terrible urgency. "Understandably, you do not want be caught between factions, *Foi'kani*, just as we try to avoid bloodshed — we left the levies alone, though they were at our mercy. But we cannot put ourselves in jeopardy."

"That we understand."

"Then simply, with no half-truth: what forces are in or near Dônshei, with their weapons close to hand?"

To answer this the man had to confer with a couple of advisors. Galt had quietly placed archers well back at either side of the road where they could reach but not be reached by the bowmen of the Dônshei Guard on the walls above; the Frontier bows were not slung but held across the saddle. Dorrmas, wrists crossed, was a man who has heard enough complicated wrangles, and longs for the simplicity of swords.

The answer that came at last was less than satisfactory. The two somewhat diminished squadrons of Kargul had ridden through in retreat a short while ago, leaving the city by the same northern route, the El'tuf road, that Tovakh had taken in early morning. More of the levies, those with horses, had gone with Tovakh. Some others remained with officers and a few men of the General Cavalry, installed at the once-famous Schools, which, though within the outwalls on the northern side, were outside the city proper, accounting for *Foi'kani*'s equivocation. Those officers, it seemed, were in much the same stance as Kizhunai had adopted for a week before Dolvid arrived, waiting for authorities to agree on who was *rabhsai*. Tovakh had probably told them, and told Dônshei, those who called themselves Rodlakh's men were a pitiable rabble, allied to the outlaw Shumat.

Finding his army admitted if hardly welcomed, Dolvid outlined the difficulties for Dorrmas. There were levies just outside the city, and Hinn, if he came, would meet the others bypassed this morning; there was no opportunity now to ride back and demand their new allegiance, nor would it necessarily bind them if the tide began running against Dolvid, though he would send another message to Hinn. When the retreating Kargul' squadrons caught up with Tovakh he might well turn back with all his army. The Dônshei Guard, unless *Foi'kani*, against all prudency, accepted Rodlakh's *rabhsayum* and rushed into renewing the ancient alliance, were their own army. All that was needed was for Bolan to come to the El'tuf Gate, and Shumat from the west.

"The makings of a great battle," Dorrmas said.

"Or a great alliance."

Riding beside *Foi'kani* Dolvid risked a direct appeal. "It would be a service the realm would not forget if the Dônshei Guard, should Kargul return, held the gates against them."

"*Bôdhrai*, Tovakh baKargul says I must assist the realm against rebels and usurpers."

"A time of choice," once again, putting a hand across to restrain Dorrmas, whose hand had twitched for his sword. "Can the *nim'* of a province far to the south speak for the realm at Dônshei?"

"Not for my realm."

While the troops passed through the curious narrow streets of the city, with many dwellings where stone was cut into the knife-edged curves of snow or sandbanks sculpted by wind, he rode to the northern side with Dorrmas and a few men. Between the road and the hills that hemmed the city in to the northwest the Schools were set among the tallest elms this side of Arnan. For centuries, before they were gradually absorbed into the *Atarlum* to parrot the glories of Ancient Owan, the Schools had been a center of learning, a rival for the *Mankh'*, and without the chantings and observances that gave that place its festering gloom. After Night and the Return, and some cunningly contrived agreements, the Schools, contrary to their original spirit, became headquarters for the *Manadilum*, Dolvid's order when he was at the *Mankh'*, the Teachers. That lasted till in Plakhsila's reign the dispute came to a head over their claimed right to teach only in the Old Tongue, their demand for orthodoxy of belief in pupils, a quarrel ended with Plakhsila's closing of all the *manal*. Though the lesser *manal* had reopened briefly in the reign of his daughter, closed again when the War of the Widowed came, for a century now these lofty buildings where the wise had studied movements of the heavens, the composition of living and mineral things, fire and metals, painting and music, had stood empty, except when used for quartering troops during wars, or storing food from an exceptional harvest. The groves of elms were dank, swathed in shoulder-high banks of nettle, and the Schools were beginning to crumble. Some roofs had gone, floors and pillars were cracking, yet surely some of the noble purpose in their original building lingered in the air.

In the largest structure still whole there was yet one more chance for Dolvid to proclaim this was a time of choice. Vakhilat, till last week a junior half-squadron of General Cavalry, was here in charge of ninety regulars and somewhat more levies, foot-soldiers who had neither gone north with Tovakh nor joined the attempt to bar the way to Dônshei. He was proud of having done nothing; Bolan's orders had put him under Tovakh's command, but since then dispute over the succession had erupted, and with no new instructions, he had told Tovakh his men could not be used against others of the realm, except the declared rebel, Shumat. "What if Tovakh told me to assail the *rabhsai*? A man must use judgment."

He saw that with other battles to fight Tovakh obviously could not spare men to take on his, and wanted to know whether Bolan was their Captain-General. Astonished by how news spread, Dolvid cut short discussion with a plain question, would Vakhilat hold the outwall here against Tovakh, if he came back?

"The Dônshei Guard defends the city."

"Not very well," Dorrmas broke in. "I've seen whorehouses better at keeping out visitors."

"The Schools, you see, command the road."

"I did right, *Bôdhrai*, did I not, refusing Tovakh?"

"The question is, whether you and your men will fight for anything." This was more pugnacious than Dolvid's way, but he saw Dorrmas had encountered a dog of a different breed, and was bristling.

"Now Kargul has left Dônshei," Vakhilat, wide-eyed, "Are they likely to come back?"

This officer was in charge of better than half as many soldiers as there were with Dolvid, badly needed unless Hinn came with reinforcements.

"He will need some stiffening," Dolvid, as they rode away.
"A whole new spine, *Bô'rai*. A spoiled brat of the — " His
mouth began *Owanil*, and he just checked it. "Of how they're
brought up nowadays."

Yes, always easy for the Others to forget the struggle was
against injustice, and that many Owanil were on the same side
with them.

He tried to explain why he could not relieve a General
Cavalry officer on the grounds of how he told his tale, without
bringing out into the open the question of whose authority held,
his or Bolan's. "I wonder whether Tovakh's orders were refused
by Vakhilat, or his men?"

In the morning he would have to ride out and meet Shumat;
it could not be anyone else. Hinn if he came, Dorrmas was told,
must be welcomed to Dônshei, and would at once become senior
officer there, while Tovakh, or even Bolan, was kept out, and any
bickering with the Dônshei Guard avoided. A close watch must
be kept on what Vakhilat did.

"His men will fight, if there's a need, *Bô'rai*."

By dusk some of the pikes and bows from the bypassed
levies were trickling back into Dônshei. Dorrmas did not expect
much from them, but he arranged them into companies again, and
marched them to the camp by the west wall. It might help
impress *Foi'kani* with the gathering royal strength.

Guthdar was anxious to find out what had become of his
brother, and was among forward scouts. In afternoon he came
riding back to report sighting fast-moving lancers, outriders of a
larger force. He did not know their tunics, no cavalry he had seen
before. Certain it must be Shumat, wondering how the reunion
would be after so many years, Dolvid went loping ahead, and on
the Irbat road where it stood away from grey-green highlands they
met. Mounts nose-and-tail they clasped hands gravely, a little
shyly.

"Dol. Or *Bôdhrai*, if that's you — your man was not sure
whether name and title went together." Noldar had reached him

before noon, shortly ending debate about what to do with the preposterous instructions brought by this other man, Vinosai, now a prisoner. "I let the one who talked sense stay free." In maturity Shumat's face had broadened, the familiar lopsided ugliness more comfortably worn.

"Before tales, are you ready to end your revolt and take allegiance to the *rabhsai*?"

"To Rodlakh *Rabhsai*, that would be?"

"There is only one."

"What does he offer? Well, curse it Dol — " a bitter anger came swiftly — "we've had promises from Kamsilat, and they've killed men, my friends. Sebhal was going to do this and do that, and he would advise us and bring Rodlakh into it — do you think I began all this to make widows at Yuvakh Din?"

Dolvid said he had seen Onebhal at Kamsilat, and that changed Shumat's direction without altering his mood; he demanded where Onebhal was now, and Sebhal with all the help they had counted on.

"Onebhal was supposed to get word to you, among other things, of Sebhal's death." Briefly he told a stunned Shumat how Sebhal had died, and how Rodlakh only heard of the plan belatedly, from Onebhal. How, certain he must after all join the rebellion, he tried to delay Shumat's invasion while collecting his forces.

"Sebhal told me he could prevent the Household from fighting, and with my troops we could force a settlement on Ban-Sila, either renouncing any part of Preference, or else recognizing the Free State of Arbhal, which Rodlakh would rule." Seeing his skepticism, Shumat said, "You know I'm not one for plotting and policy. I was against what Ban-Sila was doing, which would have ruined the Northeast, and *Sebhal* was telling me this — Sebhal Saidhans-son, the *rabhsai*'s uncle."

Dolvid confessed his belief that Sebhal from the start had meant to assassinate Ban-Sila. Shumat hotly, for Dolvid unnecessarily, denied he would ever have been party to that. "But Rheduban murdered Ban-Sila, everyone says, and your Noldar says you fought single with Rheduban and a holy man robbed you of the win. The realm has gone mad."

Correcting Noldar's account to suggest it might have been Rheduban who was doubly robbed, Dolvid again asked if he would serve Rodlakh. Painful to imagine alternatives.

His bitterness a little softened Shumat still had to recount where promises out of Kamsilat had left him. Many, if not most, of the small army, his following, were wounded, though Shumat seemed unhurt. Those who could not walk were in one of the three wagons they had with them. Something close to six squadrons were in the saddle, red-stained linen bandages conspicuous. On foot or riding pack-animals there were seventy-odd bows and about fifty pikes. They were weary, perhaps dispirited, and even the scratch squadron with Dolvid, made up of oddments from several different General Cavalry garrisons and some of the Owan Sai men, were parade-ground fresh by comparison.

Misfortunes had begun with a storm at sea scattering his fleet, washing boats ashore and driving others back: he had good hopes some had reached the shelter of Sebira Bay. Forming a lesser flotilla with the remainder he made landfall where originally planned, but in less than half strength. They were especially short of bows, though by chance the ship carrying all the spare arrows had arrived safely. Sebhal had given him names of probable sympathizers in the port of El'tuf, some miles to the east, and Shumat's messengers came back with encouraging offers of help.

There was treachery, and sixteen full squadrons of Dramal's provincial cavalry had come close to trapping Shumat at the gates of El'tuf. He successfully raided a compound at the port to steal wagons and animals as well as supplies. There had followed a zig-zag series of retreats, and this flat account and his despondent mood did not conceal the professional pride Shumat took in the skill of his maneuvers and the discipline of his men. Vinilat's troops had been reinforced by some squadrons, two at least, of Kargul.

No one so far had said anything about Dramal drawing in harness with Kargul, though what could be more natural? Vinilat, *Nim'* of Dramal, was Tovakh's first cousin.

"We spoiled them," grimly. "Dramal needs a new cavalry. I stood and fought south and east of El'tuf — Vinilat's private hunting, so a Fro' herder told us. They came at us all afternoon, but they were the ones to break it off. We had losses, too — you remember Ardi?"

"Ott's youngest." He had been in the Yuvakh Din campaign, a deadly bow. He was also Shumat's brother-in-law, of course.

"He was killed with our rearguard, when Kargul came in fresh at the end. Tovakh was nearly there himself, with fresh horse and some levies. I couldn't stand and fight a new army. They lost us when I broke out to the west and crossed the hills, and the Dramal cavalry, they say, went to Irbat and locked it up." Tovakh, meanwhile, must have sped down the good road east of the hills to stop the gap at Dônshei.

"And you went on making for Kadon Dinul?" Allegiance or none, they were all moving south again now.

"The only way to turn, and I was looking for word from Sebhal. Some people in a hamlet told us Ban-Sila was dead, and I was hoping the war was over."

Yet all this was a skirmish compared with Rodlakh's fight. Again, he offered to hear Shumat's allegiance, as a Captain in the new *rabhsayum*.

"With what to offer him? I remember years ago you said luck is part of captaincy, and without it skill can go for nothing. I have lost it, Dol. Mistakes, granted, but who would believe such a run of chances falling the wrong way?"

"It is just as well to use up all your bad luck before you have *jinzal* to fight."

"Or before I take on — who was it killed Wisdom? Ranak, Lord of the Dark, was it?"

"Hranakh."

"That's what I said," gloomily.

"But Hradhi the Healer restored Hrafi, and together they chained up the Darkness. I mean, real *jinzal*." Shumat became the first person on the Mainland to hear all about the *jinzal* armies, their probable numbers, the weapons, the spreading fear. He listened carefully, showing concern, never doubting the story.

"And with Sebhal gone, Rodlakh *Rabhsai* is captaining the West? He's not much more than a boy."

"And not much less than your age at the Gates of Narn."

"His childhood, all respect, was not mine — he wasn't clearing ground for growing when he was eight, unless he did it for fun at that place the fire was, rest Lambarr. I miss him, Dol, would you ever have predicted it? I hear he knows what to do with a lance, though. Good hands."

"And a good head. He will do well, but he needs help."

"This?" indicating his battered army.

"You have to trust me. I landed three days ago with forty men, and now Kadon Dinul and the Heartland are Rodlakh's, and I am gathering an army here." He gave the strategy; hold Dônshei and keep Tovakh bottled in the north, ride south collecting troops, if needed give Kamin-Tolagh a hard rap, and then embark men for the Colony. Shumat, shedding some of the defeated air, pursued points with eagerness. "Better, naturally, if Tovakh tries to storm Dônshei, and gets knocked out of the war. Poor old Bolan — his men, given a nudge, are going to come over to Rodlakh whether he does or not. But how long, Dol? Can't we leave Kamin-Tolagh to chance, and get our hands on Bolan's main army?"

Dolvid drew his friend's attention to *we* and *our*. The troops were drawn up, and Shumat dismounted under the Beech-Tree to offer up his sword. As he stood he said, "And so ends the Free State of Arbhal."

"Here begins the free realm of Arbhal."

"Let us wait a year or two before we hail his love of justice." An odd idea came to him. "Zhôl preserve the *rabhsai*, but what if he is killed fighting *jinzal*? You take it for your own?

"You seize the Residence and make proclamations," to Dolvid's gape. "You bestow and withhold posts and commands — "

"Under this banner. For myself, I can't tell a dog to chase a hare." Good to have someone at last he could talk to openly, but only to Âna would he confess the passing flash of a dizzying vision brought on by the innocence of his oldest friend's query.

"So justice stands or falls with Rodlakh?"

"Not necessarily. I would try for a *Moradhilum*, with Orbanak. Under Saidhan's guidance, not Tovakh's."

Though Shumat's men were tired they pressed ahead, anxious about what might be happening in Dônshei. At evening they had reached where the road ascended in a long, even, westward curve past the skirts of knobbly hills. All at once there were horsemen on the skyline, black against the darkening sky.

Soon they were seen as Household, some of Dorrmas's men. With half-squadrons of Shumat's riding well ahead of the wagons Dolvid hurried forward before there could be any mistakes about alliances. A Household half-squadron officer found him, and stammered out a report of happenings that sounded disastrous. Enemy had started coming into the city from the north side, and were not stopped at the Schools. Dorrmas had cursed the officer there and taken men, but was now believed to be captured or dead.

Tovakh was said to have come back to Dônshei, with many cavalry, but also squadrons under Bolan. The officer Dolvid was questioning said, "Him I saw, no mistake, *Bôdhrai*. He brought a lot of horse with him. The small officer from the West — "

"Squadron Galt."

"He said we should get out of the city before we were trapped."

"You did the right thing — " but loss of both Dorrmas and the city was hard. "Galt — is he safe?"

"He and his bows were rearguard, first at the west gate, then the little bridge outside. I never saw such archery."

Shumat had joined Dolvid. He told the officer with the wagons and foot to make for high ground and keep watch for enemy horse. Saying the rearguard must be hard-pressed he took most of his cavalry forward, Dolvid riding with them. They reached the head of the long slope and descended into a shallow valley, soon picking up Household men in small clumps of three, five, an entire file, all happy to discover Shumat's men were friends.

Light was dimming as they looked down on Dônshei. Here the road was closest to the hills, and fell in an undulating bend to where a small bridge spanned the Lurr, more than a mile away. Between the stream and the western wall of the city the grassed space was filled with horsemen. Nearer there were running fights, sword to sword, while over on the scrubby lower slopes of the hills men riding hard on little horses would obviously not outrun pursuing lances. Suddenly they broke formation and wheeled individually to tumble hunters from their saddles with rapid bowshots, just before that part of the field went from his view behind a bastion, a great knee thrust out lengthwise into the valley.

Shumat was calling men to him and pounding downslope to circle clear of the steeper escarpment directly facing the city. Dolvid, riding forward, saw him beat swords with a Karguli rider, unhorse a lancer, and then with his men sweep away the Kargul' outriders, who veered off looking for friends.

A huge voice bellowed, "Kargul! To me, Kargul!" and there was a glimpse between horses of the bearded and broad-shouldered figure under the light-blue banner. Enikai strode, and Dolvid came up near Shumat.

"Recall them." Obvious suicide, to try re-entering Dônshei now.

Drawing up near an outbuilding belonging to a small farm Shumat shouted, and the cry was taken up; the cavalry of the Northeast checked. Tovakh was gathering his farther down, in front of Dônshei; light was failing, the shadowy mass of enemy there impenetrable.

When, as they gathered near the head of the slope, a late arrival reported that Dorrmas was neither killed nor captured, but besieged at the Schools. Dolvid gave such a despairing look back at the city that Shumat said, "You can't," and put a hand across to restrain him, as if he had meant to storm Dônshei singlehanded.

The enemy cavalry was fading from the chase and rejoining Tovakh. From over on the right Galt appeared, his men picking their way down the embankment after him one by one. Shumat was keenly interested in the mounted bowmen.

"This is Squadron-Leader Galt, who was with us at the taking of the Residence."

"He should have been with us, at the fight there is no name for, by El'tuf. That's a hard art to acquire — they say your infants leap from the cradle into the saddle with a bow in their hands."

"We start young, Captain." Galt was equally interested in the renowned Shumat, but Dolvid wanted information about Dônshei.

Galt was sure Kargul and Bolan between them had secured the city for their cause, but said losses were less than they might have been. He had held the little bridge while others escaped, but the Lurr could be forded in marshy country just to the southwest, and Galt knew he would soon have enemy cavalry at his back. With no more friendly troops coming from the city he fell back. Most distressing, breaking out of the city they had to fight some of the Dônshei Guard, and kill several. "We could not be caught within walls," contritely, and Dolvid reassured him.

About Dorrmas Galt had heard both stories, and was sure only that the officer at the Schools, Vakhilat, did not fight, and Dorrmas went there and was seen later fighting on foot.

"Have you heard anything about the men from Kred Bakali, Hinn's squadrons?" Dolvid asked, depressed by the growth of enemies. Galt had: there had been a dispatch from Hinn which Dorrmas had, saying Hinn would make all speed to join with them.

"All speed," Dolvid echoed. From Kred Bakali to Dônshei could be done by an ordinary traveller in a day.

At the crest they turned to see the lights of Dônshei beginning to show yellow in the misty gloaming. The deeper shadow, massed cavalry, had not moved; evidently Tovakh, having regained the city, was content to hold the position originally wanted, blocking the way south.

Leaving men to keep watch on the long climb out of the city the collection of armies made camp on a broad knoll, hauling up the wagons by hand. Fires lit and watches set it was posible to start an accounting. With others perhaps yet to trickle in about one hundred and eighty of the men brought with him to Dônshei were here, well over a hundred having escaped from the city after Tovakh's entry. Virtually all Galt's bows were safe.

As for the enemy, he supposed they would gain back the levies, and Bolan take back the men Vakhilat commanded. Bolan's presence made uncertain whether Hinn's slowness had been loss or gain; the Kred Bakali squadrons might have been added to enemy strength.

"What do you make it?" Shumat asked, and they went through it together, using reports of men who had seen the enemy ride in, and where those failed, best guess. With Tovakh, allowing for losses and the four squadrons sent to Kadon Dinul, ten to twelve squadrons, all first-rate. Not less than that many with Bolan, fourteen squadrons if he added Vakhilat's men, at least sixteen if the Kred Bakali men joined him. Twenty-four to twenty-eight squadrons of regular cavalry all told.

Shumat's face was lengthening. "We might pass for eight squadrons of lances and one of mounted bows. Perhaps two hundred more, foot, bows and pikes."

"If we attacked Dônshei and the Guard fought alongside Tovakh's auxiliaries — " quite aware such an assault was out of the question — "The enemy foot, many with bows, would approach a thousand, including the levies."

Three to one at best, perhaps five to one, and the enemy had the walls. "I should have risked relieving Vakhilat. If Dorrmas or Galt here had been at the northern outwall to hold Tovakh the Dônshei Guard would not have dared fight us — we could have reentered the city, and held it with ease. I stepped into a nest of snakes at Dônshei, and we are in the very position I came to save you from."

When Dolvid again swore about the ineffectual Vakhilat, Shumat said, "Now you can see how we cursed the name of Sebhal when we had to face the whole cavalry of Dramal."

Galt straightened from his crouch. "I must see to the second watch." His voice was controlled with effort, and he walked stiffly away.

"What — ?" mystified.

"Sebhal has not been dead a month. He was a father to the West."

"To the Northeast also — a father who promises raisins and brings a whip instead."

"No doubt," icily.

"Curse it, Dol, we're soldiers, this isn't a meeting at the Residence where it all has to be honeyed. I have an opinion."

"You are a Captain of Army. Do you think I have come this far by letting others hear my opinion of this one or that one?"

"And how far have you come?"

The sarcasm wounded. Dolvid bit down on his lower lip, and held his breath. "To the end, if the commanders fall out."

Shumat fumbled in his pocket for bits of the sweet root the men of Narn chewed; he gave one to Dolvid and gnawed at the other. "You have been carrying some weight on your shoulders, too."

"Some, yes. And now where I am is cut off from Kadon Dinul, not knowing how far loyalty won with bluff can hold if things start to go wrong, if Kamin-Tolagh and the *Adanum Plakh'* come knocking — well." He was making these sound like his own sorrows. Shumat would not hear that he was cut off, recalling Dolvid had been a strong swimmer. The path by which Noldar had come might be no good for armies, but one man could slip unnoticed down to the Paowan, swim across, and hail a traveller on the Great Stone Road.

This, leaving them all here, was not a real possibility to discuss. Dolvid began talking about bows where, numbers aside, they should be a match for the enemy. All of the bowmen with Tovakh or Bolan were levies and auxiliaries, no regulars, whereas Galt's mounted bows were beyond compare, and so in their own way were the archers of the Northeast using their Gabhani longbow; Dolvid had seen them at work in '28. There should be a way to make use of the speed, power and range of both sorts.

Galt's men, Shumat objected, were mounted, but his were foot, effective where there was cover or enough pikes in front and cavalry at the flanks to protect them. This was open country, and to march foot-bowmen into a plain full of lances was murder.

"No," agreeing. "Tovakh must come to us."

"He has no reason to. Why should he not sit where he is and wait for our next move. We can't turn back north, where would we retreat to?"

Tovakh would not sit in Dônshei, Dolvid suggested, because he was Karguli and in love with cavalry, because the *péfrapravádal* regulars were by far his best troops and only reliable ones, because he saw the realm tilting towards Rodlakh and wanted a swift win, and finally because he was no Shumat, renown already won before his twenty-third birthday. He recalled the victory feast after the Narn campaign, when Petakoi had embarrassed everyone demanding Tovakh's petition for a captaincy be considered. Tovakh was past forty then, in his mid-fifties now, steeped in the glory and bitterness of Kargul's wars. For all he knew this was his last chance at fame, and that was not going to be won by a successful defense of city walls.

Shumat said grinning he did not see how Tovakh would dare go against so many persuasions. "If I had the option I would meet him tomorrow where we encountered him today, the long slope out of the city, somewhere near the crest, so his *pefral* would be puffing when ours were fresh. There is that place — " and he described in exact detail the slopes he had seen once, with fights and chases all around to distract him; Dolvid had forgotten that talent of Shumat's for memorizing the shape of land. It meant that if only in hope plans could be made for tomorrow without need to look over the terrain again. They could make an early start.

While dawn was an uncertainty Galt's men killed three scouts, all men of Kargul by their tunics. Dolvid pitied them, arrows through their throats before they knew there was anything stirring in the misted shadows where they peered. Galt said contemptuous words about men not taught not to put themselves against a morning sky; this habitual belittling of adversaries was how an otherwise generous-spirited man managed to bear his talent for killing, shifting blame onto the slain. If it went well today he would need new resources of scorn: his part was dangerous but vital, and he accepted it with a thoughtful nod. Dolvid, whose plan it was, could not send him without being sure he understood the risks.

Galt was munching bread. "*Bôdhrai*, there aren't battles with no dead. I'd sooner be doing other things, and so would anyone — these madmen from Kargul, too, most would rather talk or herd their cattle, fuck their women." He grinned mischievously. "Or their boys. But we are not going to give up who's our *rabhsai* by them calling us names, or showing us what they say is law — they've come to kill us, and we have to kill them till they stop."

"But it is all a great pity."

"And a great madness. Still, I wouldn't want to be a man with nothing he would kill for, or die for, not till they show me some other world, where you don't have to care about your worth."

He went with his men in a long file, leading their horses, crouching over the skyline; their first job was to keep watch on the city from partway down the slope. Now the rest of the army began to move, no one except a few scouts mounted, the infantry close around and actually drawing the stout wagons. The draft-horses were left tethered on the knoll where the camp was, and the worst-wounded were left there, too, with a small guard of those with lesser injuries. Some who could not march could manage bows, and several of those had stayed in the wagons, wanting to be part of the battle. They, with other unwounded archers, were going to be a bait to Tovakh, but a bait that could sting.

The wagons were manhandled to the tongue of higher ground running out into the last slope, forming a natural bastion with steep sides, the front less so but still far sharper than the main incline. On its crown the wagons were secured with stakes between spokes of their wheels, and the foot-archers clambered up, joking too heartily, apprehensive. There would be no shortage of arrows; hundreds in emptied barrels were behind them in the middle of each wagon. The other infantry, with long pikes, were stationed around the rim of their bastion, backs to the wagons. The sun rose, round, soft as a rose-petal, dull in the valley mists.

Noldar came up to where Dolvid stood, to report their deployment had been seen; a patrol on the road, after watching some minutes, had ridden back hard for the city.

Galt appeared again. "Will they come to us, *Bôdhrai*?"

"I believe they have to." Galt would be taking a distant flanking position, and would not be able to see the whole field. A great deal depended on the timing of his eventual move, and he would watch for a signal from Dolvid. There was high ground on the left where Dolvid would take his stand and watch developments, a rounded outpost of the main hills. Galt and Shumat had each independently asked him to stay clear of the fighting, and he was not sure whether the tribute was to his importance or his ineptitude.

Among long, dove-grey shadows that seemed to fall from the hills Dônshei glinted like precious metal in a dimly-lighted shop. The muted sound of trumpets floated up, and in the dew-whitened space between the west-facing gate and the bridged Lurr the glitter of weapons and armor could be seen. Companies of foot, mainly pikes, were starting to cross the small span where Galt last night had held off Tovakh's troops and saved the Household men. Only, perhaps, to die this morning, then Dolvid felt his heart rise and expand as the soft gold of early sunlight touched the rooftops of Dônshei, and made colors leap from the hills. Who would not want to be saved, be grateful he had been, even for just one more tremulous, tremendous daybreak?

Over one large company of foot unfurled the white banner with the bronze border and the Bronze Sword depicted, the Royal Standard. Near Dolvid a Household man spat. "That we'll take from them."

Shumat rode up and dismounted, face set, voice calm. "Let's hope Tovakh goes on following the *Bôdhrai*'s directions."

Galt looked across tentatively, and Shumat stuck out his gloved hand. "Squadron, I hope you'll pardon unconsidered words. Sebhal's greatness will be remembered an age. No one has anything but praise for the House of Saidhan."

"The same for the brave men of the Northeast, Captain," plainly relieved to be able to smile.

"Let us drink together in Dônshei this noon."

A shake of the head. "They won't have our drink there. I would have enjoyed showing you our West, Captain."

"I hope you can."

Now the enemy was deploying in earnest, cavalry squadrons out to the right of the road, a narrower ground fringed by thick clumps of brush and bramble on a rise above where the stream for a while moved sluggishly westward, before bending back south to seek its gap in the hills. Upstream of there, nearer the city, was where the shallows were, the negotiable ford, a way to the path Vinosai must have used when coming to find Tovakh.

Shumat said, "Bolan," in a strained voice. What he had seen was the General Cavalry colors crossing the bridge; at this distance the figure beneath was not certainly recognizable, though there was nothing to suggest it was not Bolan. Shumat's mind must be running on the past, the Narn adventure, when Bolan chose him for second-in-command, beginning, notwithstanding all that had happened since, of eminence for Shumat, and for Dolvid too. What might be in the heads of the Household men who had called Bolan their Captain could not be guessed, but Bolan had never owned those qualities to inspire personal loyalty; afraid, always, his titles and renown would somehow vanish or be taken away, he stood on rank and could never be comradely with his men, as Shumat was.

"You and he have a few things to settle - " and Dolvid, by a natural association, asked for news of Manda, Shumat's wife. He was being taken on a tour of their children when Galt called out softly he should move to his assigned position now. Dolvid waved assent and good luck, and as Galt's company vanished over a brow, rode to take up his stand on the opposite side, where the banner of Rodlakh would be planted.

Shumat was busy ordering the Household formations, securing instant response from men who a few days ago were calling him a rebel. With all his experience and accomplishment there was still a good part of the boy who learned his trade on the road to Narn, while the intervening years had brought Dolvid no closer to that clarity.

From his set position he watched the fight begin, and it was like all the others he had been part of, cruel and brave, filled with skill and blundering, decided by mistakes.

Here the overriding madness, leaving aside the essential one of men using well-designed tools to kill each other over who would tax them, was Tovakh's inability to see the little fortress formed by the wagons fixed on their redoubt was nothing, a rude gesture. If he had concentrated on defeating Shumat's horse or driving it off he could have circled wide and dealt at leisure with the immobile infantry using bows of his own, followed by a charge from the rear. Instead, evidently seeing the impudent wagon-loads of archers as a personal insult, he began with a frontal assault, using cavalry to shepherd a mass of foot, levies whose lack of interest in the fight turned to stubborn refusal to take part in it, as soon as the range and accuracy of the longbows above was revealed. Less frightened of the Karguli cavalry's attempts to goad them on than by the archery of adversaries well beyond range of their small bows, the crowd of levies eddied back, clogging the center and making it harder for Tovakh to move his horse to meet sudden counter-attacks. There was a clear sight of the maddened Tovakh in his blue-crested helm, bawling commands, and at last calling back his cavalry and retiring to reform.

He retained great numerical superiority, especially counting the squadrons with Bolan, who came into the fight bringing eight squadrons against the one Shumat had set to guard the somewhat steeper slope to the left of the spur where the wagons were. At a steady pace uphill, Bolan, his face set grimly, passed right beneath where Dolvid was.

His leading squadrons were obviously the Special Forces raised, mainly for keeping curfews, enforcing dispossessions, and putting down the expected riots. Though they did not shape like real cavalry, they followed orders. Bolan's plan must be the sensible and threatening one of bypassing the wagons and falling on their rear.

Now Tovakh launched a new frontal assault, so that with the bows concentrated to the front Bolan's men got by without loss, and Shumat was forced to switch squadrons to that side, as the attack scaled the slope diagonally, and, though with losses, drove back the men of the Northeast there. The only reserve, a single scratch squadron made up from odds and ends, emerged from concealment behind a small brake of trees on the far side, and, seeing they must lose any race for the bastion where the bows were, instead moved outside Bolan to threaten a flank if he turned left.

Attention switched to the splendid Kargul squadrons grinding to bits against the redoubt, unscalable by *pefral* for all of Tovakh's bellowing. They recoiled again, and Dolvid could not imagine what had become of Bolan, then saw he had declined to offer a flank, and continued right across the breadth of the field, his men becoming an extended curve of riders, at present with no part in the battle.

With Tovakh again rallying his forces to him, sparing breath for what even at this distance could be seen as a bitter exchange of shouted insults with Bolan as his squadrons came straggling back down the slope, a lull ensued. Except for Shumat's attempts to parcel out lances fairly evenly among squadrons that had suffered losses, the only movement of troops was the continuing one by many of the fightless levies to creep farther away from where any fighting would be. The quiet was eerie after the clang of weapons, thunder and shrill of horses, shouts of men and cries of the wounded.

"Half an hour."

"*Bôdhrai?*" The standard-bearer, hedged by lancers, five each from Shumat's forces and the Household, turned his head.

"Nothing, half-squadron." It had been in his mind that within that space this battle of less than three thousand men could settle whether Rodlakh would come to reign. High morning and the wounded on the field, those who could, were taking advantage of respite to hobble or crawl for better shelter, from sun and the hoofs of *pefral*, some calling for aid or for water.

No time now for thoughts pushed down, the bleeding and dying on both sides, the many men with Bolan who would have chosen Rodlakh for their *rabhsai*, those with Tovakh who would have accepted him. Dolvid would have parleyed, this late in the day, if it had been feasible. Losses could not be assessed; those of the enemy had been much the greater, but they could afford to lose more. Especially if the captains, Bolan and Tovakh, saw there was no need to renew the battle; they could yet go over to the defensive, hold Dônshei with ease against the diminished forces of Rodlakh. That might very well be the view Bolan had been trying to urge on Tovakh, but when the cavalry of Kargul began to marshal for a fresh advance, Bolan's squadrons assembled too, crossing to the right side. Dolvid was afraid they were going to mount an attack on the position where Galt and his band of mounted bows were concealed, apparently forgotten since fighting a brief skirmish with a Karguli squadron at the start of battle. In case they meant to try forcing passage of the ford Tovakh had placed a strong company of foot on the opposing bank, but they had done nothing but watch the main fight.

Having crossed the road, Bolan, with quite enough cavalry to keep all of Shumat's busy, began a menacing advance upslope, the great *pefral* settling to their task, heads and the helmeted heads above bobbing to the steady rhythm, the lessened Special Forces squadrons again in front.

Now, surely, Tovakh meant to engage the cavalry full-force, and odds remained heavily in his favor, though Shumat's use of the slope had been worth several squadrons. He could hardly believe it when Tovakh aligned his lances wide of the remaining infantry, but so as to come at the loathed bastion, where not one enemy had been able to reach the archers, though the pikes there had been busy.

Bolan was in eights, already halfway to meeting Shumat with all his collected lances, and his part, clearly, was to prevent Shumat from supporting the bows, as he had before, with quick counter-attacks. Kargul was wheeling off in fours, a long column unravelling from the massed ranks.

"When the time comes," Dolvid told the men of his guard. "We'll be part of this." Once Galt was launched there would be nothing more to be done from this hilltop, and at the odds the ten lances here were a noticeable loss.

Shumat started a pair of weakened squadrons towards Bolan's advance, too soon, as first appeared. Nevertheless Dolvid told the standard-bearer, *Now*, and the standard was raised high and waved side to side. At once the heads of Galt's men became visible, moving out from cover on the far right.

Too many things happened at once for the picture to be coherent; watching one part of the action he would turn back elsewhere, and have to reconstruct what had happened in the interim. Shumat's charge broke Bolan's lead squadrons, not a match for regular cavalry with the slope in its favor. Then Tovakh came against the bastion, losing men to the bows, roaring men on with his fury.

But he was there with half his strength. Taking advantage of a gap that opened in the column of march Galt cut it in two, veered to shoot men down from behind, and wheeled again to greet pursuing cavalry with another volley: a half-file was wiped from the saddle like a child's chalked letters from a piece of slate.

His vanguard routed, Bolan's forces had evidently quit the field, and there was nothing now to stop Shumat, leading in person, from crossing the slope to challenge Kargul's embattled riders in front of the bastion; the close-quarter fighting turned the archers into spectators.

Freakishly, right below where Dolvid was planted, Tovakh and some of his officers shook free of the press. Unwounded, Tovakh was standing in his stirrups looking down towards the city, trying to see what had become of the squadrons Galt had ridden in among. He must see simple victory draining away. As he went crosswise over the bruised grass, bawling for riders to rally to him, Dolvid charged without a word. Standard-bearer and the little escort, though startled, followed at once, but there was no horse to match Enikai's surefooted daring on the downslope,

Yelling now and astonished to discover it, Dolvid rode for Tovakh. His sword was out, and there were not many whole lances left to the Kargul': Dolvid mowed at a man who came in his way, chopped at a shoulder and was nearly thrown as Enikai, jostled, sprang sideways like a great cat, snapping, fighting-mad as his rider.

Clash of swords with an officer, and Dolvid was whirled away to strike quickly at a fresh adversary, piercing flesh under the breastplate. The banner of Rodlakh dipped and swayed nearby; Enikai half-reared and in Dolvid's ear the trumpet voice of Tovakh roared, "To me, Kargul." Much farther, another brawny voice, surely Shumat's, was urging, *To the Banner! To the* Rabhsai'*s banner!*

He swung face-to-face with Tovakh baKargul whose sword was drawn back. At the pace his mind was stampeding there was ample room to tell himself he had not learned the lesson of Rheduban; he would never parry a blow with Tovakh's massive frame behind it.

Enikai reared straight up; Tovakh's sword-arm went back and across in instinct to protect his face from flying hoofs. As the great horse plunged down, miraculously clear of Tovakh and his mount, Dolvid, also on pure instinct, sent the point of his sword into the underside of Tovakh's arm, almost precisely the same slice into muscle he had used on purpose to end the absurd duel with Ghuradh, years ago.

Tovakh had lost his weapon, but Enikai was jostled, and in a complicated double move he was coming up on Tovakh's other side. Meaning to drag him from the saddle Dolvid leaned out; a dark sword flickered down from his left; he was down, in a ravine between cliffs of horseflesh, pain jabbing his temple, reins in his hand.

Madly, he heard the world groan. Enikai had not halted, and keeping the reins Dolvid went scrambling, toes, knees, once an elbow through a thick and darkening forest; horses' legs.

When he got to a clearing Tovakh had vanished. No one would stay with him, except Enikai, who turned, the eyes vast and growing.

A hand was under his armpit. He blinked, because his left eye tickled. Shumat was there, and the worry in his face was funny to Dolvid. "I was not dead," and perceiving that was odd, tried, "I am not much hurt."

Wrong side, proving it, he scrambled on Enikai's back. An undoubted cheer came, and he remembered the groan had been real, too, coming from Household men fighting their way to where he was jammed in a ring of Kargul riders.

Time crawled. Friends were coming from everywhere, and enemy everywhere were going away. Two Household men were holding an irascible Tovakh, and it came to Dolvid's slow clarity that incredibly they had won the fight.

"No massacre," he mumbled, "Tell them to take prisoners."

They were, he saw, waiting for his leadership, and he waved his sword at the city, hauling Enikai in that direction.

A strong hand took his elbow. He swivelled, furious, and there was Shumat remounted, holding him back.

"What are you doing?"

Shumat released the grip, put fingertips high on Dolvid's cheek, and showed them covered with bright blood. "You have a cloth?" Dolvid put his own hand to a slippery face, and it came away red and dripping. There was a broad stain on his chest.

Shumat passed over a square of clean linen. "Leave it to us." Dolvid slouched unhappily in the saddle, watching the mingled men of Household and Northeast spur forward. "Take prisoners," he bawled passionately. Shumat, who had detailed a man to be with Dolvid, waved acknowledgement.

Retreating enemy never attempted to hold the little bridge. Some used weapons to hack their way past routed infantry, but they were closely pursued. Now, in the green space between the stream and the city a strange thing happened; the retreat muddled and swirled there like water meeting an obstruction, and some were throwing down arms. The walls of Dônshei were held against them.

He was not sure he fainted. Feeling dizzy he dismounted with care and decided he could sit on the ground for a while. The man left behind changed into Noldar, who pressed a soft cloth to his head. Nearby, Guthdar was folding a fresh one, then held out a water-flask for Dolvid to drink. He was sure no one had ridden up. They were all in a little grassy hollow, under a young linden, out of sight of everything.

"How is the battle?"

"Won, *Bôdhrai*."

So far as cautious fingertips could tell the sword had taken a small slice from the point of his temple. He was very lucky.

He thanked the brothers, and remembered he must ride to Dônshei. "Where is Galt?"

"Dead."

The word was false; it could not describe anything Galt was.

Guthdar said, "Most of us are hurt, lightly or worse, *Bôdhrai*. Galt was lanced through."

"He was very brave — too brave." Noldar's face was stolid.

"He was — " and Dolvid's voice went. He sobbed without shame, pressing bloody hands to sockets where eyes pulsed hot. He had not known Galt long, but the loss had no remedy, a bitter diminution of astonishing victory, unfair and beyond reach of any consolation.

He had never lost a comrade-in-arms before, and now he understood how men in war could become implacable in their desire for vengeance. He did not really want every man of Kargul slaughtered, but could see why men who had watched friends die could singing cut down enemy as they tried to surrender.

When he had stopped but not finished weeping he remounted wearily and with no words rode for Dônshei. On the way he collected more men of Drin b'Afon. Kuno was riding with his head bowed down, shirt spattered with blood, though he seemed unwounded. As he raised his head Dolvid somehow met his sorrowing gaze, and made the grief-sign, right thumbnail to left forearm. Kuno nodded gravely, and fell in with the two brothers.

There was no more fighting west of the city. From ordering their forces and collecting prisoners, Shumat rode up as he came across the little bridge.

"You're bleeding." Dolvid pressed the cloth to his forehead again. He had a dazed feeling their troops had grown in number.

"Well fought," he told his old friend. He learned the shutting up of Dônshei against the retreating Kargul had come from the confluence of several events. At about the time Dolvid was bucketing down from his hilltop Hinn at last arrived at the south side of the city. The levies Bolan had done his best to re-enlist overcame the few Kargul' left within the walls, and became a threat to the Dônshei Guard, who, seeing the way the wind blew, scarcely waited for *Foi'kani*'s word to throw open the gate to Hinn. Men half-heartedly besieging the Schools now changed sides definitively, precipitating a mutiny among the regulars Bolan had left in reserve. "If you can call it mutiny, when men go over to their proper allegiance."

Shumat added the small news that in the confusion of the battle the prisoner, Vinosai, had vanished. On the whole, Dolvid was glad. The man could not do them any more harm, and there was nothing they could do with him. Tradition said he should be put to death, but that was a cold business.

Just inside the city gate a dirty and wild-haired but unscathed Dorrmas was conferring with a senior officer who had enlivened his tunic with a sash of copper-colored shuzi. Hinn had thickened over the years, as had the heavy-lidded, unctuous self-satisfaction.

"*Bôdhrai*, well met. The battle is won. We came in good time."

"Any time, Under-Captain, would be good for something, to bury the dead if nothing else. Better time would have meant no battle."

"Are you wounded, *Bôdhrai*?" Dorrmas came in quickly, too shocked by Dolvid's toughness to mispronounce his title.

Dolvid told him, and asked for his losses, which were small, Vakhilat's men having come over to his side.

"Vakhilat is what, a prisoner?"

"He's dead. I killed him." Dorrmas set his jaw, defying further questions. Dolvid only nodded, and Dorrmas asked about losses on the field, which he had heard were heavy.

"Less on our side than might have been," Shumat said. "Tovakh's lances were blunted by good bowmanship. Tovakh is taken. The *Bôdhrai* wounded him."

Dorrmas, if discreetly, was sizing up the Captain of the Northeast. He announced Bolan was also a prisoner, and that a *kímukan* of General Cavalry, actually acting under-captain, wanted to see the leader.

His name was Mattin, and he was from the Drin Dakani garrison, tall and lean with protruding eyes. He understood he was senior surviving officer of the forces that had been Bolan's. Convinced they were fighting on the wrong side of the cause he had led the mutiny, and been the one to have Bolan arrested. "For this act, I make no apology."

It made him uncomfortable, though. There were four intact squadrons of regulars, late arrivals at Dônshei, half of them from Mattin's garrison. They had rebelled against assailing the banner of their proper *rabhsai*, and when Bolan rode back to call in his last reserves had seized him. Mattin's proud argument was that his troops, ready to fight for Rodlakh, were neither defeated nor prisoners.

"They are nothing at all till I hear new allegiance."

In a cool and pleasant hostelry smelling of fresh straw, leather and roast meat, a serving woman to whom wars and battles were a personal affront washed Dolvid's face and neck and bound his head with clean linen. There were mugs of the pale beer preferred at Dônshei, slightly tart, and Shumat recalled his last words with Galt, who had regretted the city would not have the Froghuli drink, a fermented milk. "As if he had a premonition. He said we would never be together in the West."

Dorrmas had details to fit with or contradict the accounts of others. Mattin's men, he said, were the ones who overawed the

Dônshei Guard, threatening a massacre if the gates were not opened for Hinn.

"I was ready to give them a hand," adding with a discontented face, "I missed the real fight, up on the hillside. The only cavalry battle in my lifetime, and I was on foot, cooped up."

"But bows won it," Shumat said. "That and the *Bôdhrai*'s wounding of Tovakh. That broke Kargul's spirit. *Dônshei-Kindhri* — " only half in fun he saluted Dolvid.

"No."

"Your battle-plan."

"Not my fighting. But we do not hail a victor in a battle between brothers." His battle-plan had killed Galt.

"It had to be."

He wanted to shock these soldiers by telling truth: he would not have fought this battle, not even for Rodlakh's accession, if the real enemy were not injustice, and Tovakh in the way of sending assistance to the West. Not to be said without sounding self-righteous; instead he assured Dorrmas the Siege of the Schools was also part of the victory. "You will be Royal Master of Weapons, if you will take the post, which has lapsed since Kheval retired."

Dorrmas gave a nervous laugh at the idea of being successor to the legendary Kheval. "*Bô'rai*, I hope I'll have the, you know... "

"I do not think Rodlakh's court is going to be stiff with ceremony."

"Won't they say I came out for Rodlakh for my own advancement?"

"What is the difference? If you did not have the skill you could not fill the post. Men and women are usually rewarded for loyalty."

"Well, but loyalty doesn't begin by considering rewards. That wasn't why — "

"So you have said. Three times now — " beginning to be irritated. "In Hrafi's name, let us make Rodlakh secure as gold-giver before being fastidious about taking his gold."

"Very well, *Bô'rai*."

"And if you are at court, you could take the trouble to pronounce the dozen words of the Old Tongue you'll ever have to say. Faëdhal can instruct you, if you need it."

"Yes, *Bôdhrai*." That this had no irony in it made Dorrmas a lesser figure than he had seemed at first.

"It would in any case be *Dônsheyai-Kindhri* — " to Shumat, a correction Faëdhal would have made far sooner.

Dorrmas went off to the West Gate to join Mattin, sorting out prisoners from men who wanted to join Rodlakh's cause. A few words, Shumat predicted, would often change one into the other. He and Dolvid, not happily, were setting out for the Schools, where Bolan was being held.

They emerged into brilliant sunlight striking straight down between the close-set walls. A shock the day was only at early afternoon.

Their horses had been let wander across cobbles to where a trough was fed by water gushing through the open mouth of a stone-carved ram. As they collected the animals, the *Foi'kani* came up, breathless and on foot among four of his guard and two advisors, prominent merchants.

An elaborate salute for Dolvid. "Dônshei hails your triumph, *Bôdhrai*, in which we played some part."

"If you were ever a child, *Foi'kani*, you may remember what it was to be given a present you knew was bought with someone else in mind. If Tovakh had won, he might be more gracious."

"Tovakh never had friendship from this city, except by force of arms."

"Late in the day to discover that. If you had been with us at the start, a lot of good men would be alive, who are not. The *rabhsai* may want to reconsider whether this alliance serves any purpose. It is an ancient one, but the world has changed, and annexation might be better for his realm. For the present — " making this an instruction, "Dônshei is an occupied city."

"Dônshei is sovereign."

"Yes, under a treaty you declined to renew." The *Foi'kani*, of course, had not known then Rodlakh's men would emerge victorious, but that was true for Kizhunai and Dorrmas and all the others who had risked their lives. Dolvid got up on Enikai. "If you mean to resist occupation, call your Guard together. Our men are resting now, but they would find second wind for the sack of such a rich city."

"The Dônshei Guard is your ally. You are our guests — " He shouted it at receding backs. "Our guests!"

Shumat gave a low-pitched half-whistle.

"I have no patience," superfluously. "What use is his alliance now? We have no enemy worth considering left north of the Paowan." He was beginning to get a grasp on what they had won: all garrisons of the General Cavalry were now Rodlakh's men, and only Kamin-Tolagh remained to be dealt with. "But they are still dead, Galt and all the others."

"You don't really mean to occupy Dônshei?"

"We cannot spare the troops. But a fright may make him less pompous. Besides, we need supplies from him, and I shall seize them if he will not find goods to sell."

They caught each other's eye. Last night supplies were not a subject discussed, though both knew that at this season of the year, barred from the city, Shumat's small stocks, with twice the mouths to feed, would soon run out, especially in a countryside where the barns had already been emptied by Bolan's and Tovakh's armies.

The sleeve of Bolan's outshirt was ripped away and his cheek had been scratched, whether in the battle or at his arrest no one asked. This small building among the Schools was of later origin and better-preserved than some. The room had plain stone walls and was bare except for a couple of benches, and a two-legged table attached to the wall, with a slab of slate for top, chipped here and there at the edges; a strong odor of candle-wax, and a faint one of horse-dung. Men of the General Cavalry were guarding the door, and there was one inside. Dolvid sent him to fetch food for the prisoner.

Bolan's eyes were dead as sea-stone, eyes, suitable for a man whose oldest nightmare has come true; his men would not follow him into battle.

"Those I trained personally did their duty," meaning the Special Forces, whose losses had been greater than any other squadrons, even Tovakh's. They had been last to stop fighting, and none of their survivors would be enlisted for Rodlakh.

"Tovakh!" with bitter contempt. "What a fool. A brave fool, granted, but after all his bragging, what a fight to choose. There was no need; we could have stood on the near bank of the Lurr and let you come at us. You had to have the city, and the ridge you were on meant nothing. Is he alive? Someone saw him bleeding."

"He has a small wound," Shumat said.

"Fools and drunks come safe home."

"He supposed he had to bring the fight to us," Dolvid suggested. "He could see Dônshei was ready to come over to Rodlakh."

"But wouldn't have, would not have dared to, if they hadn't seen the cavalry of Kargul pounding itself to death against your rock."

"You may be right."

Bolan grumbled on for a while about Tovakh's idiocy. "What now?" He looked up brightly. "I'm a traitor, is that it? Other officers said Rodlakh — I would have been for him, too, the moment we had a ruling. It is all in how the law is interpreted, and *g'Asalladh*'s envoy said Rodlakh was out of the succession. Shâl's balls, I am a soldier."

"You have sat in Council for fourteen years. Even a soldier should have enough law to know the reigning *rabhsai* cannot change the laws of succession on his own, not even if he has *g'Asalladh*'s approval."

"Have I not served *rabhsayum* loyally for all my grown life?"

"What did you expect would be your reward after Kargul won?" genuinely curious; the coalition Bolan belonged to could only have lessened his power.

"Oh, for that matter, what does Rodlakh promise you?" He showed some animation. "The estates he takes from the Families? If there's anything left, after he gives land to every half-ape from the West."

Shumat made a censorious sound with his tongue. "Residence Quarter rant, Bolan. You ought to see by now that men of our birth don't become pure Owanil by using the same names they call us behind our backs — lazy mongrels, dirty beggars. You give help to those who judge people by race, and when they're safe in power, you'll be a half-ape, too. Ban-Sila would have found that out, too late."

This part of the debate Dolvid was too shamed to enter: what Shumat said was undeniable, and to be Owani was hard at these times. Faëdhal was the only Owani he could bring to mind who neither shared the contempt of the Families for the Other Races, nor felt guilty over being one of the privileged people. Aëlu, too, perhaps.

The guard came back with food for Bolan, and Dolvid, unable to invent any further errands, simply sent him outside with the others. He could do that, he was *Bôdhrai*. He was imagining the terrible moment when Mattin told Bolan he was a prisoner of his own men.

"We had food at the inn," Shumat said when Bolan offered to share.

"The three of us, hah?" after a minute's chewing. "You remember Irbat in twenty-eight, the inn there, what was it called?"

"We were speaking about it." He wished they had not come. Nothing here but regrets.

A drink of pale wine. "It may sound like the romances, hah, Dolvid? but I've always tried to do my duty as well as I could."

"You will be consoled by that in retirement."

"I am forty-three, Dol."

"You will have your estates. I do not anticipate the *rabhsai* will want to proceed against either you or your property." That it was possible was a shock for Bolan, but there would be no reason for detaining him once the *rabhsayum* was secure; Bolan was a nothing, a commander who could not command. There was no employment for him even with the West fighting for its life.

"Curse it, is mutton all they know here?" throwing down his table-knife. "Listen, Dol, I can still serve *rabhsayum*. I have always known what was owed the realm."

"And Bolan," unable to resist.

"After Narn, after they gave me the Household? That was the end of my ambitions, but later on there was another appetite for honors I had to satisfy, as you better than anyone can appreciate. How is the *rabhsai* going to feel, surrounded by officers who change sides when the mood strikes them, this, these officers?"

"I have accepted Mattin's allegiance." The name Bolan could not get out of his mouth.

"*You* have?" cocking his head, trying to work out Dolvid's hold on Rodlakh. He would have wanted to discuss their unexplained visit to the Residence and the failure to assassinate Ban-Sila, but Dolvid cut him short, asking if there was anything he needed for his comfort.

"They have my sword," defiantly, then with his little laugh: "I would wish to offer my allegiance."

Dolvid swallowed hard. "I cannot hear it."

"I know the plans of Kargul."

"So do I. They have failed."

The nervous laugh again. "This is the new, iron Dolvid." He was desperate for silence not to fall. "You just came from Kadon? How is Khalú?"

"I did not see her. Well, Khelagh says. He visited me at the Residence." That was sure to trouble Bolan.

"It's from him she gets it all. They despise failure, as you very well know. I wish I had been killed in the fighting — I was at the head of my troops. I didn't quit the field, except to fetch more men, and they stopped me from returning to the fight. They can't say I ran."

"No one would, who remembered the Gates of Narn." Did Shumat think Dolvid had been unduly harsh?

"Who'll remember that? They'll always bring up Dônshei."

"No, no." A little shamed by Shumat, Dolvid joined his consoling mood. "You will always be *Narnai-Kindhri*."

"You know, *Bôdhrai* — " with strong emphasis on the title. "Khalú will want to change again."

No answer; it was too grotesque for words. Bolan picked at what might be steamed parsnips. "Don't forget what you were when I found you at Irbat."

"I never have." He had been on the brink of starving when Bolan had made him an advisor to the Narn Campaign. A debt long paid, but it would go on troubling Dolvid. "We shall speak again."

viii

Bloodlines

Dônshei, or a good part of its citizenry, took to the streets to watch the army ride out. "A pity," Shumat said, "there is no time for — that." He raised a gloved hand and gave his warm, off-center smile to a spray of brightly-dressed young women. The muscular ugliness, it seemed, had not lost its peculiar attraction. "Some good sport to be had here in twenty-eight, if I remember."

"As I remember, you declined any of *that*, your heart then being in mortgage to Manda Otts-daughter."

"What did my heart have to do with missing good sport?"

"So you were asked."

Shumat frowned. "Odi's armband, you're right. Dol, would you rather be the most powerful man this side of Arnan, or a lunatic of twenty-two?"

"I was not the one refusing half the lovelies of the Heartland."

"Oh, that is true. What became of the one with a name like Daënakh's lady — Linoi? Lenayu?"

"Linaëyu. She is Khelagh's wife. She became my mother-in-law." He cackled to see Shumat blush over his lapse of memory.

On the curving rise out of the city they could take in the magnitude of their victory. Household men escorting wagons and the slower-moving infantry had left earlier; Hinn for now would stay at Dônshei (no longer called occupied); his dealings with *Foi'kani* would make a fine clash of vanities. Hinn's job was to care for wounded, round up stray soldiers, and guard the Kargul' prisoners, kept here out of harm's way. Accompanied by one of Shumat's officers Mattin had taken a squadron north, to find what was left of Bolan's army, and bring about peace if there was still fighting with the Army of the Northeast, yet with all these deductions, all losses in battle, Dolvid could send eleven

squadrons south under Shumat, and come back to Kadon Dinul
with more men than when he set out.

"Kargul has no hope now of defeating us. They can only
waste our time." He would assemble shipping at Owan Sai; if
Shumat failed to find Kamin-Tolagh, or if there could be a truce,
those squadrons would ride west to Nambalus, to be met by the
ships. The whereabouts of Kamin-Tolagh remained a mystery;
they had intercepted Tovakh's final attempt to communicate with
his son, replete with scrawled curses.

"Does your wound give you much pain?"

"Hardly any." His eyes had suddenly stung with tears, and he
did not know why now. Not pain, but for the men hacked and
bleeding on the battlefield, for Galt. These sadnesses kept coming
over Dolvid, and there did not seem to be any healing.

"Do not start a fight with Kamin-Tolagh before doing
everything you can to negotiate."

"You have said that, four times now."

"I begrudge every death, not only that it wastes men who
could be fighting *jinzal*. You must make every effort to — "

"Go yourself and talk, if you don't trust me. I'll do every last
thing I can, but I'm not going to get my own men killed while
trying to show this buck-rabbit lordling we are men of peace. Go
yourself; they miss me in Narn."

"Easy, easy — " trembling at the brink of reciprocal anger.
"I ask your pardon."

"Easy! Well — " Shumat clamped his mouth shut. "Dol,
Bôdhrai, you have not always been such a burr in the boot."

"I have not always had this job. You realize I am to blame,
or largely so, for every death and every wounding at Dônshei?"
He had to accept that.

Shumat started to compare a captain's job, but admitted, "A
field commander can always tell himself he fights in a way to
spare lives. You have everything that's mine, Dol, but not my
envy."

After thought, "Why don't you come south and see it done
right? Kadon's safe, with Kizhunai and Dorrmas, and fresh
troops."

"And Faëdhal. So safe I can do what I was afraid to before
— go and see *g'Asalladh'*. Parley with Him."

"At Treaty Stone."

"I shall see Him where He will see me. I would guess the
Mankh'. I am sure He has always said I would come back there
some day." This was in part his own private joke.

"I can't think of anything I would be more afraid of — and
g'Asalladh' has no reason for disliking me."

"I am afraid, but it has to be tried."

"You just said you weren't afraid, with Kadon Dinul safe."

Awkwardly, he had to explain the different fears without
sounding intolerably vain. If he had been lost before it would
have meant catastrophe for Rodlakh's cause. Now everything
needed, except this, could be done by others.

"Don't go. He is not a forgiving man, by all accounts."

"I have to. For help to go quickly to the West, blockade of
the Strait must be lifted. We cannot send fleets through the
Shoals, and in Nambalus we shall already be well to the south."

"You think you can persuade Him?"

"When He hears about the *jinzai* army, how can He refuse?"
He might demand some concessions, but He would have to see
His plans for Orbanak, with Kargul defeated, were dead. It could
not be believed any man would refuse an alliance against *jinzal*,
hoping for the death of Rodlakh — particularly when *g'Asalladh'*
understood if the *jinzal* were not stopped in the West, the Island
might well be next.

Shumat suggested he could write *g'Asalladh'* to the same
effect, a tempting alternative, but an exchange of letters might
take a week. Face to face it could be settled in an hour.

"You can be dead in a minute."

For answer Dolvid risked annoyance by going through the
plan once more. If he failed to return from the *Mankh'*, Shumat
would hear the news from Faëdhal. Once Kamin-Tolagh was
dealt with, however that ended, every available man must be
embarked for the Colony with adequate supplies, prepared to fight
their way through the Strait if the blockade was not lifted.

Shumat refused to be distracted. "Can't you send someone else to debate *g'Asalladh'*?"

"Why could you not instruct someone else to direct the cavalry at Dônshei?"

He made a puffing noise. "In a fight things happen that can't be foreseen. You cannot instruct for what you don't know is going to happen."

"You have answered yourself."

Sarnak woke Dolvid. "Raining, on and off, *Bôdhrai*. Funny-looking sail in the Estuary, sure to be that toothache Alkmas. If he drowned in the Shoals no one on Arnan shore would ever need to buy vinegar again."

He dressed in haste, hoping Alkmas had come back from the Colony with news of Rodlakh, if not word from him. Arriving after dark at Owan Sai and hearing Kadon Dinul was calm, he had bedded down at Perimas's quarters so as to get things started here, the collecting and preparing of ships suitable for carrying troops and their mounts. Waking, he was dull, head throbbing steadily.

Down at the basin Perimas was already waiting, huddled inside a cloak. The boy Torr bobbed up the steps to wind line on a bollard. His appearance suggested the gusts of wind were bringing not cold rain but a fine spray of pot-grease across the ruffled Estuary. Moving to the edge of the slimed stone quay, Dolvid looked down to see a well-wrapped Alkmas at the tiller, as oarsmen were making fast.

The pigeon-chested fisherman clambered up. From his waterproofs he produced a bulky packet of documents, also wrapped in oiled shuzi against the wet. "News, to say the least, out of Kamsilat. The beauty-boat is here again. One over, one back, that's fair."

Anxious to read Dolvid might have ignored the cryptic greeting, except it insisted on explaining itself. From the boat's afterwell emerged a head shawled in a blanket, the slender top half of a young woman, hands clutching the covers red-knuckled with cold. His throat closed as his heart paused, and then he saw the hair was long, dark only with the damp, the bronze hair of Kamin-Tarú.

"What is this, Alkmas?   By whose authority have you brought her here?"

"If you've met the lady you know she has her own authority. She asked me to take her just as we set sail, dead of night. I may be fast-messenger to the realm, *Bôdhrai*, but she's my boat."

So it was, and Kamin-Tarú had never been a prisoner; he begged the man's pardon.

Kamin-Tarú allowed an oarsman to hand her onto and over the weed-smeared steps.   Her hand went up for him to take, deathlike with cold. "Oh, Dol," she whimpered in misery.

"*Asayu*," grimly, helping her across the final slimed step.

"Hug me." He could not reject her shuddering form. Pulled tight against him, her nose was a cold coin pressed to his cheek.

"Come, Tú. I am not much warmer, and I have dispatches to read. There will be a hot drink at the Commander's quarters — and a fire, Perimas?"

Perimas started to say there was no fire lighted, then recognized a polite command. He had a horse here, and went hurrying on ahead.

"Don't punish Alkmas, do not be upset with me."

"I am not upset with anyone." Tight-lipped Dolvid strode along, the packet of letters burning his hand, any distraction maddening. As they walked Kamin-Tarú kept up a kind of mournful *kolukezh'* of complaint, excuse and regret. Kamsilat all at once was a war-camp, she had not known the boat would be so small, the crossing so rough, the weather so bad. She did not mean to annoy him, and she had no change of clothes with her.

"Tú — " he pitched his voice carefully to soothe them both. "We'll get you some dry clothes, and I shan't be angry if only you will be quiet for a few minutes. Tú?"

Perimas was having no luck kindling soggy peat, and Dolvid was on the verge of breaking up a good chair when a servant remembered an empty barrel. While Perimas went to find warm drinks, the sound of splintering wood promised a fire quite soon. Obedient to the letter, Kamin-Tarú's lips pressed tight together as she hunched on a stool by the cold hearth, lovely hair lank. Cold was not what made his hands tremble as he opened the packet.

Puzzling that the outer sheet, from Saidhan, had been written at Banakit. It was brief.

> Bôdhrai: *The* rabhsai, *as you will see, is safe so far. The enclosed dispatches, his and my earlier one to him (which he instructs me to forward) tell all the news. As I am, the* rabhsai *will be encouraged by your triumph at the Residence, your dispatch having gone to him in the West.*
>
> Bôdhrai, *we must have help, though I confess misgivings, bringing more men where there seems so little hope. But your news may be a better omen. Doleni now commands at Kamsilat and will see to all forwardings. Raëdh give you a good road and Hrafi ride beside you.*

All this was in the looped, even hand of a scribe, while the signature was a script once fine the gnarlings of age had made tremulous.

Dolvid, mystified, took up and sliced open the thick letter from Drin Navuna. Soon he realized who it was taking dictation from Rodlakh, and felt a guilty new fear; he had assumed Âna was safely clear of the fighting, but done nothing to keep her so. Once she was at the Frontier, her return there was easy to have foreseen.

That gloom remained a separate one as he read through Rodlakh's level account of breaking the encirclement at Shâl Mines, and the terrible journey back to Drin Navuna, the night-encampments in the open, guarded mainly by fire and well-chosen terrain, but their numbers steadily diminishing.

Flames were now leaping in the grate. A new butterfly, blood pulsing to uncrumple her wings, Kamin-Tarú threw off the fishy blanket and dazzled Perimas with her eyes as he brought warm, spiced *raminat.*

He read through Âna's terse story of the siege at Drin Navuna, and was with her in the noise, dust and anxiety of the fortress, rejoicing with her at Rodlakh's safe return.

Referred to Saidhan's earlier dispatch he came to the shocking news of the fresh *jinzai* army threatening Banakit, and there was a copy of Rodlakh's reply, ordering the start of what he called the Long Retreat. Both the map and his recent sight of these places were in his mind; he could picture the long thread of hard road the army must keep unbroken, and the wide Vale of Banakit, town all-but defenseless against any force that could pass the Lunu Tezh' Gate and cross the placid Navu. The road would be clogged with farm-wives, children, slow-moving carts, the wounded and infirm, and Rodlakh had to hold off this new enemy while the withdrawal was accomplished, then slip the last of his defenders out before the Vale was overrun. That Âna was caught in all this was an impotent terror for Dolvid, which he did not so much master as dodge, so as to keep his head clear. Having seen Vonni's Jaws he thought not even *jinzal* could force a way from the westward, so long as there were defenders to shoot bows and roll rocks from the clifftops.

Yet to move, in effect, the entire population behind those defenses, while *jinzal* tried to gnaw the Colony in two, was a giant undertaking, perhaps impossible. In the heart of catastrophe it was astonishing Rodlakh took time to dictate a short treatise on correct cavalry tactics against massed *jinzal,* and after that the long dispatch took an odd, drunken turn that must come from great fatigue, and momentary safety in the midst of many anxieties.

> *Do all you can to send help; Kamsilat will be kept open.*
> *In such a time it is good to have and to have had such*
> *friends. Âna thrives on war.* (No, on these brief
> respites).

When will I have some word about your mission? You can tell Galt he is missing the fight of his life.

Âna is getting pen-cramped. (long ago) *My mind will not let go the prophecy of the True* Rabhsai *who comes out of the Farthest West — must my reign be the one to see it come true? I dare not guess where we might next meet, or how.* (but we shall, we shall) *Get us any aid you can, and go with my love.* (mine, too).

The *rabhsai*, who had taken the pen to make a few minor alterations, must have seen Âna's interlinear comments. He signed the message simply *Rodlakh*, no title.

"This is serious," fatuously, not to anyone.

"Now there's a right fire," Alkmas remarked as he came in.

"How soon can you return to Kamsilat? You will be well paid."

"Through the Shoals? I thank you." After collecting his foul blanket, he made a feint of walking away.

Dolvid let him warm his hands, then told the man his journey was of extreme importance, perhaps the difference for the realm between life and death.

"Well, long as it is not anything that matters. Who is it can't fetch his woman now?"

As before, Alkmas's boat would lead a larger craft, again with Sarnak at the helm. Dolvid was sending archers, levies who had come by barge from Dônshei Bridge yesterday, and also the remnant of Galt's squadron, nineteen fit men, though others should recover from their wounds. Only eight of the men of Drin b'Afon were still whole.

Noldar, their new leader, said, "You are dividing us, *Bôdhrai*. Some are lying sick at Dônshei, and four others up at Kadon." They were the ones wounded in the Residence fight.

"Five, also, are healing at Kamsilat, the wounded from the Island. You'll have a reunion."

"If any of us live."

"Your *rabhsai* needs you. You are paying the price of your skill — " This was bitter in his mouth. "It happens in big wars, the best soldiers are sent over and again where there is most danger." If he went on with that, he would soon be weeping again. Instead he outlined for Noldar the military situation in the West, with *jinzal* past Drin Navuna, and Rodlakh racing for Banakit.

"On our farmlands, *jinzal*?" Guthdar said. "We should have been there."

"*Bôdhrai*, Galt said we would stay by you till Rodlakh was in his Chair," Noldar said.

"Rodlakh needs you more." If the retreat to Vonni's Jaws succeeded, it was not clear how great numbers of additional men, cavalry in particular, could be useful on that narrow front. The seventy they were sending, all bows, were no army, but their arrival could encourage the Colony as a sign the Mainland was gathering help. As he observed to Sarnak, dispatching mainly foot-archers would make space in the hold for some of the supplies brought down from Dônshei Bridge, food and feed collected for Bolan's northern campaign — Dolvid wondered if the oats of Arlimas were among the many sacks.

"If we are not to be the *Bôdhrai*'s guard," Guthdar said. "He must find one. He is too ready for danger, pardon me."

"So Galt said Sebhal's lady said," Noldar put in to soften his brother's temerity. "Others have a use for his life, if he has not, she said."

Flattered but puzzled by Aëlu's solicitude, he told the brothers if his plan for today worked, the battling here would be over; Rodlakh was in personal command in the field, and needed more guarding than anyone.

With a firm-chinned expression that came from Galt, Noldar nodded.

Kamin-Tarú was dozing, being baked by a fire more than one barrel had stoked when Perimas came banging in. "*Bôdhrai* — I ask pardon — "

"These are your quarters." The man was enormously excited.

"One of our warships has docked. I hope this does not cause trouble. They followed your orders exactly."

"There must be others to keep watch."

"Oh, yes. This was the night-duty ship, and overdue, already relieved, *Bôdhrai*."

"And — ?" Why did reports have to be wrenched out of men, dandelions from clay?

Perimas, calming a bit, said near dawn the warship had started to pursue an unidentified vessel. With no chance of catching it, they had turned back, and were right in the path of another, sailing west. As instructed they stopped and boarded her. A ship of the *Atarlum*, and there was a brief clash with a few of the *Adanum Plakh'*. "The ship, as you ordered, was released and made to go back to the *Mankh'*." Perimas approached his climax. "*Bôdhrai*, we've captured, or it may be we have set free — " he faltered at the brink.

"Come."

"We've got the Lord Orbanak *bi*-Arbhai-Navu. He was being sent under guard to the Island, at *g'Asalladh'*s orders, just as you feared."

"But not with *g'Asalladh'* — " a stupid question, that news would have come first. "Orbanak is here, at Owan Sai? Perimas, you don't know! This takes away the teeth of the *Mankh'*. He will be mad with rage, *g'Asalladh'*."

Dolvid's shout as he hugged the astonished soldier roused Kamin-Tarú, who shifted and yawned. The Patriarch must somehow have heard about Dônshei, Dolvid's return in greater strength, and been afraid of an armed attempt to seize Orbanak from Him.

"You gave written orders, *Bôdhrai*," Perimas said, aware of cases in the past when the wrath of a Patriarch could bring trouble from *rabhsayum*. He obviously had no idea what his ship had accomplished. Now the Patriarch controlled no rival claimant anyone would acknowledge. In unfeeling practical terms it meant if Rodlakh were killed, Preference would not return; the twelve-year-old Orbanak *Rabhsai* would be set in a *Moradhilum* with Saidhan at its head. The last authentic argument against riding to the *Mankh'* had also vanished.

The boy was slight, small for his age, pale-faced and nervous, mouth twitching into smiles that soon faded. Habitually he glanced aside before speaking as if afraid of being overheard, though there was not much danger of that; his voice was a whisper. In face he was most like the brother who had come between the late and the present *rabhsai*, Lambakh, his pupil, killed in the Tan Lughsai fire. But Lambakh had been quick on his feet, strong, with no shyness about giving his views, even at this same age. Dolvid was curious to see whether Orbanak's mind had been made captive in two years divided between Ban-Sila and Ban-Sila's mentor, *g'Asalladh'*.

"Where is my brother now?" he whispered.

"Rodlakh *Rabhsai*?" Surely news of the elder brother's death had not been kept from the boy. "He is in the Colony. There is war there."

"Then it is not true? *G'Asalladh'* told me he could not be *rabhsai*."

"*G'Asalladh'* is mistaken." The gross impiety seemed not to shock Orbanak, and that was encouraging.

"He said, he had made war on Ban-Sila *Deghi*, and that meant I would be the new *rabhsai*."

"How does that seem to you, *biRabh'loi*?"

"To me?" The boy put tongue to lip, tasting the novelty of being asked his opinion.

"You have been taught some law."

"I have learned some of Ban-Sila's will, which used to be law, and is not anything, now." He showed some spirit. "Rodlakh is grown and he could rule, he is a good fighter. If he had really made war on Ban-Sila he would have won. You are not *g'Asalladh'*'s friend?"

"I serve your brother, the *rabhsai*."

"Ah." The boy's eyes searched him, looking for something to trust. Dolvid thought how mysterious children are, even the straightforward ones. Whole continents of feeling could remain undiscovered, and guesses about how they saw events were almost always wrong. He said, "You were with Rodlakh in the South for quite a few years."

A realler smile came. "He knows the names of trees, and taught me how to hold a sword. When I was a child we went right to the edge of the Ní-Tilagh without any guards, and made camp there. Did you ever warm your *raminat* over a camp-fire, a small one? Anyway, *g'Asalladh'* only wants me to be *rabhsai* so He can be *rabhsai*. Rodlakh would be better. I do not know anything about taxes."

While Dolvid was explaining the laws of succession Kamin-Tarú woke once again, and flushed from the heat moved to a more comfortable chair farther from the fire. Hair spilling over her face she watched with one green-glinting eye.

"If they made me *rabhsai*," Orbanak declared. "I could make decrees. I'll abdicate, and Rodlakh can be *rabhsai*. He knows almost everything, I think."

With what he hoped was tact Dolvid recounted some of the danger Rodlakh was in. Kamin-Tarú stretched out a hand, and surprise was unreasonable when the boy went to her, letting himself be held loosely in the loop of her arms, head against her breast. Understanding enough of the position he said, "Then I do not have to go back to the *Mankh'*."

"Not if you don't want to."

"Want to!" Kamin-Tarú reproached. "Who could ever want to go to that great gloomy place?"

He reopened the dispatch Alkmas was to carry, so as to add this late news, keeping the telling brief, though he kept seeing fresh ways arrival of Orbanak changed the game. The Families, for example: anyone opposing Rodlakh would have to do so in declared disloyalty to the House Arbhai-Navu, no longer in pretended fidelity to the absent other.

Originally, he had planned to smuggle Orbanak into the Residence, taken from here in a closed wagon, all for safety's sake. Conspiracy and intrigue made for bad habits; far better, Dolvid now saw, to have Orbanak ride openly, so no one could say he was an unwilling captive of Rodlakh's supporters. Discreetly guarded there was no reason the boy could not go all over the city and be seen by everyone.

Yet it was a curious threesome riding under the Beech-Tree banner at the head of a half-squadron, Dolvid, Orbanak and Kamin-Tarú. The rain had blown away, chill and misery were baked out of Kamin-Tarú. Her smile was back, but not the same, being mainly for Orbanak, whom she treated as an equal; an open question whether she was ignoring the boy was twelve, or that she was not.

"That's a handsome dagger." A ceremonial one, with jewels on the hilt, worn at the waist in front.

"It was made for me, by the best craftsmen of Ninkufu."

"But that is not where the best knives come from, the South. They come from Upper Dakbân. At Inilun Barabhi I have knives from there."

"I have, too, far longer than this, a real weapon. *G'Asalladh'* did not let me carry it."

"There is no such knife. You're fibbing."

"There is. You cannot say that to me. I am *biRabh'loi.*"

"And I am grand-daughter to the *Nim'* of Kargul." Laughing she reached across to tousle his hair. The pallid face was livelier now. Orbanak was losing his heart, while Dolvid tried to imagine how Kamin-Tarú would be when she discovered her mother was a captive at the Residence, her father defeated, wounded and a prisoner at Dônshei.

Not till they had passed through Harbor Gate and were on the Avenue was Orbanak recognized. A woman noticed the boy and called out his name, pointing. At once, several women, all with the plaited bags they carried on market days, were waving and calling.

"You may wave," softly, as Orbanak hesitated whether to. Till they reached the Residence steps they did not go half-a-dozen paces without some shout of welcome, a salute, recognition moving by a process of contagion never fully understood. Within an hour the whole city would have the news Orbanak was back at the Residence under his brother's flag.

At the Steps Dolvid was assailed by an irate Dorrmas, who had heard he had sent archers to Kamsilat. Madness, he said, to take men from defense of the city. They had word the *Adanum Plakh'* had been reinforced with four squadrons of Kargul which had never attempted to enter the city, and were therefore intact, while no one could be certain Kamin-Tolagh had not circled wide to the eastward of Kanzan Tâl, and would now come down on them here. Dorrmas begrudged a single bow.

Dolvid thanked him politely for his opinion, increasing annoyance. Dônshei, he told him, had been fought principally to obtain forces for the *rabhsai* in the West.

"You could throw away all we won there. We've been scraping together every man we can arm — "

"*Kímukan!*" Dolvid barked. "This is not the place." He sidelong indicated Kamin-Tarú, who had caught her brother's name and was frowning to follow the discussion. Nevertheless, her eyes were taking measure of the compactly effective Dorrmas. "Perhaps you would give a hand to Kamin-Tarú baKargul, our guest." She was willing now to be helped down, though at Kamsilat Dolvid had seen her dismount with about as much difficulty as her brother had.

Already before they reached the Great Doors there were questions about styles of swordplay, and she was flattering Dorrmas with her gaze, not making him conscious he was slightly the shorter. Having turned aside one assault Dolvid did not see how to avoid Dorrmas's renewed exasperation, instructing him to take care of Orbanak, to see Rhunilat about his rooms in the Personal Suite, and arrange a twenty-four hour bodyguard.

"Is that all, *Bôdhrai*?" Now his correct pronunciation had some parody in it.

"Am I going to see you again, *Kímukan*?" Kamin-Tarú said.

"*Asayu*, I am where my orders take me."

"Here at the Residence," Dolvid invented, "The Great Families are the special concern of *Kímukan* Dorrmas. I wish a private word with you, but then he can be your guide to this great cavern of a palace."

"I thank you, Dolvidh." Kamin-Tarú was complacent as a cat, and Dorrmas had lost his sour face as he waited for Orbanak.

"I thank you, too, *Bôdhrai*," the boy said, putting out a hand.

Dolvid reminded him he was the *biRabh'loi*, and if he wanted the bakers to make their apricot tart, always good, he had only to say so.

Orbanak nodded, and he and Kamin-Tarú parted casually, as children do.

Yet she was exactly her mother when she heard about her father's wound, the resigned nod, the pursed lips seeming to imply such things will happen to those who play with knives. Rheduban's death she brushed away as expected, sooner or later.

"I have to give this news about your father to Petakoi *Asayu*."

Kamin-Tarú moved her head as if cobwebs had brushed her face. "And is Dorrmas coming to me? You told me I would be able to look for Tam."

"Your brother is in the field somewhere, with a dozen squadrons of *péfrapravádal*."

"That is because he has heard there is war in the West. Everything Rodlakh does, he wants to do."

"I think it is because of Kargul, and their grudge against Arbhai-Navu."

"It ought to be settled between Tam and Rodlakh, like Tobhsila and Saidhan. This time it would be otherwise, though. Tam is the best lance in the whole realm."

"Tú, it ought to be settled — " He finally spoke the word in his mind since winning Dônshei. "In alliance. They would do better matching lances shoulder-to-shoulder, against the real enemy. You could help bring that about."

"You will use me as a hostage?" She seemed oddly pleased at the prospect.

"Hostages are not a part of this *rabhsayum*. You will be riding to find your brother, either with me, or someone else — "

"With Dorrmas?"

"Perhaps." Not his first preference; Dorrmas showed hothead signs never predicted.

"Is he married?"

"With sons. His wife wears the sash, I am told."

"That is her foolishness. Are you afraid to fight with Tam?"

"If he fights, he will lose. We have more horse, and too many bows."

"Bows!" She wrinkled her nose. "A weapon for beasts, Tam says, not a thing for one man to use against another. Tam is not going to be hurt. Before he ever came north I went to see a *raf'yalu* in Yuvat, and she burnt all his dooms, sword, knife, lance, arrow and hoof. He wears the charm under his shirt. I do not begrudge the money."

When he explained he wanted her to carry a message to her brother with terms for peace, and, more generally, that Rodlakh had no ill-will for Kargul, she laughed, saying it was foolish. "Once I am out of your hands, where is your bargaining?"

"No bargain, Tú. An honorable parley. I would trust you to carry that message, if you will."

"You could compel me. You are a gentle man." She put her hands on his shoulders, and frowned. "I would much rather go on a journey with you than with Dorrmas... "

He chuckled at her perplexity. "But Dorrmas is new, and if we do go south you might not have another chance at him. We shall travel together, Tú, unless — " Unless he failed to come back from the *Mankh'*, was the thought. "Unless I am detained, which is not likely."

She brightened out of brief gloom. "How did you know? About Dorrmas?"

"Magic. No, I have been through it myself." She spoke as if he could, in any case, have stopped her from doing what she wanted. She was grateful, even admiring, and with it all there was a faint pout. Just as at Kamsilat when they plotted against Rodlakh's virginity, he was too ready to give her up.

Petakoi did not flinch. "Wounded? Captive, his men disarmed, and you were afraid to let him come to Kadon Dinul?"

"I was, *Asayu*, and am, so long as your son remains in the field against us. If you desire to go to Tovakh at Dônshei, I can authorize that journey."

She did not respond to that, asking where her husband's lodgings were, and whether his wound gave him pain. As Dolvid answered, Tovakh was not the man to say so. "He was very brave in the fight. He is reasonably comfortable, as much as a caged mountain-lion can be."

Even steel Petakoi had to allow a faint smile for this allusion. "If I did desire to go to Dônshei would you spare men to escort me?"

"The journey would not be permitted without an escort, *Asayu*."

"Even in chains you fear us."

"If fear is the word. Your house, *Asayu*, exulted in use of Aëlu as a hostage, so as to nullify Sebhal's army. I have not sent word to your son telling him to lay down arms in return for your safety, or his father's, or that of his sister, who is with us here at Kadon."

Petakoi's power lay in what she knew, and she hated to show surprise. Recovering, she asked why they were keeping Kamin-Tarú from her.

"We are not keeping her from, or making her go anywhere. She can come when she wants."

"*Bôdhrai*, you will tell her I command her to come at once."

"I'll tell her that is what you said, *Asayu*."

"The reason you do not use hostages," Petakoi hardly blinked. "Is that Kamin-Tolagh would not believe your threats."

"True, but Kargul's are always believed. We have our memories. Hard adversaries who count on our softness cannot be trusted — as you say, even when in chains."

"One moment, *Bôdhrai* — " he had turned on his heel, and Petakoi, unoffended, called him back. "Our daughter came here from where?"

"Kamsilat."

"But you do not take hostages."

He explained how Tú had come to Kamsilat on her own, and was never restrained, how she might have left sooner, but the Patriarch, Petakoi might have heard, had closed the Strait.

She was dour. "She has given my son a great deal of anxiety. She ought to be whipped."

Our daughter, my son. "Is that the only way Kargul can show its affection, with the lash? While Tú is under the care of this *rabhsayum* she is not going to be harmed."

"The *rabhsai*, the man you would call our *rabhsai* — Rodlakh Lambarrati, does he also call our daughter Tú?" Petakoi's mind was visibly turning to new opportunities.

Amused, he told her he understood Rodlakh, though he had many responsibilities, had done so, and Petakoi cited all she and Dolvid had in common, their Owani blood, his training at the *Mankh'*, her birth on the Island. He did not answer that he had cut across a corner of her family lands, pursued by the *Adanum Plakh'*, after a raid on Drin b'Afon.

Her foundations laid, she asked him, between what ought to be friends, whether Rodlakh and Kamin-Tarú might be a match.

"For the looks, *Asayu*?" This was teasing. "They are both tall and well-made, handsome together."

"You are not a village magistrate, and we are not talking about some country couple to be judged by eye. Could this not be an accommodation, even the end of all the old grudges?"

This, at present, was a distraction. It had its attraction, no matter what Saidhan laid down about the need for a Mixed *rabhsayu*, but could be discussed only on one condition. "If this were to be put to the *rabhsai*, *Asayu*, would Kargul desist from all acts of war?"

"Would your forces desist from theirs against Kargul?"

"Willingly." This readiness caught her off-guard a little.

"It would need," slowly, "the participation of *g'Asalladh'*, who has firm views as to the succession."

Yes, it would be absurd to betroth her daughter to a man her ally the Patriarch wanted to humble. "They may be less firm than they were — " not explaining about Orbanak's release. He told Petakoi he intended in any event to confer with *g'Asalladh'*, and if Kargul joined in a declaration no rival claimants to *rabhsayum* would be entertained, the views of the *Mankh'* might be of some value.

"You want surrender first and then negotiation, *Bôdhrai*."

It was slipping away. "Why does it always come to this with baKargul? If we begin by doubting Rodlakh's true title, what is the object of discussing Kamin-Tarú's match with the *rabhsai*? I had hoped we were going to deal honestly, for once."

"Is it honest dealing to grab so quickly for a truce you know would favor you, giving you more chance to build your garrisons?"

"*Asayu*, it occurred to me it was horrible to have men killing each other while their overlords discussed wedding-feasts. Kamin-Tolagh's situation, with or without a truce, is desperate, his father beaten and our strength growing. The most he can do is to cause further deaths before he is defeated. We could save the realm from that."

Petakoi's smile was corrosive. "We all have our realms to save, do we not. For me, illiterates and hairy goat-herds in posts of ancient Owani power is no realm at all, worse than none. I had just as soon see *jinzal* in the Residence."

She was wasting his time. Dolvid had half-enjoyed this high-style fencing with a skilled adversary, almost approving some of his own rant. Petakoi meant what she said, and only a battered, weary army stood in the way of *jinzal* in the Residence indeed. He had been seduced by vanity, the dream of solving all questions with negotiation, always at the center of it all. What it was, this hint at marriage, was one last toehold for Kargul, in case all their schemes and the *Mankh*'s came, or had already come, to nothing.

"*Asayu*, I must ask leave."

"If I do not give it?"

"Would you force me to be discourteous?"

She went smoothly into the Old Tongue, to say, "*You see virtue in these antique hypocrisies, Bôdhrai? In a show of respect to a captive foe? Yet you strive for the extinction of Owan, womb of all such graces.*"

Futile to lecture this resourceful woman on Froghuli hospitality, the dignified courtesy of a poor Gabhani farmer, the gentleness of a fighting-man like Galt, the radiance of Âna, called *mongrel* in this very spot by Petakoi. In ordinary language, he said, "What is truly good in Owan can survive, as gold does, perhaps stamped with new faces, new virtues we never thought of."

"New evils, too. I would not have expected this chronicler of past crimes, this exile, this husband to Bolan's wife to be sentimental."

"He would not have anticipated there being so much to admire in someone who can do so much harm."

She actually laughed. "My leave, *Bôdhrai*, before you corrupt me with your virtues. A very Owani kind of corruption, let me say."

Everything took longer than it ought; he was beginning to doubt he could start for the South today, even if it all went smoothly at the *Mankh'*; there was no certainty the Patriarch would receive him at once.

Faëdhal was found on the main staircase. His wings continued to spread; the sword-wearing week as Dorrmas's advisor had increased rather than changed him: there might now be two Faëdhals in the same lean body. Now, for instance, the familiar one was strongly urging Dolvid not to risk the *Mankh'*, to send someone else, while the other very sensibly went through a mental list of questions as to his intentions in case he did not return to carry them out.

Faëdhal reported they had released Rheduban's killer, at-Zhâlai, this morning, as instructed in the message sent last night from Owan Sai, enclosing a note for *g'Asalladh'*. "He was, to my eye, more than dubious about riding to the *Mankh'*."

"I am not surprised. By the Treaty he was going into the hands of the only power that could punish him for the murder. But he has taken my note. Where else would he go?"

They had come to the large sobriety of the Oak-Wall Chamber. "A strange deed." Faëdhal pursed his lips at the spot where Rheduban had died. "But treachery takes precedence over all other learnings, does it not, at the *Mankh'*. Do not go, Dolvidh."

Dolvid was thinking how none of the close acquaintance of Rheduban had condemned or regretted the killing. "It is sad there are creatures born good for nothing but pain and death, till at last they are killed. *Jinzal.*"

"In many ways," judiciously, "he very much resembled a *jinzai*, as all reliable reports describe them, though to be sure, nimbler on his feet."

No quarrel. "Even a hint of the *tra'munu*. When his eyes first came on me I could hardly lift my sword." But he did not want to talk about or relive that fight. They passed on, coming to the door to the Private Audience Chamber.

Faëdhal would not let go. "This, in fact, was running in my head, because of that curious old document you sent me by way of Norlum the stablemaster — curious, indeed, if not so very old. It is, I judge, of Kanavakh's brief age."

"It came from a boat believed to be Kanavakh's." With his mind on nearer and farther things, it took an effort to recall what document Faëdhal meant, the one he and Rodlakh had plundered from the chest, before sending the boat to its grave in Arnan.

"Ah. Then perhaps after all one might dig up a shred of sense among all the gibberish. The style is most odd, and the subject even odder." Faëdhal had pulled out a flat wooden box and lifted the lid.

"Kanavakh was beyond odd himself, and the earlier Gabh'Owan rulers used a dialect or manufactured variant of the Owanilú, from the Island *Mankh'*, in private writings. But there is no time now for rummaging in history."

"Yes, yes, a horrible man, a madman. Nevertheless, if the truth could be, as it were, skimmed out, there might be a clue here to the mystery of Lost Plakhan."

Caught. Five minutes, surely, could be spared for a matter where Rheduban, *jinzal*, Lost Plakhan and his brother Kanavakh were all in some improbable way juxtaposed.

Faëdhal shuffled sheets. "These are some notes I made. Not, I must hasten to add, a proper idiomatic translation; the usage is most obscure, and the use of the Script highly individual. You will no doubt be able to suggest improvements in some of the obscurer points."

Besides the sketched translation in Faëdhal's precise and graceful hand, there was what he said was an exact copy made to preserve the fragile original from too much handling. That, too, was now carefully spread beside the other pages.

At first it seemed incomprehensible, a document for them to pore and wrangle over, as in the old days.

`Men say my name is Hurtful,' was Faëdhal's rendering of the opening. Well, but Dolvid preferred the reading he had made standing on a gravelled spit beside Rodlakh, `They call me cruel.'

`Hranakh is Hradhi, Hradhi must be Hranakh.' That
could not be altered, and was mad enough to support the idea the
writer was Kanavakh in person, blasphemously muddling Wise
Minister and Lord of the Dark.

`Blood whitens (cleanses?) blood, in blood shall I ?gild
my blood.' Coming on that Dolvid was almost ready to throw the
thing up as nonsensical raving, when his eye caught the word
jinzai, in the next paragraph of Faëdhal's draft:

`What hurt should I do when Plakhan my brother gives
life. To his lady small jinzai came, which he ?quenched,
discovering. Hence shall I be Rabhsai, since he in grief
(illegible).

`Yet in my blood sends again.

`G'Asalladh' has said it is outwoman (?) who had blood
jinzal took. Grant this, O Aëlovoi! My self son Plakhval is small
of mouth (speaks little?), and Vonavu is great again. G'Asalladh'
has said, one lonely clan of Kufshei bears these taints (?) begun
in lusts of soldiers of Shaël. Long known in the Manadilum.

`The stallion must hold our blood unmixed, the mother
longfathered of this same. Thus says g'Asalladh'. Maëdhi makes
his word come inside.'

"Not laghi, Faëdhal," Dolvid said, "it is leghi."

"Is it?" He peered at the copy. "Ah, yes. Very possibly."

"It is the same in the original."

"Yes, yes. Where there is so little to make sense, the
obvious can become obscure. It would be `Maëdhi let his words
be true,' then."

Faëdhal, with Dolvid, was convinced the writer was
Kanavakh. "Might it not be, then, that his brother Plakhan lost all
heart for the realm when his beloved bride was killed by jinzal?"

"That is not what it says: `the outwoman who had blood
jinzal took.' I suppose `outwoman,' van'naëdhu, to mean the bride
of Plakhan, whose blood was partly of the Western tribes. But
jinzal do not take blood when they kill. They tear flesh." They
were doing so now, while scholars quibbled over the incoherent
words of a long-dead maniac, but he could not banish conviction
this had something to do with present troubles. The hair on his

forearms rose as a possible interpretation began to come to him. Notion coalescing he read on, and began trembling so much the sheets rattled together.

"`...when Plakhan my brother gives life — ' You have a stop there in the copy, and it is only mildew. Listen: `Why should I not be cruel? When my brother Plakhan fathers a jinzai child upon his bride, and seeing what it is, smothers it.' Then again, here, not yolan, but yi-olan."

"Yes, yes," Faëdhal nodded, `he would be.'"

"`It would be — ' in fact, `Yet it would still be in my blood.'"

"Which I suppose may be taken to mean he shared the same blood with his brother?" Faëdhal's only weakness as a translator had always been a refusal to adduce meanings from context. He had an added disadvantage here, never having read at the Mankh' library, where the young Dolvid had labored with page after page of the longwinded Island Patriarchs with whom this synthetic aristocratic variant of the Owanilú had begun. With something to go on, Faëdhal began making better readings, though the real sense of what they were translating seemed not to strike him.

"This passage clearly means g'Asalladh' reassured Kanavakh it was not the blood he shared with his brother that was to blame, but that of the outwoman, the bride from the tribes. But then, `Plakhval my son is small of mouth.'?"

"Kanavakh must have been apprehensive his son would be born with jinzal features, like his brother's. Or, no — this must have been written shortly before the birth of their daughter, Volsivu; `Vonavu is great again — ' that is to say, pregnant for the second time. This, then, was in late 2561 or early 2562, the year Volsivu was born. The son, Plakhval, was already alive before Plakhan went on the Bride-Quest. Kanavakh is saying, `No reason why my coming child should have the face of a jinzai. Plakhval does not.' And the then-Patriarch has reassured him this strain is to be found only in a single clan of the Kufshei tribes." It drifted into Dolvid's head that Kamin-Tarú had talked about a scandal to do with Rheduban's mother having some tribal blood.

"But what is this about `beginning in the lusts of Shaël's soldiers'?"

"Something to do with the First Empire, and how *jinzal* came into our history."

"Dolvidh!" Faëdhal was severe. "We are speaking, surely — Kanavakh, I mean, surely is — of a somewhat *jinzai*-like appearance, as with Rheduban."

"No, I think not — " solemnly, struck with the awe of it. "I believe this is the true secret of the birth of *jinzal*. Here, not *stallion, sire*. And, `a mother of the same ancestry.' He says when a woman whose Kufshei blood is already mixed with Owani mates again with Owani — "

"The children are *jinzal*? But — "

"The sons only. It must be true, it solves all the old riddles. If *jinzal* are freak male offspring of a cross-mating, it explains why in all the centuries no female has ever been seen, no *jinzayu*, and how the *jinzal* manage to survive though they have never been known to mate. Also, it clarifies how the tribes of the West all say the Empire of Owan brought the *jinzal*, whereas our accounts all agree the *jinzal* came out of the West. Both could be true."

Faëdhal had an objection. "This says the sire must be `our blood unmixed.' I take that to mean — " clearing his throat apologetically — "*Lekh'Owani*. But ever since they first appeared *jinzal* have continued to appear. How could they have been fathered by unmixed Owani blood all through the Night of Owan and down to our own day?"

When listening to the story of the brothers Thuladh and Dhunival about the men who controlled the *jinzal*, plainly men of Owan, Dolvid had hated the notion of a tide-pool left behind when Empire receded, but now he could not see any other solution. Somehow, living unknown to the realm in the remote West a settlement of Owanil, men and women, had kept their bloodlines pure through all the centuries, except those men who, mating with women of this one Kufshei tribe, fathered *jinzal*. "I could not see how it was possible, but here Kanavakh says it had long been known in the *Manadilum*, and the Teachers would never make a mistake over something like this." Past and present were muddling painfully; this was an excess of news.

"But if these, ah, left-behind Owanil troubled to keep their own bloodlines pure — " Faëdhal too was struggling.

"It can only mean that for many centuries they have bred *jinzal* by design. In the beginning they must have seemed an accident, but when they solved the riddle they must have seen if they could ever tame and train the *jinzal*, they could have an army no one could resist."

"But who could ever desire such an army?"

"To conquer our lands — reconquer, as they would say, lands anciently theirs? To maintain their rule forever, in a subjection of terror? This must have been, for half an age, the only ambition of this settlement. You and I and Rodlakh have the bad luck to see its harvest."

"This secret, if indeed we have it right, was formerly known, it would seem in both the *Manadilum* of the *Mankh'*, and in *rabhsayum*. What a pity the shame of Plakhan, as it would seem, kept it concealed. If the realm had only learned about this breeding place, we might have gone in great strength, years ago, before the *jinzal* had grown to such numbers, and, ah — "

"Exterminated them, yes. But how many of our tales mention *Lunu Jinzalladhiyu*, the Valley of the Jinzai-Fathering? We have always known, Faëdhal; it is just that we did not want to believe."

Cool for a mid-spring day, but the rain had gone away, and the assembling of his escort, saddled horse held at the foot of the Steps, brought together a small gathering of the inquisitive. He was known by sight now, and heard mutters and whispers of "*Bôdhrai*," and "Rodlakh's man." Faëdhal had been instructed in policy, many documents given him for safekeeping. Shumat in the south had the military plans, and would be seconded by Kizhunai, Acting Captain of Armies (an invented title, which could not require confirmation in Council). Nothing was left to keep him from the *Mankh'*, unless his fear did.

Closer to hand his name was called, and he saw a slender woman, somewhat apart from the small throng, come towards him. Not tall, certainly not meanly dressed; Khalú. A pikeman barred her way, and Dolvid called the man off.

Speaking his name again she reached to grasp his wrist with her small hand. The pikeman, not altogether reassured, was still hovering.

"I am told Bolan is wounded, and a prisoner. Dol, I must see him."

"He is a prisoner, not much wounded. Tovakh was wounded. I regret you were not notified; I have been very busy." Pulling on riding-gloves he continued down to where Enikai was waiting, while Khalú sidestepped, leaning urgently. Petakoi would not have praised his courtesy now.

Made of subtle changes, the difference in her was great. To judge by eyelids she had been weeping, but the eyes were clear, less round than he remembered, the corners drawn out a little. Soft sides of her face had planed away to leave in relief the fine, high, tapering bones; short of thirty she was altogether more arresting in her looks than half-a-dozen years ago. He had forgotten the fascination of the small, slightly rounded, faintly projecting front teeth.

The boy holding Enikai was shivering in a thin shirt, and Dolvid dismissed him.

"And you were wounded."

"Not much. Too many are dead."

"Dolvidh, I must see Bolan."

"He is not here." This was unnecessary, coming out of the deep well of rancor spilling over into his brain and his guts. He was ashamed.

"I was told he was brought to Kadon. Dolvidh?" He remembered that tone of reproach, one half of his name a dagger-thrust, the other curling up into a wheedle.

"Not quite. He is at the Bronze Residence." Another thing to displease Dorrmas, who complained Bolan was harder to guard there, easier for determined men to rescue. A dismissive *What men?* had ended that discussion. Bolan was to be made adequately comfortable, and his guards were Shumat's soldiers. A last precaution and a last compassion not to use men formerly under his direct command.

Yet Bolan in regular communication with the Families could be a great nuisance; Khalú could not come and go as she chose, potentially as her father's courier. "Would you share his captivity?"

She stared and looked away: the question, with *exile* instead of *captivity*, had come up before.

"That was not the same," tongue suddenly thick. "Bolan will be released quite soon, and he will be allowed to remain here in the Heartland."

"Can I not see him?"

He had pushed through an imagined barrier, and was going to be all right. "Yes, I think you had better do that. I am going that way; you can ride with me now."

She thanked him seriously, but laughed when he grasped her small waist to lift her into the saddle. She was still no heavier than a handful of kitten.

"You have become very mighty." From the unaccustomed sidesaddle position she glinted down some of the remembered mischief.

"The world turns." Looping the reins past her he swung up.

"What will become of Bolan? He has not done anything wrong." A half-squadron, twice the men he had ordered, fell in behind. If there were wondering glances as he moved off down the Avenue he ignored them.

"No, just his duty. He told me."

"What are you going to do to him?"

"I am not going to do anything, and do not see why anything will be done to him. While the war lasts, he will be held. Bolan will not be harmed any more than he has harmed himself, I can pledge that." In his nostrils the remembered scent of Khalú was keeping him edgy.

After several breaths she said, "Then that is all finished."

"Unless your friends of Family succeed. Nothing would save Bolan from his allies."

"But the rumor is, you won completely, beat Tovakh and Bolan in an hour. If that is true, my father says, you are Rodlakh's *rabhsa'dhanai*."

"Your father was not at Dônshei. Bolan will tell you. He'll lay stress on the mutiny of his troops, the folly of Tovakh. On the field, bows won it, and Shumat, and a man named Galt."

She snuffled. "Galt? Who has a name like *Galt*?"

"A brave man, my friend. He is dead."

They were coming down the hill to Harbor Gate. Riding in at the head of Household men one of Dorrmas's officers gave a jaunty salute. With the perplexing business of the *jinzal* haunting him Dolvid wanted to be left alone to think.

"Bolan's men would not fight? That's dreadful."

"For a captain, the finish."

"You are not certain Rodlakh is to reign?"

"Khalú, I am nearly sure." He had warned her once and now he made it plain. "If the crowd Bolan has been allied to manage to snatch the victory, there will be an order for Bolan's release. If you hear Rodlakh has been killed or Shumat defeated, Bolan should not waste ten minutes, but get out of Kadon Dinul, go to the Northeast, to Ninkufu — somewhere far off. Do not forget to tell him."

At the gate he was pleased to see the strong company of bows busy changing their strings after the rain. He passed through the gate and set out across the wide square, for what might be the last time.

"Dolvidh — "

"Yes?"

"Have you no feeling left for me?"

"Only anger," he confessed.

"It was not just that you were determined to be on the wrong side of the *rabhsai*. You were a stranger I did not know."

"I never said justified anger."

"There was no one who agreed with you, the things you said and wrote. I was warned you were defying the *rabhsai*. But for Bolan, you might have been sent to the Island. Now they will say you were in the right, all along — the world turns, but how could I foresee this?"

"Khalú — " They had ridden to the side-entrance of the Bronze Residence, and one of the escort dismounted to hold Enikai's head. "Exile did not prove me wrong, and victory will not make me right. It may become a fashion to decry Preference — it was once before, in the reign of Banak and Laluvoi. That is not bad, we need fashions in virtue. But there always have to be some aware what justice is, who do not have to wait for fashion to tell them. Otherwise we are all a flock of geese."

"You never change. I ask about you, and you tell me about Banak and Laluvoi, your Three Great Mysteries, the realm, justice for all."

"Yes." And the same with Âna. That was him, and he could not find or invent a different Dolvid.

She waited while he instructed the guard. She could stay as long as she wished, overnight, a week if she wanted, but if she left she was not to be readmitted without new orders.

"You are saying I can have only one visit."

"No, simply that you cannot come and go, I am sorry, Khalú. There will be food, and you can send for clothes. If you can't stay, see Faëdhal about your next visit."

"I'll stay," defiantly. "Why not? Now Bolan is out of favor the Residence Quarter will not be nice, and Arbhu Hills is dreary till it's summer. Nobody comes there now, except a few old men."

That strongly reminded him of something or someone else. He had no time.

His foot was in the stirrup. "Dol — "

"I cannot stay." He could never be back from the *Mankh'* early enough to begin a journey tonight.

"Will you marry again? Have you got a special friend?"

He made a slack gesture. "I am glad to see you so well."

Very quietly, thinking of it only now, she said, "If I stay by Bolan you will respect me again, for that. Do you know I always saw everything through your eyes?"

"You said long ago: even if I had not been exiled, we would have been apart." He meant this to say he did not blame her for not going into exile with him, but in the cool voice he kept to, it came out as a needless brutality. Khalú opened her mouth to say nothing, and turned away swiftly, his order in her hand, to go into the Bronze Residence. He knew she was weeping.

After so much he was taking to the *Mankh'* road again with a horse he had come to admire. Lordly Enikai would not be pleased to be matched with an aging piebald (now long dead), short in the wind, coughing on wet days.

The escort was dismissed, and as he mounted the bank to skirt the road-barricade archers there cheered him. He waved, still trying to work out his feelings on the meeting with Khalú. Chiefly, it seemed, simple relief; the encounter was bound to come, and now it was over.

Now. If the origins of the *jinzal* were accurately described in Kanavakh's hectic scrawl, how had the mystery persisted so long? Accept the solution, once known, was forgotten with so much else in the long age of the Night, but it was four centuries since Plakhan went off forever, and the secret was known then, according to Kanavakh, in the *Manadilum*, from which the present Patriarch came. That was also true when Kanavakh wrote his account, ga-Owan-Alladh XIV, who, like this Patriarch, had been Head of the Teaching Order, *Menadhi*. If that Order had known so long, why had there been no laws, warnings, or, as Faëdhal said, an expedition to stamp out the breeding-place of the *jinzal*?

Abstracted, he halted Enikai. Khalú's complaint about the dreariness of the Arbhu Hills came back to him, and he recalled now where he had heard something almost identical: Kamin-Tarú. She said the same about Peframi in the western corner of Kargul: no one ever came there except *atarlal*, and after a few days they

rode on. Rode on, a striking choice of words; a woman of Kargul
would, he was sure, speak of heading east and north for the
Heartland as riding *back*. These *atarlal* rode on. Yet south and
west quite soon would bring them to Kargan baDulfu, the greatest
range of the six provinces, hemming in Kargul along the south
shore of Arnan, and reputedly impassable.

When the frightened traders Thuladh and Dhunival had
escaped from their post overlooking the Lunu Jinzalladhiyu the
first road they had come to, unlike all the later ones, which struck
out to the northeast, for Drin Navuna and the Colony, had run
almost due east, best-finished of the roads they saw, a well-
established route. Cowering beside that road the brothers had
been almost in the southward foothills of Kargan baDulfu.
Peframi, where the *atarlal* rode on, was on the other side, an
arduous journey, probably, but Dolvid now had no doubt there
was a way through the mountains. For men of the *Mankh'* to
come and go, to and from Lunu Jinzalladhiyu.

He discovered his escort, notwithstanding orders, had been
following him at a distance, and the officer now caught him to ask
if there was anything wrong.

"This," sickly, "was to be the glory of Old Owan restored."

"A shoe, is it, *Bôdhrai*?" The man was glancing down at
Enikai's feet.

"Nothing. I have changed my mind, I am not riding for the
Mankh'." What did he have to say to men who bred *jinzal*? He
was trembling as he turned Enikai. At his most rancorous he
could never have believed the *Atarlum* so evil.

The Long Retreat

As foreseen there was grumbling among ordinary soldiers when the order was given to abandon the Causeway defenses, which might very well have held; hard to convince them they would eventually be doomed by capture of faraway Banakit. Withdrawal from the fortress was accomplished with greater ease than expected, and Rodlakh said the enemy here was holding back, confident these men would be trapped when the road was cut behind them. Before riding on he reinstructed resignedly obedient squadron officers that retreat must continue at a steady pace no matter what the *jinzal* did or failed to do.

For Âna who went with the cavalry it was all fleeting pictures, that ride, unnaturally clear. Unmeaning details were burned in; roadside flowers, a woman carrying her cripple son, the broken wheel of a cart which must somehow have continued its journey, carrion birds flapping above crags. Late in the day, short of Kreshavu, they encountered a fast-messenger going west. Rodlakh pulled his squadron to the side so he could open dispatches forwarded by Saidhan.

He gave a vast happy whoop; soldiers riding dourly past turned their heads, grins coming. "He has done it, Dolvid! This was written at the Residence — the Residence, Âna."

Now she heard in brief about the landing at Owan Sai, the winning-over of Kizhunai, the Residence fight and death of Rheduban. "There he was at fault, challenging single-fight with companies of men standing by. I do not question his skill, but avenging Sebhal was not his particular duty, and no one is proof against accidents. Where would our plans be if he had been lost?"

Her face hot from knowing she, not dead Sebhal, had caused that duel, she did not speak. Rheduban's death gave no personal satisfaction; she was glad the realm did not have him in it any longer, and could vividly recall the reasons for wanting revenge, but not the feelings. Perhaps she did not dare bring those back.

When it came to Dônshei, he shook his head. "I would have dealt with Kamin-Tolagh first."

"Tovakh seems to him the nearer threat, and he hopes, as he says, to add Shumat's forces to his own. He is not sure he has the troops for meeting Kamin-Tolagh — " startled by her own clarity.

After reconsideration, he nodded, admitting Dolvid was probably right, especially if he could prevent Bolan and Tovakh from marching on Kadon. His own choice of Kamin-Tolagh might be because he was hungry for a worthy human adversary, a fight with honor and honors to be won. "Except they are bigger than any jackal and fiercer than a weasel, this is only vermin-killing."

"*Rabhsai*," ardently, "If there is fighting at Banakit you must not be so much in the thick of it."

"Very well." She knew he was lying.

The evening calm in Kreshavu contrasted with the turbulence of the road below. A single half-squadron of cavalry remained to chase looters, not much of a task if *jinzal* were coming here, but the gloomy hostel-keeper, boarding his windows up, loading some last treasures onto two packhorses, remarked, "*Asai*, if the world was splitting in half, there would be some hanging about hoping to strike gold."

Âna was saying silently, *Here I was happy*. The emptied town made her shiver, and she would not spend the night there, preferring to be below at the cavalry-post. Sad past bearing to picture uncouth *jinzal* shambling through these streets beneath the slender trees.

Next day there was Fifth Bridge, where she had been reunited with Dolvid. The compound was now a way-station for refugees, and Arvat was here, trying to see to the fair distribution of bread and cooked meat, of which, for the moment, there was an abundance, many having killed off livestock rather than see animals shrink and perhaps die on the long road.

"*Deghi*, how far are we to retreat? Can *jinzal* ever come here?" She saw Rodlakh stiffen at the question, a sore-spot. Many obviously believed they were yielding too much ground without exacting a price from the enemy, and those who had left their farms were bitterest about this. But Arvat's concern was not that; he shyly explained there was a young woman in his special care, newly widowed, with a daughter of less than two. Âna saw her just before riding on: the mother must have married at sixteen, and surely was not twenty now, small, pretty, very trusting of Arvat, who might at last have found his reason for growing up — here, Âna went by Sebhal's opinion of the man, forever the boy who had escaped his father's murderers. Rodlakh told him to send mother and daughter to Kamsilat, where Arvat must soon be arriving. When the *rabhsai* added his hope they would not have to retreat farther than the port, Arvat had the face of someone not sure whether it is a joke.

Here where the road was wider the refugees, though slow, kept moving, with no need to flatten against a wall while the cavalry nosed its way past carts and pack-donkeys. Rodlakh said, "If only there is no holdup at Fourth Bridge, we can do it." News from Banakit was that all troops available had gone up into the Lunu Tezh' Gate to slow the enemy there.

She remembered food; there was no name for the place where they stopped to rest and eat. Rodlakh mentioned Arvat's young woman, and from there was a simple step to, "That question you promised to consider... "

Not yet, to herself.

"Have you?"

"Not as I would like, with some quiet for thinking in. Nothing familiar is left in the world for me. You do me great honor."

He made a face at the convention. "Not if you do not think you would be happy."

She heard perhaps the start of a reconsidering of his own. The proposal had been nothing if not impetuous. "We might both want to give this some more thought."

"It could not be more in my thoughts than now. If I do not marry you, I shall stay single."

"If — " she began, and cancelled that. "When you come into your power, *Deghi*, you will have your pick of Six Provinces, and a long life for regretting haste." She at once perceived idiocy: as *rabhsai*, married or single, he had no need to deny himself any pleasure; if he wanted he could have, not just his pick, but all the realm's beauties. But his father's attachment to Saëdhu had been a lasting wonder, a mystery to the cynical.

"Will you marry me, if I live?"

"You — " coming back to an earlier discussion, "You must stay away from so many risks. You have already spent ten times the luck of both your grandfathers put together — "

"A war-leader belongs at the head of his men."

"Before, you were just a war-leader. Now there is hope at Kadon Dinul, the realm needs you alive."

"Well, if you would promise me a future worth staying alive for — " He laughed as he said this, she did not. "Well then, seriously, how can I ask others to do what I will not? It is my manhood."

"What about responsibility? What others cannot do, you can. If the *jinzal* are beaten, but Rodlakh killed, all your dead will have died to save the realm for Preference." Intent on her point she was surprised by tears that trickled down her face. He gently took her chin in one hand and wiped her face with a kerchief. "Well, I shall not take so many risks," he said, and stood, helping her up. "If we can hold them back at Banakit it will be mostly a bowman's affair. With this shoulder I cannot do much with a bow."

Kreshavu's desertion had been strange; the Vale of Banakit was eerie. Not one-tenth of its people were left, almost all in the town. With humans and livestock even birds seemed to have abandoned the farms; the absence of small sounds struck the ear.

In the town shops were shuttered, houses boarded up, while small detachments of cavalry clopped through bare streets. By Saidhan's orders some smiths remained, a wheelwright, and harnessmakers, busy with repairs, would be among the last to leave. Two hostel-keepers and some who had drink-shops had elected to stay, and there were as many weekwives as there had ever been. Their prices were said to have gone up.

As Rodlakh with Âna came to the town residence on its low fir-set hill, a sleepless Happ was at the door. "*Rabhsai*, I am more than glad to see you."

"Where is Saidhan *Asai*? Resting?"

"Far from it." Happ indicated the southward hills. "He has ridden for Lunu Tezh' Gate, with the last cavalry to arrive here."

Rodlakh was out of the saddle so tigerishly Âna thought he was going to assault the anxious Happ. So did Happ, who took a step back. "*Rabhsai*, he took up a lance. He said he carried one in four reigns, and would not fail a fifth. The men were very heartened."

"I am sure they were."

"*Deghi*, he said a senior commander was needed to direct the defense, till you came."

Rodlakh looked as if he would grasp at the man's shirt, but merely left his right hand spread on Happ's chest. "You are senior enough, but he knew you were not competent. Did any new reports come in to make him do this?"

"*Rabhsai*," Happ was masking anger now. "He said our troops were too scattered."

"His hands," turning to Âna, and near tears. "He cannot hold a weapon properly; his thumbs are too stiff. I am going after him."

He stayed just for *raminat* and some cold food, and would not listen to Âna, who wanted him to sleep.

"Happ is going to need some goading," soft-voiced. They were in the room where suits and criminal cases were judged, panels of mellowed wood, with highbacked chairs and a long oak table. "He has to keep the road from clogging. I hear there is already half a mile of people and animals waiting to cross Fourth Bridge. Happ must make some order."

"He — "

"Yes, I was far too harsh with him — I'll apologize before I go. Saidhan's unwisdom is not his fault." Rodlakh said more about the need for some fast-riding patrols to watch for stray *jinzal*; what was called the Gate was a number of larger and smaller ways through the hills.

She was alone again, watching survivors tramp through, counting wounded brought back from the Drin, waiting for news from everywhere. Leaving, Rodlakh had touched a hand to the left side of his tarnishing breastplate, to signify his vow to stay out of the forefront of battle. She might have believed it, if Saidhan had not ridden out.

From the west she heard the *jinzal* had been left behind at the Causeway, but later there was word archers of the rearguard had turned and fought when overtaken by the *jinzai* advance. As planned, Sixth Bridge, the wooden one the near side of Kreshavu, was broken behind the retreat. Rodlakh, who rode in strained from lack of sleep, was encouraged they had succeeded so far.

Saidhan remained in the field, annoyed he had been thought fool enough to ride into battle at his age; he had remained well back from any fighting, and Rodlakh conceded he could hardly be ordered to safety.

Here, without walls, the increasing *jinzal* forces could not be held; at best the cavalry could kill the foremost and retreat again. Losses were not small, and once past the Gate in strength *jinzal* could be in Banakit in three hours. Saying the last of the cavalry might be closely pursued, Rodlakh found reliable officers to take charge of the two minor wooden bridges across the Navu near Banakit, to have them destroyed behind the last of the retreat.

From the last shopkeeper to board up his doors she had bought a fat little bottle of tawny wine, but Rodlakh had no time for tasting it. Her disappointment when he was gone became a deeper distress when she saw his careful instructions about destruction of the bridges must mean he himself intended to be with the final rearguard.

Arvat came to show her new-made fire-arrows sent up from Kamsilat. The shafts could be set burning with a glowing tinder-cord, and could not easily be put out. "These were commanded by Dolvid. Old learning has its uses, as he would say."

"I think he would say, learning is its own profit."

"That's a fact," Arvat did a tolerable exaggeration of Dolvid being didactic: "I am not asking you to learn this for my sake, but suggesting you do so for your own."

"Was he right?"

"You did not know him then, did you? At the Bronze Residence? He is changed. Then again, he is just the same. He laughed more then — I remember him and old Faëdhal cackling over something only they could read — some bawdy tale, most likely, would you say?"

"I would guess you were the one hunting the bawdy tales."

Arvat gave her a sharp look, and she wondered whether she really did go in for pointless provocation. At this meeting Arvat had not till now shown a sign of being aware she was a woman; evidently that was hard for her to support, and she had put out her false signal. If anything he repelled her, and she certainly was not seeking a renewal of his inept advances, all words.

Not shifting his stance Arvat moved his voice closer. "All you hear now is Rodlakh *Rabhsai*, his skill at war, his friendliness. I wish I could be with the *rabhsayum*. Oh, the Colony has been good to me, but now we've got a *rabhsai* for all the people, Kadon Dinul is the spot to be, would you say? It is my home. My sister is there. I would like to have a place at the Residence."

"So would Rodlakh."

Arvat opened his mouth, but recognized the unanswerable. They were up on the walls of Banakit where a watch could be kept southward. From time to time Âna saw horsemen or imagined *jinzal* in the narrow band of farming on the right bank of the river.

"Here they come," but Arvat was pointing at the westward road, at last empty of refugees. Approaching was the rearguard of the Army, mainly bows. Soon they were coming into the town, dirty, dishevelled, some with wounds, almost all cheerful to be here ahead of the *jinzal*. They sang songs, shouted boasts to the few there to hear them. Idmas, an officer remembered from the day she met Dolvid at Fifth Bridge, said they had felled many *jinzal* with archery, but in one stretch where the road doubled back, descending, had lost some men to *jinzal* bows. But the *jinzai*-masters had kept their advance cautious where any turn could be an ambush, and the confines of the road meant they could not send their companies charging at weak spots. Now the pursuit was very distant, presumably trying to find a way to restore Sixth Bridge, cut behind the retreat. "We could have held them," he insisted, and when Wanildhai arrived, upright and detached as if riding for recreation, he concurred, though he added *jinzal* were good climbers, and eventually might have worked their way past any defenses. "Better at Vonni's Jaws," he told Happ's ceiling. "Massed bows on a narrow front, we'll pile *jinzal* dead ten deep. The *rabhsai* needs a hand?"

The orders, as Happ repeated, were for the main force to continue to Fourth Bridge; it was Âna who said bows already at the two small bridges could be reinforced, to be sure of stopping any enemy that might outrace some of the rearguard. Rodlakh's desperate parting instruction, that even at cost of abandoning some of the last defenders, the bridges must be broken if there was any danger the *jinzal* would take them intact, was an order sure to be disregarded if the *rabhsai* himself was among those last.

Midday came and went, time crawling in the dead town. Messengers had been sent to find the *rabhsai* and tell him withdrawal past Banakit was nearly complete, but no word came back.

Mid-afternoon, cavalry began coming into view on the bare brown hills beyond the farmlands, twenty and thirty-man remnants of full squadrons, riding hard. Though a better general view could be had from the roof of the official residence in the middle of Banakit, she could not bear to be so far from the crossings, and with Idmas and a clump of war-weary bowmen made the short ride eastward to where some sixty bows were already crowded by the near end of the flat wooden bridge, low to the full river. On the far side were lancers, and as they came down to the rough span *jinzal*, heads working hard, appeared higher up beyond trees, the terror they spread never lessened by familiarity.

Doggedly horsemen who had once reached safety turned and labored back uphill to join a counter-attack. In accordance with what Rodlakh had written about tactics the cavalry no longer made massed charges but rode in open order, never afraid to give ground to draw single *jinzal* out of the pack. But this must be a small body of enemy outrunning the main mass, and after losses on both sides they were recalled by trumpets. More cavalry came into view, and soon Saidhan rode down to the bridge, face grey with fatigue. He held his back straight as ever, though the shoulders drooped.

In a knot of officers and men he rode over the planking, and seeing her called out, "The *rabhsai* is safe. So far," gesturing back. Men under the Red Blossom banner were trotting down.

Rodlakh came just ahead of the last of all contingents to reach the bridge; not a dignified arrival; some of his squadron were interspersed with advancing *jinzal*, and he shouted for axes to begin their work in earnest; a start had earlier been made.

He swung back away from the bridge, and many *jinzal* were now in sight, some on the track, others trampling through farmland. Had they made straight for the bridge there would have been a hot fight to hold them off while supports were hacked away, but their masters, cloaked men above with their trumpets and whips, halted them to reassemble companies.

When his *pefrai* had one hoof on the bridge, Rodlakh turned to gaze upstream. The bridge there, over a mile away, could not be seen for trees and the slow curve of the Navu, but in sight was a strong band of *jinzal* heading for that point, and clearly they would reach there ahead of cavalry contingents disentangling from fights higher up. Rodlakh, raising a hand, began to turn, evidently with the idea of taking his squadron to this new danger-spot, using the riverside track, its whole length threatened by approaching enemy. Âna, mounting to the near end of the span, screamed, "*Rabhsai*, no!

"They have a hundred bows there," less frantically when he turned, questioning. He gave another look, nodded, and let his hand drop. His smile was deeply sad as he rode to Âna, axes now trembling the bridge.

"You are not wounded again?"

"My fool's luck is holding. This is my third mount. What about the other bridge?"

An hour ago, she told him, they had burning pitch ready to be poured. With the last of Rodlakh's squadron across, their own bridge was tottering. At the last a company of *jinzal* came at their best crushing pace, and the leaders were on the bridge when they were met by a hammer-blow of arrows in giant, swooshing volley. Following *jinzal* stumbled over the abruptly dead, and with a last burst of chopping, hammering and furious kicks the bridge tipped, a middle section breaking away to float slowly downriver. A puff of smoke upstream, followed at once by the leap of flame, meant the other bridge was gone.

Amid cheering Rodlakh confided, "We shall not be beaten. We have killed over two hundred, and unless they have ten thousand they will never see Kamsilat now."

No joy was in this; he was too tired and had seen too many deaths. But then he was among the men, hailing Idmas, slapping the back of an archer, laughing at coarse jokes, calling out names. It came from Sebhal, but of course the Army of the West would never again be the one Saidhan had recruited and Sebhal led. Officers who had grown up in that army, like Edarron, were dying, and those who lived, if Rodlakh was right and something survived, would make new traditions of their own. Who would ever say *I learned my trade with Sebhal* when he could boast, *I fought in the Great Jinzai War?*

The last lap through and up out of the Vale of Banakit was a strange affair, with the rearguard of the Army moving on the road, *jinzal* companies within a long, speculative bowshot on the far side of the river, neither any immediate threat to the other.

Across Fourth Bridge the army would actually be back on the same side of the Navu as the enemy, but the road went steeply up while the river, turning north, plunged into a gorge; on that right bank was broken, rocky ground and then a fissured wall of rocks; the only practical way to continue eastward was to cross and recross the river.

Rodlakh, having made sure the compound was evacuated, sent Âna across ahead of him, taking up a stand by the entrance to the bridge, to see the last of the Army pass by. On the bridge and slopes overlooking archers were already posted.

Near the top she drew aside for a last look back at the Vale. Her mind unexpectedly, with that entire inward reliving that goes beyond memory, was on that night ride to Kreshavu. It became a painful longing, but how could she regret the passing of joy when its whole substance was transience? She was still baffled at how time's texture had failed, and they had not gone on loving, lesserly, perhaps, but made of the same stuff.

Saidhan was across Fourth Bridge, bestowing congratulations like a triumphant prince. He looked to her ten years younger than when she had told him her news at Kamsilat, and he mourned his losses.

Idmas was near her again. He was yet to invent a proper way to address a friend of the *rabhsai*'s not herself of high birth.

"Madam," he tried. "Your pardon, they say we're going to defend Vonni's Jaws, sit still and kill *jinzal*? Well, it might be Saidhan *Asai* could be persuaded his place is at the Great House."

He meant she might influence Rodlakh to make it so. "He wanted to share your hardship and danger, *Kímukan*." She turned to look at this serious-faced officer Dolvid had called conscientious.

Who genuinely tried not to go on, but his feelings were too strong. "He fusses us. The old should be told when they — " and now Saidhan was approaching. Idmas straightened to give a salute.

"*Kímukan*. You will be with the rearguard?"

"Behind the last pack-animals, *Asai*, with the true rearguard behind."

"You have your men together?"

"Those that can still ride, some thirty-four." Idmas indicated them.

"Close order, hah? No straggling."

Patiently, Idmas assented. About to ride on, Saidhan turned back. "I am told there has been a great killing-off of animals and building of fires at Vonn. There will be hot food for everyone. You are waiting for the *rabhsai*?"

This was for Âna. Down below, Rodlakh was crossing, helm slung at saddle-bow. "If *jinzal* had names and champions, that is one whose feats of arms would be sung for a thousand years." Eyes glistening pride, Saidhan rode on.

Idmas was adjusting equipment. "I was not up in the Gate," he muttered. Contradictory ideas might both be true.

Coming up the hill Rodlakh had seen Âna, but his gaze was past her, a tense mixture of emotions on his face. Threading past long lines of ascending troops, a small file of Frontier archers were jogging down. She recognized the Tan Lughsai men, who were supposed to be on the Mainland with Dolvid. "Galt's men?"

"Noldar's men," voice taut. She did not understand and Dolvid did not seem to be here.

"I forgot — " pulling a sheaf of pages from inside his shirt. "You have not seen the latest."

She had heard messages from the east had been carried to Rodlakh in the field, and was eager to see them, but he was greeting Noldar, and then his brother.

"*Rabhsai.*" An elaborate royal salute went with Noldar's first speaking of the title. "They say there is fighting, with *jinzal.*"

"And with men, I hear. You are in good time with your bows. One man we shall miss." He put hand to his heart.

"Not Dolvid," she managed to ask without screaming, but Noldar was agreeing, "Aye, and for more than his bow, *Deghi.*"

"Dolvid is wounded," Rodlakh told her. "Not badly enough to prevent his writing." Noldar touched the point of his forehead on the right side, and held up finger and thumb to show by how much the *Bôdhrai* had escaped death.

"With Shumat, he has had a big win at Dônshei. Bolan and Tovakh were beaten, and both are prisoners. The General Cavalry is mine. Galt was killed."

"Oh, Galt." She would have supposed him indestructible. Tears came to her eyes.

"I would give a lot of the realm to have him alive. Dolvid writes he would miss loss of a hand less." She nodded, and was truly saddened by Galt's death, but her tears were of relief.

"Better, they have snatched Orbanak out of the Patriarch's hands. He is installed at the Residence, and Dolvid says despite g'*Asalladh's* best efforts *there is no stauncher Rodlakhani than your brother, uncoerced.*"

He briefly outlined Dolvid's view the Patriarch would now be obliged to lift the blockade; aid, food and fresh fighting men, could very soon be on their way, especially if a truce could be arranged with Kamin-Tolagh.

"If we do stop the *jinzal* at Vonni's Jaws, hunger is soon going to be a worse enemy. What do you say? With his father defeated, can Kamin-Tolagh be convinced?"

Âna was amazed by the reversal of fortunes, and Rodlakh's calm. True, he had spent half a day with the news, struggling with closer worries, but she did not see how it could be done, short of sorcery. "How can I say?"

"Give me your ideas. You know the man and I do not."

Belatedly he grimaced at a poor choice of words and almost allowed one of his old blushes. She was not troubled. "There are at least two Kamin-Tolaghs. If he is in his father's helm that day, he will defy what he believes his father would defy. If his personal squadron or a new bed-friend are nearby, he will do what he thinks they might see as brave and generous. His sister could persuade him."

"So Dolvid has decided. You know Tú went back to the Mainland with Alkmas?"

"I hope she enjoyed the company — " with a sour mouth for the fisherman's remembered quirks. "She is with him now?"

"He intends to use her as a courier, a go-between, trusting to her goodwill."

"The goodwill of Kargul?"

"If he can go with her himself, she might do all he asks. She was very taken with his manners at Kamsilat."

Âna merely took note of that piece of news. Rodlakh had not mentioned this before when telling about Kamin-Tarú; men were greatly different, but did not differ greatly, not when it came to those pleasures.

Now he told her what might keep Dolvid from travelling south with his embassy, the planned confrontation with g'Asalladh', not summoning Him to the Residence, but going to the *Mankh'*, alone, probably unarmed. By now, this had happened, and nothing could be done.

"What concessions might g'Asalladh' demand for opening the Strait?" distracting herself from other anxieties.

"Dolvid hopes it will be enough to tell Him about the *jinzal*. But I would endorse any agreement that brought us allies. If the *jinzal* can wait us out, our food cannot last forever. The Strait must be opened, or forced."

"He would never bargain away justice. He has higher regard than you for your own honor." She was determined to keep her passion down.

Rodlakh's placidity was very determined. "I do not see much honor in a *rabhsai* who would let his realm be destroyed rather than compromise. I would choose death for myself if it was that or live half-slave, but I cannot make the choice for everyone else."

They were moving now, horses side by side. "It is with the declaration Preference is dead that so many good men have been won to your cause. Shumat would still be in revolt."

"All we are sure of is that Dolvid put himself at risk. Let us save our fears; there may be fresh news at Kamsilat. But it would be a hard choice. Will you despise me if I say I am glad he has to make it, not me?"

"No." She did not think many men would make that admission.

"*Jinzai*-killing, though I loathe it, is work I was born for. Or the planting of trees. Simple acts where there is no third way. Oh, but Âna — " As if catching up with what he had forgotten he reached for her hand and kissed it. "I have missed you, these bloody days."

"I have missed you."

"Sebhal was wrong. Men who ride to war should not know a woman. I worry about your safety, but want you to be near me."

That she could not answer. He worried about her safety, while performing, Saidhan said, feats of arms for an age. If there was conceit, its innocence excused it.

He looked straight ahead. "I shall sleep in Vonn tonight, and we might find a real bed. Would you share it with me?"

"That would please me, yes." No time for living on hopes.

Back, hilltops hid the Vale of Banakit. Readily in his mind, she said, "I cannot bear to imagine those brutes ransacking farms and houses it took so much love to make. So much life."

"Better the houses than those who built them. All these lands have been cleansed before, and can be again."

She approved of hope, though her imaginings brought the opposite. If after cleansing another Night came, life after life went only to postponing defeat. "We have to build what we can, between ruin and ruin. What else is there?"

That puzzled Rodlakh, whose visions of triumph were less equivocal. But it is all a rearguard action, all part of the long retreat. No building had stone hard enough or joined well enough to outlast time; had she not seen the decaying stump of a great seaport, across the stream from the fishing village of Voruni? She had seen how the outwalls of Kadon Dinul, razed, became formless boulders in the Gardens of Kamzhinu, falling to pebbles, wearing to dust, blowing away. Rodlakh's good luck was to observe the growing and shaping; in a plausible vision she saw that if they lived out this war her part might be to offer consolation when all his hopes, as they would, came to nothing, the bitter comfort of acceptance, her sadness worn smooth by familiarity.

She shook herself and made him stare by laughing out loud. She was twenty-one, had seen and done unimaginable things, endured through evils and dangers, and was friend to the two best men her age would know. Standing, stretching in the stirrups, she turned her face to Rodlakh. "I want to get to Vonn," an unanxious, pleasurable urgency in her voice. "To be in bed with you."

Kargul

Kamin-Tarú asked again, "Where, then, are we to spend the night?"

He had thought at first they could reach Kred Bakali, going hard on the Great Stone Road with its *ôdul* to mark the way after dark, but then saw it would be too long a ride tonight. "In the Arbhu Hills," he told her. "The estate of Khelagh." When Dolvid had sent a note asking if he and his escort could be quartered overnight at the country villa, celebrated for its sumptuousness, his former father-in-law had expressed a deep sense of honor, perhaps with some irony — or it might be his messenger had mentioned Kamin-Tarú would be in the riding, no mere *Bôdhrai* of dubious parentage, but a daughter of the Great Families.

Surer unintended irony was in late arrival of a letter from g'*Asalladh'*, a distasteful blend of outrage and conciliation, inviting Dolvid to the *Mankh'* for a *free and frank discussion of the differences that lie between the* Bôdhrai'*s interests and Our Own.* That phrase, with its refusal to recognize Dolvid as an agent of Rodlakh, its bland assumption he would be flattered, was very much the man he had known as *Menadhi*, and the signature was in his remembered hand. He had dictated an answer, masking revulsion, regretting he was called away on the *rabhsai*'s business, hoping they might indeed meet, 'when present annoyances are disposed-of.' He now had not the slightest doubt the *Atarlum*, or at least the Teaching Order, had for centuries been breeding *jinzal* deliberately, and the bright-cloaked riders who controlled the *jinzal* were of the *Atarlum*. The part Kargul played was harder to define; Kamin-Tarú knew nothing about it, else why would she in all innocence have dropped the clue that let Dolvid put the puzzle together? That her Island-born mother, Petakoi, would be part of the scheme was more than thinkable, but Dolvid was not sure about Tovakh, and continued to hope Kamin-Tolagh knew as little as his sister. Otherwise this was a wasted journey.

Concerning him, a message had come belatedly, having gone north, narrowly missing him at Dônshei Bridge, to catch up with him, five days after it was written at Kanzan Tâl. Kamin-Tolagh with a number of squadrons was now in the Paowanu Loi (which he would call the Kovilanu), not stopped or seriously challenged crossing the Nanakh, but at Kôbh Crossings the General Cavalry, reinforced from Kanzan Tâl, had declined to let him pass without authority from Kadon Dinul, whereupon Kamin-Tolagh had withdrawn and vanished. At this point in the dispatch he recognized news stale before it was sent; the commander at Kanzan Tâl had seen no sign of the Karguli cavalry for several days, and was asking for new instructions — which by now had arrived with Shumat.

It remained a puzzle, and by this time Kamin-Tolagh could be anywhere. Though it was hard going to bypass Kanzan Tâl to the eastward, and unless the command there had decided to let him pass he was most probably somewhere south of Shelum with what was estimated to be at least six to seven hundred first-rank cavalry, more of his own men than Tovakh had commanded at Dônshei, scarcely fewer than Shumat's forces and the garrisons put together.

"We cannot afford another Dônshei."

"Thunder-face, you will bring back the rain." Like a beaten dog the drab clouds had gone crouching away to the southeast, and afternoon was dying with thin ripples of high cloud.

Last of all these delays at Kadon had been most pleasant; Sett came limping into the Residence, having been in the city three days. His boredom with Burantal had become unbearable when he heard about Dolvid's arrival, and now he had come for authentic news and to be allotted some task. Given the newly-coined title Agent to the *Rabhsayum*, he was sent to Owan Sai to take charge of assembling shipping and supplies for the relief of Kamsilat, with more money advanced from the Treasury than had been spent so far on everything else. Sett knew Perimas, and was confident they could work together.

"We shall ride on after dark, then?" Kamin-Tarú persisted.

"The road is easily followed. I would not ask this, but we must find your brother before war breaks out again."

She looked at him blandly. "I have not complained. I love riding at night, if I am with someone I enjoy." She was a born rider, flowing with the movement of her mount.

"Dorrmas? He is a good soldier?"

"He is a swordsman even your brother would admire."

"A Mixed," no more than a statement.

Lanterns were bobbing from the big, low house, Khelagh's retainers arming, the ring of a challenge, and then a voice known but not expected here, Linaëyu. She stood within the pillared vestibule, lighted by pale *ôthu*, and he was dismayed at how much seven years had aged her. More than should be for a woman of Owani blood unmixed; Dolvid added up years, then smiled at his own innocence; Linaëyu might well have lopped something from her age when they first met. Still feline, she now evoked a satiated tabby drowsing in front of a fire, and the eyes, narrowed by the puffiness of her eyelids, bore out the notion. She had plumpened, and the arms that once had excited him with their white litheness had small peaks of elbow planted in soft pads of flesh, throat and chin with all their taut danger gone, a slack bowstring.

With others of Family she and Khelagh had adopted the welcome-cup. She passed the cup first to Kamin-Tarú, while Dolvid observed the beringed bluntness of fingers on the goblet of hammered metal. For an instant when it came his turn they wrapped around his hands, but there was no curiosity left in them.

She made flattering talk of the kind she once despised, and later when they sat for food in cushioned and tapestried comfort of a lesser hall she preferred for intimate gatherings Linaëyu spoke blandly about past years, apologizing to Kamin-Tarú that two old friends were reminiscing together. Tú was, if this was possible, bored and fascinated at once; the allusions to people and events she did not know or care about were tedium for her, but behind the masked yawns there was an animal alertness to tone and manner; she was assessing what Dolvid and Linaëyu had once been.

"You have received, I hear, your niece Absivoi." She too was determined to assert the relationship, divorce notwithstanding. "Is she not charming?"

"She is well-mannered for her age."

"For any age. Power agrees with you; you have never looked so splendid."

Kamin-Tarú wriggled. "Isn't this the house I have heard of, with baths in the style of Ancient Vrobhan?"

"It is, *Asayu*. Khelagh will be pleased its fame has gone so far as Kargul."

Yawning openly now, Kamin-Tarú stood. "Could I be shown to a bedroom? I have not slept properly since — oh, the night before the night I left Kamsilat. How many nights is that, Dol?"

"Too many, *Asayu*."

Linaëyu put her in care of a steward who had been haunting the shadows, and soon came back. She smiled benignly at Dolvid, who had also stood up. "I do not want to count the nights since we spoke."

"Alone, past two thousand. You rode out to warn me about Ghuradh's challenge."

"Even now, you will not take care. Or anything else, will you? Poor Khelagh has not the least idea what to do with you. He does not believe in incorruptibility."

Into his head flashed the vivid picture of an autumn afternoon when he lived on the Court of Nasilú (it must have been a few days after the great victory feast, when they had met and bedded promptly) and Linaëyu came to visit him for the first time, kissing him and beginning to take off her clothes, smiling smugly and saying not a word till she was lying naked on the bed. This, it could be proved, was thirteen years ago, but for the life of a feeling it had been yesterday. In the world outside there was nothing left of those afternoons, all swallowed up by what Bronal called *the soundless, gliding shark, voracious time.*

She laid a metal-weighted hand on his forearm. "Do you remember a little minstrel-girl at Bolan's feast? You wanted her so much."

"Linaëyu, I have writing to do before I sleep, and I must make an early start tomorrow."

"I must not forget the burdens you carry." After a cool look for the steward she herself showed Dolvid through polished and clothed ways to his wide bedroom. He was depositing his saddlebag on the writing-table when Linaëyu said, "You have seen Khalú?" With his back to her he noticed the voice was the same, its softly furred texture.

He told her about today's encounter, and judged it was not what she was looking for. She said, "The Karguliyu child's room is next door down."

He thanked her for the information, and she drew herself up. "No one ever said I was grasping."

She was not joking. That preening note was unlike her, yet familiar; Khalú, always hungry for praise, had habitually supplied such invitations. He had seldom seen anything of her mother in Khalú, and now there was resemblance at last; Linaëyu was taking after her daughter.

"Will the bronze-hair be the *Bôdhrai*'s next wife?"

"Linaëyu — "

"The Heiress in Kargul is not beyond reach of a *Bôdhrai*."

"We are riding on the realm's business."

She laughed, a sound woven into all his adult life, plashing of water on a summer's afternoon. "Same Dolvidh. That is why Khalú was so determined to marry you, no doubt, because you would never say anything about next year. Or even next week."

Unwillingly his interest was caught. "Does she say that?"

"No, I guessed. I suppose you were the same with her as you were with me, but she was younger and had to have revenge. It takes years to learn to be a saddle-filly, stabled and forgotten when the ride is over.

"I could say, same Linaëyu. Why is it a woman who takes pleasure where she finds it needs to call the man a robber when he does not offer eternal devotion?"

"Pride." Her turn for the door had only been a feint. "You were an idiot. For your sake, I would have left — this." Her arms included house, lands, position. "I would have left Khelagh, left my children for servants to care for, if you had once said, be with me."

"Memory is lying to you — " and was about to bring her to tears. "You would talk about running away to join a band of Froghul herders, and in the same breath be surmising what some new Household officer had in his breeches, say we would tire of each other in a month."

"True, for you. You would have left me for a supple child with green eyes and a round bottom. But I still like you."

"And I you." The lie was slight and gracious; he could remember the existence of a Linaëyu he liked — and could be honest with.

Breaking off the fencing-match she simply told him an extraordinary secret, to do with the men who had come to set fire to his work at the Bronze Residence, when his edition of the *Song of Tales* was almost ready. Possessing no evidence he had always blamed the Patriarch, then *Menadhi*. With the incident practically forgotten, it was odd, now he knew about far worse crimes, to learn the man was innocent, that Linaëyu had sent and paid them.

"That was a thousand years ago. Of course, you did it for your daughter's sake." Khalú had been both jealous of his work and deeply apprehensive about the challenge it threw down to the *Mankh'*.

"For Khalú's sake, yes. That is how I explained it. No one said you slept so near your work, nor that you would be there that night."

He nodded again. A moment had passed, and he was not, after all, going to tell Linaëyu about Âna. She might have given him his answer already: Âna would marry Rodlakh because all Dolvid wanted was a saddle-filly, forgotten after the ride. He did not see that in himself, but Linaëyu was the woman who had known him best.

"Let me advise the *Bôdhrai* on one thing. Do not be too quick to show your contempt for the Families. Rodlakh may need them more than you think, and if he makes his peace with them, you will be alone."

He thanked her, though it had nothing to do with any real future, and less with *jinzal* threatening Banakit. The air was neutral, and they could say goodnight.

He wakened sourmouthed, fully dressed, the sky scarcely lightened. Muddled, he vaguely remembered leaving documents to rest his eyes before getting ready for bed. He wondered if Kamin-Tarú knew they had rooms next to each other, why she had not come to wake him. She had been exhausted, of course. His candle had burned away, and it was nearly dawn.

Though the Owanil relished saying baths such as Khelagh's were `in the style of Ancient Vrobhan,' most did not really believe they could have existed so long ago, the childhood of mankind, before the Empire had learned to close a keystone arch, to make a spoked wheel. The historian knew better, and was sure Khelagh's were a lesser imitation of antiquity, when the slave-served cities of Vrobhan made Shaël's armies gape with awe that soon turned to destructive envy.

These remained luxuriously pleasant. Dolvid soaped and cleaned in a smaller bathhouse where the deep bronze bath must be labored over by servants; he could see not a trace of green in any crevice of the deeply worked metal. Next came a place with couches of polished stone, air kept warm and dry by fires out of sight. From there broad steps of reddish stone led down to the main bath, flagged irregular edge, here and there tufts and sprays of green plants, making it like a natural pool, though lined with gleaming white marble. At several points there was a trickling inflow of warmed water, and somewhere must be a constant outflow. Large windows were high up on the walls; the arched ceiling, hundreds of small glazed tiles, hid *ôdul* in niches.

The shallow steps led into the glistening water, steaming faintly, deep enough to reach his chest. On the far side brass rings were set in stone, and he grasped two to let his body float up, ache ebbing from his muscles. His head wound was well scabbed and he had not troubled with a fresh dressing. The windows were brightening; this was the southeast corner of the villa set on ground that fell away steeply behind, so that coming cross-country it was up on a green knoll.

Sun was slanting in when he clambered out of the water beneath the windows. There were more smoothed stone benches, but Dolvid, taking a towel the size of a bedspread, patterned in red and gold, lay down on rush matting. Shapes of light wriggled on the ceiling, water turning from silver to pale gold as sun outdid the *ôthu*-light.

Humming, someone was coming down the steps from the dry room. Twisting his head he saw Kamin-Tarú, barefoot and with her rich hair loose to her shoulders. She was wearing nothing but a simple shift of the white material called teased linen, by some process drawn out to be as fine as finest shuzi, or nearly so; it fell lightly from breast to knee, tracing hips and the molded belly. She had just removed a waist-tie, and used it to gather up her hair, eyes on the shimmering water. She had an expression of open-eyed pleasure, and her youthfulness touched him. Pointing a toe to go down the steps she glimpsed there was someone on the opposite side, squinting and shading her eyes.

She seemed pleased to see who it was. About to take off the shift, with a sly half-glance under lowered lids she spread herself face-first into the water, and stood with the wet linen clinging to her nacreous body. Dolvid propped on elbows, then knelt up, as she gave her high laugh, and went sliding full into the water, gliding with a quick wriggle of hips. Dolvid slithered back in, and she, with an effortless turn back under herself, darted sinuously back to the steps, fingertips stretching out.

Might as well enter the hawk's domain, and he would feel no clumsier there, working elbows for wings and watched by its soaring denizen. He floated, then waded across, while she like a child at the shore squatted on the steps, bottom touching water. As he arrived she was standing again, face held with a tremulous earnestness she was enjoying, her body clung about with the odd paradox of nakedness enhanced, the inexplicable excitement of her being covered but in no detail concealed.

"Tú." He reached out with his hands.

She bobbed down as if in abject deference. "I have caught a water-snake." They struggled together, wrestlers for a fall. Nostrils flaring she wanted to couple in the water, but he led her to the far side, and they climbed out dripping and breathless. The sodden shift was peeled away, and on the matting he spread a pageantry of towels, purple, rich green, gold, crimson, skill of the Heartland dyers to frame their nakedness, dance in his eyes, receive his plunging face as joy made a long, a long journey into gratitude.

After she said, "Tam's face." Startled, with Kamin-Tolagh never far from his mind, Dolvid rolled over. She pointed to a roundish patch of light wobbling over marks in the ceiling where the curved tiles joined. "It was him. It changed," when he failed to see the likeness.

"How do you know my brother's face?" To ask this she had to push his hand away from her lips, but he did not stop marvelling at their softness.

"I have seen him, at Kadon Dinul, and elsewhere." Peering through an aperture that pierced the Oak-Wall carvings, from behind an inadequate screen of weeds above his exile-house by Shemugrân. Âna had said something about that occasion, or about Kamin-Tolagh's annoyance Rodlakh had done something he had not, passing through the marshlands.

He raised on an elbow to kiss Tú's cheek. "We ride by the Arcades at Bathrâd today. I'll buy you any present you like."

"No need for presents. You have pleased me, too."

He did not explain, filled with tender gratitude for her body. But the reward was for something else. She had said Tam wanted to do everything Rodlakh did. Quite obvious where he would be found, if he did not drown first.

Shumat said, "They may be fierce enough, but we can't get within a lance-length of them."

"My brother has a plan, depend on it. The *péfrapravádal* of Kargul know when to fight."

"We saw them fight at Dônshei," Shumat agreed. Even when Kamin-Tarú was not speaking his eyes kept wandering from Dolvid, going to her eyes or her breasts.

"Do not talk about Kargul as if we were monsters."

He bowed from the waist. "Only the blind could do that." A dozen Kamin-Tarús in the realm would bring back the Blossoming Age, every man striving to be a poet. Nothing ever heard from Shumat remotely approached that courtly response.

They were riding together, Dolvid and Shumat with Kamin-Tarú, and a large contingent of lances, out of the deep hollow of Kanzan Tâl. On the eminence and spreading a long arm of ramparts along the eastward ridge, the immense fortifications dominated, and in the changing light the stones ranged from a powdery yellow through honey to a warm brown-gold, giving the name, *Danulurai Plakh'*, the Great Golden Walls. Between these ramparts and the shores of Entun' Shelum the town spiralled down, houses clinging to the slopes, many narrow streets with steps, amid small apple-orchards and steep vineyards. This was the gateway to the Heartland, a gate slammed more than once in the face of Kargul in the three wars fought with *rabhsayum*.

Not far south and the road climbed again, mounting higher than the hills to the right, so there was a sudden view of Shelum's expanse, deep blue and calm under a fleecy sky. Soon, coming down a little, the ways divided. Leftward the Royal Way continued its long journey south, for Nivu Din and Kir, the waste emptiness of Ní-Tilagh, before reaching the southern enclave of

Ninkufu and the city of Thenimala on the warm sea. The riders took the lesser branch, rightward, the road that followed at a distance the shore of Shelum, before striking out for Kôbh Crossings, way to Zelkova and all the province of Kargul.

"We've kept a strong guarding force where the road, they say it's the Nambalus road, crosses the smaller stream."

"The Lovu." Though a long way from the hollow where Dolvid lived out his exile, this was the threshold of that country.

On the far side of the Lovu Shumat's men had caught sight of Kargul' patrols, though not identifiably of Kamin-Tolagh. The officer most often seen was said to be Yenughai — Shumat was tentative with the name; his years in the Northeast had increased his uncertainty with words of the Owanilú.

"Yenughai," Kamin-Tarú confirmed. "Tam says he could have been a better soldier than his brother, but he is too fond of wine."

She said *brother* as something they knew, and when asked changed it to half-brother; Yenughai had the same father as Rheduban, but his mother, she said, had no out-blood, and Yenughai had a man's mouth. "He is not handsome, and has a dowdy wife. Perhaps he will want to fight you because of Rheduban. He hated him, but men often want vengeance for kin. I am not a man."

"If this Yenughai wants to challenge Dolvid — " while his eyes endorsed the last — "he'll have to let us come nearer than he has so far. His patrols don't stand to parley or fight." He had not followed them far for fear of a trap; there was also the possibility Kamin-Tolagh was trying to draw him westward so he could slip past and reach Kanzan Tâl.

"Does that mean he would take Kadon Dinul?"

"*Asayu*, he cannot take Kanzan Tâl. He will break his lance against the Golden Walls."

"They would cower behind their walls? Shoot their bows at the *péfrapravádal* of Kargul?" She had been impressed but not pleased by the large companies of archers with the long Gabhani bow. "That is no way for a man to fight."

"*Asayu*, I love sword and lance as much as any lordling, and some are worse with them than I, but we would rather hold Kanzan Tâl with bows than lose it with chivalry."

She pouted just detectably, less over *lordling*, perhaps, than because her adversary was attractive to her; Mixed by Mixed she was losing the power to dismiss all Others as less than human. What would it do if she knew the *Atarlum*, home of every Owani virtue, trained bows for use against cavalry, bows carried by *jinzal*? He had not yet told that to anyone, not Shumat, not Faëdhal, who remained puzzled (if relieved) that Dolvid had not after all gone to the *Mankh'*. How ridiculous to recall his certainty the Patriarch would lift the blockade of the Strait when He heard about the *jinzal*.

In the Colony, counting days, the Long Retreat had either succeeded or must fail.

"When Kamin-Tarú rides forward with me, they will have to stand and parley." She moved her head archly, and it might be that as her brother neared she wanted some distance from Dolvid. At the Arcades, sadly diminished, with everything else that served travellers, she had been a delight; half the booths were empty and barred, but there remained plenty to distract Kamin-Tarú, who darted about, holding up articles for him to see. After as much treasure-hunting as he would allow, she chose a small book of tales to remind her of Dolvid. Bolan, who knew Bathrâd well, had once called it a townful of bad bargains, and the book would have cost less in Harbor Way, but Rodlakh's treasury did not dicker.

While Shumat dropped back for a word with his officers she said earnestly, "When we meet with my brother, you will not call me Tú?"

The promontory enclosed by the loop of the Lovu where the high-arched bridge led from emptiness to emptiness, was a hilly region, road winding through overgrown slopes, the way ahead seldom visible for above a hundred paces or so. The scene could not be more different from that of Dolvid's exile, yet he felt he was coming home; if he could find a path off to the right, keeping the westering sun in his eyes tonight, tomorrow morning his long shadow going ahead would show the way to the stone hut five years had made his own. Farther west again would lead him to Âna's country, the broad hinterland of Nambalus.

"What are you smiling at?"

"There is no such place as Arlemirrstead." Her brother would understand quite well. Dolvid was thinking too that Konat and Asana could learn a lot about their own daughter to surprise them.

"Tam and I had many secrets we kept from my father Tovakh and my mother." A disconcerting gift, and luckily she did not know she had it.

With their small escort behind, one riding proudly with the Beech-Tree, a man of Narn somewhat sullenly bearing the blue-edged standard of Kargul, Tú recollected her childhood at Inilun Barabhi.

"In the rushes beside the Inilu we had a secret house, woven of rushes itself. You could be looking at it and not see it. Tam was clever with his hands, always. He taught me how to cut a reed-pipe. We were good allies, and that saved us many whippings."

Important in her short life, she spoke as if it was many years ago, and had lasted summer after summer, though that was hardly possible. Then Kamin-Tolagh, she said, fell in love with war and weapons, and did not have any relish for their game where he was Shâl *Nim'raibakim-dhanai*, she a highborn lady of Vrobhan. His new companions were mostly soldiers' sons, and there was a day she came to the secret reed-house to find them mounting a siege under Tam's captaincy. In the final assault the flimsy citadel had been levelled.

"When I wept," bitterness undiminished, "he laughed. I hit him, and he and his new friends rolled me in the mud, and a good gown was ruined." Nor had she forgotten the crowning injustice of being punished for it.

Her face softened. "When he was sixteen, and had his wish to ride with the *péfrapravádal* of Kargul, we were friends again.

For my thirteenth birthday he gave me a new robe of shuzi. My lady mother was furious. A bride-gift, she said, not proper for brother to give sister. But I saw he remembered the fight we had, and was saying he was sorry. The gown he spoiled in the mud was only linen, but the same color as the new one — "

"Yellow," with certainty, coming out of half-attention.

"So it is, I have kept it always, although I outgrew it. No wonder your *rabhsai* wants you as his *Bôdhrai*, if you are a seer."

"Here come our welcomers." Both relief and anxiety, to see cavalry of Kargul coming down onto the road from the densely-grown embankment just ahead. Two full squadrons; one, divided into files, quickly enveloped the six riders, four of them all the troops the *rabhsai* could call on, this side of the Lovu. Shumat hated being told to keep his men on the far side, but would follow orders; it was likely Kargul kept concealed watch on the bridge, and Dolvid wanted them to recognize his small riding as an embassy, not suspect it as bait in a trap.

Bright-cheeked, without helm, a round-faced young officer confronted him. Hedged in by lances, the standard-bearers and the two others sat uneasily.

"You are our prisoners," the squadron-leader announced. "Kamin-Tarú *Asayu* is set free."

"Do not be such a big baby, Pivrekhan. Do I look like a captive? This is the *Bôdhrai* Dolvid, and he is here to parley with my brother."

Pivrekhan pulled in his chin pompously. "I know of no arrangement for a parley. Kargul is at war with the usurper Rodlakh and his followers." This was the boy Rheduban had wanted, the one Kamin-Tarú had bedded as proxy.

"Where is my brother? Where is Yenughai?" She easily won the brief battle of eyes.

"At the farm, our headquarters." That meant Yenughai; Kamin-Tolagh was afield with his own squadron.

"We shall ride there," Kamin-Tarú decided.

Terribly young for all this responsibility, Pivrekhan allowed that Dolvid could come, unarmed. When he rose lifting his left arm to show the empty sheath, Pivrekhan said he meant escort, too, but the escort had come as far as they were meant to, and would return to the bridge over the Lovu. Pivrekhan started to object, and Dolvid swiftly warned him not to take any action to jeopardize the coming talks, where the stakes were much higher than the freedom of four soldiers.

"I have not said they could not go. We shall send an escort with them part-way. Kargul knows when to fight and when to parley."

Kamin-Tarú smothered a giggle.

A prosperous-looking farm, the farmhouse large, having grown outwards from a modest start, serving on as central living-quarters. There they met Yenughai, whose rank was under-captain.

He had a long face, the only resemblance to his half-brother. Yenughai was shorter than Rheduban, and younger, though he was balding. Under thick brows the eyes were dull, with none of Rheduban's mad fire. When Kamin-Tarú told him her brother must be found and informed who was here, Yenughai's expression of grinding tolerance betrayed that he had dealt with her before. He respectfully informed her this man was of Kargul's most persistent enemies, companion to and fellow-plotter with the usurper Rodlakh.

Kamin-Tarú asserted her height, and told the man she had just come from Kamsilat, where she had enjoyed Rodlakh's hospitality, and had journeyed all through the Heartland with Dolvid, treated with every courtesy. Dolvid had never shared the fear she might (as Shumat said) become Kargul's five-day heroine by claiming to have led him into a trap, and handing them his head. His only doubt was that in the field among soldiers her authority might not carry. A largely personal concern, since he had given her a letter and other documents that could put the case to Kamin-Tolagh, but since being spared his visit to the *Mankh'* had restored an attachment to his own survival.

Even more burdened by command than Pivrekhan, Yenughai slowly decided he could send word to Kamin-Tolagh in the field, but made no move to begin. He told Dolvid he must submit to a thorough search; Kamin-Tarú would have objected but Dolvid said, "Willingly," before she could speak.

When he again urged no time be lost in informing Kamin-Tolagh, Yenughai demurred: night would soon be coming on, and this country was unknown to them. In the morning —

"We have saddle-lanterns, have we not?" Kamin-Tarú said.

"*Asayu*, yes, but the way Kamin-Tolagh *Asai* took — "

"My brother will be overjoyed to learn I am here. If he discovers he could have had the news twelve hours sooner, he will be quite angry. For myself, if there is any unnecessary delay, next birthday I shall ask him for something of yours not of much consequence, but you will miss it, and your wife." This was cool and unemphatic enough to shock Dolvid into realizing he had begun to sentimentalize her; all Kargul's cruelty — say, all the world's — had not died with Rheduban. She was plausible to Yenughai; he left the room, main one of the original house, and could be heard barking out orders which caused audible stir. With no one important left to witness it, Kamin-Tarú quickly kissed his cheek, and said she would see him when her brother came.

After Dolvid had gone to a side-room and stripped off his clothes for sullen, careful soldiers to examine them and him (one even took in his hand the Beech-Tree token on its chain, and peered at both sides as if it might conceal a weapon), he dressed, went back, and found Yenughai with his booted feet up on the table. Told the man was truly unarmed, he laughed, pulled up another chair, and poured wine, also refilling his own cup. A pale wine with the unmistakable tang (clean sea air) of the upper Peframi Gorge.

"Some news, Under-Captain, you may not yet have heard, about your brother."

"Rheduban was my half-brother." Dolvid took note of the tense. Yenughai wiped his mouth with a kerchief. "Everybody has heard, even the fat farmer here. He was killed at the Residence, by a friend of Rodlakh's. It's true, isn't it?"

"It is true he is dead."

"You are Rodlakh's friend." After a large gulp of wine Yenughai took inventory of Dolvid's probable strength. "It could not have been you."

As exactly as he could Dolvid described how Rheduban died, and the actual event did not seem to evoke any emotion in Yenughai. "I cannot fight an *atarlai*. Are you a religious man, *Bôdhrai*?" He made Raëdh's sign before reaching for the wine-flask.

It began a long evening. Kamin-Tarú did not come back; she might have gone with the messenger to look for her brother. A few soldiers came and went, and Pivrekhan at the door announced there was a meal ready. Yenughai, drinking steadily, did not want food, and kept Dolvid by him, hungry and faintly sick, though he was only sipping the wine. The wound in his forehead throbbed, and he was enormously bored. He wished Kamin-Tolagh would arrive.

"Rheduban could not help it. Not his fault, he should have been smothered in his cradle. He loved to torture me when I was small. Yet he was my half-brother, *Bôdhrai*, he had his worth. He painted, what about that? Vivid little, what-do-you-call-them, tiny paintings?"

"Miniatures?" trying and failing to imagine those fingers clamped on a brush.

"Ah — on ivory, also glass. So small you could not believe it — an *atarlai* taught him. I have no patience for those skills. You are not drinking your wine."

"I do not have much head for wine, not on an empty stomach."

"You do not care for the wine." Ignoring the hint, Yenughai cradled his flask, their second, closer. "Well, if the wine is not good... "

"It is good." taking a token sip. "The wines of Peframi Gorge are praised everywhere."

"Ah, you know Peframi. My country, the river of wine. Everyone knows Peframi, hah?"

He began to show signs of getting sleepy, and Dolvid helpfully refilled his cup as soon as empty. Unfortunately he also forgot or chose to discount Dolvid's version of Rheduban's death, and said he would have to fight him. "You killed my kin. It may be different in the Colony where they have half-apes for soldiers. I have wished Rheduban dead, or that he never lived — where I ride I am pointed out, Rheduban's brother. No, I ought to thank you, but it is a question of kin. You have to fight me." He was near tears.

"I shan't. My business here is too important."

"Then I'll kill you. You have a brother? Why did you, man of Owan, join with the mongrels to kill my brother?"

"Half-brother," Dolvid corrected. Though he did not pick up or go for a weapon Yenughai went on pugnaciously insisting on a fight, bragging of his prowess with sword and lance. As threats grew more bellicose the manner of speaking them continued to lose energy. "You must fight me, *Bôdhrai*; the honor of Kargul demands it." His chin reached his chest.

Dolvid sat quiet till slow snoring began. He was not sure there was even a guard mounted; little movement could be heard.

The main building for most of these larger farmhouses followed a similar pattern, with smaller rooms and closets opening off a corridor between big dayroom at the front and kitchens, scullery, often dairy at the back. Here the kitchen was huge, and when Dolvid arrived there he joined a strangely assorted company. The farmer, fleshy but not fat, and his short wife, both Mixed, with a son of about twelve; seated with them at the enormous table the two soldiers who had searched Dolvid, and the Squadron-Leader Pivrekhan. At the bread-oven there was a plump, pretty girl, a niece or cousin of the farmer's, being assisted by a flushed, dishevelled Kamin-Tarú, complacently playing peasant. She gave a smile and said there would be bread and pies, and a message had come back saying her brother would be there early. Dolvid sat at the table and wondered what he was doing here, while in the Colony they were fighting for life. Nevertheless, the browning bread smelled very good.

"You must get up," a voice bawled at his ear. "And fight me."

He cursed that he had slept so long; full light, and Yenughai was up and dressed, accompanied by the same two men. The deepened lines down his cheeks were only signs of his drinking last night. Chiefly, like many a drunk, Yenughai was boring. But he could be a dangerous bore, if Dolvid gave way to exasperation.

The very stupid soldier, the one who had examined Rodlakh's token, thin, with a pocked face, had his sword out, very near Dolvid's ear as he swung out of the narrow wall-bunk. Ignoring it, he said, "Is Kamin-Tolagh here?"

"You must fight me or die."

"No. Where is Kamin-Tarú *Asayu*?" His boots on, but not laced, he stood, and moved in the direction of the earth-closet.

All three followed him, Yenughai saying loudly Dolvid need not think of appealing to the House baKargul; Kamin-Tolagh *Asai* would never interfere in a matter of revenge for killing a brother. Dolvid was not allowed to shut the door to the earth-closet, relieving himself while Yenughai's harangue went on. Hard not to turn, and harder, if he were otherwise occupied, when another blade, Yenughai's own, came ringing from the scabbard.

It was worrisome. Never having heard of Yenughai before yesterday, Dolvid was confident he would win with swords, but it would be a poor start to the conciliatory mood he hoped to establish.

In the scullery, closely shadowed by the trio, he found water with the chill off, good enough for hands and face.

"If you won't fight you are a coward, and deserve to die." Yenughai's sword kept making little jabs, too near the throat. Back in the kitchen, seeing there were bowls of yellow milk on the table Dolvid took a chunk of last night's bread, dipped it, and munched. The farmer's pretty niece was there, sidling at the edges of the room to stay far from the soldiers with their drawn weapons. When, lifting an apronful of crumbs, she reached the door, Dolvid got up and opened it for her, and thus was in time to see Kamin-

Tarú in early sunlight ride into the enclosed farmyard, scattering hens. She was cloaked in blue on a dark *pefrai*, and did not see Dolvid, swinging her mount about with a high wrist, and looking back through the arched entrance.

Some soldiers in the yard surmised what this meant, and there was a general fastening of tunics. Kamin-Tarú must have ridden out to watch for her brother, perhaps to the next rise with its clump of small maples, and for some reason did not want him to know she had. Her free hand was beside her cheek, twisting a strand of hair.

In full gear, breastplate under his yellow-lined cloak, Kamin-Tolagh came through the archway. Without a word he halted by his sister, and each stretched out a hand so that fingertips touched, then palm met flat palm. The hands slid up till each held the other's upper arm, and their eyes were joined. This had a melancholy poetry, and when both dismounted it was pleasing to see them hug like children, Tú reaching up with her whole body so her chin could be over his shoulder.

He had not seen her, and before last night could not have had any word of her, since she vanished from Inilun Barabhi, but did not demand explanations. Leaving their horses they came hand-in-hand for the door. The plump, pretty girl, having emptied her apron for the chickens, was caught in an enchantment, fingers to mouth. Greeting Dolvid, Kamin-Tolagh had a spare hand to pat the girl on the bottom as he passed, something which Kamin-Tarú conspicuously failed to see. There was a sound of swords being discreetly resheathed.

In the dayroom Kamin-Tolagh took the largest chair, and his sister half-sat on the arm, one foot on the floor. He sent Pivrekhan for food, meat and some green things. "I have been in the saddle since dawn was a rumor, and the house where you spent your exile, *Bôdhrai*, is not well-stocked with food. I had the last of your *raminat*."

"I am honored," but there was pain here he could not explain, unless simple nostalgia for that simple life.

"I have seen better hide-holes than that loose hearthstone of yours," genially. "What you have written about Laluvoi is mostly good, but there is more to be said on Kargul's side."

"I shall be glad to listen to any suggestion," adding silently, *but not now*. In all imaginings of what might be discussed he had never included his history.

"The *True Song of Tales* was better."

"I am amazed you have read it, *Asai*." Or admitted doing so.

"At risk of losing my skin. At seventeen, to forbid me to read a book with battles in it — you might as well tell a cat not to watch birds."

His sister's eyes were very wide. "Did Dolvid write the stories about Odi Kukkuk and Okseti Jester?"

"*Asayu*, I made new translations, and arranged them in better order. The existing versions were very poor."

"Aye, short-measure, like everything from the *Mankh'*." Dolvid was gladdened; this could have been thrown out as bait, but the small reproving sound the sister made gave it authenticity.

"Here I was, reading Dolvidh's history of the War of the Widowed, and a messenger comes groping through the night to tell me the very man was here with my sister. This man — " he turned to her, "is going to show me the way through Shemugrân."

"There is no way for horsemen." Having waited more than long enough to be asked, Dolvid sat without leave.

"You led Rodlakh through. Don't try to tell me you did not."

"On foot, *Asai*."

"Mudding about like a peat-cutter, and now he wants us to call him *rabhsai*! But there must be a way to avoid a fight at Kanzan Tâl. Tobhsila fought there, his worst mistake."

It was time. "I am not here to help you assail Kadon Dinul, *Asai*. I am the loyal servant of Rodlakh *Rabhsai*. A fight can be avoided by not riding north. You have no reason to; Kargul can no longer win."

"Because you have recaptured the Residence?"

Here the pretty farm-girl reappeared, and the soldier with the pitted face, carrying plates and dishes of food, which they laid out on a side-table. Kamin-Tarú said, "I have made bread, Tam," and went to fetch some, while Kamin-Tolagh got up and moved to where the food was.

While he ate Dolvid recited all the recent news, for Kargul uninterrupted disaster. Counting those beaten at the Residence and Dônshei, four bottled up at the *Mankh'*, eighteen squadrons at the least were gone, and so were their only available allies, the cavalry of Dramal. Most troops under Bolan's erstwhile command were now prepared to resist Kargul.

While Kamin-Tolagh shook his head over defeat, he was astute enough to see the worst blow of all was the freeing of Orbanak, whose loss to the *Mankh'* left Kargul with no excuse for war but their own ambitions.

To make space for thinking he asked for details about Dônshei, not understanding how it had been lost with such a superiority in horse. Briefly, Dolvid told him how the battle had begun and developed, how the little redoubt of bowmen had come to obsess Tovakh.

"Bows," Kamin-Tarú, scornfully, coming back with half a loaf.

"My father always said bows shooting from cover must be engaged — but to come against them on a narrow front with nothing but cavalry? What we needed was infantry with some fight in them."

"Worms crawling in the mud."

"No, Tú," her brother disconcerted her. "It is good to love *pefral*, but we cannot let our loves blind us."

"You should make friends with the captain from the North." This was sarcastic, but exactly what Dolvid was aiming at.

"He would be worth meeting."

He might mean in battle, but Dolvid said, "You could see him today. He is camped not six hours from here."

"In what strength?"

"Adequate."

"Does he have thirty-two squadrons? Any other cavalry needs to be two-to-one where Kargul does not let archery decide its fights."

Noting he had just declared his strength at eight hundred *péfrapravádal*, Dolvid told him Shumat certainly had the men to retire in good order to Kanzan Tâl, which, with every fortified city of the Paowan, was bristling with bows. "There is no town north of Kôbh you can capture and hold."

"Then you claim to have won the war. Is it usual for the winner to come and beg for a parley?"

"There is no winner when men of the one realm kill each other."

"I have not let my troops be taken in flank by dwarfs on midget ponies, that was my father. What does Tovakh say about ending the fighting?"

To the overture from Dolvid he had said something very coarse. "Your father, as I do not need to tell you, *Asai*, can be hard to reason with. Besides, he believed Orbanak was safely in the hands of *g'Asalladh'*."

"But you want me to surrender, with my squadrons intact? Perhaps I cannot take Kadon Dinul, but I can strike here and there in the Heartland, and Rodlakh can't call himself *rabhsai* till I am defeated in the field. You know that."

"To what purpose? To the same end as Tobhsila, in the end, with nothing gained. By ending the war now you could win back what he lost."

This was his most daring use of his plenipotentiary powers. At the end of the War of the Widowed with Kargul on its knees, under threat of the complete deposing of the House baKargul (Banak had vowed to make Saidhan the new *nim'*), the province had been stripped of its easternmost quarter, the fertile land between the rivers Nanakh and Kôbh, in three wars launching-place for savage Kargul' raids, haven to which their riders returned. With its new name, Paowanu Loi, it became an honorary princedom for Banak's son Lambarr when he reached sixteen, and he in turn started what was intended to be a custom by reserving that title for the sixteenth birthday of his second son, the boy who became Ban-Sila (his eldest, Tholat, was titular *Nim'* of the Paowan altogether). But at the same time its loss had become another festering sore for Kargul, a perpetual excuse for all their plots against the realm. Time, Dolvid offered, to heal that wound.

Kamin-Tolagh was instantly alert if untrusting. With his mother captive and his father disastrously defeated there was a chance here to become hero of his province.

"But surely the only reason for war is to gain what could not be won by peaceful means."

"And honor. Being Heir in Kargul has its demands, too."

"At Burantal, *Asai*, you can see puppet princes of the Guild, and they have no will; they have to do what their parts say, move when the Master pulls a string. Men have choice, or else the world can never change; all of us must become exactly what our fathers were. Or our mothers." He bowed to Kamin-Tarú, who made a sour mouth at the notion of becoming Petakoi.

"You offer to give back Kovilanu to Kargul — for what? As the price for peace?"

"In simple justice, once Kargul earns the realm's trust."

"What about when the minnow, Orbanak, is sixteen, and wants his toy realm. Is he not going to be Prince of the *Paowanu Loi*?" speaking the hated name with bitter emphasis.

"He is not a minnow," Kamin-Tarú protested. "I have met him. He is a good boy, but he has been with old men too long. He needs feeding."

"He can grow fat on Karguli territory, if his brother has his way."

Dolvid was beginning to understand the ambiguous note in Âna's voice when she spoke about this young man (who, in that big, curtained bed — and there was no reward in that line of thought): he had wit, neither as hamfisted as his father's nor sinister like his mother's, and he had better grasp of the realm and its affairs than could have been predicted — although Dolvid would never have made this journey without some hope for his brains.

"This is a very old realm, *Asai*, and in its whole history only two, both in easy living memory, have held that title. Some other honor can readily be found for Orbanak."

"You say. What does your *rabhsai* say? Is that why he stays in the West, so he can come back and have never heard a word about treaties made in his name?"

Annoying, but it might be encouraging, too; if Kamin-Tolagh wanted guarantees it meant he could seriously contemplate an agreement. "Rodlakh *Rabhsai* has given me the powers to make this offer. But beyond that he is convinced it was never Banak's intention to separate Kargul for ever from some of its best growing-land. As you do, he calls the region Kovilanu."

"Once our threat is removed, why would he give it back? How can you show me his good faith?"

"His good faith!" No need to pretend indignation; it could not be hidden. "What word has he failed to keep? He would not harm his brother when he had him in his power, and he would not use Lady Kamin-Tarú as a counter-hostage, even having seen good blood spilled rescuing Aëlu. In that abduction Kargul sided with the *Atarlum*."

"I never did!" Kamin-Tolagh was vehement.

"Your lady mother hailed it as a splendid stroke."

"She told you that?" He could not imagine how else Dolvid knew. "My mother is from the Island." He shifted uncomfortably. "She is a faithful daughter, but the One Way is not always my way."

Again Kamin-Tarú made a small noise of reproach. For her, calling the *Atarlum* old men who did not know how to take proper care of Orbanak was not to challenge the virtues of their faith. He became more certain only one of this ruling family could know about the breeding of *jinzal*. Tovakh probably believed (and had often told his son in private) that with Petakoi's close ties to g'*Asalladh'*, the *Atarlum* could be made to serve the aims of Kargul.

"That is understood, *Asai*. You want to fight honorably in war, not plot and connive."

He was about to offer him more war than his goriest dreams, but Kamin-Tolagh was not pleased. "You seem to know us very well. We were fools not to hire you before Rodlakh could."

This intended insult could not be let pass. "I am afraid I would have been beyond the means of Kargul — "

"He is a seer, Tam," midway between teasing and awe.

"Rodlakh *hired* me with a compliment: he knew I was with him, and trusted me to trust him. That is hard to outbid, *Asai.*"

"Well, but you did not have much to lose." He had just spent a night in the hovel of Dolvid's exile, and Dolvid, knowing this lord could not understand the struggle there had been to make him leave it, was obliged to laugh.

"I never approved of this closeness with the *Mankh'*, never." His eyes defied his sister to recall otherwise. "You lend a hand there, you are lucky to get three fingers back. According to them your *Song of Tales* overpraised the Gabhanil, but Shumat is a more famous fighter than I am, and at the gates of Kadon I crossed words with a better swordsman, a Mixed, than I shall ever be. Since coming north I have met Mixed women, too, and they may not be lettered... " He shook his head, and Dolvid knew, with a catch at his throat, Âna was in Kamin-Tolagh's mind.

"She was pretty, you mean, and you were not bored after two beddings. Wisdom!" the archness was affectionate, and for a moment Dolvid was sharing the reed-house by the banks of the Inilu.

"Skill of the body is a kind of wisdom," sententiously. "But there was more." He shook his head again, and it was a joke Okseti Jester, clown of the Gabhanil, would enjoy, if a girl deceiving Kamin-Tolagh with a pretence of stupidity convinced him intelligence and virtue might be found among the Mixed.

"So. We promise to stop fighting, you release my mother and my father, and give us back the Kovilanu, is that the proposal?"

Dolvid was happy to leave a subject physically distressing to him. This, now, was the risky place where he revealed the danger Rodlakh was in. "I am asking for more, *Asai.* Alliance, in which you can yet win honor for Kargul."

Kamin-Tolagh, blank, observed alliances were made by two, but against a third; Kargul till now had only one enemy. "Who would this alliance fight?"

"*Jinzal.*" If Dolvid had guessed wrong, and all this house was in the secret of breeding the creatures, this was the end of his embassy. He told about the great armies of *jinzal,* showed him copies of passages from Rodlakh's dispatches, and saw it was news; no one could have simulated the shudder Kamin-Tolagh gave.

"This crazy tale has been heard before. Is it true?"

"Kamin-Tarú can tell you, even Kamsilat is preparing for war."

"I do not understand this about the second *jinzai* army threatening Banakit."

Dolvid took charcoal from the grate and made a rough map, showing how the fresh forces from southward would cut the Colony in half, to leave Kamsilat virtually undefended, the Army of the West unsupplied. "That was the last news I had. If the Long Retreat did not completely fail, Rodlakh with at least some of his forces is in strong defensive position — here." He showed about where Vonn would be.

"That is the only way to Kamsilat?" putting in words a question that had nagged quietly at Dolvid.

"Except for a little-known and far longer way, following the wide northward loop of the Navu, and coming down through the forests. I trust Rodlakh will not altogether neglect watching it."

"When was this account of his sent?"

"Seven days ago."

"And nothing further? You did not speak to my father about this?"

"The dispatch came when I returned from Dônshei."

"And you would rather bid for squadrons your bows had not mauled. My mother?"

"No. Petakoi *Asayu*, despite Dônshei and our firm grip on Kadon Dinul, notwithstanding our removing Orbanak from g'*Asalladh*'s control, prefers to pretend there is still a dispute over the succession. If there were, it would make no difference now, not to Kargul." Revolting to know that in reality Petakoi must hope and believe the *jinzal* would make her husband's defeat meaningless.

"My mother stands out for principle, for a *rabhsai* blessed by g'*Asalladh*'."

But Kamin-Tolagh, Dolvid objected, had accepted joint-captaincy of the Household from Ban-Sila. "The laws of succession are just as Faëdhal recited them to you at Market Gate. If Ban-Sila was *rabhsai*, Rodlakh is *rabhsai*."

"If he is alive," but again Kamin-Tolagh came up against Orbanak now in other hands. He grinned. "It is all eagle's milk. I said so to my mother, who is quite sure if g'*Asalladh*' says the sky is the ground, we shall all fall up. If Banak could never be *rabhsai*, why was all Kargul at Kadon Dinul, giving his grandson the royal salute?"

"I am empowered to hear your allegiance."

"It is not that easy, *Bôdhrai*. This is a difficult business."

"At this moment there are men struggling against *jinzal*," prodding him. "Every minute is of value." He had a secondary proposal, where Kamin-Tolagh, if not an alliance, would assent to truce, and allow relief for Kamsilat to pass through the great Karguli port of Zelkova, a day's ride from here, and a day closer to the West.

"My father talks on and on about strategies and his own prowess, and in the end, if you are telling the truth, sends cavalry plodding uphill against bows he cannot reach. And now I'll be *failing to uphold the honor of Kargul* if I do not smash the rest of our *péfrapravádal* against the Golden Walls."

"If we allow the Colony to be destroyed, the *jinzal* will not stay on that side of Arnan; the men who lead them can also put them in boats. Maybe nothing we do can stop them, but certainly we cannot afford to war among ourselves when the whole realm is in danger. Simply your undertaking not to invade the Heartland would free General Cavalry and Household troops for the Colony."

Kamin-Tolagh,   frowning,   only   perfunctorily acknowledged this. Picking at the bread, he said he wanted time for reflection, and to hear his sister's story, and suggested they meet again for midday food. "The beef here is passable, though not Karguli, and there is some good wine, if Yenughai has left us any.   He drinks for the loss of his brother and has been anticipating that grief for many years."

Kamin-Tarú said, "Will Shumat not be anxious for some word?"

Kamin-Tolagh, with a wave of magnanimity, said a Karguli rider would carry Dolvid's message, under a flag of truce. Finding a small square of parchment, Dolvid scribbled a note.

"You understand, you must not tell him — oh, you are a man of honor, I trust you."

"You may read this. I have said nothing but that I am in no danger, and you and I are still talking — " proffering the note, but he now declined to look at it.

No one accosted him as he wandered, stopping at the stables to see Enikai was being properly cared for. A squadron of Kargul, soon to ride out on patrol, was having food in the shade of the maples, and he shared some of their wine, coarser than the one drunk with Yenughai. With him and Pivrekhan for examples Dolvid had not been impressed with the officers of the Kargul' cavalry, but as at Dônshei he found the common soldiers much the same as any, though coming, as most did, from remote western mountain-valleys, they had quaint ideas about the Heartland. Some of them obviously saw the Mixed they had met so far as only a branch of the Owanil, far too human to be the half-apes of Other Race they had heard about all their lives;

when told the farmer's niece was quite typical of women they would see they were quietly skeptical. But when their squadron-leader had them form up their discipline was impressive, and they were all tough, big-shouldered men.

Alone, he chewed on some problems not discussed with Kamin-Tolagh. When the Kovilanu was ceded to the Paowan some Kargul' farmers had sold their lands there, and some purchasers had been Others, who might feel justifiably nervous about return to Karguli dominion. There would have to be guarantees against their dispossession, and as *rabhsai* Rodlakh would have land to compensate those who felt impelled to leave. But after some sixty years some hardship and heartbreak was inescapable.

How life would be in Kargul for Other Races might depend on who ruled there; unthinkable Petakoi could stay wife to the Heir, *nim'* for every practical purpose, if her complicity in breeding the *jinzai* army could be proved. Quite likely Tovakh would seek divorce, once he found out the truth, that Petakoi, from the beginning, clean contrary to what Tovakh believed, had been using Kargul to further the aims of the *Atarlum*. If he could be prevented from killing her.

Dolvid smiled sadly to reflect on all the difficult and dangerous things to be accomplished before any of these futures were worth thinking. Going back to the house he took some squares of parchment from his saddlebag, and began making a detailed record of everything that had happened since leaving Shumat.

Pivrekhan, round-faced and flustered, came to him, well short of midday, to say Kamin-Tolagh would see him again. On his way into the dayroom he passed the pretty niece, and Kamin-Tarú was just telling her brother, "You choose quarters with every comfort." Her mouth was drawn down sardonically; Dolvid had heard women comment on their husbands' womanizing with exactly the same mixture of distaste and unwilling admiration.

Kamin-Tolagh had new resolution. "True men fight their own battles. You fought with Rheduban, I should go against Rodlakh, and let that settle it all."

"All what, *Asai*?" This change of directions was shocking and nonsensical, but not a reason for losing hope, not with Kamin-Tolagh's mind running on personal glory. Dolvid insisted if he killed Rodlakh it would cause wide mourning, but change nothing; opponents of Preference would rally around Orbanak, and Kargul would still be in a war it could not win.

"Besides, he is too busy at present."

"If he is alive." Kamin-Tolagh said again. "All the giants are gone; Tobhsila's remembered only because Saidhan is still with us, and he is the best part of ninety."

"What is too near our eyes may be unclear. If the realm can live, your grandchildren will hear about Rodlakh who with a handful of men tamed the citadel at Drin b'Afon to rescue Aëlu, and who fought the Short Retreat and the Long. To them, this will seem an age of giants."

This had some cunning, but Kamin-Tarú stole the effect with, "*All* his grandchildren?"

"While Kamin-Tolagh did nothing," This in his new mood of lament. "Watchman's work in the Heartland, and a campaign he was too softhearted to ever begin. I could challenge Shumat, that is a name worth beating."

"He would not fight you. He knows he is needed. You would do better in harness, Pir Kallikuk and Plakhat Gabh'Owan."

"Banak and Saidhan," giving an apter pairing of Mixed and Owani, one Dolvid had not dared cite. "Like Shumat, Banak was the seasoned campaigner, but the Owani dealt the last stroke."

"By treachery," dutifully.

"Nonsense, Tú, it was a fair fight; don't believe something just because it is said a thousand times at Inilun Barabhi."

She bridled, but all at once his mind jumped to the *jinzal* and the men who controlled them, whether the legend of the True *Rabhsai* could be real after all. Exactly as in the first genuine talk he ever had with Âna, and again with Rodlakh, Dolvid attacked the very idea, arguing Lost Plakhan had voluntarily renounced *rabhsayum* for himself and his heirs in perpetuity (then, with Âna, he had not known those heirs might have included some *jinzal*). "The masters of the *jinzal* are renegade Owanil, trying to make use of the *Rekh'Rabhsai* tale," he said, true as far as it went. He was prepared for further evasions, but Kamin-Tolagh did not linger.

"Look, the Colony road, as you explain it, is a tunnel, or like three tunnels between towns, and Rodlakh should by now be stopping-up the most easterly, between Banakit and Kamsilat, is that it?"

Not a bad description in the strategic sense, and it showed his mind moving in the same direction with Dolvid's own.

"You land a thousand, two thousand cavalry at Kamsilat. What do they do? Two thousand more to be fed, and no space to deploy them."

Dolvid took the map sketched earlier, and southward of the Colony indicated the Lunu Tezh' Protectorate, the Grân River flowing down from the farther side of the hills pierced by the Gate. "Here is the lake, En'tesh. Here, the mouth of the Grân, just across narrow waters from the westernmost part of your province, *Asai*. Arnan-going ships can navigate to the head of the lake, where most settlements are."

This was bound to be seductive to someone looking for feats to duplicate. One hundred years ago in one of his famous early exploits Great Banak, starting at the town now named for him, had led eighty men from the Colony through the hills into what was then the almost unknown Valley of the Grân, down to the shores of En'tesh.

Seeing what was in his mind Kamin-Tolagh objected; if the *jinzal* had come through the Lunu Tezh' Gate in the opposite direction to Banak, they could also have turned south, into the

Protectorate. Dolvid argued there were no large armies there; the chief aim of the *jinzai*-masters would be not to capture territory but to destroy the Army of the West. They might well leave a guard at the Gate, but main strength would surely be sent against Rodlakh.

"How long would it take, a march up the Grân Valley and to the Gate?"

"Banak took eight or nine days, but had to cut his own trail. The ways are more open now."

"And there would be more than eighty men." Kamin-Tolagh put his finger on the spot that represented the second city of the Colony. "You would hope to retake Banakit while most of the *jinzal* were trying to break through here at Vonn."

"If Rodlakh is right, and Vonni's Jaws can be held, the relief force could cut Fourth Bridge behind the bulk of the *jinzal*, or fill the bridge with bows, and the entire enemy could be trapped in a few miles of mountain road. They would starve."

"You make fighting *jinzal* a simple sport."

Soberly, he agreed, he had made it sound too easy. They could not tell the full numbers of the *jinzal*, and as the dispatches reconfirmed they were a terrible enemy. If further large numbers came from the West, the relief expedition could be the one trapped between armies, and there was no strength of cavalry that could be certain of fighting out.

"A man is a fool to pick a fight with *jinzal* if he does not have to."

Dolvid studied his palms, and was afraid this journey had been a waste. He should have made sure the garrisons were prepared to resist, and left with Shumat and a scraped-up dozen squadrons three days ago. Karguli kin-feeling might be too much to overcome; if Yenughai had been so dogged about fighting over a half-brother he loathed, what were Kamin-Tolagh's struggles as he contemplated, if not joining, at least failing to impede the enemies of his House, who had already disabled his father and made his mother captive?

Hard to tell how much Kamin-Tarú had followed. Often near a yawn while strategy was being discussed, her expression often failed to reflect what was being said, eyes straying from window to fireplace and back to table. Now she said negligently, "Our father would understand a truce made for the sake of our mother's safety, and his own."

That reed-house again, a child's sophisticated proposal for escaping punishment. There was no sign Kamin-Tolagh heard. Abruptly he said, "Oh, you can count on your truce, *Bôdhrai*. No question of Kargul attacking the Heartland while I command its cavalry, so long as the Kovilanu is ours again."

So, casually, he had won the most he had ever dared hope was possible. Kamin-Tolagh's offhandedness came less from a failure to appreciate the importance of this step than from his preoccupation with the other. "Alliance. I have to sleep on that. You might want to rejoin Shumat."

"I shall wait, *Asai*."

Sleepless, he heard the hiss of a steady rain. In the dayroom a single weak *ôdu* gave enough light for him to start a lantern.

His ink was mixed when Kamin-Tolagh came in. He was in a blue dressing-robe, hair standing out from his head like Rheduban's. "*Bôdhrai*. What are you writing?"

Dolvid told him, a message to go north by fast-messenger. "A fleet is collecting at Owan Sai, and has to be started south. We shall have to embark at Nambalus — "

"Nambalus? A small port for this business, and you won't find supplies there." And Kamin-Tolagh, unprompted, suggested the fleet come to Zelkova, where an army could rapidly be embarked, extra ships readily found, food and feed obtained, if Rodlakh's treasury had the price.

"Can we send our squadrons through Karguli territory without conflicts arising?" Zelkova was only a short ride within present borders.

"If Kargul rides with them. We shall go to Zelkova together, you and Shumat and I."

"And embark together?"

He was standing, and made his odd gesture of pouring from one hand into the other. "If I go it will not be as Shumat's under-captain. He is the older campaigner, yes, but I shall be Kargul's commander."

"The three of us together will concert strategy — " foreseeing some lively debates.

"Also," and words came Kamin-Tolagh must have rehearsed in his mind till sure they were right. "You and I will pledge to this truce, and sign our names to its conditions. As for allegiance, I am Kamin-Tolagh Tovakhati *bi*-baKargul, descended from Talbhan, whose wife was Filadhu, daughter of Plakhsila *Kímukoi*. You have my word for this alliance, but I pledge allegiance only to the *rabhsai*'s own person, when we stand together at Kamsilat, or wherever it may be." He dropped the lofty tone. "He may yet want to fight single-combat with me."

In the morning Kamin-Tolagh left his senior officers to round up the squadrons and get them started, so he could ride to meet Shumat. In the dayroom his sister armed him, as she had Dolvid at Kamsilat. Outside when they prepared to mount she whispered to Dolvid, "I am pleased you are to be friends after all."

Mounted, Kamin-Tolagh, very solemn, did what Dolvid knew from marionette-plays, but never expected to see in real life: he held up his sword two-handed in front of his face. "*Ul da-kindhral*," he intoned. "We shall conquer."

When the main fleet began anchoring at Zelkova Sett was among first ashore, limping down the quay to grasp Dolvid's hand. "Is Alkmas here? Is there new word from Kamsilat? Is the *rabhsai* safe?"

Yes, and yes, and yes. Alkmas had come back to Owan Sai when the fleet had already sailed, then overtaken and passed them in his faster-sailing boat, bringing new dispatches, another thick document, this one not in Âna's hand.

Dolvid unfolded it again so as to give Sett the outline of the Long Retreat, the fighting near Banakit and how a wounded but still effective Army of the West had come to Vonn.

> `*Vonni's Jaws have teeth again,*' Rodlakh wrote.  `*While we were fighting at the Gate we had men building walls, breast high, from boulders and slabs of loose stone, across the road, with a gap to be closed behind the retreat and eighty to a hundred paces between walls. Bowmen on the cliffs above command the entire length of the cleft, the bend in the road across the face of the cliff where the Jaws begin makes the enemy siege-weapons useless here.*
>
> `*I do not see how Vonn can be reached from the west so long as defenders have food and drink and can shoot arrows. We have beaten off the opening assaults.* Jinzal *were killed trying to scale the cliff, and many trying to knock down just the first of our four walls. It was damaged, but will cost hundreds of enemy lives to destroy. While* zhin'pefral *could then be set up, they would be directly beneath piled rocks and boulders on the cliffs, and Âna reminds me we now have fire-arrows, too. One saving joy, among many sorrows, is to have had Âna beside me.*'

"He would not always have said that," Sett observed.

"She will be *rabhsayu*, I think."

Dolvid read, "`She is very brave, tireless, always cheerful; we must not let her out of our sight again,* Bôdhrai.'"

"Little Âna."

Imaginably now, Rodlakh could become *rabhsai* indeed. Losses, he wrote, had been heavy in the open field, where they had not had enough cavalry, but now they were behind walls again, and could kill at least twenty for every one lost; *jinzai* archery was very inaccurate.

> `Kamsilat is saved, unless there are huge new armies of* jinzal *left in the West, or unless they can starve us out. The long path to the north which comes down into the forests of Kamsilat is known only to those who have studied the Colony's history, and I do not see how the enemy can find it, though we maintain a watch. Sit still, kill* jinzal *remains the motto.'

"What about food?"

"Rodlakh wrote on the assumption I would persuade *g'Asalladh'* to lift the blockade, as also that the *Mankh'* might be helpful in arranging a truce with Kargul. As is, the Strait, if still defended, will have to be forced so as to bring supplies to Kamsilat, but meanwhile the relief expedition will have to carry every scrap of food and feed both men and horses will need, for a minimum of fifteen days."

"How many? Will you have enough cavalry?"

A face of unknowing. They would have about three thousand, cavalry with some horsed infantry — archers who rode to battle, not mounted bows who fought in the saddle. The Karguli contingent was growing; Kamin-Tolagh, outwardly concerned over the safety of his mother and father, was using unchallenged authority with unmistakable relish, not troubling to consult his aged grandfather, the titular *Nim'*. By drawing on various garrisons he brought his sixteen squadrons up to twenty-four. That was exactly the legal number for the entire provincial cavalry: everyone had always known Kargul maintained more *péfrapravádal* than the law allowed, but not over twice as many, as now was clear. Some were still left for ordinary escort and guard duties, with eighteen squadrons in the north accounted for.

Part of this Dolvid told Sett, but he was worried by the phrase in this last dispatch about *those who have studied the Colony's history.* If the *Atarlum* bred *jinzal*, and of the *Atarlum*, the Teaching Order, who knew as much about any history?

Sett was puzzled by the same passage. "He says he can't see any way the Vale of Banakit could be recovered, and Vonn might be the new Frontier. I am no strategist, mind, but what about this northern way?"

"That is how the Colony must have been reconquered after the Return. I suppose he cannot foresee being able to supply such an expedition. Or he sees the *jinzal* as too strong for years to come."

Sett nodded thoughtfully, and Dolvid was unconvinced: it was as if Rodlakh wanted to put the northern way out of his mind. He would be warned again in his reply; Alkmas must sail again and soon; already more than five days gone since Rodlakh had written.

There would be nothing in that message about the complicity of the *Atarlum*. Dolvid was unsure why he had not shared that secret, even with Shumat. He had saved it for a final argument, but it was too large and terrible in his mind to be used, as his original instinct had been, to bind even some friendly with the *Mankh'* in an alliance of sudden rage to sweep the *Atarlum* out of existence. He wanted a face-to-face talk with Rodlakh before lighting a fire that might be harder to put out.

"If you had told me when we first came to see you I would soon be docking a fleet at Zelkova, I would have said you were mad. I'll say this, the Kargul' seem a lot better to me since you did for the toothy one, but wasn't Tovakh — "

"Not here." History, unless he wrote it, seemed as determined as Yenughai to forget the one decisive act of at-Zhâlai's life.

"But Âna said Petakoi — "

"Hush." Mounted, Kamin-Tolagh was picking his way along the quay, and now quite near. In only a few days it had become surprising to see him apart from Shumat.

Getting down, he let Dolvid present Sett. "Master, if you had told me a week ago I would be welcoming a fleet under royal colors to this port — Are the needed supplies aboard? There is food and feed here, but Shumat says we sail tomorrow."

Sett made a face, but brightened when told that meant only the troops for the Lunu Tezh' and their necessities, not food for relief of Kamsilat

"Oh, then, for the expedition, supplies are ready, yes, just as they came down from Dônshei — what you captured from Bolan and — " Sett shut his mouth, and started a loud blush.

He picked himself up. "Not beef as good as you would get in these parts." Covering one mistake, he threshed into another. "Across the Nanakh here the Paowanu Loi farmers generally have food to sell, at a price."

"That land," Dolvid said, "as it used to be, is the Kovilanu once again."

On the whole Kamin-Tolagh was amused, and with a proprietary air asked Sett his professional opinion of the port. Its situation was a spacious one, on the broadest reach of the Kôbh Estuary, fed also by the waters of Nanakh, an expanse of water ample enough for a lake or inland sea. The mountains that gave Kargul its name were here at their farthest from Arnan, many miles to the south, and Zelkova's hinterland was green and undulating, port spreading along the rim of a wide bay.

Sett had been here in former years, and spoke admiringly of the machines that moved cargoes, the double ramp of the chief waterfront granary, where the weight of a filled hopper was used to return the empty one. Shumat, Kamin-Tolagh said, had also been impressed, and was having drawings made to see whether the machine could be copied for Narn.

"A port I have not seen, *Asai*. I have always sailed Arnan, you see."

But Shumat would hardly see Narn again, or remain there long. If the war was lost presumably they would all die somewhere in a desperate last fight, and if victory somehow came his place would be at Kadon Dinul, Captain of Armies.

"So far, Kargul is not Karguli enough for him.   I promised to show him some of old town, its drinkshops. It has to be tonight, if we're sailing tomorrow."

A little stiffly, on the grounds of work, Dolvid declined to join them, and reminded Kamin-Tolagh there was to be an evening meeting of officers at and above the rank of squadron-leader, to settle the order of embarkation and march. The three leaders should get together half an hour earlier. "Good, *Bôdhrai*. Kargul will be there."

As Kamin-Tolagh rode away Sett said, "He has not demanded freeing of his mother and his father as the price of this alliance?"

"Their freedom is not what he wants, not just yet. He might be forbidden to ride, then, and lose his chance of fighting beside Shumat."

"How does that sit with Shumat?"

"He has good sense. At the moment, he may be a little flattered." Sett gave a swift look, hearing something more in the tone.

He should be glad, was glad the two had taken to each other so warmly. Quarrels between captains, each leading large forces, could mean disaster, and yet his reservations could not be simple jealousy over a friend. Certain Kamin-Tolagh with his breastplate on would not willingly listen to the suggestions of a penman, a civil official, Dolvid had hoped Shumat would be the steadying influence.

"We must be sure he holds to a plan, once made," he had told Shumat. "Against *jinzal* there won't be any room for visions of heroic deeds." He was recalling too, the dreams that had kept Kamin-Tolagh south of Shemugrân while his war was being lost in the north.

Shumat told him he had to trust the captains in the field, whose business was fighting, that Tam meant to fight, and his officers would follow him. Dolvid felt rebuked, but would not have minded that, except all the influence was so far going the other way; true, Kamin-Tolagh had questions about tactics in the Narn campaign, the handling of horse at Dônshei, but that was flattery, too, and Shumat, after wearing his well-earned fame so many years, was fascinated by Kamin-Tolagh's dash, his lordliness, the vain poses so exasperating to Âna. The more Shumat laughed and made excuses for Kamin-Tolagh's airiness, the more pompous he could observe Dolvid becoming, and he hated it. Uneasily he knew it would come to matter; there would be a point where he and Shumat would have to overrule Kamin-Tolagh's impracticalities. Nothing could be done now, and tomorrow they would be sailing the long coastline of Kargul, each in a different ship.

Aloud, to Sett, he wondered whether his plan was the right one. He could not see any other course, but it would be the third day, earliest, before they could reach the head of En'tesh, that hidden lake, and then seven or eight days more, with so many men, till they could hope to look down into the Vale of Banakit. No dispatches could reach them, and that would mean not less than fifteen days with no word of what Rodlakh was doing.

"He will come through, fighter that he is, and Âna — she is not going to die." Sett's eyes glittered, and he sought an easier subject. "What do all these porters and loaders do when there is no work for them? You can always hire them when you need them. They have small plots of land, I suppose, or work for farmers."

He remembered hopeless years in Irbat. "I would go hungry."

Simplicities

"Are you not lonely here?" Aëlu asked. Here was nowhere Âna had ever expected to see Sebhal's wife, Sett's house, looking out on the port and the mouth of the Navu.

She had spoken with Aëlu at times since halt of the Long Retreat at Vonn had let Rodlakh insist she come down here to Kamsilat. Âna had not managed to overcome her feeling of awe; even in breeches and a rough shirt Aëlu was herself, gracious without being cold, imperturbable, not aloof. In her presence Âna always felt faintly dishevelled, or as if her nose might soon need wiping.

Worse, she was formidably capable, and had made herself responsible for feeding and shelter of the homeless flooding Kamsilat. Âna had overheard her one day making an officer of the Army proud to be bullied into getting latrine pits dug for the large encampment out near two-mile stone west of the city.

"Why won't you join us at the Great House?"

"*Asayu*, my gratitude, but I am not ready for that." That sounded as if she was saying no invitation was needed, so she added, "The *rabhsai* told me I could go there when I wished to," which made it worse.

"It would save the *rabhsai* some steps — " this was subtly humorous, and no malice could be detected. "He prizes your advice."

"So he tells me, *Asayu*."

"I wish you would use my name, Âna." Obvious Aëlu knew she was failing to strike the right tone; her smile was taut. It was awful. No one ever called her condescending. Ordinary soldiers, Galt and Noldar for two, had adored her, while Âna believed herself free of the tendency, not unheard-of among Others, to detect slights where none were. Why, then, was the air so stiff between them?

"You were with Sebhal when he died?" Aëlu, at the archway that led to a small, pleasant flagged courtyard, could not possibly know the little figure of carved soapstone she was looking at was Sebhal's favorite.

"His last words were for you."

"So Dolvid told me."

"It is true."

The cool light of Aëlu's eyes rested on her. "I'm sorry. He managed at the end to deprive us both. I wish I were not so shy of you." She gave a laugh, as of embarrassment. "Less so, now, perhaps, now I have said it. But you are a woman who *causes*. I am the sort who waits."

"I never made him do anything. He was Sebhal — " not altogether enjoying being made responsible for what a man did, leading or goading him.

Aëlu made it better. "He was Sebhal, and your strength is your own. Do not listen to me. Pregnant women can talk nonsense."

Âna's frown of curiosity, wondering whether she meant herself, was misunderstood. "Oh, yes, Sebhal's, if there is a child, and I am nearly sure there is. It could only be his. Wearing sash is not wise where the man is in love with danger, but when I was *nôd'yanu* I used to dream of one man who would be all men I admired. Sebhal came — " her hands portrayed sufficiency. "But he was my dream, his dream was not mine. Dolvid — "

"Yes?" Almost a jump; this talk of more than one love had put him in Âna's mind.

"Nothing. He said things about not recognizing our desires when they come. He is more wise than happy; Rodlakh misses his advice. You really must come to the Great House."

It did not quite follow. "Who else knows about your child?"

"No one. It is not certain, yet. But I am quite sure. A boy, wouldn't you say?"

A nod. "Saidhan *Asai* should hear about it. The morning after the ride to Vonn, he was too stiff to remount; he said,

`What's left for an old nuisance to live for?'" His exasperation, standing baffled beside the stirrup, a new enemy, made it too painful to answer.

"War. That is left, and the need for boys, to be taught to fight. But you are right; I must tell Saidhan."

Rodlakh too might have been put off-stride to encounter Aëlu here, but he had several errands for his brief stay in Kamsilat, and was too glad to find one of those he had to see to worry about where. Added warehouses on South Shore had been made ready to house refugees, and he wanted the camp by two-mile stone moved. No one knew why that site had been chosen, except there was a stream, and the camp now had several hundred inhabitants.

Aëlu objected to marching small children, the aged and ill, down through Kamsilat to the harbor for shipping across the Estuary, and reminded him there were ferry-landings on the Navu not far from two-mile stone. It would mean using smaller boats, but she calculated each boat could manage the return trip, downstream loaded and back up empty, in under an hour, the whole crossing accomplished in half a day.

"This is already decided?"

"Do you have reasons against it?" At least when the subject was business, the former gingerly manner with her was entirely gone.

One objection was that people exhausted by their flight from danger soon became attached to a place that seemed safe. She had been there for the sick and wounded, and knew how soon people had found neighbors, made their habits and customs. They wanted their real homes above all, but till that came they would much rather stay put.

Rodlakh pointed out many more could sleep dry in the warehouses. But his real argument was that the camp, on level ground almost under the eaves of the forest, could not be

defended if even a small number of *jinzal* found a way past Vonn.
Aëlu assented gravely. "I'll take the news there myself."
"Isn't there someone you can send?"
"Not that I would wish this on."
"Shall I ride with you."
"No, *Rabhsai*, rest while you can. I shall find an escort."
Âna, amazed by Aëlu's calm at not having asked, wanted
to know if there was danger *jinzal* might reach Kamsilat. There
was no reason to think so except the feeling the Jaws were being
held too easily; officers in the Army of the West were saying
forcefully they should not have retreated so far. Attacks still
came, but in much smaller numbers, and in yesterday's fighting
only eighteen *jinzal* dead had been certainly counted. If the
enemy captains had determined on a long, wearing war, it was
foolish strategy in a position where not much harm could be done
to the defenders, and the numbers the Army was facing appeared
reduced beyond what could be accounted for by casualties; where
had the missing *jinzal* gone? Yet the outposts in the north, and
their patrols, had nothing to report.
"If they come?"
"Kamsilat was never built for a siege, but we are doing
what we can. What supplies we have left will be gathered in
buildings we can defend — Great House, barracks, the granaries
by the docks." Already men were boarding up windows, leaving
slits for archery.
"All those who do not hold weapons will cross to South
Shore. If the worst happens, survivors can be taken off by ship."
"Survivors."
"I am speaking of the extreme case, which we are not
likely to see. Even if the whole *jinzai* army came, they could not
have enough numbers to surround all our strong places. Cavalry
could make sorties, and keep ways open — " he waved rather
vaguely. "Till help comes." He went to the window where Âna
spent so much time. She realized Aëlu had left, and was not sure
just when.
They discussed the blockade of the Strait, the assumption
it was now or soon would be lifted. Rodlakh emphasized the

time it would take for *g'Asalladh'* to send new orders to his men in the far south of Kamanta. But Âna could not see why *g'Asalladh'* Himself, or a high-ranking representative, would not sail with the relief ships to get them through.

"Allow some space for men and supplies to be put together. I wrote that supplies were more urgent, and they could be sent under minimal escort. How many days?"

"Since your last message? Nine. Fourteen since Dolvid's planned visit to the *Mankh'*" — keeping it all factual.

"Well, what happens on the Mainland must happen; we cannot change it. You don't really fear for Dolvid?"

"No," she lied, keeping step with his mood.

"To our knowledge he has accomplished things anyone would call impossible. He will come through."

"You're tired." He had yawned, and suddenly she saw the face, lifeless with lack of sleep.

"I have to see Saidhan and Arvat, and I am riding back to Vonn tonight."

"Are you needed there so much, with the defenses holding?"

"More than ever. The bowmen must not imagine we are feasting at Kamsilat while they shoot their fingers raw."

"I have bread here, and some white cheese."

"I shall eat in the saddle." He had lowered to the arm of a stout wooden chair, and groaned slightly as he stood again. A last glance to the window. "Still no word. I want you to cross to South Shore."

"There is work for me on this side. Who is going to read your scribble to Saidhan? Is Doleni *Asayu* leaving?"

"She says, when *jinzal* are in her main hall. At least sleep at the Great House, so you can leave with the others if it comes to that."

"Very well." She surprised herself in acceding so casually; was she influenced by the revelation that Sebhal, at a time when he was her only glory, had managed to make a child with Aëlu?

"Good, come now. Or when you can; you will want to gather up some clothes." He kissed her rather seriously, and she saw why she had been so hesitant. Her move, practically speaking, was acceptance of his proposal. She was consenting to be *rabhsayu.*

Next morning Arvat woke the Great House with news brought racing through the forest from the north. Long files of *jinzal* had been sighted descending on the narrow trails above the valley. In a grim mood, Rodlakh rode back that afternoon. Not a sail was to be seen on Arnan.

"Some day," Shumat said, "I'll come back to see the shores of En'tesh." Next to Dolvid he was looking down on the deep lake from one of the network of trails, each with its close-packed line of moving horsemen, that climbed northward from the head of En'tesh on the right, the westerly bank of the Grân River. The whole history of Lunu Tezh' could never have seen the water so burdened with ships, mainly crowded at the north end, though away from the gushing, tumbling inflow of the river. A small crowd had gathered to watch the hurried disembarkation, and the military commander introduced himself, an Owani with nominal rank of *kímukan*, but not the troops to sustain it. He was under the command, again nominally, of the Captain of the West, but his reports went, if anywhere, to Kadon Dinul. With his half-dozen regulars and such levies as he raised at need he could not attempt much beyond keeping order in the string of Froghul' habitations, now threatening to grow together into a single, straggled city along the eastward shore of the lake, where the slope was less steep, and deep bites had been taken out of the dense growth of brush and stunted trees. He had no news about *jinzal* in large numbers or small, but admitted he had abandoned patrolling beyond a half-day from the lake, after a death and two eighteen-year retirements had left him even worse shorthanded, with, he said, more chance of being named next Captain-General than of getting replacements.

With no real sight of the settlements the expedition started north, crossing the thundering Grân on a long, arched bridge made entirely of wooden struts lashed together with cord. On the far side the overgrown shore fell straight to the water.

Beaming, Kamin-Tolagh urged his mount close enough to shout something delighted and incoherent about parts he had never dreamed of seeing. He gestured to the north as if treasures and feasts were waiting. Shumat called back a caution about the hard journey ahead, but was grinning. "Mad," he confided, an expression of admiration.

A short way beyond the falls where a trail wound in from the west was a small, rickety village devoted entirely to fishing, with a partial dam of wicker across the river to trap fish. With the villagers Dolvid tried out his crude Western Froghulú, and was taken to the head-man, who in turn led him to the well-woman.

"Why well-woman?" Kamin-Tolagh hastened to join the small delegation to her house. Obviously there was no need for a well here, but those with the gift of finding water had been held in honor when these people's forebears were wanderers in drier lands. "Now, the title signifies wisdom. Some of them prophesy or have healing skills." Dolvid was hoping only for news.

"Tú would have wanted to be here — these things interest her." Kamin-Tolagh's hand went inside the neck of his shirt, where a small goatskin bag hung on a rawhide cord: it must contain a pinch of ashes from each of the `dooms' burnt for him when Kamin-Tarú consulted the *raf'yalu* of Yuvat, an emblem of each weapon, fragments from an arrow-shaft and from the haft of a lance, a sword-shaped stick, a sliver of hoof, and so forth.

The practice, long condemned by the *Mankh'*, was thought to be dying out.

The well-woman in her dim-lighted house on stilts beside the river seemed at least one hundred, though the Froghul aged quickly, women in particular going from youth to apparent age without much in between; she might be no more than fifty. She spoke about "new *jinzal*, shining-chest *jinzal*," knuckling Shumat's breastplate to point her meaning. When asked about armies, she laughed, showing good teeth, and said there were *jinzal* not a day away, but *jinzal* were *without campfire*, as the Froghu' phrase was, too wild for such things as cooked food, or armies.

Shumat thought the breastplated *jinzal* might have been deserters, but *strays* might be a better word. By Rodlakh's account the brutes, notwithstanding their drilling into armies, their use of weapons, were too dull-witted for an idea like desertion, but any detached from the army might well wander aimlessly, not knowing which way to go. But Kamin-Tolagh was sobered, and bowmen were brought forward to ride with the vanguard.

The first *jinzai* Dolvid ever saw was a dead one, stretched beside the way where several trails bunched together into a rough road. Some days dead the corpse had a dozen wounds, enlarged by the cutting-out of arrows for further use, and a good part of one shoulder had been gnawed away by some beast. If there had ever been weapons or a breastplate they had been stripped away as prize. Even in death and smelly decay the size and muscling were formidable. Heavy arms with their stone-clawed hands were shorter than was said, and it might be the crouched posture when they ran was responsible for the common belief *jinzal* arms hung well below the knee; the legs were thick, shapeless, with muscles like rope to carry the weight of the deep-chested torso, hunched back and huge neck. Strange such massiveness could ever come out of a union between the usually slender Owanil and one of the wiry little tribes of the West.

Knowing Froghul' customs, it was still a shock to see they had apparently carried off one trophy, the organ everyone mentioned when describing *jinzal*. An older one, dried and preserved, had been shown in the village when they asked the headman about *jinzal*, the great unmeaning yard with its shrivelled bag.

"Why is this left at roadside?" Kamin-Tolagh asked.

"It is their way with a dead enemy, to frighten others."

"But *jinzal* are not frightened by their own dead, any more than ants are, or crows."

"A custom is a custom. When you speak about wisdom, you make Maëdhi's sign — " touching a forefinger to his breast. "And would, even talking to a man you knew had no clue what it meant." Kamin-Tolagh opened his mouth and closed it again, accepting the parallel, though clearly an Owani practice was different altogether.

They pressed on up the river-valley, slope sometimes steep, always left to right, here in the Grân Valley. Many streams went spurting for the river, and these must often have been obstacles, before the best spots for crossing had been joined by paths. It was also too early in the year for the worst of the biting insects Banak's men had been maddened by in late summer. Not guided by any recognizable landmarks the relief expedition had no more idea than Banak's what distance they had covered, but though their direction often veered, there was no fear of being lost, so long as the main slope persisted, and the gleam of the Grân could be glimpsed deep below. For a stretch the trail would be broad enough for three abreast, and then where ground was broken by mossy boulders or matted corpses of large trees the ways would divide again, and often leading their horses they went among thick growths of fern and laurel, blackthorn and whitethorn, dogwood near blossoming and dark river-birch, their tracks raindrops on a windowpane, moving towards eventual reunion. They called constantly to each other when divided; the multiplying trails helped make up for the slow pace, yet Dolvid was anxious, aware pack-animals and rearguard could hardly be less than three miles behind the leader, usually Kamin-Tolagh.

When night came, senior officers went sidling back to make sure this distance was closed up as much as possible, while the foremost trampled out a camp-site on a relatively open curve of the valley, between two tributary streams. As darkness deepened their watchfires made a diminishing arc, the glowing blade of a sickle.

Among those gathered at the fire where the commanders were, it was good to see Onebhal, who had arrived at Zelkova just in time to embark in one of the last ships to untie. After leaving Kamsilat he had been too late at Irbat to send word delaying Shumat's expedition, and had ridden all over Dramal, evading enemies, always just missing friends, till, having started for Kadon Dinul, he got news at Dônshei, and turned south at last. His failure to warn Shumat was in the end to the good; without his landing Tovakh would have been at Kadon Dinul in strength when Dolvid arrived from the West.

Shumat was unusually eloquent about the changes prosperity had brought to the Northeast, his own simple and settled life there; perhaps he could sense it was coming to an end. When Onebhal said he had thought his journeying days were over, Kamin-Tolagh remarked again how his sister would have enjoyed seeing so much that was new.

This was curious; one reason at least for her absence had been his threat to beat her with his own hands if she tried to slip aboard one of their ships; their parting was hot tears and bitter words, though Dolvid, for one, would be surprised if Kamin-Tarú did not embark with Sett when he left for Kamsilat with relief supplies in a day or two.

"*Bôdhrai*," unknowingly echoing his mother. "What did the *rabhsai* have to say about my sister's arrival in the Colony?"

"He called her *cousin*, and hoped for friendship between Arbhai-Navu and baKargul."

"Did he admire her?" A trap-question. Either yes or no would be troublesome.

Shumat said, "Now you are asking whether Rodlakh *Deghi* has eyes," and might be the only man in the realm who could say it and sound innocent. Kamin-Tolagh shelved the subject, while Dolvid pictured a greater surprise waiting for him, if they ever reached Kamsilat: Âna.

Next day was much the same, but later they came to an inhabited vale, where a main tributary of the Grân flowed. Huddles of houses here were too small to be called villages, and what must be the entire population stood in silence to watch the passage of this unprecedented riding. Dolvid's Froghulú, as always, was greeted with astonishment, though he could barely follow one word in five of the local dialect. He understood there had been *jinzal* sighted at outlying farms; some people had been killed, a *jinzai* wounded, and tracked till the trail of blood gave out.

"Chase them, lords, chase them away," his informants called after him.

The riding crossed the small river by log bridges low to the water on crude rock cairns, and often washed away, to judge by debris. The real climb began. Beyond slopes studded rather than matted with growth brown hills rose, steep and disheartening. The worn slots of the trail left the course of the Grân, and now they could ride, not pushing their mounts despite temptation to hurry, keeping in mind there would be fighting ahead. In the lower country men had often chanted or sung, troops of the Northeast bawling out ribaldry from Narn to answer a scurrilous Karguli song, or both joining in a well-known one from the Heartland, but now it seemed they felt too visible, and even talk was subdued. Shumat had dropped back to somewhere near mid-column, and Kamin-Tolagh was riding tight-lipped, as if he had not realized weary and inglorious travel in featureless country would also be part of war. Not far behind, the round-cheeked officer, Pivrekhan, was equally taciturn, and as Kamin-Tolagh did gave signals to his squadron with three negligent fingers instead of whole hand held rigid. Pivrekhan's hand was unfortunately rather stubby, no match for Kamin-Tolagh's elegance, and that was true for Pivrekhan's hair, too, tight-curling and wiry, though its owner went without helm, and leant back in the saddle, trying to make it swing free as Kamin-Tolagh's did.

"Shumat, *Bôdhrai*, agrees with my view." Kamin-Tolagh found room to swing out of line and halt for a moment while they had a mouthful of cold *raminat*.

"Does he? " This was a continuing discussion over best use of cavalry against the enemy, presuming an open field. Dolvid, relying on Rodlakh's dispatches, had remarked they would have to depend on the initiative, courage and sense of officers at squadron and half-squadron level, provoking a lecture from Kamin-Tolagh, based on principles ascribed to Larghai, on the effectiveness of massed cavalry in battle.

"He says he is not bringing more than a thousand horse so far to throw them away in spoonfuls."

Dolvid declined to duel with an absent Shumat. "We shall debate this fully when we camp tonight. There cannot be any misunderstandings, and I have some writings I want you to see."

He meant Rodlakh's treatise, written at Drin Navuna before the Long Retreat, but Kamin-Tolagh was in a new mood. "Freighanai," to his sad-faced squadron officer. "Have you ever read a book about sporting?"

"Sporting, *Asai*?"

"With women. Did you never read *Virgins of the Mount*, or *Interrupted Sleep*, those books with the interesting drawings?"

"Oh, that. I've seen some, *Asai*, yes."

"Is that how you learned?"

"Fucking, *Asai*? From a book? My father took me to the *margú* on the Zelkova road. I learned doing it, you could say."

Kamin-Tolagh kicked his horse. "Exactly."

Late that day, having crawled like ants up a huge bare slope scarred with water-channels, they came to a strange spot known from descriptions, a broad shelf projecting from the mass of hills, a sparsely-grassed plain where there were many small, round, ice-cold pools of unknown depth, black water always in faint motion from below. A few dozen poor goatherds made their home here, and Dolvid took a present of linen and some dried fruit to their cluster of dwellings, something part hut and part skin tent, obtaining a very detailed account of the various trails between here and the Lunu Tezh' Gate. The army had done very well to be this far north so soon.

The westward routes, he relayed to Shumat and Kamin-Tolagh, did not climb as high as those farther east, but the easterly way, though straighter, was considered by the herdsmen the longer journey — that would mean, driving goats, and they admitted it could be otherwise with big horses. It might be better to divide forces, the pack-train taking the lower way, under Shumat with all his assorted squadrons, Kamin-Tolagh leading the cavalry of Kargul the steeper way. The enemy, Dolvid argued, not anticipating any large army out of Lunu Tezh', would rush all forces to oppose the division first sighted. If one was engaged in the narrows of the Gate the other might either come to its support, or take the opportunity to strike straight for Banakit, as circumstance dictated.

Shumat objected the two armies would be out of touch, but using the travel times provided by the goatherds and improving them for the better pace of even loaded pack-ponies, it was hard to see how they could possibly be above a few hours apart, coming to the several passes of the Gate, so long as they did not lose their way.

Kamin-Tolagh noted a further advantage of splitting their forces, that it would mean a less extended line-of-march, making quick deployment easier if an enemy was encountered. He also made the sensible suggestion that two men who knew the way, one each, could be borrowed from among the herders.

"I'll go with you, if Kargul will have me," Dolvid said.

"Kargul is honored. So long as it is understood the disposition of troops is only mine."

Dolvid had come to this meeting in a dour mood. Returning from conference with the goatherds he had stopped to speak with some men from the Burantal garrison, and got the news the woman Svondais, Rheduban's adept in the *Epranda*, had been dragged into the street and killed by a mob when Rheduban's death was known. Not all cruelty came from Kargul, he knew that, but was distressed both by unnecessary act and the boasting tone of its telling. Making war on *jinzal* had a deceptive simplicity about its choices.

Cheered a little by Kamin-Tolagh's acquiescence in dividing the army, he knew a fight could not be shirked on a question that might be the difference between defeat and victory.

"Shumat is with me. Any man of sense knows the heavier hammer breaks more stone."

"In principle. We did not have the numbers at Dônshei, but massed attack is best against a massed enemy. They have to be broken."

Rodlakh had observed the large target provided by a mass of cavalry was a gift to *jinzai* archery with its long range but indifferent aim. Dolvid repeated this, while opening his saddlebag to find the copied dispatch, adding some calculations of his own, that even the slowest archer with the range of the *jinzal* could shoot five effective arrows before cavalry could close.

"If they stand till the charge hits them," Onebhal said.

That was just the point; all notions of war took into account an element absent in *jinzal*, fear; Rodlakh said when twenty *jinzal* charged and nineteen had been struck down by arrows, the last one kept coming forward.

"Look — " Kamin-Tolagh turned to Shumat. "We have the strength to charge on a front of sixty-four lances two squadrons deep; no one has seen that weight of cavalry in a generation. Our men are trained to hold their places — we'll sweep the *jinzal* from the field."

Dolvid had the sheets now. "Rodlakh writes — "

"Writes!"

"*Asai*, the *rabhsai* has been in the field against *jinzal* for three weeks, leading cavalry in person. He watched men die for lack of proper tactics, and wrote down what he had learned, not knowing whether he would survive, not wanting others to pay the same price for the same lessons."

"But you learn from doing." Kamin-Tolagh repeated, word for word, his dialogue earlier with Freighanai.

Shumat failed to laugh. "Exactly, I said," Kamin-Tolagh repeated, trying in fading light to carry Shumat with him.

"The *Bôdhrai* is not just a book-soldier. He led a charge at the Pass of Perus. He made the general plan at Dônshei — "

"Yes, but it was a fluke, your wagonloads of archers. My father should have brought torches and burned them where they stood. The cavalry on the field, you handled that."

"In a way I never could," controlling old exasperation over soldiers who always wanted to fight the last battle but one.

Kamin-Tolagh began again about practical fighters. Onebhal wanted to recall events at the Pass of Perus, fourteen years ago, but Shumat was there quicker. "Who do you think wounded Tovakh at Dônshei, and began the rout?" Was it possible that for the blink of an eye he had forgotten what Tovakh was to Kamin-Tolagh?

Time stopped. Dolvid till now had tactfully omitted this detail, uncertain how it would affect the alliance: he'd had more than enough of aroused Karguli kin-feeling.

"If you had killed my father, *Bôdhrai* — "

"The small wound I gave was due mainly to Enikai."

Another silence. "I can see I shall have to give more respect to your horse."

"He has not generally been given his due."

"You have not wounded any others of my family?" Kamin-Tolagh's humor was verging on the hysterical. "My mother, you say, was well when you left her? How is it Kamin-Tarú calls you gentle? My House will never forgive me this alliance."

"Yes, if we win," Shumat, bluntly.

"I know very well, *Asai*, what you are risking. All the more reason why we must not waste lives on tactics for some other war." Quite true. He and Shumat could die, and if there was ever history again it would say they had done what they must, but for Kamin-Tolagh the only redemption was victory (and even there he would be defeating, among others, his own mother).

"I don't understand how you can be against massed horse." Kamin-Tolagh was more judicious having lost Shumat's automatic agreement.

By now a lantern was needed to read what Rodlakh had written. The thesis was clear and simple; it was only a manner of speaking to say weight of cavalry broke an enemy. They might ride down the front rank, but fear did the breaking, as those behind saw what was happening. That was with men; *jinzal* would charge or they would stand, but seldom turn and run, and without fear to be spread a charge against them was like riding into a forest of pillars; some were knocked down, but the others were unmoved.

"Pillars that can kill," Shumat said. "What, then?"

After watching the bravest batter themselves to death as part of massed charges that ground down to a halt, Rodlakh had recognized squadrons and half-squadrons must be used, coming at the enemy from one side then another, not giving the enemy bows a chance to do damage, using the speed of *pefral* to avoid being entangled in the general fights that were always lost. He could have used a thousand mounted bows like Galt's to sting and retreat, turn to sting again, but lances, he said, were effective so long as they knew enough not to drive on into the enemy mass.

"It's true, naturally," Kamin-Tolagh grudged, "single squadrons charge at better speed, and can change direction quicker than a large body of cavalry."

"And retreat faster. He emphasizes and repeats twice, there is no dishonor giving ground to this enemy. He saved something from Shâl Mines, he says, because he learned to keep the men who direct the *jinzal* not knowing which way to face, refuse a fight on a restricted front, strike at flanks and pull away. *If their archers can be killed first, so much the better,*" he read.

"Listen, son-of-the-water — " punning on Shumat's name as a word in the Owanilú. "What do you say? Every squadron riding for itself? This will be ordering a whirlwind."

"I like to have control, but I am not going to see good men die for the sake of good formations. What do you say?"

"We need to call all *kímukanal* and squadron-leaders together in the morning, before we part company. Perhaps the *Bôdhrai* can favor them with a brief reading." Irony persisted, but Kamin-Tolagh meant what he said.

This was a bare and baffling country, every expectation of a vista from the next summit thwarted by more brown domes, color unvarying except where outcrops of stone showed whitish, near-black or pink. Sparse tracings of thorn, a vinelike growth criss-crossing pebbled ground, a slender dry and tattered weed, grey-green, completed the sights of these arid uplands, a roof of the world where the cavalry moved steadily and their shadows went gradually from left to right as day progressed. It was not hot, but gusts of cool wind were just as parching as sun, and the men were glad of full waterbottles. The drink the horses had at the deep, cold sockets of their camping-place would be the last, either of their lives, or till they tasted the Navu.

Kamin-Tolagh was reflective, talking about his province, about women he had bedded. Hard to bear if Âna was identifiably included, but Kamin-Tolagh never got that far, and what he did tell was a dreary recital of detached features, hair, breasts, hips, actions, with nothing to make their possessors real. Later, Kamin-Tolagh turned to his sister, and his hope she would take a husband before too long. Not immediately, he amended, and he hoped she would demand good birth, but not someone too proud. He should not be too much absorbed in his lands, but no idler, either; a soldier would not do for her, nor anyone over-learned; she would be unwise to marry youth, but a man in middle life would never suit her. Kamin-Tarú, naturally, would never take sash, yet a husband who did not care whether or not she kept to him would be a poor prospect.

"As you say, *Asai*, your sister is very young." He did not get an answer to this, but Kamin-Tolagh seemed more cheerful.

Their shadows slender, stretching away to the right, they were descending by stages, down a long slope then up a shorter one. Outriders came cantering back to report that from a height not three miles on they had looked down into slotted gaps with the green of a broad lowland visible beyond; Lunu Tezh' Gate. They had removed themselves from the skyline as soon as they realized where they must be, and no enemy had been sighted.

"Let us see for ourselves," Kamin-Tolagh suggested, and with Dolvid, their herdsman guide, and a small escort, went forward to look for a route to take them deep into the narrows of the pass, shielding them as much as possible from any watchers. Expecting an encounter at any second, they came down into a blind valley, a long trough that led nowhere, space where a thousand men and their mounts could make camp with hopes of being undetected. They climbed the left-hand slope where it was easier, and it had seemed from there they would have an open run down to the Gate, one of the wider openings, without long windings between threatening heights, column strung out dangerously. But the complex foldings of this country had fooled them; instead of a clear slope down to the Gate they were looking across another narrow valley, at a long ridge extending from massed hills. Rightward it tapered down, crowned by bushy growths.

Their guide, whose only ambition was to leave them and go back, gave a complicated description, understood as meaning the broad opening through the Gate would be found beyond the next ridge, but his people drove their animals a narrower way, a mile or so north and east, which could be reached by a circling route from the entrance to this closed valley. A scout was sent, and Dolvid sat with Kamin-Tolagh, their horses just below them on the slope, discussing the next move.

Kamin-Tolagh urged if they pressed on they might be through the Gate before dark. Not much before, Dolvid maintained, and they would have to make camp on exposed ground; it would still be a three-hour ride to Banakit, and there were many reasons not to arrive there fatigued at the end of a long day; they would be unable to spy out enemy dispositions and might be involved in night-fighting where men could lose their way, all the advantages of their intelligence wasted. Besides, supposing they got through a night camped on the farther slopes, it would mean charging uphill if they had to come to Shumat's assistance in the morning.

Scouts came back to report the narrow cleft, nearer than their guide had said, was unguarded. Far below they had seen the glint of the Navu and the houses of Banakit as windows caught the last sun.

Kamin-Tolagh pulled urgently at Dolvid's sleeve, flattening to the ground, and motioning at the opposite ridge. Where it began to decline there were dark, solid shapes, not bushes; shapes moving slowly up the crest. Then the sun, though not visible from where they crouched in shadow, must have found a gap between hills, and tawny light knifed across to outline the farther ridge in gold, thinning the screen of bushes. Dolvid now could see helmed heads and sharp weapons, rounded shoulders. The *jinzal* were taking up position, but as far as could be told their backs were to the watchers.

"It is true," Kamin-Tolagh murmured, so first acknowledging any doubt. The glow faded, leaving shapes blurred and indistinct once more.

Well below the skyline, men keeping watch above, Kamin-Tolagh put forward the guess Shumat was somewhere quite near, that his army had been spotted, the *jinzal* part of the defenses being prepared against him. It would also explain why other ways had been left unguarded, if the *jinzai*-masters, amazed at Shumat's numbers, made the natural assumption it was the entire army, and rushed all their companies to fight it.

Dolvid had expected Shumat to be farther to the south and west, where the path beyond the Gate led down to the crossing just the far side of Banakit, but Kamin-Tolagh's reading would explain why all the *jinzal* on the ridge were facing the wrong way. Indeed, if here was the broadest, straightest way through the Gate, Kamin-Tolagh's whole strength was in the rear of a force meant to take Shumat in flank, as he came down to engage other *jinzal* that would surely guard the pass itself.

"But not tonight. He went to your school of prudence, *Bôdhrai*. He will be camped and resting. He'll want a good look in the morning before he tries for the Gate."

Useless sending men looking for Shumat's army in the dark. A watch must be kept, but morning would bring opportunity for upsetting enemy plans.

While the main squadrons were flowing into the dimmering valley, Kamin-Tolagh said, "You judge Rodlakh is holding Vonn?"

"I hope he is."

"Kamin-Tarú said he was tall, courteous; I had heard that elsewhere."

"Did she mention how touched he was she came of her own accord as a counter-hostage for Aëlu?"

"Yes, yes; Rodlakh if he is alive is young Banak born again. Would he want Kamin-Tarú for his partner?"

Dolvid kept amusement invisible; Tú as the new Laluvoi! Yet he did not think any less of Kamin-Tarú knowing she would be bored numb by ten minutes of the statecraft that was food and drink to Laluvoi, even when she was ninety. "Your mother asked if Rodlakh and Tú could be a match. I offended her, I'm afraid, saying they looked well together." But with what he now knew, he was the angry one, Petakoi toying with him, certain there were *jinzal* on the march.

"My mother would marry Tú to a *jinzai* — no insult to Rodlakh — " for once hurriedly, Kamin-Tolagh tried to correct an impression Dolvid in his surprise would not have noticed: "I mean only to say she wants Tú safely married. Would Rodlakh have her?"

"No." Distracted; his turn to omit diplomacy.

"Is something wrong with my sister? Not her lineage, surely?"

"Would Kamin-Tarú want to be *rabhsayu*?"

"You mean, he has already picked a woman."

"Yes, he has," not meaning such a harsh tone. Kamin-Tolagh, who might understand better if he knew who the woman was, let it drop. Night was settling itself in small noises, restlessness of horses, murmur of voices kept low by command. Kamin-Tolagh had opened his shirt to finger the little goatskin bag. "*Bôdhrai*, Dolvidhai, you might get a theme for a tale-teller from this: a man spends his boyhood yearning for his chance of glory, and when it comes... "

He could not go on, but Dolvid presumed to speculate. "I do not believe heroes of old were without fear. If heroism was not knowing fear, any *jinzai* would deserve a *frela'olu-rai* with Larghai. History ought to teach us men who were afraid could still go forward. I have ridden in battle and loathed it, but this enemy cannot be reasoned with; we can either fight or run. We have to fight."

"Or run, as you say. I am not so much afraid of *jinzal* —
"

"Aren't you? I am — " but knew he would have to be a part of the fighting, or find a way to live with shame.

"Yes, only a fool would not be. But I fear fear most. I am not going to be remembered as the coward — is that a use of your history?"

"Boasting, too," recalling the men last night, outbidding each other in what they would do facing *jinzal*.

"What if boasting fails when put to the test?"

"It always does. Boasts are not what we are, but what we wish to be. They hold us as oaths do, because we are more afraid to break our word than to risk death. Ridiculous, but true."

Kamin-Tolagh took this in. "Great Hrafi, I am muddled, but I would not change that for your clarity. Powers need mystery to remain powerful, not so?"

"Mostly."

"What moves you, if you see how everything works? I would far rather be fooled."

"So would I." His powers were being overestimated by Kamin-Tolagh, who nonetheless was showing depths that could never be guessed from his everyday posturing.

"You had better sharpen your pens. Poor bastards in some battle a hundred years from now will be told to remember Kargul at Lunu Tezh' Gate. They will never learn about the fear, or be allowed to guess it."

Rodlakh and Saidhan were differing. "Our aim," Rodlakh said, "is to kill *jinzal*. Nothing else."

"That is what I say, and we can kill more defending the bridges."

"We can't defend the near end of First Bridge against *jinzal* coming from the north. All our men between there and Vonni's Jaws will be doomed."

"But if the *jinzal* ignore the bridge in their greed for Kamsilat, we shall have bowmen in their rear."

"The *jinzal* are not going to come down to the road and then turn for Kamsilat, not when the forest can bring them almost to the courtyard of the Great House. Our best bows will be needed here."

Saidhan's exasperation was like a sneeze. "To shoot at the same *jinzal* they could kill with less cost in Vonni's Jaws."

"Grandfather, I am not going to let the *jinzal* defeat us in installments, first Kamsilat with too few bows, then the men left behind to be crushed from both sides. No."

"Very well," with all the signs of being reasonable. "But you are talking about giving up a place as strong as Vonni's Jaws, and opening the road for their artillery to come down and knock down Kamsilat, one stronghold after another."

"Vonn is not a strong position from eastward, and once the defenders were trapped, I doubt they could be relieved, even when we get our help from the Mainland. If they were not overcome, they would starve."

"I do not say leave all the defenders there. A hundred men could be found, good bowmen, who would be proud to be part of a rearguard. War is trade with a different name, and that's a good bargain: they could kill a thousand before they were done."

Rodlakh wearily rubbed at his face. "I cannot make those bargains."

"Poh. We know men are going to die. Open battle is a lottery, but when you have volunteers willing to give their lives — "

"Saidhan, your principle is sound, but I cannot think that way." Rodlakh, Âna would have wagered, had never addressed his grandfather by bare name; the old man blinked a little.

"Practise does not make me like war any better, but if we have to have battles, every man has a right to the same coward's hope as I have, that he won't be killed or maimed."

"Captains have to make hard choices," remembering the Ní-Tilagh.

"Yes, and if I knew holding Vonni's Jaws a little longer was the difference between victory and disaster, I might call for volunteers. I might. As it is, I am not certain we will not lose Kamsilat in a fight where just a hundred bows would change the outcome. No." He made sure his sword was free in the scabbard. "We shall stand together, all with the same hope of relief."

Saidhan's face was easily read; though tempted to cite his extensive experience, three times the years Rodlakh had lived, his equally old devotion to the House of Banak would make him submit to a plan he hated.

Rodlakh was going west to begin withdrawal from the Jaws, and gave instructions all shipping must stand at anchor out from the port, or be moored on South Shore; the *jinzal* must not capture any vessels.

Saidhan heaved his chest, still sure he was right. "Aëlu should cross, also. All her orphans are on South Shore."

Both men turned on Âna, who looked pointedly to where Doleni sat immovable.

As everyone said, the Great House was not a fortress. From this room over the rear courtyard they could see how the gate had been strengthened with timbers; a wagon loaded with rock could be trundled into the gap and its wheels knocked off. Benches and barrels along the base of the wall gave archers a platform to shoot from, and all lower windows were boarded up and provided with slits. Nearby, the barracks was also prepared for defense, though a good half of the remaining cavalry, under Wanildhai, was in a makeshift camp up near the light-tower, from where charges might be launched if opportunities came.

"The *jinzal* seen up north have been in smaller companies. If I had a thousand added lances, we could strike at them as they come out of the forest." He mocked himself with a grim laugh. "In my last to Dolvid I said we had not much use for cavalry. True when I wrote it. What can he be doing? Why no word?"

"We are not even sure — " If he was a captive at the *Mankh'*, there was no assurance Kadon Dinul was still for Rodlakh.

"Well, we can only go on fighting. Help may yet come."

"Must come."

Just before he rode word arrived a squadron-strength patrol had clashed with *jinzal* not twelve miles from the Great House, losing nine men. Shaking his head over the casualties, Rodlakh saw he no longer had enough horse for patrols far afield; the outlying farmers and woodsmen had already come into Kamsilat, and only the road counted now. Âna came down to West Gate to watch Rodlakh with his own squadron ride. These partings were not becoming any easier.

Morning was cool in the hills, a wind gusting from the yellow east. Men roused, most serious but some with taut jokes, wetting lips from water-bottles, munching at bread and dried meat. Some gave hay to restless horses, while others worked at their harness, wiped mist from swords, wound throats with long strips of cloth, bound wrists with leather. Officers who kept the lore of old campaigns went among the younger soldiers advising them to empty their bowels now if they could, to save discomfort when the enemy came in sight. As the cumbersome beast, army, stretching itself, blinked into fuller waking, there was bantering between squadron leaders about who would be first to run from the battle they knew was near. Again, soldiers of Kargul were much like any others, shrugging away danger or predicting as direly as they dared, licensed clowns forcing their long belches and doing grotesque, shuffling imitations of *jinzal*, while serious soldiers powdered the hafts of their lances with resin, lined helms with straw, used knives to cut excess from a bootlace. Some, elaborately casual, drifted near for a look at the senior officers, perhaps hoping to read their fortunes in Yenughai's sober face, the flourishes of their Kamin-Tolagh, or smaller gestures of this creature, *Bôdhrai*, who had dropped among them bringing a banner depicting a Tree.

While horses were being saddled and squadrons formed up Dolvid went with Kamin-Tolagh to last night's vantage-point. The sharpbacked ridge was touched with cool light, intervening low ground left in deep shadow.

"Where will you ride today?" A startling question; yesterday's book-soldier today invited to ride with the *péfrapravádal* of Kargul.

"Your plan seems best." Some of the squadrons would be here under the skyline, while Kamin-Tolagh led others through the narrower way to the east. After giving him an hour's start, the force here would cross the little valley, and see what enemy there was to be fought on the opposite height.

About to quit the crest they saw movement on the next ridge. A long line of bobbing heads was moving farther up its spine, thrust of the muzzle mouths now easily seen. "Bows," Dolvid said, recognizing the long shape that stuck up higher than heads.

Light was improving. The line of *jinzal* moved up till the head of the column halted almost opposite where the watchers were. A horseman was directing them, leaning posture unmistakable, though the mount could not be seen. Without a glance behind he turned his creatures to face the other way. More heads, till the *jinzal* had formed at least a double line, though there might be more, out of sight on the farther slope. Dolvid counted eighty heads, and was sure he had missed some.

Kamin-Tolagh at once increased to ten the number of squadrons that would assail the ridge; he would have made it twelve, equal halves, but Dolvid, convinced there would be larger forces barring the pass, urged him to have enough men with him to be able to come at their rear. "Once through, the slope is bare. If you get a way down from the summit, you can look to your left for a pass blocked by *jinzal*." There was also the chance he might still have a clear run for Banakit.

They clasped hands, and without warning the spirited Kamin-Tolagh returned, the one first seen riding up to the house by Shemugrân. Cloak and hair swirling he ran to where Freighanai was holding his horse, and with that fluency Dolvid envied was into the saddle. He swung to pick a way through waiting squadrons, leaning over to swap jokes with his men. Yet he conveyed the plan to his officers, and soon the larger part of the cavalry was moving, winding off into fours, a long column circling up a stony slope in the dazzle of rising sun, soon beginning to pass out of sight.

The squadrons Dolvid was with had three regular *kímukan*, and were commanded by an under-captain, Yenughai. With these officers, he went back to their watch. In brighter light the double line of *jinzal* archers was in plain view, crouched. Added to Rodlakh's idea that in gaining the weight and discipline of an army the *jinzal* gave up some of their individual strength, a lost alertness; untrained the creatures were unlikely to be taken by surprise, famous for the constant swivelling of their heads, this way and that, on the short necks, but now perfectly still.

To a subdued Yenughai he pointed out the ramp-like curve of a gentler way to scale the ridge, down to the right, and suggested that while six squadrons fanned out to take the shortest distance across the low ground, the remaining four might make for that place and circle back along the crest.

"Then we had better spread the squadrons out a bit, and pack them in under the skyline till you give the word, *Bôdhrai*." Yenughai's appearance was changed today; several days away from his last wine he was firm-jawed, clear-eyed, but grim, like someone who felt worse about being better.

When the time-wick had smoldered away two-thirds of Kamin-Tolagh's head-start there was the hoarse sound of horns or signal trumpets from beyond the farther ridge. Mounted, Dolvid urged Enikai up a few paces to where he could see *jinzal* archers standing, fitting arrows to their strings; clearly battle for them was imminent.

He turned to Yenughai, and gave a nod. No chance to change his mind; the cavalry was at once on the move, he was part of a storm that grew of its own forces.

Coming over the crest, mounts straining, the mass somehow sorted into regular fours, squadron after squadron, gathering speed. In the mounting fury of the charge with the racket of drumming hoofs, jangling harness and the snorts of *pefral* it was astonishing the enemy did not hear and turn to face them, but as Dolvid found when he climbed their ridge, they had noise in front of them. The nearest *jinzal* turned hideous, snarling faces only when the foremost cavalry was almost on them. One went down under the hoofs of Enikai, and jabbing with his sword Dolvid was near one of the men in bright cloaks, blue-green worn over a plain tunic. He struck out with his whip and the lash curled across Dolvid's upper left arm. He would be bruised, but scarcely felt it, hauling Enikai around as the man dropped the whip and went for his sword, never drawn as Dolvid drove his own home to the hilt, and felt the weight a moment before the body slid from the blade.

In the next wide valley there were incomprehensible events. Dolvid could allow himself only a brief, astonished impression, a dense band of *jinzal* in jogging retreat kept together by cloaked horsemen, and another company of *jinzal* moving up from the right where the sweeping curve of the wide pass was, running hard, not breaking formation. Beyond them were cavalry under the Beech-Tree banner, and it could be seen Shumat's forces were deploying with calm deliberation, not attempting hot pursuit of the retreating band.

Other than bows the *jinzal* on the ridge had no weapons, and while snapping teeth and clawing hands were horribly powerful, the unexpected assault put nearly half out of action before the others knew there was a fight. Some stood bewildered, ready to charge but not knowing where to, while swarming cavalry hacked down others in front of them. But Dolvid saw a rider of Kargul dragged from the saddle by a *jinzai* with a lance already buried in its great chest, and rode to the assistance of another man grabbed at by a big *jinzai*, huddled behind the right leg of the rider, who tried to twist free. Dolvid scythed at the bunched neck, feeling toughness of muscle and bone as his blade bit through breastplate-strap and rough shirt. The head turned, and he felt the true *tra'munu*, a sudden slackness of sinew and weakening of will as glaring eyes met his. He fought to break the gaze, and the other rider, coming free, had room for a backhand slash that staggered the brute. It was the boyish-faced Pivrekhan, and together they beat the *jinzai* down with flailing swords.

Such fights were happening all along the ridge, the *jinzal* greatly outnumbered, but dangerous, tough beyond belief. Below, where the long fall to the Navu valley was checked by a level stretch and even a low mound, the retreating *jinzal* had halted now and turned, a blast on one of the short trumpets Rodlakh had described bringing heavy pikes to the ready, their masters working a prearranged plan, oblivious to what was happening above. A second company was coming to form up beside the first, and farther over yet a third.

In defense of the pass it could have exacted many lives, if Shumat had been the only attacker, and a rasher one. The slope of the ridge was steeper this side, and from its safety the bows could have poured volley after volley into the ranks of the cavalry as the standing *jinzal* below checked their charge.

Turning back to bloody nearer business, added half-squadrons of Kargul were coming into the fight, choosing their spots. To a nearby *kímukan* Dolvid panted out that with things in hand here men could be disengaged for a powerful downhill run at the formations below, timed for when Shumat made his attack. That would be soon; he had his squadrons set, and apparently they were going to come as successive hammer blows, beginning at the farther end. The officer at once started calling men back from pushing along the ridge to where fighting remained hot, and signalled a half-squadron seeking an enemy.

With their masters all down or vanished, a few of the *jinzal* here returned to their instincts, making wild single charges, some of the wounded trying to crouch away into cover. Dolvid wished for an enemy that could see its position as hopeless and lay down arms; no mercy was possible for creatures that could kill while dying of twenty wounds, but he could not forget these were monstrous offspring of human mating, no more unnatural than he was.

Squeamishness left him when above the ankle he was gripped by a *jinzai* hand, the huge head of one left for dead coming up, trying to get teeth into his leg. Not meaning to, he came out of the saddle, and the stagger of Enikai nudged him nearer the *jinzai*. Terrified of teeth he brought his sword down flat on the creature's head, and it was like hitting stone. Enikai, making a circle, stamped down with both forefeet, and the *jinzai* rolled away, still trying to fight. Dolvid stabbed out again and again, and a rider came to plant a lance into the brute's middle. Yenughai said, "You owe me a fight, *Bôdhrai*." Without reply, Dolvid dropped his sword and went to the writhing body to drive his long knife in behind the ear. His dreams of pity would have to wait.

Enikai's smooth flank had been scored by clawlike nails; there was no blood but the hide was torn. Perhaps, in his pain, he would as readily have trampled Dolvid, but now allowed him to remount without objection.

Below the ridge Shumat had sent the first of his squadrons from a distance of three hundred paces, a second and a third soon after, to make a staggered line of bristling lances. The *kímukan* spoken with had assembled men from anywhere to make up nearly two squadrons, and was poised to charge where the slope was least difficult. Now, one of the shiny-cloaked *jinzai*-masters pointed up at the ridge, first sign they knew they had been deprived of their supporting bows. Then, well behind the mass of *jinzal* but closing quickly, more cavalry, much more, and Kamin-Tolagh was in front, cloak and red-brown hair streaming in sunlight. His squadrons were coming upslope, but he was aiming to his right so he could cut back and gain speed across the level.

Nearby fighting took Dolvid's attention, and when he could look down again there was no connecting this scene with the last. The main *jinzai* formation was gone. Struck successively and repeatedly from three sides, it had broken apart and spread over all the field, knots and huddles of *jinzal* ridden about by stabbing lances and slashing swords. Largest single stand of the creatures was now some forty, with no bows, cavalry circling, striking again and again.

Conviction came their masters, if any were left, would have done better to turn the brutes loose; the training that kept them in close ranks was a disadvantage against well-handled cavalry that struck and retired and struck from another side, giving them no direction to gather for a charge. The ferocious killer that would attack anything alive had been made into a weapon, still powerful, but one that had to be aimed at an enemy, and here enemy was everywhere.

Dolvid saw Shumat standing with his reserves, ready to direct fresh troops where they were needed. Giving Pivrekhan, again nearby, the job of finding Kamin-Tolagh, he designated a small hillock where the commanders would meet to confer, as yet outside the fringes of the fighting.

Onebhal as Dolvid rode up shouted some words about the Pass of Perus. Shumat was spattered with blood, and no longer had a lance.

"What have you been up to?" Dolvid saw he was stained too, like Shumat with enemy blood only. They swapped brief tales riding together to the little mound, while a hundred paces away fighting raged. Shumat had encountered *jinzal* early yesterday, astonished when the enemy, after a clash, retreated in good order before their flanks could be enveloped. They had remained just out of reach, and were there in the morning. Clearly their purpose had been to draw him northeastward, into this particular opening of the Gate, where the trap with archers was set. Unsupported, with odds of only three-to-one, Shumat might have been in difficulties, though he made plain he would never have mounted a charge against *jinzal* directly under the threatening ridge, and had begun only when he caught sight of the fighting there. "How was it?" he asked, and Dolvid said, "This."

Odd to be on the edge of a battle they could watch as a spectacle; eight or a dozen *jinzal* would gather and mount a charge, but their target was elusive, and time after time a flank attack would kill and disengage as the *jinzal* turned, with a fresh half-squadron ready to assail the new flank.

Kamin-Tolagh cantered over with his winded standard-bearer. He was proud to say he had two uncommitted squadrons on the far side of the pass, left there to guard his rear as he turned to join the battle; he agreed to exchange them for some of the bows, and to finish what was rapidly becoming a slaughter, while Shumat rode for Banakit. Shumat told him to maintain a watch on the pass, intending to bypass any small contingents of *jinzal* so as to arrive at Banakit ahead of all news. If the town was seriously garrisoned there were not enough men with Shumat, but any forces spared from the main fight must have been sent to defend the Gate. He would leave men to guard the pack-train, a mile or so to the rear.

"We shall see you at Fourth Bridge," Dolvid told Kamin-Tolagh, and how to find it, adding it might be defended.

Kamin-Tolagh, mastering a state akin to ecstatic drunkenness, nodded understanding. His eyes, filled with the recollection of last night's admission, met his. "You saw Kargul ride, *Bôdhrai*?"

At brink of the valley Dolvid's heart rose, and at last he let himself at least imagine success. North and east naked rock rose, guarding the way to Vonn and Kamsilat beyond. Left, higher mountains were hard and clean-edged in the early sun; far to the north the hills were blurred grey, and in between was the soothing green of the Vale of Banakit. Shumat said it seemed a dream, and he too was remembering an older campaign, when, after the harsh wilderness of Naëni they came to the fertile hinterland of Narn.

"All the same — " referring to his earlier claim of wariness against traps, "I am glad you found the bows before we did. Not a bad tactic, but too elaborate. They would have done better to occupy the mound in one mass, bows to the center, and defy us to move them. These *jinzal* are not for subtleties."

Emerging from the official residence, weapons in hand, were not *jinzal* but men, all of them in the dragonfly cloaks. The cavalry with Shumat had fought *jinzal* to reach Banakit, at the restored bridge across the Navu, on the pleasant stretch of road where Dolvid had raced with Rodlakh and won Enikai, and again inside the town, whose gates stood open and unguarded. They'd had losses and were angry, and they came like a flood through the fir-trees of the low hill to chop down the enemy. Of the retreating remnant three died in front of the door, two others slipping inside. Shumat already had men encircling the building; no one could escape.

Both Dolvid and Shumat were with the first through the door. Inside, a robed man, large, weaponless, tried to bar the way with outstretched arms, and before any order could be given he has been sworded down. Only Dolvid knew he must be of the *Atarlum*.

An armed man was killed in the plain room with the high-backed chairs, used for hearing law-suits, where Dolvid and Rodlakh had sat to write dispatches on their ride for the Frontier. Cowering in the magistrate's chair another robed man wailed his surrender. "Stop them," Dolvid said, and Shumat rapped out a command. His men fell back, points ready.

The deep blue robes the man wore were like those used at the investing of a *rabhsai*. Threatened, he stammered out, "*Ul Rekhi-Rabhsayin owal.*"

"He says he is the True *Rabhsai*," Dolvid informed Shumat, while Onebhal, who knew some Owanilú, said, "Ha. *Jinzal'asayit on.*"

The True *Rabhsai* made a sour mouth. He was not the ancient man for some reason expected, but about his own age. For appearance, he had been chosen well, except for the stature, which was ordinary. But the long face with its sloped brow and slender curve of nose above wide mouth with lips both flat and thin could easily have belonged to a descendant of the Gabh'Owan line, as depicted on coins. Even more, a face from earlier ages, a stone-carving from the First Empire.

Oddly, when he reached that point Dolvid knew the man, or had known the boy he once was. His name was Dravadhi.

He was a pupil at the *Mankh'*, a year or so ahead of Dolvid, almost a full *atarlai* at the time of his abrupt departure.

As a student Dravadhi had been slow, and what small notoriety he enjoyed Dolvid had given him. He was called Shâl-face.

The *Mankh'* was a large building and an old one, very often restored and added-to. Over what once had been a portico, now closed, hidden in a deep inlet, Dolvid had discovered stone faces carved in relief, miraculously preserved from the earliest building. One he decided must depict Shaëlai (later called Shâl I), since it wore the high crown of Vrobhan, the empire Shaël' conquered to begin his own. By far the most vivid of the carvings, a hawklike, pitiless face, skin taut across high cheekbone, almost a pulse at the veined temple: fascinating in itself, but there was also a resemblance to their own Dravadhi, and the nickname, Shâl-face, had stuck. If anything, twenty years had made the resemblance more striking.

A puzzled Shumat agreed to take his soldiers and search the rest of the house, and alone with Dolvid the robed man repeated, "*Ul Rekhi-Rabhsayin owal.*"

The pronunciation was as taught, though not always spoken, at the *Mankh'*. Dolvid laughed. "What do they call you now, Dravadhi?" in ordinary speech. "Plakhat IV? Shâl one-beyond-the-Last? You have lost your Kred' Taknai whine, at least." This was meant to incense Dravadhi, whose accent, from the south of the Island, had lingered stubbornly.

Uncertain whether he recognized Dolvid now, he was astonished to hear his name, yet at the start seemed determined to bluff it out. After silence he quavered, "They have all left me."

"Would you expect better, of those who would unleash *jinzal* against their own countrymen?"

"You think that is what I wanted? Just travelling near the beasts is a nightmare; I've had them night and day for two months, never knowing when one might turn on us."

"Dravadhi, much better men than you have been killed by your *jinzal*. Do not ask for tears from me. You will not be harmed, not now, if you answer my questions."

"Dolvidh — " Success in recalling brought him some confidence. "The traitor. I cannot speak. I have taken Greater

Oaths." That in itself was an admission, since the Oaths could only apply to *Atarlum* business.

Dravadhi as a prisoner might help solve many mysteries. Most things Dolvid wanted to learn could wait; all he wanted now was information about the *jinzal* armies.

It took very few threats. Except for those left to guard the Gate, all the *jinzal* had gone east, Dravadhi said. Not for the attack on Vonni's Jaws, which had fallen three days ago, but east for the taking of Kamsilat. Many other *jinzal* which had gone north ten days before were already in Kamsilat, which Kemunai said could not withstand a siege. Kemunai was captain of the men who commanded the *jinzal*.

About numbers Dravadhi was vague. He was sure there were still many *jinzal*, though Kemunai was upset about losses at Drin Navuna, again at the Jaws. Dozens had been lost, with some officers, when one large band went wild and attacked another.

There were fewer to begin with than the five thousand Kemunai had wanted; some had to be slaughtered when training failed, and mock-battle cost more than expected. But there were ample numbers, Dravadhi insisted, citing Kemunai, for the taking of Kamsilat, and after that of Kadon Dinul.

"There are no others to come from the West?"

"Not trained. Some were at Drin Navuna, also here, hunting the back-country for men in hiding, but Kemunai had them all brought in. He says, destroying the Army of the West is what counts."

"What a loathsome cockroach of the *Mankh'* you have become, Dravadhi." He had almost sympathized with a man forced to become *Rekh'Rabhsai*, to have *jinzal* as his entourage, but that was all gone now, as he heard the flat voice, sorry only for Dravadhi, speak about the brutes hunting fugitives for food, gathering to smash Rodlakh's army.

All discipline, all the anxiety over Kamsilat, were needed to put off questioning Dravadhi about *g'Asalladh'*, about Petakoi, the details of *jinzai*-breeding. There could be no satisfaction in having made right guesses when the answers, here as on the road for the *Mankh'*, made him sick.

He told Dravadhi he would soon have to decide between his Oaths and his desire to live; he was going to dictate a full account after the war was won and Rodlakh safe as *rabhsai*.

"Rodlakh is dead."

Dolvid felt his heart pause. "How do you know?"

"It happened days ago, before they took Drin Navuna." He went on to describe how the *rabhsai* had been give a thigh-wound not even such a great hulk of a man could survive.

"Nolimas," when he regained his breath. Dravadhi, hearing the man who captained the Army of the West had been mortally wounded, must have muddled it, but the false news hung in the air as an evil odor.

Recalling Shumat he said Dravadhi must be kept under close guard, and kept alive to the last. "We shall take him with us."

"Where?"

"Kamsilat, and soon."

Kamin-Tolagh said, "Can we risk travelling by dark?"

The day was westering as they gathered at the near end of Fourth Bridge, left wholly undefended. The watering of horses had taken up time, men resting in watches, some tending wounded, others on the lookout for enemy. Once the last squadrons of lances had shepherded in the bowmen and supplies the wooden bridges by Banakit had been broken again, to delay return of any small bands of *jinzal* there might be, left up in the Lunu Tezh' Gate.

"Do we dare not to?" Dolvid said. It was a plain road, if defended perhaps impassable by night or day, but if they delayed till morning they could not be at Kamsilat till late, and the city may already be desperate. The stone-throwing *zhin'pefral* would be there by now.

"What about this Vonn?"

"Past halfway to Kamsilat. We could rest there a few hours before dawn, if everything goes as it should."

That was not Kamin-Tolagh's meaning. His men had captured one of those in charge of *jinzal*, badly wounded. He could barely speak, and when he did used what Kamin-Tolagh called 'some form of the Owanilú,' but had told about terrible losses in Vonni's Jaws. If it could be held by men against *jinzal*, Kamin-Tolagh argued, why not *jinzal* against men?

Dolvid's worst fear; he had doubted Dravadhi's talk about the "fall" of the Jaws; far likelier, the position had been relinquished when the *jinzal* found a way to Kamsilat from the north. But Shumat said, "Then we must break through, at any cost." He predicted *jinzal* would make poor defensive fighters, unlikely to remain still behind walls, and most of their archers would have gone to the assault on Kamsilat.

"You have been there, *Bôdhrai*. What about the women?"

"The women?" — thinking first of Âna, then Aëlu, Doleni, but that was not what Kamin-Tolagh meant.

"I'm ready for a bouncing. After the battle my prick was higher than my lance."

Shumat nodded sagely. "It does that to some."

"Then let's get to where there is some *trosinai*." The word meant *sheath, scabbard*, but used in that collective way was a vulgar term for women. A military decision had been oddly reached; they would go forward.

At that quarter-hour between dusk and night when the light briefly was a solemn blue they had already climbed high into the hills, when forward, where bowmen were interspersed with lancers, there was the ring of weapons. Pressing ahead Dolvid found the vanguard had a captive. Onebhal was holding a seized sword and sheathing his own, while three others held a cloaked and helmeted rider whose hand was bleeding. He seemed young.

Questioned in the Owanilú and threatened with being dropped over the precipice to the right, the man unwillingly repeated the message he was carrying to Under-Captain Iliukh at Banakit. It was from Kemunai, their commander, and heartened Dolvid, being evidently the reply to news of sighting Shumat's approach. Far from sending back the reinforcements Iliukh demanded, Kemunai told him he had more than adequate strength, and should hurry his fighters, especially bows, forward to Kamsilat as soon as the new enemy had been dealt with. The men, he emphasized, were needed.

Dolvid asked cunningly, "Why does Kemunai not summon the bows from his rearguard?"

"You have heard my message," sullenly, his Owanilú so reeking of *Mankh'* that it seemed sure Kamin-Tolagh would detect it. "What rearguard? The only rearguard is with the Under-Captain."

"Who, with his rearguard, is dead." He must have been one of those killed at the official residence.

What the young man thought, riding near the rear of the column, bound beside a bound *Rekh'Rabhsai*, could not be imagined. But it was good to hear the enemy was short of bows, and unless he was a wonderful liar Vonni's Jaws would be uncontested.

Less welcome, the man had insisted with all losses the siege was going well for Kemunai, the remaining defended places closely invested, soon to be taken. The quays were said to be occupied by *jinzal*. Relief supplies would be unable to land.

"If they could, only live men can use them," Kamin-Tolagh said, urging the vanguard forward.

At the Jaws they risked lanterns to find their way through wreckage of fortifications breached and thrust aside by the *jinzal*. A rearguard of twenty, Shumat said, could have held them a week. Speculatively, he wondered why Rodlakh had abandoned so strong a position, then answered himself; "He must have needed the bows for the defense of Kamsilat."

The moon had set and the hamlet when they reached it was eerily quiet. A few windows had been smashed, but as at Banakit there was not much real destruction; this was an enemy with little interest in looting.

"Aye, and they clean up a battlefield better than jackals and vultures," Kamin-Tolagh, with a shudder.

Shumat, in a section where they could make themselves reasonably safe on both sides, decreed a three-hour rest for everyone. Kamin-Tolagh was for riding on, but stumbling through these darkest hours would not bring them there much sooner. "We don't want fighters half-asleep in the saddle," Shumat said. "How we fight in the morning is going to decide this war."

In the last of the hills above Kamsilat they halted again and had food while the columns closed up. The road here was broad enough for forming fours, and they would become eights once First Bridge was crossed. Neither Old Bridge nor New had been guarded, but in that threatening country a *jinzai* straggler had leaped from shadows and killed a man before being overwhelmed.

The scene was incongruously pleasant, air light, scent of the evergreen trees reaching them, quiet stirred by the sound of cavalrymen ambling into position, not enough noise to scare birds coming in hope of crumbs. High morning.

"How far?" Shumat said.

"To the bridge, half an hour. To Kamsilat, under two hours, not allowing for fights on the way."

"You have seen the town," Kamin-Tolagh said. "You have any thoughts on the order of battle?"

"What can I say? If it is true *jinzal* have closed in on the Great House, we should not meet many in the countryside. Again, I think we should ride in half-squadrons, one ready to assist the other. It would be good to envelop the city, north and west," closing his eyes to make the picture clearer. "Where the road runs straight for the river, short of two-mile stone, there is a naked ridge off to the left — by naked I mean without trees; it is grassed, running back to where the forest comes closest to the city; there are some small houses at the end, among trees. We should send some squadrons along that ridge to circle down to the city: grazing land right up to the west wall, so cavalry can spread out on both sides of the road and converge on the gate. The Great House is hard to miss, off to the left on a low rise."

"Don't you admire how he begins with *what can I say*? And where will you ride today, *Bôdhrai*?"

"Don't ask him, Tam. He'll tell you some place he can observe the fighting and end up wading through blood to his thighs. He relishes this business more than a penman can admit."

"Dorrmas told my sister he would have killed Rheduban, but for the little *atarlai*."

"Dorrmas knows better." Dolvid recalled the surge of maniac joy when he charged downslope at Dônshei, the pleasure of how a sword-hilt mated to the hand. "But that would have been easier than killing the Rheduban we all carry inside — or the *jinzai*."

Shumat was puzzled, and Kamin-Tolagh shook his head.

He tried to scramble out of hopelessness. "If you will take the left, including the ridge we spoke of," to Shumat. "I shall go with Kargul again, if I may, on the straighter way to the city."

"Kargul is honored," Kamin-Tolagh, with a straight face.

The squadrons Dolvid would ride with were at the rear of the column. He gripped Shumat's hand. "I shall see you at the Great House. If the bridge is held, force it, but do not stay to kill. There are good men behind you, and you have to reach Kamsilat before they hear you are coming. Good hunting, friend."

"And a safe day's end."

Kamin-Tolagh, coming back to be sure the officers all understood the objectives, grinned when he saw the Beech-Tree floating above Dolvid's head. "If that is going to be with Kargul again, it had be better with my lead squadron. When Rodlakh looks out a window he will have something to gape at, Beech-Tree and Lion flapping side by side."

"You will ride under Rodlakh's colors?"

"If you will permit it."

"Gladly."

They too clasped hands, and Kamin-Tolagh went off with the standard-bearer.

Pivrekhan was near, and the rosy face was discontent today.   He complained he had wanted to be with the lead squadrons, to kill *jinzal*.

"There will be enough for everyone."   Even with complete surprise yesterday their victory had been a brutal affair; he could not imagine anyone still wanting more.

Pivrekhan's belief, as further grumbling revealed, was that Kamin-Tolagh had specifically excluded him from a position of honor, whether the young officer thought he was being punished for once having bedded Kamin-Tarú, or saw it as part of a general undervaluing of his worth. Dolvid said, "But good men are needed here, too. We follow the leaders, and choose fights where our help is needed most."

"My thanks, *Bôdhrai*, but I see what is going on." Defiantly, Pivrekhan unslung his helmet from saddle bow, and for once put it on his head; when they started forward at a walk he moved his squadron with a regulation stiff-hand signal.

Dolvid was astonished, then ashamed of the feeling. Leaders acquired the habit of speaking about *the troops*, and easily forgot every man had a life central to himself; sobering to consider and impossible to take account of; no wonder armies tried hard to make every soldier the same as every other.

The pace moved to a steady jog, rhythm soon containing them; this, too, had power to make them something other than just men riding together, both lesser and greater. Dolvid, as often, let himself worry on the question of armies, and how these men next to him would have brought terror to the Heartland in the service of Preference if they had been ordered to, not for any personal gain. It remained an enigma, this power to collect men and forge them into a weapon to do the will of others; belonging was needed, but a separation, too: there had to be an other for enemy. That was why the realm must be Arbhal, a name that Narn and Zelkova could both ride for.

There was some jostling as they were forced to halt a few hundred paces short of the last slope down to the bridge, and there was agony in being so far back, unable to see what was happening ahead. After restless minutes they started forward again, and as pace gathered, rounding the curve, they saw First Bridge had been to some slight degree defended; bodies of four or five *jinzal*, each shot with many arrows, were lying on or near the bridge, and in the approach they passed the lifeless body of a General Cavalry man, struck by a thick *jinzai* arrow. Then they were drumming on the heavy timbers of the bridge, the river swift and rock-torn far below.

Day was clouding and Dolvid felt a speck of rain in his face, though sunlight dappled tree-clad hills to the north. Soon they were in woods, road curving between ferny banks, and no enemy sighted.

For half an hour the steady, downhill pace continued, an easy trot. They came out of the trees, heading south of true east, on the long stretch that led almost to the Navu, clouds heavy over somber hills on the far side of the river. Lead squadrons began doubling into eights fanning out from the road, pace at the center slackening a little so wings could come up level. An unforgettable sight, watching the precision of the Karguli cavalry as they formed a block of eight squadrons four abreast, two to right, four left, two on the road, setting the pace.

Now there was a small rise, and from the top be could seen Shumat's formations, less precise, in two unequal parts, Onebhal leading the lesser, and veering leftward to mount the curving ridge he had mentioned. At this distance nothing could be seen moving there, but Kamsilat rose, Great House plain, the colors flying too distant to identify.

Where the road swung back to parallel the bend of the Navu they came on *jinzal* at last, used as draft-animals in teams, each under direction of one mounted man, hauling wheeled *zhin'pefral.* Enikai raised his slender head and gave a war-cry, answering perhaps a signal Dolvid had given without knowing. The leading wing-squadrons quickened pace, rapidly gaining on the still-unwarned *jinzal.*

In these last two miles he lost any coherent picture. A few small, scattered bands of *jinzal* moving for the city were caught from behind or turned at bay as the cavalry overtook them; one half-squadron was surprised by a band of the creatures that charged from cover to topple many lancers; too distant for the forces Dolvid was with, but he saw a pair of Household squadrons hurrying to help. Then the road went into its shallow cutting, and when it emerged he could no longer see any of that fight.

Where *jinzal* were already overwhelmed by numbers Dolvid kept urging his section on, hoping to arrive at Kamsilat as an unpleasant surprise for the besiegers. With three squadrons he bypassed all skirmishes, and near the gate came up to Kamin-Tolagh, ready to storm into Kamsilat with a squadron and some oddments.

All together they made for the open gate, and as they did a company of *jinzal* with pikes rushed into the gap. Lances were down, clashing and splintering, horses rearing with shrill voices. As few as forty *jinzal* broke the front of the charge, and showed how tactics with massed cavalry would have failed elsewhere. Riders were going down, and more lances came into the gaps. Another squadron arrived at the gate, and thrust from behind a single-pointed wedge drove into enemy ranks. Kamin-Tolagh, lance gone, made powerful mowing sweeps with his sword, and burst through at the farther side of the gateway, instantly wheeling to beat down a *jinzai* from behind. How he or his mount had come through whole baffled Dolvid, who was in a jam between two horsemen. Enikai, not liking it, gave a surging bound as yet another Karguli squadron came crashing into the rear of the fight, and the lines of stabbing, gnashing *jinzal* bent and broke. As on a great wave, comrades wounded and whole, empty-saddled *pefral* and the shards of lances, battling *jinzal* and *jinzal* maimed were carried on the surge through the gateway into cobbled space beyond. Like Kamin-Tolagh, Dolvid came clear, finding room to wheel and with a butcher's chop nearly sever the arm of a *jinzai* making a thrust for Pivrekhan, whose lance was held uselessly above his head with no space for bringing it down. He, letting lance go, drew his sword and with a continuous motion slashed at the *jinzai*, yet standing after Dolvid's stroke. The men of Kargul were cheering themselves on, and with fighting on the wane in the fields formations raced each other for the gate. Perhaps, after all, there was a use for the weight of massed cavalry, so long as the *jinzal* had no bows, and the cavalry were ten to one *jinzai*.

Kamin-Tolagh, already disentangling troops from a fight that was won, called out, "Staying well back I see, *Bôdhrai*."

"Can you make squadrons?" Formations were a muddled wreck, but losses had surely not been so great. The last remaining *jinzal* here had been backed up the steps of the large covered market just right of the gate, and now the troops hung back, daring them to charge. Men were pressing through the gateway, shoving and shouting.

Kamin-Tolagh swiftly collected over a hundred, forming fours wherever they found themselves. He loped to the head, and they moved off at a steady walk. Dolvid hailed officers to see to ordering of more formations, and rode after Kamin-Tolagh.

He hurried through the straight-sided cutting that took the road through the Great House grounds, the pathways on the little bridges overhead. Leftward he could hear sounds of fighting, and once the thud of a *zhin'pefrai*.

In the space where the gates to the Great House opened on a meeting of ways there was absolute confusion. The largest of siege-weapons, the giant bow Âna had described, now mounted on a wagon, had overturned, probably as it was being swung to join an assault on the front of the Great House, or the barracks next door, whose road came down beside the fenced grounds. There were dead and dying *jinzal* here. Many of Kamin-Tolagh's company had continued on where main road began its descent to the harbor, but Kamin-Tolagh had circled back with a few men to engage a clump of *jinzal* archers on the mound beside the broken gate to the Great House grounds. Across the toppled siege-engine Dolvid saw new *jinzal* come into the fight, charging down from the Great House, pinning Kamin-Tolagh's men against the grassy hump, which they had little choice but to mount, having displaced the archers. Other *jinzal*, passing in front of the engine, came at the flank of the men with Dolvid.

He had a cold feeling they were being defeated by their own tactics, divided and hemmed in where their speed and intelligence meant nothing. Again the fighting was furious, and from a corner of his eye he was aware of a rush of movement up on the skyline where the barracks were. More *jinzal*, no doubt, leaving their siege to join this open fight.

No longer very open, fresh cavalry arriving, the jam by the front of the fallen artillery-piece so tight no weapons could be used, not lances, not swords, not even *jinzai* teeth.

Lurched sideways he suddenly had no near adversary. Over the heads of the *jinzal* pressing in on the mound, he saw Kamin-Tolagh's horse founder, going down on its front knees, the rider wrenched sideways from the saddle, thrusting madly at the *jinzai* that went for his throat. He vanished, and on the mound the banner of Kargul swayed to and fro, mast of a storm-tossed fishing-boat.

Enikai staggered under the terrible blow of a broken pikestaff used as a club. The great horse recovered, shaking himself, and Dolvid kicked out at the *jinzai*, which slid away laxly, already lanced in the back.

He was just in time to see horsemen charging down the barracks road, cavalry of the West. He shouted Rodlakh's name as the *rabhsai*, riding hard but upright, tossed away an unused lance, flashed out his sword, and struck at the enemy huddled around where Kamin-Tolagh had taken his stand.

Riders of Kargul had broken through the press at the back of the overturned siege-weapon, and came at the rear of those same *jinzal*. Some turned, snarling, and Dolvid glimpsed that Rodlakh had done what no one willingly did, dismounting in the midst of *jinzal* wounded and whole, to cleave at the brute hunched where Kamin-Tolagh had gone down. The *jinzai* rolled away, and Kamin-Tolagh was there on hands and knees, face and hair splashed with blood, sword grimly held as he pushed back into a kneel. Enikai swerved, and in front was a *jinzai* with pike levelled at one of Rodlakh's men. When next he could face front Rodlakh was lending Kamin-Tolagh a shoulder, leaning over as he jabbed defensively at a badly-wounded enemy. The two tall men stood straight, and neither, perhaps, knew who the other was. Their two banners were fluttering together nearby.

Abruptly fighting ebbed. Dolvid, having captured an empty-saddled *pefrai* rode over to the two, just as they turned to each other.

"My thanks, *Rabhsai*," teeth together.

He smiled. "Kamin-Tolagh baKargul. A good season for your visit to Kamsilat."

Dolvid dangled reins for Kamin-Tolagh as Rodlakh looked up. "How can you be here so soon? from westward?"

Not with his usual grace, Kamin-Tolagh was clambering into the saddle. "Would you have us ride away till you are ready for us?"

When Rodlakh had remounted and the laugh was gone Dolvid saw how grey the face was. "Household scattered the siege of the Great House. Otherwise I could not be here. The warehouses and granaries are besieged."

Kamin-Tolagh was leaning forward, hands at saddle-bow, and there was a long bleeding gash at the left underside of his chin. Fumbling under his shirt he found a kerchief, and made a sling, as was sometimes done to poultice a swollen jaw. As he made to go forward both Dolvid and Rodlakh caught at him. He shook head and shoulders angrily, and redrew his sword. Fresh forces, some of them Shumat's, were descending from the barracks, bypassing what was left of fighting here. Everyone was converging on the harbor.

The battle for Kamsilat might yet have been lost in the narrow alleys and passages near quayside, where riders were forced to meet *jinzal* head-on. But bows inside the boarded-up warehouses were deadly, and the last big fight was in the wide, flagged space where wagons came, and on the terms of the cavalry, here where there was riding-room. More were coming down through the town, and every charge begun by the *jinzal* was answered by flank-attack. Kamin-Tolagh was crazed, riding into the thickest of the fighting, hammering at the brutes with a tireless sword-arm. Rodlakh was everywhere, too, but his face was set for a hateful business, while Kamin-Tolagh whooped and shouted as he slew. Men were still dying, and this powerful enemy could be defeated only by death.

On the far side of the main fighting was a strange sight, lines of *jinzal* in step-by-step retreat, harried by Shumat's cavalry. The creatures were shielding a knot of the bright-cloaked riders, who bawled orders, using whips to keep the *jinzal* from either charging or breaking apart; evidently their intention was to reach the quays. One, with a crested helmet, must be Kemunai, the commander. Finding a squadron-leader with some men for the moment unoccupied, Dolvid rode down between the two largest warehouses, threading a path through the dead there. He saw there was just one small vessel moored at the far end of the docks, and then the men he had brought launched a bold attack at the retreating *jinzal*. As they turned, snarling, Shumat, on the far side in person, was quick with his own attack. Horses and *jinzal* fell, the path of the retreat was littered with dead, but the main clump of enemy held fast.

Wishing for bows he heard planks being ripped away from low windows in the nearest warehouse. Among men emerging were Frontier bowmen, some of the survivors of Drin b'Afon. He shouted to Noldar, who nodded, organizing his archers so rapidly that Dolvid, grabbing at shoulders and sword arms as he had seen Shumat do, had to show the squadron-leader the cavalry must be held back to support the bows and give them a clear field. Noldar's wary men advanced in ten-pace rushes, their shooting grimly effective.

The retreat faltered. *Jinzal* were falling and some with wounds were near the end of restraint training and whips could impose. On the left horsemen hit again at the crumbling formation, and now a half-dozen *jinzal* came at the stinging bows. The archers, after a last volley, ran for safety, and the cavalry was in a new, fierce fight, circling and stabbing.

Men the retreat had shielded abandoned their command and made a bolt for the quays and the one boat. Shumat's men were tangled with large bodies, and the *jinzal* were out of control, snarling and snapping at each other, at anything alive. One caught the heel of a retreating officer and dragged him from the saddle. Startlingly, another of the cloaked men was knocked down by an arrow. Turning, Dolvid saw it was from the short bow either of Noldar or his brother, both up on bollards and already with fresh arrows at the string.

Menaced by their own *jinzal*, two of the men gave up trying to reach the boat, and made a run for the cliff path. They would not get far; cavalry with Wanildhai was descending there.

Last of the officers was the crested helm, and the presumed Captain Kemunai dismounted quickly and knelt to untie the boat. He was interrupted by a wounded *jinzai*, crawling to snatch at his legs, but thrust it off with his sword. None of the cavalry was close, and in the shore breezes it was a very long shot; an arrow from Noldar passed near. Kemunai turned for a last jab at the *jinzai*, and went stiff, then limp.

As the body crumpled on the jetty it could be seen he had been knifed by a man standing in the boat. Tall, loose-jointed, he climbed up on the quay waving both hands and bawling, "Don't shoot."

"Sarnak," Noldar said. Dolvid laughed with him, but his gaze was going beyond Sarnak to open water, and the estuary was filled with sails, ships flying the colors of Kargul. The relief-supplies had come.

In the broad court on the far side of the warehouses bows shielded by what was now an overwhelming preponderance of cavalry were deciding the last concentrated action. To no one Dolvid said, "At a price, we won."

A little later he gathered with the captains where the horse-troughs were, a few stone benches shaded by trees, opposite the granaries. Rodlakh rode close to assist Kamin-Tolagh, blood-soaked kerchief stuck to his face, and Dolvid felt nausea or perhaps a sour hunger, weariness keeping him stiff. No one was elated. The welcome Rodlakh gave Shumat, their first meeting, was warm but abstracted, and Shumat had the look of a man whose day's work is not finished. He soon went to make plans with Wanildhai (who knew Kamsilat) to carry the hunt through the streets, till there were no live *jinzal* left.

Rodlakh was weeping, not bowing his head, tears rolling down. He and Dolvid eased a weak Kamin-Tolagh from the saddle, and sat him on a bench. Enikai, sides heaving, lapped in the trough nearby.

"Âna?" frightened by the tears. "She is safe?"

"Âna, yes, she is at the Great House. So is Doleni. Saidhan is safe, and Aëlu is across the river, and you and I are safe. Very many are not." Nearly inaudibly he said, "So many good men."

Dolvid nodded, and felt trembling of his own. Kamin-Tolagh turned up his smeared face and put a hand inside his shirt to clutch the goatskin bag. "Tú's charm," lips scarcely moving. "Sword and knife, lance and arrow, club and hoof. Nothing about teeth. They never thought of teeth. I could not break the clench." He achieved a shadow of his jauntiness, to say, "Not sure I wanted to. Better my jaw than my throat."

Eyes half-closed he added, "And better to win."

"Yes, better to win." Rodlakh failed to smile.

xii

Respite

Rodlakh said, "Shumat now regrets his thoroughness.
We might have saved a couple of dozen *jinzal*, if we could have
made them dig pits for us." Disposal of *jinzal* dead was a large
job. Behind the Great House draft horses were dragging corpses
to where lime-pits were being dug.

"With their need for food," Dolvid, lightly, "they would
have had less to bury." Âna made a disgusted face.

She had given him the story of the siege at Kamsilat,
jinzal, repulsed by archery and by brave sorties, mindlessly
charging again, thrust back from the windows of the Great House
itself. The *zhin'pefral* might have meant defeat, but no more
than two ever were in position and working at once, and above
half, as believed, never reached Kamsilat. Âna trembled again
with joy when she described how the cavalry came, more
horsemen than she knew existed, to strike at the attacking enemy
just when hope was at its lowest.

Onebhal was dead. He had deliberately offered a flank to
draw out reserves of *jinzal* held at the edge of the forest, and was
killed without ever reaching the Great House, fourteen years after
reprieve at the Pass of Perus. Worse ends could be imagined: a
worthy object had been accomplished, and he had escaped
decrepitude.

The enemy had been beaten and annihilated, yet by many
tiny margins. If Rodlakh had hesitated over the Long Retreat, or
declined to abandon Vonni's Jaws, if arrows had run short or the
masters of the *jinzal* wasted fewer troops in ill-conceived
assaults; if their trap at Lunu Tezh' Gate had even partially
succeeded, it would have been catastrophe instead of triumph.
When Dolvid considered how Kadon Dinul had been taken and
Dônshei won he lived his apprehensions over — and then he had

almost ridden to undoubted death or captivity at the *Mankh'*. In his absence, it was unlikely Kamin-Tolagh would have become an ally. Dolvid had almost settled for the truce: all the men Shumat could bring together would not have been enough, and Kamin-Tolagh's own presence had been indispensable. And the courage of unnamed men; if a single squadron had refused to ride against *jinzal* or had broken and run, it could have infected an army.

Alkmas, another of the necessary parts, was missing, not seen since he sailed from Zelkova with messages Rodlakh never saw, of encouragement and approaching help. Sarnak, who had come back through the Shoals from Owan Sai arriving just ahead of the supply-fleet, insisted Alkmas was too much of a wart not to turn up again.

Dravadhi was wholly cowed from witnessing destruction of the invulnerable *jinzal* armies. Dolvid, wanting all his story, shut himself up with the pathetic True *Rabhsai*, and so missed some history he had wanted to see, Kamin-Tolagh's meeting with Âna.

She had half-dreaded it, but only half, and would never forget his look when, face bandaged, he came into the dayroom where she was sitting with Rodlakh, Saidhan and Doleni. Aëlu and Sett were also there, but Kamin-Tolagh froze in mid-greeting, bewildered beyond dreams.

He recovered enough to make deference to the *rabhsai*, who stood to take his hand. "I am glad to see you up. Can we offer you a meal? Food was sent to your room."

"The beef was Karguli." Sett's breach in etiquette made Saidhan frown, but Kamin-Tolagh said, "And very good. I guessed where it must come from. That is why I got up — who could possibly need better than the beef of Kargul to put him on his feet?" Distracted, he could achieve only a weak imitation of his courtly style. His eye strayed again and again to Âna, and there was no doubt he recognized her. With her hair worn loose and scented and campaign clothes succeeded by a soft green gown of her own, she was more his Âna than the one her friends had chiefly known in the past weeks.

Sett was telling Rodlakh how quality of beef could be judged, and about the hard bargaining of farmers, who might have been selling their wives, to hear their laments over the prices he offered. He had taken minimum commission, and would welcome an audit. The supplies, in ships under colors of Kargul, the Patriarch's expected ally, had passed without challenge through the Strait.

"You did well," Rodlakh told him, and Âna thought he did, too, not to show boredom with the topic.

"*Rabhsai*," Kamin-Tolagh said, "You saved my life."

"If I did," displaying his own aptitude for ceremonial, "you were where your life was in danger for a cause that makes us brothers."

"I cannot be your brother before I am a subject — " putting his hand to his hip, but there was no sword there.

"Take mine, Kargul," Saidhan stood to reach where sword and scabbard were hung on the wall, and proffered the hilts.

"A fine old blade." Kamin-Tolagh admired the chasing along the ridge, as he bared the ringing steel. An idea came into his mind, and he arched his eyebrows. Saidhan nodded gravely. "That was the sword. Take it, keep it, as a pledge from your house to mine. Old memories can lose their bitter taste."

"To me, *Asai*, the rancor of my Kargul has never been quite true. How can there be honor, if only fights we win are called honorable?"

"It was a fair fight, you know."

"I never questioned it."

Someone had, Âna knew, the winner's son. Great heroes might do better not having sons to be twisted out of shape by impossible envy, then guilt over not giving perfect admiration.

Saidhan was saying, "You call your house the House of Talbhan, as we call mine that of Sainat. But Sainat's wife Rintavu was Talbhan's sister; we are both the House of Tebadh, their father. Cousins should be friends."

Throughout, Kamin-Tolagh had never stopped stealing quick, puzzled looks at Âna, as if next time it might not be true. Now he concentrated on ceremony, kneeling to Rodlakh and offering the sword. When his allegiance was sworn he took back the weapon, slid it into its sheath, and bowed his acceptance to Saidhan.

Unable simply to put down the buckler he glanced at Âna. Aëlu, not aware of the full story, but with an intuitive grasp of the tension, rose quickly. "Let me, *Asai*," and she deftly helped him arm, and then to disarm again, doing it with a light touch Âna admired, nothing that could ever be mistaken for a promise.

Rodlakh said, "You would remember Lady Aëlu, I think, and the Lady Doleni. Here is Âna Konats-daughter."

"Daughter of Konat," as she made deference. Kamin-Tolagh would no longer have to believe Dolvid's knowledge of Kargul plans was based on unearthly powers.

He tried a small test. "*Udh' un danamo an ke-budradhi udhal,*" returning a half-deference.

"*Asai, bi-amit adh' un danamo.*" It could even be true, the pleasure of meeting again, if pride would let him be forgiving. His eyes were inward, and she could not yet tell. He might be remembering (she certainly was) how his intervention had saved her from death, the morning of Ban-Sila's murder, and how he took her to where, as he now could guess, she was able to bring news to the Colony, causing the imprisonment of his mother, defeat of his father. What saved Âna from shame, that she had not insinuated her way into the Residence, that he had picked her from the fields like a cabbage and brought her there, could only make it worse for Kamin-Tolagh. Her eyes appealed to Rodlakh, who turned casually back to the table, while Âna drifted to the far end of the room. Saidhan frowned, but said nothing.

Kamin-Tolagh followed. "I would seem to have been a wonderful fool," between teeth.

She saw dusky color come into his swathed face. "Not so, *Asai*, but it is not the worst you could have been. I had no plan, but was bound to seize the chance."

Her turn, she judged, to flush, as interest in her womanhood came back to his eyes. He would marry her as the alternative to killing her, the only other way to lock away his mistake in judgment. She tilted her head slightly in Rodlakh's direction, and Tam touched the bandages on his face, drawing in his lips. "The bargain was good," voice low but grating. "In the end, I had the best of it."

They would not be friends, and she had been insane to expect it, with a man of his pride. He would have to go on believing all women but his sister were unworthy of trust. Yet this insult made it easier to remember other slights, how he and his family had talked about her as less than human, and only mad Finú had been kind. Though she had done her best to seem stupid it rankled to remember Rheduban explaining ivory, or this man telling her what venison was.

The air was noticeably cooler when they came back to the main gathering. Kamin-Tolagh, courteously but now with a glint of steel, reminded Rodlakh his father and mother were being held under guard.

"They will be freed as soon as word can reach the Mainland. I hope they will both be signataries to the agreement we draft."

"*Deghi*, I have to make my own peace with them first."

"Oh, yes, you will be censured when they sit at a feast and they hear the *Frela'olu-rai Kamintolaghi*, hear you called *Jinza'dakradhi, Kamsilatai-Kindhri*. They have wanted a captaincy for your house, and you will be Captain of my Household, if you will take it."

"I understood Captain Kizhunai — "

"We have a new post for him." Dolvid had recommended the Captain-Generalcy should in effect be two distinct commands, a Captain of Armies for the field and a Captain-

Counsellor for administrative business, Shumat and Kizhunai respectively.

"Shumat is a soldier anyone would be proud to serve with." It went out without even a ripple, and so, Âna reflected, a couple of weeks, a small death-struggle, undo prejudgments of an age, and the Heir in blood-proud Kargul is glad to endorse a Mixed at the head of all the armies. Shumat was laboring on, and there was conjecture about an expedition across Landegh to reach Lunu Jinzalladhiyu, and extirpate the last traces of *jinzal* and *jinzai*-breeding.

Saidhan was being goaded towards his rest by Doleni, but had something yet to say. "That's a soldier's soldier. The parts of war that bring no glory or titles or songs, they need rare qualities, too. A boy should be taught that, growing up." The covert glance for Aëlu told Âna she had kept her word and confided in him. The war had left him with a tiredness he might never get rid of, and perhaps he had made up his mind he would live to see the last of his grandchildren — or a first great-grandchild, as his eyes now went to her.

"Come, now," Doleni said.

"Now you," Saidhan told Kamin-Tolagh. "If I do not flatter myself, put me in mind of a soldier named Saidhan at your age — eh?"

"You were less handsome," Doleni said. Kamin-Tolagh's hand went back to his bandages, while Saidhan said, "Hush. When I mean, you were a baby in the South; we did not meet till I was past thirty."

"If they had told me your looks were in their decline, I might have tried someone else."

"I know, I know." Their hands joined in familiarity, which did not exclude affection, and they went out together.

"I wish my sister could be here," suddenly.

"She is here." Sett spoke, almost forgotten. "At Kamsilat, that is to say, *Asai*. She would be at this House, but she is not sure her brother has thought better of threats he made — I am only saying what she says, *Asai*. She insisted on sailing with the supply-fleet, then spent the night — " he was near drowning in loud blushes. "She was eager to come here, but, well, I told her, nonsense. That she could not," he finished in a small, doubtful voice.

Leave was given to Kamin-Tolagh's back, as Sett offered to show him the way to his harborside house.

When Dolvid came in he said, "Sett and Kamin-Tarú?"

He meant, bedded, but Âna had weddings on her mind. "No, he'll wait for Morulis Untimarrs-daughter to grow up, and when she does, run to the ends of the realm." She was the younger, prettier of the two girls at Burantal.

"While Orbanak would wish to grow up fast enough to claim Kamin-Tarú."

Rodlakh made fun of the idea, then quite seriously said it would be a good match for the realm's sake, to forge a link between *rabhsayum* and baKargul.

Dolvid saw he now had to tell all he knew, guessed and, questioning Dravadhi, had confirmed about the breeding of *jinzal*. He was still cautious about publishing the secret, but assumed Âna could share anything the *rabhsai* knew. Aëlu had gone to oversee food distribution for the refugees on South Shore.

For one who was going to be passed off as True *Rabhsai* Dravadhi's grasp of the realm and its powers was appallingly limited; he had been taught what to do and say at his investing, but not who his friends would be; he was unsure what Preference decreed, and only knew *ga-Yalum* by name as something to do with the *Edhrodilum*; he was astonished when Dolvid told him the practice of consecrating fields to the service of Edhrodi could be a way of taxing Mixed farmers into extinction. Mainly, he was frightened, caught between the power that had controlled his life from boyhood, and the nearer one with the strength to vanquish *jinzal*.

One point he was clear about; as suspected, breeding and knowledge of the breeding of *jinzal* were confined to a small inner circle of the *Atarlum*; the Patriarch and certain of the *Manadilum*, the Teaching Order. They'd had a former True *Rabhsai* in readiness, a much older man, but he died, and once Dravadhi was made his replacement he was sworn not to tell anyone what he had learned, not even the Head of another Order. He had heard the name of Petakoi *Asayu* very often, but could not tell anything about her part in the scheme.

When Dravadhi spoke about being sent into the dusty and parched Farther West so he could fulfill prophecy, Dolvid felt the start of a familiar tingle, a quickening of his pulse. One last was left of the Three Mysteries he had wanted to solve for more than half his life. The reason Lost Plakhan rode out of history had turned out to be closely conjoined with origins of the *jinzal*, and so too, he was all at once convinced, was the most recent of the puzzles, happenings in the Ní-Tilagh in 2876 that had led to extinction of the Gabh'Owan line: an attack by *jinzal*, loss of the Bronze Sword, the astonishing speed with which Kargul received and responded to events. In Kargul, then as now, the overlord had an Island wife, then as now the Patriarch had come to the Seat from the *Manadilum*. There might never be any confirmation, but he knew as fact those *jinzal* had been trained and were controlled by men.

"The Bronze Sword," to Dravadhi. "You were to receive it at your investiture?"

"From *g'Asalladh's* own hands — " Dravadhi's Greater Oaths had long been mislaid. "I have seen it, Dolvidh. It is heavy, and must have been beautiful, but it is very battered."

It could also be guessed who Dravadhi's bride would have been. Her brother had said their mother would marry her to a *jinzai*, then why not a ruler *jinzal* had brought to power? But Dravadhi's smirk when questioned about Kamin-Tarú, whom he had never seen but heard described, would have brought him instant death from Kamin-Tolagh.

To ensure his rule, the True *Rabhsai* was to have had in reserve a thousand trained *jinzal*, but all the rest would have been slaughtered after their Mainland victory. Dolvid supposed, but Dravadhi could not confirm, that for needed replacements the training would have continued at Lunu Jinzalladhiyu. As most likely at this moment: it might be some weeks before they had sure news of their catastrophe.

Rodlakh listened, and began with flat disbelief. Power for its own sake was not in his range of acknowledged desires, and without that it was hard to imagine why anyone would want to train *jinzal*. Anger would surely follow.

"Who else have you told?"

"No one."

Âna said, "Then Kamin-Tolagh fought not knowing he was warring against *g'Asalladh'*?"

"Enough for him, as for others, he was fighting *jinzal* commanded by men. I think his father would say he was right. Tovakh wants power for Kargul, but not by those means." The real crux, however, was that whatever position Kargul would have had in the *Rehk'rabhsayum* it would have received at the hands of *g'Asalladh'*, Petakoi's choice, not Tovakh's.

Quite soon came the expected yet dreaded question: why had Dolvid kept this knowledge to himself? Obvious now to him, but not easy to explain. He knew the subtleties, had deduced before questioning Dravadhi that the secret, kept within a limited circle of the *Manadilum*, would horrify most *atarlal*, as certainly the Patriarch the present one succeeded, the gentle Kamanasalladh. But to, well, to Shumat, *Atarlum* was *Atarlum*, and he was wiser than most men; Dolvid's fear was that public outrage would stampede Rodlakh into a war with the *Mankh'* that would destroy good with bad, and might divide the realm as irretrievably as Preference. Most Owanil, while they would not have spurned a realm *jinzal* helped establish, would surely share in an outcry against the breeders of the creatures, but that did not mean they would stand by and watch the destruction of the home and center of all their faith.

"We could drive the *Atarlum* from the Six Provinces," Rodlakh said. "Let it keep the Island where it began, with *jinzal* for servants. How can we not make war on people who turn nightmares loose on what it calls Yoëlladhu's Children? The home of holiness and law — it makes me want to retch."

Patiently, as one who had ample reason to despise the *Mankh'*, Dolvid began to recall some of the practical good the *Atarlum* brought to the realm; advice of the Growers, work of the Healers, the *margul*.

"Smoked eel?" sardonically. "*Raminat* and *ga-ôdul*? For the sake of not having to light a candle you would leave untouched these criminals, who someday could set *jinzal* on us again?"

"That is finished," confidently. "Lunu Jinzalladhiyu will have to have a new name. What I would work for is to make the *Atarlum* answerable to the realm, using threat of exposure to impose a new Treaty. Dravadhi in our hands, with some of the other captured *jinzai*-masters, makes *g'Asalladh'*s position a weak one. You can force his abdication, and insist the *rabhsai* in future will have a say in the naming of Patriarchs."

This opened a discussion that was not going reach conclusions that afternoon at Kamsilat, nor the questions it raised be settled this year, perhaps in this reign. That in itself was a victory for judiciousness.

They spoke about taxes, and ways of giving those not rich an audible voice in the running of the realm. They could only touch on subjects needing days of wrangling, and Rodlakh said he would summon a Great Council of the Realm, as Banak and Laluvoi had, more than a Pledging, because how laws were made would itself be a topic. Midsummer was obviously too soon, and he settled on Autumn Halving-Day.

"Spring was late," Âna objected. "In some parts they will still be bringing in the harvest."

"Zhôl's Day, then," Rodlakh said. That was between; the day of the first full moon after that of midsummer; it would fall late this year.

"It is also *Elu b'Aëlovoi*, a lucky day among old families. That is why it is chosen so often for weddings —" blundering into what his mind had been avoiding; Âna's eyes burned a hole in his right cheek.

"But I must be invested at midsummer. We cannot leave that to go stale."

"You will need the Patriarch." Dolvid forestalled protest. "No, *Deghi*. No Patriarch and all ancient customs may as well go; we do not need an investiture."

"Well, the Patriarch has to understand my *rabhsayum* will owe nothing to the *Mankh'*."

"He will be told." With no war to lose and a threat to hold over *g'Asalladh'*s head, it would be safe now for Dolvid to visit the *Mankh'*, for a discussion of all their futures.

They came back to the question of baKargul. "You say only Petakoi had any knowledge of the *jinzal*," Âna said. "But would Saidhan have bestowed the sword if he had known what Dolvid knew about that house?"

"No one was braver fighting *jinzal*," Rodlakh protested.

"Would you have given him your Household? It could be a sword at your throat."

"I have called him my brother."

"So you did Ban-Sila." An *atarlai* or a pious devotee might warn Âna she had been entered by the dark spirit of Zhunoi. She could not stop it; revulsion, one part of complicated feelings about Kamin-Tolagh, had come uppermost. "You have given back the Paowanu Loi, so raiders can gather there again, and Preference come back."

"Preference is abolished; the Kovilanu is part of the realm."

"Declared abolished. When will the cavalry of Kargul be disbanded?"

"Oh, Âna — how can I dismantle in a week the army that came to save us? Preference will die; the tide is running against it. Kargul cannot change that."

Dolvid, who had spent hours out amidst various troops trying to gather different views of the battle, mentioned some men of Kargul looked like finding wives among widows of the Colony; Kargul would begin to have Mixed families of its own.

"What about Petakoi? What are we going to do with her? Not exile to the Island; that would be a reward."

"A trial would be useless," Dolvid said. "There would be no evidence."

"She cannot go unpunished."

"I do not see how you could invent a worse punishment than the wound her son has, the scar he will have. Her *jinzal* that came near tearing out her son's throat."

"For her," Âna said, "knowing who saved his life will be a punishment, too. The point is, to be sure she recognizes her plotting is over, forever."

Dolvid should have personal resentment against Petakoi for the games she had played him, the nonsense about Kamin-Tarú and Rodlakh, the reluctant admiration he had begun to have for her resourcefulness in defeat, when all the while she was waiting for news the West had been shattered by her *jinzal*. As Aëlu had said, rancor could not stand for policy. "She is hostage for her own behavior. Tovakh would not need evidence of her conspiracies with *g'Asalladh'*; he has lived with her. He would not be pleased to see how he was used as one small standard in the big game where *jinzal* were winning tile."

"He would divorce her?"

"He would kill her," Âna said.

"If he was convinced of her guilt. And not even Kamin-Tolagh would try to stop him, or say he was wrong."

Âna searched in the unpitying face of Dolvid. "Let us try — " she began, and stopped.

"Yes?" Rodlakh prompted.

"Nothing. Silliness." She hid it away, but Dolvid could finish her thought. She dreaded how power might change them all.

g'Asalladh'

At Treaty Stone Dolvid dismissed an escort under Dorrmas. The first time he had ever come here was with his father, to look down from the top of the rise at the *Mankh'*, a dark, somnolent, quietly sinister animal sunning beside the bright Arnan. The next, he was a prisoner, after his father's death, and the beast had swallowed him.

Those years were longer than he had lived, or else the flicker of a single day: the Great Pledging in his sixteenth year, when he rode the other way, and at the Old Bronze Residence met and crossed swords with a young officer of the Household, who swore he would be its Captain someday, and managed to keep the promise. Bolan was out of captivity, and hardly anyone cared; his ambition had been so purely personal that his rise and fall in the end made very little happen. What he and Khalú would do was not public business, and surely not Dolvid's.

He did not want to arrive drowsy. A shake of his reins, and Enikai with a laughlike motion of the head stirred into a trot. Early summer, a warm day after three wet ones, and everything was at its greenest. He had always known he must come back to the *Mankh'*, measure of how far he had travelled.

He was expected; Petakoi had sulkily agreed to transmit his note, and though she would rather see him dead there was small chance anyone would try to kill him, not with Dravadhi alive and in Rodlakh's hands. But he glimpsed yellow-crested riders of the *Adanum* keeping watch from near the road, and when he came to the main gate to the Estates, flatteringly it was manned as he had never seen, forty pikes and half as many bows standing by, an entire squadron of lances formed up in the saddle. A half-squadron officer, incredulous the expected dignitary would be alone, challenged his entry, and Dolvid gave name and title. Beside the gate a pikeman was staring, and he recognized one of the men briefly held captive at Drin b'Afon; glad he had not been executed for failing to die, he did not know whether the soldier ever made the identification; in new silver-and-black suitings with Beech-Tree pendant at his breast he was hard to connect with the filthy, unkempt men of Drin b'Afon, campaign-clothes stained with blood and salt and marks of a long, hard climb.

"*Bôdhrai*, you must please give up any weapon you have."

"I came unarmed — " raising left hand so the empty scabbard could be plainly seen.

"We are to escort you."

"I know the way." Nevertheless the officer and an entire half-squadron rode with him to the stables. In this court he had often banged swords with Silnath, the father of Sunabhal, Aëlu's guard, surely killed by *Adanum* arrows on the last step of the retreat from Drin b'Afon. Over across the front of the *Mankh'* young students of the *Edhrodilum* were squatting in the sun on the low, man-made ridge above their gardens, no doubt listening to a lecture on grafting or mulch. Nothing changed here. Clang of the gate behind him had brought back the old fear of imprisonment, but he would not admit having come around to the opinion of Rodlakh, who fully endorsed no part of this expedition.

Still, the ancient, weathered stone of the *Mankh'*, its ponderousness, brought back all the dead weight of the past. Not reasonable *g'Asalladh'* would do him any harm, but was there no room for pure vindictiveness?

As ever the soft-lighted hush of the interior lapped him with a reassurance he wanted to resist. Once, this had nearly enfolded him forever, the comfort of dozing off in warm, bright water. He could not deny a feeling of coming home, yet regret was altogether false, a nostalgia for years past, not belonging to this place, nor anything that had happened here.

At the head of the central stair Dolvid nearly left the guards that paced with him, by turning the wrong way. He was called back sharply; the meeting would naturally be in rooms the

Patriarch set aside for visits from the outside world. Not Dolvid now, not the *rabhsai* himself, would be allowed to walk in a way that was *ga-dazhu*. Rodlakh in fact had lightheartedly trodden black stones of the Sacred Way at Drin b'Afon, and they were all One Way, *ga-Zhanu b'Asalladhi*. *Ga-Zhanu b'Asalladhit ga-Shaëdhu-na b'Asalladhitai ôl*; the Way of the Blessed Father is the Blessed Father's Will. *Olagh am*.

He thrust away incantations crowding in on him, spells to drain off will and leave obedience in its stead. When with *g'Asalladh'*, he had made up his mind not to use the Owanilú; the blandishing forms reserved for addressing the Patriarch would concede the question he was here to debate.

Pikemen pushed at double-doors and he was in a place he had never been, a high-vaulted room with its windows at the front of the *Mankh'*. He was led to one of four highbacked chairs, gracefully poised, padded at seat and back.

These central quarters, the Patriarch's own, had always seemed the body of the spider, crouched over the central arch. But the interior kept a careful balance between comfort and awe, retaining *mai* in an atmosphere of color and ease. The *ôdul* supplementing light from many-paned windows were all invisible, concealed in fanned capitals of a dozen pilasters, throwing their gleam into the arching vaults of the ceiling, which glowed silver with several thousand six-sided tiles of kilned glaze. The flagged floor had carpets in shades of grey and rose, lilac and tawny gold, chiming agreeably with wall-hangings of pale gold and a misted moss-color. Between hangings polished stone confused the eye, set in curves or recessed angles, warm grey and reddish-brown, exact distances hard to gauge.

He had expected *g'Asalladh'*, as a point of principle, to make him wait a while. After a minute he got up, ignoring a guard's urgent signals, and went to the window to confirm he was at the front of the *Mankh'*. He was *Bôdhrai*, with the Beech-Tree at his breast; not even in the Patriarch's lair was he to be hissed at by the *Adanum Plakh'*. It was the front, gate off to his left; he would be spared any invitation, as in rear-facing rooms, to turn his contemplation westward to the Island. On this bright but hazy day, surely, not even the most fanatical could claim a sight of the ever-white tip of Karg' Kamanta, floating in the west.

He never saw *g'Asalladh'* come in; He was there, padding from the direction of a doorless wall, and there might have been a slight click, a dull thud.

The small man was bowed beneath the overmantle, and in this even light the straight lines down his cheeks were deeply scored. Dolvid accorded him full deference, and nearly touched to his heart the index-finger that was for *Menadhi*, instead of thumb, for Patriarch.

Greeting him formally in ornate Owanilú, the old man waited for the proper response. "My thanks, *g'Asalladh'*, and the *rabhsai*'s greetings and mine to you." The plain words were jarring, and *g'Asalladh'* flinched as if Dolvid had raised a hand to him. He had aged.

"You are Our guest, Dolvidh, and We shall speak the language you choose." He indicated with a tiny hand where they would sit, and among parchment-folds the eyes were as keen as ever. "Yet it seems a pity, when so few, now — few at any time have had your command of our older voice."

Dolvid showed no reaction to the compliment. When they were seated *g'Asalladh'* said, "We can have refreshment brought in a while — *raminat*, as in the old days, although lately it has been in short supply."

If this was the contest he wanted, *g'Asalladh'* had made a poor move. "That is curious. I just came back from Kamsilat, and there *raminat* has never been so plentiful. The Lady Aëlu mentioned it to me."

"She is well, *Bôdhrai*?" A polite, conventional question.

"As well as can be expected in the Colony, *g'Asalladh'*. They have had some vexation there, as you may have heard."

In a familiar delaying tactic, before coming back to the Colony and its troubles, *g'Asalladh'* returned to his gentle lament over the Owanilú, which so few now spoke correctly or with a good accent. He might be puzzled, seeking a clue to the defeat of the invulnerable *jinzal.*

Dolvid talked about tactics, losses and courage, took pleasure in stressing the help they had from Kamin-Tolagh baKargul. "Without him, not only Colony but realm might have been lost."

"I wonder, Dolvidh. As Rodlakh's *Bôdhrai* you are bound to call his rescue saving the realm. Others, as you know very well, have other ideas of what the realm might be."

"The law will do for me."

"Ban-Sila's decree made it lawful to order the Strait closed."

Strange. Impossible for *g'Asalladh'* to be certain what Dolvid knew about the breeding and training of *jinzal*; he could not even know Dravadhi remained alive, but his determination to debate lesser points had even answered an accusation not yet made. The man must be trying to bluff his way, in the delusion he still had some power.

"The law between *Atarlum* and *rabhsayum* is the Treaty, which with everything else guarantees timely treatment for the sick and injured. We have had no reply to our request for *ramidul* at Kamsilat, where there is a great deal of work for them."

"Would you stick by the letter of a law, good for its age, that came to mean something never intended? A law to keep land in pasture, let us say, that causes a shortage of corn."

"I had a teacher once, Teacher of Teachers, who taught me not to conjecture on supposed events." He had taken the bait. "If there were such a law, would its realm contain a Dolvid Vidukhat, and would he see his world as I do?

"Words — " here he ignored, and might be only one in forty years to ignore the fluttering gesture *g'Asalladh'* made for silence — "can change meaning, but no imaginable change can give *Atarlum* the right to help destroy our best men."

"Truly, *Bôdhrai*, our best? Were there some who built splendid buildings? Had any of them found better medicines, or written books? Your work has merit, but you are here and not destroyed. Who were these best?"

Anger brought a stammer even as it fueled eloquence. "Galt, my friend, who died at Dônshei because someone told Tovakh he could grab the realm in those turnip fists of his. A boy named Truni who died at Drin b'Afon where Aëlu had been taken. Onebhal, an Owani officer who fought at Yuvakh Din in '28, and was killed near Kamsilat when he should be enjoying peace, a young Karguli squadron-leader called Pivrekhan, who is dying there now. Captain Nolimas would not have died if healers had been there; Kamin-Tolagh will have a plain scar. Scores more, killed and maimed, names I do not know."

"You, too, will have a scar, I see — " *g'Asalladh'* leaned forward to touch the wound on his temple. "The price of meddling. That has been your life since you left us, ideas half-understood, a gift for persuasion greater than your understanding, so you could always do harm beyond your accomplishments. The talents no one denies, but war is not your craft."

A disdainful mouth. "Outside of that meddling, when was your life threatened? You lived for years in exile with no other house nearby; was anyone sent to murder you?"

How had they come to here? The man retained the gift he was accusing Dolvid of, plausibility, but there was an old element of boasting, too, as he showed how much he knew about Dolvid's doings.

"Even last month when you came back to Kadon Dinul as Rodlakh's emissary, you could have had a knife in your ribs when you went strolling in Harbor Way.   But it was underestimated again, your strange power to persuade. You were not harmed then, you are safe now.   You have let your nightmares about the *Mankh'* become guide for your waking thoughts and actions."

"Sleeping, I have never dreamt a nightmare as horrible as seeing a *jinzai* tear with his teeth at a fallen victim."

"And at the death of the humblest illiterate out of the dusty West you die yourself, so you imagine. But you do not. After all the tragedies, you are here, and in a little while we shall have some *raminat*. When we first met I hoped I could be *ramidu* to heal that muddled notion of justice you got from your father. Have you not gone beyond the twelve-year-old? Children follow fine-sounding words, having had no real life to measure the words against."

Again, not by design, he was drawn in. "Then the *Mankh'* is filled with children, mouthing the fine-sounding words you teach, *Amshu ga-Radh la rava inanol owan*, how many thousand times? till behind these walls it takes the place of a real life."

"Of course," *g'Asalladh'* blandly agreed. "We need our loyal servants. For them, questions and doubts are only confusion. Speech is more easily learnt than thought, and the head obeys an obedient tongue. But we do not let them make policy. Your poet is still Bronal the lovesick?"

"Bronal was sick with *zhin'paghai*."

"*Zhin'paghai*, yes. *Ye'rekh'rakhu yi-ôl, bi frel'afoi-na ôl.*"

Dolvid did not answer, furious with himself for having invited the proverb, saying, roughly, only the Old Tongue had the right word.

"Tell me, Dolvidh," very smug. "How many men or women have you met who would know the difference between *zhin'paghai* and a trooper's itch for a week-wife? You have had disappointments — "

"*G'Asalladh'* — " wanting this excursus to end.

"If not adduced from your history it could be read in your face. You would let the world hurt you less if you once admitted fine feelings and fine ideas are for a few. Not many can talk, in any tongue, as you and I can."

Seductive as ever, this joining of assessment to sage utterance so that to be flattered was a glimpse of wisdom. But, "Are you saying because most people do not need poetry, I need not mind if they are slaughtered or enslaved?"

"I am saying you do not care, cannot ever care, no matter what you mouth about justice for everyone. In your bones you know the idea of justice is as alien to your nameless people as the crystal images in Bronal's best poems. What they want is revenge, and to be protected against vengeance of others, just as they want praise from those they slander in private, and demand honesty from the ones they cheat. They covet what others have and want laws to make their own possessions sacred. They want rules, yes, but only to restrict others — these are the ideals of greed, not justice."

"They are certainly the ideals of many Owanil I have seen." *G'Asalladh'* had exactly described the truth about Preference, behind fetid cant about the glories of Old Owan. "But, sir — " If this was the debate the man wanted Dolvid had time, and complete confidence in where he stood. "You are using one word to mean two things. Justice is the sense of fairness, which may be as rare as you say, and justice is the idea of fairness made into law. It is because we cannot keep to the one we have to have the other; laws are made to say what is right and what wrong, to balance greed against need, adjudicate claims between people who otherwise would have no recourse but weapons and force. To say we cannot have justice till everyone lives up to it is to say there cannot be any healing till everyone is well. If we were all innately just, we would never have had a need for laws."

"Always," breaking into any self-congratulation Dolvid might be indulging. "When you were otherwise the best pupil I ever taught, you had that same impatient ability, to go two steps and never see the third. Did you not learn the *Atarlum* has a use for everything? You tell me greed is the truth behind Preference — might there not be a truth behind greed? Does *g'Asalladh'* worry whether an Owani owns some scrubby bit of land?"

Here was the moment. "If I had never learned it as a pupil," closing in, "I would certainly know by now how far your *Atarlum* will go, finding a use for terror and death. I always knew the *Mankh'* encouraged Preference because it gave you power. I could never have seen how mad that dream could be till you let loose your *jinzal*. How? — " as *g'Asalladh'* blinked, "How, if you claim to stand for anything human can you raise these creatures and train them for use against men?"

"Who told you we do?"

"Kanavakh *Vakh'biSegh*." He relished saying that. "He knew about poor Plakhan's son, and wrote about it. Scraps from everywhere tell me. Dravadhi, your pathetic *Rekh'Rabhsai*, who is alive, betrays you merely by his existence."

"We had one before, who made a better figure," blandly abandoning denial. "But a half-trained *jinzai* killed him, and Dravadhi, you must admit, has the face." Pinching his lower lip between thumb and forefinger the Patriarch called for the promised refreshments by ringing a small silver bell. At once there was a click at the far end of the room, and Dolvid now saw the door by which *g'Asalladh'* had entered, an entire panel faced with smooth stone. An *atarlai* and a pair of youths in their smocks brought pastry, and a tray with a small burnished pot Dolvid remembered very well, set on a tripod over a tiny oil-fed flame.

When the servers were gone without a word exchanged, *g'Asalladh'* caressed the vessel with his fingertips, and glanced up at Dolvid, whose steady gaze acknowledged nothing.

"It was the Will of Raëdh *jinzal* come into the world."

"You do not deny He has had some assistance?"

"As well as your persuasiveness, we seem to have underestimated — what would it be?" He stooped to pouring of *raminat*. Veins of the hand were like rain-bloated worms set on a parchment to dry, but there was no trembling.

"Kamin-Tolagh would call it my luck."

"Your luck, then. You discovered we did not begin the *jinzal*?"

"The earliest would have been accidents, like the son born to Plakhan *Rhaëli*. They must have begun eleven hundred years before, when the Empire subdued northern Kufshei."

"Very good." A quarter-century melted away, and this same man was felicitating Dolvid on success in a set task. "The part those random *jinzal* played in the coming of the Night has been overstated, but they were certainly not bred by the *Atarlum* or with purpose by anyone. During the Island years the question was studied and solved, and the *Manadilum* established the exact process. Simple, once known. There is a tribe, originally of the Kufshei calling itself Man-mani, though they are not as different as they like to maintain from your Froghul. We call them *Jinz'onoyul*, the Mothers of *Jinzal*."

"And the Owanil are the *Jinz'alladhil*."

"If that pleases you." No ruffle showed, but it did not please *g'Asalladh'*. "When one of these women mates with a true and unmixed Owani, the child, boy or girl, appears normal, but all those female offspring carry the seed of *jinzayum*. The sons can mate however they wish, and there will not be any *jinzal*. But if the daughter mates with an Owani, the sons will all be *jinzal*, and that is true in turn for her daughters, and so in female line for generations — perhaps to the end of time, so long as a *Lekh'Owani* is found to father the *jinzal*. Our understanding of this was forwarded by a bleeding sickness in the ruling house of Ancient Vrobhan, which in the same way affected men, but descended through the female line. Of course, *jinzayum* dies out in a line when no girls are born. The line itself can easily become extinct after the first son; if not taken away, infant *jinzal* very often kill their mothers."

"I cannot understand why those mothers, or the fathers, did not kill their *jinzal* sons. Plakhan did, according to his brother." He tried to imitate an emotionless detachment which revolted him, but he had been at the Lunu Tezh' Gate, and *g'Asalladh'* had not.

"No doubt that happened in countless cases. But very often the mothers were alone with their sons; soldiers of Owan used tribal women for their urgent needs, but seldom settled down with them. There must have been mothers, too, who bore these monsters and would not see them as they were, not soon enough. For a little while an infant *jinzai* is not very different from any boy born large, and the difference is less to a mother's wishful eye. They are very sudden coming to their strength — or we might say, we are so slow. *Jinzal* are more like other creatures: they will never learn much, but what they need soon arrives. Think how soon a kitten can walk and begin to use its teeth and claws. Now imagine a wild-cat kitten born to a rabbit, and how surely the mother would be torn by those claws and teeth, unless she could drive out the stranger in the first weeks. She might do that; she would not be disabled, as we can be, by soft sentiment. Many a *jinzai's* mother must have been proud in the beginning of her son's size, his great organ, how quickly he could crawl and crouch, the quick coming of teeth, small at the start. You can see this to this very day with our breeding-stock. When *jinzal* grow up and the killing begins, it is the father's turn for pride."

"Men, Owanil, are proud of *jinzal* sons?"

The Patriarch laughed. "Have you never seen a man puffed up with pride about how his hound tore out the throat of a deer? Can you not see he would be all the prouder if he had fathered the hound? The trainers of *jinzal*, officers who lead them, have sons among their soldiers."

"Led. Had," correcting the tenses.

He ignored that. "You call *jinzal* monsters, and so they are, but they are monstrous fulfillment of human desires. That is why Raëdh sent them, and Maëdhi gave us wisdom to work out the mystery. They came as a rebuke to the arrogance of the Shâls, and a warning to Owan against mingling their blood with inferior peoples."

The first could be let go, but the second was obvious nonsense. *G'Asalladh'* had emphasized the father's bloodline must be Owani unmixed; asked again he recalled that when they had failed to father *jinzal* with men of the Island, they had always discovered an unadmitted mingling of races somewhere in the bloodline. Only the barrier of *Lekh'Owan*, Owani aloofness from the Other Races, had made it feasible for *jinzal* to continue so long.

The old man said, "It will be a long age before the last *Lekh'Owani*, and a dozen men can mate with many mothers."

"Don't dream it. It is finished. We have the secret now, and no more *jinzal* will be born."

"As Raëdh wills. Our purpose is His."

"What good could ever come from it?"

"Dolvidh, Dolvidhai. The *jinzal* through all their years have been a flame where courage was tested and tempered. Have not all our heroes, from Pir Kallikuk to Saidhan and now to Rodlakh and Kamin-Tolagh, been *jinzai*-fighters? All great powers are evil till we can tame them. Fire was frightening at first, it hurt and killed, drove men from their forest or grassland homes, yet tamed it makes a good servant. Poets, I think, could find a theme in use of brutal and witless *jinzal*, to turn the realm away from viciousness and rule by the unthinking."

Confronted by this muddle he had to fight for calm. "When we tame fire, it becomes life and comfort, cooking and pottery and metalworking. We do not have to use it to bring fear and death, but that is the only use for *jinzal*. Turn the realm away from viciousness! I have been part of the struggle against these brutes; it is a theme for pity — this creature that knows nothing but killing brings that with him like a plague, and to defeat him we have to become him."

"War can be a bridge to a greater peace."

"Yes, death — " angrier than ever with this man who went from Paowanu *Mankh'* to Summer Palace swathed in comforts and servility, and ordained for others the benefits of war. "Did Raëdh tell you to study evil so it could be propagated? The *jinzal* that came without help from your *Atarlum* would have been more than enough, if, which I do not believe, He sent *jinzal* to rebuke our pride and test our courage."

"Neither I nor anyone else can ever know the Whole Will, and it is not for me to question the *aën'modha*, nor, indeed, plain wisdom of those who wore this overmantle before me."

"But only a few who wore it were ever part of the breeding, not so? — coming a small step nearer some goal. "Is it not true even you, *g'Asalladh'*, would never dare proclaim openly to your *Atarlum* that your *aën'modha* tells you it is Raëdh's Will *jinzal* are to be bred? Most here would call it the work of Dark Hranakh. It is only in your *Manadilum* this work has gone on."

"You dare say what I *dare* do?" He let steel show for an instant. "Yes, beyond any other Order our *Manadilum* has been concerned with preservation. That you can testify."

Dolvid let it pass unchallenged, that crazy equation, breeding of *jinzal* with preservation of what was best in Owan. "But not the whole *Manadilum*? In my day, old at-Oradhai was not in on the secret, nor at-Keliukh — " he named some gentler members of the Order. Important, since a small group, needing secrecy, would be crippled by loss of Lunu Jinzalladhiyu, whereas an entire Order might smuggle *jinzai*-mothers to the Island and begin the breeding all over again.

"There are always those who serve, and an inner few able to judge the hard decisions that must be made for the sake of a distant good. As inmost in Rodlakh's *rabhsayum* you will learn not to burden little men with a share in large matters."

By a curious irony this *rabhsayum* had already begun it, and with the same subject. But *g'Asalladh*'s answer, with all his evasive skill, was *yes*, and meant there was no need to begin a war on the *Atarlum*, with its unforeseeable end.

They both sipped *raminat* for a silent minute, Dolvid still feeling the lapping tide of past years. "Once, you invited me to share in the secrets of your *Manadilum*. They seemed wonderful, and now I know they were as sordid as the breeding and training of *jinzal*. The murders in the Ní-Tilagh, the deception of even your best allies — how did you get Tovakh to take an Island wife? I have no use for Tovakh and his ambitions, but you let him believe his wife's friendship with the *Mankh'* was for his benefit, and all the time he was going to be nothing but a wedge to hold the door open for your *Rekh'Rabhsai* with his *jinzal*."

"Guesses, Dolvidh, guesses." A familiar admonition, but the voice had a cutting edge. "If all your suppositions were correct, how would Tovakh be harmed? He was to be given high office, Captain-General, perhaps. Petakoi saw she could serve both him and us."

"He could have been killed at Dônshei."

"He was born a fighting-man — do not judge everyone by yourself. You are Owani, of good Southern blood, and with no accidents can expect to live ninety years. If you see one hundred, there will still be books for you to read and puzzles to solve. But Tovakh? If he was crippled like his father, nearly blind, do you imagine he would want to go on? At first sign of that creeping end Tovakh would welcome quick, honorable death on the battlefield. When you see him again, ask him whether he would rather have died at Dônshei, or have sickness and slow decay yet to be faced at Inilun Barabhi. He will tell you the truth, even if a book-man cannot imagine it."

"Shall I also ask if he would prefer a wife who did not lie to him? That is an answer I can easily imagine."

He had made a breach, though change in the creased face was slight. "You do not intend to share your allegations."

"I am only a servant of *rabhsayum*; I advise. The *rabhsai* agrees these *guesses*, supported by the existence of Dravadhi and other prisoners, and some documentary evidence, might well destroy the *Atarlum* here on the Mainland."

"You overstate the case, my friend. The *Atarlum* can count on its friends, and most of the realm would be indifferent."

"Is that the prize after thirty centuries, most people do not care whether the *Atarlum* lives or dies? But you are wrong, and once the word *jinzal* is heard, old friends are going to turn their backs on you. You'll be lucky if you are safe on the Island."

"Well, when famine comes, or another Great Sickness, we may be missed."

"If the realm had no use for the *Atarlum*, I would not be here."

"The *Mankh'* is flattered." The comment was unneeded; what he said was enormously arrogant, but true. He echoed the Patriarch's implied praise of Growing and Healing Orders, and spoke about the *margul*, the *nôd'yanul*. Also the schools, the *manal*, which could reopen at once, if pledged to teach, and open freely to everyone, with no barriers of blood or language. The *atarlal* would be guaranteed protection from General Cavalry and provincial forces, and the *Adanum Plakh'* must be reduced to proper size for a Patriarch's personal bodyguard.

"Under the Treaty — "

"The Treaty of the Wind Caves is dead; *Atarlum* made war on the *rabhsai*. They were *jinzal* that came from the West, but your armies shattered at Kamsilat. A new Treaty will be negotiated."

"Not by me."

"True.   Your abdication of the Golden Chair is indispensable condition for peace."

"Does Rodlakh see himself as a new Plakhsila *Kímukoi*, with power to unmake a Patriarch?"

"He has that power. So far our *guesses* have been kept between the *rabhsai* and me — though I have written and sealed a full account which would be unsealed in the event of my death or disappearance."

"You imagine you can bring the *Atarlum* to its knees with this?"

"On the contrary. I am convinced your own *Atarlum* would demand your deposing. Those not horrified by your crimes would yet see it as a small price for peace — for survival. Even the *Adanum Plakh'* might be weary of dying for the sake of plots."

It would have been opening for rant about the loyalty and defiant strength of His *Atarlum*, the unconquerability of the Island, the friends g'Asalladh' still had. Instead the man gave a sad smile. "Is this why you endured exile?"

He was caught on the wrong foot; he could not see what prompted this. "We are not here to talk about me. I endured exile because I was exiled."

"You could have avoided it. You declined the chance of pardon when it was available — yes, yes, you opposed the policies of Ban-Sila, and giving up position and comfort is proof of your virtue. The truth is, you chose exile, out of disillusionment with men and women as they are. You prefer solitary dreams of what they might be. That is why the *Mankh'* will always be your true home."

"No disappointment with the world at large could make me despise it as much as I do this place, with its false histories of a golden realm that never was. Owani self-flattery, when the Owanil could cure half the evils in the realm simply by giving up those dreams."

"You are mistaken if you think we love even the Owanil for what they are. Only a few can understand the traditions they guard and preserve, or have the love for them you and I have. Why do you not come back with us, Dolvidh?"

He said nothing, getting less and more than he had come here expecting; there was no contrition, not even defiance, but instead this chilling admission, which seemed to say Owan was to exist for the sake of an inmost circle of the *Atarlum*, not the reverse. There could be no shocking or shaming a man who would slaughter thousands and enslave the survivors to make the realm safe for a tiny group of the elect.

"You are one of us," the old man said. "You do not see this now; the coming of Rodlakh makes you dream there may, after all, be a role for you in the larger world. A youthful *rabhsai*, and the young put their faith in ringing phrases; you see your wished self mirrored in his fervor, but that has more to do with his young manhood than with the rise of justice. Knowingly, you let yourself be deceived again, and condemn yourself to the sour entertainment of watching passion go cold, or turn aside into self-indulgence. If he is able to wield power, this Rodlakh will be somewhere between his father and his grandfather — like Lambarr easily distracted from great affairs, like Banak soon disgusted with the people, and how slowly they understand what is meant for their good, how they will always burn down the barn rather than share the corn. Banak without a Laluvoi, moreover, to curb his impatience. Oh, he will tinker with this and that for making rule more just, and end up another Banak, using words about freedom and equality to dress up a *rabhsayum* as despotic as Plakhsila *Kímukoi*, or Shâl the Fourth, and you will be tormented by your impotence to change anything. You will have smiles and endorsement in principle instead of censure and exile, but exactly the same power you had with Ban-Sila. In ten years, if he lives that long, Rodlakh will see you as a new Rhunsilakh, full of fine words, but nothing to do with real *rabhsayum*, or real ruling."

"*G'Asalladh'*, I do not think so," was all he could achieve as an answer to this stupefying vision. In the Hall of Trade, an ugly building at Irbat, there were wall-paintings he loathed, landscapes with trees that could never have grown, birds that were small, pretty and monstrous, not made into something new by the artists, but given just enough truth to be fascinatingly repellent. The recital by *g'Asalladh'* also made life-portraits that were unlike, flattering Dolvid by diminishing Rodlakh, with both remaining recognizable, so with his distaste and annoyance Dolvid was distressed to hear a whisper of self-serving agreement. Tell anyone, anyone but a passionate disciple, he is too good for his employer, and he will know it is true.

"You are still chasing marshfires. You want plowboys and scullery-maids who know their letters. If they do not have the fire in their hearts, what will that make them, except plowboys and scullery-maids who can read? Do you suppose they will turn to the lyrics of Bronal and the treatises of *Kirova-Kindhri* — or even your own *Song of Tales*? Bronal's tears are for all the world, and so you imagine compassion can be taught. Not so; songs do not live by persuasion, but because there will always be a few who already have in their hearts what Bronal can say for them. The romances ought to teach you, stupid and vicious people are not cured by books, they merely become arrogant, asking for stupid and vicious writings to mirror their own natures. Then, coddled by what they called into being, they see themselves as good as the best man or woman in the realm. Give this power to everyone, and their clamor may be loud enough to drown out all quiet voices you admire — including your own. Without a shared tradition to contain it, compassion may die, and many other virtues, so your lettered realm is tenfold as brutish as it was in ignorance. Fortunately, the *Atarlum* stands to guard the old graces."

"You stand for compassion, after bringing *jinzal* on the realm?"

A wearied gesture. "I would rather spend my last years at Lunu Midhi. The next Patriarch, as you say, will have to decide how we stand with the new *rabhsayum*; I have no further taste for debating the larger realm."

"That can be understood." The tone made unambiguous what he meant: anyone would be tired of statecraft after seeing all his schemes brought to nothing.

"Rodlakh could be everything you hope, and then you will learn what it is to be ruled by the rabble that shouts its opinions in the Avenue at Pledging. You have known solitude, perhaps, but now you will discover how much lonelier it is never to be alone, surrounded by ignorance and loutishness. For me, there is the Island, and what happens in the world outside will be someone else's dream. What is one reign? There will be other Kanavakhs to clot the Sword with blood, other Plakhsilas to champion change, other amiable, inept Lambarrs. It is only a sandbank, Dolvidhai, and a *rabhsai* who is lucky enough to get low tide and calm weather is a fool if he thinks he has tamed ocean. But the Island is its own small realm, where not much changes. It is not too late for you to join us there. I tell you as a friend, you belong with us, and always will. We might not give you a pictured device to hang around your neck, but we would know your worth without it. We could meet as we have today, as equals."

Once Dolvid had studied this man for clues to his own future, and knew he could use even anger as a calculated effect. He seemed sincere now, that was the most that could be said; he had stopped trying for the advantage, and his voice became yet softer, as if droning to itself. "At ga-Tembúrai, kept in a chest of carved stone, there is a bronze plaque, already old when Night came, described as `ancient' by a scribe of the Blossoming Age. Its meaning was forgotten, though he wrote that in the reign of Yuvakh — of Yuvakh, Dolvidh! — it was said to hold a great

power. The Patriarch Owan-Alladh' we call `Kirova-Kindhri,'
who mapped and read the heavens, could not read that
inscription, and neither could the language-masters of
Mankh'Alladh' V, who saved the Old Tongue from corruption
and decay. You, with your gift for puzzles, might be the one to
interpret this ancient mystery. Carefully kept at the Lunu Midhi
Mankh' are bundles of documents never properly sorted,
accounts from the wars with Vrobhan, many in the hand of
Bonusholi, favorite scribe to Shaëli — hm? These I could give
access to. If you want to write books showing how every tattered
tribe of the Farther West has a history to match Owan's, no one
will stop you; there can be librarians and copyists to assist you,
and more ancient writings than you have ever seen. If you do
resume that curious pursuit, never forget you are making use of
a mind Owani-trained, interpreting the observations of Owanil.
If you can show me a page, a sentence, a note in the margin of
any history of another race as generous to Owan, that says, *we
are an ancient, proud people, but no more so than the Owanil*,
I will allow others can equal our magnanimity, and be as
steadfast in the search for truth. You are far from the first of us
to praise former enemies, former vassals, and it seems to me this
very act of denial only reaffirms our unique greatness. But by all
means bring to the Island your love for every heritage that is not
yours; among your own race you can keep it intact. Met with in
the flesh, day after day, it can only sour you. The Oaths can be
waived for a *Bôdhrai* in retirement. It is not too late."

He folded his hands, and Dolvid, nearly tranced, had to
jolt himself into answer: "It is much too soon for me. Not the
benefits of war but the fruits of a just peace are what we have yet
to harvest: a poet who might have been finer than Bronal never
learned his letters, and women who might have equalled Laluvoi
have died in hunger. The realm cannot be made perfect, but it is
alive, more than you can say for your placid Island. There, bee
and beehive are fitting emblems; bees know their job and their
place, and do not have to worry about change or revolution.
Kadon Dinul, very well, can never have the quiet of Lunu Midhi,

the serenity of ga-Tembúrai; it is alive. Rodlakh may fail, you say. Not *may*, will — just as Plakhsila failed, Banak and Laluvoi failed, as everyone fails when they set out to establish perfect justice. But we can learn from their attempts, and see how they pushed chaos back, just a little — "

"Did they? Did they, in the end?"

"We need not quarrel about that. I have had the luck to have met good and kind and noble people from all races I have dealt with, but if I had not I would know our time is smoldering out. Your wax-molded mask on the Island is not Owan, and not even an army of *jinzal* can prop up a Shâl-face in the Chair of State and make him a living power. Owanil can serve the realm, not possess it. That is true for the *Mankh'* as well. Yet it is a worthy aim, to belong to a realm."

"Belong, Dolvidh? You may be the most powerful man this realm knows."

"No." He profoundly rejected that; power as the Patriarch meant the word had to be worked at for itself.

"You will admit, then, to being one of the powers? a trusted advisor to a new *rabhsai* with no experience of the in and outs of Kadon Dinul. You will have more enemies than you need, unless you find some tact."

This was delayed rebuke for how Dolvid had addressed him today, but an apparent sign g'Asalladh' had abandoned the eerie invitation. Dolvid, with a lingering regret for those bundles of unexamined texts, put down his little cup, and stood. "I should thank you, g'Asalladh'. You have told me many things about myself, though that is not what I came for." He was not sure that was altogether true.

"What it is you came for?"

He reflected. He had the abdication, assent by default to a new Treaty. What more could there be? Did he hope for repentance, even angry defiance — some sign this little man recognized the evil he had brought? He was numbed by the smallness, even the triviality of ideas that had lasted out centuries, and brought so much fear and bereavement, spoiling and death. "Three small pieces of business. Or four. What has become of Rheduban's killer?"

"Zhâlai is detained, awaiting our determination of his case. Does *rabhsayum* mean to pursue this?"

"That was my own curiosity. However, the *rabhsai* does have an interest in the whereabouts of a boat-owner named Alkmas and his apprentice, Torr, with two men of Kamsilat, his rowers when he vanished."

"Is *g'Asalladh'* expected to keep watch over such people? If that was the boat one of our war-vessels saved from running-aground in the Shoals, the crew is now at Pavani, and can come over on the next ship, if your blockade of the *Mankh'* has been lifted for good. The man stupidly drowned a number of documents by binding them to his anchor, and was saved by a lucky chance."

Probably a different, more forceful story would be heard from Alkmas. "Then I would be wrong in supposing you had rammers guarding the Shoals because a former under-warden of Kamsilat informed you that way was being used, and also brought you early news about the Battle of Dônshei?" Here, Dolvid had got it wrong; there had been additional harm Vinosai could do. Of course, like a straying cat he had made straight for his real home, the *Mankh'*; the Patriarch's silence confirmed it.

"Next, there is work at Kamsilat for not less than a dozen *ramidul* — or should I make this request of *Ramidhai*?"

"Your message will be conveyed to him."

"He should be told the request comes urgently from the *rabhsai*."

"Enough," icily, "he know who conveys it."

"Then there is the question of Rodlakh's investiture, which is to be at midsummer, together with his marriage."

"Midsummer? That is not many days to prepare." Then, "If *rabhsayum* denies the Treaty, what use is *g'Asalladh'*s part in raising the *rabhsai*?"

"*G'Asalladh'* has no part in raising the *rabhsai* — none. Come if you will, or if you do not want a part in acknowledging

him, say so. We shall in any event have the Bronze Sword,
which I hear has been found again?"

"And Rodlakh wishes me to call down a blessing?"

He seemed really to want to be asked, but Dolvid
maintained the agreed position. "He permits me to extend this
invitation."

"You are hardening, Dolvidh. Be careful; you may
become what you most despise."

"*G'Asalladh'*, I have been passed through the tempering
fire of your *jinzal*. It was, rather, a river of blood that had to be
waded, and none of the virtues of Old Owan were of any use; to
fight *jinzal* you become *jinzai*."

"You can never be free of Old Owan. Is it this Mixed
woman, who was Kamin-Tolagh's pleasure for a week, who is to
be our new *rabhsayu*?"

"Âna, daughter of Konat."

Still acute, the Patriarch had a sharp look for the
unexplained thickening in Dolvid's voice, but did not enquire; He
considered, fiddling with His cup. "Well, we shall invest this
rabhsai, bless his wedding to the farmer's girl, leave him with the
Sword. Those will be my last acts as Patriarch. Is that all your
business?"

"Unless you have more to say."

"You want me to defend my policies — or to renounce
them? You accuse yourself. You cannot make yourself care
about how others have suffered, and you hate me because I have
no need to pretend. Men of our kind do not achieve learning
except through selfishness, and that is too harsh a word; I mean
what you serve is within yourself, and can be nowhere else; you
say you serve the *rabhsai*, but it is your own opinions and
judgments reflected in Rodlakh that you follow. The same need,
above anything else, made you leave us, all those years ago."

The man got to his feet. "And I have given you a third
chance to reject me. You never understood. You have false
memory of the *Mankh'*, only remember you left in bitterness.
Your pride does not let you consider the good there was in our
friendship, and so we have been adversaries, when if we had

joined forces as I desired, all history might have been otherwise. But I tell you one last time: you will learn regret, and long for a refuge."

"I am accustomed to regrets, *g'Asalladh'*. Any choice means saying no to all others."

"The more reason to be sure you choose well."

Not yet could he try to come to terms with the monstrous charge he in some way shared blame for *jinzal*, the war, though it would come back to him often. Ratifying at last the break with the *Mankh'* had no feeling of a great watershed; there was never a chance he would go back on his choice of twenty years ago. True, there had been times when out of a distaste for decision and a kind of lethargy of emotion he had failed to recognize a point of choice. It had happened a few weeks ago, with Âna on the road for Kreshavu; he now saw and felt the crucial moment he had let slide past, when she asked for his *opinion* about Rodlakh's proposal. Then, like some conscientious idiot, he had striven for a considered answer to her explicit question, instead of recognizing the moment for saying he loved her, for offering her his life. This was not the same; the refuge he might someday want from the world would not be *g'Asalladh'*s.

Necessary to leave a lingering threat. "Let me say, *g'Asalladh'*, there are actions not satisfying as justice, nor for their own sake — that are simply policy. As that, they can be reversed, if there is danger forbearance might be taken for weakness. That an innocent wife in the Colony can be killed or widowed by *jinzal*, while Petakoi of Kamanta goes untouched, is not justice — only policy, for now. Other examples could be cited."

"No doubt." He was expressionless. "Such balancing of necessities becomes a meager amusement, as you will find out. We shall see each other at the investing, *Bôdhrai*, but not again after that, I think. You have Our leave."

The closed-in wariness of the *Mankh'* shadowed him to the stables, where it was good to see Enikai waiting. At the gate Dolvid waved at the men of the *Adanum*, who glowered back; only natural, they had to stay. Just the same there was something besides relief when the gates clanged shut behind him. Dying must echo in anything done knowingly for the last time, and his eyes blurred.

He had expected it to be different, and did not let that thought escape; it had the answer to both this journey and its feeling of incompletion. For twenty years, seemingly, he had expected to come back and see the man he had left as *Menadhi*, and quite impossibly had wanted to return in triumph, a son coming back to throw predictions of disaster back in his father's face.

A son, his father. A shock to know that for all his grown life memories of *Menadhi* had in depths of his mind been muddled with those of his real, mild, uncelebrated father, who was well-loved, but no longer well-remembered. In those earliest days here at the *Mankh'*, when Dolvid was twelve, he must have longed to turn into a new father this other small, bright-eyed man, who kept saying he was a friend and ally, but never won Dolvid's complete trust. In the years since, he had turned *Menadhi*, who became *g'Asalladh'*, into the darker side of fatherhood, so preserving his memories of a flawless actual father, just as *jinzal*, absolutely evil, allowed *g'Asalladh'* his ideal of a glorious Old Owan that could never have been. A necessary dream had brought *jinzal* into being, necessary unless you could fight free of childish judgments, and learn to accept inescapable mingling of good and evil. Even in a loved father.

At the top of the rise he paused, and started to look back. Irritated with this sentimentality he jerked at the reins to turn resolutely for Kadon Dinul, the New Residence, tomorrows. Something whirred near his head. He ducked, and there was shouting away to his right as an arrow arched to the ground behind him.

Halfway down the back side of the slope horsemen were milling, men of the Household. As they opened a little Dolvid saw a body stretched out on the ground, and the tall, slender man just straightening up beside it was Rodlakh.

With a shout Dolvid trotted down the hillside. The dead man was Vinosai, a bow beside him, four arrows laid out neatly on the grass. Rodlakh had taken a piece of white cloth from a Household man, and was wiping blood from his knife-hand. He apologized that Vinosai had been able to make one shot before they reached him.

"You should not be here, *Deghi*; this is the *Adanum*'s preserve. Who was he aiming at?"

"He lived in the Colony long enough. He was not such a bad bowman. You think you have no enemies? Playing your game with him, you humiliated this man."

Dolvid thanked Rodlakh, and had no leisure to tremble over a near escape, again suggesting they get the other side of Treaty Stone with all speed. They left the body where it lay.

"How did the parley go?"

Dolvid told him; investiture, marriage, abdication, new Treaty. Clouds were gathering again, and rain began spotting down. "One question I could not ask, *rabhsai*, about your father's death; I was afraid it might be answered." Whether the Patriarch had caused the great fire at Tan Lughsai, which, by killing, with others, both *rabhsai* and proper Heir, had brought Ban-Sila to power.

Rodlakh knew. "My mother had a slower death. Do you believe it?"

"It can never be known, but what is not thinkable, in a man who makes policy with *jinzal*?"

"I shall hammer them, Dolvid. The new Treaty will be imposed, not negotiated. There must be guarantees they can be held to, we must make them live up to their undertaking to serve the realm. If they refuse our terms, or try to evade them, we will break the *Atarlum*. Let them have the Island, or go to the

Western Ocean; if they will not serve all our people we'll do without them — borrow their skills for ourselves. It might be better if we had no other choice." Anger winding down, he looked across, as if expecting an argument.

"For the realm to learn what you and I had to learn young — not to need a father?"

"Everyone has to, in time."

They were coming back to the city. Across the road some swifts darted, twittering for shelter under the cornices of the Bronze Residence, as sky eclipsed doubly with rain and coming evening.

Âna and Dolvid

On midsummer's eve, conspiring to escape for a while from a Residence filled with guests from everywhere, Âna walked with Dolvid in the Garden-Court of Nasilú. Stars were unassertive in a sky still luminous, and a soft breeze stirred delicately-hung leaves of birches, the dark hair worn loose about Âna's face. Faint scent of roses and the sweet herbs woke pasts realler than any words. "The Owani disease," he told her, "is to create a past better than it could have been, make a luxury of longing for it. These were my apartments before I was married. There is where Rodlakh grappled Ban-Sila."

"Will you live here again, *Bôdhrai*?" The title stayed mildly funny when he and Âna were together.

"I love it here, *Rabhsayu*-elect, but my chief work will be at the Bronze Residence." As in Plakhsila's reign, daily routine of the realm would be separated from ceremonies of the court by the length of the Avenue.

"So far away." Belatedly she tried to make it a joke.

"I shall be here every day for instructions, or with documents for approval."

"You will have better freedom than the *rabhsayu*. I am watched more closely as Rodlakh's trothplight than ever as Kargul's captive." True ever since she had ridden up from Owan Sai at Rodlakh's side, in a high company which also included Saidhan and Doleni, Aëlu, Kamin-Tolagh and his sister, Shumat and Dolvid, making unknown her, she judged, subject of some speculation by onlookers. From then it had taken her several days to conclude that to wander at will through the Residence and its grounds she must be firm enough to get rid of attendants, soft-voiced enough that soldiers did not hear; between them servants and guards made a complicated, implacable mill, indifferent whether it ground away at Ban-Sila or Rodlakh, Petakoi or Âna, and she foresaw a long struggle to prevent the Residence from making her into what best fit its own ideas. When with Dolvid and Rodlakh, making policy and perhaps nonsense, she was still Âna, and never bored when she sat by while suits were heard or pleas for relief; she actually looked forward to stormy meetings of the Council. But she did not enjoy being taken prisoner by squadrons of dressmakers and hairdressers, and her temper was not improved by the excuse this would be the first wedding in the Family since Rodlakh's late sister a dozen years ago, first to create a *rabhsayu* since Saëdhu's to Lambarr, before Âna was born. Pleasure of handling rich-textured and gorgeously colored materials soon palled, and while the wardrobe of a *rabhsayu*, of course, was a part of government, she did not see why it should be, and after two fittings was grim in her endurance.

The tall, bony woman who was commander of the hairdressers was related to Rhunilat, and a celebrated source of gossip; after one hour-long session she was banished till the morning of investiture and wedding, an act which had already given her a reputation for oddity.

"They say you told her to come back and instruct you after she had ridden against *jinzal*."

"She irked me. She simpered as if I was a sweet little child."

He lightly touched the bare arm. "No crime, to be irked by the irksome." They walked a few steps under the colonnade, emerging again on the flagstone path through the garden.

"Shall I be happy, Dolvid?"

"You ask me?"

An empty-handed gesture. "You have given good advice before. At times," she qualified.

"Will there be happiness. Yes. I have heard people speak about happy lives; ask them how it is done. From my own life I can only say, there will be some good hours and days. Laluvoi once said to me life was a fraud, and she might hate

Saidhan instead of praise him, for giving her so many added years."

"*Laluvoi* said that?" Her radiance was legendary.

"Again, she suggested once she and Banak had lived in vain. The curse of hope, I suppose. Without it you would not know happiness when it came, yet everyone with hope is going to be unhappy at least half the time. Pardon me, this is no talk for the eve of your wedding."

Perhaps not, but she was avid in agreement. "That is what I saw at Kamsilat — no, at Banakit, when Rodlakh rode in from defense of the Gate. He is a different kind, you have seen that? It's good he is. He thinks troubles came into the world especially so he can overcome them — " becoming shy of her thoughts. "No victory can ever get beyond a respite, no?" putting faint pressure on his upper arm. "Better for the realm it is not you and I who are to rule it. One doomsayer is enough."

That brought on a thick pause, small stream rattling among the trees, the stir from the Residence faint.

"But I was happy at Kreshavu." She had to say it.

"So was I — " no hesitation about when at Kreshavu she meant. "As at Burantal."

"Burantal, I would have said Burantal, but I should not have been happy there." She meant, so soon after Sebhal's death.

Both an oddity and very natural she had taken this moment for these reminders. In one of the romances — Kamin-Tarú could probably name it — there was a fine lady who on the eve of her fine wedding ran away with an itinerant smith. The story was unknown to blacksmiths, but had been loved by generations of well-born daughters, not one of whom had ever done such a thing. Âna was only and properly afraid; *rabhsayum* must have for her the same sound as *Atarlum* once for him, a heavy door shutting behind, forever.

That obscurely flattered, but he saw her far more at ease with Rodlakh than she had ever been with him; the two of them made jokes and the *rabhsai* welcomed her minor insults; their small gestures did not make a world tremble, and any griefs that came would be fenced with moderation. They were all three friends, and Dolvid was clear about his part in the realm. He could make a spurious offer now, chance of escaping the rigors of eminence, and she would see at once the mortifying trap she had laid for him.

In dim light she could just read his face. "Greedy Âna. Forgive me. My mother once told me women who do not learn endings come to be hated by men. You have to be my friend — enough to have Kamin-Tolagh hating me."

"No he doesn't," judiciously. "For a while he'll wish you did not exist. He will find a cure, or two, or three."

"Sett will not be here for tomorrow." There was a connection; with the peculiar idea Kamin-Tarú would entrap him Sett had identified an urgent need to begin revival of trade with the Colony, and left for Kamsilat.

She giggled. "Would I have to call Kamin-Tarú *Aunt*?"

Plainly, marriage was sweeping through the realm; Arvat was going to make the young widow he had adopted his wife.

Âna was still with Kamin-Tarú. "I told Rodlakh he should outrace his brother, and take her for his *rabhsayu*."

"Why?"

"Thank you, Dolvidhai." She made a deep courtesy. "I can be convinced for whole minutes I am altogether honest. Why would any woman ever do such a thing? Would I admit making a case for Kamin-Tarú so as to hear other reasons why I have been chosen?"

"Were the answers to your satisfaction?" He followed her into the alien archness both of them knew would fail.

"I told him she is more beautiful, she was born to great houses and ceremony. She was his first bed-friend, and they are nearer in age; she is younger, while I am older than Rodlakh, by five hundred days. Then, it would be good for the realm if Kargul married Kadon Dinul — did I leave anything out?"

"One I can think of. About beauty, you lied."

"I have heard you did not decline Kamin-Tarú." Swiftly back into true feelings, and he could have pointlessly answered, nor you Rodlakh. He turned and kissed her lightly.

"You will be `Rabhsayu' tomorrow," he said, "Âna."

"Even now," with a wonder like fear. He could feel it, the tug between them, growing stronger. It would pass. It would pass.

"Where would there be?" and they were like two who had the same poems by heart, just a single half-line needed to match a whole realm of thought and feeling. But ridiculous and quaint, the fashion of an age long past, that their friendship and its sweetness could come to where a whole actual realm was in question.

"Greedy," again. Even now she could have held to his kiss and brought her body full against his. Stupefying how nothing was enough till we had misery, too.

They distanced a little, small motions of her hand like trying to quiet a child or to subdue wind-bellied skirts. "Will you marry Aëlu?"

"Will I?" For a notion altogether new it slid into place with remarkable smoothness; he enormously admired Aëlu. "She has said she will never marry again."

"She said that to you? You were alone?" Âna loathed the falseness of her bright mockery but clung to it. "I do not know who taught you to read women, but he was not as good as your master of languages. After Kamsilat, Aëlu asked first if you were safe. At meals she repeats your wise sayings till the whole table is yawning."

He could not imagine it, with Aëlu's tranquil self-containment. She had been reserved in their encounters since arriving here, only sign of the coming child one he had noticed before in pregnant women, a small thickening of features, so space seemed wider and the bridge somewhat flatter between her eyes. He would have less trouble believing she had conceived a baby all unaided than that she could achieve infatuation.

"A good thing for the son of Sebhal, to grow up in a scholar's house."

"Do you think I can't teach the weapons?" With Âna he would not have needed that boast before he let Kreshavu dribble away. "Son, you say?"

"Aëlu says so. Saidhan is certain — " catching at his hand again as she muttered, "I wish I could have been — " *like Aëlu*, she had almost said, not meaning altogether, that would be silly, but at one decisive moment.   One night away from Kreshavu, if she had been asked to the bed of the new *rabhsai*, Aëlu, she was certain, would have thanked Rodlakh, and excused herself. Saying, perhaps, that there was a misunderstanding with Dolvid that must first be addressed: the perplexity that for Âna became an exasperating additional argument for accepting the invitation would for Aëlu have been the strongest reason for declining it. A choice gone beyond revision, but that patience was a quality she would like to aspire to.

"Yes?"

"You and she — " instead, "have enough in common for a marriage." Reasonably, he endorsed the truth of that, while they stood rigid, two handspans apart, wrestling the irrational.

He had tried reason with himself about Âna, too, the diminishing effect of detached analysis; she was a small, pretty country girl, passionate by nature, brave, potentially infuriating in her hot opinions, by a long way not stupid, confident and shy at once, very dear to him, Âna.

"We'll be friends," teaching herself.

Before he could rule on that yellow light rushed from the doors leading to the Residence proper, and the tall figure of Rodlakh turned to dismiss his bodyguard. They did not draw apart as he came to them, smiling to see his friends were friends. Âna released Dolvid's arm and put her hands together in Rodlakh's. The regicide Dolvid looked benign.

"Vinilat kept me. He was Tovakh's ally against Shumat, and now he comes to me sweet as an overripe pear to ask a favor. He is the most tedious man in six provinces, has some grievance about Froghul' herdsmen driving their goats across his hunting-land. Dolvid, I told him you would settle it with him."

"I did, when I was fifteen years old." Twenty-one years ago to this exact day.

Rodlakh was dubious. "This could not be the same. In northern Dramal. The people winter on Dramaru."

"Yes, *Deghi*. Ka-Nam's people."

"These are your Froghul, the ones you told me about, with the girl you let go?"

"Tini-ra, yes." Nothing changed. "Vinilat has no case. Your father ruled on it."

"Our learned *Bôdhrai*," Rodlakh was confiding, "has more passion in him than he shows."

"Than he shows you." Âna's risky joke, but it got past.

"We are being sucked into a Shemugrân of suits and countersuits," Rodlakh complained. "Oh, let us get out of this city where answers are duller than the questions. Why should I not lead the expedition to Lunu Jinzalladhiyu in person?"

"That is Shumat's command, and you will be needed here."

"Kamin-Tolagh wants to go, and I don't see how I can say no. He and Shumat hunt together now. He even has Saidhan's sword."

No one failed to catch the allusion to Banak. The campaign, however, would not be one filled with glory. One of the captured *jinzai*-masters would be their guide. Extermination was the objective.

They discussed the chance Kamin-Tolagh would learn about the origins of *jinzal*, and even his mother's complicity. "If he does, he does," Rodlakh said. "Petakoi will have to make her own defense."

Âna did not want to be accused again of bias against Kamin-Tolagh, but it had to be asked, whether he could be trusted so far out of Rodlakh's sight.

Dolvid offered, "He has a new taste in his mouth, and he savors it; popularity with all races. He is recognized and cheered wherever he rides; why would he give that up?"

"If I went with the expedition — "

"You cannot, *Rabhsai*," Âna said.

"The expedition must not be delayed," Dolvid urged. "And you cannot preside over a Great Council of the Realm by fast-messenger from the Farther West."

Rodlakh moved his feet impatiently. "Curse. Land-grants, petty appointments, fair apportionment of taxes, special relief, proving title, boundary-lines and water-rights — was this why we fought Kamsilat?"

"Yes." Under his stare she held her ground. "Well, wasn't it, exactly for this?"

They drew together, portraying contentment they ought to feel. Yet their sinews kept memory of using all the strength they had against a plain evil, of finding resources beyond everyday capacity. After triumph there was rest and some joy, and there were bound to be times when they felt as Rodlakh had, out of patience with the petty concerns of the prize won in the great race. He truly believed what he had told *g'Asalladh'*; *jinzal* were too high a price for that fierceness of life, brilliant sun rimming a thundercloud, fire at the edge of doom. Somewhere, perhaps in the new struggle for a rule that was just and benevolent but needed strength to survive, they could find or make some space between bloodsoaked killing-ground and stolid pasture, between the tiger and the sheep, a land where they had no need to be either mad or too sane. Between beast and beast there was human.

Rodlakh said, "Have you seen Shumat's children?" A side-ceremony tomorrow would raise Dolvid's oldest friend to Captain of Armies.

"Poor Manda," Âna said, and in part meant, poor Âna.

"She is prouder than pigeons," Rodlakh protested, but Dolvid knew. In the Northeast Manda had deep roots, and now she had been torn out of the ground and brought to the commotion and ceremony of a packed Kadon Dinul, to be beside a husband who would leave on a new campaign in only days. She was not, as her husband affectionately said, fat as a seal, though plumper than when last seen. She was proud, yes, but frightened as well, and would have been more so but for Âna's understanding. Now she had joined forces with natural allies, Âna's father and mother, brought by boat from Nambalus, and equally bewildered by the New Residence and their daughter's rise.   Her elder brother Konir was here, too, but nothing disconcerted him; he might not have aimed so high but had always said his clever sister would do well. He was at his ease with Rodlakh, friendly with Dolvid, had taken a lesson in swords from Dorrmas; about women a sister could not tell. Konir's wife had stayed behind in the Lower Paowan.

"The boy," Rodlakh said, meaning Shudarr, Shumat's eldest. "Quick as a cat, and the shoulders on him — you realize he is a little younger than Orbanak? They should be friends. The girls, too; the little one is a wise-faced kitten, the elder is her mother to the life." On impulse he seized Âna and hugged her to him tight.

After moments he let her lean away in the loop of his arms. "Very well, *Bôdhrai*, I shall stay here at Kadon, but the court will not see much more of me than if I had gone on my own Bride-Quest."

That brought a transient chill, but Âna was not the passive Saëdhu, and would never let Rodlakh imitate his father's preoccupation with family life at the expense of rule. She would be too bored on her own account. A good pairing, with some discontents on either side, not with each other; Rodlakh adored Âna, and she was in friendship and a profound respect he'd had to earn. While Dolvid presumably must prefer, not a saddle-filly to forget, but unspoiled dream-texture of isolated times, a perfect paragraph rather than a flawed volume.

After a minute he said he must see to it those on the Steps knew their
proper stations for the ceremonies tomorrow. This was a duty of his, though it could safely have been delegated to Faëdhal, glorying in the protocol of this title-crowded episode. There was also a need to look up Master Nentirr and the others from the Marionette Guild, who were somewhere in the city, getting ready for many performances. Dolvid had never espoused censorship, but the Guild was said to be rehearsing a new scene, and with soldiers of Kargul and the West rubbing shoulders in the streets of Kadon Dinul, five injudicious minutes of a piece called *Sebhal*

and Rheduban at Burantal could undo all the work of conciliation.

Kamin-Tolagh also became a Captain-Elect tomorrow; very strange that Tovakh would be near Dolvid on the Steps, and beside him the woman who had helped breed *jinzal*, Petakoi's pride not a bit diminished by Kamin-Tolagh's scar.

Whether or not the sun shone Âna would dazzle them all in her new green gown, and no one could doubt she was a fitting bride for their young *rabhsai*. There would be some hoarse throats by nightfall. Even *g'Asalladh'* would be cheered (Dolvid could see Him smiling, and bobbing His gratification), and why not? what they were saluting was their own hope, and that or passing joy was all there was. Besides work.

Notes had to be made towards his account of the Great *Jinzai* War, avast sheaf of details collected from soldiers who had fought at Kamsilat to be sorted. When he looked back from the double-doors the couple had blended with shadows under the trees. Very little light was shed by a slender curve of new moon lifting above the archway.

The End

Arbhal

www.ingramcontent.com/pod-product-compliance
Lightning Source LLC
Chambersburg PA
CBHW020245030726
47499CB00001B/69